SHADOWBLADE

MORE TALES FROM THE WORLD OF SPELLMONGER

SPELLMONGER SERIES

Spellmonger, Book 1
Warmage, Book 2
The Spellmonger's Honeymoon: A Spellmonger Novella, Book 2.5
Magelord, Book 3
Knights Magi, Book 4
High Mage, Book 5
Journeymage, Book 6
Enchanter, Book 7
Court Wizard, Book 8
Shadowmage, Book 9
Necromancer, Book 10
Thaumaturge, Book 11
The Road to Sevendor: A Spellmonger Anthology, Book 11.5
Arcanist, Book 12
The Wizards of Sevendor, Book 12.5
Footwizard, Book 13

SPELLMONGER CADET SERIES

Hawkmaiden, Book 1
Hawklady, Book 2
Sky Rider, Book 3

SPELLMONGER: LEGACY AND SECRETS

Shadowplay, Book 1
Shadowheist, Book 2

SHADOWBLADE

SPELLMONGER:
LEGACIES AND SECRETS, BOOK 3

TERRY MANCOUR

EMILY BURCH HARRIS

All rights reserved. No part of this publication may be reproduced, stored in a retrieval system, or transmitted in any form or by any means electronic, mechanical, photocopying, recording, or otherwise without prior written permission from Podium Publishing.

This is a work of fiction. Names, characters, places, and incidents are either products of the author's imagination or used fictitiously. Any resemblance to actual events, locales, or persons, living, dead, or undead, is entirely coincidental.

Copyright © 2024 by Terry Mancour and Emily Burch Harris

Cover design by Alexandre Rito

Map by Moreno Paissan

ISBN: 978-1-0394-4845-2

Published in 2024 by Podium Publishing
www.podiumaudio.com

*To **Elizabeth Carver**,*
who has been a fan of mine for more than thirty years.
— *Terry*

---

*To my nieces **Lillian** and **Julia**.*
May your sense of adventure, creativity, excitement,
and wonder never cease.
Be brave. Be fearless. Be strong.
— *Emily*

CONTENTS

Map	ix
Chapter One *A Simple Mission*	3
Chapter Two *Silk and Steel*	31
Chapter Three *The Shadow Council*	42
Chapter Four *Journey by Sea*	59
Chapter Five *Prejestia Sea Haven*	77
Chapter Six *Sailing Lessons*	92
Chapter Seven *Shadowblade*	110
Chapter Eight *Smooth as Glass*	124
Chapter Nine *Cadena: A Not-So-Pleasant Stop*	139
Chapter Ten *The Venjanca*	155
Chapter Eleven *Maiden Voyage*	170
Chapter Twelve *Pirates!*	188
Chapter Thirteen *Shipwrecked*	202

Chapter Fourteen *Flotsam, Jetsam, and a Red-Headed Stranger*	222
Chapter Fifteen *The Shrine of the Shipwrecker*	238
Chapter Sixteen *Mariner Matros*	255
Chapter Seventeen *The Legacy*	269
Chapter Eighteen *Eyes on the Horizon*	284
Chapter Nineteen *The Witch of Manahar*	300
Chapter Twenty *Sea Lord Lancellus*	317
Chapter Twenty-One *A Duel on the Deck*	329
Chapter Twenty-Two *Planning the Mission*	345
Chapter Twenty-Three *Heist Presentation*	358
Chapter Twenty-Four *The Vaxel Anchorage and Assessment*	373
Chapter Twenty-Five *Lady Bomaris*	386
Chapter Twenty-Six *A Productive Meeting*	402
Chapter Twenty-Seven *Pirate's Provocation*	416
Chapter Twenty-Eight *Shadowblade Unsheathed*	436
Chapter Twenty-Nine *Daydream Sets Sail into the Sunset*	454
About the Creators	469

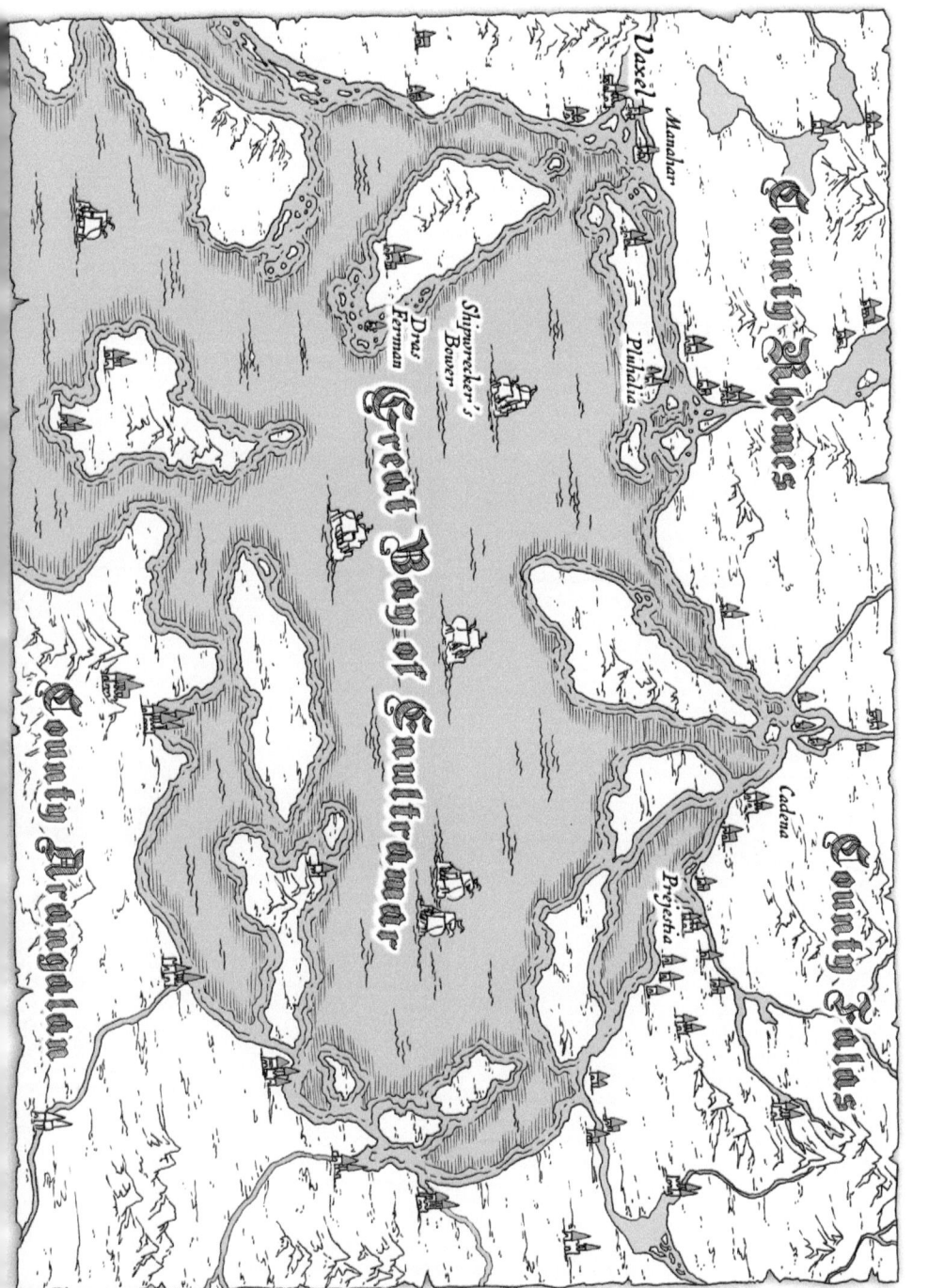

SHADOWBLADE

CHAPTER ONE
A SIMPLE MISSION

It matters not how well you planned, or how easy the heist might seem, for Fortune is a fickle mistress. Tempt her not with impulse and recklessness, nor be unprepared for the unexpected. For she will always seek to exploit your foolishness.
—from **The Shield of Darkness**,
written by Kiera the Great

NOTHING WAS GOING RIGHT, GATINA THOUGHT AS SHE RACED DOWN THE street, her green gown hitched up to her knees in a very unladylike manner. Her heart raced and her lungs heaved with the exertion of her unanticipated efforts. Her simple walk through the Warehouse District had become an unexpected game of cat and mouse.

And she was the mouse.

She didn't know where she had picked up her pursuer, and that concerned her. In mentally retracing her steps, she knew she had not been followed from the orphanage. When she had left the chapel that afternoon, she had used the back door and walked cautiously through the alley behind the stable, avoiding even casual observers. She had carefully skirted potholes, puddles, and garbage, crossing over the open sewer in the street, her nose wrinkling as she adjusted to the smell. The warm, humid night air exacerbated the stench of urine, stale spirits, and garbage. She hadn't been worried about being seen or attacked then.

Instead, her focus had been on keeping her gown clean. It was new; she needed it for this evening's trip to the Palace District and whatever other missions her parents had planned for her. It was a noblewoman's dress in the latest fashion, tailored for her by the finest seamstress in Falas. She looked lovely in it, she knew, and she had attracted plenty of casual glances from the workmen making their way home from work early and gentlemen making their way out to enjoy the nightlife. The women in the market also looked at her, either in envy or to size her up as a customer.

But this was different. This was purposeful.

Gatina felt eyes watching her soon after she crossed the street near the broken fountain where she had spent a summer perfecting her first alias. Years of training had made her incredibly sensitive to that sort of thing. The attention made her skin crawl. She didn't look around, though. Instead, she glanced at the reflection in a lamp's glass lens hanging outside of a shop. It confirmed her suspicion. The three men following her were not admirers; they were predators, she could tell at once. At first, she didn't worry, confident she could lose them in the crowded streets. Slowing her pace, she browsed the Market Day wares like any young noblewoman would as the merchants began closing up for the day.

But Gatina didn't lose them as easily as she'd hoped. No matter how long she paused, or how quickly she changed directions in the still-crowded market, they did not lose interest in following her. They split up and circled her at a flower cart, finally giving her a good look at them. One short, two tall, all three slim and wiry. Each of the pale men wore the same loose-fitting brown trousers, dirty, wrinkled shirts, and the kind of working boots donned by men who worked on the docks. And all had small blades attached to their belts. Not swords, not daggers.

Rat Tails.

Gatina recognized them at once. The long, sharp blades were distinctive: ten inches of iron sharpened into a needle-like point, with no edge, no hilt, and a pommel in the shape of a crudely wrought effigy of a rat. Only one group dared to use such a simple but deadly weapon. They were members of the Brotherhood of the Rat, the criminal organization that controlled the docks and much of the crime in Falas.

Once, they would not have dared to display the blades openly, lest they attract the attention of the City Watch. But that was before Count Vichetral had taken control of the city and the duchy. Now the Rats arrogantly strutted through the town with other bands of toughs, no longer bothering to disguise their brazen crimes. Baron Jenerard, the duchy's disreputable Master of the Waves and their patron, was frequently a guest of Vichetral in the Ducal Palace and a good friend to the usurping count. The City Watch knew better than to intervene. The fact that they were willing to openly pursue her—or any noblewoman—by daylight was telling.

That meant they were trying to either rob her or kidnap her. But this didn't seem like a simple robbery. That would have been easy enough to contend with, under ordinary circumstances. Gatina, Kitten of Night, apprentice shadowthief and heir to a legacy of centuries of magic and craft, would have no problem escaping with her purse and her virtue intact. It might even have been fun. She had frequently crossed paths with the Brotherhood and occasionally crossed swords.

But not tonight. She didn't have time for whatever games they had in mind. She was on a mission for the Shadow Council.

Gatina had a job to do, and she needed to lose the Rats quickly. It was time for some decisive action. She quickened her pace. She replayed her steps in her mind, looking for flaws. She hadn't left the orphanage more than a quarter-hour before, she guessed. She followed Shadow's instructions explicitly. Her journey through the marketplace was designed to avoid attracting any attention within the crowd—this was the busiest time of day, just before close. Bargain hunters and goodwives teemed through the stalls and carts in the square. There were hundreds of other young noblewomen and artisans' wives shopping the market. She should not have stood out in the slightest. But the market was also an ideal place to confound a pursuit, she knew. A pastry cart ahead provided the distraction she needed. She darted between the cart and the alley entrance, pushing her way behind the plump vendor, much to the man's surprise, causing him to halt and obstruct the alley with his cart.

"Ay, watch it!" he yelled, narrowly missing hitting her backside with his oven peel.

Gatina didn't answer. Instead, she recognized the opportunity offered. The unexpected baker and his cart had bought her a precious few moments' time. She used that time to cut through an alley, bearing left between two small stalls and vanishing into the shadows behind the curtains that shielded the stalls from the midday sun. That was her new plan. Hiding.

The three thugs loudly cursed the pieman and his cart, which were both moving slowly. When they emerged from the alley, they looked around for her in vain. They hadn't seen which way she went, she realized, relieved. And that bought her time enough to marshal her resolve and consider her options. When things went amiss on a mission, she knew from practice that you must take a moment and get your bearings. That was sacred doctrine on a heist.

She tried not to question the doctrine. Shadow was usually precise when it came to the heist plan, and even if she wasn't technically stealing anything this time, she was loath to depart from Shadow's rules. Indeed, she had come to rely upon his strategies with almost-religious faith after nearly two years of heeding them. If Shadow said that there would be a small hammer under a window in a temple bell tower, for instance, Gatina could rely on that fact to manifest more assuredly than a prediction that the sun would, indeed, rise in the east on the morrow.

But she also knew that she needed to be in the Palace District before the next bell, which signaled the changing shift of the guard. Ordinarily, the presence of the guardsmen would be a problem—they were hardly who a thief wanted to meet in the normal course of business. This mission was different, though, and she saw the extra soldiers as an opportunity. Half of them would be exhausted after a day-long shift and ready for supper and bed. The others would be ready for a cup or three and not yet as alert as they would be in an hour of patrolling. All that foot traffic would help her hide in the crowds.

It was less likely any of them would stop to question a well-dressed noblewoman entering the district, and more likely that they would at least stop three grown toughs pursuing a young girl and ask a few questions. But she needed to get there soon, without three Rats dogging her tail. Once she got to the Palace District, she would be safe. Her gown would blend in there. The vibrant green cotton was the most popular color of the season, according to what Mother had said after her mission to Vore. And if that were true, which Gatina was certain it was, then most of the women in the wealthier districts would be sporting a similar shade, to confuse the issue.

But here in the alley, that green gown was a liability. It attracted the eye, and the three would be searching for it in the crowd. She quickly considered her options. Her lungs were heaving as she pressed her body up against the alley wall, her mind a whir. Her choices were limited, she realized. She could strip to her working blacks, which she wore under the gown. Or she could wait a few moments and venture out, hoping the Rats had lost interest and wandered off. She still needed it to look the part and finish her mission, so the dress would remain, she decided.

But that sent her mind to the larger problem. Gatina was not supposed to be followed. Shadow had assured her that no one knew about her clandestine trip, and Shadow was never wrong about such things. There had been no contingency plan for such a situation. She had no backup, no confederate watching over her, ready to intervene. She had to improvise.

Yes, she was pursued and had to retreat—but her choice of havens was limited, as was her time. The orphanage was not an option, and it was in the wrong direction. That was the meeting location for later that night if things went according to Shadow's plan. Which they had not. And that produced an unusual amount of anxiety in the Kitten of Night.

It was not out of character, she knew, for Shadow to throw an unexpected twist into one of her missions. Doing so taught her to think on her feet and be prepared for any and every contingency. While three gang members chasing her seemed excessive, it was not out of the realm of possibility.

And Falas was a hotbed of unrest. Factions and street thugs had made the city rougher under the Five Counts in the last few years. The ducal capital was where the Shadow Council had been the most active against Count Vichetral's illegal rule, especially of late. In Falas, there always seemed to be far more going on with her missions than she was aware of, and that sometimes led to . . . complications of her own making. But this was not something *she* had done.

After several moments of intense consideration, she decided that the three Rats were circumstantial, not a breach of the Shadow Council's security. They had seen a young woman alone and unaccompanied in the marketplace and thought she would be an easy target for kidnapping, robbery, or worse.

Shadow had not spared her the ugly reality about the rise of Count Vichetral and his cohorts after the unexpected deaths of the Duke and Duchess of Alshar. Their *assassinations*, she corrected herself. Vichetral was the late Duke's distant relative and long-time rival, and he had wasted no time in consolidating his power around the capital and a ducal court that was in disarray the moment that the news had arrived from the north. With the Alshari heirs at their bloodthirsty aunt and uncle's mercy in Castal, hostages in all but name, the throne of the duchy had been left unguarded. And that made it ripe for the ambitious Count Vichetral and his rebellious cronies to take over under the pretense of safekeeping the throne—and the government of the duchy—until young Anguin could claim his position as Duke.

But Vichetral's rise had meant a stark change in policies, one that was appalling to most folk in Alshar. Everything from the arrest, imprisonment, and even execution of his political enemies to the favorable treatment of his political allies to the imposition of taxes and outrageous fees to the harassment of the common folk . . . and, worst of all, the legalization of slavery. There seemed no pit of corruption that Vichetral's faction found too distasteful to wallow in while he occupied the Ducal Palace. They sought money and power and used the most brutal methods to secure both. Only her family of magical thieves and a handful of others had opposed him in the form of the clandestine Shadow Council.

In her scant few years of working against the usurping Count of Rhemes, Gatina had learned far too much about the purely awful things going on in Falas. This was a time of extremes, and there were forces at work that she was ignorant of. Even so, she had seen much tragedy in the last few years.

Blood had been spilled. Spies were everywhere. This was an insurgency, after all; there were those who would do anything to maintain their power, and it was her duty to contest that. She had crossed blades with a number of groups in the last few months as she had undertaken one complex mission after another.

But in reflection, she understood how those encounters were almost contrived by Shadow to introduce her to each new group that had their own aspirations for the government of Alshar. One by one she had learned of several militant blocs with designs on the future of her country. Alshar had a long and complex history, she knew, and it had produced factions that had insinuated themselves for centuries to see their ambitions fulfilled. The Shadow Council, she had to admit, was only one of them.

In advancing her art as a spy and thief, Shadow had often had her contend with some previously unknown power in Falas. The capital had countless criminals and thugs who ran their own enterprises right under the nose of the City Watch and Palace Guard. The Brotherhood of the Rat was one with which she was intimately familiar, thanks to her first training mission.

The Rats ran most of the city's street crime and answered to a well-placed palace Rat, which gave them a position of prominence among the city's criminals. In turn, Vichetral had employed them as unofficial enforcers of his rule. Their role was to help keep the citizens of Falas too terrorized and weak to overthrow him. Their agents were constantly looking for easy prey after dark—like an unaccompanied young noblewoman with a purse full of silver. They would murder her out of hand if they could get away with it. Or worse. Nor could she count on the help of anyone else if that happened, unless they tried to take her directly in front of a City Watchman. That made her situation particularly dangerous.

But they were not the only ones by a stretch. The most challenging organization was the Royal Censorate of Magic. Vichetral had provided a haven to a tithe of Censors after the Castali duke—now king—outlawed the order and its charter. That almost made her like King Rard. She hated the checkered-cloaked inquisitors almost as much as Count Vichetral himself. Censors complicated things. They had brutally regulated magic across the five duchies for several lifetimes, and now it seemed as if half of them had ended up there in Alshar. The ban ended the Censors' authority abruptly. But with Vichetral's support, the Censors arrived in Alshar and began interrogating every magically Talented person to gauge their abilities and their support of the rebel counts.

Shadow was usually incredibly reliable about such important things, she knew. She had come to rely on his direction implicitly. But she suspected the mission had gone into the chamber pot instead of to plan—the three Rats were a testament to that.

She couldn't very well follow her original route with three thugs looking for her. She could take a longer path, but she worried she would be late. She had to improvise.

Fortunately, she knew where she was and that the promenade that would take her into the Palace District was nearby. Fulman's Exotic Elixirs, the wine shop that was her ultimate destination, was just over the bridge, past the second fountain. She closed her eyes and committed her new path to memory. *Take the back alleyway down to the promenade,* she ordered herself. She performed a quick breathing exercise to prepare.

The breath work calmed her, allowing her to release the anxiety that had built up from the chase. It also served as a way for her to transition back into her alias. When she opened her eyes, she was no longer Gatina, Kitten of Night, apprentice shadow thief and insurgent spy. She had become Lady Leonna anna Baskley, a Coastlord noblewoman of high estate and low character. She was intimately familiar with the owner of the name, having spent a summer sharing a dormitory room with the insufferable girl. But, as her father had suggested then, what better way to craft an alias than through an intensive study of the subject and then a practical application of the subject's behavior?

Her application had improved since the first time she'd used it, she admitted to herself, as she had set a tower on fire quite accidentally and almost killed herself in the process. In subsequent missions using that guise, she had seen success.

Lady Leonna anna Baskley emerged from the alleyway, her head held high and her attitude strong enough to deter anyone who might cross her path. That was the secret to a good alias, she knew, understanding the person she was pretending to be intimately enough to avoid any hint of suspicion she wasn't exactly who she portrayed herself to be.

She was on a mission, and anyone who stopped her would face her aristocratic fury. She was visiting a cousin in the Palace District. Her cousin worked for the Count, who was wise to employ a variety of deterrents against those who questioned his custodial rule of Alshar while the young duke-heir and heiresses were cared for by their aunt and uncle. Count Vichetral would set Alshar right.

Gatina cringed to think such thoughts, but her alias was a separate being entirely, with her own history, beliefs, and politics. She made certain she had the details clear in her mind, especially after the unexpected chase. But she was a professional. She knew her craft. When she exited the alleyway just before the promenade, Gatina dug into her small purse and removed her falsified documents, just in case she was asked. Documents identifying you had been required since Count Vichetral took power.

The gatehouse was a testament to how chaotic things had been since the Duke had died. It was new, a simple structure hastily built last summer. There had been several riots in Falas after the rebel counts took power. Gatina had been in several of them. She'd even started one.

The gatehouse was one of many now scattered across the city and served as a dreary reminder that the majority of Falas's citizens were no longer welcome in the Palace District. It had been added just after the Censors arrived. Guards were stationed inside in shifts, day and night. They kept the people where the rebel counts wanted them kept, Shadow had explained. Those who could be leveraged were kept inside the fenced district, close to Vichetral. And those they couldn't use, or who weren't needed, were kept out. Most of the citizens did not live inside the Palace District, which was designated for those who were either connected to the Duke and Duchess or who worked in the ducal government.

As she got closer, Gatina inspected the ugly stone-and-wood structure. She noticed the wide-set vertical wooden beams on the one window of the narrow three-story structure, but she wasn't deterred or concerned by it. She knew how easily she could slip through it to get in or out. She'd done it once already on a different mission.

But she was more concerned with the stone fence that isolated the district. That would be her exit strategy, she decided. It was easier to climb a fence, after all, and gave some added concealment. The gatehouse was merely her landmark. She knew the guards would think an attack or an escape near their gatehouse would be unlikely. She counted lanterns and sconces along the wall. Those would be her beacons.

When she arrived at the checkpoint, there was a line, just as she had anticipated. People were either returning home from a day of errands or leaving the wider city to return home.

When it was her turn, the older of two guards looked her up and down, glanced at the parchment clutched in her hand, then waved her through the crowd with a grunt. He didn't even ask for her identification. Sloppy, she thought. But she was gratified to see that her gown, cosmetics, and changed eye color had done the job. Her normally remarkable violet eyes were now a very unnoticeable hazel, her face was painted to make her appear older, at least sixteen, and her clothing indicated her station better than any document could. She looked as though she lived in one of the grand homes inside the gate.

She was careful as she crossed the worn stone bridge over the canal. Part of her disguise included the latest style of footwear. It was a style she found most uncomfortable. Instead of flat boots, she wore far more delicate leather shoes with a heel that pitched her forward. She hated it. It had taken her several days of practice to adjust her gait. She hadn't anticipated how much her feet would hurt or how difficult walking in the shoes would be. Instead of stopping or slowing to rest, she pressed on. Her assignment would not wait for her feet to recover, she knew.

In her guise as Leonna, she continued to stroll along the processional, her head high and a slight but tight sneer on her lips. The first of two fountains came into view. She could see the Ducal Palace. But she didn't let a trace of her disgust and fear of the evil men inside taint her expression. Lady Leonna, of course, would support order and control and profiteering, which was what Vichetral and his rebel counts had brought. Leonna supported slavery, too. Well, she *had*. Gatina hadn't spoken to her since she left Palomar Abbey. Maybe the young, reluctant mage had had a change of heart.

The Palace District looked as it always did: regal. The houses inside the gates were more opulent than those in the other districts. The status of their owners demanded that. There were townhouses, of course, built-in tidy rows with neat yards. But there were also small homes with lush gardens and trees. The houses looked as they had just after the troubles began. Then, however, mourning flags had hung from windows for the late Duke. Now, the only flags decorating the homes bore Vichetral's golden anchor, surrounded by five stars for the ruling council. She wondered if that was a mandate or by choice.

She watched as children played in their front gardens before supper, likely waiting to greet their fathers. The squeals and laughter did not distract her. She was observing, calculating. The farther she was from the gatehouse and the fence, the greater her risk. But she loved a challenge.

As the crowd thinned, Gatina slowed her pace. She was not in a hurry yet, and moving quickly would invite suspicion. She was too close to her target to get distracted. Exotic Elixirs was in that portion of the district, where the wealthier classes lived. Gatina knew where it was. And, thanks to her own surveillance, she had a plan.

Fulman's Exotic Elixirs had an alley behind it, she noted, as was common for deliveries. She stepped off the sidewalk and crossed the wide-cobbled stone street to the expensive-looking establishment. Before she entered the wine shop, she paused at the door for a last glance at other shops. She briefly considered visiting the roof of a certain spellmonger's shop. It was an alley away. But she was there on another task.

She took one last look around the street to see if she'd been followed from the gatehouse. There was no one she saw who had taken notice of her. An upscale tavern was open across the street. Her stomach cried when the smell of something delicious tickled her nose, and she realized she was hungry. She immediately suppressed the notion. The sooner she finished this mission, the sooner she could return to the orphanage and enjoy supper herself. She heard the plucking of a harp and laughter. It was that transitional period in the day when some shops were still open, as the lamplight indicated; but most were closed for the night. She saw three shopkeepers lock the doors. Then, moments later, lamps were lit above the shops.

Darkness was falling. It was time for her mission to begin in earnest: to acquire a particular bottle of wine.

The bottle painted on the sign outside was enough to indicate the nature of the business to most, but for the more literate classes, the name of the establishment had been painted in elegant Narasi script: FULMAN & COMPANY IMPORTERS OF EXOTIC ELIXIRS. Lady Leonna placed her hand on the doorknob and turned. When she pushed the door open, a tinny bell announced her arrival. She stepped inside and closed the door, allowing her eyes the chance to become accustomed to the candlelight, which was dimmer than the fading sunlight outside. She assessed the nearly full establishment with a glance.

The shop was busy that night. She knew that was good for her purpose. If people were focused on their conversations and their cups, then they were less likely to notice other things. Despite her fashionable gown, she wanted to fade out of sight. The shopkeeper was accustomed to the bell's noise, but patrons at two of the three tables were startled, though nobody spilled their cups. The barman nodded to her as he stepped away from the bar behind a velvet curtain. The small wineshop had one empty table left. Instead of sitting, Gatina walked to the counter, her steps smooth and measured, as would befit a lady of her station. And she assessed the shop's clientele as she moved.

The table of two nearest the door was occupied by two older women who had shopping baskets at their feet. They had the best seat, by the door and the only window. They looked at her, nodded, and then went back to their conversation. A man and a woman sat at the second table. The third table, nearest the counter, was occupied by three men about her brother's age, which was not unusual. Many young noblemen, sons of the greater lords who lived near the palace, frequented this district in the evening for good company and excitement. As she passed their table, one of the men raised his cup to her, in a toast meant to be alluring but which was undeniably creepy.

She was careful to show no emotion. Gatina smoothed her gown, adjusted her gloves, then placed her hands flat on the polished oak counter that doubled as a bar, though nobody was seated there. The shelves behind it held bottles of whites and reds and even more exotic varietals, though she did not care to read the labels. She was certain what she sought was not on display.

She instead used the reflection on the bottles to watch the table of men, particularly the one whose eyes she could feel boring into the back of her head. She was not enjoying the attention at all. If she could use

Leonna's own variety of magic on him, she might have done just that and started a fire at his feet.

"My apologies, my lady," the shopkeeper said when he returned with two bottles in his hands. "How might I be of service? May I offer you a cup of wine after a long day? Only a few pennies." He uncorked one and began pouring it into a glass, which he set on a tray that he quickly filled with others, red and white. "Excuse me one moment," he said, picking up the tray and serving the table of young men.

Gatina resisted the temptation to glance over her shoulder. Instead, she used the reflections in the bottles to track the barman's steps. She did see that the patrons at the smaller tables were still enjoying their cups and their conversations. The man who had raised his glass to her, the one she had ignored, was watching her watch him. When the barman returned, she leaned closer to him, to avoid being overheard.

"Apologies once more," the man said. "It has been a rather busy day. Now, what might I help you with, my lady?"

Gatina placed her gloved hands on the bar. In her more polite version of Leonna, she began discussing the bottle she hoped to purchase. Quietly. The man watching her, and she was convinced that he was watching her, did not need to hear their conversation. There were spells she could use to ensure privacy, but with the Censors in the city, she did not want to chance it.

"I've been sent by my cousin to purchase a particular bottle of Remeran red he ordered—a Tarano," she said, pronouncing the Remeran name with appropriate snobbishness. "It should have been delivered within the last two days," she began, but the barman scowled and shook his head, causing a sinking feeling in the pit of her stomach. "Have you not received the wine?" she asked, changing her tactic.

He finished wiping down the bar, which seemed to be more from habit than necessity, Gatina noted. The bar was spotless. The man flung the cloth he had been using up and over his shoulder with precision. But his lips were frowning.

"I am sorry to say that I cannot sell *any* Remeran wines, my lady. The palace issued an edict this morning impounding every shipment of wine from Remere. No warning, either. Taxing the crates isn't good enough. Each *bottle* must be inspected and assessed before it can be sold. It's been tragic for business, I'll tell you that much," he said, disgusted. "Remerans are some of my most popular vintages. I have *crates* of the stuff in back."

He tilted his head toward the curtain. "The counts plan to tax each bottle, heavily, but that's only after inspection. My shop is to be visited on the morrow. I can't sell any Remerans until the day after. If I'm still in business by then," he added, throwing up his hands in frustration.

Gatina considered her options. She *needed* that bottle. It was the entire point of the mission. She wondered if she could sweet-talk the barman into selling it to her, or perhaps raise enough of a fuss to embarrass him into the sale, or even offer enough money to secure it. Each was a reasonable approach to the situation.

Until he elaborated. "You wouldn't believe how many customers have come in, offering me triple the price to sell the bottles. Remeran is the best, eh?" He smiled at her. "But if I sell even one bottle of it before it's taxed, I could lose my entire shop to the authorities. Now, what can I get you that's *not* impounded, my lady? I have a lovely light, sweet white from Caramas that pairs nicely with fowl or pork. Three years aged. A good afternoon wine, suitable for a lady," he said, enthusiastically. "We have it—"

Before he could finish his sentence, the table of three men banged their cups on the table.

"Master! More wine!" one called, louder than needed. "And this time, don't water it so badly!"

"Why isn't there anything from Remere?" demanded the one with the mustache, acting as if the lack of Remeran reds was a personal slight. "I can't stomach another glass of Caramas! Do you at least have a decent Bikavar?" he pleaded.

"Yes, let's make it a bloody bottle," the third man growled. "Something other than this swill. And I want to see you unseal it in front of me this time!"

Their behavior seemed out of sorts in the early hour. It was only just twilight. Though she was gratified to see that he was now the focus of their attention.

The paunchy, balding barman sighed and shook his head. "As if I had time to water my wine—or survive if I was caught out," he muttered under his breath. Then he looked up and assumed a bright expression. "Of course, gentlemen! One moment, if you please," he said to them. To Gatina, he said, "Take that table, my lady, and I'll bring you a cup—on the house," he added apologetically.

Gatina's plan changed right then. Instead of buying the bottle outright, she would have to steal it.

That wasn't a problem. Stealing from him at night after he closed was one thing—the shop was proof against most casual burglars, but Gatina was a professional. But she did not want to wait that long. Slinking in through the alley during business hours presented a challenge, an exciting one, but one that posed a greater risk. She needed more information, and she wanted time to gauge the building for weaknesses. She seated herself at the last table and waited for her wine while she studied the place and sought its weaknesses.

Her alias afforded her several uncharacteristic behaviors, one of which was haughtiness. She wrapped that disdain for others around her as she sat at her small square table in the far corner. It provided an excellent vantage point for spying. And the focus of her attention was the table of young men.

A quick appraisal indicated they were relatively wealthy, likely sons of rich merchants or nobles. Each wore the latest fashion in Falas, velvet doublets of rich jewel tones with dark brown breeches. She saw they wore fine footwear made of leather, similar to what she currently had on her own feet, with a much lower heel. She suspected their shoes were far more comfortable than hers. They were clean-shaven, save for the one with a mustache, and their hair was decently trimmed.

The other patrons shifted in their seats, some casting nervous glances, others sharing looks with their tablemates. But nobody said anything to them. And Gatina quickly understood why. All three of the men had their sword belts and rapiers slung on the backs of their chairs, covered by their cloaks. Swords were common accouterments among the male nobility, of course, an indication of status and position in a society where only the nobles and their servants were permitted such arms.

But these were not the common blades that most gentlemen wore; the hilts were fashioned for a precise grip and the guards were designed to allow a full range of attacks. They were members of a "debating society," she realized, the euphemistic term for the dueling clubs that were terrorizing the artisan class or fighting among their rival clubs. In essence, they were high-born gangsters whose palace connections protected them from ordinary justice. This simple mission was again complicated.

She reasoned that she should observe and listen while remaining hidden in plain sight, as doctrine would demand. Soon enough, she would break into the storeroom. But first, a nice cup of wine and a bit of spying. The proprietor brought her a cup and a plate of biscuits as he struggled to keep the youths from disturbing his other customers.

As she dined, Gatina scanned the room. She wished she had a book or needlework or something else to serve as a false focal point. But the light in the shop made reading almost impossible, so she contented herself with nibbling and drinking her wine in dainty sips.

While she ate, she eavesdropped on the men's conversation. That wasn't hard. They were loud, joking and laughing, but they did not appear to be a threat. They were bragging and complaining in turn, discussing their fights and their romantic conquests with equal vigor. There was nothing particularly unusual about that.

Still, something about their presence nagged at her. Their behavior seemed odd, even for youthful belligerents. There were plenty of debating societies in Falas, and she'd run afoul of them from time to time. But they seemed to be waiting for something—or someone—and that disturbed her. She was alert for danger after her encounter with the Rats.

When she had ascertained that the men's banter had nothing to do with her mission, she set down her cup of unfinished wine, along with a few silver pennies to pay the bill, and left the shop. Nobody noticed the bell as she left. She slipped out into the gloom as another couple entered.

Darkness had fallen. Her alias was useless now. Young ladies like Leonna should be at home or accompanied by a gentleman at this time of day, before the dangers of the night emerged in earnest.

It was time for the Kitten of the Night to come out.

The alley was empty. Instead of stepping into it, Gatina fell in behind a group of women walking in the same direction, toward the other shops, which were closed. It was easy for her to blend in with them. Everyone was dressed in gowns similar to hers. As the women crossed the street for the next group of buildings, Gatina slipped into the alley at the end of the row of shops and backtracked to the wine shop. She was certain that she had not been noticed. There were few people on the street. She did her best to walk quickly in her horrid shoes. Her target was just ahead, the wine shop's back door. As she neared it, Gatina slowed. She leaned against a building for the second time that day. The night sky above provided plenty of shadows to choose from, and she found a spot within them. When she was certain she wasn't being observed, she began her transformation.

She bent to remove the horrid shoes. The latest fashion included dangerously high heels that had women pitched precariously forward, as if on their toes. While the shoes made her considerably taller, they also made running much more difficult, as did her developing chest, which was straining in the tight bodice that was also the current fashion. With her feet firmly on the ground, she wiggled her toes to stretch them. The short time she had spent in those heels had cramped her toes, calves, and back.

Once satisfied, she deftly unfastened the ties to her gown and silently slid it down, revealing her working blacks: a matte-black, tightly fighting garment specifically designed for passing through the night undetected. It was light enough to be worn under most dresses and was as dark as her gown was bright. Her shadowblade was sheathed on her back, under the gown. She repositioned it so that it was ready to draw.

When the soft green fabric was puddled at her feet, she stepped over it, breathing deeply and freely as she did so. The bodice had not allowed for that. Her pack, set just below her back at her bottom, had served as a bustle. She hastily removed it and dug out her mantle, her black waistcoat, and her working tools. Her light, thin boots were in special pockets on the backs of her thighs. She put them on her feet, sighing with relief. Her sore feet were happy to be back in familiar footwear. She tucked her working-black trousers into the boots and pulled the cowl up over her head.

She dressed quickly, then she rolled the gown tightly and placed it, the corset, and the horrid shoes inside her pack and slid that onto her back. She adjusted the straps a few times to make sure the pack did not block her blade. Before walking to Fulman's Exotic Elixir's back door, Gatina took the time to stretch. She reached both arms over her head and bent side to side, mindful of her sword. Then she assumed a wide-legged stance and gently lunged side to side in a fluid motion, allowing her hips and legs to loosen.

The series of movements had been taught to her by Lord Steel, her swordmaster. She began with a standing lunge and got lower and lower until her bent leg was nearly parallel to the ground. She had no idea what she would encounter on the other side of that door. She only knew she should be prepared for anything, so she wanted to remain flexible and fluid. She did not need any room for error tonight. She called forth her patron Darkness to protect and guide her and then invoked magesight.

That simple spell suddenly brought clarity to the darkened alley. Almost all magi could use magesight; it was a wizard's ability to use magic to see small things as large or distant things as close—but it also allowed her to see in the dark. She set off to examine the lock on the door and found something disheartening: the lock was simple, just enough to keep a common footpad from breaking in. No challenge. She had it open in seconds.

The wine shop's back door was wide enough to provide easy delivery access for wine shipments or meals from the tavern across the street. She examined the iron hinges and quickly produced a small vial of olive oil to treat them with—no need to be tripped up by a squeaky door. It opened without protest a moment later.

Well, maybe it will be a simple mission after all, she thought as she slipped inside and flattened herself against the wall closest to the door.

The storeroom was well organized, she saw as her eyes swept the dimly lit small space. Given the size, no larger than a stable for one horse, it had to be, she reasoned. Though she could hear noise from the common room, it was quiet back there. Against the wall opposite her she saw racks of bottles organized by variety and region. That wasn't what she needed.

Her bottle would be a special order, from what Shadow had said. A worktable and shelves were built into the wall beside the racks to the left of the curtained doorway that led into the shop. That curtain provided enough cover for her to move freely, she saw. But she also found a mountain of wooden crates, some opened, others still nailed shut. Her mind whirled as she counted. There had to be at least twenty crates from all sorts of exotic places.

This mission is vexing, she thought. But then she reminded herself of the doctrine: *All missions provide opportunity.* And this one had loads of that, she realized.

She didn't want to just randomly start opening crates. That would be risky and time-consuming. At the desk, she found a packing list with notes written on it. She needed a bottle of Remeran red, specifically from the Tarano vineyard, outside of Pelsis on the Remeran coast. It took a few moments to find the notation among the stacks of parchment—even with magesight, it was difficult to read in the gloom. According to the list, it had indeed been delivered, she saw.

Either the barman or the wine shop's owner kept very detailed records, which she found incredibly helpful. The crates were logged as they arrived, and inventory was noted. And the record-keeper had crafted a system of logging the inventory by symbols. A large star was drawn next to the notation for that particular bottle, indicating a special order.

She set down the list and found the appropriate crate. As she gingerly lifted the lid, which had already been opened, she heard yelling from the wine shop. It sounded as if the table of belligerent debaters had finally gotten a little too into their cups.

She propped the lid against another crate and began sorting through the straw used to cushion the bottles against breakage to find her bottle of wine. Urgency was required. Gatina's fingers had just grazed the neck of a bottle when she heard a crash from the wine shop's dining room. It sounded like a table had been turned over. There were loud and angry voices.

She needed to move quickly. She pulled out the first bottle and dismissed it. It didn't match Shadow's description of *twine-wrapped*. She sifted through the box and found two more bottles that did not match what she needed. Her heart was racing once again. The voices from the other room were louder. The final bottle in the box had been wedged against a corner. She realized that she needed two hands to lift it.

The twine-wrapped bottle was larger than the others in the box. Taller, at least, though narrower, with twine used to shield the delicate glass of the bottle in shipping. The label affirmed it was from Remere and had the hallmark of the vineyard stamped on the wax sealing the cork: *Tarano*.

Gatina removed it triumphantly and determined the best way to secure the precious cargo was by wrapping it inside of her discarded gown. Once that was done, she replaced her pack, tightening the straps across her chest for added security. It was then that she heard a second crash from the dining room, followed by deadly silence.

Her shadowblade was immediately in her hand. Instinct. But instead of peeking through the curtain, she turned to leave. Her business there was done. Whatever had happened there was not her concern.

Once she was back in the alley, she had planned to retrace her steps and begin her withdrawal. Instead, curiosity got the better of her. She edged around the building to the front door, keeping to the shadows, hoping to see what was happening inside.

What she saw would have been comical, had it not been terrifying. One of the debaters had the barman at the tip of his blade. And while that was not her problem, she was fascinated. She had crossed blades a handful of times with duelists. She wanted to see this man's fighting style.

However, the other patrons had seemingly had enough of the drunken trio's antics. Two men seated at different tables stood at the same time, their hands on the hilts of their own blades in a clear threat to the duelists. The companions of the two men each rushed toward the door, where the other two women had been sitting. Gatina figured that they would follow behind to avoid a fight—but instead of leaving, all four women watched with morbid fascination. The men were both taller, stronger, and older than the debater holding the barman. She watched his mates look at each other, wondering what they were going to do. It was a tense moment.

Before anything happened, the duelist lowered his blade, unwilling to strike in such a public setting. Someone was yelling that the City Watch had been called.

Gatina turned away and slunk back to the alley, almost disappointed that a fight hadn't broken out. She would have enjoyed seeing the three bullies beaten by the other gentlemen in the shop.

Unfortunately, she got to the wine shop's back door as the three duelists burst through the freshly unlocked door, stumbling, each carrying several stolen bottles of wine wrapped in a cloak.

She quickly calculated the odds of a successful fight. They had their hands full with bottles, not blades. They were clearly drunk and therefore sloppy. That made her feel better about the situation. She had not anticipated anyone leaving by the back door and chided herself for not closing it when she left and for not simply leaving once she had stolen the bottle of wine.

"Who're *you*?" one of them demanded as he peered into the darkness in surprise—the tall man who had held the wine merchant at swordpoint. Gatina cursed silently to herself and cast a shadowspell she had hung in case of a situation like this. It made her harder to perceive, and it had taken hours to prepare. But it was worth it to keep from being spotted.

"Who's *who*? What are you talking about?" a second man asked the first in confusion as he scanned the alleyway. He hadn't seen her yet, so she slunk back into the shadows to buy a few seconds' time and consider her odds. She could fight and follow the alley to the gatehouse, or she could risk the streets, where the City Watchmen were patrolling.

"Whatdayamean? Don't you *see* him?" the tall man said, pointing directly at her. Her spell had come into effect by then, but his attention was already fixed on her presence. That was bad news.

"Come on. There's nobody there. You're drunk. Time to go," the third man assured him, nervously. "We got what we came for. All Remeran reds. All with twine."

"Hope they taste as good as Bikavar," the second man slurred.

"They're not for drinking. I tell you, there's someone there!" insisted the first man, pushing his hair out of his eyes as he peered into the darkness. "Another bloody footpad!"

"You're drunk. There's no one here!" the third man said, his voice almost a whine, as he looked back and forth down the alley. "We must depart! They called the bloody Watch! Let's get out of here instead of spooking at shadows!"

A thought struck Gatina. Why were they stealing only twine-wrapped bottles of wine from Remere? How did they know that *specific* detail about the wine bottle? Before she thought better of it, she stepped forward and spoke, her voice muffled by her hood and altered by her own training. She adopted a masculine affectation and kept her shadowblade in hand behind her.

It wasn't a smart move—she had what she came for. She should have sneaked away. But she wanted to know why they were only stealing Remeran reds and—more importantly—who sent them to do so.

"He's not wrong. I'm here," she announced from the darkness. "And I want to know why you're stealing wine. You've obviously had plenty already," she said, dryly. "You've each got a full purse. So, why steal it?" Gatina had not revealed her sword yet.

"What?! Who are you?" the second man demanded. He was very much caught off guard by her presence, though it was clear he could not see her in the darkness of the alley. His hand struggled to find the hilt of his blade.

"Me? I'm nobody, just a concerned citizen. Why all the wine, good fellows?"

In response, two of them tried to draw their swords. One managed to get his blade free of its scabbard before she acted. She flicked her shadowblade to slap his dueling sword out of line.

Then several things happened at once. The one she assumed to be the leader threw his bottles to his friends—who caught them with surprising alacrity—and drew his sword and lunged at her in the shadows.

She parried his heavier blade easily. His footwork was sloppy, but she realized that he was not drunk enough to not be a threat. Gatina thrilled at the challenge now that she was in her element: in the darkness with a sword in her hand.

She dodged two more strikes he threw blindly, which allowed her to gauge his commitment and his skill. Both were strong. But he fought like a duelist, not someone who wanted to win a fight. Once she had an idea of his technique, she began to counter with strikes timed to catch him and his feet off guard, shifting angles of attack and direction. She attacked from the side and was mindful of the cargo in her pack, which sloshed every time she moved, throwing off her balance a bit.

"Bah! Who *are* you?" the man snarled as he fought in the darkness. The other two were having trouble keeping their blades and their cargo in hand as they tried to guard his flanks.

"The Kitten of Night!" she whispered as she slashed at his face. She couldn't resist, though it was breaking protocol. Thieves had professional names for professional reasons, not to spread around among their victims.

By then, the other two men had started to treat the fight in earnest, moving to try to surround her—or where they thought she was. They still stumbled, but the alley was cramped and there was only so much space between them. While all three of their swords shined in the dim light, her shadowblade had been painted matte black to keep it from doing so, making it very difficult for them to defend against. It was nearly invisible. The third man swung blindly, but the tip of his sword came uncomfortably close to her.

"Who sent you?" she demanded, as she distracted them by kicking over one of the bottles. It shattered and sent expensive Remeran red all over the filthy alley.

"*Hey!*" the second man yelled in alarm. "He's breaking the bottles! Stop that!" He swung wildly again, but Gatina sidestepped it easily and pushed over another bottle with the tip of her blade. It shattered like the first one.

But they were blocking her exit. They seemed to have her at their mercy. She was outnumbered by larger foes, but they were swinging in the darkness, while she could see them clearly enough. Gatina did not have the time to play this game. She had her mission to complete, and she'd already acquired the loot. She needed to end the fight or escape. Escape was her best option, she knew, but she couldn't bring herself to retreat. Not quite yet. But she did see a path to an exit—not through the alley but over it. Unfortunately, it was on the other side of the three bravos.

Gatina remembered the stack of empty wooden crates near the door. She scanned the alleyway with magesight and found it directly behind one of the men. Working quickly, she slipped agilely between two of the men and silently hopped on top of it, giving her an advantage in location and height. None of them even saw where she had gone.

Without hesitation, she used the pommel of her sword to hit one of the men in the back of his head, sending him sprawling. With an "oof" and a thump, he fell to the ground at the feet of his fellows. It wasn't very sportsmanlike of her, but all's fair in a rebellion, she reasoned.

Gatina quickly turned to the next nearest target. He looked around, his eyes blindly scanning the darkness for any sign of her. The remaining wine bottles were at his feet, along with his sprawling comrade. Seeing an opportunity, she sprang off the box, arching over him into a dive, knocking over another bottle as she passed. She flipped in the air and landed softly on her feet. She'd mastered that flip in the past few training sessions, and she was gratified to use it.

The duelist felt the breeze her movement brought and turned his sword to be ready. Instead of targeting him, she attacked her first target. The *clink* of her blade against his brought his companion to his side. She faced both. The third man, covered in wine and broken glass, was struggling to get to his feet.

"You never said why you need all that wine," she said as they dueled. "It looks to be about eight bottles." Gatina's training allowed her an advantage. "Are you having a party?" The swords *clang*ed and *clink*ed as she knocked away every strike at first. "Can I come?" she taunted.

"How do you... Who are you?" he demanded. "Who do you work for?"

He lunged again. She sidestepped it and blocked his friend's strike with a loud *clink*, then she pivoted and kicked the first man inside of his knee, and he buckled for a second. She danced close enough to draw blood. Her shadowblade left a narrow cut across his cheek. He cried out in pain. Instead of recoiling, he attacked again, energized, but was still having a hard time finding a target in the darkness.

Gatina knocked over another bottle of wine with enough force to splash the three of them. But she was where she wanted to be. "You don't seem like you are in a celebratory mood," she said as they cried out in dismay.

"I will be when I've ended you!" he said hotly. "Stop breaking the wine!"

"You have to find me first," Gatina said mockingly, mindful to keep her voice disguised. She had climbed the building wall and watched the two men lunge and strike at the air, until their blades *clink*ed together. "What's so special about some crappy red wine from Remere?"

The men stopped. They realized they were fighting each other. And Gatina realized the man she had knocked out was no longer on the ground.

He was standing right below her right foot. With a tug, he reached and pulled. She knew she couldn't fall to the ground and risk her own bottle smashing, nor risk getting caught. Her instincts kicked in and she planted her feet on his chest, using it to springboard from him. The poor fellow wasn't having a good day, she thought, as he fell back, gasping for air. The discovery and her landing gave the others the opportunity to circle her.

"Who sent you?" the first man demanded.

"I asked you first," Gatina reminded him, again ducking their unimaginative blows. It was clear to her that this dueling society had little experience with actual fighting. She could leave anytime now, but she wanted answers to her questions. *Why this shop? Why tonight?* It seemed odd, she thought, and far too coincidental.

Again she asked, "Who do *you* work for?" She was on the offensive until the man who wouldn't stay unconscious suddenly grabbed her arm and pulled her off-balance.

"I say you answer *our* questions!" he barked. She could smell the wine on his foul breath. She stomped a heel on the top of his arm, put her other hand over her sword hand, and rammed her elbow into his nose, which crunched with the impact.

"Godsdammit!" he swore, releasing her as his hands flew to his nose, trying to stop the blood from gushing out. She didn't wait for him to recover. That would take time. Instead, she launched herself to the nearest target, her frustration leading her blade. She was angry with herself for getting caught up in this messy distraction. It was past time to leave. She had the bottle. But curiosity won out again. She wanted answers. Did these men work for Vichetral? The Brotherhood? Some other criminal organization?

"Who do you work for?" Gatina asked. Each word was punctuated with a precise blade strike. "Tell me and nobody else gets hurt."

One of the men laughed.

"It's funny, is it? I've drawn blood twice. You have yet to land a blow. What kind of dueling society are you?" she asked, mocking them, hoping for a reaction while she continued to press them. The broken-nosed man was out of the picture. He was kneeling by the door, crying into his hands. As she moved, her foot found one of the bottles. Without thinking, she picked it up. "What's so damned special about the wine? Is it gold? Dragon's blood?" She held it with her free hand, dangling the narrow neck between her fingers over the cobbles. "Shall I smash another?"

"No!" both men said at the same time.

She smiled under her mask. "Who do you work for?"

Neither man spoke. She tossed the bottle up, her eyes on them, not it.

"No!" the first man shouted in disbelief. Gatina realized she might have leverage to use, after all. She caught it effortlessly. Part of her recent training in the House of Shadows' gymnasium included catching and throwing objects. She was quite good at it. She enjoyed lobbing balls at her brother's head. Now she was the kitten toying with the mice.

"Well?" She held the bottle above her head as if she meant to hit one of them with it. "I can do this until my arms get tired. Who. Do. You. Work. For?" Each word was punctuated with a different combination of sword and footwork. Gatina continued to attack and press her advantage. Her opponents were tired. They had been drinking. They were sloppy. They were fighting against an opponent they could not properly see. Her last strike had caught the second man in the arm. He winced. She used that time to dance closer to him, waving the bottle just within reach, taunting him. He was more concerned with the cut.

"Tell me who sent you and why the wine matters," she asked him insistently.

Hissing in pain, he looked at her, teeth clenched, clutching his wounded arm. From this distance she could smell the wine on his breath. She knew it was a risky—but calculated—move. She was poised to strike again, to draw blood a second time, when he spoke.

"I'm done with this! It was supposed to be easy! The Golden Anchors didn't say I'd get hurt," he said accusingly to his friend. "This wasn't the job I agreed to!"

"Shut up, you idiot!" his friend roared.

But she had her answer: the Golden Anchors. One of the Coastlord dueling clubs—"debating societies"—that regularly sparred against each other in the streets. Her attack had them backtracking from the pitch-black alley to the street, which would be busy with foot traffic. She would circle back down the alley, evade the third man, and make it to the promenade quickly, once they answered her second question. That would have worked . . . if it had been a simple mission. Instead, Fate delivered the City Watch.

"What's going on here?" a man bearing the golden sash of the Watch demanded when he saw the two men with their swords drawn. "My lords, have you been attacked?"

Gatina recognized the error she had made in overstaying her welcome. Instead of waiting to hear their answers, she turned and ran, prepared to defend herself against the third man or evade him entirely. But he was no longer in the alley.

She focused on her escape. The warm flood of adrenaline rushed over her body, serving as a cue to help Gatina shift her mind from the fight in the alley to a more-focused state of awareness. She saw no resistance at the end of the alley. She released the shadowspell and pushed her legs to run faster, the sharkskin soles of her boots barely making a sound. A few more feet.

Then she heard the guardsmen call after her. Their excited shouts killed their element of surprise, but Gatina could work with that. They would be looking for someone on the ground. She slowed enough that she could stop without stumbling.

She secured her blade and ran her hands along the wall of the building. She wanted to feel the surface and gauge how it was made. The smooth stones had plenty of toe- and fingerholds, she discovered, and pits where the old mortar had chipped away.

Satisfied, she began to climb. It wasn't the challenge she had hoped for, she realized, but then she banished that thought. She did not need any more challenges tonight. It was an easy climb, even with the bulky wine bottle on her back. By the time the guards had gathered at the alley's end, Gatina was already above their heads, nearly to the gatehouse and the fence. A quick glance showed her they had lit torches and were spreading out in the alley and on the main road, searching for the mysterious masked swordsman who had waylaid three innocent noblemen in the alley.

While she danced across the rooftops, she replayed the alley fight in her mind. She should not have engaged with them. If they had not been stealing bottles of wine wrapped in twine, she would not have bothered. She knew something was not right. She just hoped her instincts were wrong.

When she reached the end of the roof, she was facing the opposite street and a difficult choice. If she descended, she'd undoubtedly encounter the duelists or the Watch or both. The roof of the next building was tantalizingly near. Gatina considered her options. The alleyway was narrow, less than four feet wide. It would be an easy jump—unless she broke the precious bottle of wine. To her, it wasn't the wine that was precious. Her mission was precious. Her target was the bottle of wine, and that bottle was the thing of most value to her now. She wanted to keep it unbroken.

After a brief consideration of the different outcomes, she decided jumping might not be the wisest decision. It was the best, to keep her cargo safe. The men had not told her why they wanted to steal twine-wrapped bottles. And Shadow had not told her why that bottle was so important. Now the Watch was involved, and things were getting messy. Jumping might not be the wisest decision.

She backed up a few feet, then broke into her fastest run of the night. A quick pace was needed to gather the momentum to launch herself over the gap and keep herself in the air. The smooth and dry roof provided little drag to slow her, and for that she was gratified. Pumping her arms up and down with force also helped. The adrenaline had returned—not that it had really left; it rarely did on a mission—and it served to push her legs faster. She ran toward the edge, and before she reached it, she vaulted, her arms in front of her at chest height.

Gatina's legs continued their motion. When she landed on the other rooftop, she exhaled in a heavy but quiet *woosh*. The bottle was intact in her bag, she knew, and the other side of the roof represented enough distance from her encounter to provide some security. Other than her breathing, she made no sound as she navigated the wooden tiles of the roof. Her boots were designed to absorb and quiet noise as well as help with surface traction, which made scaling buildings easier. She didn't even bother with a rope on her descent. There was an adjacent building that was a level lower, then another. The buildings nearest the gatehouse were built like a staircase, just for her, she thought.

Gatina quickly and quietly jumped from one building to another until she reached the lowest roof. Then she climbed down. A quick glance around the corner revealed two men talking. These were not soldiers, she saw, merely two gentlemen having a discussion. Taking that as a sign from Fortune that news of her attack hadn't reached this far yet, she ran softly toward the gatehouse, mindful of the lamplight from windows and streetlamps. She should be safe now. But she did not lower her guard.

Gatina heard noises, soft at first, of men shouting and calling to each other. The closer she got to the gatehouse, the louder it grew. There was a feeling of expectation in the air. The air was heavy, like before a storm.

This had happened to her before a riot in the Warehouse District. Something was happening. Probably not something good. Instead of stopping, she pushed her legs faster, knowing that the sooner she was free of the Palace District, the safer she would be. Her heart pounded, that sense now louder than the buzz of energy. When instinct told her to wait a moment, she ducked into another alley and hid in a darkened doorway. A patrol of the City Watch marched past her hiding spot, heading toward the wine shop. She waited for a few heartbeats after they passed, then she stepped from the alley. It was past time to leave.

When she reached the gatehouse, she skirted its edge, keeping out of the light. The fence was just beyond it. If she picked the right spot, her climb would put her out onto the bridge.

Gatina rolled her shoulders, rotated her neck, and twisted her arms side to side while she evaluated the fence. It was a bit taller than she but manageable. She placed her gloved hands on the wall and began to climb. But before her boots left the ground, she sensed metal and smelled blood. Her mind screamed a warning. She didn't question it. In one smooth movement, she drew her sword and whirled around.

It was the third duelist, the one with the mustache, with his blade drawn. He hadn't seen her yet, but he surely would when she climbed the wall—that wasn't something you could overlook, even in the darkness. She used that to her advantage and launched her assault. It wasn't designed to kill the man, but it gave him a lot to think about as the shadows came alive and attacked him.

Her offensive included a series of sidesteps, striking high and low. The duelist responded reflexively, barely parrying the darkened blade as it menaced his face. The *clang*s of metal on metal were muffled by the shrubs and rose bushes that grew against the wall, thank the Darkness.

The man huffed and wheezed, still hurting from his broken nose, as he defended himself. Instead of engaging in any banter, she focused on besting him. Using the unimaginative moves that were the standard style of duelists, she pressed him back. But that took her away from the wall she needed to escape over. And that was not good.

A series of three more blows pushed him into the bramble bushes. He landed with a thud and emitted an *oof* with his landing, then a yelp at the thorns as they stabbed him. Those hurt, she knew from experience. But it gave her an opening.

She sprinted for the wall. It was a few feet away. She knew she could make it. And she almost did. She was halfway up when he grabbed at her boot to pull her down. Her sword was still in her hand. She couldn't fight him, hold on to her weapon, and climb. For the second time, she kicked the idiot hard in the face. He slumped down in a heap—finally—but the violent movement made her lose her grip on her blade. It tumbled down next to him, landing dangerously close to his already-bloody face.

"Darkness!" she swore under her breath. She could retrieve it, or she could keep going. A few more feet and she'd be over the fence.

The City Watch made up her mind for her—there were four men in their livery, bearing a lantern, entering the alley. As much as it pained her, she had to abandon her shadowblade.

She climbed, hand over hand. She was exhausted, both physically and mentally. But she pushed until she reached the top of the stone fence. There, she hoisted herself up, pressing herself flat on the fence's narrow width. She sighed tiredly and realized how uncomfortable she was with her chest smushed into the fence with the weight of a large bottle of wine on top of her. It felt extremely heavy in that position.

As she peeked over the top, she saw freedom below. The other side was empty of Watchmen, duelists, Rats, or even passerby. After a few moments, she swung her legs over to the other side of the fence to begin her descent. The bottle of wine was safely intact in her pack.

She would have words with Shadow. It was not a simple mission . . . not at all.

CHAPTER TWO

SILK AND STEEL

———◆◆———

I rarely know what my missions are accomplishing, which is frustrating. Shadow assures me that each one is important and speeds us toward our goal, but that's difficult to see sometimes. Just when I feel we have struck a decisive blow against our enemies, something else is revealed that makes it all seem pointless. Trusting in the Council and the masters is difficult sometimes. All I can do is cling to duty and tradition, knowing that eventually we will prevail.
— *from Gatina's Heist Journal*

THE TIP OF GATINA'S PRACTICE BLADE ROTATED AROUND THE CIRCUMFERENCE of the hen's egg mounted on a board with a precision born of daily practice: two hundred circles clockwise and then two hundred circles counterclockwise—every night. The goals were to keep the tip of her blade as close to the egg as possible without touching it and to go as fast as possible.

The exercise had once caused her wrists and fingers to ache painfully and had led to an embarrassing number of cracked eggs when she had first begun it under Lord Steel's direction. After more than a year of daily practice, however, her wrists no longer felt it. And she hadn't cracked an egg in months. Still, it was a daunting task that required a lot of concentration and focus. But her fencing with the dueling bravos of Falas had convinced her to redouble her efforts. The hot-headed boys she'd faced might not have been adept, but they had challenged her swordplay in ways that made her uncomfortable. She had returned to the hidden complex of tunnels and chambers her family kept and resolved to improve her skills.

"Good control," Master Steel grunted as he passed by her in the practice room. "Better than before, at least."

"I lost my shadowblade tonight," Gatina informed him, continuing the mesmerizing circles with the point of the blade without looking up. Master Steel did not tolerate "I shouldn't have done that" as an excuse.

"Swords are disposable," Master Steel dismissed. "You are not. No matter what kind of fetish the Narasi have for them, a sword is merely a tool. It was inadequate for your needs, anyway. You've outgrown it."

"You have another for me, then?" she asked, her mind silently counting the number of circles her wrist was making.

"We shall have one made to your measurements," he assured her. "A better one. One better suited to a kitten's paw. In the meantime, I have a temporary replacement in the armory."

"I can't believe I lost my blade," Gatina fumed, her jaw clenched, as she completed the two hundredth clockwise circle. She paused for a single breath before she started the exercise in the opposite direction. Master Steel smirked.

"Cat has lost three blades on his missions, now" he informed her. "And not even in combat."

Usually, such a comparison would make Gatina feel better—she and her older brother were competitive about such things. But the night's events had put her in a foul mood, despite her bringing in the looted bottle as directed, and she realized she didn't need to feel superior to Atopol. She needed to feel superior to herself.

"He was probably smart enough to avoid combat," Gatina growled as her blade went faster. "I should have been able to. There were three of them, though. Things just seemed to happen fast."

"They frequently do, in a duel," Master Steel nodded. "Against so many, it is inevitable that you will make decisions that fail. We learn from our failures; we don't wallow in them," he recited. Gatina winced. That was a common saying in his studio. "No doubt you will be replaying this episode over and over in your mind for some time to come, seeking to discover where you went wrong. That is to be expected. But to blame yourself without cause is folly."

The tip of her blade was moving so fast now that it was a blur as it rotated around the delicate eggshell. Gatina was proud of her abilities, honed over countless hours of drilling and practice there in the depths of the House of Shadows. She concluded her exercise with a flourish, whipping the practice blade up to her face in a salute before she cut the air savagely and decisively.

"Your form is improving," Master Steel admitted, grudgingly. He selected a dueling blade from the practice armory, a slender sword similar to those she'd faced in the streets. "Let's see if you can improve it further," he said as he took a classic guard position, the blade extended at her face. "Show me what you did with those bravos last night."

Gatina gave him a grim little smile and started to assume a similar posture—but then lunged at him. Master Steel's face showed no surprise as he blocked the attack and began his own.

For several heated minutes, the two combatants fell on each other furiously, the large man swinging his sword around in the style of the street duelists while Gatina danced nimbly through the net of steel he wove, her own slender blade ringing merrily as it blocked his and bit back. Unlike the foes she'd faced the night before, she knew she faced a master at his craft—and did not resort to the tricks she'd risked before. Though he was maintaining the style resolutely, his size and strength and self-assuredness would not allow for such foolishness. Master Steel would not flinch or get distracted—and would make her pay dearly for trying.

"That's it . . . higher!" he urged, as he slammed his blade down toward her head, forcing her to block with the base of her blade. "Keep your guard higher!"

"The idiots I fought were shorter than you," Gatina defended, as she whirled her blade over to strike at the right side of his body. Master Steel deftly flipped his sword down to block the attack and pushed her blade out of line. It nearly caught her off-balance, but she recovered in time to parry the next pass at her throat. But she stumbled the slightest amount as she did so, earning a rebuke from the swordmaster.

"Footwork!" he barked, and then began pressing her with a relentless attack. Gatina self-consciously regained her balance and tried to be as light and nimble as her working name suggested. It was hard—he was deceptively fast for a man of his size, and his footwork never faltered. His expression didn't change a bit as he advanced, his sword dancing around her face and shoulders with deadly speed.

But Gatina was used to this. Master Steel had tutored her in all the popular swordplay styles the dueling societies favored and had instructed her on how to overcome them. Her slender blade either blocked the blows or avoided them altogether by moving out of their path. She moved as quickly as she could from one side of his body to the other, never pausing in her attempt to strike him.

She had once feared his lessons, after she began them, for Steel was a relentless master. Gatina had exhausted herself at every lesson, leaving the session feeling incompetent and depleted after his constant stream of criticisms. But she had arrived at the armory eager for more. Despite his harsh words, she knew that she was getting to be a decent swordsman. Probably better than Atopol by now. She had come to embrace Master Steel's criticism and redouble her efforts, determined to hone herself into the best at the art.

"Good, good, never let your opponent get you face-to-face," he praised, as her aching arms pressed her attack. "Always from the sides. That gives you leave to—"

Before he could complete the sentence, Gatina dropped to the floor and somersaulted behind him, her blade tucked against her arm. She popped up behind his left shoulder, triumphantly, striking against his left side where his sword could not defend . . . until her practice blade slammed into his. He had changed hands the moment he'd seen her make the move, she realized.

"That's not something the duelists do!" she protested as she twirled out of range of his blade and took a guard position once again.

"Ordinarily, you would be correct. But you might encounter one with an original thought," Master Steel countered, shooting her a small smile behind his big sword. "The dueling societies do cling to the traditional forms, but some of them have been exposed to other styles." He lowered his blade. "But I concede that you gave an adequate account of yourself. You would have struck most of the common duelists."

"I did," she sighed, lowering her own blade. "They didn't overmatch me. They outnumbered me."

"That just provides you additional targets," he said dismissingly. "How did you lose your shadowblade?"

"It slipped out of my hand when I went over a wall," she admitted guiltily.

"Were you not wearing gloves?" Master Steel frowned.

"I was. I lost my balance. I was carrying a heavy bottle of wine on my back. That was the mission," she added before her swordmaster accused her of being a drunkard. "And . . . well, these things got in the way," she added, glancing down at her bustline. "They are throwing my balance off, even when I bind them," she complained.

"It's just as likely your growing height is to blame," he conceded with a sigh. "Your entire center of gravity is shifting," he explained. "That's only natural."

"Then it's naturally inconvenient!" Gatina huffed.

"Your mother manages to fight quite adequately," Master Steel pointed out.

"She's had more practice," Gatina defended.

"Then you need more practice," her master agreed. "Take your guard. Let's try this again. Only faster, this time."

"Ah, I love a good Remeran red," her father, Hance, said smacking his lips as he entered the armory. Gatina was taking a break after more than an hour of drills with Master Steel, rubbing her aching wrists and wishing she had time to massage the soles of her feet, which hurt far more. "They are subtler on the back of the tongue than the Bikavars we're used to. Less oaky and more acidic, with a sweetness that lingers in the aftertaste. Thanks for picking that up for me," he said, shooting a fond smile at his daughter.

"You . . . you had me risk my life for *so you could drink a bloody bottle of wine?*" Gatina scoffed in disbelief.

"It's a really good bottle of wine," Hance said defensively. "But no, it wasn't just the wine you retrieved last night," he continued, perching on a stool. "Indeed, there was a small glass vial inside that contained a message from the Ducal Court Wizard in exile," he explained. "Nine tightly rolled leaves of parchment with a coded message."

"That explains it, then," Gatina realized when she recalled the events of the previous evening.

"Explains what?" her father asked, his lavender eyes darting at her.

"When I went to retrieve the wine, it was like those duelists knew it was something special," she decided. "They had to be informed about it, somehow."

"You think they knew about it?" Hance asked, alarmed.

"It's the only explanation for how they acted," Gatina said, biting her lip. "And why there were so many Rats in the vicinity at that hour? I think someone knew about the bottle and was trying to catch whoever it was who picked it up. They mentioned Golden Anchors. That must be who sent them. I'm sure of it!" she declared.

"That's . . . disappointing," Hance said. "I don't doubt you, Kitten, but it means that we have a leak in our operation. Again," he said, shaking his head. "It was inevitable, really. I'll make an investigation. I'm glad you're all right," he added.

Gatina shrugged. "I managed. But it's clear that the Palace is starting to get on to us. We've been awfully active the last few months," she observed.

"And what does Master Thinradel report?" Master Steel asked curiously.

"A great number of interesting things," Hance answered. "He's still lurking around this spellmonger fellow off in Castal, keeping an eye on things there. He reports that the Orphan Duke is chafing at his captivity and has secured at least a certain amount of freedom from his uncle, after enduring an abysmal tournament season in Gilmora. His sisters are likewise safe and protected at an abbey in Castal. More importantly," he added, "he reports some rumors that Duke Anguin has begun to gather some political support in exile—from some unlikely directions."

"So, he might come back to Alshar?" Gatina asked hopefully. Duke Anguin was the rightful sovereign of the duchy, not Count Vichetral. Vichetral claimed that the so-called King of Castalshar—a horrid name!—Rard of Castal, had essentially forced Anguin to agree to the treaty that united three duchies under his supposed crown in order to be recognized as the legitimate Duke of Alshar. Things were getting so bad in Alshar now under the Five Counts that she was certain that the people would rise if Anguin suddenly appeared there.

"Not yet," her father admitted. "Master Thinradel has been quietly encouraging the expatriate Alshari in Castal to rally to support Anguin, should he be able to win himself free of captivity. But he is still far too reliant on Duke Rard—sorry, 'King Rard'—for support, himself. And Rard shows little interest in us. He's too busy preening on his new throne," Hance said, derisively.

"But there's hope," Gatina encouraged. She thought of how poorly things had gone for the people of Alshar in the last few years. Vichetral had invited the Royal Censorate of Magic to Alshar to help enforce his brutal rule—the checkered-cloaked warmagi were now inhabiting the Tower of Sorcery, just a few miles away. He'd legalized slavery, and now there were markets of human beings, captured mariners and tribals taken from the southern islands by force, where they were sold at auction to shipyards, orchards, and manor farms across the duchy.

That had led to thousands of commoners being left jobless and had depressed the cost of work damnably across the duchy. Taxes had risen as the Council of Counts—of whom Vichetral was the only permanent member—issued "emergency edicts," supposedly to counter anti-Alshari activities across the duchy. The Count of Rhemes was pillaging what was left of the Ducal Treasury, she knew, and was inventing new ways to enrich his coffers.

Hance sighed. "Hope. Yes, Kitten, there is always hope. But Anguin alone is not enough to topple Vichetral and his cronies. The count enjoys the support of too many Great Houses who chafed under his father's reforms . . . and who are profiting too much under Vichetral's regime to take Anguin's restoration seriously. Still," Hance continued, tossing his head to throw a shock of white hair out of his eyes, "Anguin represents hope to us. But he is still under King Rard's 'protection.' It may well be up to us rebels against Vichetral who have to persuade him to return to Falas. And that is something the Count of Rhemes will resist with arms, if need be. We would prefer to avoid a civil war," he reminded her.

"So, we keep being spies and saboteurs instead of just honest thieves!" Gatina huffed, discouraged.

"We knew it would take years, Kitten," her father reminded her gently. "A true insurrection takes time, energy, and money if it is to be successful. And sadly, Count Vichetral has the support of too many Great Houses for one to succeed just yet. But . . . among Master Thinradel's suggestions for action are some insightful bits of gossip that could well advance our cause."

"Such as?" Master Steel asked, skeptically. The swordmaster hated Count Vichetral and his pretend council with a passion, Gatina knew. Still, he was a pragmatist.

"The most pressing issue he presents is the disposition of the Sea Lords," Hance admitted, after a moment's thoughtful pause.

"The Sea Lords?" Steel asked, suspiciously.

"Yes. More than two-thirds favor Vichetral's policies," Hance explained. "But certain houses revile the practice of taking slaves. Many more are uneasy with it, for various historical and economic reasons. Others are unhappy about being cut off from trade with Farise and Remere. Thinradel suggests that we try to improve that number and makes several suggestions about how we do so. He has admirable intelligence on them, it seems. In his letter, he identified a few that may be most easily moved into our camp—even to help us actively."

"How could the Sea Lords help?" Steel asked disdainfully.

Gatina sighed. She might be just a girl, but even she understood how powerful the ancient houses of Sea Lords were in Alshar. They had founded the duchy, so to speak, long before it had been a duchy. It had been the Cormeeran-based mariners who'd discovered and exploited the protected havens of the Great Bay of Enultramar, using the far-western ports first as winter refuges from the navy of the Imperial Magocracy and then forming permanent settlements along the coastline. Long before her people had come there, the Sea Lords had ruled the waves of Alshar.

Now they composed the greatest share of the vast Alshari merchant navy that plied the seas from there to Vore, and across the Shattered Sea to the Shattered Isles and beyond. They departed eastward with cargoes of Alshari wines, olive oils, and other luxuries and brought back plenty of exotic fare to Enultramar's far-flung markets.

She had learned that they were responsible for the affluence Alshar enjoyed—and were therefore extremely important to the economy and political power of the duchy. Count Vichetral had courted them accordingly. One of the other four rotating seats on his illegal council was always occupied by one of the Sea Lord counts, she'd learned. If the Shadow Council could convert just a few of their Great Houses to their side, it would be a step closer to victory.

"They are our best option right now, cousin," Hance admitted to Master Steel. "I am not betraying any secrets when I tell you that our conspiracy is in its infancy, with no promise that it will be successful eventually. We have made a start among the Coastlords and the magi and have found other allies as we expand our reach, but we are far, *far* from removing Vichetral. Having the allegiance of some Sea Lord houses could prove instrumental."

"As if mariners and galley slaves could fight on land!" scoffed her swordmaster through his thick, bushy beard.

"It is not their blades I seek," Hance informed him, standing from the stool. "It is their influence, their purses, their keen eyes, and their sharp wits that I need. And their ships most of all. They can escape this place and visit the rest of the Five Duchies in a way that the rest of us cannot," he reminded them. "That could well prove instrumental to our ultimate goals."

"They're a bunch of drunken, conniving, uncultured mercenaries," Master Steel pronounced darkly.

"Which we need," Hance repeated, patiently. "Nor are all of them so . . . uncivilized. We have certain familial connections that may help position us to make an alliance," he proposed. "Thinradel was quite thorough in his suggestion, including the names and positions of those who are most likely to lend us a friendly ear. And some intriguing advice about how best to influence them. I plan on presenting the matter to the full Council when we next meet."

"Familial connections," grunted Master Steel skeptically.

"Not all of our houses were so reluctant to mix with Vale Lords and Sea Lords," Hance reminded Steel stiffly.

"You're talking about . . . *her*, aren't you!" accused the swordmaster.

"She's our kin," Hance said sternly. "She's family. Perhaps distant, but she's loyal to her house. And she is quite useful," her father stressed. "More now than ever before."

Master Steel was silent, but Gatina could tell that there was a whirl of emotion behind his usually stonelike face. She realized that there had to be some story there.

"So be it," he finally said with a shrug of his great shoulders. "But you know Lady Mist will not be happy about it."

There was something in the way her swordmaster spoke that implied a history she was not aware of, some story that he seemed reluctant to even speak about. That was unusual. Steel was one of the most stalwart people she knew, as unbending and strong as his professional name. It was unusual to see him troubled by anything.

"I didn't expect she would be," Hance sighed. "But I get along with her. And it's important for the cause," he reminded his cousin. "Believe me, Lady Night won't be particularly pleased, either. She gets seasick sometimes."

Steel gave a surprised snort. "You're going to do this yourself?" he asked.

"It will be a good excursion," Hance agreed. "Besides, Falas is getting a little warm for us right now, as Kitten pointed out. A few weeks by the seaside will do us some good. A little sailing, a little meeting with old family connections by the shore sounds like a lovely way to spend the summer."

"Falas does get humid in the summer," Steel agreed reluctantly.

"Besides, it's time the Cats learn about their distant kin," Hance suggested, as he paced in front of Gatina. "Learn the ways of the Sea Lords and the things you need to know to steal from them. And take their guise. They are, indeed, important to Alshar, as important as the Vale Lords and more than the Wilderlords. It will be an excellent opportunity to introduce you to sailing, as well," he added.

"Sailing?" came her brother's voice from the doorway, as if he had been summoned. Atopol was still dressed in his own working blacks, a shadow among the shadows in the corridor. "We're going sailing?" he asked, doubtfully.

"So it appears—if we get the Council's blessing. Darkness, we might do it if we don't," Hance decided. "Any problems?"

"What was he doing?" asked Gatina, confused.

"Not anything I couldn't contend with. And I was cleaning up my sister's messes . . . again." Atopol shrugged as he threw back his cloak. He knelt and presented something to Gatina with the grace of a courtier. It was a mocking gesture, of course. "Your shadowblade, o Kitten of Night!" he proclaimed. "You seem to have misplaced it. Next time, use the lanyard," he chided.

Gatina stared at the battered blade in embarrassment. It was bent, she could see. She remembered it falling from her hand as she scaled the wall, and how stupid she felt about not using the cord attached to its hilt for security. That was unprofessional. And being suddenly reminded of that in front of both her swordmaster and her master at the art of shadowthieving was . . . *humiliating*.

"I think you likely need a new blade, Kitten," her father pointed out unnecessarily, in a gentle voice.

"We've already discussed it," Master Steel assured him. "I will visit the swordsmith tomorrow."

"Don't worry; I've lost two blades already," Atopol assured her in a whisper.

"Three," Gatina corrected, in the same stage whisper.

"Are we really going to sea?" he asked his father, ignoring Gatina's dig.

"We really are," agreed Hance. "Our kinfolk keep our family sloop at one of the havens along the Great Bay. It's time you made their acquaintance. And learned some seamanship."

"It's part of our plan to convince some Sea Lords to join the conspiracy," Gatina revealed. "I'll explain later."

"No, I shall explain to Cat what he needs to know," Hance said, firmly. "You are being all too free with intelligence once again, Kitten. What you do not know—"

"You cannot tell," groaned Gatina. It was an axiom that both her parents had emphasized forcefully to her over the last few years of her training as an apprentice shadowthief of House Furtius. It was in the family's secret texts, written by their storied founder, Kiera the Great. But it was no less bothersome.

But it was true, she knew. Keeping secrets kept people alive—herself included, she reminded herself.

"In the meantime," Master Steel said as he approached the wide variety of practice weapons in the armory, "perhaps it's time to introduce the Cats of Enultramar to the art of fighting with the Sea Lords' chosen blade—the mariner's scimitar. Sometimes called a *cutlass*," he said, selecting a short, heavy, curved blade from the rack. "I think you will find it . . . *instructive*."

CHAPTER THREE
THE SHADOW COUNCIL

Misdirection is as important a tool as obscurity, when on a heist or in a debate.
—Proverb of House Furtius

GATINA MET HER FATHER NEAR THE BROKEN FOUNTAIN SHE HAD BECOME SO familiar with, the one closest to her favorite safe house, a nearby orphanage dedicated to Trygg All-Mother. Hance had purchased pies from the baker whose cart bought her the time she had needed to evade the Rats a few days before.

Hance looked nothing like he usually did, of course. He was wearing a white shirt, blue tunic, and brown hose along with a shockingly black wig that matched her own. His eyes, like hers, were a magically enhanced blue. He'd been out of the city for a few days since she'd returned from her mission to the wineshop, no doubt sharing the information with his secret contacts across the duchy.

"Ah, my lady, I have brought you luncheon," Hance said as he handed her a pie full of potatoes, sausage, and cheese. "It's savory, not sweet, Kitten," he added in a warning whisper. "I see that you benefited from your mother's shopping trip," he said, a little louder. "We match today."

She smiled and nodded. Mother had commissioned her several new dresses from a seamstress who had connections to the family, as Gatina had outgrown the gowns she'd worn just six months before. The one she wore was made from a much more breathable Gilmoran cotton, far more comfortable in the rising heat and humidity of a Falas summer. The bodice was not nearly as tight as was fashionable, but she didn't mind. It matched her father's blue tunic so perfectly it might have been made from the same bolt of cloth.

"Yes, Father. And new shoes as well. Though I must say that I prefer my flat shoes to these monstrosities." She lifted the hem of her gown and wiggled her right foot to show him the footwear. "These shoes are awful. They hurt my feet. You simply cannot run in them. The heel is nearly an inch high! It's like wearing riding boots!" she complained.

Hance laughed. "I'm fairly certain that function was not a consideration in the design of those shoes, Gatina. They are for style, not comfort. Ladies of good breeding are not supposed to run."

He guided her through the chaotic and loud Market Day crowd away from the Warehouse District. Merchants were yelling to ramp up interest in their wares to the largely illiterate crowds. Their carts were parked so close together that it was hard to maneuver, and the competing shouts began to ring in Gatina's ears as she bit into the pie.

Her father looked around at the busy market. "Shall we be on our way? It's a bit loud here," he said as if he had read her mind.

"Where are we headed?" she asked between bites.

"We have a meeting in the darkness," he informed her lightly. "I have news."

She was happy to walk with her father and to have a bit of time alone with him. It had been ages since they had been out and about in daylight, and she welcomed the interlude. Gatina hoped the coming days and weeks would bring more togetherness on their next mission, but she figured that on a ship, there would be limited opportunities for walks.

Gatina and her father took the leisurely route toward the grand Temple of Trygg, his longer legs constantly outpacing her, forcing him to slow. Once her feet adjusted to the shoes, she was able to keep pace with him. She realized they would take the entrance hidden in the dressmaker's shop owned by a cousin down to their family's hidden lair underneath Falas. She had taken that route her first time, with her mother. It was one of at least seven entrances to the hidden mansion she knew about, and one of the more accessible when she was in disguise. No one questioned why a girl would be going into a dress shop with her father.

Her great-grandfather had built the House of Shadows during the Black Duke's reign when the Shadow Council had last been active to clandestinely curtail the violent monarch's policies. Over the years, House Furtius had expanded it, and it now extended in several directions under the city. All seven of the main entrances were hidden, and only one had been shared with the other Councilmembers. Even so, accessing that entrance required that the chosen Councilmember know the ciphers and meanings that decorated the doorframe and provided instruction on how to open the passageway to the Council chambers.

That was, of course, by design. She was intimately familiar with the long-standing rule of House Furtius that you couldn't tell what you didn't know. The less that outsiders knew about the underground fortress, the better.

As she followed her father, she wondered how large the safe house was. She had only explored a tithe of it, and Atopol had said he had once gotten lost in it. She knew it contained the majority of the family's weapons and costumes they used for heists around Falas. And there were secret chambers that were a treasury of family secrets. Mother had said as much.

The passageway behind the hidden door was dark, but both shadowthieves were able to use their magesight to navigate in the gloom. She was fascinated by the House of Shadows. When they arrived at the door to the family's antechamber, where they donned their black robes and masks, she decided that someday, she would explore it all. It was an important part of her family's legacy, after all.

Gatina's new robe, like her father's garb, was made of that same matte-black material as their working blacks. Her mask was white and shaped like a kitten's face. The only part of her face left uncovered was her mouth, which she appreciated. It unnerved her, a bit, to see her father's face vanish under his mask and cowl. His was designed to cover his entire face and make him appear like a shadow, which was, of course, fitting, if uncomfortable and inconvenient. But such measures were required to keep the tight security the conspiracy demanded.

This, at least, was an assignment she had become accustomed to. She had been tasked with representing House Furtius with Hance, known within the secret Council as Lord Shadow, while her mother and Atopol undertook other assignments on the family's agenda. Mostly, that just meant standing behind him and looking formidable, occasionally running errands or bearing messages. Gatina was gratified to join her father this time. She wanted to be present to answer any questions about her mission to retrieve the bottle of wine, if they came up. She had firsthand information—and suspicions—about the goings-on in the Palace District with the debating societies.

The chamber was smaller than she remembered. That first time she had been there, two years before, it had seemed cavernous. Everything had seemed larger then, even Lord Hound, the Council's master-at-arms.

When she first met him, he was larger than life. His voice was still enthusiastic under his dog-shaped mask, but she could tell that the council's slow-moving progress had taken a toll on him. He was, of course, grayer and older, but he seemed more tired, somehow, she realized. Then again, all of them were tired from the drawn-out struggles against the Council of Counts.

It wasn't just Lord Hound. After almost three years of action, the rebellion had affected the entire Council. And, she knew, leaders often shoulder the burden of leadership differently. Her father, Shadow himself, now had lines around his eyes, small but visible, that hadn't been there before. She suspected that the tension associated with leading the Shadow Council was aging him prematurely. His hair, of course, when natural, was still that same white that was distinctive to her family, but it looked more silver around his temples.

Gatina stood behind her father as the members of the Council filed into the windowless room deep beneath the city. This was where the representatives from a few noble Houses, mostly Coastlords descended from the nobility of the Magocracy, had met and agreed, despite their differences, to unite against the usurper Vichetral and his fellow counts. Things had gone well at first. At the Council's inaugural meeting, arranged by her parents through coded messages sent to the oldest—and wealthiest—of Alshar's magical families who had long connections to Duke Lenguin, his death was fresh on their minds, and their outrage at Vichetral's power grab was strong. Everyone had seemed optimistic and enthusiastic back then.

Now she recognized that some of those members had been merely opportunistic, as well as overly optimistic about their chances of overturning the rebel government. The conspiracy had not seen much in the way of the desired results—yet. They were committed to the cause. Inevitably, some of the Council's members had become frustrated by the slowness of the progress, and she feared their commitments were waning.

She understood that sentiment. When this had begun, she did not realize how long it would take to rid the duchy of Vichetral. She had thought her parents would have it wrapped up by Yule. Back then, she was younger, untested, and very idealistic. While she clung to her ideals, she was a bit more battle-tested and wiser now, she thought. Overthrowing a government that was determined to rule in tyranny was far easier to talk about than to do. There had been losses. There had been traitors. There had been failures that had cost lives.

Yet, since the initial meeting, the Council of Shadows had grown in number, thank the gods. The recruiting efforts had been dramatically helped by the arrival of the hated Censors working for Vichetral two years earlier. The Censors had managed to use magic to track a few of their operations, trace their agents, and even foil a few plots. Imprisonment, torture, and execution had resulted, with a mere accusation sufficing to send innocent people to the dungeons of the palace. After that, a number of magelords and their families had suddenly seen the benefit of resisting the Council of Counts.

Of course, the arrival of the Censors had also complicated things. Before the checkered cloaks' arrival, contacting the older Houses had been a more-straightforward process: a coded message was sent by courier, someone familiar with the members of the chosen House. An invitation was extended, along with instructions about where and when to meet.

Each House had sent one representative—except for House Furtius. Only her father knew all the other councilmembers' true identities, by design. In addition, every member of the Council of Shadows used a code name and a mask for their meetings. Safety and secrecy demanded it, as did tradition. That dedication to secrecy had been rewarded when they saw Houses turn against their conspiracy and attempt to sell themselves out to the Council of Counts. Not one of the members of the Council of Shadows knew which details the turncoats had shared with the Censors, but their operations had suffered as a result. Traitors had been punished. In the Shadow Council, treachery was not tolerated.

The strain of organizing and maintaining the security of the Council was telling on her father. He had been trained as a shadowthief, not a revolutionary. There, in this place, he was Lord Shadow, head of the Council, mysterious leader and ultimate arbiter of the effort. Men lived and died on Shadow's order. Just as she was Kitten, agent of the Council, not Gatina anna Furtius or any number of other aliases.

Still, she couldn't fathom the thought of yet more traitors inside their Council. Previous turncloaks had faced the fierce retribution of the Shadow Council. Her parents had not told her what the punishment for such treachery was, but she had her suspicions. She did not want to think that her father—or her mother—could deliver such a severe punishment, but oaths had been sworn. Action had been taken. She didn't know by whom, and she did not want to know.

Once the Councilmembers had been seated, Lord Shadow welcomed them.

"I have news from our friend in Castal that I must share," he began. "It came in a bottle of incredibly good Remeran red, through a very convoluted channel to escape interception. Our former Court Wizard has some intriguing ideas about how to expand our efforts, as well as a warning..."

As her father provided an update on Anguin and his young sisters, she watched the members who were present. They were masked, so she could not read their facial expressions, but she could feel their emotions by how they sat, how they paid attention, even how they fidgeted. When they arrived, everyone had been nervous. Now a sense of relief washed over each of them. That had to be a good sign, she thought. If they were happy to hear about the heir and his sisters, then they must be true to the cause, she reasoned.

"I fear we have once again managed to attract attention to our conspiracy, my friends," Lord Shadow said, when he was done with the update. "As you know, Master Thinradel finds unusual channels for the delivery of his messages," he said. He paused when the other Councilmembers murmured agreement. "As I mentioned, for our most recent communication, he sent us a message in a bottle of red wine. When one of our agents was tasked to retrieve it, she was attacked by duelists operating under the Golden Anchor Debating Society. A well-known pawn of the palace, and Vichetral's spymasters."

Shadow paused again, this time for the gasps of surprise and nods of sympathy. Falas had been awash in the brash dueling societies for years now. She had learned that they had originally begun many years before as legitimate debating societies among the great abbey schools and colleges where the nobility educated their young men. When tempers flared between them, they took up the sword and worked out their philosophical differences with steel, sometimes permanently. Then they evolved into actual gangs and killed each other—and the occasional bystander—with their violent duels.

Duke Lenguin had banned and suppressed them during his reign, but Vichetral had lifted that ban at the beginning of his regime. Now they were proud young aristocrats, often without much expectation of inheritance, strutting around the capital and terrorizing the citizens with the tacit approval of Count Vichetral. They had been a persistent menace among the clergy, merchants, and the lesser nobility, worse than the Brotherhood of the Rat, sometimes.

"Of course, she defeated them handily and escaped with the message intact," Shadow continued, giving her a nod, "but they appeared to have been directed to intercept the message. The Golden Anchors work at the direction of the palace. That means they are aware of our methods, which means they had some knowledge of them, which means our security has been compromised, somehow. I am concerned that we have another internal problem."

Lord Hound pounded a meaty fist on the desk in frustration, his lips curling under his mask.

"Not another one, Shadow! I grow weary of untrustworthiness among our comrades," the Master at Arms growled. "This needs to be investigated! Master Thinradel is a trusted guide to our Council, and any communication by him is critical. I assure you; we will find out who and—"

"I trust you will, Lord Hound, which is why I bring it to your attention," Shadow interrupted smoothly. "Due to the nature of the message, we must also consider magic could be at play."

"Since the Censorate came in force, we've certainly been victim of that," Lady Wren conceded with a sniff. "We have warded our strongholds and chambers as strongly as we dare, but magic is a subtle thing."

"We must explore both possibilities," agreed Lord Hound. "I suggest we abate some of our operations until we determine the nature of the leak: arcane or mundane."

"It might also warrant a more-vigorous response on the streets." Shadow suggested. "Your fellows should enjoy that." Gatina was aware that Lord Hound was a military man, perhaps a warmage, who controlled several cells of men willing to do violence in the service of the cause. She'd worked with them occasionally. Some of them were quite belligerent. "In any case, the message was retrieved. But I agree; we have been too active in the capital of late and might want to consider relocating operations out to the provinces again. It might be wise to avoid attention, at least in Falas, for a few weeks or a month and let the Censors chase normal shadows for a while."

"I have no objection." Lady Wren shrugged. "I can scry from anywhere. It's almost the muggy season in Falas," she said distastefully.

"It's best to confuse them rather than flee from them or fight them," Lord Ox agreed. He was in charge of revenue and funding for the Council and its operations. That involved all sorts of shady dealings that kept their efforts from being discovered. "The last thing I need is to arouse suspicions and earn an audit. I can shut down most of my operations for a season or so and go on holiday. I hear the theater in Inmar has gotten quite good."

"A summer away at my country estates would provide cover for one or two things I've been working on," agreed Lady Hawk, smiling under her feathered mask. There were nods of agreement from all around the table.

"Perhaps, then, it's best that we all take the summer to see to our own affairs and work on recruitment, gathering intelligence, and raising funds for the effort," Shadow suggested. "It would give us time to regroup, reflect, and investigate this breach of our secrets."

The others quickly agreed. After a couple of years of fighting, stealing, spying, and skulking, a holiday seemed a welcome idea.

"Now to the next item," Shadow announced coolly. "Consideration of Minalan the Spellmonger as a potential ally."

An angry murmur broke out around the table. That was a name that they had been hearing more and more over the last two years, Gatina knew. The wizard who had helped put Rard on his crooked throne had produced a host of rumors and news lately. He was a sinister figure, but he also had his admirers in Alshar.

"I don't make this suggestion lightly. Master Thinradel seems very much aware of everything that is happening here in Alshar. To be truthful, it's uncanny how aware he is. I have not yet ascertained how he knows as much as he does, other than through his acquaintance with Minalan the Spellmonger."

"This Minalan, he's from the Wilderlands, isn't he?" Lord Trout asked curiously.

"He's Castali, originally," Shadow answered. "He holds a fiefdom in northern Castal now and styles himself a magelord, according to Thinradel."

"Magelord?" sneered Lady Wren. "How pretentious! There haven't been magelords since the fall of the Magocracy! The Narasi forbid it!"

"Now they allow it," Lady Hawk pointed out. "That might be one reason Master Thinradel suggests this course of action. Despite all of the wicked things people say about this spellmonger, he has done well by the magi," she admitted grudgingly.

"This Minalan fellow is no longer just the spellmonger with irionite," he said. "He has been ennobled by Rard, with more than a score of his fellows, and been granted lands—real lands, in his own name—by the new kingdom. More, Thinradel says that Rard has entrusted him to regulate magic within his frontiers in the name of the so-called king."

"He sounds dangerous," Lady Wren said, tilting her head.

"He sounds ambitious," Shadow corrected. "Now that he has King Rard's ear, it seems he has positioned or appointed himself as the voice of all wizards. It was he who was responsible for overthrowing the Censorate and expelling them from Castal and Remere, which is why they're inflicted on us. And he is apparently friendly with young Anguin. That should be taken into consideration," he proposed.

"He was associated with the assassination of Duke Lenguin," reminded Lady Hawk darkly.

"Associated with, not responsible for," Shadow corrected. "Master Thinradel made that quite clear. Indeed, from what Thinradel writes, he was appalled at Lenguin's death under the circumstances."

"He works for Duke Rard," Lord Bull said condemningly, the first time the big man had spoken. Despite his great girth and stature, Gatina knew he was a mage who hailed from the Great Vale in the northern uplands. She suspected he was Narasi. "He is advising him on magical affairs. How can we possibly trust him?"

"At least someone is," mused Lady Wren, a relative newcomer to the Council. She was younger than most representatives and had apparently come from a house of magelords. "We are not unaware of this Spellmonger. He has apparently distributed irionite among many wizards now. He is not hoarding it for himself. Our kin in Castal are quite pleased with him," she reluctantly admitted.

That produced a wave of murmuring and exclamations that told Gatina that this spellmonger was becoming an increasingly important figure. She had always considered him somewhat sinister, but apparently, Master Thinradel had another perspective.

Shadow raised his hands to quell any further interruptions. "Let me elaborate, my friends. From what Master Thinradel has written, this young man is charismatic but seems more to be in the right place at the right—or wrong—time, depending on how you look at it. We have a file on him now.

"It seems that he was in the Wilderlands when the gurvani uprising began and organized a stiff resistance. That is where he ended up after he was conscripted into service as a warmage in the Farisian campaign.

Thinradel says he personally petitioned the Dukes of Alshar and Castal to unite to stop the invasion. I am not saying he's trustworthy. He is not from a noble family—and he's Narasi." That produced a few scowls around the table. The Council was made up of Coastlords, primarily, or those closely allied with them. The Narasi were still viewed as uncultured newcomers by these ancient houses after more than three hundred years.

"But by all accounts, he saved thousands of lives and spared Gilmora a goblin invasion," he continued, his voice even and devoid of emotion. "He behaved honorably and continues to do so as Rard's advisor. And Thinradel speaks highly of him."

Lord Hound interrupted, his deep voice commanding everyone's attention. "You said he was trained as a warmage in Farise? So, he's a military man. I was on that campaign, as an aide to Loiko Venaren. There were many good Sparks who fought there," he considered. "That was a terrible time. It takes guts to assault the citadel of the Mad Mage of Farise. That speaks of a good bit of training and experience, even if he was not brought up a mage properly," he said with admiration.

"I do like a wizard in uniform." Lady Wren smiled.

"So, he is dangerous," concluded Lady Hawk with a sniff.

"He's powerful, ambitious, and rising in stature in this new Royal Court," Lord Bull said. "We, too, have heard of him. "He has a reputation as an idealist. He was trained in Imperial magic at Inarion Academy, where I have kinfolk teaching. Unremarkable student, I've heard."

"Any idea what his marks were?" Lady Hawk asked skeptically.

"Who cares what his marks were? He's bloody remarkable now if he has irionite," Lady Wren said. "That's been illegal for centuries, thanks to the Censorate. No wonder he had them expelled!"

Gatina had heard of the near-mythical irionite—a type of green amber that could somehow increase a wizard's powers tenfold or more. She had often wondered what that would be like. She enjoyed magic and was good at it, but irionite was supposed to make it quicker, more powerful, and better, somehow. It made the spellmonger more intriguing in her mind.

"If he's an idealist and a reformer, and a friend to the Orphan Duke, then he might be sympathetic to our cause," Lord Bull advocated in slow, ponderous tones. "He would make a powerful ally where we have few."

"His loyalty is still in question," countered Lady Hawk. "He might be friends with Anguin. That doesn't mean he will take up the cause of restoring him to his throne. That would put him at odds with Rard. *King* Rard." She sniffed, shaking her head. "As if we need a king!"

"Master Thinradel is still observing and guiding this spellmonger," reasoned Lord Trout. "Thinradel has shared his thoughts about how we might best help Anguin. It seems the Castali have taken to calling him the 'Orphan Duke,' and that seems to have helped create a shroud of mystery, sympathy, and even pity around him in the Castali and Remeran courts. That vision of him as an orphan, deprived of his legacy, has led to sympathy in unlikely places, as Thinradel indicated," he pointed out.

"But you can also tell the character of a man by the quality of the enemies he attracts," the portly man observed. "This spellmonger fellow has been targeted by Grendine and her yellow roses once already, from what I understand. He does not enjoy *her* favor," he said euphemistically.

Gatina looked at Lord Hound, wondering if he would hit the table again. Duchess Grendine—now the queen—had grown up in this very city, the sister of the late Duke. She had not been well liked by the court, by all accounts, and when she had left for Castal, she had become obsessed with ruling her home duchy from afar, often through assassination. She was still hated with a bitter passion by many on the Shadow Council. Indeed, holding Grendine as an enemy had united the Council in times when little else had. She was rumored to have a network of spies and assassins, and the yellow rose was her symbol.

"Well, he can't be all bad, then," Lord Hound conceded, with a sigh. "We can consider the matter. But it is not yet settled," Lord Hound declared to a chorus of nods and murmurs of assent.

The next item of discussion Lord Shadow proposed was the matter of the occupation of the Tower Arcane by the Censors. The traditional residence of the Ducal Court Wizard was only a few miles away, and it had been granted by the Council of Counts to the Censors for their headquarters. It had become a nuisance, a magical fortress inside the walls of Falas filled with the Shadow Council's enemies. Gatina hated even walking by the place. Having Censors this close to the Shadow Council's headquarters was risky, but they had navigated it thus far. Lord Hound's concerns were around safety and security.

"We are watching the place, day and night," Lord Hound reported. "Our best Sparks are on the job, seeing who comes and goes so that we might guess their plans. I have requested reinforcements here. However, my men want to attack the Censors at the Tower Arcane. They are angered by its occupation, as I'm sure all of you understand," he said. "They are eager to strike a blow."

Gatina was familiar with that situation. She had heard her parents discuss it with Lord Steel and Lady Mist, her magical-arts tutor, a number of times over wine. None of them were happy about it. Seeing the checkered cloaks come in and out of what was supposed to be a hallowed institution was infuriating. After a few cups, Lord Steel always seemed to be of the opinion that attacking might be an enjoyable way for him to alleviate his frustrations. That was usually when Lady Mist coaxed the cup from his hand and spoke of the virtue of patience.

Gatina and Atopol had discussed the value in both methods—privately, of course. It was an insult to Alshar's mages to see the Censors in the Tower, which had been used by the Duke's court wizard and, at one time long ago, by the dukes themselves. As King Rard had nullified the Bans on Magic, Count Vichetral offered these men a haven if they agreed to enforce order on his behalf. And the Censors had embraced their role as enforcers, she knew. She had heard the stories, and she had had her own run-ins with the zealots, which is how she thought of them.

"Would such action not show our hand?" asked Lady Hawk worriedly.

Lord Hound continued. "There is no reason for them to suspect warmagi are involved in the conspiracy. For all they know, most of the warmagi have opted to seek their fortunes in Castal, following several well-known mages, including my old comrade Azar," he explained. "So far, my people have been discreet here in Falas and the other cities and villages. But I caution you, they are increasingly unhappy about this situation."

"It would complicate things," Lord Shadow argued. "We are already struggling to operate in Falas—that's why we're adjourning for the summer."

"It would demonstrate our resolve," Lord Hound argued.

"It also adds pressure on us to act. But with no better goal in mind but to eliminate the Censors, we would expose ourselves to Vichetral's attention where we simply cannot bear it, right now.

"Let us conserve our strength—and watch them. We learn more from their operations—and the Council of Five—with them not suspecting us. If we can manage to stay a step ahead of them, we benefit. If we let them know we are a serious threat, they will treat us accordingly," he argued. "Don't worry, my friend; at the appropriate time, we will drive them from the Tower Arcane. But not until we are fully prepared for the consequences."

Lord Hound heaved a great sigh. "Agreed. We know not what devilry they're hiding within the tower, anyway."

Lord Shadow nodded with satisfaction. "Lastly, Master Thinradel has encouraged this Council to consider seeking support and alliance from an unlikely source," he paused, "among the Great Houses of the Sea Lords."

Lady Gull, the Council's archivist, gasped. She quickly got her emotions under control and continued to write her notes, written in code in a wispy, flowing hand. The other councilmembers did not appear to be surprised or upset. Lady Gull was associated somehow with the Sea Lords, Gatina remembered. But she wasn't aware of the specifics of the relationship.

"Yes, I felt the same way when I read the message," Shadow said, with a nod. "Ever since Baron Jenerard returned from the north as Master of the Waves, he has sought to make policy on this front. He advocates for the slave trade."

"And the Sea Lords have been in favor of it!" snapped Lady Gull.

"Not all of them," Shadow reminded her. "Just a few of the major houses who are friendly with Jenerard. We know that about two-thirds of the Sea Lords favor Vichetral's new policies. But what of the one-third that doesn't?" He paused, watching for reactions. "Of that third, there certainly are Houses that do not support slaving or piracy. And they certainly do not wish for trade to remain hindered as Vichetral has contrived."

"The Sea Lords keep to themselves, in their own society," Lord Bull said, shaking his head. "They are not to be trusted."

"Perhaps some of them are," Shadow argued. "Thinradel has some very specific suggestions of just whom to contact," he said, tapping the parchment in front of him. "He has discovered some houses that are particularly eager to see Anguin retake his father's throne and suggests some particular means by which we could woo them into an alliance that would be helpful to both and beneficial to our long-term priorities. Shall we discuss it?" Shadow asked, gesturing to the council with a wave of his hand.

Lady Gull stood to speak, her bones almost creaking audibly as she did so. "Thank you, Lord Shadow. What I have to report connects to what you've just said about . . . slaving." Her voice was strong and her tone measured, Gatina noted. She seemed to be passionate about what she was going to share but would not let her emotions take control.

"As you know, my House has some certain interests in maritime shipping," she continued. "We deal with Coastlords, Sea Lords, and foreign enterprises in the conduct of our business. We meet all *sorts* of people," she said, her voice hinting how disreputable some of those people might be. "I am always wary of dealing with the Sea Lords, as their customs are severe and their loyalties are often for sale—if they extend beyond their own companies to begin with. You must always be on your guard with them, especially about politics. If we approach them with a serious offer, we must be prepared for treachery," she warned.

"It would be a boon for them to just control the Brotherhood of the Rat—they are kin." Lady Wren sniffed disdainfully.

"Nay, the Sea Lords owe no loyalty to the Brotherhood," Lord Bull insisted. "The Sea Lords are corsairs, knights of the sea. The Brotherhood are renegades, pirates, thugs, and gangsters. There might be a few Sea Lords among them, fellows who were cast out of proper ships and havens, but the Brotherhood is not tolerated on the wharves and havens of the Sea Lords proper. They prosper only in Coastlord ports, from what I understand."

"There are many powerful Sea Lord Houses in the Great Bay," agreed Lord Hound. "They rarely turn their attention to landsmen's politics, only when it affects their ships and their voyages. More than half of the Alshari Navy is comprised of Sea Lord ships, privateers," he reminded them.

"Enough of them enjoy the new market in slaves Vichetral has created," Lady Hawk condemned.

"Not all of them have taken up that horrid practice," defended Lady Gull. "Indeed, some despise it, as it places their own ships in danger. Piracy, too, is not held in high regard in all Sea Lord havens. Perhaps enough of them to make a difference to our cause," she admitted. "Vichetral's other proposals toward maritime affairs have some of them alarmed. They seek to consolidate the profitable trading routes and transshipment ports exclusively to the larger Houses, friendlier with the Council of Five. That is to force the smaller ships to turn to slaving or piracy as a matter of necessity."

"No man likes his trade dictated by a tyrant." Lord Ox nodded sympathetically.

"I think we must reach out to them," Lady Wren proposed. "I'm not fond of the idea, but we are making little progress, doing what we are doing. We have established ourselves and have built up our network, but

I will be a grandmother before Vichetral is pushed off the throne, I think. We *must* do something."

"Then we must proceed with the utmost caution!" cautioned Lady Gull in a wavering voice. "The great Sea Lord Houses are honorable . . . until they are not. They have their own codes, their own culture, their own laws. It is difficult to gain their loyalty or even their allegiance."

"It can be bought," Lord Bull proposed.

"But will it stay bought?" Lady Gull riposted. "I have my doubts."

"Yet I think we must try," Lord Hound agreed. "With a few of their Houses in our service, we would have a far easier time moving beyond the Great Bay, say, to bring in mercenary troops to challenge the Counts," he suggested, "or gather forces to seize control of strategic ports. But who should make the embassy?"

"Not I!" Lady Gull said, somewhat shrilly. "It would imperil my enterprises and threaten my interests—and that could jeopardize our security. We would have far too much to lose if I even whispered about it with my associates," she assured.

"Master Thinradel has asked us to meet with Sea Lord families who might be open to our cause," Shadow repeated. "There is a great gathering of their councils at Vaxel, this summer, where they consider the policies of the Master of the Waves and discuss their people's business. I am prepared to infiltrate it and secure allies, if this council agrees. Thinradel has provided detailed intelligence on those Houses he thinks might be open to joining our efforts, and suggestions for what each House might contribute to them."

"We should be considering a strike at the damned palace, not mucking around with boats!" complained Lord Bull.

"The ships of the Sea Lords aren't 'boats'!" Lady Gull said, irritated. "They are oceangoing ships who provide most of our trade! They are among the wealthiest merchant houses in Alshar. They control commercial trade, maritime defense, and all manner of inland enterprises. They would be a valuable addition . . . despite their reputation!"

"Do you think you can make a deal with them, Lord Shadow?" Lord Ox asked. He was the Council's treasurer, Gatina recalled, and had perked up at the mention of Sea Lords' wealth.

"I believe so," Shadow agreed. "This isn't a fool's errand. And I don't undertake this lightly. I know the risks. But I think we must include the Sea Lords in this struggle, as Thinradel has suggested. If the Council agrees, my House will take a journey to the coast this summer and make the connections there. If we can come to an accord, I will negotiate on the Council's behalf, pending your approval. Would that be acceptable? What do you say?"

"How will you know who to trust?" Lord Ox asked. "It's a long way from Falas. You don't appear to be a mariner. You don't want to find yourself without allies. That could be unfortunate."

Gatina realized how valid his question was. She had that very same question. She trusted her father implicitly. And she knew they had kin there, distant but still Furtiusi blood. Lord Shadow, she noticed, did not share that information with the Council.

Hance was prepared with an answer. "Thinradel has provided assistance. I trust him, as should you. If it weren't for him, we wouldn't be as organized as we are now."

Lord Hound offered a bit of cryptic advice, though. "When contending with the Sea Lords, be wary of more than the sea. You might actually find the sea to be friendlier."

The Council did have concerns, of course, about the mission's safety. After a brief discussion, the Council agreed to allow Lord Shadow and his family to pursue building relationships with Sea Lords.

"Master Thinradel did warn us that anything was possible once Rard took power," Shadow said, choosing his words carefully.

The debate and discussion went on. Gatina listened, enthralled by the details. As boring and mundane as they sounded on the surface, she knew better. Often the deliberations of the Shadow Council had sent her off on a new, dangerous mission. She hung on everyone's words. As frustrating as it was to know that the tyrant Vichetral was still haunting a throne he did not deserve, she also appreciated the complex matters involving his overthrow.

To most, it was a choice between remaining under the heel of the Council of Five, as the rebel counts were known, and capitulating to the distant King Rard and his bloodthirsty wife. To others, it was a matter of seizing the opportunity to undermine Count Vichetral's attempts at administering the duchy until all was chaos and he could be removed from the throne in a coup d'état. Others felt their best hope was to rescue young Anguin, the Orphan Duke, and use him to rally the people against his usurper.

But she had learned a lot in the last few years. Her idealistic perspective had grown waned and diminished as she had become educated on matters of government, state, and commerce. Things were far, far more complex than she had thought when the conspiracy began. Loyalties were not absolute, allies were not permanent, and any action taken against the regime had unintended consequences that had to be weighed against the ultimate goal.

For three years, the Shadow Council had carefully negotiated those jagged shoals of policy, built their strength in secret, and recruited more sympathetic forces while gathering resources and weakening the enemy in subtle ways. She understood the reasoning behind the cautious approach they were taking. But that didn't make her any less impatient.

She remembered that first mission and the excitement—and mystery—it held in her mind. But she also recalled, when she was in the midst of it, that she had soon learned that patience was a crucial part of her Art.

Strike only when the time is correct. To strike too soon leads to calamity. Kiera the Great had penned that in the family's history. In her three years of being an agent of the Shadow Council, Gatina had come to appreciate that bit of guidance. She was good at being patient now. Usually.

That didn't mean she had to like it, though.

CHAPTER FOUR

JOURNEY BY SEA

Every new heist is an adventure, every new mission a chance for glory. And failure.
— from Gatina's Heist Journal

GATINA TRUDGED ALONGSIDE ATOPOL IN THE LIGHT OF THE EARLY DAWN as they made their way through the fog to meet their parents. He had been sent to retrieve her from the orphanage under the pretense that she shouldn't walk unaccompanied by an escort as either a lady or clergy at that time of day.

Secretly, though, she suspected he volunteered so that he could enjoy a hearty breakfast before they set sail. Atopol's appetite was legendary, and Sister Karia was prepared for him. She had even packed him a basket for the trip. The Tryggite nun was their former tutor, back home at Cysgodol Hall, and had known her brother since he was a baby. She could contend with his appetite.

She and Atopol wore the clerical habits from their time at Palomar Abbey, where they had spent a summer as Nocturns studying the stars with the Saganite Order. The robes no longer reached their ankles. Instead, Atopol's hung at midcalf and Gatina's skimmed the top of her boots. The length wasn't the only difference either. Atopol's was also tighter across his chest, back, and arms, where he had built muscle. Gatina's was snug across her bustline but hung loosely everywhere else.

For the trip down the river to the Great Bay, they would be using their previous aliases, which were already tested and practiced, while they were in public view. With the Censors, duelists, Rats, and spies from the Council of Counts, Falas had become too dangerous for House Furtius. Fleeing disguised as clergy was a reasonable response. Besides, they had a new mission, she knew. A new adventure and distant family to meet.

In any case, Gatina was relieved to leave Falas. Summer there was miserable, an exercise in humidity and heat that was unrelenting.

"I guess we're growing," Atopol chuckled as he tugged at the front of his robe. "I swear this habit was longer the last time I wore it. At least my shoes fit." He wore sturdy brown boots, not his working-blacks boots, which were made of a more subtle leather.

They quickly learned that it was one thing to decide to go on a long journey by sea; it was another thing entirely to plan every detail of it. A large portion of a shadowthief's life was spent looking at granular details that could mean the difference between life and death, success and failure, which their parents never failed to stress to her and Atopol. She found it aggravating but necessary. She understood why planning was needed for heists, of course, and why attention to detail was likewise essential when taking a voyage, especially by sea during a time of piracy and rebellion.

In truth, the lack of immediacy frustrated her, necessity be damned. She was a girl of action. While she recognized that having a plan usually kept her from extreme conflict, Gatina had to admit that she tended to go off plan frequently. That, she knew, was a source of contention and concern with her mistress and master. Her parents had lectured her repeatedly about the need for following directives instead of improvising in an impetuous manner. That couldn't always be helped, of course—things went wrong on missions all the time.

But Gatina sincerely believed Fate provided her with options. That was not an approved answer, unfortunately, and it had come up in many of the post-heist reviews with her parents. She reasoned that her ability to adjust her plan quickly had helped her obtain the bottle of wine and its hidden message and discover another spy in their rebellion.

Her parents had agreed but were less than pleased with her fighting the three duelists behind the wine shop, and were concerned she might have revealed too much, too soon. It had not been her first fight, and she suspected it would not be her last. But her personal danger was not their issue with her performance—it was her willingness to risk the success of the mission for a bit of unnecessary swordplay.

Gatina respectfully disagreed, although she kept that opinion to herself. She hated the young bravos who had infected the capital, making folk of all classes nervous with their violent antics. The dueling societies had become far too common and disruptive in Falas in the past year. Groups of boys and young noblemen had taken it upon themselves to defend whatever slight they saw against Count Vichetral and his council's rule or take personal exception to imagined insults as a pretext for drawing their blades, even against unarmed commoners, without concern for consequences.

"How was the meeting, Kitten?" Atopol asked conversationally as they walked toward the docks. "I wonder if our friends are as frustrated by the slow pace of the enterprise as we are."

Gatina knew she could tell him all sorts of things. Or tell him that it wasn't his news to know, but she thought that would be unkind. She preferred the direct approach. She decided on the truth, in a vague and ambiguous sort of way. It was a confusing way to communicate without revealing details, but the two had gotten used to it after living a life of secrets. Their clerical disguises gave her a template to relay the information.

"Well, the abbot discussed the same concerns with them as he did with us. Though he was not as forthcoming with them about some of the details. But yes, they are frustrated. The dog and the seagull especially so," she answered. "The seagull is wary of ships. The dog is sniffing around for vermin and wants to bark at the tower. They did approve of our summer pilgrimage, though," she added.

Atopol nodded. "Good. I'm gratified to hear that. I thought we would be further along by now, honestly. It doesn't seem that we're making much progress."

"Perhaps this pilgrimage will change that," she suggested.

"Well, we spent three days securing the supplies we'll need for the trip downriver. There should be more waiting for us when we finally get to the ship. Clothes, parchment, and we have enough elixirs and ointments to ward off all sorts of bugs and fevers. Are you excited yet?" He certainly was, Gatina realized. She nodded.

She was excited too. She had never been this far from home before, or on a ship larger than a river barge, and the thought of seeing new cities and meeting her extended family had tested her patience while the trip was being planned. She smiled and exhaled some of the air that was already heavy and humid. A quick glance revealed empty streets, at least for now.

"Of course I am excited. I didn't even know we *had* kin at the coast. No one ever talks about them. I'm intrigued to meet this 'wet sheep' of the family."

"From what I understand, there's some drama behind it," he nodded. "Something about a busted love affair. It caused some hurt feelings. But that's about all I know."

"I wonder what happened. Lord Steel is certainly unhappy about it. He's got some sort of history with this cousin. It sounds positively scandalous. Do you know anything else about it? Or about *her?*"

It was in her nature to want to know everything she could about it. Perhaps as a consequence of the secret life she led, Gatina had developed a positive love of other people's gossip. Her mother had hinted it was unladylike and a flaw in her character, but considering much of her life was spent gathering information on other subjects, learning the scandalous details of other people's lives was something she had come to enjoy.

But he had nothing interesting to share.

"I haven't heard anything," he said. "Only that they're distant cousins, that there was a marriage that wasn't exactly approved of, and half the family thinks it's a scandal. I'm curious, too. I'm guessing the Sea Lords are involved somehow. I suppose we'll learn more when we get there."

"Where, exactly, is 'there'?" Gatina asked, realizing that she was going on a journey when she didn't properly know what the destination was.

"A seaport called Prejestia, in the northeastern Bay. We'll be on the barge for a few days until we get to the Great Bay, where we've booked passage to there. After that, it'll be a long trip across the Bay to Vaxel. It could take all summer. Did you bring anything to read?" he asked.

Atopol loved to read. Fortunately, so did she. Indeed, raiding the family library before a long trip had become a tradition for them. They had spent many sleepless nights and long days in safe houses, hiding out or preparing for a heist. Having something to read in those lonely moments made things more bearable.

"I brought a book about the Sea Lords' religion," she said. "It is very informative. You might want to borrow it when I finish. What did you bring?"

He grinned and she immediately regretted asking. "I brought *A History of Enultramar* and *Sailing the Great Bay*. Both are scholarly and dry, but I think they'll be useful for the mission. The abbot said we are to learn how to sail," he reminded her. They continued their trek, their pace faster, as they approached the dock where their barge awaited them. "That should be fun," he ventured.

"From what I understand, it's complicated and a lot of work," Gatina said, shaking her head. "I just hope it's easier than riding a horse." She could smell the river and feel the slight dampness from it. "I don't think I'll miss Falas too much. Darkness, it's awfully humid already! I hope there's a breeze on the water," she added.

Atopol shrugged, his shoulders stretching his habit out until the seams strained. He noticed the ill fit of the robe. "It will be better when we're not wearing all this wool. I'm going to need a new robe soon, though. This one is too tight. How's yours, Sister Avorrita?"

Mentally, Gatina shifted to the persona of Avorrita, the awkward, bucktoothed maiden who had attended the abbey in preparation for holy orders. The guise was helpful for avoiding attention and led to them being treated with respect and deference by most passers-by—most people were respectful of the clergy, even strange orders like the Saganites. Fortunately, she was not wearing the dental prosthetic that made her teeth stick out comically. She had accidentally left it behind the last time she was at the abbey, when she and Atopol had taken their vows. She didn't feel too bad about that.

"Too hot, too heavy, and I'll be thrilled to dress . . . *differently*," she said, knowing that a new alias meant a new change of attire—not to mention a new name, a new disguise, and a new story to tell. She didn't mind portraying a nun, of course. It was handy to avoid detection when you were traveling, on a heist, or hiding out.

Each traveling Nocturn carried a satchel of their belongings, by tradition, but theirs were specially made to include the items that were needed for their Art. The bags had been crafted with hidden compartments, special straps, and other devices that might prove useful to conceal the tools needed to be a thief. When Mother had told them to pack for the weather and the occasion, they knew to bring everything from lockpicks and magical supplies to their shadowblades and heist journals. In other words, the necessities.

"There's the barge—I see them up ahead through the fog," Atopol said in his Nocturn Dain voice, as he sped up. Gatina shuddered at his pace, but she matched it, nonetheless. Her feet were still sore and had a few uncomfortable blisters from those awful shoes. Her brother grinned as they stepped onto the dock. "The sooner we get there, the sooner we can be on our way."

Gatina was glad to be going, in truth. After that last mission, she was just as ready to put Falas behind her for a while and start a new adventure. The capital city was a foggy, humid mess in the summertime, punctuated by hard afternoon rains that only made the humidity worse. She looked forward to visiting the Great Bay: the huge body of water that led to the ocean proper.

Gatina had spent the previous evening poring over an atlas of the Great Bay to familiarize herself with it. She now knew many of the major ports by name, location, and specialty. The Great Bay was the duchy's hub of sea merchant activity, the heart of Alshar's commercial empire. Thousands of ships plied its waters, and thousands more arrived and departed every year with cargoes from the inland farms, vineyards, and orchards.

She had often imagined what it would be like to be on a ship or at least see the body of water that was so essential to so many people. Though she had read accounts of what that was like, she was thrilled that she was finally going to see it firsthand. It was an entirely different style of living than she was used to, her mother had repeated over and over. Yes, this was going to be an adventure.

When they got closer, Gatina saw through the fog that their parents were also dressed as clergy. Mother wore the brown habit and wimple of a Tryggite nun. Father was dressed as a Nightbrother of the Saganite Order. Both wore wigs, she knew, and Father had enchanted his distinctive eye color. Instead of the usual dock owned by the Temple of Ifnia that they often used for excursions downriver, just outside Falas proper, they had secured transport from a commercial dock along the city's waterfront this time. She didn't know why but suspected there were good reasons for it.

"Brother Espus," Gatina said, bowing in greeting to her father and respecting his alias in public. That was a long-established protocol. You did not break character where even a casual observer might see it or overhear, and there were plenty of those lining the dock. "A billion blessings upon you. You remember my fellow Nocturn, Dain?" she asked as Atopol repeated her bow. "Are you studying the night sky along the river?"

"It is good to see fellow stargazers on this voyage," her father said in answer to her greeting. "Billions and billions of blessings upon you both. This is Sister Minelva," he said, nodding to Minnureal. "She, too, is going on pilgrimage and has elected to join us for a time. Your baggage is already aboard. The captain is eager to be under way, so we'd best get going."

The family's passage had been booked on a single-masted commercial river barge that would carry them down the river from Falas to the Great Bay, before they took transport to Prejestia. The four somberly dressed clergy were not alone on the barge; there was an assortment of travelers who had also purchased passage on the boat, Gatina could see. Mostly individual traders, pilgrims, and merchants who had business farther downriver or on the Great Bay, she guessed.

Fortunately, as clergy, she saw that the other passengers gave her family a wide berth. That was one of the other advantages of traveling as monks and nuns. People were hesitant to engage in small talk with them, in general, although there were occasional exceptions—folk with guilty consciences who wanted them assuaged, people with genuine spiritual questions who sought guidance, or those who sought to purchase divine favor with open displays of piety.

Thankfully, nobody sat near them when they took up an entire bench of the barge. Within a quarter of an hour, the dour-looking river captain had the mooring lines cast off, the polemen had pushed off from the dock, and the barge was underway with the steady current of the mighty Mandros. The river itself was so blanketed in fog that she could not see the surface—it appeared the barge was gliding along on a cloud.

In keeping with his bookish Dain alias, Atopol began reading a volume he had brought with him. That also kept strangers from bothering them, Gatina realized—very few people in Falas could read, and many had an almost-superstitious view of those who could. Bringing out an actual book was a way to build an invisible wall around yourself, she reflected. It marked her brother as a scholar as well as a priest. She saw the eyes of the other passengers go wide when Dain was so casual with something as rich and expensive as a book. Thinking that was a good way to pass the long journey down the Mandros River, Gatina bent to remove the book about the Sea Lords from her own satchel.

That was when she felt the first sense of unease. It hit her as soon as she leaned forward. The words swam on the page, and her eyes had a difficult time keeping her place. Her stomach churned. She blinked several times when she sat up, her book in her lap.

Sister Minelva looked at her and spoke for the first time. "Are you well, Nocturn?"

Gatina closed her eyes and nodded. This would pass, she knew. "Just a little queasy from the rocking of the boat," she admitted.

Her mother frowned. "That doesn't bode well," she said, quietly. "Seasick?"

"I don't know. Perhaps. I don't usually get that way," she recalled.

"It might be trying to read on a boat," her mother nodded. "Sometimes, that can bring on nausea."

"I am fine, Sister," Gatina assured. But she closed the volume and instead looked at the shoreline for a while until they had passed completely out of the city and were floating past the manors and estates that lined both sides of the river. It took a while—and several deep breaths—but her nausea passed enough to try to keep reading. She concentrated on her book, trying to absorb the information she was reading, but it was difficult. And it did not, indeed, bode well for her future voyage.

She knew there would be several more stops before the ship made its way beyond the city's outer precincts. She finally closed the book when she realized she couldn't read without her stomach complaining. It was best that she focus on silence for now—and observation.

Atopol, she realized, was likely doing the same, as she caught him glancing up a few times—skimming his book while inspecting the other passengers and crew members. She knew how important observation was to a mission, and she had spent many hours doing it herself. Indeed, her parents would test her sometimes, having her stake out a particular place and then quiz her in excruciating detail about everything she saw.

She resolved to learn all she could about the passengers nearest her and to watch the crew; it seemed like a wise way to pass the time. It was also smart to check for things that might be out of the ordinary on the ship—like debating-society members with fresh cuts on their faces, or Censors trying to disguise themselves. But the crew and passengers of the barge each seemed entirely ordinary.

She guessed the backgrounds and histories of each of them, based on little clues of their dress, their behavior, and their mannerisms. She was able to determine—or at least guess—that the crew of the barge was from significantly lower down the Mandros than Falas—their accents bore a more rural, flat tone that was used by the Rhemesmen. They were strong, hardy men who moved with purpose and alacrity as the captain called orders to them—not proper mariners, perhaps, but she did see at least two men with eye patches covering one of their eyes. She shuddered to think what might have happened to them. Another young crewman was sounding the depth of the river and the speed of the barge with a length of knotted rope. His shirt billowed up and she was able to see his flat stomach underneath. He seemed to be in excellent shape, she thought, and then blushed self-consciously. Nuns were not supposed to think such things.

Most of the passengers were only going a short way down the river, she figured out. Two of the merchants she quietly watched were clearly from Espreen, a prosperous town in central County Falas, by their hats and footwear, and by their conversation, they were headed into Rhemes on the other side of the Mandros from Falas. Gatina had ridden through Espreen once last year in a coach.

Another man looked like she thought a mariner would look but lacked the calluses on his hands that would belong on a seaman. Perhaps a clerk, she reasoned, or a merchant, by the large oilskin satchel he kept next to him. He was due to meet a man in Asilten. A young husband and wife from Falas, not much older than her brother, sat close to each other, and had the smiles and expressions of two lovers going on a holiday somewhere. Likely to visit relatives downriver, she guessed.

That startled her, for some reason. To see a boy—a young man, she corrected—about Atopol's age already married and planning his future with his bride made Gatina's head whirl. How could someone find love so young, she wondered? Was it an arranged marriage? Their clothes did not suggest that they were nobility, but they were of good quality and their baggage was well made and full. Arranged or not, it was apparent that they were newly wed and very much in love. The young man was pointing out various sights along the shore and explaining the different roles the bargemen had on the boat: poleman, flagman, pilot, and captain. He had been on a barge before—but his new wife had likely never been out of Falas.

It was fascinating to watch them, Gatina realized, as they held hands and talked quietly. To consider pledging your entire life to someone when you were only barely more than a child seemed strange to Gatina. Yet the couple looked supremely happy together. She wondered what it would be like for someone to look at her the way the young husband gazed adoringly at his pretty wife.

There was little prospect for Gatina to find such happiness anytime soon, she knew. She would be spending her summer by the sea. Learning about boats and barges, sailing and the trade of the mariner. There would be a mission, she had no doubt, perhaps more than one. Disguises. Deceptions. Not to mention the fact that her family tradition demanded that she only marry a mage of exquisite Talent and ability. That narrowed her choices for romance dramatically.

At least she was better off than her brother, she reflected. Family tradition also required that Atopol only marry the best female thief he could find. Those were few and far between, Gatina knew. Indeed, she and her mother were the only female thieves she was aware of. It was not a profession that encouraged a lot of social engagements.

Gatina tried once again to turn her eyes to her book and immersed herself in Sea Lord traditions among the six different cults of that culture. Atopol hadn't noticed her watching the sounding man, but he did offer a bit of knowledge when he finally closed his own book.

"Have you learned all the special terminology you need to know, Nocturn?" he asked, curiously.

"I'm learning about the Maiden of the Havens," she revealed, keeping her thumb on the page as she closed the book. "She's some sort of goddess of hospitality."

"I meant the maritime terminology," her brother said. "Like the front of a ship being called the bow, and the rear the stern. The left side of the ship is called the port side, while the right is called starboard. And see that, what he's doing?" he asked, as two of the bargemen began raising the sail at the captain's command. "It's called hoisting a sheet. That's what the sails are called, according to this book," he said, tapping the smaller of the two volumes on his lap. "And those aren't ropes they're using—they're called lines."

"That seems unnecessarily confusing," she complained.

"It's actually quite fascinating," he objected. "Just like astronomy has its special language, so does the sea. Everything on a ship has a specific name, a specific title, and a specific place. It actually is designed to keep things from getting confusing."

"I didn't think boats were that complicated," she offered.

"For one thing, they aren't 'boats'; they're 'ships.' Boats are smaller. And they are very, very complicated. Not like this barge. It will spend its entire life between the banks of a river. If you sail out of sight of land, however, things get complicated quickly."

By the time the barge made its stop in Lansil, on the Rhemes side of the river, the young couple disembarked and Gatina discovered that her family had the passage to themselves. They would maintain their aliases, but they could speak mostly freely, as long as they spoke quietly. The crew was more concerned with the ship's operations than the four clergy members keeping to themselves.

The barge was much larger than most of the others that she saw on the river, and most of that space was taken up by cargo—mainly barrels of salted beef and pork from upriver, destined for the markets in the Great Bay. It was the standard width, about thirty feet across, but it had to be long enough to hold five wagons, she figured. River barges had to be narrow enough to fit through the city's canals and pole up tributaries to the Mandros. It was a good size, she decided. Besides, she assured herself, her parents would not book a vessel too small or too grand to attract any attention. Time mattered, yes, but so did secrecy. This was still a mission, after all. Which made her wonder about where, exactly, they were going.

"Is the boat—the ship—we're going to larger than this?" she asked Atopol, mostly out of boredom. It gave him the chance to show off how much he'd learned, and there was always the possibility Gatina would learn something herself.

"Oh, much bigger," he assured her. "There are some actual ships that we'll start seeing as we get closer to the mouth of the river that ferry cargo and passengers from riverport to seaport. But oceangoing merchant vessels are built differently. Instead of having a flat bottom, like this barge, a ship usually has a rounded bottom, and at least one storage area below the main deck. Ships are designed for the deeper and rougher water of the Great Bay. Their hulls have to be deep enough for cargo but not so deep that they get stuck in the shallow river water at low tide. A ship must be sturdy enough for the waves, tough enough to weather a fierce squall—"

"What is a squall?" Gatina asked, confused. She'd seen the term in the chapter on the goddess known as the Shipwrecker but hadn't understood it.

"A storm at sea," Atopol explained. "They can get pretty violent. And they happen all the time in the Great Bay, apparently. If a ship isn't tough enough to survive a bad squall, it isn't worth taking out of port."

They had a luncheon in Lansil. The riverport was large enough so that her father could go ashore and find a street vendor to purchase a bottle of inexpensive wine, a couple of loaves of bread, and several skewers of well-marinated pork. Atopol graciously shared the basket of food Sister Karia had prepared, which added fresh sweet rolls, cheese, and sausages to their feast. Food was not part of their passage—and after what she saw the bargemen ate, an unappetizing watery brown stew of river fish and a few beans, she was glad for that.

"Enjoy the fresh bread while you can," her mother encouraged her as she bit into one of the small loafs. "Once we're at sea, we'll be eating nothing but ship's biscuits for days."

"Ship's biscuits?" she asked, confused.

"Hardtack," her father chuckled. "Think of them as rocks masquerading as bread. It's too salty at sea to bake bread, usually, and too damp to keep leavened bread from getting moldy within a day or so. Mariners need something sturdy enough to survive the damp conditions, so they buy ship's biscuits," he explained. "They're made with flour, a little salt, and water, and then baked three times to get all the water out. That makes them dry, and as hard as a death sentence. They keep for years if properly stored. But that's what the mariners live on. That and salt pork or beef."

"That sounds . . . unappetizing," Atopol said, staring at his loaf.

"It is," agreed their mother. "A ship's biscuit is a tasteless assault on the sanctity of your teeth. Usually, you have to soak them in freshwater or wine or ale before you can gnaw through them. But it's not the only thing you get to eat, particularly in the Bay. There is plenty of fresh seafood, and ports are close enough at hand to eat fresh fruit and vegetables on a regular basis. Not to mention spices. A decent ship's cook can do amazing things with that. It's a more-balanced offering than what is served at the abbey."

"Mariners who venture beyond the straits of the Bay and into the wider ocean have it worse," their father assured. "They can be out of sight of land for weeks or even months at a time. They get used to biscuits after a time. It's better than no bread at all."

The wind picked up as they left Falas behind. The barge was steered by the pilot while the mates manned the sheets to shift direction and guide the boat along the current. Gatina heard it *splish* and *splash* along the sides, slapping in its own rhythm. It was calming, almost too much so. She shook her head quickly to keep from dozing off.

The four disguised Furtiusi kept their conversation quiet while dining, but their parents began instructing them in some of the basics of ships and the sea. She understood the concept, of course—her work at Palomar Abbey had been devoted to creating sea charts for the duchy based on their observations and calculations—but she was learning very quickly that there was far more to the practice of voyaging than she suspected. The Saganite Order was known for its work. Their study of the constellations had helped map routes and create tide charts for mariners. The stars above were sacred for seafarers.

She reached for an orange while she listened about what the various parts of a ship were called and delighted in the sharp sweetness as it hit her tongue. It had been ages since she'd enjoyed one. That was one thing she could look forward to this summer—she knew that oranges, lemons, limes, and other citrus fruits were both common staples and often exported from dozens of ports along the Great Bay. She looked forward to the fresh fruits the journey would bring.

The wave of nautical terms was more difficult to digest. But there were certain important elements she picked up on at once.

"The captain of a ship is the absolute monarch of it," her father related. "Even this barge captain is, as long as we are underway. The ship's master has ultimate responsibility and command for everything on a ship, including the people. That includes the ship's seaworthiness, its course, the lives and safety of everyone on her, the security of the ship, the cargo, navigation, managing the crew, and keeping things as efficient as possible. The captain is responsible for discipline and has every power needed to enforce it. If he gives a command, it is followed, without unnecessary questioning. That is incredibly important to remember. You cannot argue with the captain of a ship; you must obey. Everyone's life may depend upon it."

"He couldn't execute you or torture you, though," Gatina suggested.

"He can and he might," her father assured her, "if he thinks it's the only way to keep order. He can throw you overboard or hang you from a mast. He can order you whipped, or cut your rations, or see you in chains. And there is nothing you can do about it," he cautioned. "A good captain wouldn't resort to that sort of thing unless absolutely necessary, of course. But that is not something you ever want to test."

Suddenly, the orange didn't taste so sweet in her mouth.

"And just how long is our journey?" she asked, as her eyes flicked to the barge captain. "I neglected to ask the abbot before departing."

Father nearly laughed. She saw the telltale twinkle in his now-blue eyes. "It's about two days downriver in good weather. We should have no trouble holding to that schedule. The captain has been told of the urgency of our mission to study the stars before clouds arrive and obscure the view. He knows the importance of our studies and will get us to the river delta in time. We will have a ship waiting there to get us to our ultimate destination. A small abbey on the coast." That was code for their cousin's home, she realized.

"I understand the abbey where we are headed has a few young Nocturns," Atopol offered, speaking in code.

"Yes, it does. They are about your ages, as a matter of fact. And the abbess takes care of the abbey's business thoroughly," her father reported with a grin.

"Are they far along in their studies?" Gatina asked. She wanted to know if they were magically Talented.

"One is. The other is not," he answered. In other words, one of her cousins had *rajira* but not the other. "And they both study the sea as well as the night sky. It helps, given where they live, to have a command of seafaring," he suggested. "In fact, that will become part of your lessons. How can a student of the night navigate the sea if he does not know how to operate a boat?"

Gatina was not sure what to make of that suggestion. On one hand, she thought it sounded exciting and adventurous, but on the other hand, there were serious risks with the open water, she was learning. Her book had suggested as much. Her mind raced with the problems—pirates, foul weather, the sea gods and their pantheon, of which she was just now learning: the Storm King and his five daughters: the Maiden of the Havens, the Fairtrader, the Corsair, the Shipwrecker, and the Salt Crone. Each had control over a Sea Lord's life, according to the book.

"And how is the abbess? What is she like?" Atopol asked, probing for information. "I have heard that she can be—unpredictable," he added diplomatically.

"Perhaps when she was young. But she does her duty," her father said sharply. "Abbess Beah is cut from a different cloth than the rest of us, but she supports the temple." He looked around to ensure no one could overhear, and his voice softened until he no longer sounded like Brother Espus. "I think we can talk freely. It is true: your distant aunt has a reputation for unexpected behavior. In her youth, well, she was quite the wild one. In fact, she and Master Steel caused quite a family—"

"Enough!" her mother interrupted, softly but sharply. "That is not our story to tell, nor would it benefit the Nocturns to hear it. It's only a minor bit of family drama. All else is mere rumor," Minnie admitted, "but they *were* lovers, once."

"Then they weren't," her father added. "She married a Sea Lord under unusual circumstances. They eloped. It was all very sordid."

"It had been assumed that she would wed your cousin Steel, but she didn't," her mother said, firmly, shooting a glance at her disguised husband. "That is all you need to know."

Father nodded. "It was quite the scandal," he admitted. "Beah, in her youth and probably even now, was very much her own person. She is a mage, and a good one, but she chose love over her Art and the family legacy and fled to the Great Bay. I met her when I was a boy; as a young woman, she was striking. She spoke her mind, always. She did not bend to tradition unless it suited her.

"Describing Beah is like describing a thunderstorm," he continued philosophically. "Imagine trying to capture lightning over the water. It's sheer folly. And perhaps fatal. That was the effect she had on Steel. Her abandonment of Steel led him down a dark path until he met Mist. In fact, she worked hard to gain his affection. He was distraught over the entire affair, and she was devoted to him."

"That's why when Beah left, the family gave her the nickname of the 'Wet Sheep' of the family," her mother agreed. "Perhaps not fairly, but it does describe her. She's actually quite lovely and a good mother. Your father and I have met her several times now, and we approve of the life she's made for herself and your cousins. And just because she left the family business doesn't mean that she's forgotten her duty. She maintains her loyalty to the house. But she honors her husband's legacy, as well," he said. "And that gets complicated."

Before she could stop herself, Gatina spoke. "How?"

Minnie looked at Hance and nodded as if saying *We've told them this much*, Gatina thought.

"Beah's husband came from a non-Talented family. He is a Sea Lord, yes, but he had no *rajira*. However, his family was—and is—somewhat wealthy, as Sea Lords measure things. And there was scandal on his side for him marrying a landsman. When Beah wed, she left her Art and House. She embraced the Sea Lord lifestyle and her husband's family. But her husband was forced to leave his own family's compound and strike out on his own when he wed. That worked out well for several years. They had children and a very successful shipping business. But they also had a tragedy."

At first, Gatina was lost in the romance of the tale. She, of course, knew that as a member of House Furtius with *rajira*, she was expected to marry a mage of equal or greater Talent. But to wed only for love seemed so romantic. And certainly not acceptable, according to the House rules. Beah had apparently endured estrangement from most of her family as a consequence.

Gatina looked to see Atopol's reaction to this news. She wondered if he knew anything about this scandal. From the look on his face, he did not. She felt better that they were both hearing it at the same time.

"Beah's husband, Alekandrus, set sail one day as the master of his caravel four years ago on a routine merchant trip to Farise," her father continued quietly. "His ship was caught in a squall and vanished, presumed sunk and destroyed with all hands. All gone. It happens all too often that a ship is lost at sea.

"Beah was distraught, of course. He was her world. She'd given up her own family for him. Within days, she had organized a search party and spent months searching for him. She took a smaller boat herself and hired others to scour the sea for him and his crew for any evidence of what might have happened," he explained. "But nothing turned up."

Her mother picked up the story. "Instead of fading into her despair and throwing herself into the sea or drinking herself to death in grief, as many widows of the water do in such circumstances, she rose from her grief and embraced their legacy. Though one caravel was lost, they had another and smaller boats, and she swore to keep his company going as his gift to his children someday. She's been running it for four years now, and to a good profit."

"That's awful!" Gatina protested.

"It's an inspiring story, to be truthful," Hance said. "Alekandrus had taught her how to operate the ships and manage the company. That's part of Sea Lord tradition, that a wife learns the same trade as her husband. She felt it was important to her that she learn, from what she shared in letters she sent me. She and I had a good relationship, despite the scandal," he explained. "Indeed, that's where your mother and I went after we got married, to Beah's place. We stole the *Daydream* on our honeymoon," he recalled fondly.

"Anyway, the two of them often took to the water together before she had the children, working alongside each other on voyages around the Great Bay. When their children were old enough, according to Sea Lord tradition, they were taught seamanship themselves. They serve as apprentice crewmen on Beah's caravel, the *Legacy. Alekandrus's Legacy.*"

Gatina's mother shook her head. "I thank the Blessed Darkness that your father is who he is. I could not fathom the thought of a permanent life on the water. It is far too dangerous for me. But, given this journey, well, we thought it best you both come along and learn about your extended family." She patted both of the children's hands. "And learn about seafaring. As well as the very important culture of the Sea Lords."

"So, we're to become mariners, then," Atopol summarized.

"Yes. I plan to have you both apprentice aboard Aunt Beah's boat—ship, rather—and learn how to crew. That's a practical skill you cannot fake, like a detailed knowledge of astronomy. I want to ensure that you are both able to handle yourselves in any situation. And your mother agrees with me." He looked at her and she nodded.

"The Sea Lords are a vital part of Alshar's society. But their culture and customs are very different from either us Coastlords or the Vale Lords in the north. So, over the summer, we will be living with your extended family and mingling with their Sea Lord kin in disguise. Your goals are to learn all that you can from your cousins about seafaring and their cultural beliefs, mannerisms, and religious systems."

That alarmed Gatina. She was no stranger to danger, in her line of the Art. She had scaled buildings, jumped from rooftop to rooftop, swum through sewers, crawled through tunnels, forded rivers, nearly blown her face off with magic once, and dueled with bravos and even Censors. But the open water frightened her.

The perils of the sea were severe and well known. Being a mariner was dangerous—even being a bargeman was dangerous, she realized. There were several men aboard the barge who had been tested by their craft and had paid a gruesome price. The tillerman managed to walk quickly across the deck despite having only one leg. His pants were cut off and tied up just below his knee. His left leg was missing, and he relied on a crutch to help him. But he still managed to pilot the barge.

It fascinated her, how he managed to stay upright when the barge rocked on the river. It was an impressive display of balance. And she knew how important balance was—on the water and on land. She focused on her parents and the lecture—well, it was more of a story or history than a lesson.

"These lessons are unique," her father continued, jarring her back to the present moment. "I know not yet whether we'll have anything for you two to do on this mission, but until I do, you will focus on studying seamanship. This will be a most interesting apprenticeship."

His proclamation sounded foreboding to Gatina's ears. She glanced at Attie, who nodded in agreement. And if Atopol was that enthusiastic, she resolved that she would be, too. She had no desire to miss out on an adventure, despite her trepidation about the water.

Still, Gatina was nervous about the idea of sailing. And her parents' words did little to quell that feeling. She had only been on the water a handful of times, in barges and small boats. She could swim, of course, but the thought of being trapped in the middle of a vast body of open water terrified her. There were fish, and crabs, and all manner of creatures down there below the surface, and gods only knew what else. She knew of the Sea Folk, the strange people who lived far beyond the Great Bay in the depths of the sea, and that was bad enough.

Kittens, in general, are not fond of water, she reminded herself philosophically. She knew there had to be a good reason for that.

CHAPTER FIVE

PREJESTIA SEA HAVEN

Every ship and every mariner has a home port whose comfort is unmatched by a thousand exotic destinations.
—Traditional Sea Lord proverb

IN LESS THAN THREE FULL DAYS' TIME, THE NAMELESS BARGE MADE IT TO THE mouth of the Mandros, where the four clergy transferred to the merchant ship that Gatina had nicknamed *Shadowdancer* and sailed eastward into the Great Bay. It would only take two days to make it to Prejestia, she learned, but being on a real seagoing ship for the first time was more exciting than she had thought.

The ship did not deserve so grand a name; even Gatina's inexperienced eye could see the chipping paint, the worn sails, and the weathered wood of the decks and concluded that the vessel was old and shabby. Though the caravel was actually named the *Gaillardia*, Gatina had bestowed that name on the vessel because in the shadows at night, she and her brother sneaked out of their cabins and practiced their stealth by sneaking around the deck, dodging crewmembers, and by climbing the lines into the rigging to work on their balance. It was a challenge, and there was always the chance they'd get caught, but it was also incredibly fun.

Their exercises had been inspired by watching the crewmembers swing from mast to mizzen to crow's nest in the rigging about their heads. The mariners demonstrated amazing alacrity as they raised and lowered the great sails of the ship—not just one, great square sail, as their barge had boasted, but several in different shapes and configurations. The men fairly danced on the lines between the mainmast and the great lateen sail. When she saw them, it had set her longing to climb a tree or a building, anything, really.

The caravel displaced just under twenty tons—that's how ships were measured in size, she'd learned, by the number of tons of water their hulls displaced. It had two decks and a bilge—that was the lowest portion of the ship, where the heavy stone ballast lay to keep the ship upright in storms—as well as a small pilot's deck on the stern. It was dwarfed by some of the galleons they passed as they sailed into the Bay, but after the barge, it seemed expansive—which led to the Cats of Enultramar coming out to play at night.

Besides, she needed to exercise, she rationalized. Sitting on a barge with nothing to do but read and daydream made her antsy, especially in the heavy woolen nun's habit. She had too much energy and no place to burn it off. She couldn't jump overboard to swim or practice her swordsmanship. Instead, Mother and Father had them perform basic calisthenics belowdecks, in their cabins—hardly challenging—to keep themselves limber.

On the first day, the hot afternoon sun had been filtered by the large sails and the air on the top deck was fresh and cool, so much different from the muggy streets of Falas. Gatina thrilled with the force of the wind—until she didn't. She craved it but fled downstairs when the wind whipped too hard. The salty air made her lips and her exposed skin chapped. When her mother applied a cooling balm of willow, almond oil, and lavender on her skin that night, the salve instantly took the sting from her skin. The lavender scent helped calm her mind enough that she fell asleep quickly. But when Atopol quietly knocked on the door to her closet-like cabin, she woke easily, well rested, ready to skulk around the ship a bit.

The first time she saw the sea, when the caravel left the mouth of the Mandros, it had taken her breath away. To see that much water with no land in sight on the other side made her head swim at first, though she still got used to it. She never thought that there was that much water in the world—and this was just one small part of the Great Bay. There were seas and oceans far larger, she knew.

But at night, even the comforting sight of land on the horizon was gone when she looked over the gunwales, the railing surrounding the ship. Gatina saw nothing but the dark vastness of the water under the overcast sky. It was dark, it was deep, and it promised death if it was not respected, she realized. It might even if you did respect it. For the first time, she realized why the Sea Lord cults were so infatuated with it. Like the Darkness her family swore by, it was both protective and dangerous. It deserved a sense of awe.

Being the only passengers aboard afforded them a bit of space, but they roomed together for propriety's sake. And, because they were clergy, the crew left them alone unless they had a need for a stargazer or sister of women's mysteries. All four of them, as clergy, had been invited to dine in the captain's cabin each night, and they joined him out of custom. To not do so would be rude and insulting to the Sea Lord culture—Gatina had read that in her book. The Sea Lords were respectfully reverent of the gods of other cultures. And nobody wanted angry gods or goddesses on a sea voyage.

The meals had been filling, if simple. Fresh fish seasoned with lime and cooked over an open flame on deck, which seemed risky. But the cook, a grizzled old man with sun-weathered skin and seven of his ten fingers, knew his way around the great cookpot that sat atop the flame contained inside an iron firebox. He used little wood but instead fed the flame with charcoal. Once he got the fire going, he'd add fresh charcoal only a little at a time.

Gatina watched the cook, Grohl, with fascination from over the top of her book when she sat reading on the deck on that first day aboard the ship. He chopped vegetables with a sharp *thwack* of a large knife, as careful as he could be while the boat swayed side to side with the waves and current. Initially, she wondered why he was cooking on the deck when she knew that the *Gaillardia* had a proper galley, the ship's kitchen, but she learned that Grohl wanted the light to cook by. The galley was a dark, cramped, tiny little closet of a space, and a man of Grohl's expansive girth preferred a more open environment. When two crewmen hauled a net full of fish up the side of the boat, she realized it was much easier to cook where Grohl was. He had a system, she saw. Chop everything up, throw it in the pot. Everything Grohl made was a stew.

It wasn't a bad stew, but neither was it particularly good. Grohl managed to do a good job, better than she could do, she realized, but the pale brown liquid that graced her bowl every meal was far from the fare she'd grown fond of in Falas. She did wonder if any of his missing fingers had made it into the dishes, but then she banished that thought. Grohl wasn't the only person on this ship with missing body parts.

He'd likely once been a fit mariner, but seafaring was dangerous. A man took whatever job he could get on a ship, once he'd lost a limb or an eye. She sensed it was a way for the mariners to provide a living for those who could not dance in the rigging anymore, which she found an unexpected display of compassion. It was clearly not reflective of culinary talent.

A shadow over her head drew her eyes up as one of the men climbed from the main mast to the foremast. He clung to the post, high above. Birds flew below him while he worked to adjust the sails. She covered her eyes to block the sun while she watched him. When he was satisfied, he pulled a brass spotting scope from his trousers' deep side pocket with his free hand. He flicked it open and brought it to his eye with a practiced fluid movement. Then he scanned the horizon. She was fascinated. The man was easily thirty feet above with no harness. He was holding on with his legs and one arm, wrapped tightly around the mast, his bare feet barely touching the rigging.

She knew that was no easy task.

When the mariner shimmied down and stood on the deck, she approached him, book in her hand, finger marking her page. She was in her disguise, minus her wimple as it was a risk on the boat if the wind picked up. A tightly wrapped scarf covered and held her hair back instead. She did not wear a wig, nor had she colored her hair. Father said she wouldn't need to but did not explain why when she asked. Instead, she plaited it, pulled it into a knot on top of her head, then tucked it into the scarf.

"Excuse me, may I ask: what did you see?" she asked, as politely as she could. What she really wanted to know was if he saw the coast, which had been missing from view for a while. When he looked confused by her question, she tried again. "When you were up there," she pointed.

He looked at her warily. She suspected that he was not accustomed to talking to passengers, let alone women. It was a matter of class: paying passengers spoke to the captain or the mate, not a common deckhand.

The mariner grunted and looked at her suspiciously.

"I beg your pardon, sir," she said, knowing that she had come across as forward. This man did not know her or even her alias. "My religious order studies the stars. That means I study the sky at night. I am curious as to how you see the sky during the day," she explained. "At night, the constellations guide me on my path. Those same stars have guided my order to chart maps for ships and sailors. But during the day, the blessed stars are hidden, blotted out by the bright sun. I am simply asking what you see when you peer into your scope," she said.

The man seemed older than he looked. His body was aged, even though his skin, while tanned by the sun and wind, seemed young, maybe a few years older than Atopol. He was not tall, only two inches taller than Gatina, but he was wiry and lean. His lips were turned down into an odd grimace, not a smile or a frown, and that's when Gatina wondered if he was well or not. He held up his hand and waved it as another crew member walked near—the mate, she recalled. The man saw him and joined them.

"Aye, Sister, what can I help you with?" the second man asked. This was a grown man, she decided, based on the wrinkles around the corners of his eyes and his full beard that was more silver than black. "Won't do you no good to talk to Palo here, he can't talk. No tongue," he explained. "Got caught stealing food on the dock and the shopkeeper took his own justice. Cap'n found him and fixed him up, brought him aboard, and taught him the trade," he added. "What can I help with?"

Before she could answer, Palo pointed to the sky and brought his spotting scope to his eyes, mimicking the movement. Then he motioned with both hands, one still holding the scope. He brought them together, flat, then spread them out, as if he was smoothing a cloth over a table. The second man nodded expectantly.

Gatina looked back and forth between the men, wondering what type of secret language they were speaking. But she didn't wait long for an answer.

"Sister, Palo says that he's seen land from o'erhead. I figure that puts us about another day's sailing from making port in Prejestia." The mute man nodded in agreement. "Unless the weather turns or the raiding ships stop us, we'll be there in the morn. But the sky is clear and the horizon seems safe, thank the Stormfather," he said, bringing his palms together and bowing his head. He was Sea Lord stock, then, or at least paid homage to their cults.

"Can he truly see land from up there?" she asked, skeptically.

"Oh, aye, we aren't but a jigger from land, here in the Bay," the mate assured her. "This is a light run, betwixt the Mandros and Prejestia."

"Do you think we'll see pirates?" Gatina clutched the pendant that hung around her neck, the one that indicated her position in the Saganite Order. It wasn't by accident. The idea of pirates raiding their ship both excited and terrified her.

"It be unlikely, Sister," he said, chuckling reassuringly and perhaps a little condescendingly. "We have seen no sign of activity, we're too close to shore, and we're but a small ship," he said. "We're carrying *pears*. Not the sort of thing a corsair would consider worthy of his time. Nothing to afear. And if there were trouble, we are always prepared," he assured her bravely before he turned and walked away.

Gatina smiled at Palo, who nodded goodbye and went to his other duties, leaving her to her book and solitude. But she could not focus on the book. The idea of pirates—bandits of the sea, who would take a ship, its crew, and its cargo as a matter of trade—infatuated her. Her book had revealed that many honorable Sea Lords had turned to base piracy over the centuries. It was considered a respectable, if not honorable, tradition among the culture. But so were the men who fought piracy. It was a strange world the Sea Lords lived in, Gatina reflected.

Too excited to read, she searched for her brother. He would want to know that they were nearly to port, she knew.

Prejestia came into view long before the captain called it to their attention over dinner that night.

She had learned a little about their destination in the last few days; it was an ancient Sea Lord port turned Coastlord in composition after the Magocracy conquered Enultramar. For four centuries it had been a coastal market for the lemons, oranges, and limes that grew in vast estates in the coastal backcountry, and it served as a home port for a few score merchant companies. It was not big enough to house a truly large enterprise, but it was also not so small as to be considered unimportant.

Gatina learned that it was a "captive port"—a haven that was dependent on the produce and supply of the surrounding inland country. Other ports, like Ganivet, Gavina, Vaxel, and Glavores, were considered international ports: the harbors from which the great overseas voyages to destinations in Merwyn, Vore, Farise, and the Shattered Isles began. Most of Enultramar's trade was from captive ports, she learned. Caravels and even galleons brought wine, olive oil, citrus, garum, cotton, wool, brandy, and a host of other products Alshar made to the international ports, where they were sent far, far away to be sold for astronomical prices in distant lands.

In return, those ships brought cargoes of sugar, vanilla, spices, tea, kaffa leaf, kava, and a host of other exotic wares to Alshar's shores. She quickly learned by listening to the crew and the wizened old captain that the essence of trade was simple: the farther you shipped a cargo, the more expensive it was at the destination port. Even simple things like fruit or flax could prove incredibly lucrative in a place that didn't have them. That was the essence of the Sea Lord culture and all maritime affairs. Not fishing—the mariners on the *Gaillardia* sneered at the fishing boats they passed on their short voyage. Fishermen were another breed, barely better than landsmen, according to the deckhands of the caravel. A Sea Lord turned to fishing for his living only when he was too worn and beaten by the sea to live any other way.

Prejestia was unremarkable in most ways. As they approached the small harbor, Gatina could spot the areas that had been settled by the austere Sea Lords and the far comelier portions that had been built by her Coastlord ancestors. The latter were smaller, less concentrated, and whitewashed a blistering white with gaily colored blues and greens painted on the trim. Both cultures had cultivated large docks and wharves to house the ships that plied the Great Bay, but there was a clear difference between the compounds of the merchantmen of the Coastlords and the more sparse and severe slips that housed Sea Lord ships.

Their final supper aboard the *Gaillardia* was another hearty and entirely tasteless fish stew. While Gatina thought she would never tire of the fresh seafood, the ship's cook seemed determined to rob the food of any flavor. It was filling—and completely uninspiring. She did miss fresh bread, though.

The view from the boat's main deck before the sun set that last night finally demonstrated dots of green trees on the northern horizon, peeking above billowy wheat-colored sails. There was still a lot of blue water between them and the shore, but it was apparent that they were close to land, which brought her some comfort.

And while Gatina was ready to be on land and curious to meet her extended family members, she was more excited by the prospect of the potential mission that lay ahead.

The time on the boat had been instructive. She knew now much more about how a ship operated. She understood the mechanisms and how each crew member was vital to operating the ship, from bow to stern. And that would help her as she undertook her apprenticeship with her cousins in Prejestia. Of course, she realized, she had never actually hoisted a sail—*or sheet*, she corrected—but it seemed to be run by a system of pulleys, and she was familiar with those.

By the end of the first full day aboard the ship, she had finished her book. So, she spent the remaining days on deck, pretending to read but actually absorbing everything she could about how the crew worked together to man the ship. It had been a fascinating study. She decided on the second day that life on the sea was not for her. She did not want to risk slicing her leg while fighting on deck with her shadowblade because the unpredictable waves knocked the boat off kilter. Nor did she relish the idea of fighting against the wind to reach the helm to correct the ship's course. She was strong, but she was not strong enough to control a ship this size—not without help. She shuddered at the thought of such a dangerous responsibility.

As the captain sailed the ship into Prejestia port, Gatina forgot her alias for a brief moment, she was so excited by the sights and sounds. There were barges and ships of all sizes everywhere. She saw a long wooden walkway with at least fifty docks connected to it—much larger than what she was used to in the riverport of Falas. She saw people. The walkway was still in the distance, and the people looked like specks, but she saw specks that she could identify as people, not birds. And she saw land. She missed land.

The motion on the deck brought her back to herself. Some of the crew members began gathering lines, which she now knew was what sailors called ropes, in preparation to toss them to dockmen who would secure the craft to the dock. Others worked to lower the mainsail and tie it to the boom. They did not need all of the sails to get into port. Too many sails and too much wind would take them away from their destination.

Gatina looked around and found Nocturn Dain right beside the captain on the pilot deck. He wanted to learn how to steer the ship, and the captain had taken Atopol's interest as sincere, so he had agreed to demonstrate. Gatina had wondered if Atopol would actually have the opportunity to handle the massive wheel at the helm.

For a brief instant, she was jealous, but that faded quickly when the specks on shore became more discernable. She saw faces! And she could smell more than the stench of the men on the deck. The smell of the water had changed; that was a subtle shift, but the closer they sailed to the dock, the brinier it grew in her nostrils. That led to a brief sneezing fit during which she nearly lost her scarf.

The port of Prejestia revealed itself to be a complicated maze of boats and ships as they arrived and departed. She quickly saw there was an order to how barges and ships were docked. Larger ships were on one side of the port, medium-sized ships in the middle, and the smaller ships and barges were to the side nearest the shore. She reasoned that it made sense for controlling comings and goings. Only so many could sail out at the same time. She did not see a lighthouse, at least not yet. She wondered about that. Nor did she see any guard towers. But their vessel was still a distance away.

"Nocturn Avorrita?" She turned when she heard her mother's voice. "Ah, there you are. We've nearly arrived. It's probably best that you return to the cabin to pack your belongings," she said. Her mother's voice sounded tired, and Gatina knew she had made it sound that way for an effect. Normally, Mother's voice was lilting and light. "Come now, Nocturn," she added, with emphasis.

Without hesitation, Nocturn Avorrita followed the elderly nun toward the narrow staircase they had been shown on their first night. They made their way to their shared cabin in solemn silence, as it seemed proper to allow the crew peace to complete their tasks ahead of the ship's arrival.

When they were safely inside the small room with the door closed, Minnie broke character. "I am so relieved to see the coast, Kitten. I am ready to be off this wretched ship." She sat on the narrow bed and reached underneath to remove her satchel. "Start preparing for our departure. I know we didn't unpack much, but—"

"But leave no evidence of your presence," Gatina replied by rote. It was a rule, after all. "I will make sure that nothing is left, Mother." She walked to her own bed and reached underneath, removing her small bag and opening it. "Other than fresh undergarments and my book, I did not unpack anything." Gatina stuffed her book into her bag. "Are we about to start the mission?" she asked expectantly.

"Here is neither the time nor the place for such a conversation, Nocturn." She stood and began adding her own items to her satchel. "I wager we have about an hour before we are at the dock. I thought we could have a private conversation about—" Minnie hesitated and that caught Gatina off guard. "Well, about your safety in this current climate and location."

Gatina was confused. "But I can swim!"

Her mother stopped what she was doing and turned to face Gatina, a folded nightgown in her hands. "It is not the water I'm worried about. Oh, I am, but that is not my point. It is very dangerous here. Well, it's dangerous everywhere now, but what I mean is that the ports and the access to the water pose a grave risk. The Brotherhood of the Rat is only one of the gangs that are on the lookout for easy prey to sell at a slave market. The captain was telling us last night that he's lost mariners—grown men—right off the docks and in broad daylight. If you are captured and taken aboard a boat, you very well might be gone before anyone realizes it. You could be sold at auction on the other side of the Great Bay within a few days. So, I am giving you an order, Apprentice: do *not* get captured."

Gatina sucked in her breath. Her mother's voice was as quiet as a whisper, but her tone was deadly serious. "Yes, Mistress, of course," she said, looking her mother in the eyes. "I will not get captured. I will be careful. And I will be aware."

"Good, Kitten. Now let's get ashore and off this miserable ship before that cook inflicts more of that . . . *stew* on us. I want to get changed out of this dreadful habit and into more-civilized clothes before we meet your aunt and cousins."

Gatina carried her bag up to the deck and watched the mariners with fascination as they stowed the sails and lines and prepared the mooring lines. A man in a small boat wearing a bright sash pulled near to the bow and shouted instructions to the pilot about where to dock. It only took a few moments for the nimble mariners to leap down from the deck to the dock and secure the ship to it with mooring lines. A moment later, the wide gangplank was lowered, allowing easier access to the ship. With a certain sense of fondness, Gatina prepared herself to leave the *Gaillardia*—the *Shadowdancer*.

After offering various blessings to the crew for a continued safe voyage, the four of them quickly departed and hired a handcart and a porter to take their baggage to the line of small shops that faced the pier. Once they were safely out of sight of the ship, one by one they excused themselves to a privy and changed their garb.

When Gatina rejoined her parents and Atopol on the boardwalk, nobody would have recognized them as the three Saganite clergy members and elderly Tryggite nun who had arrived moments before. Hance wore a doublet of pale gold with brown hose and a white shirt. Atopol wore brown trousers and a white shirt topped with a doublet the color of the sky before a storm—a deep blue. Both had swords on their hips—not their shadowblades but short, slightly curved Sea Lord–style swords like the ones Master Steel had shown them in practice. It seemed to be the style, she noted, as most of the better-dressed travelers along the boardwalk seemed to carry similar blades.

She wore no sword, but both she and her mother had small, wicked-looking curved daggers that were apparently worn by Sea Lord ladies on the thin leather belt that gathered her dress, just behind the small of her back.

Gatina's dress was novel to her: the type of gown a Sea Lord maiden might wear, her mother had explained when she presented it to her. The fabric was light and airy. It wouldn't get hot in the coastal climate. It was a blend of silk and cotton, strong and durable but also attractive. The blue gown was the color of the sky just before nightfall, a pale violet blue. The wimple was made of the same fabric but not as long as the Coastlord style she was used to—apparently Sea Lord maidens didn't mind if their hair was exposed. It was short and barely brushed her shoulders. She was relieved to note that the Sea Lords also did not seem to favor corsets or other binding undergarments the way that the Coastlord aristocracy was starting to favor. Indeed, her gown was quite comfortable, compared to what she wore when she was pretending to be a noblewoman of Falas.

And the shoes—instead of worthless slippers or those fiendish high heels, Sea Lords wore boots almost universally, male and female. Gatina's came to just above her ankle and were thankfully flat. They were also quite stylish, tooled leather treated with some sort of finish that shed water easily.

As Hance nodded to her in approval of her dress, he took advantage of the quiet from the lull in activity to speak.

"We will meet our family soon. I sent word a few days before our departure to let them know our schedule. They should be sending a carriage for us. We will be going to the family's estate—it's not far," he explained, "but it is on the other side of the harbor."

Gatina listened to her father, but her attention was on her surroundings. The docks fascinated her. She watched everything, her eyes scanning side to side. She was interested in all of the activities. She had never seen so many ships or mariners in one place before. There were porters and stevedores everywhere, as well as street vendors hawking their wares to the newly arrived.

The stevedores were impressive. They worked in unison like dancers, tying and untying boats and ships, loading or unloading cargo, and shouting orders or commands with order and precision in what would otherwise look like chaos. It was mesmerizing—and loud.

Prejestia's famous Citrus Market was directly across from her, where thousands of pounds of fruit from the inland were bought and sold. The colors and smells called to her. The sweetness of oranges met with the bitterness of lemon and the tang of limes danced under her nostrils. She wanted nothing more than to run across the street and buy an orange. She resisted the temptation.

She realized that her father was still talking, much quieter now, directly to her mother. They were standing closely together, as husband and wife, not as two members of the clergy. She and Atopol were close enough to just overhear. She looked over at Atopol, and he nodded as if to signal that this conversation might be important. So, Gatina focused on it.

"I am so proud of Beah for standing her ground," she heard her mother say. "It took a lot of courage to remain here with her children after Alekandrus went missing. I can't imagine what she went through." Gatina was close enough to see her mother reach her free hand to her father's and give it a reassuring squeeze.

"She is a very strong woman, just like her ancestors, beloved. I look forward to seeing her again. I just hope our mission doesn't interfere with her work too much," he said, concerned. "I know this is important, but she has a ship and a crew to be responsible for, not just her family. She's been struggling—and I don't want to be part of her struggle. Ah! I think that's their carriage," he said, pointing at the road next to the boardwalk. "There it is!" he said, voice certain. "Their crest is a combination of mage stars and a wave. The merging of our Houses," he explained as he motioned for the children to follow.

Gatina saw the crest before her father had pointed it out. The outline of a five-pointed mage star was indeed riding atop a blue wave, which had been beautifully colored in different shades of blue. The carriage itself was far cruder than the ones she was used to, and it was clear that it was used for transporting cargo as much as people. It was open, with only a flimsy bit of sailcloth covering the bed to shade it from the sun. It was drawn by a team of two sturdy-looking draft horses.

As they approached the carriage, her father greeted the coachman with a handshake and an embrace. He introduced the man—or man-sized boy, Gatina realized with a great deal of enthusiasm. He was as tall as Atopol, she saw, though far heavier-boned, bordering on portly. And his hair was as white as hers or Attie's.

"This is your cousin Jordi," he said, as the drover jumped down. "Lady Behantra sent him to pick us up with our baggage. And he'll make arrangements to see the other cargo delivered to the estate."

"Well met!" The young man grinned shyly. He had a short-cropped head of hair that was a familiar white under his cap, and a wide, ruddy face that seemed to flush and blush for no particular reason. There was a family resemblance around his eyes that reminded Gatina of her father, but his eyes themselves were a calming shade of hazel, not the violet that she and Atopol had. "We're all terribly excited to meet you! Mother has a big feed planned to welcome you properly tonight, so we should really get back and see you to your quarters," he advised. "You're Atopol, right?" he asked her brother.

"Today I am," he conceded. "You can call me Cat, too. Need help loading the bags?"

"That would be welcome," Jordi agreed. "I need to talk to someone about bringing the cargo to the estate, but the sooner we're underway, the better. There's a big galleon that should be docking about noon, and by then, all the porters will be taken."

The open nature of the carriage not only allowed a gentle breeze to blow through, but Gatina's perch provided breathtaking views of the Bay on one side and the distant cliffs on the other. The water was a greenish blue, and she could see some sort of sea life bobbing and along the top, skimming the surface. Gulls and albatrosses soared between the shore and the waves as they searched for fish or convenient piles of garbage along the docks. Their air was no longer merely briny—she could smell the vibrant aromas of land once again, realizing there was a distinct difference.

"It's amazing here," Gatina said in delight as the carriage pulled them through the colorful town. In truth, she had seen nothing like it before. She was able to spot exotic flowers the size of her head creeping up trellises. They gave off an intoxicating scent. The road was not paved, but it was hard-packed and, from what Gatina could see from her view out the window, it was nearly white. She wondered if it was sand or a sand-and-shell substance. The sun reflected off it a bit, like a looking glass.

"Wait until you see Salterpath House," Hance said. "The views are breathtaking. You can see for miles when the horizon is clear," he said, lost in a memory.

"If the weather holds," Jordi agreed grimly. "It's been a bad season for squalls already, and it's barely summer. We get at least one or two showers every day, which is fine, but when those bad ones blow in from the Bay, it's hard to see your nose in front of your face."

The mention of squalls intrigued Gatina—and not in a good way. "I'd rather be on land for one than at sea," she assured him. "It was calm on the passage from the river, and I still had a hard time keeping my balance. I can't imagine being in a storm on a ship!"

"You just need to get your sea legs," her cousin suggested. "They'll come in time. But you're right: squalls are never very much fun. The Shipwrecker never sleeps," he said, as if it was a proverb. "My sister, Pia, sort of likes them, though," he admitted with a trace of disgust in his voice. "She thinks they're exciting."

"How old is Pia?" Gatina asked, curiously.

"About your brother's age," her mother supplied. "And Jordi is about your age, Gatina. Just a few months older. Beah wanted more children, but . . ."

"Yes, Father was lost at sea," said Jordi, with a nod and a sigh. "She still holds out hope for his survival somewhere. May the Shipwrecker preserve him if she spared him," he said, fervently.

"I thought the Shipwrecker was an . . . evil goddess," Atopol said, confused.

"Evil?" Jordi asked in surprise. "She's not evil, really. There's nothing personal about a squall or a tempest. She might break your ship, but the Shipwrecker also sends the crews and boats to search for you after a storm. She protects castaways if they make it to shore. And the men dedicated to her service will salvage a ship if they can."

"You have a very complicated religion," Atopol observed.

"She's not a malevolent divinity," Gatina said, recalling the chapter in her book about the mysterious goddess. "She doesn't really try to wreck ships. But she represents the dangers of voyaging at sea."

"She's not my favorite," Jordi admitted. "But a mariner who doesn't respect her power will pay for it with his life and end up on her enchanted island when he dies, they say."

"You go to an island when you die?" Atopol asked, intrigued.

"That depends on how you die," Jordi reasoned. "If you die of sickness, you go to the Salt Crone's island. If you die in battle at sea, you go to the Corsair's. Most mariners want to die in port, so they'll go to the

Maiden's island—that's supposed to be the best one," he informed them thoughtfully.

"So, who decides how you die?" Gatina asked.

"Enough questions about religion, Kitten," her mother reproved. "Most people aren't as well read on the subject as you."

"So . . . you're Cat," Jordi said, nodding to Atopol, "and you're . . . Kitten?"

"Professional names," explained her mother with a smile. "Their grandparents gave them those nicknames when they were babies. Atopol was a sweet baby, never doing much more than sitting around all day like a comfortable cat. Kitten, on the other hand, started getting into mischief the moment she realized she had fingers and toes. Always getting into places where she shouldn't, and fiddling with things she shouldn't. That hasn't changed much."

Jordi gave both of his cousins a long, searching look. "And you are all . . . thieves?" he asked, his voice near a whisper.

"Shadowthieves," Gatina corrected. "Magical thieves. But don't worry; we don't ever steal from family. Or without a good cause. We're better than that," she assured.

"That must be interesting," Jordi nodded. "You ever get caught?"

"We're better than that, too," Gatina grinned. "Mostly. Every now and then, we'll have a close call, but . . ."

"Let's save the professional chatter for tonight, Kitten," her mother reproved. "Some things are best said in private. And over brandy."

CHAPTER SIX

SAILING LESSONS

*Within the haven's anchorage the Maiden's Grace protects
From the fury of the Father,
From the chaos of the Shipwrecker,
From the invisible hand of the Fairtrader,
From the wrath of the Corsair,
From the despair of the Salt Crone.
Blessed is the Anchor that holds us there,
Sacred is the Cup of her hospitality.*
—Sea Lord Prayer to the Maiden of the Havens

THEY HAD FINALLY ARRIVED AT SALTERPATH.

The estate was situated on the far side of the harbor, away from most of the activity, on a narrow spit of land that stretched from the cliffs to the shore. There, a large dock and a compound of sheds provided for the care of dozens of boats and a few proper ships. There was a sandy strip of beach nearby on which several boats had been overturned, and where a group of men were repairing nets and sailcloth. A path led from the compound past a small grove of citrus trees and gardens up to the main house—Salterpath House—and it was impressive.

Atopol let out a gasp, and Gatina looked up until she caught sight of the massive brick structure built into the cliffs. Excited, she peered out the window and her eyes focused up, up, and up—the house seemed to climb into the cliffside. It was remarkable to her how the beach and water could be on one side and the cliffs so close on the other.

The main house was built of whitewashed brick with limestone supporting columns at the corners. There were plenty of windows, Gatina noted, and many with real panes of glass covering them—an expensive display of wealth.

The lowest level was the largest, Gatina could see, a sprawling series of bays and additions that seemed to serve as stables, kitchens, storehouses, and workshops of various sorts. The second floor was slightly smaller, providing a wide balcony on the roof of the first, as well as a number of doors and windows that looked out over the harbor—clearly a residential section. The third floor was smaller still, and the balcony that resulted had carved limestone rails. Above the third floor was a tall, two-story spire that peeked over the cliffside and no doubt provided an excellent view of both the sea and the land.

It was a grand-looking place, in the more ornate Coastlord style, with the shutters and doors painted with the same blue as was used in the family's device, and gray slate tiles on the steeply pitched roofs. Mage stars were also part of the décor and were painted in several places. There were almost-whimsical paintings on the whitewashed walls and a few bits of sculpture in various places, but the yard in front of the place also contained some oddities: a ship's anchor, a great millstone, and a boat that appeared to have been crushed, all sitting amid elegant gardens.

As her eyes scanned the impressive building, her mind began to work of its own accord. By the time Jordi opened the door of the carriage and helped her mother out, Gatina had figured out how she would enter to rob the place.

A serving girl led them to the main entry of the house, distinctly different from the other doors that led inside, while a crew of kitchen drudges unloaded the wagon. The smell in the air was exotic—part fresh salt air, part sweet citrus and summer flowers, and part rotting fish, she noted.

The inside of the house was as impressive as the outside. The hall beyond the entranceway was strangely beautiful. A broad stone staircase wrapped up along the eastern wall, winding around to the second and third floors and perhaps beyond. The beams overhead bore simple chandeliers with oil lamps of glass. Painted filigrees of twisting vines and stylized waves surrounded every doorway. Rough woven rugs of dyed grasses covered much of the floor, while a number of chairs, benches, tables and cabinets seemed to be crammed into every corner.

But it was the window in the ceiling that captured her attention. She had never seen a skylight before, not one with thick panes of glass. It let in a tremendous amount of sunlight, she noted, enough so that the interior was nearly as brightly lit as outside. The clouds danced above, hiding the setting sun. She imagined how the stars looked at night from there. She imagined how she would break through the grand window on the ceiling without breaking its many panes.

Attie called her to attention. She had fallen behind, and she quickened her pace, mentally chastising herself for being so taken in by the home and the exquisite views. She wasn't a peasant, after all. She, too, had grown up in a regal home, though perhaps not as unique. Salterpath was just ... different from the homes she was used to.

The serving girl, whose mannerisms indicated she might be older than she appeared, pushed aside a light linen curtain and motioned them through it. Two women were engrossed in reviewing a thick stack of parchment across a narrow table as they entered. When all four Furtiusi were in the room, the serving girl announced their arrival by their actual names for once.

As a result of her training, Gatina's eyes and attention were drawn first to the room, not the people. She quickly assessed the value of items and the escape routes—three that she saw, all floor-to-ceiling doors that opened onto the balcony, and all were currently open to allow the breeze to cool the interior. Instead of the usual tapestries she would expect in a great hall, the large room featured a collection of maps hung on the open wall spaces as well as one large, beautiful painting of the seascape.

The room itself was not lavishly appointed, but she noticed several unique pieces of art and a bronze crest crossed by a pair of Sea Lord scimitars above the fireplace, unused in the summer heat. The room was full of bright green potted plants and more pillows and settees than she was used to. It made Gatina feel calm, she decided. It was comfortable and not ostentatious.

But then the people took command of her attention. The two women— one older, one younger—rose and embraced her parents warmly.

Beah was a strong, sturdy middle-aged woman with the family's white hair and violet eyes, which drank in everything they could about her and her brother the moment they landed on them. She had large hands that were callused in a way no self-respecting noblewoman of Falas would ever endure, Gatina observed, bearing several rings of gold and silver on fingers of both hands. She did, indeed, resemble her father, especially around the eyes, like her cousin Jordi. She also wore his smile—the one Gatina didn't see often but engaged her when it came out like the sun from behind the clouds—only Beah wore it almost constantly. Both were wearing it when they broke their embrace.

"Aunt Behantra, Pia, and Jordi, we take great pleasure in introducing you to our children, Atopol and Gatina," her father said proudly. "It's been far too long since we have visited you, Beah. And I apologize that I have not brought my children before now."

"Having babies makes it difficult to travel." Beah nodded understandingly. "But you're here now, and that's the important thing. How was your trip?"

"Fine, until we got to the delta," her mother supplied. "The caravel we hired for the final leg was the only disappointment."

"The *Gaillardia*? Yes, it's a wretched old hull," she said sympathetically. "If your letter had arrived any sooner, I would have sent a boat for you myself and spared you the trouble. I know the captain—nice enough, but his ship is old and needed to be overhauled five years ago. He doesn't go beyond the shallows these days. It's easy to be a good captain on still waters. But he can't afford to go any further. He doesn't trust it on the open Bay and has to make his living with these short little cargo runs along the coast. I'm glad you made it safely. But this occasion calls for a glass of brandy, don't you think, nephew?" She smiled with genuine endearment. The two were not too far apart in age, Gatina guessed; it was only some trick of genealogy that made her her father's aunt. Great aunt. Or something. "And please, call me Beah."

The four children smiled at each other as the adults congregated by the table. Pia, the girl her brother's age, had the violet eyes and white hair that were her family's hallmark. There was no sense of awkwardness, which surprised Gatina. Instead, Pia put her at ease immediately. She grabbed her brother's hand and pulled him along behind her as she crossed the space between them quickly and gracefully.

"I'm Pia. It's short for Piandrea but please don't call me that. I prefer Pia," she said, speaking in the tone of someone who was accustomed to being heard. "And you've met my brother Jordi, short for Jordanedel. We've heard so much about you from Mother! It's so nice to finally meet you!" She looked at them expectantly. And Gatina nearly spoke, but Atopol finally found his voice.

"Hello, cousins. I am Atopol, or Attie. And this is my sister, Gatina," he said, his voice smooth and even as he bowed and gestured to his sister. "We've heard a bit about you as well. A little bit."

Pia smiled warmly and Gatina felt herself relax, releasing a tension in her shoulders she hadn't known she was carrying. She wasn't a beautiful girl, but she was striking. She shared her mother's face and big smile, as well as her commanding presence. She was slightly taller than Atopol, and her shoulders were broad.

The adults' laughter brought a brief moment of silence to the cousins' introductions. But Pia was a gracious hostess. "I imagine you are both ravenous after such a long journey. Let me show you where the kitchen is. We can get to know each other better there," she promised.

Jordi nodded, his shy smile flashing for a moment and making Gatina feel comfortable. Indeed, she felt comfortable with both of her cousins, when she was used to deception and suspicion. "The kitchen has a secret supply of sweet biscuits," he revealed. "I'll show you where it is." Pia and Atopol walked ahead of her and Jordi as her older cousin led them back downstairs.

"How was your journey from Falas? Mother said you were coming on the *Gaillardia*, so we were all a bit worried. That ship is half in the Shipwrecker's halls already. She's one good squall away from the bottom," Pia declared. That concerned Gatina. She hadn't thought the ship had been that bad.

"The trip was fine, but the food was awful," Atopol answered. "Thick brown stew for breakfast, luncheon, and supper. We got fed better at the abbey," he insisted.

"It wasn't that bad," Gatina protested, although she agreed with her brother in spirit. "It was a good trip. We had a lot of fish stew, made fresh each day. I'd say it was fairly easy. Though I've only been on the water a handful of times. And I'd never been on such a large ship before. But half the crew were missing limbs and tongues and . . ."

"Well, the captain of the *Gaillardia* can't afford to hire any better," Pia explained. "He's in debt up to his throat, and his ship is falling apart, so he can't take on any decent cargo. The bottom has so many barnacles on it that it's a wonder she sails at all. If he'd gone more than a mile from shore, you'd be lucky to survive the trip. Our ship is much better," she boasted, "it's a proper caravel: three masts, over thirty tons. It's called the *Legacy*."

"*Alekandrus's Legacy*," Jordi corrected. "It's named for my father."

"The one who d— who's missing at sea? We heard about that," Gatina said, sympathetically.

"Mother thought it would be fit to rename her, to honor him," Jordi nodded. "She still holds hope that he will return someday." From the tone of his voice, it didn't sound as if Jordi shared that hope. Gatina couldn't imagine a life with her father gone, presumed dead. She wondered what her mother would do if such a tragedy happened.

As they crossed from the long hallway into the kitchen, Gatina paused while she took in the sight before her. The kitchen was whitewashed and featured more of the tall windows, shutters wide, and a few doors, one of which was open to a bountiful vegetable garden alive with reds, greens, oranges, and yellows. There were several kitchen drudges assisting an old woman Gatina assumed was the head cook preparing the evening meal. Open shelves full of porcelain bowls, plates, and glassware lined the white walls.

There was a huge kettle simmering on the fire, and the oven was being heated while the drudges chopped, kneaded, and stirred. There were bowls full of red tubers and green beans and baskets of bright yellow, green, and orange fruit that hung from hooks above another long, narrow table. This one was mounted to the wall and near a deep soaking tub. It seemed as though water came directly to the house, which was something she had only heard about. It was curious to see. She supposed it was incredibly convenient. It smelled wonderful, she decided.

"You'll really appreciate the *Legacy*, then, after the *Gaillardia*," Pia assured as she led them to an alcove and opened a cupboard. "We've spent the last year refurbishing her, scraping the hull, and replacing the rigging. She's as good as when she came from the shipwright," she said, proudly. "And she's so much larger than a normal coastal caravel. The hold can easily carry a village's supply of grain in one trip," she said proudly as she distributed sweet biscuits to them all.

"Are those cinnamon?" Atopol asked before reaching into the tin to take one. He held it to his nose and inhaled the scent. "Absolutely heavenly," he said after tasting it. "I love cinnamon. Gat, you should have one; they're your favorite."

Pia handed one to her. "I love cinnamon too," she said dreamily. I suppose it runs in the family. That bark comes all the way from Farise or the Shattered Isles."

"It's so expensive," Atopol said, shaking his head gratefully. "But so delicious!"

"In Falas, perhaps," Pia shrugged. "Here in the Bay, you can get it a lot cheaper. The farther you ship a cargo, the more expensive it becomes. A lot of crews will pilfer the barrels of their cargo and trade the odd bit of cinnamon bark or cloves or nutmeg for coin or other luxuries. There is a whole economy on the docks like that. I think Mother got Jordi from a merchantman for a piglet and two barrels of tea."

"She dramatically overpaid, then," Jordi said dryly. He laughed, which made everyone else laugh.

And in that moment, Gatina realized that she was no longer alone. One of the things about her life she didn't realize until then was how absolutely lonely it could be. It was difficult to have real friends when you had to change your name and appearance all the time, and were constantly on the lookout for Rats, Censors, street toughs, and inquisitive members of the Watch.

There, she had a family and cousins her age. Cousins were blood. And they seemed to be intelligent, witty, and friendly. She didn't have to hide her legacy of secrets from them, she realized. And that meant she might have people to talk to, specifically another girl to talk to about girl things. And mage things that were more specific to girls. And that made her very happy.

She just knew this was going to be a wonderful mission.

Supper that night was a marvelous affair; the servants of Salterpath House had clearly been admonished to make it memorable, and they succeeded. The family dined in the spacious main hall around a grand old wooden table that looked as though it had been made from old ship's timbers and then polished by magic into a glorious sheen. The stark white linens bore a bounty of colorful and delicious dishes Gatina had seen being prepared in the kitchen, with a massive ocean fish cooked whole and served on a silver platter. Wine flowed freely as their parents exchanged news with Beah at one end of the table, while their children enjoyed an animated conversation at the other.

Gatina saw how relaxed her parents were, and that brought her some joy. They were laughing, and Beah as Father joked about old stories of family members she'd never met. She had not seen her parents so relaxed since things had changed before the Shadow Council had been called into service and they'd become responsible for so much more than their family. Perhaps being at the shore was calming for them, or maybe it was the fact that they were not in disguise for once, pretending to be other people, or perhaps it was being with the extended family that had them at ease. But it was welcome to see them so peaceful.

Despite her "wet sheep" reputation among the larger House, Gatina found Aunt Beah to be incredibly kind, she saw immediately. And she had a way about her that appealed to Gatina. Things seemed to come easy in her presence, so far.

Beah also catered to tradition. At the table, for example, eight places had been set. One for each of them and one for Aunt Beah's missing husband, Alekandrus. Pia had explained that was one way they held him close, though Jordi appeared skeptical about the practice, as if he'd given up hope of ever seeing his father again. Gatina thought it was a very romantic way to remember someone, alive or not.

"One thing my children will not become is entitled," Aunt Beah said adamantly, at the start of the meal. The candles on the table played off her father and aunt's hair. Jordi and Atopol's, too. "It is something Alek and I agreed upon before we had children. He grew up working hard for all he had, despite his status, and he wanted the same for his children. And, well, Hance, you know how we were raised." Gatina looked at her father as he tipped his cup toward his aunt. "I think it teaches them the value of work and an appreciation for those who do the work." Gatina's mother nodded approvingly. Gatina remembered helping her work in the garden before the assassinations changed the duchy. And all the rigorous lessons she'd had to learn over the years.

And it had been a long few years, Gatina realized.

The bond between her father and Beah was strong, she saw. They had a chemistry between them that was more like brother and sister, like her and Atopol. Despite Beah being her great-great-aunt, the woman did not appear much older than her father and mother. But the resemblance was certainly present. Beah's hair was white and her eyes violet, as was customary among House Furtius's mages. But instead of pale skin, protected by the Darkness, the woman looked sun-kissed. She was bronze, as were Pia and Jordi. Beah's skin made her hair look natural, at least in this setting and location. Gatina was suddenly self-conscious about how pale her skin was.

Her study of Beah was interrupted when Pia passed her a platter of vegetables before she sat down. Jordi had a tray of little roasted fish, and he served that to the adults before his sister and cousins. Gatina scraped a healthy portion of baked vegetables onto her trencher while she waited her turn for fish. The vegetables were colorful instead of dull, and cooked until tender, not into mush. The carrots were a vibrant orange and the beets a deep purple. Watered-down wine mixed with orange slices, a fruit salad, and bread baked that morning complemented the delicious meal.

The subject of magic inevitably arose.

"I heard that you got your *rajira*," Atopol mentioned to Pia. "Congratulations!"

"Yes, about a year and a half ago," Pia agreed, as she spooned a thick sauce over her fish. "I've been apprenticed to Mother ever since. She's going to let me do some of the spells on the cargo this time," she said, proudly. "If it wasn't for magic, half of the citrus we carry would spoil before we made port."

"It really makes that much of a difference?" Gatina asked, curious.

"Oh, assuredly," Jordi agreed. "No one wants to haul a load of rotten fruit. Most of our competitors have to hire a mage to cast those spells. With Mother—and now Pia—able to do them, our costs go down dramatically. Do you know that spell?" he asked, curious.

Gatina shook her head as she sampled a dish of shrimp, corn and cheese in which garlic played an important role. "No, most of our training involves general magic, with some emphasis on photomancy—shadowmagic," she explained.

"I for one would like to know what is so bloody special about being a shadowmage," Jordi said, quiet enough for only the four of them to hear. "It doesn't sound particularly useful."

"It depends on what you do with it," Atopol reasoned. "I don't think it would be very useful on a ship. But if you happen to be breaking into someone's house, past a bunch of armed guards and a pack of vicious dogs, then through a locked door, well, it can prove beneficial."

Pia shook her head in wonder. "I can't believe that you two are actual thieves," she said. "When Mother told us that, we didn't believe her. But then she showed us a few tricks she'd learned as a girl. She almost disappeared right in front of us!"

"Now I never know when she's watching," Jordi added, forlornly, making everyone laugh. "So . . . what kinds of things do you . . . steal?" he asked.

"Whatever we need to," Gatina explained. "There's definitely an art to it. But we've stolen art, jewels, gems, wine, anything of value. Just before we came here, I stole a special bottle of wine. Got into a duel, too, that night," she said proudly.

"And then lost her sword before it was done," Atopol reminded her.

"What's the most impressive thing you've stolen?" Pia asked. Both of her cousins appeared fascinated about their clandestine lives, Gatina noted. It felt good to be able to talk about it openly for a change.

"A book," Gatina decided. "A very important book. It's not about what you're stealing, though, usually; it's *how* you do it. Every heist is different, of course, but once you know what you're doing, most of them are pretty easy. Take this place," she said, looking around at the grand furnishings. "This would be a simple place to rob."

"Would it?" Pia asked, surprised. "We've never had a robbery here! There are too many people, and we're too watchful for that."

Atopol and Gatina exchanged knowing glances. "I've already figured six different ways I could get in without being seen," Atopol revealed. "Kitten?"

"Eight, actually, off the top of my head," Gatina boasted. "And if there are eight, then there are actually nine. Or ten. Or twenty. Most people aren't as secure as they think they are. And nothing is secure from the Cats of Enultramar."

The admission startled their two cousins. "You really could break into Salterpath House?" Pia asked skeptically.

"If Kitten and I worked together, we could have every valuable in the place in about two hours, and you'd never know we were here," he assured her. "We once robbed a country estate in Falas, just the two of us. We took everything down to the keys to the spice cupboard. There were nine guards that night. Six dogs. Not one of them saw us or suspected anything until morning—and we were long gone by then."

"Isn't that . . . dangerous?" Jordi asked.

"No more than sailing," Gatina ventured. "A lot less, actually. It really depends on whether or not you know what you're doing."

"I think we need to get more dogs, then," Jordi said, shaking his head.

"It wouldn't matter," Gatina shrugged. "We get past dogs all the time. There are spells for that. And drugs you can put in bait."

"Sometimes, you can get away with a familiar scent and a pat on the head," Atopol agreed. "But you have to know what you're doing. We aren't common footpads, after all. We're professionals. The most important thing is to not get caught."

"Didn't you say you were caught once?" Jordi reminded Gatina. It made her blush.

"Just for a few hours," she admitted, guiltily. "Special circumstances. It was the first time we were up against another mage—Censors," she said condemningly. "But I escaped. And burned down the tower I was being held in," she added casually. "That was an exception."

"So, what were you stealing?" Jordi asked.

"People," Gatina sighed. "We were rescuing a bunch of prisoners from the Counts. The burning tower made a lovely distraction."

Pia gave her a searching look, as if she wasn't certain Gatina was being honest or not. "That sounds . . . exciting," she ventured.

"It was. And completely improvised. That was the first time I used magic in a heist, too. But sometimes, you have to be able to think quickly as your heist changes. There's always something you didn't account for or some secret passageway that wasn't in the plans. A sentry where they aren't supposed to be, or even a fat, friendly old dog that you missed when you scouted the place before you robbed it."

"Like a sudden squall at sea," Pia nodded. "You always have to be prepared for that, even if the surface is as calm as glass." She paused between bites and studied both of her cousins. "I'm guessing that this trip isn't just about a holiday at the coast, is it?" she guessed.

"There might be a larger reason behind it," Atopol suggested casually. "I don't rightly know what it is, yet, but our parents don't really take regular holidays that don't involve a heist."

Gatina knew that there were limits to discussing their lives with their cousins—discussing thieving and robbery were one thing, but she understood that nothing about the Shadow Council should come up if she could help it. It was time to change the subject.

"What training have you had, Pia?" she asked, curious.

"Just the basics," her cousin admitted. "Magesight, of course. I'm on my eighth staff of runes, and learning the chorded sequences, now. I even cast a magelight," she said proudly. "It lasted nine whole minutes. Plus some seamagic spells: weather prediction, anti-corrosion spells, and a bunch of useful cantrips. Mother keeps me busy."

"I'm so glad I don't have *rajira!*" Jordi nodded enthusiastically.

Gatina was surprised—almost shocked. "Why? Why wouldn't you want to do magic?" she asked.

"I had enough trouble learning to read and figure. Learning magic on top of that would have been torture!" her cousin assured her. "Oh, I know it's useful stuff—we wouldn't be doing as well as we are without it. Mother even makes extra coin by casting spells for other merchants in Prejestia. It can cost up to twenty percent of the value of your cargo to get proper seamagic done—we get it for free," he admitted, with a bit of gloat in his voice. "It keeps the barnacles off the hull and the sails from ripping open, if you do it right. But I'd hate to be the one responsible for that. I hope to be the master of my own ship one day," he revealed. "But I'll have to get my sister to cast spells for me. And I'm perfectly fine with that."

"Until then, he'll be learning on the *Legacy*," Pia agreed. "This will be our first major cruise together this summer. We're taking a cargo to Vaxel, clear on the other side of the Great Bay. It will be the first voyage of the *Legacy* since she got out of dry dock."

"And tomorrow," her father announced, unexpectedly breaking into their conversation from the door, "you two will go learn the basics of seafaring from your cousins. Starting at the pier. At an impossibly early hour."

JUST AFTER DAWN THE NEXT MORNING, THEIR COUSINS WOKE THEM, BROKE their fast with them, brought them appropriate clothing to change into—short leggings made of sailcloth and linen shirts—and then escorted them down to the Salterpath Pier.

"Why is it called Salterpath?" Gatina asked as she stumbled along to the docks in the twilight. "That's kind of a strange name."

"When the Sea Lords ruled this port, they traded with the inland villages," Pia explained as they walked down the path to the pier. It was strewn with thousands of seashells that crunched under her boots, Gatina realized. "This particular place was where the villages came to make salt from seawater, originally, and eventually to trade. The men who do that are known as 'salters,' and this was the path they took. So . . . Salter Path."

"My father purchased it right after he married Mother," Jordi agreed. "He thought it would be perfect for his company: good access to inland, good harborage, and close enough to river traffic to make it worthwhile. He started with an old galleon he inherited but traded it for two sturdy caravels about the time Pia was born. We've several good barques, too. We've been trading ever since," he said proudly.

Pia led them to the gate of the pier compound and gestured grandly around at the dock and the sheds. "This is our family's merchant business," she said. "These buildings are where cargoes arrive, are stored and sorted for outgoing shipments. Mostly citrus at this time of year, but we've hauled wine, oil, garum, vinegar, and even tar from upriver. But this is not what I really wanted to show you, exactly. Follow me." She beckoned.

She led them between four more buildings on the walkway, which was made of more crushed seashells, Gatina saw. "This is what I wanted to show you," Pia said. The walkway ended at a private dock that stretched more than a hundred feet into the harbor. There were six ships smaller than what they had arrived on but still sizeable, and two larger ones with three masts apiece. Even-smaller boats were clustered in the closest berths to the dock head.

There were a surprising number of people working at this time of day, Gatina noticed. "Where do these folk live?" she asked, as she hadn't seen but a few cottages along the beach.

"Mostly in the hostel," Jordi supplied. "It's a kind of bunkhouse or barracks. Half of them are crewmen. But it takes about five men on shore to put one out to sea, they say. Ships take a lot of maintenance to work properly. And we have a few," he said, as they stepped out onto the dock.

"This is our fleet. Well, most of it is ours," Pia corrected. "That caravel there hired the berth. But the other one is the *Legacy*."

"She's beautiful," Atopol assured his cousins. "And a lot cleaner than that thing we came to Prejestia in. Is that what we're going to learn to sail on?"

"Oh, we're a long way from that." Pia chuckled. "You two aren't qualified to be cabin boys yet. No, Jordi and I will teach you what it's like to be a proper mariner. On that boat right there," she said, pointing to a boat that was about twelve feet long but wide in berth. "You can't sail until you learn how to row. And swim. And a hundred other things. Mother asked us to see what you could do in the water, so that's the boat we'll start on. Let's get it out on the water."

"Do you know the most common sailing injury?" Jordi asked as they stepped gingerly into the flat-bottomed craft.

Pia shot her brother a warning look. He just grinned, and Gatina had to admit he was charming. "Jordi, no! Don't scare them! Now is not the time. Nor is it the place."

"Why not?" he asked. "Seamanship is scary. Come on, Attie; what do you think it is?"

Atopol looked from Jordi to Pia and then smiled. "I would guess it's lost fingers."

Jordi looked at Gatina. She had not planned to answer but decided that he expected her to, so she said, "Eyes. I saw a lot of eye patches on our trip here."

"Those are both good guesses," Jordi said, as he unshipped one of the long oars from the side of the boat—the gunwale, Gatina corrected herself. "But you're wrong. The most common injury on a boat is a splinter!" he laughed. "Think about it: you always see the gruesome injuries and those stay with you. But there's nothing more vexing than a splinter, is there? And those sometimes get infected. They can be hard to treat at sea. That's where a lot of those fingers and eyes are lost."

"So, if you cut yourself, see to it at once," Pia agreed, as she handed an oar to Atopol. "Don't put it off. Or they'll cut it off," she warned. "Today we're going to practice rowing out to that buoy," she said, indicating a spot on the horizon. Gatina didn't see anything, at first, until she tried with magesight. There was, indeed, a tiny construction bobbing in the waves far out in the harbor. About a mile away.

"Are you sure that's safe?" she asked nervously.

"As long as you don't sink the boat," Jordi quipped. "Does it really matter if you drown in four feet of water or a hundred? Shall we launch, then?" he asked. "I think the best way to learn is by doing."

Pia coiled the mooring line with practiced ease after Jordi pushed them off the dock. For the next two hours, the two Cats were hard pressed to learn how to coordinate their efforts on the two great oars. Even though Atopol had rowed before, that had been on the relatively calm waters of the Mandros, around Falas, not into the constant waves that they had to contend with at Prejestia. Gatina was exhausted by the time they finally made it to the distant buoy. Her shoulders ached, her hands were nearly bruised with the effort, and she was out of breath. Thrice more the boat made the trip between the dock and the buoy as their cousins critiqued their form and their effort.

"All mariners know how to row," Jordi assured them, when she questioned the merits of the exercise. "That is, you won't be able to pretend to be a Sea Lord if you don't know how. It will be a dead giveaway."

"I think they've got the basics down, though," Pia said, as they headed the boat back to the dock for the fourth time. "Let's see how they swim!"

A moment later, both Cats of Enultramar were proving they could make it a few hundred yards across the briny water to the safety of the dock. In some ways, it was nicer to swim in the sea than the river, Gatina reflected, as she kept spitting out seawater while she swam. In other ways it was harder. Her eyes stung more. You could use the waves to help push you along, though. And there wasn't as much filth in the sea. But by the time she and Atopol climbed up the ladder to the dock, they were both thoroughly spent.

"I'm considering the merits of drowning," her brother mentioned as he heaved for breath after their exertions. "Our cousins seem determined to kill us today."

"They mean well," Gatina protested weakly. "But my arms feel like limp leather, and I can barely stand." Her sailcloth shift was shedding water in a fast puddle.

"That wasn't bad," Pia commented a moment later when she and Jordi easily pulled the boat back to the dock. She tossed their boots and dry clothing onto the pier for them. "It wasn't great, but you didn't drown. I think that's enough for now. There are . . . other things you need to know about." She gave her brother a conspiratorial look. "Shall we show them?"

"Yes, I think they'd like to see," he agreed with a smile.

"Show us what?" Atopol demanded, still heaving. "You didn't dig graves for us already?"

"Don't be silly. Sea Lords get buried at sea. Come with us," Pia said, helping him up. "While we're down here, there's something you should see." Reluctantly, Gatina struggled to her feet before Jordi could do likewise. It had been as rough as a workout with Master Steel, she decided, only her feet didn't hurt. Their cousins led them to a long shed painted bright red and half-protruding out into the water. But they were blocked when they approached the door.

"Aww! She *locked* it!" Jordi complained.

"A lock?" Atopol asked, suddenly interested.

"Yes, it looks like Mother didn't want anyone poking around it," he said, disappointed.

Without another word, Atopol approached the door, examined the lock, and produced a bit of wire. In seconds it was unfastened. That seemed to impress both of their cousins immensely.

"Your mother needs to invest in better locks," he quipped as he set the lock on a post. "So, what's inside? Treasure?"

"Not ours," Pia assured them, as she opened the door. "Yours. Your family sloop: the *Daydream*," she announced as she led them inside.

"She's been here for years, now," Jordi explained. "I've only seen Mother take her out twice for maintenance. I've never sailed on her. But when the tide comes in, we're to put her in the water."

"That's . . . *our* ship?" Gatina asked, as her eyes adjusted to the gloom.

The sloop was a sleek-looking craft, about twenty-five feet long, though there was a bowsprit projecting far in front of her. It was suspended from the great wooden beams overhead by dozens of lines affixed to pulleys, and jutted out over the water as if it was just waiting to sail. Unlike most of the ships they'd seen on the dock, her wooden decks were gleaming as if they'd just been varnished. The mast was unshipped, Gatina could see, but other than that, the sloop seemed ready to sail to her unpracticed eye.

"Let's get her into the water!" Jordi said, excitedly. "She's beautiful. I've wanted to sail her since I first saw her. The tide's coming in now, anyway."

"Jordi! That's no way to introduce someone to a lady!" his sister chided. "I think it might be better to explain the terms and show them around first," Pia suggested reprovingly. "That way, they'll know what you're saying when you start barking out orders." That comment drew laughter from Atopol and Gatina, but when it was finished, she said, "Oh, I wasn't joking. He's bossy."

Atopol rolled his eyes. "A bossy younger sibling? I have *no* idea what that's like."

"Good captains are bossy," Jordi shrugged. "I will not apologize for that."

For the next ten minutes, Jordi and Pia peppered them with a litany of maritime terms, from the basics of bow, stern, starboard, and port to the names of more obscure parts of the ship, like the anchor's hawse—the hole in the gunwale it was lowered through—to the main hatch that led down to the cabins below. Some of it they had already learned. Much of it was new to them. But both of the Cats were good at detail and absorbed the terminology quickly.

"Jordi, why are ships called 'she'?" Atopol asked suddenly.

Gatina was surprised he didn't know. She volunteered an answer, beating Jordi to it. "Ships are referred to as feminine to honor the sea goddesses who guide and protect the ship."

Jordi nodded approvingly. "You're right, Gatina. Yes, and I believe that tradition holds in other religions and cultures. In the Sea Lord histories, ships named for men tend to meet horrible fates. So, we feminize them.

Even the *Legacy* is referred to as 'she,' even though it bears my father's name. Mother had it properly blessed," he added defensively.

"Shall we continue? Next, the pilothouse is where the pilot or captain steers the ship. He—or she—uses a tiller or a wheel, depending on the ship's size. This sloop has a tiller," he lectured. "Either will turn the rudder underneath the boat, and that controls your direction." He walked forward to the long, tall vertical pole. "This is called the mast and this is the boom." Jordi patted the boom, which was horizontal to the deck. "You'll see it makes a ninety-degree angle, and that's important when we get to the sailing part of, well, sailing."

"Sloops can configure their rigging in a lot of different ways," Pia agreed, "depending on what you want to do with them. They're very versatile. But they're not great haulers; there's little room for cargo compared to a barque or a caravel. This one was originally a pleasure craft, I think. It's always been somewhat of a mystery about where it came from."

"That's because my parents stole it on their honeymoon," Atopol suggested. "It was part of their first real heist together."

"That's . . . romantic," Pia acknowledged. "And . . . technically piracy."

"And would explain why Mother keeps it locked up, away from prying eyes." Jordi nodded as they climbed a ladder up to the deck. "I'd love to hear that story!"

"So would we," Gatina agreed. "Our parents' lives are largely a mystery to us. But we do get intriguing little crumbs every now and then."

Jordi bent and opened a cabinet and removed a stack of tightly coiled ropes. "You've probably noticed that there are a lot of ropes on a ship."

"But they're not called ropes," Pia added. "Each has its own name and its purpose."

Jordi nodded. "Yes. Dock lines are used to tie the boat to the dock. Those are self-explanatory. We have three very important ones for you to know. Those are the mainsheet, jib sheet, and halyard. These are connected to the sail, which is called the sheet."

Pia interrupted him again. "You've seen the sails. They're triangles," she said. "The main sheet connects to the sail. You can add or release tension, and that helps you control the sail."

Jordi walked to the starboard side of the boat and tapped a metal cylinder with handles on it. "This is the winch. Your headsail is hooked here. Clockwise. Always clockwise. That helps you control the tension."

Gatina wondered how many sails the *Daydream* had. But Jordi anticipated her question. "This boat has two sails, based on its size. The second is called the headsail and it attaches to a forestay. There are all sorts of other rope terms and we'll get to them, but for now, those are the most important."

"Don't forget to tell them the parts of the sail," Pia coached. "Oh, and in fair weather, the mainsail stays on the boat, but it is lowered and covered. That makes it quicker to take the boat out."

Jordi sighed. "Yes, the parts are called the head, the tack, and the clew. The head is the point of the triangle. The tack is the front portion, and it attaches to the bow's front." He held up a longer line to demonstrate. "This is the halyard, and it connects to the top of each sail when the mast is rigged," he explained while pulling on the rope that made a triangle.

It was all very confusing. Even after learning thievery, the stars, and magic, it seemed like a lot of new terminology to Gatina. Her expression must have been obvious to her cousins.

"I think that's enough for today," Pia finally said, after another half hour of explanations and instruction. "The tide is coming in earnest now. We should go ahead and put her in the water before luncheon. Then we can perhaps take her out this afternoon, if Mother approves."

"That's when the real lessons begin," Jordi agreed. "Learning all this stuff is easy. Knowing how it all fits together and conspires to get you from one side of the Bay to the other is the tricky part. Now," he said, enthusiastically clapping his hands, "you girls let loose the portside, and Cat and I will do the starboard lines. Ready?" he asked, expectantly. "Heave to!" he called when they didn't answer quickly enough.

"See what I mean?" Pia asked in a hushed voice, as she and Gatina took their positions at the pulleys. "He's bossy. But he'll make a great captain someday, if the Shipwrecker spares him. And I don't kill him first," she added.

CHAPTER SEVEN

SHADOWBLADE

A Captain's judgement is absolute. Perhaps wrong, but absolute.
— Sea Lord proverb

THREE LONG, EXHAUSTING DAYS LATER, OVER AN EARLY LUNCHEON OF CHEESE, bread, prawns, oranges, and watered wine, Gatina listened with interest as Aunt Beah described to her parents the increase in piracy and other hazards brought on by the rise of Count Vichetral and his rebel dukes.

"It's clear, what they're doing," she said indignantly, as she buttered her bread. "They're trying to monopolize as much trade as possible under a few Great Houses and force the rest of us to take up arms just to survive. If we can't make a profit on fruit, wine, and olive oil, then we'll be forced to hire on as privateers with that awful baron and his cronies!"

"That's why we're here, Beah," Hance assured his aunt. "Our intent is to discover which Houses are unhappy with Vichetral and ally with them against him."

"There are plenty of those. Of the smaller sort. It's scandalous," she continued, her voice deep with condemnation. "Do you know what happens to a ship when you take it into battle? Even if you win, you lose. You can take more damage in one fight than in a decade of trading. And you lose *people*." She sniffed. "It's bad enough that there are so many more pirates now. Most are just opportunists who think they can make some quick coin with a little casual murder at sea, but since Duke Lenguin died, they've been as thick as fleas on a dog's neck!"

"It's been a rough few years," her mother agreed sympathetically.

"We've fared better than most," Beah conceded. "We kept to harbor and only sailed the eastern end of the Bay since the Duke and Duchess died. But you can't make a living on that, not really. The big international ports are in the west, mostly. Finally, I decided to just sail the barques and put the *Legacy* in dry dock for a year to save money. She needed it, but now I need the coin. So, we'll head for the Vaxel Anchorage with a hold full of citrus and make a penny or two. This trip should put us aright," she assured. "And I can introduce you to plenty of Houses who aren't happy with that damned count!"

Gatina stifled a yawn. Father had allowed them to sleep in late today. The previous few mornings, either Pia or Jordi had woken them just before sunrise for more sailing lessons. They had become very familiar with the *Daydream*, as they'd helped launch it and prepare it for the journey across the Bay.

But it had been exhausting. Gatina had never felt so tired. There was so much to do, from raising the mast and rigging the sails to checking every line and every sheet on the ship for rips and frays to stocking the sloop with provisions and supplies and tools and so many sundry items that Gatina wouldn't think would be useful . . . until they were. On that third day, when they woke, Father told them that they were not sailing today. She almost cried, she was so relieved.

Instead, they would be working to create their aliases and disguises after breaking their fast. That was welcome news. She had not realized how tired she was or how exhausting seafaring left her. She was used to a rigorous training regimen, but hoisting sails and lines worked her muscles differently than climbing or swordplay. It wasn't that it was more difficult; instead, she decided, it was a new and exciting challenge. One that left her sore in places she hadn't realized could actually ache. But they did.

She shifted in her chair and rotated her torso, using the chairback as a brace to look over first her right shoulder, then her left. She repeated the motion slowly several times until her back made a small crackling sound, releasing the tension she had been carrying there.

"Kitten, that's not very becoming at the table," her mother reproved.

"But it *hurts*," Gatina complained. "It all hurts. My *eyelids* hurt," she insisted. "And my hands are completely raw," she said, offering them up as proof. "My legs ache, my arms are about to fall off, and my back—bloody Darkness, my back—"

"It's good you'll be working on the ship instead of pretending to be a passenger," her mother added, teasing as she sat down at the table. "You've become as coarse as a mariner. You'll fit right in."

Pia tried to keep her laughter hidden with her napkin, but she couldn't. As soon as the girl started to laugh, everyone else laughed with her, including Gatina.

"I am sorry, Aunt Beah," Gatina said. "I'm a poor guest. I have become far too comfortable here. I suppose I feel at home."

Aunt Beah smiled widely, showing her very white teeth, and nodded. "Don't worry, lass. We don't keep things overly formal at Salterpath. Besides, if you're working on a ship, you're not just a guest. You do fit right in. And from what Jordi has said, you and your brother have both taken to seafaring better than most inlanders."

She glanced at her son, who was shoveling a chunk of bread into his mouth, dripping with preserves. Shaking her head at him, she said, "I'm looking forward to shipping to Vaxel. I'm looking forward to *working* again. Real work, not just casting spells and making schedules. And we'll be making port just around the time of the Vaxel Anchorage and Assessment—that's a big festival. I'd love to see that again!"

Gatina caught the especial emphasis the woman put on the word *working*. She knew what Beah meant; they all did. She'd taken responsibility for the entire company since Alekandrus's disappearance. From what she understood, the business had even expanded until Duke Lenguin was killed. It was hard work—but it didn't seem like work compared to being at sea, to her. That's where all of these folk seemed to want to be when they were ashore, Gatina reflected.

"Tonight, I have invited Captain Armandus for dinner. A proper Sea Lord captain," Beah said, proudly. "He is Alekandrus's brother. He'll be mastering the ship—I'll be owner-aboard and navigator. But I want you to get to know him before you're initiated into the crew."

And that was how Gatina discovered that she would be participating in yet another religious order as part of a mission.

"An initiation?" she asked.

Aunt Beah paused before taking a sip of her wine. "Yes, did your cousins not tell you about it? All apprentice seamen must be initiated before they can take sail for the first time. Don't worry; it's merely a formality. Under the moonlight and on the water. That was the only way you're permitted to serve as crew," Aunt Beah explained.

Sea Lords were superstitious, Gatina had learned from both her books and being around the coast for a few days. Very superstitious. So much so that they had to be initiated before Gatina and Atopol could depart Prejestia as crewmembers aboard *Alekandrus's Legacy*. Indeed, there were all manner of superstitious rituals they undertook. Anything from launching a new ship to burying the dead at sea.

"It's not unexpected, though I did try to circumvent it," Aunt Beah said, apologetically. "My crew is trustworthy, but I don't want to alienate them, family or not. Don't let it worry you. It's a simple rite of passage. Both of your cousins have completed it. We can help you or answer any questions you might have."

She looked at the four children when she spoke. And her tone allowed no room for debate. Gatina had quickly learned that what Aunt Beah said was the law at Salterpath.

But she had also observed that the woman could be unpredictable. Not given to flights of fancy, but wildly driven. Gatina decided that her aunt was guided by things Gatina just did not understand. "Your parents have opted to have you both travel as crew, Atopol and Gatina. I trust that Hance has created appropriate aliases for you?" Gatina recognized the look she gave him. It indicated that she expected an answer.

"Yes, Minnie and I have outlined aliases for them," her father assured as he wiped his hands on the fine cloth napkin before placing it beside his trencher. "We put in a good deal of thought for them. Kitten, you will be Maranka, a maiden of Prejestia. You are new to seafaring. You've secured your first post aboard *Alekandrus's Legacy* for your maiden voyage," Hance said.

"You are an orphan, but you are not alone. You have your brother, Martijne, who has looked out for you since your mother's death. She had a flux and never recovered. Atopol, you have worked on smaller ships before. You will be protective to an extent—a watchful eye. But not overly so. Once Maranka *quickly* proves her worth on the ship, you'll be able to relax unless you're at port, obviously."

Gatina met her father's gaze when he looked at her. She understood the assignment—and what it implied: stay on the mission, do the work, and learn everything she could about the ship. "Beah has always been generous to orphans who choose life on the water," Hance said.

"That is true," Beah nodded. "I do support the temple of the Maiden of the Havens. I give homage to all of them, of course, but that one holds a special place in my heart," she said, quietly. "Tonight, Armandus will join us, and he will meet you both. Your parents will, of course, have aliases, as is wise. Vichetral seems to have agents even out here. We don't want to cause *too much* trouble," she laughed.

"Can we count on this sea captain?" Minnie asked, nervously.

"Armandus has my trust. He's family. But he's no mage. Even though he knows there is something more going on, I suggest you keep to your aliases for tonight," she decided. "It will be good practice for Pia and Jordi, as well."

Hance nodded in agreement. "I will become Lord Hamanthus, and Minnie will be Lady Elletia. Maritime-minded Coastlords," he said, motioning for Minnie to speak.

"Those are personas we have used in the past with great success," she agreed. "We are Coastlords from County Falas pursuing new business opportunities for our estate out on the Bay. Our estate produces wine, a little oil, and flax. We are traveling to visit my lord husband's distant family in Vaxel to see about grape varieties we might cultivate to improve our wine business. We will pick up our yacht, the *Daydream*, on the way to Vaxel, and the *Legacy* will tow it to our destination. We are traveling in a convoy to avoid pirates," she added.

A knock at the front door and the arrival of one of the servants interrupted their casual meal and conversation. The young maid appeared to be between Gatina's and Pia's ages, but Gatina couldn't say for sure because her skin was aged from years in the sun. The girl carried a long narrow box and curtsied in front of the table.

"Mistress Beah, this has come for the gentleman," she said, nodding toward Hance.

He stood and took the box, thanking the girl, who quickly began to clear off the table. Excitedly, he set the box on the table and began to pry it open, using his dagger. He'd pulled it out so quickly, Gatina hadn't noticed. Mother glanced at Gatina and then back at the box. And that's when Gatina realized this was *something important*. She also sensed metal. Whatever was in that box called to her.

"What is it, Father?" she asked, wondering if it was another bottle of wine or more cryptic notes from Castal, where this mysterious Master Thinradel lived. Gatina reached for a slice of orange while she watched and waited for an answer.

When her father had finally loosened the lid, he pulled it off with little effort and set it aside. She continued to watch but only saw fabric inside the box. Her father used his dagger again, slicing into it and splitting it down the middle. That's when it got interesting. She leaned closer to get a better look. That's when he reached inside with both hands and gently lifted out a long, thin black scabbard. Gatina saw that it was a solid matte black. She sucked in her breath. This might be something very important, indeed.

Hance held it parallel to the table, then he set it down with reverence and turned to her. "Gatina, this is for you," he said. "Master Steel has sent your new sword. He had it made for you, based on your measurements. Your mother and I are proud to present you with your very own shadowblade. We know you will use it justly."

Minnureal smiled at her daughter. "I can only hope you are able to keep this one in your possession."

Hance and Minnie both laid their hands on top of the scabbard. They closed their eyes and spoke together, blessing the blade. "May Kiera the Great guide you in your endeavors. May she keep you hidden in the Blessed Darkness. May the Shadows greet you like an old friend. And may Duty keep your fight on the right path."

Gatina sucked in her breath and held it. They were words of ritual, straight from the *Shield of Darkness*, Kiera's own heist journal. She was both excited and terrified. This was really happening. She was receiving her own personal shadowblade, not just using one from the armory. And she vowed then to never lose it again, unlike Attie. Then she exhaled.

She saw that Pia and Jordi were fascinated by what was happening. And when she looked over to Aunt Beah; the woman smiled at her, approvingly, and she wondered if the woman still had a shadowblade. Or if she practiced shadowmagic at all now.

When Hance and Minnie stood, Minnie took Gatina's hand. Gatina stood beside them. She had butterflies in her stomach. She was not nervous. She was elated.

"Gatina anna Furtius, it is our pleasure to present you with this shadowblade," Hance said. "This is a testament to your dedication to the Art and your study of the Craft." He and Minnie removed the sheath and held the blade aloft, before re-sheathing it.

Minnie spoke next. "Gatina, I am proud of the woman you are becoming. I know you will do amazing things in your life and live up to the expectations Kiera the Great set for you."

Her parents picked up the sword together and handed it to her. She accepted it without hesitation. She stepped back from the table and drew the blade from the scabbard, examining it closely, mindful of its razor-sharp edges. The metal was stained black as the night, to avoid the reflection of any light. It fit her grip perfectly, with a hilt covered with sharkskin. The metal didn't burn her palm, either. It was exquisitely balanced, she realized as she tested it in her hand.

"It is a fine blade," she said simply when she realized that everyone at the table was waiting for her to say something. "I am sorry. It's not often that I find myself at a loss for words. You've managed to surprise me," she added, honestly. She set the blade on the table and embraced her parents one at a time. "Father, Mother—Master and Mistress," she corrected, "I thank you."

Hance smiled and spoke. "It was time for you to have one of your own, Kitten. Don't forget to name it. Now, if you'll excuse us, we have a few items to discuss ahead of this voyage." He addressed all of them.

The silence around the table was awkward and she felt like she was part of the cause. She looked at Pia and Jordi and thought about asking if they had swords, too, but decided against it. Instead, she suggested the four meet in the library after she put her shadowblade in her bedroom.

As if reading her mind, Pia suggested that Gatina try it out. "There's plenty of room in the side yard. I am not suggesting a duel, but if you'd like to get acclimated to it, you should. Then when you're ready, come find me in the library."

Jordi laughed. "Why are you always in the library? There are loads of things I could use your help with, including gathering our supplies for this trip." He looked over at Attie and said, "She's always in the books." He shook his head, got up, and walked toward the back of the house.

Gatina lifted her shadowblade and examined it. She held it horizontally to gauge its weight—perfect balance. It was a bit heavier and a little longer than the one she had most recently used but still short enough to fit across her shoulders or on her hip. It would not take much practice to adjust to it, she knew. She placed it back into the sheath.

Atopol watched her, a smile on his mouth. "It really is a fine blade," he agreed. "Steel outdid himself on that one. Have you given thought to a name for it? You should," he suggested. She knew his own custom blade had been named Cat's Whisker. A good name.

"Not yet," she admitted, as she got used to the weight of the new sword. "I'm sure something will come to me." Gatina picked up the sheath and looked at her brother as she stood. "Shall I try it out?" she asked, nodding to the door. If Attie wanted to chat, they could do so outside, she reasoned. She motioned for him to follow her.

Outside, on the side of the veranda away from the view of the shell-packed road, Gatina practiced one of the sequences Master Steel had taught her. After ten passes of that one, she started another.

"I am a little bit nervous about the journey but not about this initiation," she admitted as she worked her way through the routine their sword master had drilled into her mind. "Sea Lords have tons of rituals and ceremonies and superstitions."

"Let's hope there's no ritual tattooing." He smirked as she danced with the new blade.

"I am also excited. It's a mission. And it's an adventure." She moved into that same routine in the opposite direction, careful to avoid cutting down any of the shrubs or heavenly-smelling flowers. "I'll need a good blade at sea. The Stormfather and his daughters are formidable. Not that I'm scared," she added quickly. "Are you nervous about it?" she asked, hoping to gauge his level of discomfort. She was more apprehensive about the open sea than she was about the deities.

He was silent. A sideways glance let her know that he had heard her, based on the expression he wore. Attie often thought through questions, whereas she jumped in with answers and improvised.

"I am more nervous about the sea than pirates or goddesses," he decided. "Between the weather and the fury of the Stormfather and the possibility of pirates, it seems a lot could go wrong very quickly," he sighed, gloomily. "It's good that your blade came when it did. You'll want to practice as much as you can on the land in case you need to use it on the water."

As Gatina completed her routine, she wondered if Aunt Beah would mind if she borrowed an egg or two. Attie was right; practice was good. And it had been weeks since she had last lifted a sword.

"We should speak with Pia and Jordi about that. They can help us with this initiation. I would like to know what I'm getting myself into," she said as she sheathed her blade and gently slung it over her shoulder. "It feels so much lighter, even though it's longer."

Attie nodded. "It's an entirely different thing to have a blade that's made for you and not just taken from some dusty armory. You'll adapt. It won't take long. I did it with Cat's Whisker," he said as they walked toward the veranda and the front door. "Some things just take a little getting used to."

Gatina found Pia in the library at the large oak table in front of an unfurled map, not a book as Jordi had predicted. Pia looked up from her study. "All finished with your practice?" she asked. When Gatina nodded, she smiled. "What was it like? Better than the practice blades, smoother?"

"Much. It's like wearing perfectly broken-in shoes instead of stiff, tight, and uncomfortable ones," she said, deciding she would need a better analogy. "That's not quite right, but it's close."

Gatina found herself wondering if the Sea Lord gods played a role in the crew initiation. Her book had been light on the common rituals of the divinities and had instead focused on theology. She assumed that if they did, it would be symbolic. The more she thought about the Stormfather and his daughters and what they represented, the more nervous she got.

Not about the mission. About the sea. It was dangerous and anything could happen. And that was both thrilling and terrifying. But first, she wanted to know about the initiation.

"So, what should I expect tonight?" she asked hesitantly.

"It's not so bad," Pia assured her. "Like Mother said, it's mostly a formality. One of the things you do before a voyage. Uncle Armandus is kind of gruff, but he's not cruel. He'll spare you any real embarrassment."

"So, no crawling through bilgewater stark naked," Gatina nodded. "That's a relief."

Her cousin laughed, not in a mean way, Gatina realized, so she laughed too.

"Not yet," she conceded. "That's for more advanced voyages."

"What's so funny?" Jordi asked when he and Atopol arrived.

"Girl stuff," Pia said, shutting him down quickly.

Atopol shook his head. "Don't worry; you *don't* want to know," he assured Jordi. "But I want to know what to expect with this initiation."

Pia and Jordi looked at each other, and Gatina wondered if they were about to be truthful or spin a tale. Jordi had a knack for exaggeration; she had noted that when they fished on their first sailing lesson.

"It's a formality, like Mother said," Jordi said. "Just meeting the crew, taking an oath, signing the logbook. Years ago, when our parents were our age, it was more serious. A blood oath, I think, but it's not like that now. You basically repeat what the captain says." Gatina was visibly relieved, something he noticed. "You *were* worried? It's nothing. You're both magi. You've done far more dangerous things! How did this scare you?"

She shrugged. She didn't have an answer. Instead, she asked, "Is that a map of the Great Bay?" She could better see what Pia had been studying, and even though it was upside down from her vantage point, she had studied reading that way. "Is this where we are sailing?"

Pia motioned for her and the others to walk around the table so they could see the map from the correct side.

"It is. We are *here*." She pointed to the peninsula where the dock was. "And we'll be traveling out this way to Cadena, then Pluhalia, where we'll take on cargo from a couple of other ships." She traced the route with her finger. "If the weather cooperates, the first two stops will take a few days. I would wager that Uncle Armandus will have us stop longer in Pluhalia for supplies. But then straight on to Vaxel."

Jordi groaned when she said that. "I don't like Pluhalia. We stopped there last year. There's too much trouble there," he said.

"There's trouble everywhere these days," Pia sighed. "But that's the proposed route. Don't worry; Uncle Armandus will get us there safely. He's just the captain we need."

Just before dinner, the family sat on the veranda, watching the ships come back to port. The setting sun was casting brilliant shades of pink and orange across the sandy beach and the Bay. Atopol, Gatina, Pia, and Jordi had joined to seek a total of eight silver coins. Even though Jordi had no shred of *rajira*, he was very competitive and smart. Gatina quickly found him to be a worthy opponent in the hunt.

Mother had hidden the coins on the veranda and inside the house, on the first floor only; she had already explained that when she advised them of the rules of the game. As far as Gatina knew, she was the only one who could sense metals, and that gave her a distinct advantage. She had not counted on Jordi following her so closely. It was irritating, and she recognized instantly how she must aggravate her brother.

While searching for her third coin, Gatina was drawn to a flowerpot hanging from one of the veranda's posts. She knew she would need to climb to reach it. Instead of scaling the post, she went to the second floor and stepped through an open door onto a balcony. The view was even better, she instantly realized.

She saw three great ships sail past the cove. They were massive, far too deep to land at Aunt Beah's dock. The rudders would be stuck in the sand. The water at the dock could handle small barques, sloops, and caravels, but not big merchant galleons. Aunt Beah's largest ships were docked in the village proper.

Pia and Atopol's laughter from somewhere in the house reminded her of the task. She crossed the narrow balcony and squeezed through the wooden railings. Hand over hand, she hoisted the flowerpot up with little effort. When she could reach inside, she did and was rewarded when her fingers closed around the small cool coin. Gatina lowered the pot down as she pulled it up.

That's when she heard Aunt Beah talking about the pirates. She didn't mean to eavesdrop—but she didn't not mean to, either. There was just something about hearing the word *pirate* that made you want to listen.

"... heard that pirates or raiders were spotted off the Prejestia strait," she was saying. "Ships of war, flying the Corsair's banner. They could be honest privateers," she reasoned. "I wouldn't worry about it, usually, but with everything going on, I want to be prepared. I got word after luncheon when I went to the storehouse. I've sent word to pull my crew and ships in, the ones I could reach."

Gatina flattened herself to the balcony and got as close as she could to the railing. She wanted to hear this. It was valuable information.

Her father's footsteps were nearly silent, but she knew the sound of him pacing by heart.

"Will this impact our plans, Beah?" he asked, concerned.

After a silence long enough to make Gatina wonder if they knew she was listening, Aunt Beah answered.

"It might. We may need to take another route. I'll leave that up to Armandus. He's a worthy captain. He'll know what to do. I wouldn't worry about it much, though. Between us and the children, we'll be magically advantaged. And the *Legacy*'s crew is formidable, for a merchantman. I don't want to put my ships or my family at risk, but a ship you don't sail might be safe in port, but it's useless," she concluded.

"So, when will we depart?" her father asked as Gatina guiltily climbed down the wall. She didn't wait to hear the answer. Gatina realized that their voyage might be met with more than adventure. And she was very relieved to have her new shadowblade. She resolved to practice with it more before they set sail.

Later that day, after Gatina had completed two runs of the egg-circling routine—with her aunt's permission, of course—she found herself staring at a very plain and dirty dress that she found spread on top of her bed when she returned to her room. Her deckhand clothes, she realized. Once she had secured her sword, Gatina picked it up and shook it out to get a proper look. And she instantly regretted it.

The tunic was massive, the size of a mainsail or at least a picnic blanket, and was made from the coarse cloth used to make sails. It would swallow her. The men she had observed on their trip downriver had worn pants and loose-fitting tunics. She hadn't seen any women aboard. She assumed she would wear trousers, as the men did. So, this tent-like dress in her hands left her with a feeling of dreaded disappointment.

Granted, it was cleaner than what she had worn in her disguise as Lissa the Mouse in Falas. It came with a wide leather belt with a plain bronze buckle. She tried it on, and with a great deal of struggle, she got the belt to fit around the voluminous tunic. It was like wearing a flour sack, she decided. Worse than her nocturn's habit. And it did even less for her figure.

It was part of her alias, and she knew not to argue about it, at least to her parents. But she wondered how a skirt this large would allow her to hoist lines and sheets without also hoisting herself.

She tossed the dress back on the bed and walked to the desk, where a basin and bowl had been left for her to clean herself before dinner. Gatina wasn't that dirty. She had been swimming each day in the ocean, coached alongside Atopol by their cousins, who were both grueling taskmasters and expert swimmers. The lessons there included stamina in the water, treading for extended periods of time, and how to use the water's current to their advantage. She was a good swimmer, she knew that. But her cousins took swimming to a new level. Master Steel was exacting in his sword lessons. Pia and Jordi were worse.

"Blades can kill you slowly or quickly, just as the water can. The difference? In the water, you don't know you're dying," Jordi had told her on the first day.

While she dipped the washing cloth into the basin, Gatina reflected on that. She'd never been cut. But she had been tumbled in the water. The memory washed over her. She had been young, six maybe. They were in the river for swim lessons with Sister Karia and Mother. The water had been still, and she was practicing her retrieval skills. One of them had thrown brightly painted stones into the river for her and Atopol to find and bring up.

It was similar to the coin game. She loved to beat Attie, even then, she remembered, smiling as she washed the right side of her face. But she hadn't paid attention to what was behind her. A larger boat had picked up wind and was rocketing downriver. Or that's how it seemed to her younger self. As she dove down, the boat passed by and sent a ripple of waves in its wake. Those waves hit her hard and she lost her equilibrium. She tumbled over and over in the water and didn't know which way was out or up. Fear flooded her for a moment as she relived that sense of terror and helplessness.

Her pulse quickened as if she was running for her life, and her breathing came in shallow gulps. She was in a panic. And that was not acceptable to her high standards. Gatina looked at herself in the looking glass next to the basin. She wasn't judging herself, but she stared into her own violet eyes and addressed herself.

"You are safe." Her tone was firm. She repeated that sentence four, five times. And in seconds, her breathing calmed, and her heart no longer pounded in her ears. She had braved the sewers of Falas, after all, not to mention forded the mighty Mandros River across a slippery chain. She now knew how to gauge the waves before going underneath them. She could manage the waters of the Bay, she reasoned forcefully. And her heartbeat slowed.

Now that she was not in a panic, she studied her face in the looking glass in her chamber. The clean side and the dirtier-than-she-thought side were both turning a shade of bronze. That dirt was actually not dirt. It was the color the sun was turning her skin. She had never seen herself with sun-kissed skin, at least not that she could remember. It was novel.

"You are . . . *Maranka*," she told her reflection. "Orphan and proud to be going to sea like a proper Sea Lord lass."

She decided to keep her hair color, like Beah's and Jordi's. It worked there, on the Great Bay. But her eyes would need to be darker, she decided. Gatina closed her eyes as she spoke the spell that affected her eye color, and after the telltale tingle, she opened them and did not recognize the maiden she saw. Her eyes were green now. She didn't like it or dislike it, but it was something she could use for her alias, Maranka. That was something she knew she must know inside and out.

"Hello. I am Maranka. Thank you for allowing me to join your crew, Captain Armandus. Mistress Beah, no, Lady Beah has told me much about you. She has helped me with my constellations. I hope to be of service to the ship. No, that sounds forced," she said as she practiced her alias in the glass. "I look forward to the voyage. I am excited to learn— No, no. Thank you for allowing me to apprentice on this fine ship." She nodded, finally satisfied. She was ready for sea.

Or so she thought.

CHAPTER EIGHT

SMOOTH AS GLASS

The start of a voyage is always the most hopeful part.
—Sea Lord proverb

When Gatina left her bedroom an hour later, she was transformed into a white-haired, green-eyed orphan with an affinity for the sea and her head in the stars. Maranka descended the staircase and made her way, careful of her voluminous dress, to the library. It was empty. Instead of sitting down, she walked to the table where Pia had been studying the map. She found Prejestia, then she traced the route to Vaxel. It was not a straight line. Instead, it looked like Mother's curvy handwriting. Each port was notated with a large dot. By the time she had committed the dots' names to memory, her brother and her cousins had arrived.

Pia took a look at her and shook her head. "Oh, my, you are not wearing that correctly. Let me help you." For a moment, Gatina was mortified that she had mucked up her costume. "Don't worry. This is nothing you would have known. I put it on this way the first time too."

Pia began pulling at the dress, lifting up the long bits of fabric and tying them around Gatina's waist, under the belt, not as tightly as a corset but tight enough to give her some shape but also the freedom to move. "There's so much fabric, but this style of dress was actually designed with a purpose in mind. The way you tie it allows you to carry the tools you might need aboard the ship," Pia explained. "And it also provides you a bit of modesty if the dress gets wet while you're working; maybe a wave crashes and splashes you or maybe there's a storm. With it tied up, you are able to not show anything you shouldn't." She smiled at Gatina. "And the fabric is sheer and lightweight, so it will dry quickly, even when it's wrapped."

Gatina caught sight of her reflection and was surprised by how much tying up the dress did for its functionality. She had her shape back again, which was reassuring, but she could see how and where she could tuck in daggers, tools, and even a small coin purse, should she need it. Or maybe where she could hide loot . . . but *that* was not this mission, she reminded herself.

Pia wore a gown in the Sea Lord tradition, a long skirt with a tightly fitted, high-collared bodice in a pale violet with a matching short jacket over her shoulders. Her hair was plaited down her back. Jordi wore trousers of a light tan and a white tunic with an ornate vest over it.

He fussed at his boots. Gatina had learned early that her cousin preferred bare feet to shoes. He had told her that it gave him better footing on deck. She wondered if he had tried the sharkskin boots like she wore with her working blacks. Atopol, like Gatina, was dressed as a deckhand. As Martijne, he wore simple trousers and a shapeless white tunic.

Captain Armandus arrived a quarter hour after Pia's instruction in seafaring fashion, according to the water clock in the library. When Aunt Beah finally led the man to the study, Gatina and the others stood to greet him.

The feature about Captain Armandus that Gatina first noticed was his size. He was a big, hulking man with incredibly broad shoulders. His dark beard hung halfway down his chest, and his long hair was pulled up into a long braid down his back. He wore a coat of blue with bronze buttons over his starched white shirt and black trousers. He sported Sea Lord boots of black leather, with bronze studs holding them closed.

His bearing was one of absolute authority, as If he were already aboard the ship and underway. His dark eyes seemed to see everything at once, she noted, and she had no doubt that he was criticizing everything he saw in his mind. He reminded her at once of her swordplay instructor, Lord Steel, in both his unwavering scrutiny and his demand for perfection. This was a true sea captain, Gatina decided at once. No, a Sea Lord, a man who was only a guest on land.

"This is Captain Armandus," Beah announced as she led him in. "He will be captaining the *Legacy*. It will be up to him whether you two will be permitted to apprentice to his crew this voyage. This is Martijne and Maranka," she introduced. "The apprentices I spoke to you about."

"So, you want to be mariners, do you?" he asked searchingly. His voice was deep and had a bit of a croak to it—there was definitely a bit of the accent she associated with Sea Lords to his speech. She'd already picked up a hint of it from her cousins. "Why, by the Father of Storms, would you want to do a damfool thing like that?" he asked, incredulously.

"I want to be a fit mariner," Atopol started to say.

"Son, you will address the captain as 'sir' or 'captain' *always!*" he barked, raising his voice slightly.

"Sir, I want to become a fit mariner, and perhaps a steward or navigator one day!" Atopol—no, she reminded herself, he was Martijne now—said confidently.

"You think you have the brains for that?" he demanded.

"I want to find out, sir!" Martijne assured him. "I won't know until I try."

The captain grunted at him, as if he doubted the lad but appreciated his sincerity. Then his eyes shifted to Gatina—to Maranka—and she felt as if there was a crossbow aimed at her head.

Much to her dismay, despite her attempt to portray Maranka as a proud and confident young lass seeking a life at sea, Gatina found herself more intimidated by the man's stare than she had ever been by a duelist's sword. When she stood in front of him to introduce herself, she found herself tongue-tied, which was very unlike her. There was something powerful in those dark eyes. Dangerous, perhaps, but what thrilled her more than the danger they implied was the unwavering sense of control they presented.

She barely came to his chest, which was broad and well-muscled—she could tell that from the fit of his clothing. She looked up at his shoulders, his neck, his chin, his mouth, and finally found his dark eyes, which resembled Pia's. She felt so small compared to him. But she knew she must speak. Gatina fought to get herself, and her voice, back to normal.

"Hello, I am Maranka," she squeaked, which was also unusual for her. "Sir!" she added belatedly.

She used her curtsy to wrestle her mind into action before saying, normally, "I thank you, sir, for taking me on as an apprentice. Mistress Beah shared kind words about you."

"*Kind?*" Armandus asked, amused. "That's not a word generally associated with me or my command. I must be going soft. So!" he continued, "you want to be a fit mariner, too?"

"At first, sir, but I'd like to be a navigator someday. Or perhaps a quartermaster," she offered.

"A girl has to know how to read and figure for that," he said skeptically.

"I can do both, sir," she answered. "And I know the constellations already. I can figure tides, too."

"Hmmm," he said, studying her. "Just a little bitty thing, aren't you?"

"It makes it easier to dance the rigging, sir," she suggested. "And I don't eat much."

"Well, I guess you won't make much of a *thud* when you hit the deck, then," he said, with a sigh. "I don't often take girls on voyage with me," he added. "They can be trouble on a ship. I don't expect that will happen with your brother aboard, but I am still cautious. Are you going to be trouble for me, Maranka?"

"Not if I can help it, Captain!" she assured him. "I'm a hard worker. I just want a chance," she pleaded.

"Hmm. I suppose if Beah speaks for both of you, I can be persuaded to give you that chance. It's always taking a chance to take on a couple of squids on a voyage. It gives me a chance to teach them properly. But if there is one spot of trouble, I'll put you off at the next port with no arguments. Do you both understand?"

"Yes, sir!" the two siblings agreed in unison.

"Good. As long as we have an understanding. You'll be paid standard wages for first-timers. Squids," he corrected himself. "Do you need an advance?" he asked, curious.

"We have what we need, Captain," Martijne assured him. "No need for an advance."

"Good. I don't like my crew owing me money. It makes things awkward when it comes to discipline. You'll be paid out half your accrued wages at each port, and the rest when we finish the voyage. Understood?"

"Yes, Captain!" they answered in unison again.

"Very well. We will meet tonight on the deck for your initiation oath. Bring your entire kit with you. We may not sail tomorrow, but I want you ready to. Be warned: we're sailing with my niece and nephew, too," he reminded them. "They'll be treated just as you are: no better, no worse. There is no family at sea, only crew," he said matter-of-factly. "Even though Mistress Beah owns the *Legacy*, she will be under my orders too."

"Armandus, I thought it best to introduce you to our passengers," Beah said. "Lord Hamanthus and Lady Elletia are traveling to visit family. We'll be taking their sloop in tow and running in convoy. They're looking for new opportunities in Vaxel and elsewhere."

"A pleasure, my lord," Armandus said, with a stiff bow. "My lady. Have you sailed before?" he asked, his tone and demeanor changed completely.

It wasn't that he had become more deferential, Gatina decided; he had just controlled his natural tendency to take command.

"Yes, Captain," her father said, affecting the accent of the Falasi nobility. "My father was an avid yachtsman. He left me my sloop, the *Daydream*, and I've taken it out a few times. Never as far as Vaxel, of course, but I thought that it would be prudent to make such a voyage in the company of experienced mariners." Hance's dress matched his speech; he was bedecked in a Coastlord-style doublet of bright green, with yellow hose and exaggerated shoulders. Her mother was likewise garbed in a gown of dark burgundy velvet. Both had dark brown hair and hazel eyes.

Before further conversation could occur, the cook rang a bell to signal for dinner. It had been agreed that the four children would serve the meal and then dine in the kitchen, which greatly appealed to Gatina. They rejoined the adults after the meal on the veranda, once they had cleared away the table. And that was when the topic of the initiation took place.

"Don't worry, you two. I just ask that you give your firstborn son to a life on the sea," the captain said seriously. Gatina gulped. But then Armandus laughed. "I am teasing. It's a brief customary ceremony. It's for the crew to meet you. I promise, it's painless. But don't count on the voyage to be," he said ominously.

AFTER DINNER, GATINA AND ATOPOL WALKED TO THE DOCK WITH PIA AND Jordi, each of them carrying their baggage in a sailcloth duffel. Hers was heavy not just with the extra clothing she'd been given but all of her thieving gear: working blacks, heist journal, tools, and shadowblade.

Gatina saw that the docks were active, though not as hectic as during the day. Aunt Beah's shipping facility was busy day and night. Torches and lamps lit stations along the dock and onboard several ships as they were prepared to get underway. There was less light as they walked to the smaller storehouse, then near-darkness. She had to use magesight to find her way. They passed by the slip where the *Daydream* was docked. When they reached the far side of the storehouse, they were greeted with a torch-lined path that led up the gangplank to the *Legacy*. She paused to observe before she started up the ramp. That's when she saw Aunt Beah, Captain Armandus, and the rest of the crew. They were waiting for her and Atopol.

In hindsight, Gatina realized she put far too much worry on the ritual, which really was nothing at all, just like Jordi had said. Captain Armandus introduced her and Attie to the crew's quartermaster, Seksus, and the bosun, Taruk. It was a small oath-taking ceremony, with Aunt Beah serving as their witness, which Gatina understood to be a sign that she was verifying or vouching for them as good people. When they had promised to obey orders of their superiors unto death, support the captain in all ways, be fair and friendly to the crew and not steal from them, and to report faithfully for duty at the appointed hour without fail, the captain had them sign each of their names in the logbook as apprentice mariners.

Gatina almost giggled at the mention of theft. While she would never steal from her fellow crew, it amused her that there was a provision against it. When that was over, Captain Armandus gave them their assignments for the journey.

"Martijne, you will be deck crew, serving under Taruk. Maranka, you'll be working as an assistant to our navigator, Beah. Both will be on first watch. She'll be both our navigator and owner-aboard. As such, she is second in the line of command. Then Seksus, the quartermaster, and Taruk. All can give you orders, which it is your duty to obey. All can answer questions." He nodded at Seksus.

"Aye. I am more than ready to answer questions," Seksus agreed, his voice gruff but gentle. "I won't do the work for ye, but I shall help as I can. One important thing to note: tomorrow before you set foot on the ship, remember to step aboard with your right foot and only your right foot. 'Tis bad luck to do otherwise. And as this is your first journey with us, your new crew prefers that we start it off as safely as possible."

Gatina remembered Jordi explaining that the quartermaster had risen from the ranks of the crew to his office—or "came up through the hawsehole," implying he'd made it to the office by climbing up the anchor chain instead of the gangplank. He had been a fit mariner since boyhood. Jordi said the man was nearly thirty years old, but he looked much older. His skin looked like tanned cowhide, thanks to the sun. He was tall enough that Gatina needed to tilt her head up to see him. His eyes were green and his hair pale sun-bleached blond. Not full Sea Lord blood, then, but he certainly acted like it.

After a brief moment of what Gatina would characterize as nervous laughter, Captain Armandus formally introduced Taruk. Gatina quickly ascertained that the bosun was a man of few words.

"We cast off at second bell, with the tide," the muscular dark-skinned bosun said. He was a half-head taller than Seksus. "Best arrive by the first bell. We will need to finish loading the supplies and bring aboard our passengers' trunks. This is not a terribly long journey, but we want to have ample supplies laid in. If we aren't ready to depart by the second bell, then I'll have you scrubbing clean decks and coiling lines until your fingers bleed," he promised.

Captain Armandus clapped Taruk on the back. "Yes. At second bell we sail. Best get a good night's rest. It'll be the last one you get for a while."

THE NEXT MORNING, GATINA AND ATOPOL APPEARED ON THE DOCKS BEFORE the first bell, their early arrival met with approval by Seksus and Taruk, who were already hard at work preparing the ship to depart.

The first thing Gatina noticed after she stepped aboard the *Legacy*—remembering to use her right foot—was the largest orange cat she had ever seen.

This wasn't an ordinary cat. It was the size of a small satchel, and its fluffy coat was the color of an actual orange. It was quite friendly. It greeted the crew by butting its wedge-shaped head against shins and winding its body between each mate's legs. Its tail was as long as if not longer than the length of its body, and she quickly learned that the crew treated this cat with absolute respect. She remembered that it was good luck to have a cat aboard a ship, for catching rats and other vermin who might infest the hold.

As a cat lover herself she thought of it as a good omen. She was one of the Cats of Enultramar, after all. But she stopped herself from rushing to pet the cat because she knew she shouldn't be that excited by the sight of a cat aboard a ship. She resolved that she would get to know the big orange predator at some point.

Their cousins were already aboard and were detailed to explain the duties and responsibilities and introduce them to the other members of the crew.

In addition to the captain and the crewmembers they had met the night before, the *Legacy*'s crew included a cook and two other deckhands. She was relieved to see that the cook, a salty old pipe-smoking woman named Remena, had all of her fingers and both eyes. She was just as happy to know that cooking duties would not fall to her or Atopol. They were not well suited for that role. The idea of chopping up vegetables and cooking over an open flame on a wooden deck in the middle of the water seemed daunting.

The two senior deckhands, Nus and Caden, were fit mariners who had crewed the *Legacy* for years, and they expertly prepared the sails and oars to cast off. All four of the apprentices were kept busy dashing around the deck, securing loose items and coiling lines as they were loosed.

The *Legacy* had three decks, which was a bounty for a caravel her size. The lower deck was largely the cargo hold, which was already half-packed with lemons, limes, and oranges from the surrounding estates, as well as barrels of wine from the vineyards that were so plentiful in the eastern Bay. They would be filling up the rest of the hold on their journey, she learned. Just above that was the oar deck, with more cargo space, storerooms, a workshop, and a tiny galley. The four small cabins were in the aft section, where the captain, Beah, and her parents would stay when they were on board.

The crew were billeted in the forecastle deck, a cramped space in the bow that seemed barely large enough for the cat. By tradition, Pia explained, male members of the crew were assigned to the port side, while the females were given the bunks on the starboard side. Also by tradition, the more senior mariners were stationed nearest the little door that led out to the main deck. That put Pia and Gatina farthest away, deep in the narrowest portion of the forecastle. While there were no bulkheads separating the two sides, each mariner had a curtain of tattered sailcloth between them and the others to afford the smallest amount of privacy.

Gatina stared at the narrow board with the thin pad that was to be her home for the next few weeks with skepticism.

"I'm supposed to sleep on that?" she asked Pia in a whisper as her cousin stowed her belongings into a locker. There was one for each of them, bolted to the deck to keep it from sliding around in storms.

"You can try to find a bit of sailcloth to make a hammock," Pia suggested, nodding toward the fit mariners' quarters on the port side, where they had done just that. "But don't worry; by the time you lay down to sleep, you'll be so tired, you won't even notice how hard the bunk is. Besides, you won't be here very long. Each watch is four hours long, with an additional two for dogwatch. There's a lot to do on a merchantman."

Gatina sighed. "I slept in a box bed back at the abbey. This doesn't look much bigger. And far less comfortable."

"Comfort is something you should forget about at sea," her cousin advised. "Not even the paying cabins are comfortable. The captain's cabin isn't much bigger than your bunk, and Mother's doubles as the chart room. As the lowest crew, we get the worst accommodations. But this isn't too bad," she consoled. "It's just us and Remena in here. The boy's side is going to be more crowded. You'll get used to it," she assured.

"I've slept in worse places." Gatina shrugged as she opened her own locker.

"Do you think you remembered everything?" Pia asked as Gatina set her small satchel on the bunk. "Once we're underway, it will be too late to go back and pick anything up. You're stuck until we make port."

Gatina shrugged. "I hope so," she said. "Mother had me pack a sewing kit, parchment, ink, soap, pins, rags, a looking glass, and other things she thought I'd need. I guess I'll just have to improvise if I forgot anything. I suspect Seksus won't be as kind as you and Jordi were when we took the *Daydream* out. I don't think he likes me," she confessed.

"You will do fine," her cousin assured her. "Seksus is always like that. Just do as you're told and do it quickly. It's one thing to practice in a harbor, another to be at sea. This will be challenging, but you can do it. And Jordi and I are here to help you. By the time we get to Vaxel, you'll be ready for your own boat. And don't worry about Seksus. Worry about the cat. If the cat likes you, the crew will follow."

Before her parents boarded and after everything had been loaded, Captain Armandus called the crew together around the mainmast to discuss their voyage.

Gatina discovered that included the proposed route, schedule, watch, and duty assignments. Hers were thankfully easy. She and Pia would be responsible for the lines when the sheets needed adjustment, maintenance of the deck, as well as assisting Beah with navigation if she required it.

Among other duties, Atopol and Jordi were responsible for setting the fishing nets and sorting and cleaning the fish for each day's meals. All of them, Gatina learned, would be required to stand one night watch—called the fire watch—every three days in addition to their other responsibilities.

More foreboding was the announcement about the course chosen. Captain Armandus shared what Gatina had already overheard Beah and her parents discuss.

"Warships have been recently seen on the Bay," he revealed. "Pirates, perhaps, or privately contracted warships for convoy duty. Either one could be a problem. I think our risk is low, as we're not carrying valuable cargo and are too small to concern them, but each of you bears responsibility for the ship's safety. If we get threatened, we will attempt to flee. If we're forced to fight, we'll open the weapons locker. But don't let it concern you overmuch," he advised.

When the giant orange cat wrapped itself around Captain Armandus's legs, he bent down and hoisted the cat up onto his shoulders. "And everyone is also responsible for Ginny's safety," he said. "She keeps us protected."

He scratched her chin. He set her down and she immediately made a line for Gatina. But instead of wrapping herself around her legs, the cat stood on her hind legs and pawed at her.

"You'd best pet her, Maranka," the captain advised. "She's taken to you and that's an honor." She did as she was told. Ginny rubbed her head against Gatina's hand, her purr audible to all. Ginny abandoned her and found her brother. He knelt and was nearly knocked over when she head-butted him. The captain gave a rumbly chuckle. "That's that, then. The cat accepts our apprentice mates. So, they will get the honor of cleaning her sandbox. Let's get ourselves sorted and prepare to launch," he said, dismissing them.

"Maranka and Pia, please join the captain and me in the cockpit," Aunt Beah said. "We need to review a few points on the map."

Captain Armandus led the way with Ginny following closely at his boots. She hopped up onto his large, wide wood table, where a chart of the Great Bay was open. There was an array of charcoal pencils, rulers, and a compass set to the side, serving to hold down the map.

Aunt Beah moved the compass to another corner of the map. "We are here, and we will be sailing westward toward the port of Cadena. We will stop there to drop off a few barrels of wine and pick up a few crates of oranges. It should be an easy leg. I don't anticipate it taking more than a full day to arrive." She traced the route with her finger, as Gatina had done the night before.

"After that, our next stop is in the port of Pluhalia. And listen to me, girls," she said, her tone serious, "be cautious in that port. You must stick together. Pluhalia is not the safest port, especially for young women. It's frequented by slavers. If it were up to me, you'd stay on the ship." She looked at Captain Armandus, who shook his head. "It has been decided that you will be allowed shore leave, a brief one. We will be there by tomorrow evening, give or take a few hours." Beah lifted the map and pulled out another. "Beyond that, we may have to improvise a course, but this is our final destination, Vaxel. That's where the Anchorage and Assessment will be. That's where we'll be selling our cargo and picking up more to bring back."

Gatina already knew that Vaxel was their destination. But as far as she knew, the captain did not know that she knew that. He also, as far as she knew, did not know that this trip was part of a mission set into place by her father and the Council of Shadows. Gatina wondered if he'd been told that information. She had not thought to ask after the man's politics, but that would not have been appropriate as a disguised apprentice.

The captain frowned, but only briefly. "I'd prefer to skip Pluhalia altogether if we could. It takes time to make port, and there are better ones that make it more worthwhile elsewhere. But the passengers want to stop there, for some reason, and it will give us a chance to take on more citrus from the south. It will slow us down, but we're going to be at a crawl as it is from towing that damned sloop behind us."

"Oh, I think it will be fine, Captain," Beah assured him. "We can keep our schedule. I'll chart the course with Maranka tonight, just to verify that. But I can't imagine it would add more than a day to the trip," she said.

"Every day costs more coin," the captain warned.

"They're paying passengers," Beah argued. "And they paid in advance. We won't lose anything by stopping in Pluhalia. And I've already arranged a cargo transfer there."

"Bloody Coastlords," the captain muttered under his breath. "So, you think these two will be smart enough to learn to navigate?" he asked, glancing at the girls.

"Pia has managed before," she assured. "But she needs the practice. I want to show Maranka how to chart tonight. Now get to your stations and prepare to cast off," she ordered. "I'll find you when it's time to stargaze," she added.

Dismissed, Pia led her to the main deck, where they found Jordi instructing Martijne on the finer points of knot-tying as they prepared to sail.

That was a vital skill for a mariner, she knew. Thankfully, tying knots came naturally to her. She was relieved to find that several of the knots with which she was familiar were like the style Jordi was explaining—but there were many she'd never heard of. Indeed, there seemed to be a different knot for everything on the ship, each one fitted for its specific task. Pia wasted little time jumping in to lend a hand in the instruction. Jordi was demonstrating the knot on a cleat, which was how this particular ship would be tied to the dock.

"I am familiar with this one," she assured them, "though not around a cleat." She deftly measured the line as she would for climbing, the distance from her arm to her nose. Then she took the tail and crossed it over the other strand, then whipped the line underneath and through the loop and pulled it out the top. She left it loose, as she would for climbing.

"That's very good, Maranka," Jordi said. Gatina smiled. She knew it was good. It was the first knot she had learned, and she had been using it for years, long before she knew of her family's clandestine activities. "Do you remember the bowline?

Gatina looked over at her big brother, who smiled and nodded. She willed her fingers to be as nimble as possible as she worked to beat him at tying the knot. "How's that?" she asked.

Pia nodded. "That's not bad at all. Now, why might you need to exercise caution when using this knot?"

Atopol spoke before Gatina could answer. "The bowline might not hold," he said.

Jordi clapped him on the back. "Right. If the rope is smooth, it could slip. How about the right angle?" he asked.

After she completed the task quickly and was satisfied with her knot, she said, "This knot is used to secure heavier items, such as cargo." *Or loot*, she thought.

"That's right," Jordi said. "Mess that one up and you could get a barrel of wine to fall on your head. We've seen that happen when someone figures 'If I can't tie a knot, I'll tie a lot' instead of doing it properly. Now let's get these sheets ready to raise when Captain Armandus gives the word. The tide is rising," he observed. "It won't be long now."

The four of them labored together as they had earlier in the week. Working as a team, they had everything ready to hoist in a few minutes' time. Based on the direction of the wind, they would not be ready to raise the mainsheet until they had left the harbor, Gatina decided. She suspected Captain Armandus would use the tiller and the crew would use the oars or poles to get off the dock and then take the *Daydream* in tow.

She saw several pairs of long wooden oars mounted to the ship's side rails. She did not relish the idea of rowing. Indeed, the very thought of it made her back ache.

When her parents boarded the ship in their disguises as Lord Hamanthus and Lady Elletia, the *Legacy*'s newest crewmembers had worked up a sweat under the hot and bright summer sun. Gatina barely noticed them boarding, but she did see them as they went belowdecks to find their cabin.

At last, Captain Armandus gave the order to ready the ship. She joined in when the rest of the crew gave a hearty "Aye, aye, Captain" as a response. The bosun called to the dock crew, who unlashed the mooring lines and pushed the ship away with long poles.

"Oars!" Taruk called out in a voice that was used to shouting orders. Obediently, the deckhands pushed the long oars into the water after securing them in the oarlocks, and Taruk began calling a cadence to time their strokes. At first, Gatina didn't think they were having any real effect—how could six oars move such a large mass as the *Legacy*? But slowly, the ship moved out into the harbor until it was freely floating. By the time he was finished, the ship was drifting.

"Ship oars!" commanded Taruk, just as Gatina felt her arms were going to fall off. "Prepare to launch the gig!" That was the smallest boat, one of three, that the *Legacy* carried with it, Gatina had learned. The other two were a longboat large enough to ferry cargo and a slightly smaller boat useful for taking passengers or doing maintenance on the hull.

It didn't take long to deploy the gig, and not much longer for Taruk to row a line over to the *Daydream* and secure it to the bow. With the sloop empty and the sails furled, it wouldn't be much of a drag on the *Legacy*, Gatina figured.

"The wind is picking up. The captain will call for the mainsheet soon, I suspect, once we get the sloop secured in tow," Pia said, looking up at the cloudless sky with a discerning eye. Her hair whipped in her face as a breeze picked up.

The four secured the oars to the sidewall. Gatina looked at the dock behind them, at the flurry of activity as the morning got underway for the port city. Carts of cargo were being wheeled out, ready to be loaded aboard ships. The crews of fishing boats carried traps and nets for seafood onto their boats. Some were already returning to the docks with their morning's catch.

"Cap'n wants that mainsail up as soon as the gig is back aboard," Seksus directed her as she watched the bosun row back. "He'll be watching, so I want it to go as smooth as glass. The wind is rising. I'll whistle when 'tis time. Just you listen for it," he said, turning to go toward the helm. "Won't be long."

"Aye, aye," she said in response. She did not realize how often that expression would tumble from her mouth that first day.

When the whistle came a few moments later, she was ready—or thought she was. She'd practiced raising the sail on the *Daydream*, but this was a much larger and ungainly sheet that required four people to raise. She could probably complete several flips across it, had it been stretched on the ground.

The crewmen danced up the rigging and released it, while the apprentices hauled on the lines to secure it. It seemed to take a lifetime to unfurl and hoist it slowly up, hand over hand. Gatina was warm and her heart was pounding from the exertion. Sweat ran from her hairline into her right eye, but she couldn't stop to wipe it away or the sheet might slip. It was hard work, and it took a bit for them to coordinate their efforts, but it was a good skill to practice. *After all, what was the point of having a yacht if they were not able to sail it?* she thought.

She dipped her head into her armpit to wipe her brow while she continued to pull the line down and send the sheet up. Bending her neck made her aware of just how hard her muscles were working. It wasn't that different from climbing a wall using a rope, she decided, and it was nearly as challenging. The wind had started to pick up, and that caused a drag on the sheet. It was as if the wind was fighting the sail instead of cooperating.

When the mainsail was finally hoisted and secured, she wiped her brow with the back of her hand. And in moments, she regretted that decision. The salty sweat from her brow trickled onto her palm, which was raw and red with chafing from the rough hemp ropes. The sting was a slow burn, and as soon as she realized her mistake, she quickly dabbed her palms on her dress.

Atopol winced in sympathy and held up his own rough-looking hand. She looked up and groaned. "I miss my gloves," she admitted.

"We can't use gloves," he reminded her. "None of the mariners do. Jordi told me Beah has a salve for tender hands, though. But you've got to build up your calluses," he reminded her. "Sea Lords don't have soft hands."

"At least we're underway," she said as she looked up at the mainsail full with the wind. It was a steady breeze, she noted, and was propelling the *Legacy* across the harbor. But it wasn't enough to raise many waves, she was thankful to see. Indeed, the harbor's surface was smooth as the *Legacy* set sail, pulling the *Daydream* behind her. Even though she was already exhausted, it was a beautiful morning for sailing, she decided, as she scanned the horizon.

"Enough daydreamin'!" barked Seksus, interrupting her reverie. "Get the foresail raised, or we won't leave harbor until low tide! Move it, you luggards!" he shouted.

Gatina sighed and hurried to join her brother at the foremast. The *Legacy* was, indeed, underway, as was her first real voyage.

CHAPTER NINE

CADENA: A NOT-SO-PLEASANT STOP

It is not leaving port that makes a successful voyage; it's entering port.

—Sea Lord proverb

ONCE THE SAILS WERE RAISED, THE *LEGACY* MADE GOOD TIME, ESCAPING THE harbor well before the tides changed. The hectic pace of the crew slackened as the winds of the Great Bay filled the sails and propelled the caravel forward. The bosun called to raise the colors as soon as they were clear of the harbor, and soon, Gatina was hoisting the large standard that depicted the wave and mage stars that the *Legacy* flew to the top of the mainmast. Under that banner was a smaller red one emblazoned with a stylized lemon, advertising what they were shipping.

The rest of her day was filled with drills: fire drill, boat drill—in which they lowered and raised all three boats—grounding drill, weapons drill, and collision drill. She learned her station for each one, and each one was run several times until the crew satisfied the bosun that they were proficient. By the time Seksus piped for luncheon, Gatina was exhausted. It felt as if she had done a full day's hard labor, and it was not yet noon.

She was relieved of her post after the meal, and she dragged her way back to the forecastle and threw herself into her bunk when Pia informed her she had time for a quick nap. As promised, the hard board and thin pad felt like a featherbed to her tired body. She did not rise until Pia shook her awake for her next shift.

That first night, when the *Legacy* had sailed beyond sight of land, Gatina reported to her great-great-aunt for a lesson in stargazing. She was surprised to find Beah sitting alone on one of the well-worn wooden benches on the pilot deck.

Aunt Beah was staring out at the Great Bay as if she could see something, perhaps with magesight. Her hair danced gently around her face in the wind, framing it like a wimple of nightshades. The stars overhead offered a little light, which reflected on the waves the way a candle would off a shiny object. The clouds hid the moons, but every now and again, the coverage thinned, allowing for the silvery light to dance down. The *Legacy* swam smoothly under the guidance of Captain Armandus, who was on watch on the tiller.

"Is there a problem, Mistress?" Gatina asked, a little concerned by her expression.

Her Aunt Beah did not look at her but continued staring out at the sea.

"No, Maranka. Sitting here still like this reminds me of my life before we lost my husband," she said wistfully. "I do not regret any of my life. But sitting here like this . . . Alek and I used to do this every night. I still miss him." Beah shook her head. "I'm sorry. I was distracted, Maranka. Yes, I think you are correct in your timing. Now, what do you make of the clouds in the sky and the breeze on the water? Are we due for a storm?"

She glanced out of the window at the overcast. There were a few holes through which the stars peeked. "Not with those clouds, I'm guessing. Too thin to be storm clouds," she offered.

"You're right; I don't anticipate any squalls tonight. But perhaps a little rain. I suppose it's time for you to help me navigate the stars and plan our route. Now, what does your Saganite training suggest to you?"

"That it's a poor night for viewing the stars," she observed, looking up at the partially overcast sky.

Beah chuckled. "Mayhap. But we don't get to pick our weather. We need to know where we are, where we've been, and where we're going, no matter what the weather does. Let's start with figuring out which direction is north."

Gatina looked up at the stars and worried she wouldn't remember her astronomical training. Instead of worrying, she sighed deeply, closed her eyes, and willed herself to recall the guiding constellations. When she opened her eyes a few moments later and looked up, she saw the Triangle, partially obscured by clouds.

"That's north," she said, pointing toward the three stars. "Which means that's south, that's east, and that's west. This time of year, the Crab should be rising, just behind the Circle and just ahead of Agtron."

"So, what is our heading, would you guess?" Beah prompted.

"West by northwest," Gatina ventured.

Beah nodded. "Well done. How fast are we going?" she asked, curious. Gatina looked confused. "I have no idea," she confessed.

"We use a length of knotted rope to determine that," she explained. "The knots are at regular, predetermined lengths based on the curvature of the planet. And we use the water clock or the hourglass to determine the exact duration of the reading to determine our speed. I'll show you the math tomorrow, but that's how we figure out how fast we're going.

"And if we know our current location, our speed, and our direction, we can plot out precisely where we are on a chart. That's vitally important," she assured. "Without that knowledge, we'd never be able to get anywhere once we were out of sight of land." She unrolled a large sheet of parchment and showed it to Gatina. It was an intricately drawn chart of the eastern Great Bay.

"See? Here's where we started, in Prejestia. We've been averaging about seven knots—that's seven nautical miles an hour," she explained. "The chart tells us it's only twenty-eight miles between Prejestia and Cadena. So, theoretically, we should be able to make port in only four hours. Why will it take longer?"

"The tides," Gatina answered at once. "During low tide, we'll be fighting to push forward. If it's a greater low tide, then it will be even harder. That's when both moons line up and give the tides an even-greater tug than normal."

"Correct!" her aunt agreed, pleased. "Time, tides, and wind are the factors we need to contend with to navigate. We must take regular readings to ensure we're on course, and constantly check to make certain we haven't strayed. Once we get to the mouth of the Mandros, it will be even harder because the outflow of the river changes the amount of salt in the water, and that has an effect on our speed too. And, of course, we'll be working against the Northern Current. So, even though Cadena is close by, it's a bit of a struggle to get us there. Still, we should sight it by dawn, at this rate. After Cadena, we'll break for the open Bay, where the current won't be working against us and the winds are stronger."

"How do you figure position if you can't see the stars?" Gatina wondered aloud.

Before her aunt could reply, they were both misted by raindrops. The cool water was gentle at first, but it quickly became a pelting. "A lesson for tomorrow," her aunt said, standing and quickly rolling up the chart. "Best we take cover before we're soaked. Navigators and their charts should stay dry. If we take ill, the voyage is doomed. Let's go up to the pilothouse, and I'll show you the water clock and the compass. Those are essential to navigation."

Dodging raindrops, Gatina dutifully followed her aunt up the ladder. It occurred to her that she hadn't seen her parents all day long, even though they were all on the same ship. That seemed odd to her, but they were all under aliases, after all. Maranka wouldn't have any reason to see the paying passengers. She was too busy learning how to sail.

THE NEXT MORNING, IT TOOK PIA FIVE ATTEMPTS TO ROUSE GATINA. SHE was soundly sleeping and not ready to get out of bed. Her cousin tried several times before threatening to dump water from the fire pail onto her head.

Gatina's shoulders and upper back ached from the previous day and night's labor. The sudden shower had everyone rushing to lower and secure sails and lines and anything that might be picked up by the wind and carried off the deck. It hadn't blown up that way, but that was the way the crew had prepared.

It was the fastest she had ever seen that many people move. The fastest and the most organized. They followed Seksus's orders as he barked them. She knew she had done well enough, but she had expected herself to do better and be quicker. She just did not have the strength or the stamina to perform as well as the other crewmen, and she felt disappointed that the other deckhands had to assist her when she came up short. Even though it was her first little shower at sea, she did not like to ask for help.

But today was a new day. When she heard the sloshing of water, Gatina sat up quickly, careful not to bump her head in the cramped quarters. She tossed back the thick wool blanket and swung her feet to the floor just as Pia prepared to toss the cold water onto her head.

"Fine, I'm awake!" she grumbled as she eased herself out of the tiny bunk. Gatina suddenly missed her bed box at Palomar Abbey, where it was cozy, dark, and spacious.

"Where's Beah?" Gatina began her morning preparations, which included stretching and moving through a series of exercises designed to keep her muscles from cramping and her body limber. Lord Steel had taught these to her, along with the many fighting sequences. Given the cramped space, she did not dare to use her blade to practice those. *Maybe on deck tonight,* she thought.

"Mother is with your parents and Captain Armandus, breaking their fast. And probably planning our trip into Cadena," Pia said. "We made port before first bell." The girl had returned the basin to its spot and watched Gatina. "Your mother brought a gown for you. Going into port in your deck clothes isn't proper. I think you're going to be changing your alias for the day." Pia worked a comb through her dark hair before she pulled it on top of her head and secured it with several long hairpins.

Gatina crossed the room and pulled the gown off the peg on the wall where it had been hung. It was a less-affluent version of the finer Sea Lord gowns she'd seen, in a pale blue that didn't suit her. There was a dark wig under the dress, too. She held the gown at arm's length and caught a glint of steel tucked into the waistline. She quickly removed a small, curved dagger no larger than her pointer finger. The sheath had been sewn into the gown. Smiling, she replaced it.

"What's wrong? It's not a snake. It won't bite you," Pia teased. She began to remove her nightdress and work her way into her own undergarments. "I have to wear one too. Honestly, I'd rather wear the simple shift. It's too hot for all of this." She rustled the crinoline petticoat the Sea Lord ladies preferred, and grimaced.

"Won't the crew wonder why we're dressed as Sea Lords instead of—"

"They don't ask questions once coin has changed hands," Pia answered, cutting her off. "They already suspect that there is more to this voyage than lemons and limes. And they won't be on deck to see you. They've already begun to take on cargo, and that will take their full attention. You'll like Cadena. It's reasonably safe, compared to some places. You have nothing to worry about other than seeing new sights and maybe tasting some exotic food."

"How exotic?" Gatina asked, as she stripped off her ship's dress. She was already growing tired of the biscuit-and-porridge diet at sea.

"Cadena is known for its skewers of marinated meats and vegetables roasted over the coals. And its spices. Absolutely delicious. Though Jordi would have you believe that the pastries are better."

BOATS AND SHIPS WERE COMING AND GOING, THEIR SAILS JOCKEYING FOR HER attention as the two girls left the forecastle for the main deck. The water was a deep greenish blue in the morning sun. The bosun had already rowed over to the *Daydream* to anchor her in the harbor so she wouldn't interfere with the docking and loading.

Gatina heard the shouts of crewmembers from ships alongside theirs, as well as the *clickety-clack* of overfull wains and carts being pulled or pushed atop the docks. Her pulse quickened as the *Legacy* pulled alongside the dock. She looked around, expecting to see Atopol and Jordi help tie the lines as they moored the ship, but she couldn't find them among the crew.

She returned her attention to the city in the distance. It seemed a fairly typical coastal Sea Lord port, though it was cleaner than some they had passed. There was stark, four-story square tower that slightly tapered as it rose, a traditional Sea Lord stronghold overlooking both the harbor and the town. Tall white buildings stood in the distance, some with tributaries or canals leading small boats directly to their private docks.

She saw flags on several buildings, but from this far away, she was not able to make those out until she used magesight. With magic to aid her, she could discern the spires of the old haven that sprawled around the main fortress: the complex dedicated to the Maiden, the tall spire of the Storm King, and a small but well-built building devoted to the Fairtrader, complete with the sign of gilded scales.

There were plenty of other flags, but she was distracted by a gentle squeeze on her elbow. Her mother and father had arrived, with Atopol and Jordi trailing behind them. Gatina realized that was why she hadn't seen them on helping tie off the boat.

Everyone was dressed in decent Sea Lord garments, with boots, blades, and wide leather hats indicative of their status as nobility, however minor. Aunt Beah joined them a moment later. She, too, wore a gown, but she was bareheaded and her hair remained free. Captain Armandus, who was manning the pilothouse, looked down at them with a frown. These weren't the apprentice deckhands he'd signed on, he was no doubt thinking, Gatina guessed.

"Lady Maranka, I do think that gown is lovely on you," Mother said. "I also hope you are not without resources." Gatina understood instantly what she meant.

Smiling, she spoke, altering her voice to match that pattern of the Sea Lords. "Yes, my lady mother, I am prepared and found this gown to my liking." She placed her hand over the concealed dagger behind her back.

The gauzy wimple and stray hairs from her wig tickled her shoulders when she moved.

Fortunately, the days she had spent in the sun had given her skin a sun-kissed look, which helped her appear more like a Sea Lord under her wig. Nobody there seemed to be concerned with Beah's pale hair, she'd noted. Pia and Gatina's gowns were similar; Gatina had noticed that as soon as they were both dressed. Their gowns were different from the style worn in Falas, too. Instead of long sleeves and a tight bodice, these sleeves ended just before their elbows. And, to Gatina's relief, the bodice was loose and relatively breathable, which she was sure would be helpful in the humidity.

Before they left the ship, Hance huddled the family together to explain the objective in Cadena.

"Cadena is a midsized port but it's one of great importance," he began. "This is one of the best locations in the Great Bay to purchase more fresh citrus, specifically lemons. We need the lemons for our cargo."

Gatina looked at her father and wondered if he was speaking in code. *Lemons?* she thought. Those were available in Falas—for a fee—as well as in Prejestia. She looked to her brother, who showed little interest in the lemons. He had spied a pastry cart parked at the end of the dock.

"More importantly for you," Hance continued, "this is one of the better Sea Lord ports. There are more authentic Sea Lords here doing business than most places around the mouth of the Mandros. So, this is your opportunity to study them. Learn the cadence of their language and their accents, and study their mannerisms and the way they interact. Details," he emphasized. "They aren't like Coastlords. They have a very specific culture separate from the rest of the Alshari. Do your best to learn it.

"Now, Minnie, Beah, and I will be arranging for a cargo delivery to the *Legacy*," he explained. "Don't linger. We won't be here long. You four have a few hours to explore the port. Be back by the temples' noontime bells. Captain Armandus wants to sail soon after so that we can continue our journey. This is only the first stop of many," he reminded them, looking at Gatina, "and we do have a schedule to keep."

Cadena was alive with activity, bright colors, and boisterous noises, Gatina quickly saw as she and the others separated from their parents. And the food smelled amazing. The scents overpowered those of the ocean—and crewmembers who were in need of a bath. She saw the vendors as soon as they left the dock. Carts were set up along the wharf where they cooked and sold their goods to porters, stevedores, mariners, and merchants—everything from the meat skewers and pies to pastries and cheeses she had never seen in her life to carts selling weak ale.

When they reached the end of the dock, Jordi convinced them to visit Cadena's best sweets shop. Pia said it was a street over from the main street. Gatina followed behind Atopol, who followed Pia, who said she knew the quickest way there. Jordi was at Gatina's heels, keeping the cousins together. He reminded her of a herding dog, the kind they had back at Cysgodol Hall to keep the sheep from wandering too far. She didn't make the comparison in a mean way, of course. He was dedicated and intent on his task. Neither wanted to lose them in the crowd.

"Is it usually this crowded?" Gatina asked Jordi. There were rows of people walking down the cobblestone street. It was people-watching at its best, she realized. She saw everyone from the wealthy to the destitute. A great many of them were, indeed, of Sea Lord stock by their clothing: mostly men in short jackets, leather breeches, low boots, and wide-brimmed leather hats. Some of them wore blades on their hips. She heard laughter, shouting, crying children, and calls for alms.

Jordi shook his head. "No, this is odd. It is a very busy port, but this is more foot traffic than I've seen. There must be something special happening today. I hope they're not all headed our way. Oh, wait, here's the cut-through." He pointed, and Gatina caught sight of Atopol and Pia turning off the street at an alley. The shortcut brought them out just outside the sweets shop's door. But before they went inside, they saw another crowd start to gather. "I wonder what that is," Jordi asked, his voice loud enough for Atopol and Pia to hear.

Before anyone spoke, a team pulling a cage fastened atop a large wain drove past them. The cage held at least thirty men, she saw in horror. As it rocked along, the men closest to the wooden bars reached out or tried to squeeze through, with no luck. Some looked nearly dead, Gatina saw, their eyes staring vacantly at the well-dressed foursome. All were filthy and had sunken cheeks. Some bore tattoos of anchors.

She wondered if they had been mariners or maybe pirates before they had been captured. They looked like they hadn't eaten in a long time. Behind the carriage, a group of young boys and girls walked in a line surrounded by armed guards. The children's hands and feet were bound, their little legs barely able to keep up the pace.

"Are those prisoners?" she asked her cousins quietly.

"Slaves," Pia said, her voice low with condemnation. "Taken prisoner from the open sea and headed for auction. So many, too! Some of them are mariners!" she realized, appalled.

"Slaves?" Gatina asked, shocked at the information.

One boy stumbled. Before he fell, the boys on either side of him each pulled him up. A guard yelled to keep moving. The child's face tore at Gatina's soul, and his expression of suffering burned into her mind. He couldn't have been more than five, if that. She lost herself for a moment, intent on helping the child. She reached for her dagger, instinctively, and stepped toward the guards. Atopol stopped her and pulled her into the sweets shop just as the boy fell and the same guard began to beat him.

"Gat, no!" he whispered harshly into her ear. "You cannot help any of them. You *cannot* risk all of us in trying," he said. He had his hands on her shoulders, holding her still. Rage and adrenaline were waging an internal war. She wanted to act. Her conscience demanded it.

But she knew he was right. When he pleaded with her to look at him, she did. He had dropped his Sea Lord accent, which was a lilting, slower-paced speaking pattern. "This is the misery that Vichetral has brought on us. But you cannot help them. Not this day. But you will. We will. I *swear* it."

Her mind told her he was right. Hells, she *knew* he was right. She closed her eyes and practiced her breathing. By her fourth round of slowed inhalations and exhalations, her cousins were on either side of her, ready to help Atopol should he need it. Or maybe to help her. She wasn't sure. When she opened her eyes, she nodded at her brother once. And then he relaxed.

"Don't worry. We'll get all of that sorted soon enough," Jordi said. "It's bad for business all around. But for now, consider this your assignment."

"Yes, you're to learn how Sea Lords live," Pia reminded her. "So, let us show you," she said, taking Gatina's arm in her own and walking her fully inside the shop. Once inside, Gatina heard Atopol exhale slowly.

"Oh, my. How much time do we have?" he asked.

"Not long enough," Jordi said reverently.

The shop was long and narrow with floor-to-ceiling shelves and heavy tables holding glass jars. Inside the jars were more varieties of candies, cookies, and other sweets than Gatina had ever seen in her life.

"Cadena is a terminal port for a lot of the sugar trade," Pia explained. "Ships all the way from Farise or the Shattered Isles bring the big loaves in by the ton. Some of it gets sold here, where they turn it into . . . magic," she said as her brother and Atopol began to select what they wanted.

They had spent most of their coin on sweets within moments. Gatina was not in the least surprised. And, though her heart still ached for the little boy, she had to focus on this mission. She had to learn how Sea Lords behaved. So, she observed the other patrons in the candy store.

There were several groups of children, ushered around by mothers or other caretakers. The smaller children, maybe four or five years old, stared at the shelves in silent awe. The older children tried their best to very loudly convince the adults to "just buy one piece" for them. The adults wore frustrated—no, exhausted, she decided—looks on their faces, as if wondering how they had ended up in this particular shop. And the oldest of the children had their own money to spend, as Atopol and Jordi had just done.

"I bet that candy won't last them through the night," Pia whispered.

Gatina laughed. "That's not a bet I wish to take, cousin. I would lose."

Pia insisted they find one of the skewer stands before they returned to the boat, but before that, she suggested that Gatina and Atopol see some of the temples. "It will help you with your aliases and your mission. Or at least I think it will. Cadena is one of the oldest of their settlements on the Great Bay. You'll learn a lot here."

Gatina thought it was a sound plan. She was familiar with the temples of Trygg, Huin the Tiller, Duin the Destroyer that the Vale Lords worshipped, and, of course, the Saganites. She knew religion was one of the most authentic means of learning about someone's culture.

Pia led Gatina, and Atopol and Jordi brought up the rear in case either got separated. She took them back through side alleys as they wound their way up the hill then down. Gatina had seen some of the flags overhead from aboard the *Legacy*. The first temple they found bore a pelican and scales on its flag.

"The Temple of the Fairtrader," Pia announced as they entered the compound. "Patroness of merchantmen, navigators, quartermasters, and counting men. I suppose she's a worthy first place to start."

"Does that extend to slavers?" Gatina asked, quietly.

Pia made a face. "The Sea Lords traded in slaves in antiquity," she conceded. "The Dukes of Alshar put a stop to it. Until now. The Fairtrader doesn't support the trade, but she doesn't condemn it, either. Cargo is cargo. Her invisible hand does not discriminate."

Gatina wondered just how fair the goddess was, given the slavers they had just seen.

The building didn't look much like a temple to Gatina; it lacked much ornamentation on the exterior—there were few statues, shrines, or fountains, like the temples in Falas she was used to. What there was seemed understated. The one idol she saw near the entrance depicted a middle-aged woman with a serious expression on her face and the distinctive Sea Lord wide-brimmed hat, holding a brass balance scale with coins on one side and a barrel, a crate, and a cargo net on the other.

Pia ushered them inside, and Gatina's attention was immediately drawn to the maps painted onto the smooth walls inside the large building. The maps were richly limned in a flowing style, brightly colored, and resembled sea charts of the Great Bay and of faraway places like Castal, Remere, Farise, and Merwyn. They stretched over her head in bright blues and greens, punctuated with red lines delineating trade routes. Here and there, the artist had added little pictures of sharks, whales, nymphs, and leviathans in the waters.

She found the details fascinating. It was similar to the map Captain Armandus had in his cockpit but less exact and far more vivid. Animals—oxen, colorful birds, large cats, boars—were included on the largely blank landward side, and the most well-known Sea Lord havens and all of the ports were displayed and labeled, even the tiny port where her family's boat was moored. She was surprised to see that it was a Fairtrader temple, but it made sense. Her parents were merchants, she supposed, depending on how one viewed commerce. The murals led them down a wide hallway where she could hear shouting. Gatina started to be alarmed.

"That's normal," Jordi assured her. "It's where they conduct their business. The Fairtraders are responsible for all of the Sea Lord banking and trade. And on days when ships come to port, like today, it gets rather loud."

The main sanctuary of the temple looked like no other she'd ever seen. Instead of a centralized shrine or altar as the focus of attention, there were a myriad of tables and stools on which sat scores of merchants and businessmen engaged in commerce. Well-dressed young women served brandy and tea from a side table, while austere-looking priestesses wandered through the crowd, observing and occasionally stopping to witness a document or arbitrate a dispute. Pipe smoke hung thickly in the air, creating a surreal haze in the light that streamed in from the high-placed windows.

The four of them stood against a wall and watched the frenzied chaos unfold in front of them. Merchants were making payments. Crewmembers wanted their pay. Sea Lords came to settle their bills. Clerks were studiously writing down the results of the transactions. And auctions of cargo and even ships were being held, which produced the most shouting as interested parties voiced their bidding. The high ceiling was domed, which made it seem even louder.

Gatina watched it all, fascinated. She wondered how anyone could think amid this noise, then she realized what a prime target this would be for a heist. But that wasn't her mission. She settled for scanning the room. She noticed guards bearing long, impressive-looking scimitars standing discreetly near every Fairsister, the title of the women who joined the order. Guards were also stationed at the doors of the hall.

The Fairsisters' robes reminded her of the Saganites. They were a dark blue with hoods but short-sleeved. The Saganites wore gray or black. The Fairsisters wore necklaces with medallions stamped to resemble a set of scales and measures. Some carried abacuses with them, or pouches with parchment, ink, and pens. Some had large brass seals that they used to certify documents that had been agreed upon and signed. Along one wall was a group of scribes wearing short blue coats who were able to write out agreements and contracts for the illiterate among the crowd.

It was a temple devoted entirely to commerce, she realized, the main purpose of the Sea Lords' devotion to the sea. She overheard voyages being discussed at one table, proposals for trade alliances at another, and a lively discussion over commissioning the construction of a new ship at another. The *clink* of glasses of brandy or cups of tea was present, but the men and women here weren't focused on the refreshments. This was a place of raw commerce, where hundreds of thousands of ounces of gold were being exchanged, she realized.

She listened carefully to the various accents and the cadence that was particular to the culture. It was rolling in emphasis, like a ship on the waves, she realized. She focused on it intently until she could begin to pick up some of the nuance.

She also saw how the Sea Lords bargained—though not all of the patrons were Sea Lords, by any means. She saw Coastlords and common merchants aplenty, as well as a few Narasi Vale Lords making business arrangements far from home. Bankers and counting men seemed prominent, usually dressed in darker coats or doublets and almost universally well fed. It seemed quite the contrast to the half-naked, starving slaves she'd seen in the street not an hour before.

She wondered if one of these men were responsible for the human cargo outside. If their sale at market would be casually written down next to orders for lemons or casks of wine. The idea sickened her.

Suddenly, she was done with the Fairtrader's Shrine.

WHEN THEY LEFT THE TEMPLE, PIA LED THEM BACK TOWARD THE WHARF. The sun was high overhead, and Gatina realized it might be time to get back to the *Legacy*. But before they made it to the food stands, Pia veered to their left. When the others had gathered around her, she spoke. "I wanted to point out those two temples," she said, nodding in their direction. "Don't stare or anything. The one with the eel surrounding a pear is the Salt Crone, the goddess of death . . ."

"And medicine, magic, and revenge," Jordi added. "Handy if you need any of those things . . ."

"But otherwise avoid it," Pia finished, shooting a look at her brother. "It's intensely depressing. The other is the Maiden's Haven. That one there, the one with the golden anchor and cup on the flag. Best you avoid that one, too, right now. It's a little livelier than the Fairtrader's Shrine. More wine and ale, less tea and brandy. That's where most common mariners come when they're in port. They're not unsafe, just unsavory. I thought I should point out their flags so you'd know."

Gatina looked at Atopol, who shrugged. "Thank you, Pia. Do we have time to eat? I'm suddenly ravenous." She wanted to be sure to taste some of the food that smelled so amazing before they had to be back on the *Legacy*. She was already growing tired of the rations at sea. The dreaded ship's biscuit had become a staple of her diet, and she was issued two of the rock-like cakes every meal.

"Yes, come on, I know just the vendor! It's on the way!" Pia said, excited, as she took Gatina's arm once more and raced with her across the wide street to the wharf.

Jordi and Atopol were taken off guard but quickly caught up as Pia ordered six skewers—two fish, two shrimp, and two sausage, each with vegetables. There were skewer merchants in Falas but nothing like this variety. Gatina heard the meat sizzle when the sticks were held over the flames of the portable grill on the cart. She watched, fascinated.

The man and woman who owned the food cart worked well together as a team. When one moved, the other moved in tandem, which made it quite interesting to watch as they cooked. When it was finished, the woman took Pia's money—two copper pennies for the skewers—and the man handed her the sticks atop a piece of unleavened flat bread. There were three different sauces available to drip over it. Gatina spotted a space where they could stand, eat, and watch the ships arrive and depart.

As good as the food was, however, she barely tasted it. The memory of the little boy in ropes being towed behind the slave wagon was still far too fresh on her mind to let her enjoy such pleasures. Gatina hated suffering. She hated it even more when it was the willful result of greedy men.

THE LEMONS THAT BEAH HAD PURCHASED HAD BEEN DELIVERED, ENCHANTED for freshness, and loaded into the hold with the other cargo. It was traditional, Gatina learned, to celebrate a successful day at port before getting underway again. That night, they enjoyed an early dinner of freshly caught fish and roasted oysters, vegetables, and fruit cobbler on the deck with the entire crew; a small barrel of strong beer was opened in celebration. Gatina, once more in her deck clothes, asked Captain Armandus about the caged men. Atopol's meaningful glance at their father told Gatina that he had already mentioned it to him.

Before Hance could speak, Captain Armandus explained it. Not that it really could be explained, in her mind.

"That was likely the most recent group of mariners captured at sea to be sold for labor, lass," he said sadly. "Remerans, mostly, from what I saw. It's tragic. Pirates and slavers capture ships out beyond the shoals and take the crew, passengers, even captains hostage for ransom. Or they raid coastal villages far away and round up peasants. They either pay their way out or they are sold or they work the orchards or vineyards or even sold up in the Vale to pay off their ransom." He reached for his cup and took a long pull. It was his third mug, Gatina realized. "Few are able to escape from such servitude."

"It's a travesty of commerce," Beah agreed. "Human beings are not cargo!"

"It's horrible business," the captain agreed. "And bad for all other business," he assured, grimly. "It makes an honest mariner into a predator of his fellow man—and prey to slavers himself. You can thank the bloody hands of the Coastlords for that. Those damned rebel counts in Falas who stole the throne." There was an undisguised note of condemnation in his voice that firmly established the captain's political position to Gatina's satisfaction.

"They were even selling . . . *children*," Gatina said in a near-whisper.

"Aye, sell them young and you can exploit them their whole lives," the captain grumbled. "If they live. And eventually, they forget that they were ever free. It'll be a blessed day when such evil is banished from the Bay. No respectable man would ever engage in such a foul trade."

Later, as the mooring lines were cast off with the rising of the tide, Gatina stood at the rail and looked back at Cadena, where lamps and torches from the docks reflected in the shimmering waves. Suddenly, this voyage didn't feel like an adventure anymore or even a mission. There was something more serious at play now. She began to see why her parents were so violently against Vichetral, his quest for power, and his betrayal of the legacy of their friend, the late Duke.

"Something amiss, Kitten?" her father asked quietly, as he appeared out of the darkness next to her.

"The slaves," she admitted. "That's amiss. That was one of the most horrible things I've ever seen."

"It was." Hance nodded. "And things have gotten so bad that Beah found out that the Fairsisters are starting to take payments on ransoms in advance once again."

"In advance?" she asked in disbelief.

"It's a kind of insurance. That's where a mariner can pay a set fee to the temple, and in case he's captured by slavers or pirates, the temple will ransom him back. That's some of what the activity was in Cadena today when the slave ship arrived. Of course, sometimes that takes years to arrange, but a smart mariner will pay the fee every time he's in port and even get a special tattoo to mark his policy. If he shows up at a slaver's market, he can get ransomed immediately, sometimes . . . if the Fairsisters are paying attention. Sometimes," he repeated.

"That's barbaric!" Gatina exclaimed. "It needs to stop. I thought things were bad in Falas, but today, what I saw—"

"That's what people do to survive, Kitten," he explained. "And it is barbaric. And tragic. But we live in a world that is often cruel, filled with wicked men whose greed exceeds their humanity. They lack morals and ethics, and the rest of the world suffers as a result of their weakness. We may be thieves, but our morals and ethics keep us from being monsters. We steal for a cause. Or for the art of it. And never from those who cannot afford to lose their valuables. We take a risk every time we do so, and that makes us consider such things carefully before we plan a heist.

"Slavery, on the other hand, is pure domination of the vilest sort. Where one man forces another into chains at swordpoint and robs them both of their humanity."

"We should do something about it!" Gatina insisted.

"We *are*, Kitten," her father soothed. "We saw this on the horizon the moment Duke Anguin died. And we took steps to counter it. But greed and wickedness are great forces in the world. Too many men are too willing to succumb to their own weakness and indulge in it, and the profits are high enough to assuage what conscience they might have left. You might think you can fight it by being brave and whipping out your shadowblade and acting daringly, but that wins a small victory at best. In order to counter that kind of wickedness, you have to think in bigger terms. That's what your mother and I are doing with the Shadow Council," he explained.

"Which has seen us on a boat in the Bay, hauling lemons!" she said frustratedly.

"And has brought us to a lemon merchant in Cadena who was the contact to the Sea Lord House that Master Thinradel directed us to," Hance answered. "We will be picking up our contact along the way to Vaxel. And he may well have the resources we need to start making a real difference in this struggle."

"I understand," Gatina said, though she was far from satisfied with his answer. Sometimes, she really did want to whip out her shadowblade and just start stabbing wicked men like the slavers and pirates in the world.

It seemed so much easier.

CHAPTER TEN

THE VENJANCA

The Fairtrader is the patroness of trade, commerce, and quartermasters. She is the goddess of maritime life's commercial realm. Her symbols, the scale and the pelican, are indicative of the balance needed in considering and executing wise monetary decisions. It is said her invisible hand is at work in every transaction.
—*from* **Sea Lords, Their Cults, Religious Customs, and Traditions**

THE BRILLIANT RED, PINK, AND ORANGE SKY AT DUSK GAVE WAY TO SMOOTH seas for overnight sailing as the *Legacy* cast off, took the *Daydream* in tow, and made its way into the Great Bay near midnight. Gatina was exhausted from the previous night's exertions—the captain had her and her brother and cousins climbing the rigging to help raise the mainsail—and she found the waves' gentle rocking of the boat to be soothing. The sound of the water thumping on the *Legacy*'s hull created a background noise that became a lullaby.

But her sleep was fitful—her dreams were filled with the images she'd seen in Cadena, and they were a source of great discomfort. Thankfully, just before dawn, Pia woke her early for her duty shift on deck. Land was already out of sight on the horizon, she realized as she tumbled out of the forecastle as the sky began to lighten in the east. She didn't realize why her cousin had awakened her early until she saw her father standing there in his cloak. In a moment, Jordi and Atopol joined them, looking just as sleepy as she did.

Father had all of them awake at dawn to run around the main deck while the rest of the crew slept. Only the fire watch and the pilot were awake at this hour. It was not a leisurely pace. Instead, he called out tempos—fast, slower, speed burst—and directional changes. After what seemed to be an eternity, he had them stop and begin sword practice—with practice blades.

"I want you all to be used to the boat's unexpected shifts," he explained. "Balance is essential to a swordsman. The sea betrays that. In order to fight on a deck, your sense of balance has to be prepared for the swell of the waves and the listing of the deck. Wooden swords are a better choice in this instance until you're used to it. Now face your opponent and begin."

Gatina found herself paired with Jordi. She did not mind. He was a novel opponent. She already knew Atopol's tells and which way he would attack. It was good to have someone new for sparring. And Jordi was formidable in his way, she realized as she sized him up while he swung the practice sword a few times. He was only two months older than her, but he was nearly a head and a half taller, with broader shoulders and a much longer reach. Beah was tall and, based on Captain Armandus's height, she suspected that Uncle Alekandrus was also tall. Pia was the same height as Atopol.

Gatina suddenly felt a bit insecure about her own height. But only for a moment. That's all it took for her to find an advantage in her match against Jordi.

Her height—or lack of height—gave her the opportunity to duck in close to him, under his outreached arm, and tag him in the back with her wooden scimitar. The short, curved blade the Sea Lords favored was very different in style from her shadowblade, or even the dueling swords she'd faced in Falas. They were designed for slashing, not stabbing. They barely had a point on them, and you had to get very close to land a solid hit. Scimitars were all edge, it seemed. A second and third bout led to her cousin making wide, wild passes in the air, which she easily ducked under and scored a hit apiece on his leg and his sword arm.

She switched to Pia, who was more challenging than Atopol—who had just beaten her three to nothing in his own bout. She had better control and better footwork, Gatina noted critically. She was more cautious with her strikes and far more deliberate than her younger brother. Pia never attempted a strike unless she was certain she could land it.

By the third bout, Gatina began to respect her as a tough opponent. Not as tough as Master Steel, but tough. Gatina still bested her thrice. By the time the crew began to rise for the morning shift, all four were breathless but wide awake. And their cousins had a much-higher opinion of the Cats of Enultramar.

"Where did you learn how to fight?" Pia demanded as they stowed away the wooden scimitars.

"We have private tutors—for swordplay and shadowmagic," Gatina revealed. "I've been studying since I was nine. But Sea Lord blades are hard," she said apologetically. "Too short, too heavy, and too slashy. I prefer my shadowblade."

Her cousin nodded. "That's the new sword you got back home. It doesn't look like much."

"It's designed to be useful for our . . . profession," Gatina explained. "Sharp as a razor along the tip and the first third, and strong as possible for thrusting. Short enough not to become a burden but long enough to extend your reach in a pinch. When it's in its scabbard, you can use it as a kind of stepladder when you put your toes on the guard. It's enameled black so it doesn't reflect light in the darkness. It's designed to be used to wound, not to kill," she pointed out. "Just enough to get away."

Pia looked around the *Legacy*'s deck. "There's no place to get away to on a ship," she reminded her cousin.

"You make a fair point," Gatina nodded, realizing that she was correct. "I shall practice with the scimitar more."

It was a full week's sailing to their next stop, the island port of Pluhalia. Gatina's—Maranka's—days became routine.

Her first shift began at dawn, where she would grab a ship's biscuit soaked in ale to break her fast before helping trim sails, splice lines, repair fraying sailcloth, or swab the decks with seawater. That was not one of her favorite duties, but the heavy mop she wielded strengthened her arms and shoulders as much as climbing the rigging.

She noted her balance was greatly improved—she'd gotten her "sea legs." She used the swabbing as an opportunity to practice her swordplay exercises, the ones designed to strengthen her core muscles the most. It was an exercise well suited to that.

She also noted that the hectic pace of life at sea slowed down once you actually got to sea. Once Beah had set a course past the busy mouth of the Mandros and into the strait between the mainland and the island of Norisla, their pace was steady. They had to tack the sails against the westerly winds every hour or so, but that became routine by the third day. Gatina thought nothing about ascending the rigging and dropping the topsail if more speed was required. Indeed, she found herself at home in the ropes and spars of the rigging, taking a moment of rest in the shade of the sails while she worked.

She soon got used to the endless horizon stretching around the ship. Knowing where the *Legacy* was on the chart helped ease her anxiety about actually seeing land. Indeed, there was something peaceful about being in the crow's nest at the top of the mainmast, looking out over the endless sea. Even with magesight, she couldn't see land . . . and she was fine with that. Looking out over the open ocean gave her a sense of peace she didn't know she needed. It was like the sacred Darkness that happened every night. It was something sublime, something spiritual to look out over the waves and see nothing but the sea.

They passed other ships on their voyage, ships destined for ports in Sulisla or Predariba to pick up cargoes. There were also ships eastbound in the strait, headed for the Mandros and its many riverports. Captain Armandus made certain anytime another sail was sighted that someone went up the mast and gave it a thorough inspection through the small brass spyglass. There was a certain tension aboard until the ship in question was sighted and her colors examined. Due to her slight figure and her nimble performance on the rigging, this duty fell to Gatina more and more.

"He's worried about raiders," Pia confided after one such trip up the mast when she identified the flag of a merchantman from Petxina.

"I thought they wouldn't go for a mere merchantman carrying lemons," Gatina pointed out, troubled. Indeed, on the secondary mast line, there was a standard that advertised the cargo the *Legacy* carried.

"Commerce flags get faked all the time," Pia argued. "And towing the *Daydream* makes us a valuable target on that basis alone. But don't worry," she urged. "Uncle Armandus knows what he's doing. He's sailed the Great Bay and beyond since long before I was born."

Still, the fifth day out, the call went up from the forecastle. "*Sail, ahoy! Port side, aft!*"

"Get up there, Maranka," Captain Armandus ordered her, concerned at the news. "Take a look and see if we need to be worried." He paused a moment and gave her a searching look. "Use your magic eyes, if you can, and tell me who is tailing us."

Gatina gasped. She had given the man no indication she had *rajira*.

"What? Captain?" she asked, confused. That earned her a stern stare from the man.

"Do ye think I'm blind?" he demanded with a snort. "You were no more raised in the Maiden's Haven than I was raised in the ducal palace. I know ye are a scion of Beah's house, not my own. You're a mage, like she and her daughter. So, use your Talent to see if we need to flee or fight," he urged.

"Aye, Captain!" Gatina said, flustered, as she mounted the rope ladder that climbed the mainmast. She had thought she had been pristine in presenting her alias as Maranka. Either she had failed in her alias, or Captain Armandus was keener in his observations than she suspected.

Once she was perched on the tiny platform known as the crow's nest, she was able to scan the horizon for the specks sighted from the deck. It took little time, with magesight, to find the blot that had inspired the call. She stretched her abilities to the maximum to sight the craft, a three-masted caravel that she recognized as a traditional Sea Lord design, not the heavier galleons and clippers of the Coastlord merchant houses.

Indeed, as magic brought the sight of the ship closer to her attention, she spotted several concerning details. For one, the lack of commercial banners on her secondary line. Ordinarily, a merchantman would boast about the cargo they carried with a series of flags, in addition to the standards they flew describing their home port and their allegiance. This ship had neither, which was disturbing.

More, it had a protected forecastle, with solid gunwales instead of a simple rail. The sort of thing that archers could hide behind in an attack. There was also a heavy ballista on the deck, she saw, a piece of artillery almost every warship boasted. The stern was raised, she noticed, not only protecting the pilot's house but providing an elevated platform from which attacks could be performed.

That was a warship, she decided. She might not be well versed in seamanship, but there was no doubt in her mind that the craft was geared for battle. Gatina took a moment to look for any identifying signs; she quickly saw the ship's name across the yellow-painted bow in Narasi, along with the screaming figurehead that rested under the bowsprit: a woman with a fearful grimace brandishing a sea axe in her arms. It was not a hopeful sight.

"Ahoy!" she called for attention to the captain and bosun, on the deck below. "Warship sighted! The *Venjanca*, by name! Geared for battle! Running on our course off the port stern!"

She could hear the captain's snarl from her perch above. She stayed at her vantage point until the bosun called her down. By that time, the *Legacy* had changed course.

"The *Venjanca*, you said?" Seksus, the bosun, asked when she slid down the line to the deck. "She's well known in the Bay. A raider," he explained, uneasily. "Associated with House Venjancar. One of those filthy crews from Farise. Mercenaries. Pirates. Nothing but gangsters on the water," he scowled.

"Are we in danger?" Gatina asked,

"Captain thinks we're too close to Predariba," he explained. "That's a big port, a ducal port. This route is too busy that close to port. Too many witnesses. We're not valuable enough to them to take the risk of another warship coming after them. But Captain has ordered a change of course, just to be safe."

The next few hours were tense; Gatina and the deck crew had to return to the rigging several times to help trim the sails so that the ship could tack away from the pirate. Beah worked furiously on plotting a new course that would make it difficult for the larger, slower ship to catch them. The bosun even rowed over to the *Daydream* with a couple of hands—including Atopol—and put the sloop under sail. Both ships were nimbler that way and could protect each other at need.

By afternoon, there was no sign of the galleon, and everyone started to relax. The cook added some additional dried beef and peas to the luncheon meal—a stew far, far better than the ones they'd been served on the *Gaillardia*. The old woman had a knack for it, and while none of the shipboard meals had been fancy, they had been tasty.

The change in course added half a day to the journey, but everyone agreed that the delay was worthwhile; no one wanted to have to flee from a pirate or, worse, have to fight them. The sighting spawned a score of stories by the older crewmen, however, about the maritime criminals who had haunted the Great Bay in the past and in the present. They were often tragic and morbid tales, but they fascinated Gatina.

Pirates skated the edge of the law in Sea Lord culture, Gatina found. Piracy was forbidden under their codes, of course, and punishable by death in some cases. But the need for warships for the fleets of the duchies had created a demand for armed privateers who flew the banner of a duke and worked in his service. When that need was done, it wasn't difficult to convince a captain to raise the black banner instead and take for himself what he had once done on behalf of a duke. Other times, lightly armed barques or caravels would take a target of opportunity if they could get away with it.

The only real strategy against pirates was to run and, if unable to do that, to fight. That rarely went well. Pirates usually depended on overwhelming smaller ships with arrow machines, rock-throwing engines, and large boarding parties. It was rare that a merchant vessel had the manpower to defend against that.

The entire episode cast an ill light on the Sea Lord pantheon, in Gatina's eyes. She reflected for days about the role of the Corsair, the war goddess of the Sea Lords, and how according to her book she didn't exactly condemn piracy. Indeed, there was a kind of backward glory in the practice, according to her cult. Many of the captains and great lords of the Sea Lord culture had occasion to fly the black flag at some point in their career, and in certain circumstances, it was even considered a noble endeavor.

Ordinarily, the Corsair was supposed to embody the spirit of maritime warfare. But she was disturbingly vague on the purpose of that warfare.

By contrast, Gatina had a growing respect for the Fairtrader, the goddess of commerce. The entire Fairtrader order was devoted to the commercial aspects of maritime life, she recalled from the book she had read and from the recent trip to the temple in Cadena. The goddess ruled the markets in port and insisted that trade be fair. Her cult was charged with supervising all manner of trade as well as the regulations surrounding the construction and running of a ship. Sea Lords flouted her rules at their peril: a proclamation by her priesthood could bar a ship from trading ports.

Gatina reflected that Aunt Beah was the embodiment of some of the Fairtrader's aspirations. The goddess as described in the book was usually portrayed as a middle-aged woman—like Beah—and meticulously accurate with business details. Aunt Beah was also a navigator, and the Fairtrader was the patroness of pilots and navigators. Gatina thought of Aunt Beah any time she heard the Fairtrader's name invoked. By tradition and according to myth, the Fairtrader and the Corsair did not get along very well, even though they were technically sisters.

A few days later, they came within sight of their next destination: Pluhalia.

Unlike Cadena, Pluhalia was not on the mainland but on the southern side of one of the long, stony islands that ringed the Great Bay. It was a true Sea Lord haven, with little Coastlord influence despite its importance as a trading hub for the western Bay. As the *Legacy* came closer to land, she could see why her ancestors hadn't bothered with the place: it was a long, lonely expanse of rocky hills filled with scrub brush and very few trees. Where she could see settlements, they were fishing villages or lonely-looking farmsteads grazing a few sheep and goats.

But Pluhalia's harbor was one of the better ones on the Bay, deep and wide and protected from storms by a smaller island that occluded the winds that blew in off the Great Bay from the south. She could see the bright beacon fire from the top of the mast that morning, a light built at the height of the tallest spire in the port. Within an hour, they passed a warship patrolling nearby—bearing the ducal naval standard of Alshar. It had looked so similar to the *Venjanca* at a distance that Gatina found her heart in her throat for a few moments.

Its strategic location made the port popular with long-distance warships and merchantmen. Pluhalia had a reputation as a rough and wild place as a result. It was an international port that saw ships from everywhere in the world dock there. Its strategic location for local trade also filled it with smaller ships who came and went with the tides to fill the holds of the larger vessels. It was a mariners' town, she'd heard, and all manner of frightful things could happen there if you weren't careful.

When her father sent them to get ready to go to shore in Pluhalia, she had worked up a sweat swabbing the decks clean and really wanted nothing more than to jump into the Bay for a quick swim. But there wasn't time for that. She would have to settle for a quick wash with the basin of water in the forecastle.

She slipped on her Sea Lord gown and wig as the ship was led to the dock by a pilot boat. The little dagger on her belt caught her attention. On impulse, she slipped her shadowblade under her skirt, strapped to her thigh, just in case. Aunt Beah was already on deck, dressed and ready—including a scimitar at her hip and a large leather satchel slung over her shoulder.

Gatina heard Beah and Captain Armandus talk about the shipments they were to pick up. He was worried that their change of course had taken them off schedule.

"Don't worry; things like this happen," Beah assured him. "If we have to sit in port a few days, it will be worth it if we can get to Vaxel for the Anchorage with a full load. We've got three different shipments to pick up here," she reminded him, as Pia emerged from the forecastle.

"It's your voyage." The captain sighed in resignation. "I'm just trying to get her to where you want her to go on time."

"We still have time," she insisted. "Girls, you're going with me today," she said, loud enough to be heard. "We have business to conduct." She handed the satchel to Pia and looked over the two of them before she led them down the gangplank.

Aunt Beah wore a Sea Lord gown the color of the limes that grew in the woman's garden, accented by a colorful orange bodice that displayed an impressive amount of cleavage. It was a stark contrast to the plain dress she had worn when navigating—tan with an apron over it to hold her spyglass, charcoal, and mapping tools. Her white hair, still loose but freshly brushed, sent wisps around her face to dance in the breeze.

"I've got three vendors to meet with today if they arrived on time," she explained to them as they prepared to depart. "All from the southeastern part of the Bay. The *Legacy* will take delivery of thirty loads of citrus fruits; we will sell the last four kegs of wine and forty barrels of olive oil at market," she declared. "If we get them to Vaxel in time for the Anchorage, we can get thrice what we paid for them." Gatina's ear detected a note of worry in her voice as her aunt scanned the docks for ships she knew. "I just hope prices are high enough here; that wine and oil is my profit margin."

"Is that why that revealing dress, Mother?" Pia asked pointedly, a smirk on her lips.

Beah turned around and surveyed them both, head to toe, before answering. "I need the best price I can get," she replied, glancing down at her revealing gown. "Bright colors make people better disposed to you. And yes, Pia, sometimes it's not the lemons or limes that give you the best price; it's the melons. These merchants are still usually men. Which is one reason why I'm bringing you two with me. You both look young and lovely, and that is going to make them more inclined to want to give me a bargain. That's just good business," she assured them.

"Besides, I didn't want to leave the ship alone without anyone to watch my back. This port is not safe," she warned, ominously. "And it will be good for you to see how a business deal is done. Are you both carrying blades?" she asked as they began walking down the chaotic dock. Porters and sailors were everywhere Gatina looked. They barked orders or pushed cargo in large handcarts. Gatina was getting used to the activity on a busy dock.

"Yes," she and Pia said in unison.

"Good. Try not to stab anyone unless you have to. But if you have to, stab them hard."

The harbor was large—far larger than Cadena. It was split into four separate sections, two frequented by the larger galleons destined for distant ports and two used mostly by smaller caravels and barques from the local region. That meant a lot of walking, searching for signs, and asking directions until they found the first merchant on their list.

As they walked past the docked ships, one in particular captured Gatina's attention. Indeed, the sight of it startled her: The *Venjanca*.

The galleon was large, far larger than the *Legacy*. It was clearly a warship, the first Gatina had ever gotten close to. The trim was painted a garish yellow, with streaks of black and pockmarks from arrows and crossbow bolts on the hull that demonstrated it had seen battle in the past. The crenelated forecastle and the big iron ram on the bow gave the ship a menacing air, and there were several tarpaulins on the deck that likely protected larger weaponry from the weather.

But something else caught her eye. The glimmer of light off a long, narrow blade worn by a crewmember who was walking along the rail of the ship. A sentry, she realized. The sight of that made her more nervous than any threat of danger from the port.

"Aunt Beah, that's the ship we saw in the strait!" she said in a harsh whisper, nodding toward it. "Have you seen it before?"

Her aunt looked over at the *Venjanca* carefully and gave it a quick appraisal. "I have not. It's designed as a merchant ship and started her life that way. Built in Remere," Beah said as her eyes scanned the ship. "Probably in Lumia or Brucoli. About twenty years old and ten years past time for her to be refurbished. The forecastle defenses, the ram, and the weaponry were added later. She was probably taken at sea as a prize," she added sorrowfully. "A sad fate for a grand old girl like her."

"And they'll just let a pirate ship dock in a regular port?" Gatina asked, surprised.

"If she's not been charged with a crime, she's just another warship under the law," Pia explained. "What law there is," she added ruefully.

"Pluhalia has dozens of warships here," agreed Beah, as she studied the ship more closely—likely using her magesight. "Some in the service of the duchy but most not. They come here looking for work as escorts—against pirates, ironically. Or Castali commerce raiders if they sail beyond the straits and into the ocean. They're maritime mercenaries until there has been a complaint. And some of these brutes don't leave anyone alive to complain," she added darkly.

She paused to give it a more thorough look. "And that, girls, is a *Rat* ship. Take a close look at the flags. They're supposed to be ducal standards. And they *appear* to be normal Alshari flags, but if you look off to the right side, what do you see?"

Pia answered first. "The Alshari device is reversed," she realized. "So, it only looks like ducal colors from a distance. Clever. Very subtle," she said.

Gatina squinted up at the hull; the sun was beating down on her, and that obscured her view. But then she saw it—a familiar-looking sigil scrawled on the side of the hull in paint that was just *slightly* different than the faded yellow of the rest of it. A rat's head with a long tail behind it. If you didn't know where to look, or what to look for, you'd miss it entirely.

"It *is* a Brotherhood ship!" she whispered in surprise. "They actually have *ships?*"

"They've always been pirates at heart," Beah agreed as they began walking slowly away from it. "It's just easier to be a thug on the land, until lately. They've always had a few ships dedicated to smuggling, and now slavery and piracy. I don't think they would have been so bold before Duke Lenguin was killed. I caution you to avoid that particular ship and especially its crew. Absolutely horrible people," she said. "I would not be surprised to find that they're in port to pick up slaves."

Gatina shuddered. The idea of Rats and pirates this close to her did not sit well. She had hoped for a reprieve from the Rats, especially after her alley chase in Falas. She resolved to follow her aunt's advice.

Aunt Beah nodded, satisfied, and they continued to walk with purposeful steps away from the dock and toward the long line of businesses facing the harbor. "My first contact is just ahead," Beah said as they neared a four-story gray brick and stone building. There was a sign bearing a pelican with a net full of unidentifiable fruit in its beak as well as printing in Narasi and Old High Perwynese declaring RENNEL & HOLSGAR, BROKERS.

"Remember, don't say anything you don't have to," she reminded them in a whisper. "Just smile a lot and look pretty. He likes pretty young girls," she assured them.

"All men like pretty young girls," Pia complained.

"That's their fault, not ours." Her mother shrugged.

In the center of the room, on a raised circular platform surrounded by a low-fenced wall, Gatina saw a very grizzled and disheveled-looking man of Coastlord stock standing behind a trio of trestle tables. His sleeves were rolled up and his hair, graying with a hint of white at his temples, stood up and stuck out. He looked out over the room with tired eyes. When he spotted Beah, those eyes lit up and he waved her up the platform. Beah smiled in return—a far-bigger smile than was warranted, in Gatina's opinion. The old man walked around the table and unlatched the small gate.

"Lady Beah! Ah, my dear lady, it has been ages since I've seen you!" he said, greeting her as an old friend, which Gatina determined that, indeed, was the case.

"Master Rennel, it is good to see you again! Aye, two long years," agreed Beah, giving him a short bow before an embrace—one that the old man clearly enjoyed. "It's been four since Alekandrus went missing."

"Oh, I know, I know," he said, shaking his shaggy head sadly. "I do miss him. Good captain. Terrible tragedy. But I see you have brought, let me guess, your daughter and . . . an apprentice?" The smile he wore lit up his eyes, and Gatina wondered how often he saw friends in his line of work.

"That is a very astute deduction!" She laughed, a bit more exaggerated than the occasion called for. "This is our daughter, Pia, and this is our new apprentice crewman, Maranka," she said as she presented the girls. "They're on their maiden voyage. I thought I would bring them by and teach them how the lemons get squeezed," she said, giggling with undue enthusiasm.

"Yes, yes, I have your letters," Rennel said, returning to his table and a pile of parchments. He leafed through them until he found what he was looking for. "You were looking for thirty loads of lemons, limes, and oranges from . . . Glavores?"

"They do have some of the largest lemons in the Bay," Beah agreed, pulling her own copy of the shipping orders out of her satchel.

"Aye. I have some news for you, then. No need for the papers yet," he said, disappointed. "We've had several delays. Those ships from Caramas have not arrived at port, I'm afraid. That's one reason why my office is in such a state," he added, waving toward his desk. The trestle table was covered with a large map decorated with ship markers.

"It's been the poor weather," he explained, his voice raspy and his eyes tired. "The storms in the south put everything behind. My staff and I are working to adjust a score of schedules to compensate. I fear all the ships will arrive at the same time, and we won't have space to dock them. But not to worry, my lady; they'll arrive soon," he said as he rubbed his head. Gatina realized that was why his hair was so messy.

"How soon?" Beah asked, her voice and demeanor calm. "I have deliveries to make to my customers," she added. "We need to be in Vaxel in time for the Anchorage."

"Well, at least two days, maybe three, from what we're hearing. I've sent skiffs out to survey their locations. But I know the *Sea Bell* limped into Dras Ferman with a broken mast two days ago. We should hear back soon from the rest," he said encouragingly.

"That's going to put us in a bind, Rennel," she admitted doubtfully.

"I know, I know," he sighed, running his fingers through his hair. "I can't do a thing about it, though."

"Can you make me a good deal on some wine and oil, then?" she asked, pouting. "Four kegs of Bikavar, six years aged. And fresh olive oil from this year's pressing in Igri," she proposed.

While the two of them haggled, Gatina looked around the cluttered office at the numerous charts, graphs, and maps that hung on the wall. A great slate board listed this week's arrivals, with scores of ships and their schedules, she noted, and indeed the *Sea Bell* was listed as late, moored at Dras Ferman. The other two merchantmen had question marks next to their arrival.

Aunt Beah was mostly silent on the short walk back to the *Legacy*. Gatina could not read her face. Much like her father, her Aunt Beah was excellent at hiding her emotions, and her face became a smooth mask. Pia, on the other hand, wore hers on her face in the form of a frown and a sullen expression. But Gatina could tell that the news wasn't good.

When they were aboard the *Legacy* once more, Beah explained the predicament to Captain Armandus and Hance and Minnie. Armandus had granted a brief shore leave to his crew, so they largely had the ship to themselves.

Gatina listened and observed. She wanted to see how her parents took the news. Beah's brave front remained, but the captain's demeanor shifted from relaxed to calculating when he heard the news.

"It's an unfortunate situation," Beah explained. "It will take a week or more for the *Sea Bell* to install a new mast. And that cargo is already paid for. So, I propose that I take the *Daydream* and a few of the crew to go to meet the ship in Dras Ferman. That's a day's sail and a day to get back. We can take delivery of the cargo there while the *Legacy* waits here for the other two ships to arrive. We should be able to get back in time to ship out to Vaxel."

Gatina watched her parents while Aunt Beah made her suggestion. Their faces were unreadable, of course. But it was clear that there wasn't much choice.

"Where is Dras Ferman?" her mother asked, curious.

"It's a small island off the east coast of Tauler Island," Beah explained. "Not much of a port, but a popular place to bring a broken ship into. There are a string of islands and shoals around it, but Dras Ferman is safe to reach."

"Aye, it's an easy voyage," Captain Armandus conceded reluctantly. "And that sloop should be swift enough, even loaded. Aye, we can hold here a few days. I'll have the bosun prepare the *Daydream* for sail. I don't know how many crew I can spare, if we're to get the other two loaded aboard," he added skeptically.

"I'll take the apprentices," she suggested. "It only takes a few to sail the sloop, and they could use the practice. Better than them lingering in Pluhalia, getting into trouble."

"Agreed," sighed the captain. "Just be wary, Beah. You'll have to cut straight across the Bay if you're to make good time. I think your plan is the correct course. But I want you to take one of my experienced men as a precaution. It's not that I doubt your ability to sail," he added quickly, after Gatina saw her aunt's eyes flash at him. "I would not rest easy knowing I had not made the offer. For my brother's . . . sake, please take Seksus."

The prospect of such an adventure thrilled Gatina. Being at sea on the *Legacy* was an adventure, she recognized, but she was not as much fun to work as the crew. Besides, the *Daydream* was her family's own ship and she had barely sailed her.

"Agreed," Beah said with a sigh. "Have him ready the *Daydream*. We'll sail with the morning tide."

"Will that give us a chance to see the port, Mother?" Pia asked, anxiously.

"Only for the afternoon," she conceded, after some thought. "Pack your duffels before you go. And stick together. I want you back aboard by dusk. And stay out of trouble," she insisted. "The last thing I need is a visit from the Shore Patrol because someone opened their mouth to the wrong mariner."

Pia smiled, grabbed Gatina's hand, and pulled her toward the forecastle. "Let's hurry! Before she changes her mind!"

"Why do you want to go ashore so badly?" she asked, confused.

"You'll see," she promised. "Jordi and I have been here before. It's rough, but there are a few things to see . . . and we just got our pay," she reminded her. "We might as well take advantage of it."

"But isn't it dangerous?" Gatina asked.

"Isn't stealing things? Come on! I didn't think she'd let us go at all!"

Gatina hurried behind her cousin, caught in her enthusiasm. If Pia felt secure enough to go ashore, then there wasn't any reason she shouldn't, she reasoned. She still had her shadowblade strapped under her dress.

What could possibly go amiss?

CHAPTER ELEVEN

MAIDEN VOYAGE

The Corsair's ilk are hard as iron, when at sea, and no normal force can stand lightly against them, but once ashore they oft become petulant and drunken examples of the worst sort of mariner. They become demanding bullies who feel assured of their own superiority not just to common mariners but to every other Sea Lord, no matter their rank.

—from *Sea Lords, Their Cults, Religious Customs, and Traditions*

As the foursome left the dock to head for the market, Pia pulled them close and warned them again to be careful.

"People go missing here. Stay together. Jordi, don't go running off because you saw something shiny. And you two remember your aliases. You are Sea Lords, no more, no less. Proud, but mind your own business. We'll head through the docks and to the market," she proposed. "It's not that far."

Gatina found the warning to be odd and a little overbearing, but she nodded in agreement nonetheless. They wove their way through the busy docks until they came to a gray cobbled street, then followed Pia into the very crowded market district. It wasn't that far away, as Pia had said, and it was alive with loud voices, some disgruntled by the storm delays, she could hear. It was a lot different from Cadena. The streets smelled like spirits and urine. Strongly.

As they neared the food carts, she got the scent of fresh-cut oranges overlaid by flowers and fish. An odd combination but better than the briny smell of the water or the sweaty smell of the people surrounding them.

This was larger than any market she had seen, even in Falas, the capital. It stretched as far as she could see. The vast space was dotted along all the sides by the tents and carts from which vendors sold their goods.

There were tables and seating areas—blankets—in the center. When Jordi took her elbow and guided her forward, she realized that she had stopped and that Atopol and Pia had gone on without her. She mentally berated herself for a moment, until Jordi spoke in her ear. "Impressive, isn't it? I had the same reaction the first time I saw it. You could wander through this market for days, and it's always different. But we should catch up to the others. There's safety in numbers."

While Gatina let him swiftly guide her, she admitted, "I've never seen so many vendors!"

He chuckled. "They sell everything in Pluhalia. And I mean everything." He nodded toward a tent selling charms against wood rot. "That won't keep your boat from rotting," he whispered as they walked past. "And everyone knows it. But people buy it anyway. That old man's been here for as long as I can remember."

They found Pia and Atopol at a pie cart where her brother was negotiating a four-pies-for-the-price-of-two deal with the shy young daughter of the vendor. He handed one to Gatina—apple, a favorite—then he had their cousins select their own. They ate while they walked and gawked at the enormous market.

It was easily thrice as large as the biggest market in Falas, she realized. And the fare was far more varied: canopies protecting huge pyramids of brown sugar loaves, barrels of treacle, or strange round nuts the size of her head vied for her attention with huge bolts of cloth, wooden cages full of brightly colored birds, and jewelry and hair combs made of shimmery shells from distant beaches.

"They really do sell everything here," she remarked, as she passed a group of old, deeply tan women bending to make baskets being woven on request.

"The market at the Vaxel Anchorage is supposed to be twice as large," Pia nodded. "Of course, that's as much a fair as it is a market, and it's only once a year. This place is like this all the time."

Every section of the market seemed to have a vendor selling brandy in little cups, or sugar spirits from barrels, or brandy, wine, ale or beer. By the time the second bell had been rung, they had only seen a tithe of the market. She knew they would need to make their way back to the *Legacy* soon enough and thence the *Daydream*.

Just as she was about to suggest they consider returning, she found a vendor who had baskets filled with brightly colored pencils and tiny bottles full of inks of various hues. She eagerly spent most of the coins in her purse on a number of them. She was still trying to finish her special deck of cards and figured that she could work on them in her off hours to alleviate her boredom.

Package in hand, Gatina was excitedly turning to show her cousins—but before anyone could speak, a series of shrill barks caught their attention.

Gatina looked at her brother with concern. They followed the sound of the barks and found an older woman trembling, standing between a raggedy wire-haired graying dog and three menacing mariners who did not appear to be much, if any, older than Atopol. All three bore scimitars and wickedly curved daggers displayed brazenly in their sashes. They were laughing and mocking the old crone and seemed to have some interest in the dog.

Before she could rush in and insert herself into the situation, her brother put his hand on her arm, restraining her. She looked up at him questioningly, but he shook his head.

"This is not something to rush into, Maranka," he said, stressing her alias name. *"Bide!"* he urged quietly.

Pia nodded. "Wait to see what's happening before—"

Before she could finish her thought, the smallest of the three snorted and shouted at the woman.

"Get out of our way, you hag! That mutt stole my pie and I'm going to teach it a lesson," he yelled. "And maybe you as well."

"It's just a little *dog*," the woman pleaded, her voice unfazed by the man's threats. "It don't know any better!"

"But *you* do, woman!" the man in the middle sneered angrily, clearly enjoying the confrontation. "It's yours. You likely trained it to steal for you! And you probably ate some of my mate's pie!" He raised his hand as if to strike her.

The woman did not flinch. Instead, to Gatina's eyes, it seemed she planted her feet more and stood her ground. The dog darted just behind her, still snarling but now trying to hide in her skirts. It wasn't a large dog, but the mutt barked as bravely as a hound on the hunt.

A crowd started to gather, mostly vendors and shoppers, but a few older mariners watched with interest, their hands on their hilts or grasping their staves. No one wanted to involve themselves with drunks at the market, but they were keen to watch the altercation and defend themselves.

The smaller man lunged for the dog, but he was stopped by the third mariner, who held his arm.

"Maiden's Mercy, Baramel, is it worth all this—over a bloody *pie*? It's just an old woman and her dog. Just buy another bloody pie and be more careful," he suggested, his voice calm.

"I been eatin' biscuit for *days* now and paid good coin for a pie I didn't eat!" the one apparently called Baramel demanded. "I want some justice, Darrick."

"Aye, I like justice!" the second man said with a wicked grin.

"Stow it, Gondefar!" Darrick snickered. He was the most handsome of the three, Gatina saw, and seemed more patient, less drunk, and far more rational. "You're the last rogue to be speaking of justice! Do you want the bloody *Patrol* involved?" he demanded. "You're a warrior of the waves, by the Corsair, and you're about to strike some old hag at market? You're better than that. Not worth your time," he soothed. "Your purse is heavy with prize money, and you've spent thrice as much on grog as on that pie. This is no worthy challenge for you, mate."

There was silence for a moment. It seemed to last an eternity. Everyone involved, even the dog in question, was still with expectation.

Then the mariner who had been wronged pulled away from his comrades and lunged at the woman, shoving her aside. The push sent her to the ground, where she hit the packed earth with a hard *thud*. Baramel tried to kick the dog, but it bolted to its mistress's side and began growling at the mariner menacingly, to protect his mistress from Baramel and now Gondefar, who had joined his friend. The old woman had not gotten to her feet before she was surrounded. The dog lunged at Baramel and latched on to his calf with a quick but strong clamping of his jaws.

"Godsdammit! Get off, you stupid beast!" Baramel said, angrily kicking his leg out in an attempt to dislodge the dog and draw his scimitar at the same time. He was, fortunately, too drunk to either keep his feet or draw his blade. Indeed, his comrade Gondefar had to hold him up and keep him from falling, while the handsome third pirate, Darrick, looked on and laughed and shook his head.

Gatina watched in astonishment as the dog valiantly held on.

"Attie!" she whispered, pleadingly. Instead of answering, her brother shook his head sternly, frustrating Gatina. She knew he would think this was not their problem. They might make it worse for the old woman. But she also knew that failure to act when she was certain that they could indeed help, was a much worse crime. She wanted to act, to protect the woman and her dog.

While the one man dealt with removing the dog from Baramel's leg, the handsome mariner stood over the woman menacingly.

"If you can't control your bloody mutt, you'll pay for my friend's food!" he demanded. His large hands began to probe the woman. She had curled herself into a ball on the ground and used her forearms as a shield to protect her head as best she could. "Where is your damned coin, woman?" Suddenly, he no longer seemed rational, Gatina saw.

"Call the Patrol!" someone from the crowd cried. "It's those bastards from the *Venjanca*, starting trouble!"

That startled Gatina—these men were indeed pirates, then. When the man began groping at her waist, the old crone kicked at him, blindly but hard enough to get him in a sensitive spot. While he was doubled over, sucking in shallow breaths, Baramel kicked hard enough that the dog went flying off his leg. It hit the side of a cart with a sickening thud and a yelp.

By now, a crowd gathered around and had created a circle, watching in both fascination and horror. A few men started forward to intervene, some with blades on their hips and others bearing quarterstaffs. Beating an old woman was one thing, Gatina knew, but kicking a dog brought a special kind of furor from bystanders. Gatina imagined herself rushing into the crowd herself. She must have flinched, because her brother tugged her arm.

"Baramel, what in five hells are you doing?" Darrick pleaded when he concluded the old hag had no coin. "She's penniless. It's a dog. And now the bloody *Patrol* is coming!"

A murmur rippled through the crowd. Before he could say anything else, the man called Darrick walked to his friend Gondefar, put an arm around his shoulder, and said something into his ear—Gatina could not hear it, nor was she close enough to read his lips, but it was enough to bring the brute to his senses. Next, Darrick went to Baramel and helped him to stand up straight, limping on his injured leg.

"Back to your business!" Darrick commanded the crowd as he aided his wounded crewmate. "Just a little difference of opinion. No need for the Patrol. No harm done," he soothed, still heaving from the old woman's kick.

The crowd parted as the arrogant trio pushed their way through, walking toward Gatina, Atopol, and the cousins.

Gatina watched as they got closer. The two ruffians looked at their feet, but Darrick had his eyes ahead. She doubted either man felt ashamed by their behavior. There would be no consequence for them, she knew, if they left before the Shore Patrol arrived. She still wanted some sort of justice for the woman and her dog.

Atopol pulled her just out of the way of the men as they walked past—when Gatina saw an opportunity she couldn't resist. Her hand darted forward, and almost on reflex, her nimble fingers sought the prize. It happened quickly, too quickly for either the pirate or her brother to react. And in that few seconds, she managed to relieve Baramel of his coin purse and make it disappear into her dress as she pretended to stumble.

"How dare you!" she snarled at the trio of mariners in her thickest Sea Lord accent as she whirled on them. "Who do you think you are to beat up an old woman and a dog? The Maiden watch your vile deeds! *Vile!*" she spat. "And then to walk into *me?* Ruffians! You should know your station. The Patrol should see to you!"

Gatina had not thought her actions through—ordinarily, you don't call attention to yourself when you just picked a purse, much less confront the victim of the crime. But she was a slip of a girl and these were three much-larger foes. A bit of feminine anger and judgement of their bullying was appropriate under the circumstances, she reasoned.

Darrick looked her up and down as he tried to drag Baramel along. Gondefar started to speak, but his more sober friend interrupted his angry retort. "Sorry for that, Mistress," he said, sincerely and with a growl of respect. "We're taking our mate back to the ship now. No need to raise a fuss with the Patrol. We sail tonight; we'll be gone by the morrow," he promised. "The Maiden's blessings on you all; have a safe day!" he called to the crowd.

He held her eyes for the briefest instant. They were dark and gorgeous. She could not look away or break the gaze. She felt lost for a moment. When she recognized the awkward silence, she mumbled words that felt fuzzy on her tongue.

But they had continued on by then, away from the market and toward the docks. Darrick eyed the crowd anxiously. They might have been pirates and brigands, but they were also outnumbered badly by the marketgoers. In moments, they had disappeared through the crowd.

Gatina felt Atopol's eyes on her. She felt strange. "What in the hells was *that* about?" he asked, confused.

"It's time to go!" Pia insisted, eyeing the crowd worriedly, scanning for more trouble. People were already helping the old crone to her feet, and the dog seemed unwounded, though his mouth was ringed with blood. Jordi bent to pet the beast and praise him for his bravery as well as feed him the crust of his pie.

Gatina jingled the stolen purse in her dress just enough for her brother to hear. "Justice," she answered, quietly. "I like justice."

"You just robbed a bloody pirate," he pointed out warningly as he realized what she'd done.

"Nonsense. He lost his purse in the struggle," she dismissed. "It happens when you go drinking at the market and you're uncareful." She walked over to the battered crone, who was weeping over the mutt, and passed her a few coins from her own purse. "Maiden's blessing," she wished her quietly, as the woman's bony fingers closed on the money. She quickly walked away before she could say anything.

Pia took Gatina's arm in her own and began to walk back toward the docks, taking a slightly different path from the three mariners'. Under her breath, so Gatina alone could hear her, she said, "That was very brave of you, Maranka. And yes, I saw. Stupid, yes, but also brave. Shall we get out of Pluhalia without further incident, yes?"

Gatina looked ahead, careful to acknowledge Pia's advice without speaking or showing any emotion. It was one thing for Atopol to think she had been irresponsible. She was accustomed to that. But Pia's opinion mattered.

"Of course," Gatina agreed, clutching her package of inks closer to her. "I think our work is finished for the day."

"He was rather handsome, that one," Pia confided. "And he looked right at you. I don't know whether to be angry or envious."

"But did I get the *accent* right?" Gatina asked, desperate to change the subject. "Did I come across as an authentic Sea Lord?"

"I don't think anyone had any doubt," her cousin agreed. "You look and act like one now—brassy, bold, and willing to get into a tussle. Even the way you gave that crone alms was well done. Now, whether that was the wisest course of action is another matter."

"One must occasionally take risks to further one's art," Gatina suggested airily. "If I can convince a pirate, I can convince most others, I think."

"I think you overestimate pirates," Pia replied quietly. "They're not the smartest of fellows, as a rule. But you convinced everyone else."

"Well, it was a good chance to practice and teach that drunken oaf Baramel a lesson," Gatina rationalized. "I picked his purse while I yelled at him. It was quite satisfying."

Pia's jaw dropped. "You . . . *picked his purse?*" she hissed in a whisper.

"It seemed appropriate," Gatina agreed. "It's the prize money of a pirate. It's fair game. I haven't stolen anything in weeks, and it was just too good of an opportunity. And it did give me a chance to converse with Darrick," she pointed out. "He does have very interesting eyes . . ."

"And now he knows your face," Pia observed, alarmed at her cousin's theft. "What if he—"

"He knows *this* face," Gatina corrected. "I have hundreds, at need. Don't worry; I doubt they'll even notice it's gone until they get back to the *Venjanca*," she predicted.

As it turned out, she was wrong. As they were in the process of exiting the market, they spotted the three mariners speaking to the red-sashed Shore Patrol, along with an irate merchant. Apparently, Baramel had indeed realized his purse was gone and decided to steal a sausage from a vendor's cart on his way back to the ship. He'd been nicked, and now Darrick was having to buy his comrade out of trouble once again.

That was indeed very satisfying to see, she reflected, as she passed them by.

THE *DAYDREAM* HAD BEEN IN THE FAMILY SINCE HER PARENTS WERE MARRIED. Gatina had once suspected that the small sloop had been a wedding gift. But her father had explained he and Mother had stolen it.

The ship was single-masted and single-decked, and it had a second deck on the stern below the tiller. It lacked a forecastle, but the long bowsprit served as a second mast for additional foresails. It wasn't as wide as some sloops she'd see in the harbors, Gatina reflected as she rowed toward the yacht. It also wasn't as grubby, as it had not been used to haul cargo.

The *Daydream* had been safely stored against the weather in one of her aunt's boat sheds for years. It had new sails and new lines and had been thoroughly and meticulously maintained before she had been launched this summer. It carried two boats, a longboat, and a gig, both splendidly painted—the longboat even had a temporary mast and sail that could be employed if needed. But Gatina loved the lines of the vessel, even from afar. Indeed, the white-painted hull and the tasteful gilded trim made it quite a handsome ship.

Most importantly, she was *fast*. When her aunt and parents made the decision for Beah and the children to make the relatively short run to Dras Freeman, using the *Daydream* was the obvious choice. The shallower draft and the extra sail would speed the sloop along almost twice as fast as the heavier *Legacy*. Beah would be captain, with Seksus the bosun as second-in-command. Pia would serve as cook as well as taking watches with the rest of them. Gatina would try her hand as navigator, under her aunt's watchful eye. And though Atopol and Jordi would be the primary crewmen, that did not absolve the girls from the hard labor of setting the sails.

The sloop was a fraction of the size of the *Legacy*, by tonnage and length, which made it easier for the smaller crew to manage. It also had only two great sails—mainsail and headsail—which made for a little less work. It could, theoretically, be sailed with a crew of just three, but Gatina was glad they weren't depending on that. More hands made a faster pace. The *Daydream*'s shallow draft made it faster and less likely to get hung up on any shoals or coral reefs on the route, which was known for both. And it had enough space in the hold to accept the shipment they were chasing.

This should be an easy voyage, she knew. An excellent means of testing the lessons that she and her brother and cousins had learned thus far on their journey. If they performed properly—and the daughters of the Storm Lord didn't intervene—they should be back in Pluhalia by the time the *Legacy* was loaded and ready to sail.

Before they boarded the *Daydream*, her parents had taken Gatina and Atopol aside for a brief goodbye and to express their concerns. This was, after all, the first time in the voyage that they would be out of their parents' protection. Her mother had pulled Gatina into a tight hug, whispering in her ear.

"Be safe, be brave, and may Darkness protect you," she said, before kissing her on top of her head fondly.

"From what Beah says, this is a quick run. Two days there, two back at most," her father reminded them. "Try not to fall overboard or get shipwrecked or anything, if you will."

She'd packed up almost everything she owned in her duffel, including her working blacks and her shadowblade. At least on the *Daydream* she would have a tiny cabin to share with Pia, not the smelly forecastle. And, before she left the *Legacy*, she found the fluffy ginger cat and gave her head a goodbye scratch. The cat purred and Gatina took that as a positive omen.

By the time they boarded the *Daydream* where she lay at anchor, her aunt, Seksus, her brother, and cousins sprang into action on deck to get the sails unfurled as the tide went out. Atopol and Jordi discussed the type of sailcloth used and why it was good for speed while they raised the anchor. The sheets were special, he informed them, treated with wax to help water bead off it, which made it less likely to get weighed down in rain.

Afterwards, she helped plot their position on the chart. That was easy—they were still in Pluhalia—but she had to chart the route to Dras Ferman. She ended up proposing a course that would take them south, directly across the Bay. Aunt Beah gave her an approving nod when she presented it to her for approval.

Captain Beah, Gatina corrected, mentally, as she addressed the crew after the ship was underway, the twilight winds filling the sails. Seksus stood quietly behind her as she explained the purpose of the voyage to each of them and detailed everyone's tasks along with her expectations of how each of them would be completed. Exacting expectations, Gatina quickly learned. This would not be a fun or free-spirited trip. This would be hard work. More like a mission than a mere cruise.

"Our goal is speed," she explained. "We're crossing the Western Bay, which is trickier than our home waters by far. We've been blessed with a favorable wind from the south. We'll sail through the night and tack as we need to, so don't get too comfortable in your bunks. This is your first true voyage without an experienced crew," she reminded them. "This is a very serious responsibility you and your cousins are undertaking, and there is little room for error. Our business depends on getting to Dras Ferman and back as fast as we can." she explained, the tone of her voice serious.

"Navigation should be fairly straightforward," Beah continued. "Accepting the freight will be quick too, and we can have the fruit loaded in the hold in short order and return to Pluhalia immediately.

"There will be no exploration of the port. There will be no leave. And certainly no confrontations with drunken mariners on the docks. We depart the moment the cargo is aboard. Am I clear?" She looked at each of them, though Gatina felt her cheeks flush as her aunt's eyes lit on her. Apparently, the story of their run-in with the *Venjanca* crew had made it to her aunt's ears.

Seksus spoke next.

"The trickiest tasks will be monitoring the water for shoals, and hidden shallow-water threats around Dras Ferman abound," the bosun reported. "The port has a harbor that's deep enough, if you follow the buoys, but everything around it is a hazard. Obviously, *Daydream* is much smaller than *Legacy*. But it's just us out here. We are the entire crew. We must be mindful of sandbars and reefs. Even with our shallow draft, that's still a danger that would further delay the voyage. If we have to, we have poles and oars to help, but it'll be the Shipwrecker's Mercy if we don't have to use them."

"Agreed." Her aunt nodded. "Atopol and Jordi will be in the bow, charged with ensuring we avoid sandbars when we arrive. Jordi has a keen eye for these things. Atopol, you're on fire watch tonight, followed by Pia at midnight, after she prepares our supper. The rest of you get what sleep you can. We're at twelve knots already now, and by morning we'll be flying, with this wind," she assured.

A chorus of aye, ayes seemed to satisfy the captain, who dismissed them.

"The sky looks good; wouldn't you agree?" Gatina asked Pia while her cousin started a fire in the galley's tiny stove with magic. It was actually far better designed and had more storage than the slightly larger version on the *Legacy*, she noted. "And there is a good wind," she observed.

"The wind is on our side and the sky does seem clear," Pia agreed as she filled a kettle with water from the cistern. "But that can change in the blink of an eye in the Western Bay. But I wouldn't worry about that too much. This trip should be quick and fairly easy. And this ship is the perfect size for the job. She's a joy to sail," her cousin assured her, as she began dumping strips of dried beef and beans into the soup pot. "Of course, these waters are also well known for raiders who hide in the shoals and prey on the wine barques coming up from Caramas, so . . ."

"That sounds like the Shipwrecker's own blessing," Gatina said sarcastically in her Sea Lord accent, earning a grin from Pia. "Here, I'll chop up the onions for you," she offered. "I'm getting hungry."

BY THE TIME THE SUN HAD SET, THE PORT OF PLUHALIA WAS NO LONGER visible behind them. The *Daydream* had indeed found her stride, and the wind was guiding her at a pace quicker than Captain Beah had expected.

She had said as much in the pilothouse after supper, when Gatina went to check their course and take the tiller so that her aunt could eat.

They were making good time, she saw as she checked the chart. Beah had ordered two additional foresails hoisted to take advantage of the brisk wind, which only added to the *Daydream*'s speed. Beah secured the tiller and took the time to show Gatina how to sight the brass sextant and use it to determine their position more accurately, once the stars had come out, and how to use the small water clock and hourglass in the pilothouse to gauge the time. Both were important to establish where they were and where they were going.

Gatina went to bed afterward feeling a little lonesome. She already missed her parents, especially because they had spent so much time together in the past few months. Even on the *Legacy*, it was as if they were strangers much of the time, leaving her and Atopol to their duties while they plotted in their cabin. Now they were an entire ocean away from her—for the first time, she and her brother were on their own.

By midnight, when Gatina stumbled back up on deck with Pia to relieve Atopol, she was gratified to see that they were well on course, according to the charts. She was pleased when Beah once again approved the readings she took with the sextant, the log cords, and the water clock. That was the type of problem she enjoyed solving, after learning about mathematics at the abbey. As the excitement wore off, though, both her eyelids and her arms became heavy with exhaustion. She was very thankful when her aunt told her that she could go back below the deck to sleep.

"Nobody can concentrate if they're asleep on their feet," Beah said as she ushered Gatina out of the cockpit. "Seksus will take the next watch. I'll need you all well rested by dawn, when the winds will change. For now, the weather's calm and the winds are steady. We couldn't ask for a better night," she assured.

Night watch was always a cause for concern, in Gatina's mind. Indeed, the most dangerous time on a ship was overnight when the vessel was at sea, Captain Armandus had explained to her on her very first fire watch. The ship didn't stop sailing just because you were sleeping. Someone had to be awake and rested to handle anything, at any time, that might come up in the darkness. She fell to sleep thinking about pirates, monsters, squalls, and even leviathans that might be lurking in the night.

The cabin door opening did not wake her when Beah came in. But her aunt reaching for Gatina's shoulder to give her a gentle shake awake led to Gatina rolling over, her little dagger in hand. She had forgotten where she was. Thankfully, her aunt caught her wrist and woke her fully before anything could happen.

"While I am glad to see that you have such keen reflexes, Gatina, in the future, I would prefer not to see that so close to my person," Aunt Beah chided. "Next time, I will be sure to knock louder to rouse you."

"Sorry, Aunt—Captain," she amended, putting the knife away. "I was having unwholesome dreams. It was just reflex."

"I understand, Kitten," Beah soothed with a yawn as she slid into her bunk. "You've got another hour until dawn, when you'll take up your watch from Seksus. We are on course; do try to keep us that way. I just want . . . a little nap . . ." she said as she closed her eyes.

By the time dawn broke over the Great Bay, the boys had retired to their cabin after setting nets from the stern. By midmorning, the nets were full of good-sized fish. The *Daydream* was on course. Gatina consulted the chart and confirmed they were making excellent time. Indeed, they should arrive in the early afternoon, at this pace.

She actually felt a surge of power as she commanded Jordi and Seksus to trim the sails for a tack to keep them on course. Her hand felt light on the tiller as she kept it steady. She was controlling the entire ship, and that was a heady feeling. Better than riding a horse, at least, she reflected.

By the time Captain Beah had returned from her slumber, the sun cast a bright, warm light over the Bay and the deck. Before she broke her fast, she checked Gatina's readings and the course log, and she praised her for her work.

"We're ahead of time," she announced, when she finally looked up from the chart. "Which is good. Did you feel the air change?" she asked.

"The air?" Gatina replied, confused. "I was more focused on the water and the sky," she admitted.

"And you did well," Beah admitted. "We made excellent time, and I've never seen the *Daydream* sail faster—we're at fifteen knots now.

"But you must pay attention to the *air*, not just the wind," she lectured. "When the winds shifted westerly, the air started feeling more humid," her aunt explained. "That could mean a sudden squall this time of year. But we're close enough to Dras Ferman, so that shouldn't matter. If we have to, we can ride one out in port. But we'll be there just before high tide, so we should be able to sail in with no problems. Now fetch me a bowl of porridge and then prepare to make landing," she ordered. "I want this to be as quick as we can manage."

When they were not adjusting the sail, they were cleaning the deck, checking the fishing nets, and making sure things were secure in case of storm. She joined Jordi in lashing some lines that were fraying, which she found easier than swabbing the deck when Seksus ordered her to. She thought it was already quite clean, but the bosun insisted. As she mopped, she caught sight of a spot of green in the horizon. *An island?* she wondered.

"Ahoy! Land!" she called out to the pilothouse. "Starboard bow!"

Fortunately, Beah was intimately familiar with the region and had anticipated it and already adjusted the route a shade to the west. "Aye, I saw it, I saw it," Beah assured. "It's a good sign. That should be . . . Andregarus Isle. That's one of countless islands out here. There's a reef around it that could tear us apart. But it does mean that we are nearly to Dras Ferman," Beah explained.

THAT AFTERNOON, THE *DAYDREAM* ARRIVED AT DRAS FREEMAN. IT WAS NOT an easy arrival.

The tiny port was relatively shallow, by mariners' standards, a small strip of town on the eastern side of the odd-shaped island, near to the one bit of harbor deep enough to permit more than a skiff's passage. There were shoals and reefs lurking all around it, making it a challenge to even position the sloop properly to take advantage of the turning of the tide and enter the single channel to the port. Brightly painted buoys guided their way.

"This is the challenging part," Beah explained as she checked the chart. "This region is called the Shipwrecker's Bower for a reason. Indeed, Dras Ferman wouldn't exist at all without them. It's a port of necessity, not of convenience. It's the closest haven to the Western Bay proper and the first place you can land in an emergency that won't shred your hull. That's why the *Sea Bell* put in here. I need all of your eyes to get us through these shoals. Plenty of men have been marooned out here because they didn't pay close-enough attention," she cautioned.

It took nearly an hour from when they passed the first of the harbor's buoys until they were able to navigate through the trickier parts of the shoals to the tiny port, where a man in a gig directed them to a vacant slip. There were three other ships in port, two barques and another sloop, and a caravel smaller than the *Legacy* anchored a few hundred yards from the docks. The harbor wasn't deep enough to even handle a large caravel, much less a galleon or frigate.

But the number of merchant barques that plied the seas between Caramas and the central Bay made it a vital port in its way.

The port itself was dingy and weathered, she observed. Despite the stretch of subtropical trees behind it, the village lacked much liveliness. There were some workshops, a blacksmith, a tiny market, and a line of cabins along the shore but not much else. The only temple she could see was a shrine to the Shipwrecker, where three longboats were beached against the need to rescue or salvage a ship. The locals hadn't even bothered to whitewash their homes, much less paint them—and many of them seemed to be fashioned of cast-off timber from ships, she noted.

One of the barques had a broken mast, Gatina saw—no doubt the *Sea Bell*, the ship they were seeking. When they finally had the *Daydream* moored to the dock, Beah and Atopol left to speak to the captain of the unfortunate vessel. Seksus, as second-in-command, had been charged with preparing the *Daydream* for its immediate return to Pluhalia, and ordered them to prepare the hold for cargo.

"Honestly, there is not much to do," Pia said as she opened the large hatch, after her mother left the ship. "We have food, water, wine and can depart as soon as the cargo is loaded."

"Do you think it will slow us down?" Jordi asked worriedly as he looked at the sky.

"Not overmuch. I think it's only a few loads. Not enough to matter to a swift ship like this," she assured.

Gatina was half-listening to her cousins while she scanned the tiny port. A longboat was ferrying cargo from the caravel, she saw, and she watched with interest as shirtless men worked quickly to roll casks onto the dock after it was moored. The enormous barrels thumped along the wooden planks so loudly, she could hear it from the *Daydream*. The men worked with deliberation and purpose as they rolled one barrel after another down the dock. She was amazed by how large their muscles were.

Pia noticed that Gatina's attention was elsewhere and looked to see where. "That's a lot of . . . wine," she said, her voice low.

"It sure is," Gatina answered absently as she stared at the half-naked mariners. "Big, thick, meaty . . . wine. Wonder where it's going."

"I have a few suggestions," Pia said, her attention captivated as well.

Jordi looked over before he offered his assessment. "That's a Glavores ship," he said as he squinted at the caravel. "That probably means that sickly sweet red swill they drink in Caramas. I'd say they're taking that to Sulisla or eventually maybe to Falas. They're probably selling a bit to keep their load from being too heavy before they cross the Bay. A ship that size holds a tidy profit in that wine, maybe enough for the entire season. Oh, look, our shipment is here. I'll set up the crane!"

Reluctantly, Gatina tore her eyes away from the mariners and focused on the task at hand. Her aunt and brother had returned on a longboat that had already been loaded with sacks of lemons and limes, all within massive rope cargo nets. She greeted the two men poling the boat alongside with her aunt and brother.

Working together, Pia and Gatina joined their brothers in hauling the great nets aboard with the help of a line affixed to a pulley system at the top of the mast. It didn't take long to pull the cargo up, with the help of some counterweights and the two mariners from the *Sea Bell*, and then move it slowly through the air over the hatch. In less than an hour, all four great cargo nets full of citrus were loaded aboard the *Daydream*'s hold.

Before they left, Beah shook the Sea Bell mariners' hands. "Thank you for your help!" she said, gratefully. "I thought this load was lost for certain. Now we'll be able to keep our schedule. And please give my regards to your captain," she said. "I would do so myself, but we need to depart if we're going to make it back to Pluhalia."

"Aye, best to hurry," the older of the two mariners agreed, squinting at the sky. "Storms are a'-blowin' in. I can feel it in me bones. Yon caravel is leaving on the tide to get ahead of them. Best be safe," he warned. "You don't want to get caught in the Shipwrecker's Bower in a squall."

As soon as they'd departed, Beah ordered the lines cast off, perhaps a little alarm in her voice as she called out the commands. Indeed, the wind *had* shifted, and it tasted different to Gatina as she moved to raise the sail.

Captain Beah returned to her spot behind the tiller, while the boys each took up positions on either side of the bow with poles to gauge the depth below the water. Once she was satisfied that she was clear of reefs or sandbars, Beah called down for the foresail to be raised.

Gatina took that moment to return to the cockpit to double-check the route she was charged with navigating. She climbed the rigging to help guide the sloop through the harbor until they were safely beyond its dangerous shoals.

And that's when she noticed the shadow of a ship on the horizon. It was approaching them—and the port.

"*Ahoy!* Sail on the port bow!" she called down to her brother, who repeated the report loud enough for Beah to hear it. Gatina took a moment to look more closely at the speck on the horizon, using magesight to see it more clearly. It was a much, *much* larger vessel than the sloop, she saw, a full three-master, and it appeared that all of their sails were set.

"What is it?" Beah called up from below, as she made her way to the port rail.

"A big one," Gatina replied, loudly. "A caravel, I think." But it wasn't the size of the ship that drew her eyes, or its gleaming white sails. It was the shadow of black whipping above its deck.

"Captain, is that the Black Flag?" Gatina asked, her voice a little shrill in alarm. Gatina felt the chill dance down her spine as she spoke. She knew that the Black Flag was a very, very, *very* bad sign.

Her aunt did likewise, peering at the horizon and no doubt using magic to bring the distant speck into focus. "Shipwrecker's Tears!" Beah swore loudly. "Yes, Maranka, it is. All hands! Black flag! *Black flag!* Crack one more sail, and let's be quick! If we can make the buoy, we should be able to outrun her! As quick as you can!"

Gatina hurried to her station on the mast, assisting in raising the second foresail to add to the sloop's speed while her heart raced. When it had caught the wind, she slid down to the deck and went to the pilothouse for more orders. Beah was looking concerned as she peered over the rail at the approaching ship.

"That indeed is a raider," she pronounced grimly. "The damned *Venjanca*, of all ships. That yellow stain on the water we saw in Pluhalia." She lowered the scope and consulted the navigation map. "I'd say we are too small and fast to draw their attention, but only the Corsair knows what their intentions are."

"You think they followed us?" Gatina asked, alarmed.

"Doubtful," Beah said, after a moment's thought. "But there's a lot of traffic coming up from Caramas towards the Vaxel Anchorage this time of year. Plenty of merchantmen they can prey on and damned few ducal frigates to stop them. But we can outrun them, even loaded down," she assured Gatina. "It took them a half-day more than us to cross the Bay. We can outpace them nicely if we keep the wind. They've got more sail, but we can tack faster than they."

"And . . . if we don't?" Gatina asked fearfully.

"Let's not discuss such an unpleasant possibility until we have to," Beah decided. "But just in case, have Seksus break open the weapons locker."

Gatina felt a sense of fear in her belly, down deep. She held her breath for a moment, long enough to force herself to calm down, then she exhaled slowly.

That caught her aunt's attention. Beah gave Gatina a confident look. "Don't worry. To be truthful, I'm more concerned about the summer squalls than I am about that pirate ship. Those storms are what delayed both shipments to Pluhalia. So, I'm glad we didn't tarry in port longer than necessary. We'll be long gone before that ship arrives." Her aunt nodded in the direction of the *Venjanca*. "She's too big to enter Dras Ferman. But she can anchor at the port mouth and blockade it if she's a mind. I would not care for any of us to be in port when trouble starts. I have a bad feeling about that."

"So, you don't think they'd chase us?" Gatina asked, relieved.

"Fortunately, we are a smaller ship. To their eyes, we have little value compared to what the port holds. Did you see the caravel accepting casks of wine?" Gatina nodded. Beah shook her head. "That's a lot of value. They might be in for a bad night, but we should be able to get away. But be sure the lemon flag is raised," she reminded her. "No need to make ourselves look like more than we're worth."

Certainly, pirates wouldn't waste time with lemons, she reasoned. But Gatina wondered about how much value a well-built sloop would have. Not to mention an older woman who was an experienced navigator, a competent bosun, two young maidens, and two strong young men. How much value might that represent to slavers? She recalled the miserable stock heading to the slave market and shuddered.

But she kept that to herself. She did not even want to put that thought into words.

CHAPTER TWELVE

PIRATES!

The Shipwrecker is the most feared of all the Stormfather's daughters by the Sea Lords. She brings calamity wherever the winds take her. She is as capricious as the winds and as treacherous as the reefs and shoals, and feared above all others save her dread father. Her mercies are hard-won, and her cult are little better than scavengers on the sea. She is a deity of chaos. Indeed, the goddess is hells-bent on destruction, in whatever shape it should appear.
—*from* **Sea Lords, Their Cults, Religious Customs, and Traditions**

CAPTAIN BEAH DISMISSED GATINA TO HER BUNK AFTER MIDNIGHT, CLAIMING to be too concerned about the encroaching clouds and the lurking raider to sleep herself. When Gatina returned to the deck after her too-short four-hour nap, she looked up, expecting to see the sun's brilliant shades of pink peeking through the sky in the east. Instead, she was greeted by a blast of unforgiving wind and the shock of cold rain.

The sun was most certainly overhead, but she could not see it. The surf had picked up dramatically, and the ship had begun rocking as she sped ahead of the storm. The calm weather they had experienced during their trip had given away to the storm her Aunt Beah had been worried about the day before. Immediately, her sailcloth deck clothes were soaked through by the spray and the rain. Gatina wished she was still sleeping in her warm bunk below deck. This would be a very wet day.

As Gatina hurried to the *Daydream*'s cockpit, she rolled her shoulders a few times then she swung her arms back and forth, all while her head was down to avoid rain in her eyes. She did not see Atopol, who was making his way onto the quarterdeck as she was coming out. She accidentally ran into him as the ship rocked, knocking him off-balance and nearly onto his backside.

"Sorry, Attie!" she said as she reached out to steady him. "When did it get so stormy?"

"Since dawn," he replied tiredly. "The water's grown choppier in the past hour. My mariner instinct tells me that it's going to get very wet today," he advised, then went into the quarterdeck. She noticed that he was wearing a cork belt. She also noticed that the rain had stopped. For now. The wind, however, was blowing in hard gusts.

Gatina surveyed the sky once again, this time with a more intense focus on the clouds approaching from the west. They were very dense and much lower today. She hadn't seen the sky look this dark since they'd left Falas. She felt the charge in the air that usually meant a storm was coming. The wind had shifted, and it was cooler, less humid.

The next breeze that hit her sent chills down her back. She hugged her arms to warm up and climbed the ladder to the cockpit. The chart was spread on the small table, and Beah was examining it. She looked up when Gatina approached, her eyes bleary with weariness but sharp with worry.

"Ah, you're awake. Excellent. The boys can get some rest now," she said, rubbing her eyes.

"Where are we?" Gatina asked as she peered at the chart.

"We're still on course and racing ahead of this storm. Thankfully, a tailwind is pushing us—we're making sixteen knots right now," she said proudly. "We might just be able to skirt the edge of it, if Seksus is right. He's sailed this region before. I already had him loosen the lines and prepare to strike the sheets ahead of this storm if he isn't right."

Gatina glanced outside, where the rain had started once again. "How long until we know?"

"It's likely just a summer squall, not a proper gale," she suggested. "They happen all the time in the southern waters of the Bay. I don't expect it to be too bad, but I also never assume it won't."

Pia popped her head into the tiny navigation cabin. "I just heard from Seksus. Storm coming?" she asked, worriedly. She had three cork belts in her hands.

"Good idea," Beah said, taking a belt from her daughter and handing the other to Gatina. "But I think we can—" Before she could continue, they all heard shouting. It was indistinct, so all three left the cockpit and went out on the quarterdeck. Seksus was at the starboard rail, a spyglass in his hand.

"Ahoy!" he repeated. "Sails off the starboard bow!" he yelled, his voice hoarse in the wind.

Immediately, all three of the women began using magesight to see what he had spotted. They all saw the same thing at about the same time.

"By the Maiden's crusty armpits! That's bad, *very* bad, actually," Beah murmured.

Indeed, there were two sets of sails on the horizon: one belonging to a caravel, another to a larger galleon—a very familiar-looking one. The caravel was sailing ahead of the raider, whose black flag hung like an angry stain from its mainmast, but it was clear that the galleon was slowly catching up with its prey.

"It seems the pirate ship we saw in Dras Freeman has decided to attack the caravel out here in the Bay." Beah sighed gloomily.

"Will they be able to escape?" Pia asked, concerned.

"It depends on whether or not the captain is a better pilot than the raider," Beah answered. "They're both cracking a lot of sail. But it looks like the galleon is gaining," she said gloomily. "That's bad news for the merchantman. The good news is that they aren't going after us."

"Is there anything we can do?" Gatina asked, concerned, as she studied the pursuit.

"Not unless we want to attract their attention," Beah said, shaking her head. "That's something I want to avoid. As long as they are determined to take the caravel, we should be safe."

After weeks at sea with little to see but waves, the drama unfolding on the horizon was captivating. For the next hour, they watched in fascinated horror as the two ships tacked, maneuvered, and tacked again in front of the strong storm winds. It was a kind of morbid race, Gatina decided, a game of cat and mouse on the increasingly swelling surf. She and Pia rooted strongly for the caravel, of course. But every time the two ships tacked against the wind, the galleon seemed to close a little bit more.

"I don't like their chances," Beah admitted an hour later. The rain had picked up, forcing them to stay in the shelter of the pilothouse. "They're almost within bowshot now. If they close any further, they'll be able to strike at their rigging and force them to slow enough to board."

"Can't they fight back?" Gatina asked worriedly.

"They're outnumbered," Beah said, shaking her head. "A caravel that size has a crew of twenty or thirty mariners, at best, and likely half that. The *Venjanca* just as likely has twice that many. They can fight, but it's not probable they'll win. Their best chance is still outrunning them. Or hope the squall overtakes them both and they recover before the raider. Now, as witnesses, we can swear out our testimony of the attack to the authorities when we're in port, but that's hardly consoling for that poor ship and its crew."

True to her prediction, the *Venjanca* gained on the caravel until it was close enough to launch boats to board the craft. Gatina watched in horror as three longboats were deployed from the galleon, crowded with men. Some of them used great sea bows, weapons made from laminated horn, to launch volleys of arrows against their prey. Many of the arrows landed harmlessly in the hull. Some of them did not. She saw men fall into the rough surf or crumble to the deck of the caravel.

The merchantman had defenses, of course—they saw several mariners use crossbows to attack the raiders in the boats below. But there were too few, and it seemed that every oarsman who fell was quickly replaced. As they neared the hull, they threw grappling hooks over the rails and heaved great bronze sea axes into the side of the hull. The heavy three-pointed spears provided a means to secure the attacker's boats to the side of their victim.

Soon, the pirates were climbing up ropes to board the caravel. Men were being tossed overboard. Others were fighting. A lot of them were fighting—both pirates and mariners. She saw steel hit more steel and winced.

"They're attacking!" Pia said, her voice filled with horror.

"Pirates," her aunt agreed sadly. "I suppose it was good of them to leave the port alone, but to attack in such weather is appalling. It's poor form."

With her magesight, Gatina was able to see clearly for several hundred yards. And what she saw was merciless. The raiders had resorted to fighting the sailors hand-to-hand. The pirates were used to using brute force, as she remembered from the incident in Pluhalia. The merchantmen were not. They were fit, from what she could see, but they were not fighters.

One after the other, they stood to the pirates and the pirates knocked them down. It was a free-for-all on the deck, sheer chaos. She could only imagine the adrenaline coursing through their bodies as they fought for their lives.

Gatina found it difficult to watch a battle she could do nothing about. The pirates had sea axes as well as swords, and the weapons were devastating when they finally made it to the main deck. The caravel's colors were struck soon after. The merchantmen continued to fire their crossbows and defend themselves with their own scimitars, but they were outnumbered and out-skilled. The defenders retreated to their quarterdeck, keeping their attackers at bay with poles and axes, but they were losing. Soon, they were jumping off the ship, though some were thrown overboard.

"And so she has fallen," Beah said sadly. "She'll be taken as a prize now and either sold to another raider crew or to a disreputable broker in one of their secret ports. Waste of a good ship!" she condemned.

"There's a lot of them in the water," Gatina pointed out. "Captain Beah, what happens—do they drown or do the pirates fish them out to sell them as slaves?"

Beah sighed, weary. "In most cases, the pirates will wear down the sailors to the point of exhaustion, take them captive, and either ransom them or force them into slavery," she said. "That seems to be the case here. If they lose too many of their own men, they'll sometimes recruit new conscripts from the survivors. Of course, they're usually required to execute their own surviving officers as a proof of loyalty, but some men are willing to do that and turn pirate rather than keep their honor and become a slave."

The three watched another two men go overboard—one by choice and one by a boot to his back.

"I pray there are no women on the ship," Pia declared. "And that the Rats don't make their way to the *Daydream*."

"They're going to be occupied with taking over a prize ship just in time for a squall," Beah pointed out. "They won't have time to chase after us."

Another four were forced overboard as they watched. Gatina noticed that some of the men never resurfaced, which made her wonder if they could not swim. Others tried to put as much distance as they could between themselves and their captured vessel. That was difficult when the surf was sporting six-foot waves.

"Can't we help them?" she asked her aunt quietly. "Isn't that the right thing to do?"

Her questions were met with silence. Gatina felt her cousin's eyes on her, as if she was measuring her worth.

"I think we should help them," Pia agreed, as if it was the most logical thing in the world to suggest. "If it were us—"

But Aunt Beah interrupted her before she could continue. "Absolutely not. There's precious little we can do for them except get ourselves captured along with them. Those are not just pirates. They're Rats. Slavers. If we slow down to pick up survivors, we risk our ship and our lives. We have our own ship to contend with. You two tend to your duties and forget about that poor caravel," she ordered.

The wind began to pick up as if it was fueled by the emotional storm on the *Daydream*'s deck. It whipped across Gatina's back, sending yet another chill down her spine as she and Pia were sent to the bow when one of the foresails suddenly ripped. That made it even more difficult to wrestle the torn sheet from the rigging, as the winds whipped it around. The surf picked up even more dramatically.

But then the sun poked through the clouds for a moment, as if some stray god was trying to give her hope. That warmed Gatina up for a few minutes—until another blast of air mixed with heavier rain doused her again.

She listened to her aunt and did what she was supposed to. But her magic-enhanced eyes remained focused on the sailors that were floating in the Bay, trying to escape the longboats that were circling the captured caravel, collecting what survivors they could. She watched as several were dragged from the surf, some still trying to fight before they were stilled with blows from the pirates' truncheons.

At least the pirates were not having an easy time of it. The water was even more violent now, thanks to the wind. That allowed some of the mariners to escape easy capture, if they were strong-enough swimmers. Some were even trying to make it to the *Daydream*, they could see, which made their fate all the more terrible.

Alas, within minutes, the sun had again retreated behind the dark clouds. Gatina was certain those men would drown if nothing was done. Pia, apparently, thought so as well.

"They're trying to reach *us*," Pia realized. "We could probably launch a boat and get to them before the pirates do," she reasoned when they both returned to the cockpit.

"And put ourselves at risk!" Beah dismissed. "If we slow our pace any more, we could be next—or get caught in the squall. We cannot afford the delay."

"Mother, if we don't go, they'll *die*," Pia insisted, her voice deadly serious, as Gatina looked between her cousin and her aunt, gauging the level of emotional turmoil. She could see that Pia was terrified for the men and that her aunt was equally afraid of trying to aid them.

"You will address me as Captain, crewman," Beah said sternly, reminding her of her place on the ship. To her surprise, Pia ignored the warning.

"But we can help them! What if one of those poor mariners was Father? Did he have a chance to escape his fate but didn't because no one helped him? You know it's the right thing to do, Mother," she reproved.

Beah looked shocked and angry by her daughter's defiance . . . but though the reference to her lost husband clearly stung her, it also had an effect.

Pia pressed. "Gatina and I can launch the gig and try to get as many as we can before the storm hits," she reasoned. "Then we can get them aboard when you tack the next time. It's better than letting them die at sea like that. You know we can do it!"

"And if you do, *you* might die," her mother replied sharply. Gatina knew both women were correct. She also knew that Beah probably wanted to save the men, if they could before the storm picked up. "I will not lose another family member to this godsforsaken Bay!"

"Would you not try to save me?" Pia argued. "That's what I'm trying to do for them!"

"Godsdamnit!" Captain Beah swore, glaring at her daughter. "Fine! Take the gig! See if you can fish out any of them, and we'll pick you up on the next tack. Go ahead and get your brothers on deck. But you'd better hurry; you have precious few moments to get to them before the raiders or the storm. That squall will be on us sooner than you think now that we've lost a foresail. If you have half an hour to do it, you'll be getting a miracle from the Shipwrecker!"

Pia hugged her mother quickly. Beah held on to the girl tightly before pulling Gatina into the embrace, too. She heard her aunt whisper something, but she was not sure what she had said. It was barely audible, and her words sounded foreign. Gatina wondered if it was a spell of protection, a prayer, or maybe one of the Sea Lord customs. Pia gave her mother a grateful look and dragged Gatina out of the cockpit before she could change her mind.

"That's the first time I've ever won an argument with Mother," she revealed as they descended the ladder to the main deck. "I hope I don't regret that. Help me get the boat in the water! We're going to attempt a rescue!" Pia called to Atopol as she worked with Jordi to lower the gig.

It was small, but it was sturdy enough to hold at least four adults. Gatina felt confident that she and Pia could handle it. Gatina's fingers flew as she worked to release the rope around the cleats securing the boat to the side of the *Daydream*. She heard the gig *plunk* into the water below just as a gust of wind sent a wet, salty spray into her face. The surge immediately tried to carry it away. Only the mooring line kept it from being lost at once.

"I can't believe she's letting you do this," Jordi said, shaking his head as he looked at the gig bobbing wildly. "You should take a bow, just in case," he advised.

"Fetch it for me," Pia agreed as she secured her hair with a bit of the torn foresail. Gatina cut a scrap herself and did likewise. The way the wind was blowing, the last thing she needed was to try to row with hair in her face. By the time she was done, Jordi had returned with a small but powerful crossbow and a leather quiver full of iron bolts. He handed it to his sister with a certain degree of ceremony . . . along with a short boarding scimitar.

"Just in case," he explained. Atopol was right behind him.

"Kitten, take this," Atopol said, pushing her shadowblade into her hands. "If you get a chance to stab a pirate, you should take it."

"This is a really poor idea, isn't it?" she asked her brother as she strapped the blade to her back and secured it over her shoulder. She immediately felt better with it on.

"Oh, one of the worst," he agreed sagely. "You're probably going to die. But it is amazingly brave of you."

"We should really be the ones going," Jordi said darkly as he handed each of them an oar.

"We need you to hold the *Daydream* and pick us up," Pia countered. "Just watch for us. We'll be fine if you do."

"I'll not tell you what I think about this foolishness," Seksus said as he approached them. "But if the captain said you could . . . well, it's brave of you, no matter how stupid. Here, take these at least," he said, handing Gatina two more cork belts and a coil of line. "If you can't reach them, at least throw them these. That will give them a chance. Not much of one, but a chance."

Pia gave the rope ladder a strong tug before tossing it over the side. It slapped against the side of the boat. "Jordi, we might come back on another side, so be ready to toss down another line. Or another ladder.

Hells, be ready for anything," Pia called out before she descended the rope ladder. There were a harrowing few moments, but soon, she had pulled the gig back to the side of the hull and managed to steady it enough for Gatina to throw the two oars and the crossbow to her.

Gatina wiped her face with her dress and nodded to her crewmates before following her cousin. The familiar flutter of excitement and fear had made its way from the pit of her stomach to her arms and her legs by the time she dropped into the bottom of the gig. She was doing something incredibly dangerous but under the supervision of her slightly more experienced cousin. She was glad her parents weren't there—she didn't think they would have allowed the unnecessarily risky plan.

"Let's go!" Pia called as Gatina found her seat in the wildly rocking gig. The swells were at least six or seven feet high now, each one tossing the gig against the hull of the *Daydream*.

"Here." Pia handed her the other two cork belts. Pia wrapped one belt over her shoulder, across her chest, while Gatina did the same. "The one at your waist will keep you afloat. The ones over your shoulders will keep your head above water. Don't drown. Don't fall overboard. Keep your wits about you. Don't trust the water," her cousin preached as Jordi cast off the mooring line from above.

The waves pounded the side of the gig as Gatina took an oar and began paddling madly, working in tandem with her cousin. It was a titanic effort to push the tiny boat up and over the waves, the hardest rowing she'd ever done. She worried she wasn't able to keep pace with the larger girl, but she put every effort into each sweep of the oars as they made their way across the water to the two embattled ships. Flotsam filled the water around them now, as the damaged rigging and other debris from the battle was cast or blown overboard.

"There they are!" Pia said, after ten exhausting minutes of rowing. "I see them!" she shouted, excited. "There, do you see them?" Gatina nodded a reply and continued to paddle furiously toward the two men who were bobbing along top of the waves. It was difficult to see, as the rain was picking up and the gig wasn't stable, but Gatina saw two bobbing specks in the sea that magesight told her were escaping mariners. "We can get those two closest to us, at least!" Pia suggested.

"Let's try!" Gatina agreed, her chest heaving with the effort. The swimming mariners saw them, it seemed, and began swimming madly toward their tiny boat.

"We're nearly there!" she yelled so that Pia could hear her over the wind, which had picked up considerably as they rowed. The evening before had been peaceful. Gatina had not realized that such a calm night would bring so treacherous a storm.

When the gig got close enough, Pia shouted to them to get their attention. They couldn't hear her, but the prospect of salvation was enough to inspire them to redouble their efforts.

Pia tossed a line over the side and the men each grabbed it. Then, hand over hand, they made their way across the final few feet to the side of the gig. The mariners were a lot larger than she thought when she saw them on the ship, Gatina noticed, worried that she and Pia would not be able to help them into the boat.

Thankfully, desperation brings its own inspiration. They were more than able to haul themselves up and over the side of the boat, doing so with such skill that the gig took on very little water. Both of them collapsed onto the bottom of the boat as soon as they were aboard.

Satisfied, Pia nodded to Gatina. "Back to the ship!" she commanded as she began to row.

The pair looked waterlogged, but otherwise they seemed hale, at least to Gatina's untrained but appraising eye. They were alive and seemed uninjured, at least.

She dipped her oar into the water and fought to match Pia's efforts, but the current was so strong now that they nearly went in a circle twice before straightening the gig's course. Halfway to the *Daydream*, the two refugees came to their senses enough to take over rowing duties.

Gatina was relieved. She never would admit being unable to handle herself, but rowing against the current was exhausting. There were more heads bobbing in the surf, trying to make their way to the safety of the sloop, she saw. If they went back out, she knew she needed to conserve what strength she had.

In a few moments, the sailors had the gig back alongside the *Daydream*. Jordi had been watching for them. The ladder was already lowered. One at a time, the men climbed up to the deck.

Before the Gatina could follow them, Pia grabbed her arm. "There are others out there!" she shouted, pointing back toward the caravel.

Gatina looked over her shoulder and activated her magesight. She saw three more men had jumped into the water. "We can't take three!" she said, looking at the size of the gig. "Can we?"

"Shouldn't we try?" Pia asked just as her mother peered over the side.

"What are you waiting for?" Beah screamed over the rail. "Get up here! The storm's nearly on us!"

"There are more men out there, Mother!" Pia yelled as she pushed the gig away with her oar. "Don't worry! We will make haste!"

"Pia! *Pia!*" her mother shouted . . . but they were already away.

"I couldn't hear what she said; could you?" Pia lied with a grin as they both put their shoulders into the oars.

"The wind's too loud!" Gatina agreed. "I think she told us to go back and save more!"

"That's what I thought!" Pia laughed as they kept at their strokes. It was even more difficult now—the swells were nearly eight feet, by her eye, and the specks on the surface were tossed up and down with each new wave. But the girls were once more paddling toward the caravel and the doomed mariners. Gatina tried to ignore the increasing amount of water in the bottom of the boat and concentrate on rowing. At this point, they were powered by adrenaline. Indeed, Gatina hadn't felt this alive since she had dangled from the great cargo crane above Falas.

A bolt of lightning flashed overhead, just beyond the sloop. It wasn't terribly close yet, but it was near enough to motivate them. The thunder that clapped several long seconds afterward rattled Gatina, enough that she pushed her arms and shoulders even faster in her strokes.

Unfortunately, they weren't the only ones speeding toward the mariners. When Gatina paused from her labors and checked their progress, she was pleased to see how far they had gone. She could see individuals on the decks of both ships now, and at least three swimming survivors making their way toward the gig. More importantly, they were close enough to the struggling survivors to see their faces.

But she could also see one of the *Venjanca*'s longboats was also heading for them.

"*Pia!* Trouble!" Gatina called into the wind. Her cousin looked up at her, then behind her, where she saw the boat. She turned back to Gatina, wide-eyed.

"Throw them a line!" she yelled, taking Gatina's oar. "Let's not get closer than we have to!"

It became a race between the tiny gig and the much-larger longboat. There were only a handful of pirates in it now—most had boarded the caravel already—but they had twice as many oars as the gig. They began closing the distance between them and the survivors uncomfortably fast.

Every wave seemed to bring the swimmers closer but also brought the longboat closer. One of the pirates had raised a sea bow and begun firing. She didn't know if they were shooting at the gig or the swimming mariners, but it couldn't have been easy to shoot on such an unstable platform. The arrows went wide of their mark, thankfully, as the boat came within shouting distance of the men.

"Come on!" Gatina urged them, as she tied one of her two cork belts to the bowline and tossed it as far as she could into the water. "Hurry! They're closing!"

The men needed no urging—the arrows the pirates were lobbing were getting closer and closer. Indeed, the longboat pulled aside the slowest of them before the fastest could grasp the line. Their boat slowed as they pulled the struggling man over the gunwales of the skiff and beat him unconscious with a cudgel.

Another pirate raised a bow and fired an arrow toward them. In a lucky shot, he struck the man next nearest the longboat in the back of his skull. The sailor's eyes went from excitement at the promise of rescue to blank. In seconds. It was a sight that Gatina would never forget. He had the loveliest green eyes. He slipped under the bloody waves and did not rise again. He had been claimed by the Shipwrecker's Bower, she knew.

When the last survivor saw his mate's fate, he swam even more frantically to reach the boat, diving below the waves to avoid being shot. Gatina invoked the protection of Darkness under her breath as she realized just how close the pirates were now. She grabbed the crossbow, fitted an iron bolt to it, and, bracing the frame on the bow of the gig, she waited until the bobbing boat lined up with the approaching longboat.

Perhaps the Darkness had heard her and answered. When she pulled the lever, the bolt sailed unerringly across the water, skimmed just over the side of the longboat, and buried itself in the back of one of the cutthroats. She could hear the man scream over the roar of the wind.

"You got one!" Pia exclaimed as she paused her rowing.

"He's got the line!" Gatina pointed out, as the last mariner grasped the line she'd thrown. As he crawled along it, both girls pulled it as fast as they could. The longboat was getting closer and closer, making every moment more anxious.

"Gatina!" Pia shouted as she stopped pulling the rope and instead tied it off to the bow. "Row! I'll get him in! We need to get away from them!" Her voice was shrill. The last mariner was, indeed, nearly at the gig. More arrows came from the longboat—indeed, one *thunk*ed into the wooden bottom of the gig, directly between the girls.

That sudden appearance gave Gatina a renewed burst of energy. She bent the oars with all her might, straining to pull away from the larger boat.

"I've got him!" Pia said triumphantly behind her a moment later. Gatina glanced back as the man pulled himself over the side. She also watched in horror as a final arrow from the longboat found its range . . . and pierced the right shoulder of the mariner from behind just as he came aboard. He moaned and fell into the gig. Had his body not interceded, however, the shaft would have taken Pia directly in the chest.

"*Row!*" Pia screamed as she helped the man get settled, and strapped her second cork belt around his waist, being careful to avoid his wound. Then she picked up the empty crossbow and started to wind the powerful windlass, an expression of fierce determination on her face. "*Row!*"

Gatina strained to hear her cousin over the roar of the wind. That wasn't just the wind, Gatina quickly realized. It was also pounding rain, and it was coming directly toward them in a hazy wall that swept over the galleon, then the caravel.

She snapped her head around and got a glimpse of the pirates who were in pursuit of their gig. Their boat was atop a wave but closing fast. It would be on top of them if they didn't move faster. That gave Gatina access to a well of more adrenaline than she had ever felt in her life. She braced herself and planted her feet firmly into the gig's deck. Her arms took control, using her fear as energy.

A moment later, she heard the twang of the crossbow, and then Pia grabbed one of the oars.

"I got one, too!" she said proudly as she began to stroke. Gatina matched her cousin's pace. "It was a lucky shot, but it hit a leg, I think!"

Gatina wanted to ask her cousin if there was some sort of spell they might use to protect their boat or themselves, but she did not get the chance. The relentless storm sent a swell of water, and the gig rose to the top of the next wave. At its height, Gatina could see the sails of the *Daydream* in the distance. It seemed much farther away than she thought it should be, and in a direction she didn't expect.

"They're tacking," Pia huffed. "If we can make it to their next tack, we'll be fine!" she assured. Gatina nodded and kept rowing. She tried to put the roar of the rain and the blistering winds out of her mind and focus entirely on pushing the gig through the turbulent water.

They were fleeing the storm more than the longboat now. Indeed, the curtain of rain had nearly obscured the enemy boat the next time she chanced to look. Both boats were being battered by the waves now, which were more than ten feet high in the wind. But the gig was pulling away. No one was shooting at them anymore. They were almost out of danger.

Unfortunately, a moment later, she felt the unexpected crunch of the gig's hull on something solid. The wood splintered beneath her feet, and for a brief instant she saw a gray expanse of rock burst through the bottom. The gig disintegrated with the next wave, and despite her attempt to grab Pia's hand, Gatina slipped under the pounding surf.

The Shipwrecker had taken them.

CHAPTER THIRTEEN

SHIPWRECKED

The patroness of salvagers and rescuers, the Shipwrecker's cult nonetheless includes an unwilling congregation: the shipwrecked. Those who find themselves cast away by the force of the capricious goddess are involuntarily included in her cult, and are subject to a number of customs and traditions that can entangle them for years. For the Shipwrecker is not merely a storm goddess but a mistress of curses.

—*from* **Sea Lords, Their Cults, Religious Customs, and Traditions**

GATINA DIDN'T REMEMBER MUCH OF THE NEXT FEW HOURS. THE SHATTERED gig spilled her, Pia, and the wounded mariner into the sea, setting her scrambling to keep from drowning. In those desperate moments, she managed to retain her grip on her oar, which may have saved her life. Her cork belt kept her from slipping below the turbulent surface, but the wooden oar gave her arms something to cling to and kept her head above the waves . . . mostly.

The storm continued to rage around her, and once she was certain she wasn't in immediate danger of drowning, she looked frantically for signs of Pia or the wounded man. She called and called, but the rain, the wind, and the thunder conspired to carry her voice away. Nor could she spot any sign of her companions. The interposing waves and the sheets of driving rain reduced her vision, and she was unable to concentrate enough to manage magesight. In the space of a very few minutes, she was carried away by the currents.

Her universe became limited to hanging on to the oar and trying to keep the surf from overwhelming her. It was an endless moment of emergency and required all of her energy and determination just to stay alive.

There was nothing but her and the angry sea now: no sails in the distance, no fellow human beings, no sign of life anywhere. Still, she hung on to the oar and clung to the hope she would survive.

She didn't know exactly how much time had passed during her hellish struggle, but by the time the rain slacked and the belligerent clouds from the squall receded, the sun was already setting. The winds and waves resumed a more reasonable presentation. By the time the first evening stars began to appear on the eastern horizon, the surf was almost gentle and the wind no more than a stiff breeze.

And still there was no sign of life.

She didn't know where she was. She didn't know which direction the *Daydream* was in. She had no water, no food, and only her cork belt, her oar, and her shadowblade still strapped to her back. She was as alone as she could possibly be, in the middle of the sea.

As night fell, she tried her best to orient herself with the familiar stars overhead, and that occupied her for a time. She used the Triangle to determine where north was, and she picked out the western horizon as the constellation of Agtron the Angry Octopus rose in the east. From what the chart on the *Daydream* had read, she recalled that the closest landmass was a series of uninhabited islands and sandbars to the west, northeast of Dras Ferman. She started slowly kicking her way in that direction.

Despite her predicament, she was not tempted to give in to despair. Kittens are fearless, she reminded herself. When she rested, she floated on the oar and picked out the constellations above, like old friends watching over her. The darkness of night itself was a comfort, compared to the mysterious danger of the sea.

Soon, the little green moon appeared low on the eastern horizon—it was waxing gibbous, she noted, though the larger white moon, Caluna, was in its new phase, leaving the green satellite the only one in the sky. That meant that the tidal forces of the two would not compound and make the seas rougher, she reasoned. That was good news.

But her astronomical observations served to remind her of the friends she'd made at Palomar Abbey and the adventures she'd had there. She wondered what they were doing at the moment and guessed they were having less-exciting lives than she. None of them had ever seen the little green moon, to her knowledge. She counted herself fortunate in that.

That led her to speculating about her friends at the orphanage, the few she'd managed to save from a life and likely an early death on the streets of Falas. Her fellow nits were no doubt sleeping in comfortable beds now. She was speculating on what each of them might be doing when the stars began to be covered by more dark clouds from the west.

It wasn't a squall but a steady rainstorm that blotted out both stars and her ability to see the ocean in their dim light. The surf was no higher than four or five feet, but she could see nothing beyond her immediate area. The sea and the sky had both turned to darkness—the Blessed Darkness, in nature incarnate, she realized. There was no light from anywhere, just inky blackness around and below her, and fuzzy darkness above. For an hour, she just clung to the oar and tried to keep her spirits up before the rain finally slacked. She made a game of collecting mouthfuls of rainwater while mentally reciting the Stormfather's daughters' names.

Gatina's mind began to drift into all sorts of unlikely places, her imagination producing a gallery of images: her special cards, the faces of her friends, passages from books, songs she'd heard, the intricacies of picking locks, and scores of other fancies kept her from losing hope.

At one point, as the waters became even calmer, the surface of the sea broke unexpectedly, and something emerged from it. Gatina was confused and startled by it and stared at it intently to determine if it was real or something dredged from her imagination.

The nearly spherical thing turned toward her, revealing two large, deep-set eyes in an inhuman face. Clumps of seaweed clung to part of its head, she noted, a mockery of proper hair. Gatina was at a loss until she recognized the beast: a nymph.

Supposedly, the peaceful natavia sealife was considered sacred to mariners, like porpoises or sea turtles, she remembered reading in some book. Nymphs were long, wide, fat-looking creatures with large, bulbous heads. They could grow to the size of a large boat, she recalled. And there were legends that made them kin to the great leviathans who roamed the Shattered Sea and the Shallow Sea beyond the Great Bay.

"Well, hello there!" Gatina called to the strange creature, still not certain if she had dreamed it. It did not answer—which would have convinced Gatina that she had, indeed, dredged it from her imagination. But it did blink its great eyes at her as if it was surprised. It seemed to give her a long, searching look, as if it was staring at her soul. Then it quietly descended back beneath the waves.

After that, Gatina's weariness made her start to worry about surviving until dawn. It seemed as if she had floated endlessly. She did her best to rest in a kind of half-doze, her head on her hands, floating on the oar but never quite falling asleep. She was surprised some unknowable time later when her bare foot scraped across the top of a shoal.

Frantically, she scrambled for purchase with her toes while she searched around. It was still some time before dawn, she could see, but when she mustered her determination and concentration enough to use magesight, she detected a long, low mass on the horizon. It might be land, she reasoned, or it could be the Shipwrecker playing with her senses.

Either way, it was a direction to start paddling toward.

Intense, blazing heat woke Gatina the next morning.

Her skin was burning and sticky. Her throat was scratchy, and her mouth was dry and tasted of salt and sand. She was on her back on an uneven and prickly surface. There were rocks under her, she knew, some digging painfully into her side. And there was sand. Both were abrasive, uncomfortable, and blessedly solid.

She jolted when she felt something tickle her toes—a beastly looking crab was investigating them. She kicked at it reflexively, sending it scurrying away.

When she opened her eyes, she regretted it immediately. The sun was so bright that it hurt. Groaning, she covered her eyes with her forearm, then she tensed her body to make sure she could still move it and feel, outside of the heat. She wiggled her toes and her fingers, then moved her head from side to side. Everything seemed to be working, which was a huge relief, and she exhaled a breath she had held in.

Unfortunately, that led her to a violent coughing spell and copious amounts of bay water coming up and out.

Gatina rolled onto her side to help with the coughing fit and, hopefully, to regulate her breathing. She practiced the breathwork Lady Silk had drilled into her skull. *"Inhale slowly, to a count of five. Hold it for ten counts. Exhale for fifteen counts."* She imagined her tutor clapping out the time. And that helped. Instead of panicking, Gatina was calm. She was alive, seemingly unhurt, and she was on a beach.

Gatina pushed herself into a seated position. She covered her eyes before opening them this time. She looked down at herself. Her dress was torn. Purple bruises dotted her legs and her arms. She felt stiff, but lying on the sand and felt good because the beach was blessedly solid. Her cork belt had cut into her back and her ribs, but she found no fault with it because it had also kept her alive. The hilt of her shadowblade had pressed into her neck, producing a crick, but beyond that, she was physically well.

She sat up and stared first at the ocean, from which she'd been spared, and thence to the beach, which caused her heart to race. All she could see were sand and water in front of her and on either side of her.

From her spot, Gatina scanned the sand, looking for signs of anything she could use. She quickly saw she was on a beach at low tide. And she noticed the crabs that had been tickling her toes. As her eyes adjusted to the bright and unforgiving yellow sphere overhead, she saw was not alone! Sprawled on the beach not a hundred yards away was the familiar sight of Pia, unconscious but moving somewhat. The realization that her cousin was with her—and alive—led to another wave of panic and relief.

Gingerly, Gatina pushed herself from the sand into a squatting position. Her aching muscles began to register official complaints. She did not want to move too quickly only to fall over. So, she fought to remain calm as another wave of panic began to wash over her. She had to trust that Pia was not hurt.

She forced her body to stand, albeit haphazardly. She was wobbly and staggered as she crossed the burning beach to reach Pia. Her bare feet protested the searing heat, but she had to get to her cousin. She concentrated on the girl instead of the pain. And while she focused on crossing the sand in front of her, Gatina she saw the stretch of vegetation beyond the beach, and even a hill climbing toward the center of what had to be a tiny island, the top obscured by fog. She was surprised by how peaceful it was there, wherever *there* was.

She took a brief moment to thank the Blessed Darkness for saving her life. Her patron deity had landed her in a glorious place, and for however long she would be there, she would also be grateful to be alive. But she also knew she had work to do if she wanted to *stay* alive. That included making sure that her cousin was alive and unhurt. She only hoped the older girl had far more experience in situations such as this.

Gatina counted the steps. Pia was one hundred fifty paces away from where she had awoken. And, unlike her, she was facedown in the sand. Gatina fell onto her knees, relieved to see that the girl was breathing. She was afraid to touch her, afraid she might be hurt. Instead, she spoke to her.

"Pia? Pia?" Gatina asked, first softly, then louder. "Are you injured? Can you hear me?" She observed a shift in her cousin's breathing pattern and took that to be a good sign. Gatina reached out a nervous hand and squeezed her cousin's shoulder gently. "Pia?"

Pia rolled onto her back with a groan, startling Gatina enough that she fell backward onto the sand. And that led to a bit of sand landing on Pia's face, which led to a brief spell of six sneezes.

Gatina tried to help her sit up, but Pia brushed her off.

"No, I am fine, I'm awake . . . I'm *alive*," Pia assured after the sneezing ended. "Sore but otherwise hale. What about you?"

Gatina looked at her cousin to confirm, performing a cursory review of her body to make sure there were no open wounds or broken bones sticking out. She was relieved to see only bruises just like she sported. Instead of answering her, she tackled Pia in a tight hug, causing the girls to fall onto the sand.

"I am fine, just bruised up," Gatina said. "It was a rough night. But thank the Blessed Darkness, *we're alive!*"

Pia reached over and squeezed Gatina's hand. "We are fortunate, Kitten," she agreed. "I have no idea where we are, but I am thankful we are out of the water. Being on land greatly increases our chance of rescue and of survival."

"It certainly reduces our chances of drowning and being eaten by sharks," Gatina conceded.

The two lay in the sand, just enjoying the fact that they had survived. They had made it to land—somewhere—and they were together. But once the novelty of being alive began to fade, the seriousness of their situation started to set in.

Gatina sat up abruptly. "How can they find us if they don't know where we are?" she asked, a hint of panic in her stomach. In fact, Gatina's mind began spiraling into a circle of despair.

She realized she was terrified, now that she had survived her ordeal at sea. More than when that awful Censor captain had captured her and she accidentally—on purpose—set the tower ablaze. Even though her aunt was nearby—somewhere out in the Bay—she and Pia were alone on an island in the middle of gods only knew where with no food and no water and only a faint hope of rescue.

"Gatina, calm yourself," Pia said firmly as she sat up. Her voice was level but very serious. Matronly, almost. In fact, it was a tone Gatina had not heard before. Pia sounded like Aunt Beah.

"I'm *perfectly* calm," Gatina argued. "We're just stranded on an empty beach, barely alive, and no one knows where we are. That's a cause for concern."

"My mother is a *mage*," Pia reminded her. "Your parents are magi. Your brother is a mage. *We* are magi. Mother will stop at nothing to find us; believe me. She hunted for my father for almost *two years* before she finally returned home. It is our job to remain safe until she does find us."

"How can she find us if we don't even know where we are?" Gatina countered.

"I guarantee that *somebody* knows about this island," Pia soothed. "People have been sailing these waters for centuries now. It's called the Shipwrecker's Bower, remember? Her devotees patrol these waters, looking for people like us and wrecked ships to salvage. It happens frequently here. And they are duty-bound to rescue all castaways. I promise you others have been here before."

"And probably died here," Gatina pointed out.

"Some, perhaps—if they didn't keep their heads. But the Shipwrecker protects those who do. In fact, I bet that there is already a shrine to the Shipwrecker on this island, someplace. There's bound to be. We will find it. But we won't find it if we panic, nor will we find it if we do not take care to keep ourselves safe."

Gatina looked at Pia curiously. "What do you mean? A shrine to the Shipwrecker? Do you mean like a temple or an altar?"

Gatina couldn't imagine a temple being out there, but the idea of a shrine gave her hope. She remembered hearing the sailors talk about their many superstitions. Then again, they also talked about impossible places they visited, talking porpoises, and people with their faces in the middle of their chests.

"There might be an altar involved, but that's secondary. A Shipwrecker's shrine is a way that castaways honor the goddess for preserving them," Pia explained. "The tradition is that anyone rescued from a wreck builds a shrine to the Shipwrecker and leaves an offering that could help a future castaway: water, food, even medicine and tools. If we find it, it could save us. Of course, we'll have to leave offerings when we're rescued," she informed her.

Gatina looked at the belt of vegetation at the edge of the empty beach. The only things other than her cousin that she saw were sand, trees and water. It was absolutely desolate but also peaceful and beautiful. She had never found herself in a situation such as this before. There was nothing nearby.

She considered what she knew. Instead of giving way to more panic or allowing the fear that kept bubbling up in her to take hold, she breathed and took stock of the situation. Family doctrine indicated that you make the best of your situation, no matter how dire, and that was what she was determined to do. Pia was right. *Nothing good comes from panic*, she had often heard her mother say.

"I'm just afraid," she admitted quietly.

Pia nodded in understanding. "I am too. But you survived that storm last night. So did I. And we are together. We are alive. We are uninjured. And we are safe at the moment." She pulled Gatina into a side embrace. "And if we want to stay that way, there are crucial things we must do."

Gatina nodded. She knew they needed basic things to survive, water most of all.

"We need water, but not from the Bay—that's too salty and will not help us. We need to find a spring or a stream, if there is one on this island. If not, we need rainwater. I'm sure we can find it. There have to be puddles from the squall. And there is bound to be junk washed up we can salvage and use. We can go look together." Pia stood and reached a hand down for Gatina, who gratefully accepted it.

To her surprise, as they started down the beach together, Gatina noticed debris washed up on the beach that she hadn't before. The squall had pushed all manner of junk onto the beach, and some of it was bound to be useful. There was driftwood in plenty, and within a few minutes, they'd also found a few other bits of useful trash: a round bung from a keg, Gatina's oar, a scrap of fishing net, a few pieces of torn sailcloth. They collected it all together.

"There's our poor gig," Gatina noted as they walked by its shattered remains a few hundred yards from where they'd come ashore. "Or what's left of it." The small boat had protected them and carried them through the storm, but now all that remained were shards of the boat's port side, the bench, and a few large chunks of wood. There was a length of rope half-buried in the sand under it, they discovered.

"We can certainly use that wood to make a fire. Even though it's hot now, I suspect it will be cooler at night. We can use the wood for a signal fire to alert passing ships, too," she suggested. "Or maybe shelter. And rope is always useful." Pia turned around fully and scanned the horizon. "Oh, my," she said, surprise in her voice.

Gatina whirled around, unsure what to make of it until she, too, saw what Pia had seen. From this vantage point, much more of the island was visible to them. There was a lush forest of green-topped hills behind them. They weren't particularly tall hills, but their emerald finery and gentle slope, enwrapped in a mantle of sea fog, made a beautiful scene.

"Blessed Darkness," she said, understanding Pia's reaction. "That *is* spectacular."

"Well, we can't eat the view," Pia said, after a few moments of reflection. "Let's start with water. Or a fire. Or both."

She doubted they would need to search long to find firewood. The trees stretched up the central hill toward the sky like a staircase. There should be plenty of wood within, not to mention the driftwood that seemed abundant on the shore. She wondered if the Shipwrecker's shrine was on top of the hill. She hoped not.

"You don't think the shrine is up *there*, do you?" she asked, frowning.

Pia shook her head. "Well, at least not *all* the way up there. It needs to be accessible to people down here," she said. "We should probably start our hunt for water first. And maybe for food. And gather dry wood for a fire." Gatina watched her cousin study the landscape. Pia was puzzling something out, she could tell. She recognized the expression. It resembled her father's when he was trying to figure out a problem. Gatina did not prod her to action.

She got the sense that whatever she was doing, it was important, and that she would speak when she was ready. Gatina occupied herself with fashioning a sled out of the sailcloth, rope and a few pieces of the broken gig to carry the rest of the odds and ends that had washed ashore. She realized they would need a way to move firewood, and she knew that dragging it would be far more practical than carrying it.

When Pia was ready, so was Gatina. She had managed to pry smaller boards off their skiff, and she had found some bits of dry driftwood. All of that was in her sled. Pia nodded in appreciation.

"That's very smart, cousin," she said approvingly. "I think we need to mark this spot as best we can and mark our path once we are up higher. This area will be flooded at high tide," she reasoned. She pointed to the dryer, whiter sand nearest the forest. "That's where we'll do best to build a campsite. Where it's dry and will be shaded by the forest in the afternoon sun."

Gatina's sled was heavier than she thought, but she managed until they reached a slight incline. Fortunately, her cousin noticed. Pia grabbed the rope just below Gatina's hand. That made the work much easier and faster. When they reached the shadow of the trees, they stopped pulling and collapsed.

"This looks like a lovely spot for a camp," Gatina said. She lay back on the sand, which felt refreshing and cool, thanks to the canopy of shade from the trees at her back.

Pia laughed. "In truth," she agreed. "I'll find us some water once I catch my breath. You make camp."

While Pia searched, Gatina used one of the bits of driftwood to dig out a circle in the sand and create a deep depression. It was easier than finding rocks or shells, she realized, to make a proper fire barrier. She was already shipwrecked. The last thing she needed was an out-of-control fire on top of that. But she wanted to get it set, to be ready for the inevitable night. She was caught off guard, laying out the driftwood, when she heard Pia's shouts.

Alarmed, Gatina drew her shadowblade and ran toward Pia's voice.

Gatina found her several hundred yards farther up the beach, waving her arms over her head excitedly. As Gatina got closer, her cousin pointed to the sand. But Gatina had no idea what she meant until she was within twenty feet or so. That was when she saw the arrow.

The closer she got to Pia, the more surreal the situation seemed to her. There was a long arrow sticking out of the sand. Except it wasn't, exactly. It was actually sticking out of the shoulder of a man who had collapsed on the sand: the mariner they had tried to rescue.

Thankfully, he was still breathing, though unconscious. He was lying on his side, curled up into a protective ball. He was also both incredibly pink from sunburn and pale from the blood loss that had stained his shirt and the surrounding sand.

"Maiden's Mercy, he's alive!" Pia squealed excitedly. "Careful; help me turn him over," she directed. "I think we can get that shaft out of him."

"Do we move him and then remove the arrow or remove the arrow first?" Gatina asked. She wasn't sure they could move him without removing it. The pain might be too much. She knelt, not knowing how to help him. She had little medical training other than cuts and bruises.

"If you try to pull it without a bandage, he could bleed to death," Pia pointed out. "It goes through cleanly, without hitting his lungs or any major arteries," she reported, after examining the wound. When she touched the protruding head on the front of his shoulder, the man winced and moaned. "There's no way to move him with this here."

"Break it off, then," Gatina suggested, handing her cousin her sword.

Water and fire were their immediate needs. A wounded sailor was not. But the Shipwrecker had decided otherwise, Gatina realized.

It was a miracle that the mariner was still breathing, Gatina recognized. The arrow went through the muscle of his shoulder from behind and it looked as though it had pierced a chunk of muscle—but it had missed bone. It did not appear to have struck anything vital. She knew they couldn't move him without causing extreme pain, and she was pretty sure her cousin didn't want to do that, but he had to be moved. He was fortunate to be alive. He had somehow ended up on this island and in their path, she realized.

Pia exhaled and nodded. "I need you to hold him steady and tightly while I break the arrow off so that I can pull it out," Pia said. "Thank all of the gods that he is unconscious. Because this is going to hurt like seven hells."

"We did rescue him—or tried to," Gatina reasoned as her cousin prepared to do what she wouldn't have dared. "I suppose we should keep trying."

"It is custom that we render aid to those in need," Pia explained firmly as she used the shadowblade to snap the wooden shaft of the arrow close to the head. The mariner moaned painfully. "The Shipwrecker's Truce declares it. That's the custom that we have to follow."

Gatina looked at Pia and nodded. She had no idea what the Shipwrecker's Truce was.

"He's a handsome fellow under all that sand," Pia observed after she threw the arrow shaft aside. "That was the hard part. Now we have to remove the rest of the arrow from his shoulder."

Based on Gatina's cursory examination, she determined that he was no older than her brother. He had very few facial wrinkles—mostly around his eyes. His scraggly beard concealed a strong jaw. But when she felt the man's face, it was clammy to the touch. She frowned.

"He's feverish, I think," she reported, frowning.

"I don't doubt it. It's been hours since he was hit," she reasoned, as she propped him up with her knee.

She helped Pia open the man's ripped tunic to check the severity of the wound. They found a well-muscled chest and wide, strong back. She could see his abdominal muscles, too. He had a lean trunk, that of a man who was active and worked hard for a living. She noticed that Pia had paused the examination, so she glanced up and caught her cousin simply staring at the man. She thought that was odd. Perhaps she sensed something more to her cousin's inspection than mere necessity. Before she could ask, Pia began ripping the shirt from around the arrow.

"We need to get this out of him," she said with a grunt as she exposed the wound—and the fragment of arrow still in his shoulder.

Gatina, of course, had come to that conclusion already. He had been shot through the back of his shoulder, and the arrow came through the front.

"It will be easier to remove it here and while he's unconscious," Pia decided. "We can make camp here, I guess. We're high enough away from the tide."

After some discussion, Gatina ran back to the place where she'd started to make camp and undid all the work she'd done. In a few moments, she returned to the beach, laden with all their scant possessions. She used her blade to hack much of her sailcloth skirt away and presented it to Pia as a bandage.

"I need you to hold him as still as you can," she directed. "I'm going to pull the arrow all the way through," she explained. "I think that's the best way to go."

Gatina placed her palms flat against the man's shoulder to brace him. the nimble fingers of both of her hands around the bloody arrowhead, close to the man's shoulder. She could feel a fresh drip of blood spurt from the wound. Then she scooted her knees closer to his chest and pressed them into it. "Ready," she said, looking at Pia.

Pia's face was grim, Gatina saw. But her mind was made up, even though she seemed nervous. "I've never done anything like this before," her cousin confessed. "But this seems like the right thing to do."

Gatina nodded. "I think it's the only thing we can do," she said.

Pia exhaled loudly and said, "On three. One. Two. *Three!*"

Gatina held him and tried to brace the man as best she could while Pia pulled the protruding arrow through the wound. It did not go easily, alas, and their patient groaned loudly in pain each time she attempted to remove it. It took several attempts and a good bit of effort. Gatina felt bad for the poor man each time he moaned. But she also knew he would feel better without a sharp bit of wood and metal piercing his body.

Finally, with one great pull, the broken shaft came free in her cousin's hands.

"Maiden's Mercy!" Pia swore, wiping her brow with the back of her arm as she pressed a folded wad of sailcloth into the wounds. Sand and sweat and a bit of the man's blood dripped down the side of her face, along her hairline. "That was one well-made arrow." Gatina held up the bloody prize for her inspection. "Looks like a clean snap—no splintering, which is good for him."

Pia ripped off a portion of her dress and placed it on the sand. . "Let's lay him down gently," she said. "I . . . I don't think we should move him just yet."

The man exhaled but was no longer grimacing. He remained unconscious, which was, indeed, a mercy.

"All right, I suppose this is home now," Gatina decided, and set to remaking their camp.

"We need water more than ever now," Pia said quietly as they quickly erected a makeshift shelter with the oar, the bit of sailcloth they'd recovered, and a few bits of driftwood. "If he doesn't get some soon, I don't like his chances."

"We need a fire—to alert any ships," A fire might help," Gatina suggested.

"I'll start one while you look for water," Pia said. "We should probably dry our clothes and make sure we are able to stay warm, in any case. We don't know how cool it gets at night."

Finished with their shelter, Gatina stood. "I'll go find water. I make no promises about finding other wounded castaways," she pointed out, her voice light.

"Honestly, it's a good sign that we found him," Pia considered. "And it's even better that we could help him. The Shipwrecker will find favor in that."

"I'm not feeling particularly well disposed toward that particular goddess at the moment," Gatina grumbled. Using the cantrip she had learned at the abbey, Gatina started a fire in a newly dug pit and piled it with driftwood until it burned brightly.

"Don't say that!" Pia admonished. "The Shipwrecker saved us from drowning. We're protected by her truce."

"Pia, what is this truce? The Shipwrecker's Truce? I think I read about it," she explained.

Her cousin was busy tying her shift between her legs, to fashion some sort of unusual but practical garment, Gatina saw.

"It's a sacred custom," she said simply. "It's a truce between castaways that regulates your actions while you're stranded. But it's also a promise to the Shipwrecker."

"What kind of promise?" Gatina asked suspiciously.

"First, none of the survivors can fight. Ideally, everyone works together until they're rescued—even sworn enemies. You share all food and water equally—though the injured and ill get priority. You render aid to any who need it. You offer shelter to whoever requests it. And you cooperate to send signals to anyone who might see you and send rescue."

"That seems simple enough," Gatina reasoned.

"It is," Pia assured. "The Shipwrecker's Truce is twofold. It dictates that no castaway can deprive another of anything they need from the shrine. The second part means nobody can attack another—not unless they want to face a dire curse. No sane mariner wants to get on the Shipwrecker's bad side," she said, shaking her head.

"Why not?" Gatina asked, mystified.

"According to the lore, those who are shipwrecked and deserted must build a shrine when they are rescued. If there is already a shrine, then they must leave offerings there. The offerings, or tribute, are to both the goddess and the next castaways." Pia bent down to check the man's fever. Then she continued her lecture.

"But the last part of the ritual says that anyone who has been shipwrecked is *cursed*, even if they're rescued."

"Cursed?" Gatina asked, skeptically.

"Yes. But don't worry. You have a year, from the date of your rescue, to avert it. After that, you're marked. It's bad luck to carry you on a ship until the curse is lifted. And the only way that curse can be lifted is by completing a series of sacred tasks that end with the ringing of the Eight Bells." Pia walked away from the campsite. "Then you won't be bad luck to sail with anymore."

"That . . . sounds complicated. What kind of tasks?" Gatina asked, concerned.

"Don't worry, I'll fill you in on that part later. We have more important things to deal with now. Like finding water."

The girls spent most of the rest of daylight taking turns exploring both the beach and the wilderness behind it while the other watched and tended the wounded mariner.

Their efforts resulted in some unexpected bounty: a glass wine bottle someone had discarded overboard before it made its way to shore, two long staves of a barrel, and another, smaller piece of sailcloth. The forest yielded a handful of blackberries, dry wood for the fire, and a leafy bough they used to shield their patient from the elements.

Pia reported that there were signs of wild boar and other animals, should they need to hunt. As neither of them had ever hunted before, that seemed like a daunting prospect.

Most importantly, Pia had found a puddle filled with rainwater and filled the bottle with it. They were able to get a few swallows down the throat of their patient before refilling it once each for themselves. That, the berries, and a few clams they'd discovered and toasted over the fire were enough to satisfy the growing emptiness in their stomachs.

Gatina sat in front of the fire that night and considered her predicament as Pia searched for crabs on the beach. She had wanted an adventure when she sailed with the *Daydream*, but this was not exactly what she had in mind. She didn't feel like a capable apprentice shadowthief; at that moment, she felt like a miserable girl with only the slimmest of hopes. She missed her brother and her parents, even her aunt and cousin Jordi.

As tired as she had grown on the ship, this was not an ideal situation. She was on land, certainly, but she had no idea where in Callidore this land was, other than out in the Western Bay, somewhere in the Shipwrecker's Bower. Her aunt had said there were countless unknown, nameless islands there. This had to be one of them.

She wondered if she would ever see her family again. She began to second-guess herself. And her cousin. Should they have gone out at all to help the mariners? Should they have gone a second time?

No, she knew that they had done the right thing. Their actions had saved three lives. *What could be more righteous than that?* she wondered. Her conscience was clear. She quickly dismissed her imagination's suggestion of a dire fate in store for them. She had faith. Blessed Darkness had kept her safe at sea in a storm, so there was hope, she reasoned. And there seemed to be something to this Shipwrecker, she reflected.

The campsite, as basic as it was, was sufficient for the moment. They had shade from the trees, water from the rain, and the possibility of ample seafood if they worked to catch it. There were most likely more berries and other fruit deeper in the forest behind them. Gatina thought about foraging for berries. During her summer at Palomar Abbey, she had worked in the garden. She tried to remember which berries were safe. The three blackberries she'd eaten had been delicious, and she started to crave the taste again. But she did not want to leave the wounded man alone, in case he woke.

So, she studied the land. There was nothing on the horizon that she could see. She pivoted and looked at the trees behind her. She couldn't tell what types of trees the forest held, but she could see that the hill was steep. If there was a shrine was up there, it would take at least a day to reach it. She thought it would be impractical to put a shrine atop a hill, especially if wounded or exhausted folk needed to reach it. She hoped her cousin was correct.

She noticed a few trees that were similar to what her aunt had at her house in Prejestia Village, the wide-leafed trees. Gatina thought those might be useful for shelter. She checked on the unconscious man's wound again, then walked toward the edge of the tree line. She vowed to be quick, but the farther in she went, the more her instincts took over and led her to a clump of spiky aloe plants.

She remembered that aloe was useful for wounds and burns, so she delicately broke off several leaves and tucked those into her smock. On her way back to the campsite, she came across a cluster of wild orange trees. There were only a few ripe fruits hanging down, but they were high out of the reach of whatever animals grazed here. She accidentally kicked an orange that was on the ground, overripe and recently fallen. That was fortunate. Gatina knew she did not have the energy to climb a tree.

She picked up the fruit and found three more nearby. Those went into her smock, which she tied around her back a second time to create a pouch.

When she made her way back to camp, Gatina found Pia pacing around the fire.

"Where were you? I've been waiting here twenty minutes. I was worried about you, cousin!" Pia said accusingly as she checked on the mariner.

Gatina felt a brief sting of shame. "I'm sorry. I didn't realize I was gone that long. I thought it would be smart to look for leaves and maybe some fruit," she said as she dumped out the bounty she had gathered. "I found aloe and oranges."

She looked at her cousin, who grinned at the oranges. "That's kind of what got us into this mess, isn't it?"

Gatina laughed, then asked, "Did you find water?"

Pia victoriously held up a large conch shell, almost the size of a serving bowl. "I found water *and* a drinking container along the beach. This is the largest conch shell I've ever seen. It's perfect," she said as she tilted it up to her mouth, tipped her head back, and demonstrated with a long sip. "And there's a little freshwater stream about a half-mile down the beach that's cleaner than that puddle. It'll be easier to help him drink if the water is wholesome," she reasoned.

She passed the shell to Gatina, who took several long pulls from it. The shell was cool, nearly cold, and heavy. The water was the best thing she had ever tasted. Even better than Drella's pies or a fresh, crisp apple.

After they helped the man drink more water, which led to a bit of spill and an improvised method involving a bit of Pia's dress dipped into the shell, Pia spread aloe on his wounds and his face. Her search had also yielded a brace of large crabs she had caught by throwing rocks at them. They didn't have as much meat in them as she expected, but the flesh inside their shell was delicious after they toasted them over the fire, especially with an orange for dessert. A few morsels kept the pangs of hunger at bay.

"So, cousin, what is this Shipwrecker's Truce Curse?" Gatina finally asked as she licked her fingers clean of crab. "You said it was a promise. What do you mean?"

"Well, it's pretty clear. First, none of the survivors can fight. Ideally, everyone works together until they're rescued—even sworn enemies. You share all food and water equally—though the injured and ill get priority. You render aid to any who need it. You offer shelter to whoever requests it. And you cooperate to send signals to anyone who might see you and send rescue," Pia explained.

"That seems simple enough," Gatina reasoned.

"It is," Pia assured. "The Shipwrecker's Truce is twofold. It dictates that no castaway can deprive another of anything they need from the shrine.

The second part means nobody can attack another—not unless they want to face a dire curse. No sane mariner wants to get on the Shipwrecker's bad side," she said, shaking her head.

"Why not?" Gatina asked, mystified.

"According to the lore, those who are shipwrecked and deserted must build a shrine when they are rescued. If there is already a shrine, then they must leave offerings there. The offerings, or tribute, are to both the goddess and the next castaways." Pia bent down to check the man's fever. Then she continued her lecture.

"But the last part of the ritual says that anyone who has been shipwrecked is *cursed*, even if they're rescued."

"Cursed?" Gatina asked, skeptically.

"Yes. But don't worry. You have a year, from the date of your rescue, to avert it. After that, you're marked. It's bad luck to carry you on a ship until the curse is lifted. And the only way that curse can be lifted is by completing a series of sacred tasks that end with the ringing of the Eight Bells." Pia walked away from the campsite. "Then you won't be bad luck to sail with anymore."

"That . . . sounds complicated. What kind of tasks?" Gatina asked, concerned.

Pia sighed. "Well, we need to ask Mother to be certain, but I don't think the tasks are too terrible. Mostly things like saying the right prayers on the right day, honoring all six divinities in some little way, drinking a cup of Maiden's Blood at sunset—"

"Maiden's Blood?" Gatina asked, wrinkling her nose.

Pia laughed. "That's a mixture of cheap, strong red wine and seawater. The old salts swear by it. But it is pretty nasty. I say it's worth any price if we're rescued; wouldn't you agree?"

Instead of answering, Gatina quietly considered what Pia told her. To her, it sounded silly and childish, but in her brief time working on a ship, she had learned how seriously mariners, particularly the Sea Lords, took their ancient superstitions. Perhaps there was something to it. Besides, who was she to snub a superstition? If her own patron divinity had seen it fit to save her from nearly drowning, then who was she to judge another religion?

"Well, I suppose we should try to find the shrine tomorrow, shouldn't we?" Gatina suggested.

"It would be helpful," Pia agreed, glancing at their patient with concern. "His fever is getting bad. The aloe you found might help, but if his wound gets infected, that could kill him."

Gatina considered. "The climb up those hills would take a day at least. The shrine must be somewhere along that way—you wouldn't put it on the beach, nor in a dangerous forest. Perhaps not at the crest—I can't imagine that anyone would build one so high up—but somewhere high enough to protect it from the tides and the storms."

Her cousin looked past her, up to the steeper hills looming in the twilight. "The next time I go for water in the daylight, I will scout and see what I can find," Pia said. "The island doesn't seem terribly large, but distance can be deceiving. If there is a shrine, it must be nearby."

Gatina's response was interrupted by the rumbling of her belly. Pia took note.

"Do you think you could also find some more food?" Gatina asked with a laugh. "This supper was lovely, but I haven't eaten more than a mouthful since our last meal on the *Daydream*."

"We'll find something," she soothed. "We'll make a proper search tomorrow. I'm going to fetch more water from the stream tonight. Just keep the fire lit through the night. Hopefully, some passing ship will see it."

Gatina added more wood to the fire and noted that she had plenty to get through the next few hours.

While she waited for Pia to return, Gatina gathered more leafy boughs to add to the shelter. The skies were clear, but she understood all too well now just how quickly a squall could blow up. She wanted the wounded mariner as protected as possible.

She layered wide leaves on top of each other. Then she pulled two longer sticks from the wood pile and set those on top, parallel to each other. She ripped more strips off her shift to secure the leaves. Thankful she had her shadowblade, she removed it from the sheath at her back and used it to punch holes through the leaves. She wove the fabric through and secured it to the sticks.

Gatina reached down and tugged her makeshift tent closer to cover the man. She propped it up over him, using more driftwood to brace it. Satisfied by her work, she sat under the lean-to and had a very long sip of cloudy rainwater from the wine bottle. Afterward, she followed Pia's example and gave their patient more water, using the fabric as a sponge.

She was gratified to see that he drank more of it than spilled down his face.

"I do not know who you are, but I am thankful we found you," she murmured to the unconscious man. It was nice to just talk. "Maybe Pia's right. You might be a sign from the Shipwrecker herself."

That's when she glanced back up at the hill behind them—and saw a light.

It was midway up, far back from the beach—but it was unmistakably a fire. She stifled a yelp of surprise and used magesight to take a closer look. Alas, it was too distant and too high up to make out any details. But one thing was clear.

They were not alone on the island.

CHAPTER FOURTEEN

FLOTSAM, JETSAM, AND A RED-HEADED STRANGER

> *Though there are six major cults in the Sea Lord pantheon corresponding to the six major divinities, the folklore of their culture is replete with many and diverse demigods, cultural heroes, and chthonic monsters. Some are mere lackeys of the six major divinities, while others are personifications of the forces that do not quite fit easily into their theology. Some of these are representations of common forces that impact their lives. Others are quite strange and unusual to the eye of the outsider.*
> —from **Sea Lords, Their Cults, Religious Customs, and Traditions**

GATINA WOKE AT DAWN, SHIVERING ON THE COOL SAND. FOR A BRIEF moment, she had forgotten where she was, and she started to panic. She did not hear the waves slapping against the side of the ship she'd gotten used to in the past weeks. Instead, she heard the *clickety-click* of crab claws nearby, then birds singing their morning songs and the hum of insects.

And she was cold. The breeze that blew in from the Bay was cool and had kept her sleep from being fitful. But the sand under her body was sucking the warmth from her. Once she remembered that she was stranded on an island somewhere in the middle of nowhere, her mind was awash in other dire reminders.

The wounded man needed her attention in order to stay alive, she realized blearily. The fire needed to be tended for both warmth and a rescue signal. It had died out overnight, she saw when she finally opened her eyes. She added wood and watched as it began to smolder. She waited until the first orange flames began to rise before she checked on the wounded mariner. She was relieved to find him breathing steadily, though his skin remained hot to the touch. She woke her cousin to alert her.

"It's morning," she said unnecessarily when Pia came awake. "Go warm up a bit. And check on our patient," she added wearily. "He's alive, but..."

Pia sat up quickly, then got to her feet. She was cold, too, and warmed her hands gratefully over the fire before bending down to check on the man.

"He needs water," she decided. She stood and stretched. "Let's walk down the beach to the stream and get freshwater and see what else we can find. I want to show you where it is. It won't take long. He'll be fine until we return, I suspect. Maybe the Shipwrecker will grant us a boon on the way," she said as she picked up the conch shell and they made their way down toward the water's edge.

"Six fried eggs and a rasher of bacon would be nice," Gatina suggested sullenly.

"Anything is possible." Pia shrugged.

As they walked, Gatina kept her eyes trained on the distant horizon, scanning for any sign of any ship that might be passing by. While there was no sign of a ship, she discovered that there was plenty of debris lining the beach, swept in from the tide. Her cousin saw it too. Gatina looked at her and they ran in the direction of something that looked like a lump of off-white fabric.

Gatina reached it first: a large, stained, and torn swath of sailcloth balled up and strewn with kelp and sand. From its size, it was far larger than the scrap they'd recovered previously, enough for a real shelter.

She made out a bit of tawny-colored rope and realized it still had its line attached—another prize. It was wound tightly around the folds of the sail. She knew both would be helpful for their camp. She might be able to fashion a full tent for them, which would provide real shade. But when she bent to lift it up, it was heavier than it should be. Something was weighing it down. Something metallic. The buzz of metal called to her, ringing in her head as it often did. Her unusual gift hit harder than it normally did. Probably because she was hungry and tired, she reasoned.

She sank to her knees and used her hands as shovels to move the sand off the sail. Then she dug underneath and tried to lift it, but there was still something holding it down on one side. Frustrated, she reached for a shell and used that to help her move more sand. When she had cleared off more, she sank her fingers under the fabric, trying to feel what might be holding it in place. That's when she felt the pull of the object.

When her fingers danced across its surface, it was round, smooth, cool to the touch. She continued to dig and then she gave it a tug. The force of its release nearly knocked her over and sprayed sand everywhere. But this was a true gift from the Shipwrecker, she saw: a battered copper kettle, the kind that most ships carried. It was plain and unadorned and had several dents, but it seemed to be without holes when she brushed the encrusted sand away.

"Now, *that's* a find!" Beah said excitedly when Gatina presented it to her triumphantly. "We can carry water with it and cook a few things properly!"

"I wonder what ship she came from," Gatina said, as she bundled up the liberated sailcloth.

"Probably some poor barque too far from port that got caught in the squall in the Bower," Pia guessed. "Their misfortune is our blessing. If that pot made its way here, then it's likely other things did, too."

They spent the next half hour scouring the beach for more prizes. Indeed, it appeared that some unfortunate ship had been wrecked, or at least damaged, and had contributed some of its contents to the island. Using her ability to sense metal, she quickly discovered a wealth of debris buried in the sands. After a diligent search, she stood up and gathered the items she had found. Pia met her next to the copper kettle, lifted her dress at the hem, and dumped out her treasures from her makeshift basket.

"I found all sorts of flotsam! Look!" she said as she began holding up the odds and ends. "Spoons and a cup! An empty wineskin! Two bottles! And this odd little box," she said, holding up a square wooden box that fit into her palm. "I found a basket, too, but it was all caved in and ruined."

Gatina looked at her, confused by the term even though she had heard it before. "What did you call that?"

"Flotsam. It means things that were not deliberately thrown overboard," she explained. "Other than the sail and pot, did you find anything?"

Gatina nodded and showed off her own finds. "A belt buckle, two bronze buttons from someone's coat, a rusty knife blade, a boat cleat, two brass rings that came from Darkness knows where, and a . . . *something*," she said, shaking her head at the odd bit of iron she'd unearthed.

"That's a chain plate," Pia explained, after examination. "It's used to secure the mast to the hull. That's bad news for whoever lost it. I don't know what we can use if for, but it's . . . *something*," she agreed.

"We have enough vessels to bring back plenty of water now," Gatina pointed out as they rinsed the empty bottles out in the surf. "That should help keep our patient from drying out."

"I only wish that this skin had actual wine in it." Pia sighed. "His shoulder is getting infected. Alcohol is a natural disinfectant. Without it . . . I don't know how long we can keep him alive," she admitted.

They made their way back to camp with fresh water in the newly cleaned pot, the bottles, and the wineskin. Their patient was just as they'd left him, propped up in the shade of the shelter, in front of the fire. Pia hurried to his side, careful not to spill any of the water. She picked up the bit of fabric she had torn from her dress earlier and dipped it into the pot. Gatina watched, fascinated that her cousin cared so much for a stranger. She realized that Pia was very good at caregiving.

"How did you learn to do that—healing?" she asked.

Pia moved on to sponge the man's brow, cleaning his face and neck. "Well, I don't know that I ever really *learned*," she said, pausing her efforts to answer. "I suppose I just picked it up over time. I just paid attention when the physicker came to see to someone's wounds or illness. It's what Mother does for us when we have a fever," she explained as she daubed his brow. "I hope this helps to cool him down. It works for us. It helps bring down a fever."

When she finished wiping him down, she lifted the conch shell to his mouth and encouraged him to sip. He did, but he still did not wake, Gatina saw. She also saw the worry cross Pia's face quickly.

"Well, it's all we can do. With the Salt Crone's blessing, he'll heal," she said. She reached for the aloe leaf Gatina had found.

While Pia busied herself with applying aloe to the man's wounds, Gatina began her own project—creating a stronger shelter for the three of them.

She stood and tossed the fabric out in front of her, thankful that the breeze helped by picking up the end and unfurling it. When it landed on the ground, she put rocks on the three points. She was happy to see that it was a sail and it had very little damage, a few small tears and one puncture. Overall, it was intact. And based on its size, it was likely the foresail from a midsized vessel.

Once it was dried out, she was satisfied that she could use it to craft a better shelter. She spent an hour arranging and rearranging how it hung over the mariner, using the oar and a few sticks from the forest to finally create a shelter that would provide shade and shed the rain, as well as break the winds if they weren't too strong.

Pia gently strummed the taut rope that supported the structure. The shelter vibrated but showed no signs of collapse. She clapped her hands in victory.

"This works! You did well!"

"It's enough to keep him from being exposed to the elements," Gatina conceded. "Now, if we can just get some food to fill that pot..."

"I want to stay near him today," Pia said, looking at the mariner with concern. "Keep water in him, at least. I'll see if I can't find more fruit nearby."

"I'll keep looking for more... flotsam on the beach," Gatina suggested. "Maybe I can catch a few more crabs or find a barrel of spirits or something. It stands to reason that if a ship went down, there might be more debris further down the beach. Besides," she admitted, "I want to look for that shrine if it exists. I thought I saw a fire up on the hill last night."

"A fire?" Pia asked, concerned.

"Yes, a fire." Gatina sighed. "We might not be alone here."

"Be careful, Kitten," Beah warned. "There are some islands with tribes on them—descendants of castaways and criminals who were marooned for their crimes. Some of them have been rumored to eat... *people*."

Gatina was aghast at the notion. "You can't eat *people*! Eating people is *wrong*!" she gasped, disgusted at the very thought.

"Yet it happens." Beah shrugged. "Just be wary of anyone you meet. Native tribes don't usually obey the Shipwrecker's Truce," she warned.

Just then, their patient let out a slow sigh, which immediately got her cousin's attention. Pia went to check on him. "He seems to be doing better after a drink," she noted, cautiously. "You go ahead and start your scavenging. I'm going to talk to him while he sleeps. That helps sometimes," she said, staring at him hopefully.

As she made her way down the beach, Gatina was amazed by how peaceful the island was. When it was quiet and calm, it truly was a beautiful place. And despite the circumstances of how she had arrived, she welcomed the calm. As far as she could tell, the beach was empty. She heard no voices and saw no footprints or signs of life anywhere. She supposed that was good. Footprints might indicate danger. Pia's tale of savage tribes of cannibals had made her a bit jumpy.

Unfortunately, most of the debris she found along the beach was rubbish: bits of rope and netting, shreds of sailcloth, broken glass that had been smoothed by the tides and the sand, odd bits of wood that were clearly timbered planks from some ship. But she did find a few more things she thought might be useful. Part of a brass lantern, though the glass was missing, a small lead weight, and what might have been part of a whetstone. She wondered if the Shipwrecker's blessing ended with the treasures she and Pia had found earlier.

Gatina did find several good-sized sticks, so she gathered those as she went and stuck them upright in the sand as markers to make sure she didn't get lost. She reasoned that she could take them back to the campsite on her return trip. She also found beautiful shells, an army of sand crabs, and bits of driftwood along the beach. But she didn't see much more in the way of useful flotsam.

The water was calm today, she saw, but the waves still crashed softly on the sandbar that seemed to ring the island at low tide. While she walked, Gatina found peace in that sound. She marveled at how different they sounded when she wasn't clinging to an oar for dear life. Her mind began to drift back to that terrible night.

Though it seemed long past, she remembered it was only the day before that she had been shipwrecked. They had not been on the island for that long. Yet time seemingly stood still there. There was no one to tell her what to do, no enemies lurking behind every bush or wave, no mission to fulfill save keeping herself alive.

Instead of becoming sad, Gatina found the positives in her situation. For the first time in a long time—since before Duke Lenguin was assassinated—she was relieved of the responsibilities she had carried. Politics didn't matter there. Duty didn't matter. Her family's struggle against Count Vichetral and his cronies seemed far away, as if they had happened to someone else.

Her new responsibilities were simple. She and her cousin were alive. They had shelter, food, and water. And they'd managed to save the life of a wounded man. She took solace in that. Helping others made her happy. Her life had become incredibly simplified by the squall, she realized. As she walked down the beach, she could not help but feel free, no longer a thief or a mage but simply a girl on a lonely beach, enjoying nature and searching for something to put in her growling belly. It was a primal feeling but one she realized she relished.

Gatina could not help but wonder how long it would be before they were found. She missed her family, of course, and hoped that her brother and parents and her cousins were hale and healthy. As much as she loved adventure, she loved her family more. She missed them. But she did enjoy the fact that—for once—it was just her and nobody else save Pia and the injured sailor.

She'd discovered in her older cousin a friend she didn't know she needed. She'd had others, and good ones, too, but none of them knew the entire truth of her life the way Pia did: her strange family, the secret profession they practiced, the intricacies of magic, the legacy that they carried. Pia knew it all, she understood it, and she even lived her own version of it. After all, Pia and Jordi were the children of a marriage between a Coastlord family of magi and a Sea Lord captain. As complicated as Gatina's life was, Pia's was just as strange.

Soon, her mind focused on the possibility of a Shipwrecker's shrine located somewhere on the island. The shrine could be anywhere, of course, and several times she stopped her walk and investigated the openings she saw in the forest that blanketed the interior of the island. They seemed to be game trails, mostly, but even a few hundred feet within the forest, there was no sign of a rock cairn, a cave, or a shelter that might conceal a cache of supplies.

Instead of panicking, Gatina used deductive reasoning. To her mind, the shrine had to be close to the beach to be accessible but far enough from the shore to be protected from the waves and wind. Higher ground would be logical too. Likely someplace near a natural source of fresh water. Anyone who was shipwrecked would want to be close to the water source, she reasoned.

Gatina continued, stopping briefly to dip her shell into a tiny stream to get a sip of water. And as she wandered, she came across something very curious. She found the remnants of a campfire.

She walked toward it cautiously. As she neared the fire circle, she got a sense that it was recent. She could smell the scent of woodsmoke, and the tiny pit of charcoal and ashes on the beach had yet to be disturbed by the Grand Tide—the periodic result of both moons being in the same section of sky at the same time.

It was no longer warm, but the tracks around the area were still visible and the driftwood stacked nearby was dry. She examined the tracks closely. It was hard to tell in the beach sand, but there seemed to be several sets. Someone had washed ashore there, she theorized. They'd built the fire, then moved on to a better position. Not the sort of thing the theoretical cannibal tribes might do, she reasoned.

But something that tugged at her from the sand near the fire suggested perhaps an even-worse scenario than natives hungry for human flesh. A broken arrow shaft, complete with metal point. It was identical to the one they'd removed from the mariner's shoulder.

She quickly scanned the area, her hand tightening on her walking stick, primed to react if needed. Her mind raced. What if there were Rats on the island? Had the longboat that had chased them suffered the same fate as their gig? Could the survivors come ashore there, even as she and Pia had?

That could be disastrous. Especially if their ship were to find them first.

A quick search proved that there was no one there. Gatina sifted through the area near the fire to check for anything she might use. She found nothing. Whoever had lit that fire was long gone. She knew that if others were on the island, they should be bound by the Shipwrecker's Truce, according to Pia. No harm could come to her under that truce—in theory. That gave her a modicum of peace. Still, she did not trust any Rats. She resolved to move on in search of the shrine.

She continued to survey the area along the beach where the high tide had receded, in hopes of finding anything useful. She went so far as to wade into the water up to her ankles, which provided her feet with a welcomed cool relief from the hot sand, the landscape in front of her shifted from a wide and straight beach to a curvy and shaded cove. As she rounded the bend and walked toward the cove, she stopped silently.

About twenty feet ahead of her, she saw someone. And from what Gatina could tell, that person appeared to be a young girl who was splashing in the water. Whoever she was, she wasn't a pirate. Or a cannibal savage. Certainly not a threat, and perhaps the indication that there was a settlement somewhere nearby.

Excited by the prospect of another person on the island, Gatina began walking toward her. She called out and waved as she closed the distance. She left enough room that either could quickly walk away if they chose. Despite being a shadowthief known for her stealth, this was neither the time nor the place for sneakiness.

When the girl heard Gatina's greeting, she didn't run in fear or cower at the sight of her—she turned around and smiled. As she got closer, Gatina saw the girl more clearly. She wore a curious expression on her face, but that gave way to a broad, slightly bucktoothed smile that Gatina found relieving and oddly inviting. This was a friend. She knew it in her soul. She could not explain how she knew it; she just did.

That was when Gatina exhaled. She had not realized that she had been holding her breath. But the girl's smile set her at ease. Truce or not, being shipwrecked after seeing the Rats shoot unarmed men had her on edge. But this girl looked like no threat. In fact, she realized, the girl was younger and a good four or five inches shorter than she.

But Gatina had questions—including, foremost, *Where are her parents?*

The girl wore a short stark-white shift that appeared to be clean and in good repair. And over her shift she wore a dark green cloak the same shade as the sea in a storm. A storm like the one Gatina had just survived.

The girl's long red hair hung in two messy braids above her ears. Each stuck out as if birds had nested on either side. Or as if she'd been on horseback through thick brush. It was comical-looking, but Gatina had both the presence of mind and social awareness to not laugh. She found it an unusual style, but given their circumstances, she didn't question it. The girl's fair skin was free of sunburn but dotted with a constellation of freckles across her nose and cheeks.

But her eyes were what struck Gatina. The girl's eyes mirrored the deep green of her cloak, nearly the same color as emeralds.

Gatina saw that the girl wasn't simply playing in the water. She was actually digging for clams. She held a shell that she used as a shovel and a basket woven from branches.

"Hello!" Gatina said closing the remaining distance that separated them. "Are you shipwrecked too?" she asked, her eyes searching the rest of the cove, which was empty. Of course, she had a lot of questions for the girl but didn't want to overwhelm her. Maybe she was the source of the campfire, she reasoned.

"Hello! I am called Pippa," the girl said amiably. "What's your name?"

The girl's directness caught Gatina off guard. She answered honestly, not with her alias.

"My name is Gatina," she said as she crouched on her thighs to bring her down to eye level with the girl.

"Would you like to play a game, Gatina?" Her green eyes sparkled in the sunlight, and she sounded excited. "I haven't had anyone to play with in *ages*."

Gatina considered the question. While her goal was to find the shrine, this girl might be able to tell her where it was. Playing a game with her was an excellent way to build camaraderie so she could ask her questions.

"I would love to play a game," Gatina decided. "Are you all alone on the island?" she asked, hoping her question came off as conversational, as she had intended it.

Excited, Pippa clapped her hands. She picked up a stick, knelt in the sand, and drew a grid in the sand. "Let's play noughts and crosses. You can be crosses," she decided. "You go first."

Gatina knelt beside her and reached for her own stick, marveling at how many sticks were readily available on this beach, and set to work. While she wanted the girl to open up to her, this *was* a competition, and she did not want to lose. This was also a game she had played since childhood. She beat the young girl quickly.

Instead of being sad about losing, Pippa was excited. She used her hand to wipe their marks clear and drew the grid again. "Let's play again!" she suggested.

Gatina noticed that Pippa had not answered her query. So, she tried again. "Have you been on the island long?" Gatina asked.

Pippa considered the question, biting her lower lip. "I suppose so, but it depends on how you look at it," she finally said. "I've been here as long as I've been here."

"Are you alone?" Gatina asked, figuring that perhaps the girl had lost track of time.

"No!" Pippa laughed. "You're here with me!"

"You could join us if you are," she invited. "It can sometimes be frightening to be on your own," she added, keeping her voice gentle as if she was talking to a frightened child. Pippa didn't seem frightened at all, however. Gatina made her cross mark in the center of the grid.

"I don't mind being alone," Pippa admitted. "I've been alone much of my life. Oh, except for my horse and my monkey. But they aren't here right now," she conceded. Gatina thought that was a bold claim, the kind a young child might make in order to impress an adult. Pippa made her mark in the top right corner. Gatina countered with one in the top left.

"Where are your parents?" Gatina asked lightheartedly.

"My father is lost at sea," she said matter-of-factly as she studied the board. "My mother . . . well, this is her island," she admitted. Pippa drew a circle beneath her first mark.

Gatina won the game with a third *x*, in a diagonal cross with the other two.

"Oh, you're *good* at this game," Pippa said. "Let's make this interesting, shall we? I challenge you to the best of ten games. The winner gets my basket of clams. And the loser gets whatever you have there." She motioned to Gatina's bundle. "I was going to cook these for dinner, but this is the most fun I've had in ages," she admitted.

Gatina looked over at the basket and saw that it was full. She imagined clams cooked in the pot over the fire and how delicious that would taste. And that got her stomach grumbling, and she realized just how hungry she was. She agreed quickly.

She won the next two games. When they began their third game, Gatina tried her questions again. "Are you a castaway too?" Pippa shook her head. "Oh, how long have you lived on the island? We only just arrived."

The girl looked at her quizzically. "I don't know. It's my home. One of them, at least. It's a nice place. I like it here. It's very peaceful, quiet," she said while she leaned back to consider Gatina's most recent move, a cross in the upper right corner. The girl quickly blocked it with her own nought.

"It is indeed. It's actually beautiful here," Gatina said, hoping she had not offended Pippa. "But you're not alone here, are you? I have my cousin with me. She's back at our camp." She hoped she struck a conversational and caring tone with her questions.

Gatina's new friend looked at her through her hair. Her braids crossed in front of her, covering her face. Instead of finding it unnerving, Gatina found it mysterious. "I am never really alone," she replied, which added to the mystery. "Mother is always watching over me."

"Oh. Well, I suppose that's good. My cousin, well, she sent me on a mission. I'm looking for a shrine or a temple so that I might pay our respects. Have you seen one?"

Pippa nodded, excited. "Yes, there is a shrine just over that hill." She pointed to the mountain behind them, and Gatina wondered if there might actually be larger ones on the island. "But the others might have already found it," Pippa said. "I don't know if anything is left."

Gatina let the girl win that round. Then Pippa won the round after that, and that was when Gatina realized that she was very good at this game. Gatina shifted her strategy. She had a second mission now—to win the clams. But she also needed more information about the shrine.

"Is there a path to the shrine?" she asked. "Have you been to it?"

"Of course I have. I know where to find the shrine," Pippa said, her voice soft. "I practically grew up here," the girl said matter-of-factly. "It's up *there*." The girl pointed to the center of the island. The hill that Gatina had seen the fire on.

"Follow this cove and you'll see a path," Pippa explained as if she was singing a song. "It's situated in a lovely spot. Mother was very impressed. She likes a good view. Why do you want to find it? Are you in a hurry to leave the island? Why? There's so much to see here. Oh, look, I won! We are tied!"

She bounced up and down happily, clapping her hands. Her words came at a rapid-fire pace with little spacing between. Gatina wondered how the girl managed to catch a breath. But now Gatina had an idea of where the shrine was. She also felt like she owed the girl an answer. But she didn't want to offend her.

"It's not that I'm in a *hurry* to leave," Gatina explained. "I rather like it here. But I have obligations."

When Pippa looked at her questioningly, Gatina felt obliged to offer a more-thorough answer.

"There's political turmoil back home," she explained simply. After all, she knew that the best stories contained a grain of truth, and she wanted to keep things simple for the child. "My family and I are trying to fix that to make things better for everyone." She hoped her explanation was satisfactory. She did not want to continue answering questions along that line. She had a code, after all. Gatina drew the next board in the sand. And when she looked up, she was shocked to see the girl appraising her the way Gatina would appraise a mark.

"Your worth is not measured in your accomplishments. Instead, your worth is measured by how you face the storm," Pippa said while Gatina studied the grid. That was far wiser than she expected from an eight- or nine-year-old child.

"Did your mother tell you that?" Gatina prompted. "It's very wise."

It was her move. And she really wanted those clams.

"I must have heard it somewhere," Pippa said with a shrug. "I hear lots of things. All the time. People just say them, and then they go into my ears. Sometimes they get stuck there," she said, as if it annoyed her.

This time, Pippa's voice was less childlike and more mature, like Gatina's mother and aunt. And that caught her attention. Gatina realized that something was very unusual about this situation.

"That sounds pretty useful," Gatina offered.

"Thankfully, I have big-enough ears to hold a gracious plenty," Pippa said, tugging on them. "But if I get too many trapped in there, I have to say a few to make some space," she reasoned. "It's the really big ones that are the hardest. Like *'Perseverance in the face of adversity is a virtue!'* That's a hard one to get in your ear. It clogs things up. I'm glad it's gone now."

She sat and silently considered Pippa's words.

"You must be the wisest girl in the world," Gatina suggested.

"Was that wisdom?" Pippa asked curiously. "I don't think I'm the wisest girl in the world, though. The *strongest* girl in the world? Of course. Everyone knows that. But I'm not generally known for my wisdom. Are you the wisest girl in the world?" she asked suddenly.

"Me? No, not at all," Gatina assured her. "But I might be the sneakiest girl in the world," she considered. "I'm awfully good about hiding and sneaking around without anyone noticing. Everyone knows that."

"I didn't, but I do now," Pippa agreed. "I suppose that could be helpful. So, if neither one of us is the wisest girl in the world, I wonder where she is. Who is she? Who is this girl? *Where are you?*" she demanded suddenly, yelling at the ocean.

But before Gatina could speak, her new friend broke into a smile. "Your mission will be successful, I think." Pippa's voice was so quiet that Gatina barely heard it. The words were like a whisper carried on the breeze.

Gatina paused from making the final move, the one that would put her in the lead of the game.

Confused, she drew the last cross and asked, "I'm sorry, what did you just say?"

But Pippa did not answer her. She redrew the board and started the next match.

It was when they were halfway through that game that the girl spoke again, though she did not repeat what she had said earlier.

"What is so important in the wider world that you would leave such a peaceful place?" the girl asked, changing the subject.

Gatina thought about the question while she began a series of strategic moves to win this round. After she had won the game, Gatina would be ahead by one match.

"I do not wish to see others suffer," she said, speaking from her heart. "And I certainly do not wish the fate of the masses to be controlled by tyrants," she added.

"Tyrants are the *worst*," Pippa agreed. "Except for lawbrothers. They're pretty bad too." The girl studied Gatina, who was preparing their final game board in the sand. As the game began, she asked, "Do you know about the rules of the Shipwrecker's Shrine?"

Gatina met the girl's eyes and shook her head.

"It's simple, really. Those who are rescued from the island are required to complete tasks," Pippa explained. "Most people can't be bothered, but they should. The last one is the easy one. If you get that far, Mother gives you a present. Like the Chapel of the Eight Bells. You never know what you'll find when you're done."

"Like what?" Gatina asked absently.

"Maybe a monkey," she suggested matter-of-factly. "Or a horse. Or a parrot. Maybe a husband. There's probably a husband just waiting there, lying around like no one wants him, like a three-legged cat or a wheel with a spoke missing. It happens all the time," she assured.

"My family legacy says I have to marry another mage," Gatina revealed. "It's complicated."

"I'll let Mother know," Pippa said as she made her move. "That might be helpful information."

"Well, I suppose my cousin and I shall just have to leave, then, if there are husbands just lying around," Gatina suggested, enjoying the silliness of talking with a child for a change. She made her move and won the game.

Pippa cleared off their game board while Gatina considered what she had said. "Don't worry about your cousin. She's already met her husband," she added.

Gatina looked at her new friend curiously. "Are you a prophet?" she asked suddenly. She knew little about prophets, other than that they were condemned by the Censors and shunned by most respectable mages. But it was possible that this little girl was touched with *rajira* somehow and could glimpse the future. Or she could just have a wild imagination.

The girl laughed, and the sound filled Gatina's heart with joy. It was such a happy sound almost like a song. "No, I am not. I am just the strongest girl in the world playing the sneakiest girl in the world for a basket of clams. And you are up one game over me," she reminded her.

Gatina cleared her head and focused on playing the game. She won the next two rounds and the basket of clams. Instead of getting upset, Pippa laughed and clapped her hands.

"That was fun! I don't regret not winning. You have been a challenging opponent, and those clams were fairly won," she said, as if she were a noble jouster graciously conceding the contest. She lifted the basket and handed it to Gatina.

Even though she had won the game fairly, Gatina felt bad about taking the clams from the girl. She had no idea if this girl had anyone else on the island, and she didn't want the girl to starve over some silly contest in the sand.

"It *was* fun," Gatina agreed. "It looks like there are plenty in that basket for both of us. Let's split the clams," she said reasonably.

Pippa's face lit up at the suggestion. And when her new friend smiled, Gatina felt like she had seen a goddess herself.

"I like you," Pippa said while Gatina divided the clams between her basket and the girl's. "Thank you for playing with me. You know, I think I want to give you a present," she decided.

"Oh, the clams are quite sufficient," Gatina insisted as she rose and brushed the sand off her knees. "Thank you!"

"Oh, hush; if I want to give you a present, I'll give you a present. Girls *like* presents," she reasoned. "I know I do. But what to give you . . ." Pippa asked as she bounced to her bare feet and looked around the empty beach. Her eyes lit on a boulder, one of several that had toppled onto the sand in some previous age.

"Ah! I know! An *anchor*!" she said, triumphantly.

"An . . . anchor?" Gatina asked, confused.

"Yes, yes, a while back, a gale brought a bunch of flotsam and jetsam to the island and dumped it on the beach because that's what gales do. I don't know how the anchor got here, but I saw it once. It's buried under that boulder," she said, pointing. "I'd like you to have it."

"An . . . anchor?" Gatina repeated. "Well . . . thank you, I suppose. I don't know what I'll do with it, but . . ."

"It's the thought that counts," Pippa assured her confidently. "Here," she said, striding over to the giant rock. It was twice her size and had to have weighed hundreds of pounds.

To her surprise, the girl bent and acted as if she were lifting it up . . . only, to Gatina's astonishment, the boulder moved quite easily. Indeed,

Pippa flipped it over as if it was a wicker basket. Then she plunged her hands into the sand. In a moment, she withdrew a heavy bronze anchor from the sand. It was more than three feet long and another two feet wide at the flanges. Yet the girl pulled it out with more ease than Gatina had enjoyed when extracting the arrowhead from the shoulder of the mariner.

"You . . . you really are the strongest girl in the world!" Gatina observed in astonishment.

"And you really are the sneakiest girl in the world," Pippa complimented her in return. "There you go: one slightly used anchor. You can take it with you, if you can. Or you can leave it here to visit. It must get awfully lonely," she reasoned, patting the heavy, discolored anchor like it was a dog. "You never know when you're going to need a good anchor."

"And you just . . . just found it there," Gatina said, staring at the girl, the anchor, and the rock.

"A while ago. It's not the most unusual thing I've found," she boasted. "I once was walking through the darkest of forests, hundreds of miles from the nearest living soul, where I found an artificial leg. Things like that happen to me all the time," she assured. "But I must be off now, Gatina. Enjoy the clams!"

Gatina turned away for a moment, glancing up at the hill Pippa had said was where the shrine was. When she turned back around, she saw that the girl had left behind both her bundle of junk and her basket of clams. She picked it up to go after her friend, but Pippa had vanished. The anchor was still there, as well as the recently moved boulder. But the girl had gone.

It was only then that Gatina noticed only one set of footprints in the sand near the spot where they'd played crosses and noughts. Her own. Otherwise, there was not a sign that she'd been there.

Her mind was filled with confusion, and she thought she might be going a little mad.

Where had the girl gone? How did that anchor get there? Who moved that boulder?

And where had the clams come from?

CHAPTER FIFTEEN
THE SHRINE OF THE SHIPWRECKER

While the chaotic nature of the Shipwrecker is undeniable, there is another side to the divinity which encompasses mercy, accountability, and cooperation in the wake of her divine vengeance. Once the storms pass and the survivors make it to shore, her wrath turns to charity. The customs surrounding her worship are absolute. Her cult is responsible for searching for survivors, rescuing them from the sea, providing aid to them, and seeing them returned home. This mercy might seem uncharacteristic from an outsider's perspective, but the Sea Lords see it as merely a different aspect of the goddess, one that makes the Shipwrecker both feared and adored by the maritime class.

*—from **Sea Lords, Their Cults, Religious Customs, and Traditions***

GATINA'S ARMS WERE FULL, BETWEEN THE BASKET AND THE OTHER ITEMS SHE was pulling behind her as she made her way from the cove to the campsite. She couldn't run, because she did not want to lose a single precious clam, nor did she want to leave behind any of the jetsam she had found. She was nearly certain it was all useless, but in case she was wrong, she'd rather have too much than too little.

She wound her way beyond the stick markers she had left in the sand during her exploration, realizing that she had traveled a longer distance than she thought. But when the last stick was in her sight, the events with the red-haired girl replayed in her mind.

Her encounter with the strange girl really had been unusual, if not unearthly. She knew that. But meeting a husband? That was the furthest thing from her mind. She had far too many adventures ahead of her to worry about a husband. Besides, she thought, the family doctrine dictated the type of man she must wed. Unless she followed her aunt's path and eschewed her legacy, he was to be a mage of great power, a brave and fearless man worthy of her family's lineage. But she quickly shut off that line of thought and any other thought of nuptials. Adventure and restoring the duchy would be her priorities, she decided, not romance. You just could not mix that sort of thing with married life.

Gatina was reluctant to mention the little red-haired girl to Pia unless she had to. She didn't know why she wanted to conceal the strange meeting, but it seemed like a good idea. It was just too odd and far too difficult to explain. Under the circumstances, they had much more important priorities.

When she arrived at their campsite, she called out to her cousin so that she would not be startled. Pia was sitting under the makeshift tent, studying something in her hands. As she got closer, Gatina saw it was the small box her cousin had found amid the flotsam during their earlier hunt.

"There you are! Did you have any luck? You were gone for ages. I was starting to get worried," Pia said, a note of concern in her voice.

"I wanted to go as far down on the beach as I could," Gatina said, plopping herself next to the fire. "I found this stuff. And some clams," she said, nodding toward the basket. "And an anchor. I left the anchor behind," she added.

"Probably a wise choice," Pia agreed with a chuckle. "While you were gone, I got the box open! Look what was inside!" Pia raised a hand and waggled her fingers. "Puppets!" Pia declared. On three of her fingers were tiny little figures with faces and clothes. "How fortunate and fun is that?"

"Puppets?" Gatina asked, confused.

"A lot of Sea Lord ships have a box of puppets," Pia explained. "On long voyages, someone—usually the bosun or the purser, or sometimes a chaplain—will perform little shows for the men on deck during clear nights."

Gatina stared at her cousin. "You mean the mighty Sea Lords, masters of the wave, intrepid explorers, adventurers, and corsairs . . . watch *puppet shows* for entertainment?" she asked, skeptically.

"It's an old tradition," Pia defended, holding up the box of puppets. "There's not a lot of room on a ship for, say, an orchestra or a play or a dance recital, so you make do with . . . puppets. Usually about the Storm King and his five daughters and their various minions, or a famous captain or pirate, or . . . well, lots of things. It beats staring at the sea all the time," she reasoned.

That was a bit of a shock to her imagination, Gatina admitted to herself. The idea of grown men wiggling dolls on their fingers for amusement just seemed . . . odd. Besides, food was more important than fun. Gatina hoisted her basket. "How about a basket of clams? I hope you know how to cook them."

Pia snorted. "I live at the seashore; of course I know how to cook them. About twenty different ways. The easiest is to roast them over the fire until they open. And we won't have just clams, either. While you were gone, I went to gather more wood," she explained excitedly. "I found a couple of yam plants and dug them up. And some more oranges. And I found a mess of berries, too. I mashed some up and mixed that with water and was able to feed our friend," she added. "What else did you find?"

"Probably just a bunch of junk. I'm not sure if any of it is very useful, but I didn't want to leave it behind, on the off chance one thing would be of use," she explained as she dumped out her finds. "But I did have luck in my hunt, other than the clams. I think I know where the Shipwrecker's shrine is."

Pia nearly dropped the clams. "Where? Did you find it?"

Gatina took the basket from her cousin, as a precaution, and walked toward the fire. "No, I did not find it. Not yet. But I . . . met a little girl who told me where it is. She also gave me the clams. Well, she wagered me for the clams."

Even to her own ears, Gatina knew the story sounded incredibly farfetched, and she regretted revealing the strange meeting. But it was the truth.

Pia looked up from the clams. "You did *what*? With *whom*? You found another castaway on the island? Where is she? Is she safe?" she demanded, concerned.

Before she could continue, Gatina interrupted her.

"She's safe, I promise. She seemed pretty healthy. She might live here—she was pretty vague about that. But I also found evidence of other people. There was a recent campfire farther down the beach—dry, not wet—but it was deserted by the time I found it. I think those castaways arrived around the same time as we did. The little girl told me that they had probably already found the shrine."

"What about her family? Did she mention a village or settlement where she lives?" Pia asked hopefully.

"Not . . . quite," Gatina admitted. "It was strange. We just played a game. And I won the clams," Gatina added. She had hoped her answers would pacify her cousin. They did not.

"You wagered a little *girl*? For food? Where did you find her?" Pia wore an incredulous look on her face, which seemed nearly bronze from the time spent in the sun.

"Well, yes, I did. I was off looking for the shrine. Then I found the campfire. Then, in a cove, I found this girl hunting for clams," she explained matter-of-factly. "So, I asked her about the shrine. She said it was somewhere up that big hill." Gatina was surprised by Pia's questions. She was more interested in finding the shrine than the girl's circumstances. She had seemed healthy and had a strong survival sense, or at least that was Gatina's initial feeling. As their conversation continued, though, she knew something was *very unusual* about her new friend.

"She was in the cove," Pia repeated.

Gatina nodded. "Yes, she was in the cove. Gathering clams." At the moment, she was more concerned with eating the clams. "How should we cook these? I'm starving and I'm sure you are, too."

That distracted Pia—momentarily. She looked in the basket. "We need to clean them off. We can do that by soaking them in more seawater. They'll need to soak in fresher water for a bit, too. When it's time to cook them, we can use the pot you found. They'd be better with milk and a few potatoes, but we can try them with the yams," she suggested.

Gatina helped Pia tilt the basket to dump out as much of the older water as possible. Then they dumped the entire basket into their cooking pot and filled it with a bottle of seawater. "The salt water will draw out the sand. And we need to get the sand off these before we cook them," Pia explained. "Otherwise, it will be like eating sand."

Gatina's stomach grumbled loudly, which made her wince. She smiled. "I am very hungry," she admitted. "But I've eaten enough sand of late."

"I caught a few fish with that bit of net, and more small crabs, too, if you're really hungry," Pia said. "We can make a stew with them, the clams, and the yams."

For the next half hour, the two merrily prepared what food they had for a meager meal, with Pia stopping periodically to check on the health of their patient. He had taken water thrice today, her cousin reported. And the shade of the shelter had kept him from sweating it all away. She hoped the smell of the stew that was cooking would help revive him.

Gatina greedily accepted the food when her cousin handed it to her in one of the cups they'd scavenged from the beach. It wasn't a lot, but it was cooked, hot, and delicious—her stomach did not mind. The crab was salty, likely from the seawater, she reasoned. She knew they did not have any other seasonings with them. The clams were gamey and chewy, but she ate them anyway. The yams were sweet, but mushy when cooked. The berries made for a sweet end to the meal.

While Gatina ate, Pia busied herself by continuing her interrogation. "So, you did not find the shrine; instead, you found a girl who wagered with you?"

Gatina, who had a mouth full of fish, nodded. She swallowed, which hurt because her throat was dry. "Yes. And she told me how to get to the shrine. Then the girl said there might be others already there. It was kind of a . . . warning."

Pia sucked in her breath. Gatina understood. If there were other castaways, perhaps the pirates from the *Venjanca*, then that did not bode well. While she knew anyone might be shipwrecked, Gatina had a suspicion that they might be sharing the island with the very people who had shot their patient. And who wouldn't hesitate to treat them poorly.

"So, there was just a girl wandering the beach with no parents, no village, no settlement?" Pia asked skeptically.

"That's what she said. She mentioned her mother but didn't act as if she was around at the moment. And she seemed to be very familiar with the island. She couldn't have been that much younger than me. About eight or nine."

"Don't you think it was strange that she was here alone?" her cousin demanded.

"Well . . . yes," Gatina conceded. "But the entire meeting was strange. This entire island is strange. What was I supposed to do? Torture her until she revealed where she lived?"

Pia was silent for a moment too long, by Gatina's estimation. When she met Gatina's eyes, she wore a concerned look, as if what Gatina said had finally sunk in.

"So, you wandered down the beach to a cove and came across a girl. She wagered you a basket of clams in a game—"

"It was noughts and crosses," Gatina supplied. "We talked while we played. And after she told me where to find the shrine, she asked me why I would want to leave the island."

Pia sucked in her breath.

"What?" Gatina demanded. "I just explained that I had to go back and set some things right, is all," she assured.

"Did she ask you your name?" her cousin asked, not looking up at her.

"Well, yes," she admitted.

"What did you tell her?"

"Gatina," she said. "Because that *is* my name. It's kind of silly worrying about my alias on a deserted island. I couldn't help myself. I answered honestly," she insisted.

Pia nodded sagely and her questions came to an abrupt end.

Gatina filled in the conversation with her own commentary. She found her cousin's silence a bit unnerving. "I suppose it is rather strange," she admitted. "But she seemed untroubled by being stuck here. I suspect she lives here on the island somewhere," she concluded. "I offered her half the clams after I won. Then I turned around and she was gone."

Gatina knew she probably needed to explain that she wasn't simply gone. The girl had vanished. She didn't mention how the girl had lifted a boulder. The story was strange enough as it was. She didn't need her cousin thinking that she'd gone mad.

"Where did she go?" Pia asked, a very serious look on her face.

Gatina raised her arms in a shrug. "I don't know. She was just gone," she said. "I looked for her, but she was gone."

"What did she look like, *exactly*? What color was her hair? What did she wear?" Pia asked her questions in rapid succession, not allowing her enough time to answer one before the next was spoken.

Gatina considered Pia's questions, knowing that her cousin also found the entire situation to be strange. But, she reasoned, nothing bad had happened. She also welcomed the rapid questions because she very much wanted to talk about what had happened.

"Well, she had red hair that was braided on either side of her head," Gatina said. "These were not decorative braids, the ones a maiden would wear to a party. These were disheveled and uneven. Very messy. There were bits of twigs sticking out," Gatina said, trying her best to not sound overly judgmental. She watched Pia, studying her facial expressions while she spoke.

"Is that all?" Pia asked, her eyes wide in disbelief.

"Her eyes were a deep, vibrant green. Like the color of leaves after a spring rainstorm. She wore a cloak. She was dressed rather strangely for being shipwrecked on an island, to be honest," Gatina said. Judging by her cousin's stillness and now-sheet-white face, Gatina surmised that this was very serious. "What is it? Does this mean anything to you?"

Pia nodded quickly. "Yes. Continue. What else happened? Did she say anything?"

Gatina thought about it before speaking again. The girl had said plenty, some of which was passing conversation. But other bits of what she said were—well, just odd and a bit offputting and frightening. Gatina began to sort through the items she had found on the beach, sifting useful items into a very, very small pile.

"Well, when we started to play our game, she was engaging and funny and seemed to enjoy my company." She paused as she replayed the conversation in her mind. "We talked about the island—its beauty. And I asked if she knew where the shrine was, and she told me about a path. And she was fair," Gatina decided. "She did not cheat me in the match, and she paid her wager." She paused, considering all the girl had said. "In fact, I would say she was more than helpful."

"Like where the shrine was. And she gave you clams," Pia repeated.

"I won the clams, but yes," Gatina admitted. "It was a little . . . unusual. She said some things that gave me pause," she said. "I worried she might be—"

"Be what?" Pia asked suspiciously.

"Someone who dabbles in prophecies," Gatina said, worried to admit it. But before Pia could ask anything, her mouth took over and she blurted out what the girl had said.

"She told me that I would meet my husband at the Temple of the Eight Bells, whatever that is. And she said that you have already met yours. She said she was the strongest girl in all the world."

That made Pia gasp and clutch Gatina's arm so hard it hurt.

Neither girl spoke for a long few minutes. Gatina was frustrated, as if Pia was keeping a secret. Or she really did think she was going mad and just didn't want to admit it. She tried to change the subject by opening up her bundle of salvage. "It really is a lot of rubbish, isn't it?" she asked, disappointed at the pile of useless junk in front of her, though knowing that her words carried a double meaning. "No wonder the girl didn't take them when she left."

"So, a red-headed girl with braids wagered you in a game of crosses and noughts in a cove for a basket of clams and a pile of junk. She made a few predictions about your love life—and mine—told you where the shrine was, and then just bid you a good day before she disappeared?"

"She vanished," Gatina agreed simply. "People don't just vanish, right? Oh, Cat and I do, I suppose, but a little girl? She had to come from somewhere. Or how would I have gotten those clams?"

Pia looked at her cousin quizzically. "Perhaps she's a shadowmage too. No, she's too young to have *rajira* yet. Or . . ." She trailed off.

"Or what?" Gatina demanded.

"Or perhaps she was some goddess or spirit," Pia suggested, her voice awestruck. "Something magical. Or unearthly. Or divine. Right?"

Gatina thought about her cousin's question. She had wondered the same thing after she couldn't find the girl. "Or, perhaps, I'm going stark mad," she proposed. "Doesn't shipwreck do that sometimes?"

Pia nodded. "It has been known to happen. People talking to inanimate objects, seeing things that aren't there, inventing imaginary friends because of lonesomeness. I suppose we should hurry up and find that shrine. Else we might both go mad eventually."

After they checked on their patient and made sure he was comfortable and safe, they set out. They took the waterskin and Gatina's shadowblade, which was still tucked in the harness on her back, then headed down the beach in search of the Shipwrecker's shrine. Gatina led her cousin to the path she had taken.

"I thought it was a good idea to mark where I went just in case I got lost. But I suppose this whole island is one big circle," she explained.

Pia picked up a stick. "I think it's smart. Besides, now we have walking sticks."

As they rounded the cove where Gatina had met the girl or the goddess, this time there was no sign of her, but their game board of crosses and noughts was still drawn in the sand next to the lost anchor, sticking partway out of the sand.

"This is where I met her," she said. "And that is the way she told me to go." Gatina pointed away down the cove. "She said there was a path that's more direct and easier to travel."

As she looked up at the hilltop behind her, Gatina noticed smoke rising from about halfway up. "Strange. That was not there when I was here earlier," she said with a frown.

"It's likely the others, whoever they are, unless it's the girl," Pia said, her hand tightening around the walking stick she had chosen. "Do you think we could just go up the hill through the woods? Or with the path to be smarter?"

Gatina didn't think hard about that. "When a possible goddess tells you to take a certain route, that's probably what we should do," she said. "Besides, she said it would be faster."

Pia exhaled slowly and nodded. "Those are very good points. Let's go find that path."

They walked around the curve of the cove, and the path was exactly where the red-haired girl had said it would be. It was marked by a bough of branches that created an ethereal entryway of small white and yellow flowers on vines entwined around its branches. The flowers bore a sweet, subtle scent that reminded Gatina of honey.

Once they crossed under the archway, they found the path was both smooth and very well marked for being in such a desolate location—more than a simple path for wild game, she decided. A stream trickled down alongside it before it emptied into the cove. She was thankful to see it. She stopped long enough to empty the wineskin, rinse it, and refill it. She took a long sip and passed it to Pia. "That's the best drink of water I have had in a long time. Maybe since we left your house."

Pia's sip was even longer. But she nodded her head enthusiastically in agreement before refilling it and capping the skin.

They kept a steady pace as they climbed the steep path. Gatina was glad they had elected not to climb up the hill through the forest—it appeared a far more difficult route. As it was, she knew that she did not want to walk down the path in the dark, even with magesight. It was steep enough and covered with enough rocks to break an ankle in an instant if you took a wrong step.

Instead of tiring after so many days of limited food, Gatina found the climb to be exhilarating. She was excited by the prospect of what lay at the top of the hill. There could be bread, or there could be other food. Or maybe there would be—well she didn't rightly know what it would be, but she was excited by the prospect of finding out. It was a shrine to a confusingly violent and benevolent goddess. It had to be interesting.

But the nearer they got to the top, the thicker the plume of smoke rising from the hill grew.

Pia noticed it too. "They must be trying to signal a ship for rescue. They'd have a far better vantage point to spot one from up here. And the smoke would stay thicker for longer," she reasoned.

As they neared the crest of the hill, the path became less steep, evening out to a gentle incline and widening to a kind of plateau. Gatina motioned for Pia to be quiet. She heard voices—faint but unmistakably male. Laughter, in fact.

"Let me scout ahead," she advised her cousin, whispering in her ear. "I'm apparently the sneakiest girl in the world."

"You're the shadowthief," Pia mouthed with a shrug. "I'll stay here until you send a signal."

Gatina was confident that she was far better suited to the element of surprise than her cousin. She looked around until she found a good vantage point atop a rocky outcropping that afforded her a view of the relatively flat cliff ahead. Indeed, it widened into a kind of clearing hugging the mountain to the north.

Gatina pulled her cousin into the greenery where she would be concealed from anyone coming down the trail. She sneaked to the base of the outcropping and scaled the boulders until she could peek over the side and get a view of the clearing ahead without being seen.

The clearing was very small, no more than twenty feet in diameter, nestled into a grotto on the side of the hill. She immediately spotted the shrine in the middle—and it was not what she expected. It was a crude, wooden hovel no more than ten feet wide and ten feet long, made of dead boughs and roofed with long-dried bracken. She had seen sheds better constructed.

The shrine was not the permanent stone structure that she had imagined. Instead, it seemed haphazardly built, more like their beach shelter than a religious building. It was set in a natural concavity in the side of the hill, where it was protected from the elements. Several boulders sat in a rough circle around the hovel.

But it was unmistakably the shrine. The symbol of the Shipwrecker—a broken mast—was hung at the peak of the little roof, crudely painted on a plank from some ship. The shrine itself was small, simple, and peaceful.

But what was outside of the shrine was the exact opposite. There was a fire burning, she could see, a great conflagration of bundled twigs and dried ferns, creating a roaring fire and a thick column of smoke overhead.

Three men lounged around the fire, laughing, drinking, and talking jovially. While Gatina could not see their faces, she guessed from their voices that they were younger and had not yet been made harsh by life at sea. She began to use magesight to take a closer look at her fellow castaways.

They were closer to her age than her parents', she noted. They sat with slumped shoulders, relaxed and resigned. There was a sense of desperation about them and a sense of sadness behind their joviality. As she saw their faces further with her spell, her heart sank. They were, unfortunately, familiar.

Two of the men she recognized from the market in Pluhalia: Darrick and that scoundrel Baramel. Corsairs from the *Venjanca*. The third man she did not know.

"Darkness!" she swore under her breath. *Pirates.* She wondered if they would adhere to the Shipwrecker's Truce or persist in being scoundrels. But the allure of whatever supplies might be within the shrine was too powerful. They had to make an attempt for the sake of their wounded mariner.

She held up three fingers to her cousin, and then pointed at the three castaways. Pia nodded in agreement. Taking a deep breath, she pulled her shadowblade from the scabbard she had not taken off since she'd left the *Daydream* and landed on the desolate island. She moved slowly and silently through the brush, on the other side of the outcropping from the path. In moments, she was just outside of the clearing. Close enough to smell the fire, and nearly close enough to smell the pirates.

Instead of stepping free from the shrubbery and surprising them, Pia loudly called out and announced their presence first.

"Hail, good fellows! We invoke the Shipwrecker's Truce, and under that truce, we seek what we might need from her shrine!" she called in a strong voice.

Her voice made the three castaways jump in surprise at the unexpected call. Darrick leapt to his feet, a cudgel in his hand. Gatina was nearly close enough to one to stab him, she realized, but he did not see her. She felt superior for that. She did not even have to use a spell to hide when her opponent was so inattentive.

But while Pia's announcement caught the trio off guard, it did not seem to otherwise trouble them. When she stepped into the clearing, they each stared at her in wonder. Her cousin's greeting announcement had clearly caught the three off guard, but it had also cautioned the three against danger. After all, invoking a truce wasn't exactly announcing an attack, Gatina reasoned. While they had not anticipated company at the shrine, it was not so farfetched for another castaway to claim its sanctuary, she reasoned.

"It's a lass!" Darrick, the most handsome of the three, observed as he lowered his cudgel.

"A castaway," Pia corrected proudly. "I claim right to visit the shrine under the Truce," she declared.

"That's an interesting idea," Baramel answered, scratching his scraggly beard as he eyed her cousin carefully. "One might think that those who found it first might—"

"Shipwrecker's Truce!" insisted Pia forcefully. "It's the custom!"

"More of a general guideline than a custom," Baramel said, taking a step closer to her cousin. From the looks of it, they were quite comfortable where they were and weren't inclined to share their fortune without consideration.

That was something Gatina wasn't going to allow to happen. She stepped forward, and suddenly, her shadowblade was at Baramel's throat.

"I believe the lady claimed Shipwrecker's Truce!" she hissed, tapping his Adam's apple firmly. "Hands where I can see them. I insist!"

"Ahh . . ." Baramel said, raising his hands in surprise.

"Two lasses, then," Darrick said, chuckling at his friend's discomfort. He had a knife at his belt and a club in his hand but had not changed his demeanor at all. "I suppose we've been blessed by the Breaker of Masts, haven't we, lads?"

He sounded brazen, bold, and confident. Almost charming. But he was Darrick. A Rat. She gave her cousin a subtle nod, though the edge of her blade did not move a bit from Baramel's throat. She received one in return. That meant that Pia knew these three were not just mariners. They were Rats and pirates. Likely the very same pirates who had shot their wounded mariner with an arrow.

The most unexpected thing that happened, however, was how Darrick responded.

"Of course we will honor the Shipwrecker's Truce, as all wise men do," Darrick agreed, his voice pleasant and smooth. "Under that truce, you are safe to come and go without fear. We shall not harm you, my ladies," he pledged as he dropped his club. Indeed, he bowed to them like as a gentleman might before he returned to his seat. As he did so, he shot a look at his friends. And that prompted both to also bow—difficult for Baramel to do with a sword at his throat, but Gatina permitted the courtesy without cutting him.

The three men had built a decent-sized fire, and there were still a few small fish being toasted over it on sticks—as well as a pile of fish guts and bones. The remains of their meal lay scattered on the ground at their feet, just in front of the shrine. And that irritated her greatly.

She was not particularly religious, but given the strange encounter she had just had, and the strong feeling that was gnawing at the back of her mind that the girl she had wagered with might actually be a goddess, their behavior offended her. Truce or not, she was not happy to see any of them. She hoped she and Pia could make quick work of their visit.

"Thank you." Pia nodded. Gatina reluctantly lowered her sword as her cousin walked toward the shrine. Darrick apparently noted Gatina staring at their food.

"Are you hungry? My ladies, we have more fish," Darrick offered. "There is plenty to be caught, if you know how. The table settings might not be up to your standards, but the fare is quite good." He pulled one of the fish off of the fire and offered it to Gatina on a wide leaf. She suspected that it was part of one of the hospitality rules invoked during the truce. Truthfully, she did not care. She was starving despite having just eaten. And it did smell good. The clam-and-yam stew had been just a few mouthfuls, and her stomach was already complaining. She took the leaf warily from Darrick with a small nod of gratitude.

Pia studied the small collection of supplies left in offering to the goddess, selecting a few things from within, while Gatina ate a few bites of the fish with her fingers.

"I think there are a few things we could use from here," Pia suggested. "We have a wounded man back at our camp, and this brandy will help," she said, holding up a small glass bottle.

"Take it," Darrick agreed, graciously.

"The brandy?" Baramel whined. "You're just letting them—"

"We drank the spirits last night," Darrick dismissed. "It's only fair they get the brandy, if they have a wounded man to tend."

"You wounded him," Gatina reported, eyeing them coolly. "You shot him in the back. He might die," she accused. As she ate, she watched Darrick, careful to not stare at the man. Unlike his mates, he wore his shirt. The others were shirtless, and both were bronzed and sinewy. They each bore the battle scars of sword fights and other injuries. She found that unsettling.

"And you shot our mate Gondefar in the leg, and he *did* die!" Baramel informed her. "He drowned when the longboat capsized."

"The fortunes of sea." Darrick shrugged. "I didn't like Gondefar much anyway. The man snored like a tempest."

The third man quietly listened to the discussion, watching both parties carefully. He had bruises on his face and hands, but Gatina realized he didn't look like the other two. Or act like it.

"You're the one they captured!" she realized.

"Yes, he was our prisoner, until we were shipwrecked. Now he's covered under the truce too. No man may hold another in bondage if they are both castaways," Darrick related.

"You're very conscientious, for a Rat," she said, her eyes narrowing.

"Ah! My lady has heard of our society! Then you should know that we brothers are oathbound to strictly keep the Shipwrecker's Truce. Our noble order was born of a shipwreck, after all, and we owe the Shipwrecker as its mother. Sentimental of us, perhaps, but we keep to our rules."

"What is your name?" Gatina asked the captured mariner, as Pia returned with a handful of items from the shrine.

"Genver. I was the bosun on the *Riadan* before these bastards took her. And me. You said Matros was alive?" he asked hopefully.

"Matros? That's his name?" Pia asked curiously. "He's still unconscious. Yes, we removed the arrow. Gods willing, it will heal, if it doesn't become more infected. Did you know that there are ship's biscuits in there?" she asked the pirates.

"Yes, but half of them were moldy," dismissed Baramel. "We'll tuck into them if we need. We'll probably go hunting first. I've had enough biscuit already in my life."

"I took a few," Pia admitted. "They'll help Matros heal. Hopefully, we can keep him alive until we're rescued."

"That might be sooner than you think," Genver reported. "We spotted a sail a few hours ago. That's why we smoked the fire."

"Just because we saw them doesn't mean that they saw our smoke," Darrick reminded them. "And they aren't obligated to stop. It's custom but not an obligation. Likely we'll have to await a patrol. Are you ladies thirsty?" he asked. "I wouldn't want to spare you any hospitality. There's a sweet spring behind the altar."

"We refilled our bottle from the stream, Darrick," Gatina assured him curtly. He was looking at her strangely.

"I am sorry," he said. "I don't mean to stare, but you seem familiar to me—though I admit I've never seen a girl with lavender eyes before."

Gatina flushed, realizing her eye-color spell had worn off. But she was more embarrassed that he recognized her anyway. She had hoped that he would not remember her at all from their brief encounter in Pluhalia.

"Then we probably haven't met," she dismissed. "Beah, do we have what we need? Can we go?" she asked, irritated. She used her aunt's name instead of Pia's.

"I think so." Her cousin nodded. "Thank you for observing the truce. And if we see anything on the horizon, we'll let you know."

"Until then, it's a simple life of hunting, fishing, and enjoying each other's company," Darrick said cheerfully. Baramel gave them a lecherous look. "Are you girls feeling lonely yet?"

"I'm not terribly good company," Gatina said, raising her shadowblade a bit.

"That's a strange-looking sword you have there," Baramel observed evenly, as he studied her blackened blade. "Do you know how to use it?"

"That is something you do not want to discover," Gatina replied dryly.

"Do you want to take a look inside, Maranka?" Pia asked, gesturing to the shrine. "You might see something I didn't."

Still keeping her blade in hand, Gatina nodded and ducked her head inside the small enclosure. Up close, the shrine still wasn't what she thought it would be. She had had the idea in her head that it would be a permanent structure, but the wooden posts that held up the thatched roof were poorly secured at best. Inside, apart from a flat stone set for an altar, it bore little resemblance to a religious shrine and more to a very unorganized storeroom.

Apparently, there had been many shipwrecked victims who had contributed over the years. A few torn rolls of sailcloth, some rope, a half-dozen bottles—many of them empty—a few items of clothing, some rolled-up bandages, fishhooks, spools of thread, and a cork filled with needles decorated the altar. A decrepit basket filled with knife blades, arrowheads, spoons, and flints had been left next to it as offerings. All useful things if you were stranded there, but nothing of real value.

There were stranger offerings, as well: a piece of slate, a child's toy horse of painted wood, and a chipped cup of delicate, beautifully glazed ceramic were tossed into a corner along with a tiny bench and a broken stool. A haphazardly wrapped ball of string sat atop a small keg of moldy ship's biscuits. There were a few bags of herbs and a couple of battered old pipes arranged on an old banner bearing the sign of a wine cask. And there was a stack of dry wood near the door, along with a couple of tar-soaked wads of cloth—to make smoke, she realized.

As she was poking around behind the wood, she spied a better prize: a large, green glass bottle with a cork sealed with wax. It had apparently escaped the pirates' notice. She quietly pulled the cork out, and her nose was assaulted with the scent of powerful spirits—sugar rum, she recognized. She fought back a cough. Better than brandy for their wounded mariner's wounds, she recalled Pia saying.

"Look what I found!" she said, presenting the bottle to her cousin excitedly.

Pia accepted the bottle and took a sniff before corking it and handing it back.

Suddenly, Baramel produced a blade—no, she saw, a Rat Tail, the long iron shiv that was the Brotherhood's signature weapon of choice.

"That needs to stay here," he motioned for the bottle. "I have need of it. It's mine."

In an instant, Gatina had stepped between Pia and him. Her shadowblade was in her hand and at his throat once again before he could stop her.

"We have a *truce*," she calmly reminded him. "You had your chance to seek your aid from the shrine. Now it is our turn."

"It's fine!" Pia said exasperatedly. "There's enough for both of our parties. I can pour what I need into one of the empty bottles and leave the rest for you," she soothed.

Darrick grabbed the man by the shoulders and pulled him back. "What are ye thinking? You can't do that! Shipwrecker's Truce!" he reminded him angrily. Darrick took the man's blade from him.

"My apologies," he said as he turned back toward the girls. "Our friend just likes his drink. It's a comfort in these distressing circumstances. By all means, take what you need. You have nothing to fear from us, on my word. Continue."

Pia nodded gratefully and returned to the shrine for an empty bottle. Gatina lowered her blade but did not sheathe it. She had expected treachery from the men. She still did.

"I am certain our crewmates are looking for us," Darrick said in a friendly voice as he returned to his seat on the log next to the fire, embedding the Rat Tail in the log. "We did see a sail—it's probably the *Venjanca*, our noble galleon. The prospect of rescue is there. Should you wish to take it," he offered persuasively.

Gatina's blood froze in her veins. She suspected that such a rescue would likely end in slavery or worse. Pia confirmed her suspicion.

"The Truce ends with rescue," she reminded them. "I'd rather take my chances on the island than risk a rescue from a corsair."

"Surely, you have people who would ransom you quickly," Darrick suggested.

"And people to avenge us viciously," Gatina assured them. "They're searching for us too." Nobody spoke for what seemed like several long minutes but was probably only a few seconds. Then the pirate sighed.

"Well, 'tis just a thought. I felt obliged to offer you rescue, under the terms of the truce. But I'm sure two sturdy lasses like you will do fine here on this desolate island, slowly starving to death and going mad with desperate loneliness."

"That's preferable to being rescued by a ship full of murderous Rats and slowly tortured to death," Gatina sneered.

"We kill only when we have to," Darrick dismissed. "Rarely for sport. The Corsair frowns on such things. It's bad business. We're reasonable men. I'm certain we would prefer your company to your corpses," he said casually, eyeing both girls.

And that was when Gatina realized that truce or not, this was a very dangerous situation and Darrick was a very dangerous man. Before she could speak, her cousin responded.

"Thank you for such a *kind* offer," Pia said, her tone both smooth and polite. "But I am certain our crew is looking for us as well. For now, we will make the best of our situation and fare as well as we are able. With the truce as your bond, we will take what we need and be on our way. I left the rest in the shrine for your consumption. I don't think we will be needing further discussion."

"That concludes our business here," Gatina agreed. "Pray do not try to find our camp. As I said," she informed them as she slid her shadowblade smoothly into the scabbard on her back, "I am *not* the best of company."

CHAPTER SIXTEEN
MARINER MATROS

The Salt Crone is perhaps the most misunderstood of the Sea Lord pantheon. Oft dismissed as a mere goddess of death and witchcraft, upon further study, this peculiar deity has complexities and subtleties that belie her simple guise as a hunched crone. She is, first and foremost, a goddess of healing, and her cult specializes in that sacred task. She manifests the knowledge and wisdom of the elderly Salt Wives that live on the margins of Sea Lord society, widows who have accumulated centuries of folk remedies and folk magic that are surprisingly effective. Within her purview are the astonishing number of medicines that are available to the Sea Lords, as well as the knowledge to prepare and use them in a way that heals and restores their patients. Or kills them.
—from **Sea Lords, Their Cults, Religious Customs, and Traditions**

WHEN THEY RETURNED TO THE COVE, GATINA WAS CERTAIN THE PIRATES had not followed them. But, as a precaution, she obscured their footprints, wiping away any trace of their presence, and they walked back to the camp in the surf to obscure the direction they went. Better to be prepared, she thought as she stared out over the Bay.

"It really is beautiful here," she said to Pia, who had paused to take in the view and scan the horizon for ships at twilight. The cove was shaded, and the water that lapped the shore was gentle and cooler. The sun was beginning to set, and magnificent shades of pink and purple clouds dotted the blue sky.

"It's . . . magical," Pia agreed, smiling. "Metaphorically speaking."

Gatina exhaled, still troubled by the encounter at the shrine. "I cannot believe he recognized me," she admitted. "I look nothing like I did in

Pluhalia." To have someone see through your disguise was disconcerting and unprofessional to a thief. But Pia was untroubled by it.

"That was odd," she conceded with a shrug. "I wouldn't be concerned, though. He's not smart enough to make the connection. Once Mother finds us, I doubt we will ever see him again." Pia patted her on the shoulder, then pulled her into a hug. "Thank you for being ready to protect me. If you hadn't been quick with your sword, I don't know how well they would have kept the Truce. I should have paid closer attention."

"I just did not trust them. I never trust the Brotherhood of the Rat. Treachery is in their nature."

"That Darrick behaved like a gentleman. He was steadfast about the Truce. He sounds educated," Pia reminded her.

"Darrick spoke well, mayhap, but the other one? He's the sort who won't think twice about breaking a rule if no one is looking. In fact, I was a bit nervous up there even with the Shipwrecker's Truce invoked. They seemed like they might break it for a moment."

Along the way back, Gatina collected the sticks she had set earlier to mark her path. There was no point in marking the way to their camp for strangers—or the pirates. Besides, she knew they would need the wood for their fire. She gathered as much as they could carry, grateful that the sand was cooler on her bare feet at this time of day. It had been painful earlier. She had thought the cobblestones in Falas were bad until she arrived on the island.

As dusk fell, they arrived at their campsite. Gatina was disappointed to see that the fire had burned out. But she knew she could quickly start it again, and besides, she reasoned there had been no one to tend to it while they were away. Pia deposited her burdens and checked on the mariner—Matros was his name, she reminded herself.

He was still unconscious, and Gatina watched with interest as her cousin cleaned his wounds first with water, and then with a bit of bandage soaked in the spirits. He moaned when it made contact with the wound, making Pia wince in sympathy.

"Poor thing!" she sighed, as she left the wad on the wound. Then she began removing some of the things she'd taken from the shrine before examining his wound closely. "It's starting to fester," she reported, wrinkling her nose. "He's still feverish. But I have a remedy for that, I think," she said, pulling a single ship's biscuit out of the bundle. It was completely encrusted with mold.

"You're going to make him *eat* that?" Gatina asked, skeptical and appalled.

"No, no, but I found the moldiest ones in the barrel," Pia explained. "It's an old ship's surgeon's trick." She began to grind the disgusting pieces of hardtack between two rocks, then mixed it with water. "I'll make a poultice with it and put it directly on the wound. It should help keep the wound from festering further."

"Moldy ship's biscuit? Are you sure?" she asked as she worked to get the fire going again, using the smaller sticks her cousin had gathered earlier.

"The more mold, the better. Trust me, I've seen it work," she promised. "While I'm doing that and putting a clean bandage over it, why don't you fetch us more fresh water? And . . . perhaps find something for us to eat?"

Gatina agreed, and once the fire was burning brightly, she took the copper kettle and the other empty bottles down the beach to the stream. Along the way, she tried looking for crabs with magesight but saw none of any decent size. She settled for digging up a few clams from the beach who revealed themselves, and then waded into the water up to her waist with her sword drawn.

Darrick's reminder that she knew how to fish had galled her, and the flavor lingered on her tongue. While she didn't have time to do it properly, Lord Steel had occasionally set her in a stream or river to practice thrusting through the resistance at the water at riverfish as training. There was no reason she couldn't do that here.

It took some patience and a few failed attempts, but eventually she managed to stab a decent-sized flatfish the size of a serving plate behind its gills when it swam too closely. Fish stood out in magesight if they were close enough to the surface, she had learned. Another few minutes of stabbing the water yielded a second fish, almost as large as the first.

It had been challenging, she realized. Her control over her new blade was getting better. And she found stabbing fish both a useful exercise and unexpectedly satisfying. If she couldn't stab pirates, they were a worthy substitute.

By the time she returned to camp, it was dark, and they had to clean and cook their catch by firelight while they heated up the water. Pia had foraged a few wild onions and mushrooms from the nearby forest, and added them to the pot while Gatina plopped bits of fish into it along with the clams.

"I did get a few biscuits that weren't molded," Pia revealed. "I scraped them good and crushed them. We can add the crumbs to the pot. They'll thicken it up a bit," she proposed.

Gatina had not paid especially close attention to Drella during meal preparation other than to steal bits of vegetables and apples. She could toast bread over coals and boil water, but that was the extent of her knowledge of the art.

"Are you sure about that?" she asked skeptically.

"It will be fine. Hunger is the best spice," Pia answered.

Before the stars began to shine, the soup was finished. And, while it was not the best thing Gatina had ever eaten, it was far from the worst. The biscuit crumbs added a bit of body to the otherwise watery stew, and the onions added some much-needed bite to the dish.

"It's different," she decided as she ate her portion from the earthenware cup with their salvaged spoon. "But it's also tasty and filling. It's better than the stew on the *Gaillardia* was," she conceded.

"We should ration it, I suppose. And save some for our patient," Pia suggested.

Gatina was saddened by the thought of spending another night on the island as a castaway. She knew the longer she and Pia remained on the island, the less the likelihood of their rescue—at least by the *Daydream*.

"I should check his wounds again," her cousin decided. "He probably needs more water, too. Maybe a sip of brandy. For medicinal purposes," she rationalized.

Gatina followed her, curious to see how he was healing, and a bit eager to learn from Pia. Their patient was propped in a sideways, half-lying position. They had rotated him throughout the day to keep him from becoming too stiff. His shirt, tattered as it was, remained on his shoulder. But he was protected from the strong sun overhead during the days, thanks to their tent, and took water when a bottle was held to his lips. But he seemed to have shifted while she had fetched water, Gatina thought.

"Has he moved on his own?" she asked.

Pia tilted her head and looked down at him. "Yes, I think he has," she agreed as she sank to her knees in the sand beside him. "His fever is down, too."

Her cousin tore off some clean bandage, placed it over the flask's uncovered mouth, and tilted it enough to soak the cloth. Then she wiped it over the man's chest and back, carefully but thoroughly. The mariner groaned when the liquor-soaked bandage touched his cuts. Gatina noticed that his eyes winced in pain.

Pia paused her hand near his face as if she'd just had a thought. In a stroke of wisdom, she held the brandy-soaked cloth under his nose, much like smelling salts.

Gatina stood at the ready. She had brought the wineskin full of water to offer him a drink. To her very untrained eye, his wounds did not look deadly. Most of them had scabbed over, she saw, and had been scrubbed clean by the seawater. He would definitely have scars, but that was better than the alternative, she reasoned. But she wasn't sure how much blood he had lost or how dehydrated he might be. She did know that they had done their best to aid him.

"I think this is helping," Pia said of the bandage she held under his nose.

"Well, that seems promising," Gatina agreed, noticing his eyelids flickering. "Perhaps he just needs more rest to recover," she suggested.

"Maybe so. The body heals in mysterious ways," Pia said. She uncapped the flask and poured a trickle of brandy over the man's lips.

"Matros," she called to him in a soft voice. "Matros, wake yourself!"

This time, he coughed violently as the liquor touched his tongue. Gatina was startled. She had been ready to offer the waterskin but nearly dropped it. The man had been silent until then—no more than a moan, even when they had removed the arrow from his shoulder. But when he abruptly opened his eyes, Pia nearly fell onto her backside.

When he coughed again, Pia quickly reached to Gatina for the water. She recovered her position, then offered him the skin. "Be calm, be calm," she said, soothingly. "You are safe. Here, have a sip."

The man blinked a few times, likely trying to adjust his vision. He took several pulls from the wineskin, with Pia supporting the back of his head and neck.

"Be still," her cousin cautioned. "We found you on the beach. We've been taking care of you. You are safe," she repeated.

"Wh—where are we?" the man gasped, his voice harsh and raspy.

"On an island in the Shipwrecker's Bower, best I can tell," Pia informed him calmly. "My cousin and I had tried to pull you from the water."

The man finally broke his gaze into Pia's eyes to look past her. He nodded to Gatina.

"Yes! I remember! Rowing to get us like you were sent by the Maiden! Then you both have my gratitude, and I am in your debt," he said weakly. When he tried to sit up, Pia shook her head.

"Stay down," she said forcefully. "You've lost a lot of blood. You're going to be weak on your feet if you try to stand too soon."

The man looked at her cautiously and questioningly before he obliged. Gatina scooted closer, joining the two of them on the ground next to her cousin.

"We removed an arrow from your shoulder. It missed anything vital, but you have been unconscious for several days," Pia explained. "You need to get your strength and heal before you try to walk."

Now that he was awake, he could tell her if any other part of his body was injured. "Does it sting or burn, like an infection has set in?" she asked.

"Nay. I feel like I've been shot by a bolt, is all," he said hoarsely.

Pia laughed. "And so you have, Mariner Matros. My name is Pia. This is my cousin, Maranka. We found you on the beach and—"

"I know, I know," the man said, shaking his head. "Pirates; my mates and I tried to fight back. There were too many of them, so I'd wager we were unsuccessful." His voice trailed off as he remembered the events. "But you saved me from certain death," he added softly. "Two maidens sent to nurse me."

"She's the nurse," Gatina assured him. "I just keep the pirates away."

"Then she is my goddess. More brandy?" he asked hopefully.

"Just a sip," Pia said, uncorking the bottle. There wasn't much left in it, Gatina saw. "There isn't much. We took it from the Shipwrecker's Shrine. But a sip might help," she decided, and held it to his lips again. "And then water—as much as you can drink," she insisted.

Gatina avoided the strong urge to roll her eyes as she passed the water to Pia, who helped him drink.

"I'll get him some soup," Gatina suggested. "I'm sure he is starved—or delirious."

In truth, she was surprised by the man's instant ease with both of them. They had never met him before—not formally. And while the circumstances were strange, of course, he seemed very sure of—no, she corrected, *comfortable* with himself. And with them.

It came easy to him, that comfort. But it was not proper, at least to her sensibilities. Pia, she saw, did not seem to mind. While Gatina busied herself with dipping some of the watery soup into their shared cup, she thought about the man's reaction to her cousin. She had not expected him to be so transfixed by Pia. He had not stopped staring at her during the examination. She heard them talking and laughing. She wasn't jealous, exactly, just confused by the reaction.

She returned with a portion of the soup and more of the berries Pia had found.

When Matros tried to sit up, Pia shook her head and put a hand on his chest to keep him in place.

"I will help you, Matros," she insisted. "But I don't want your wound opening again. Your fever has broken, but you're a long way from being healed."

"It hurts like a . . . well, like I got shot in the back," he chuckled—then winced.

Matros's laugh was pleasant enough that Gatina found herself smiling despite her irritation at the situation. He was very attractive in a rugged sort of way, she noticed, now that he was awake. She already knew he was well muscled and broad-shouldered, but now that his eyes were open, Gatina saw that they were kind and very green—not as green as the red-haired girl's, but green.

Thinking about her friend's eye color reminded her of what the girl had said—that her cousin had already met her husband. She reasoned that Matros might not be the intended, but given their situation, it did seem both likely . . . and strange.

Gatina watched the pair surreptitiously, trying not to make them self-conscious. Matros was still very weak from both his injury and his recovery. He ate the stew hungrily, remarking that he hadn't had a morsel in days. He thanked them profusely for his care while he ate, praising various gods and cursing the pirates who'd injured him in one breath. They revealed that some of his attackers had also been shipwrecked on the island and let him know that his comrade Genver had survived and was reasonably well. Matros seemed very pleased by that.

"Genver's the smart one," Matros decided, as he finished the last of the stew. "He's paid his dues against his ransom, unlike a lot of unlucky fellows. He'll be redeemed as soon as they make it back to port if he doesn't escape first. He's a good bosun who's been sailing for years. You say that your ship will be searching for you?"

"My mother is captain, our brothers are hands, so I think it quite likely," Pia reported. "That's why we've kept the fire going at night."

"It will be hard to see, unless they sail close to the beach," Matros observed.

"My mother is also a mage," Beah said proudly. "She has locating spells, I know, and will not stop until she finds us."

"That's excellent news!" Matros agreed. "Now, can I get some more of that stew? And then I need to, ah, get rid of some of the water you've been giving me," he said sheepishly.

Ordinarily, she might have been suspicious of his intentions on general principle. Gatina knew that she and Pia could easily subdue him if they needed to, but they were completely at ease with each other. It seemed an unlikely thing to worry about.

After he ate, she and Pia helped Matros to his feet. He staggered at first. Gatina ran to the woodpile to fetch one of the longer branches for a walking stick. Once she and Pia were both certain he would not fall over, they allowed him to take care of his needs. When he returned, the trio walked to the beach with him between them, as a precaution. Matros was unsure on his feet, and the sand, while packed, was still uneven. They sat under the stars with the fire at their backs. High tide had gone, and the Bay was still.

As the birds grew quiet, they settled into a comfortable silence.

After a few moments, Matros asked, "How did you two come to be sailing way out here?"

Gatina was unprepared for the question. Neither she nor Pia had discussed a way to answer that sort of thing. She relied on doctrine: the closest answer to the truth was the best—and the easiest. Pia looked over to Gatina, and Gatina nodded. After what they had been through, she figured it was safe to be honest.

"We sail a merchant caravel out of Prejestia, in the east. We're taking a cargo of citrus to Vaxel, for the Anchorage, and had a Coastlord couple convoy with us in their sloop. When our schedule was interrupted by storm, my mother borrowed their sloop to make the connection with our vendor at Dras Ferman while our ship waited on two others back at Pluhalia," she explained.

"Ah, that pretty little sloop we saw in port." He nodded. "And you decided to take on a raider? A full galleon? With a *sloop*?" he asked in disbelief.

"We weren't trying to fight them," Gatina argued. "We were just trying to rescue as many of you as possible before the squall hit."

"Our ship was near your caravel when the pirates attacked," Pia explained gently. "I convinced Mother to launch the gig in an effort to rescue those of you who had jumped off your boat. We were able to rescue two of your crewmates. Then we went back for the rest who were in the water." Pia reached over and squeezed Matros's hand. "But the pirates shot them both. When the storm came, we got knocked off course away from our ship, then hit a shoal and wrecked the gig." She paused long enough to shiver from the memory. "It's by the Shipwrecker's good grace alone that we woke up on this beach."

Nobody spoke for a few minutes. It was hard to believe all of that had happened in such a short amount of time. She and her cousin had rescued sailors, survived a punishing storm in a small boat, and had been tossed around the waves so much, she did not know sea from sky. Then they woke on the beach and found a wounded Matros. And she had played a game with a girl who was most likely not at all a girl but instead a scion of a goddess—the very goddess who had saved them from death. So much had happened, and Gatina remembered it had only been two full days since they had arrived.

"We did find the Shipwrecker's Shrine on the island," Gatina volunteered. "That's where we found the brandy and bandages, and a little sugar rum that we washed your wound with. That's where the Rats are encamped. And your friend Genver. But they honor the Truce, so . . ."

"Of course they did." Matros nodded. "They're Brotherhood of the Rat, you say? Nasty fellows. They're little better than real rats. They haunt the docks of Glavores, coercing small ships to smuggle for them, make loans to mariners who should know better, and run press gangs to kidnap drunken sots to crew their own craft. No better than thugs and bandits. But they're oddly strict about some things. The Shipwrecker's Truce would be one of them. It's said that she protected them when their original company was cast away, somewhere in the Shoals of Sinbar. They would be damned if they broke it, and they know it."

Gatina sat close enough to her cousin and their patient that she could hear them but far enough away to afford them some privacy, too. Matros was explaining what his life as a journeyman mariner was about to Pia, who seemed enrapt at his story. She wanted to give her cousin an opportunity to get to know the man she had saved, and it was clear that there was some interest in Matros's green eyes as he stared at Pia in the starlight.

She had little interest in such tales. She knew what a mariner's life was like now. Fighting pirates was not something she desired to experience. Rats on land and Censors were quite enough for her. Instead, she looked at the stars overhead. She quickly recognized the Triangle and Agtron the Angry Octopus, the constellation Aunt Beah had told her to keep in sight as they sailed to and from Dras Ferman. That one seemed brighter than usual.

Gatina leaned forward, elbows on her knees; she lowered her eyes from the sky to the water's surface. And she saw a light in the distance. A very, *very* pale dot of light. Gatina used her magesight to see the unseen, bringing the image on the horizon closer. That glimmer of light was a ship—in the distance. The very far distance. As she studied the ship's size, she was convinced it was the *Daydream*.

"Pia! There's a ship!" she cried excitedly. Gatina sprang from the sand. Pia looked out and then at her. "There, under Agtron!"

"What? I don't see anything . . ." Matros said, confused.

"Magesight," Gatina answered. "We can see in the dark and see far-away things with it. Among other things."

"How can you be sure that's the—" her cousin asked. When she didn't finish her thought, Gatina assumed Pia was using magesight.

"How can you be sure that's even a ship?" Matros asked. His voice reminded her that she couldn't be truthful fully.

"It's *my* ship. I *know* it," Gatina insisted as she began tossing the smaller sticks onto their fire. "Come on! Let's get this fire blazing! Make it a real beacon!" she said, dumping all the firewood onto it.

"I think you're right, Gatina!" Pia said, joining her in throwing on the heavier branches, careful to not smother the flames.

Matros had not joined them. Instead, he remained seated, leaning his head on his walking staff, staring out over the Bay, watching intently. Finally, he heaved a great sigh and a chuckle.

"I do believe you are both correct," he surmised. "There *is* a ship out there!"

The heat was intense as the fire grew taller than both girls, but it was well contained. Gatina had made sure it would not spread, between her spell and the stones she had placed around the perimeter. She had no desire to be nearly set on fire again. The blaze was large enough to be seen for quite some distance, she figured, and was bright enough to be reflected on the waves. She trooped back into the forest to look for more deadfall, seeking anything that would burn brightly. This might be their only chance, but it was a good one, she reasoned as she hauled a leafy piece of deadfall back to the pyre. Especially if Atopol was watching—which she was certain he was.

The time seemed to pass slowly. Too slowly. Gatina felt as if they had been waiting for months, not hours.

"Why is it taking so long?" she lamented to Pia.

"The shoals and sandbars," her cousin reminded her. "And it's low tide. Though she has a shallower hull, the *Daydream* can't risk coming too close. She should be able to make the passage safely by morning," she offered.

Matros considered that answer, then suggested, "Your captain's likely worried about the tide. She doesn't want to ground her hull—not here. She'll wait, if she's wise."

Gatina sucked in her breath, remembering the *Daydream* still had a spare boat. She and Pia had taken the gig, but there was still the slightly larger skiff drawn up on the deck. She exhaled when she visualized where that boat was situated. Someone was waving a torch back and forth on the deck.

"Our brothers will be here in the morning," she predicted confidently. "Darkness will protect us until then."

THE THREE OF THEM KEPT THE FIRE BURNING AS BRIGHTLY AS POSSIBLE DURING the night while they considered their options. The problem was what to do with the Rats on the mountain.

The customs of the Shipwrecker's Truce were clear. The cooperation and agreement to aid ended as soon as rescue arrived. They both agreed they would not rescue the two Rats—once they were aboard a ship, the Truce was over. To do so would invite catastrophe aboard the *Daydream*. She could imagine Darrick and Baramel finding some way to try to overpower the small crew and take the ship themselves. She was not about to let that happen. Instead, Gatina agreed she would return to the shrine and leave what they had not used, as custom dictated, and deal with the cosmic consequences as they arose.

"If you go, Matros will want to go with you—to defend your honor," Gatina said simply as she took their castaway treasures and put them in the copper kettle to carry. She was certain of the truth of that statement. "He's not nearly well enough to even handle the hike, not to mention a possible fight, not yet. Besides, I have more experience—and training—as a shadowmage. And I don't say that to take away from your abilities or skills. I'm just apparently the sneakiest girl in the world. Sneaking around is what I do," she stressed.

"So is stealing," her cousin said. "This is not stealing."

She was right, Gatina knew. This was returning items that had not been stolen without alerting Darrick and his mates. "No, it's almost stealing in reverse. I'm breaking into a shrine to put something back. But it is most definitely sneaking."

"I suppose the question is do you go now or wait until we determine if that boat is really the *Daydream*," her cousin said, relenting.

"I suppose I'd best go now," Gatina offered. "I should be back in an hour or so. You stay here with Matros until they've launched the skiff. And don't let them leave without me," she warned as she stood with the kettle.

Pia had no argument for that. Giving her cousin a final appraising look, she headed back up the beach to the cove, enjoying the night air and the throb of the surf in her ears. She looked fondly at the anchor the little girl had pulled from the sand on her way—if it hadn't just been her imagination. Climbing the path up the hill laden with a clanking kettle was more difficult than she'd anticipated, but she managed, filled with the hope of rescue.

Once she came to the clearing, she paused and examined the pirates' camp carefully with magesight. All three mariners were asleep—they had set no watch—and their fire had died down to embers. Indeed, they were all snoring lustily. When she saw the empty bottle of spirits near Baramel's head, she realized why. They must have finished the bottle last night, she reasoned.

Stealthily, she stole through the messy encampment, skirting the edges to keep from waking the drunken pirates. Silently she placed the copper kettle on the threshold of the shrine, gave a quick prayer of thanks to the capricious goddess, and was turning to leave when someone grabbed her left arm.

Her shadowblade was in her hand in an instant. The darkened blade whirled around and nearly stabbed the man who'd grabbed her. Her heart was racing—she was not used to anyone sneaking up on her.

The hand proved to belong to Genver, the captive mariner. His eyes glanced at the sword but quickly returned to Gatina.

"Take me with you!" he pleaded, mouthing the words in a whisper.

Gatina debated for only a moment. It was clear that the man was unhappy with the company of the pirates and had understood her return to the shrine for what it was: a signal that rescue had come somehow. Gatina regained control of herself and nodded, sheathing the sword and motioning the man to follow—quietly.

The two Rats did not stir as they passed by, but Gatina insisted on silence until they were more than halfway down the hill.

"How did you wake up?" she demanded in a low voice when she knew they were out of earshot of the two.

"I was awake all night," Genver assured her, as he followed her down the steep grade. "I just pretended to drink and made sure they got my share when we passed the bottle. And then I pretended to sleep. I was just about to steal away to seek your camp when I saw you in the firelight."

Gatina silently cursed herself—she hadn't employed any shadowmagic to obscure herself, because she hadn't thought it necessary. She would not make that mistake in the future, she vowed.

"A good plan," she conceded. "We sighted a sail a few hours ago. We think it's our sloop. Matros woke up just at twilight," she added. "His fever is broken, and he's on the mend."

"Good news." Genver nodded.

They quickly made their way back to the beach encampment, and Gatina didn't bother to smooth away their footprints. When they rounded the final curve in the beach, the sky had already begun to lighten in the east. They were gratified to see a boat drawn up on the beach—and her brother and cousin Jordi waiting for them.

She broke into a run the moment that she saw her brother, and then threw herself into an embrace. She felt her big brother's arms around her and felt safe for the first time in days.

"You finally came for me, Cat!" she said, laughing. "I knew you would!"

"I was worried I'd never see you again, Kitten," he said. "Father and Mother would be awfully upset if I managed to lose you."

"It was just one little shipwreck," she dismissed. "We survived. So did a couple of the Rats, unfortunately. They're passed out drunk on that hill," she said, pointing in the distance. "This is Genver, the bosun of that poor caravel that was attacked," she said, introducing the man. "And that is—"

"Matros." Jordi nodded. "Pia already did the introductions. How are you, Maranka?" he asked, emphasizing her alias.

"I'm well, Jordi—it's good to see you, too," she assured. "I bet your mother has been beside herself with worry."

"She hasn't slept since the squall," Jordi reported. "She's been casting spells and ordering us to search all these islands. This was the fifth one we sailed by when we saw light from the fire. Atopol was sure it was you and launched the skiff the moment it was light enough to see."

"It's best we get you all back to the *Daydream* before Captain Beah swims here herself," Atopol agreed. "Rescuing you put us days behind schedule. We're going to have to fly to get back to Pluhalia, as it is."

"Then let's go before the pirates wake up," Gatina said, nodding, as Pia helped Matros into the skiff. "I had a lovely time here, actually, but I suppose it's time to get back to work."

CHAPTER SEVENTEEN
THE LEGACY

The sea is endless. Yet still two ships may meet.
—Sea Lord proverb

THE SKIFF WAS LARGE ENOUGH FOR ALL SIX OF THEM, THANKFULLY. Designed to ferry cargo or supplies back and forth to the sloop, it boasted three benches and two sets of oars, allowing them to power through the rising tide and get beyond the break before the sun was truly risen over the horizon. Jordi and Atopol took one set, while Pia and Genver took the other. Gatina took the tiller, steering the little craft squarely toward the gleaming lines of the *Daydream*. After the last couple of days, she would have been happy to climb aboard just about any old wreck to get away from this desolate place, but the fact that her family's sloop was the one rescuing them was particularly pleasing.

"I hope we can keep the current on our side," Atopol said as he and the others began to row.

"Watch for the shoals," warned Matros. "They're particularly bad around here, if memory serves. And watch for that damned galleon, too."

"Oh, we passed them yesterday," Jordi assured. "They were headed in the opposite direction. It looks like they claimed that caravel as a prize, though," he added apologetically.

"I told the captain to stay in Dras Ferman until after the squall," Genver complained as his shoulders strained at the oar. "He wanted to keep his schedule. Shipwrecker has her own schedule. Now the damn fool has lost his life, his ship, and half his crew," he condemned.

"Are you all right, Kitten?" Atopol asked as he rowed. "You've been through a lot—even for you," he acknowledged, which she found gratifying. "Shipwrecked. Saved a man's life. That's quite an adventure."

"And pirates," she reminded him. "Some of that same crew from Pluhalia. I've discovered I'm not fond of pirates." After a moment's silence, she answered his original question. "Yes," she decided. "I am just fine. For the most part. I saw the green moon, while I was swimming to shore," she reported, pleased. "And I saw a nymph. It came up right next to me."

"A nymph?" Matros asked with interest. "That is lucky! They rarely come into the Great Bay. It's considered a sign of fortune to see one at all. They've been known to help stranded victims in the water, like porpoises. They say they live for a thousand years," he mused.

"Perhaps that's what protected me, then," she reasoned.

"Or it could be the moon," Genver suggested. "It's called the Crone's Eye, by the Sea Lords. To see it in the sky alone is considered good luck, too."

"It's not the Crone I'm concerned with, actually," Gatina decided. "It's her sister the Shipwrecker. What do you know about the Shipwrecker's Curse?"

Genver chuckled. "Oh, I wouldn't worry about that, much, lass. You have a year to expunge it. Most of it is silly little superstitions, anyway. Find a chapel, make an offering, drink some Maiden's Blood, ring some bells, and you're fine. In my experience, the Shipwrecker isn't exactly a stickler for details."

"You might want to ask Aunt Beah," Atopol suggested. "She knows all about that stuff. And Pia will need to perform the same duties. I'm sure Aunt Beah will have some advice about it," he offered as they neared the side of the *Daydream*. "But let her hug the stuffing out of you before you ask her. Our aunt has been rather preoccupied with finding you both, and she has only gotten more and more distraught," he confided. "I fear she was sinking into despair. After losing her husband at sea, this might have been too much for her . . ."

"Mother is tougher than that," Pia said confidently.

"You didn't see her," Jordi countered somberly. "I suppose if it was just losing you, that would have been bad enough, but to lose you both at the same time . . . after giving you permission to do something dangerously stupid . . ."

Gatina understood his meaning. If Beah had also lost Pia and her . . . she did not know what to say to that. Nor how her parents would have responded.

"She was nearly ready to give up, especially after we saw the pirate ship," Atopol agreed. "But I convinced her that we should continue. I *knew* you were there—so did Jordi. He is not a mage, but his instincts are as good as one. Aunt Beah has a lot of good location spells in her head, but I have a few myself. I told her you'd be here."

"How did you find us?" Gatina asked, wondering exactly that. He grinned.

"Your blade. Mine is made of the same metal, by the same swordsmith. I was able to use mine to scry for yours," he explained. "Like attracts like, after all." That was a popular and important rule in magic, she understood. "I improvised until I figured out how to do it. It was a rather interesting process."

"You'll have to write it out for me." She nodded. "It sounds useful."

"Well, it gave me a general direction to search. To locate you, to be more specific," he said, excited. "I was afraid you might have lost the sword at sea, but as we sailed, we were able to triangulate the readings from the spell. Aunt Beah charted out the readings and saw that this was the most likely island on the maps. Then, as we approached this island, I saw the smoke. Then it got dark, and we saw the fire."

Gatina nodded. "I saw a ship off in the distance. Then I used magesight and I recognized our sloop. That's when we piled all the wood onto the fire."

Atopol continued to row the skiff forward. They were close. She could make out the ship's familiar outline just ahead, even without her magic.

"I am eternally grateful that you continued to look for me," she said. "The past few days have been an adventure. And I will tell you all about it. But not now." In truth, despite sleeping on the island, Gatina found herself exhausted. "I am exhausted—and . . . sunburned!" she realized as she stared at her forearm. It was a vivid pink.

"I'd wager that you're absolutely starved, too," Atopol said between loud huffs as he rowed.

"We did well enough," she reported proudly. "We caught fish and crabs and clams. And Pia found berries and oranges and yams in the forest. When we found the shrine, we were able to take some hardtack. We made a kind of soup," she said. "But yes, I'm very hungry."

Her brother exhaled loudly as he rowed. She could tell that something was bothering him. He took in a breath as he pushed the oar forward and let it out as he pulled. Something seemed off with him.

Instead of making her ask, he volunteered what was bothering him.

"You should know that Aunt Beah was ready to abandon hope and sail back to Pluhalia. She was worried about missing our meetup with the

Legacy," he explained. "She was considering making the connection and coming back to search for you later. But I knew you were out here," he said confidently. "I convinced her to try one last island."

Gatina sucked in her breath. The admission shocked her—and hurt her feelings. Family was family. The code was the code. You never left someone behind on a heist. And even though Aunt Beah was no longer active in House Furtius, she was still a family member. As was Pia. What Atopol said was unfathomable. She could not imagine her parents doing such a thing.

"Don't blame Mother," Pia urged as the skiff pulled next to the rope ladder leading up to the deck. "She feels like she wasted two years of her life trying to find Father, and she regrets it. But she'll never admit it aloud. She keeps second-guessing herself about that. And blaming herself for not finding him. It's sad," she said quietly.

WHEN GATINA CLIMBED THE ROPE LADDER TO BOARD THE *DAYDREAM*, AUNT Beah pulled her into a fierce hug. She momentarily forgot what Atopol had said about her aunt's mental state—because at that moment, Gatina was safe once again. Even though she had only known the woman for a brief amount of time, she *was* family. And she looked terrible.

Somehow, she realized that the woman wasn't merely being practical in her desire to quit the search. No, it was self-preservation, she decided. Aunt Beah had already lost her husband to the sea. Gatina supposed that she could not comprehend losing her daughter and niece as well.

An intense feeling of warmth spread in her body, a sense of relief. It began in her chest—happiness at the rescue and reunion, then it washed over her body when she realized that she truly was safe and rescued. It overwhelmed her. It felt like she had just had a too-hot sip of tea that was spreading from her throat to her stomach then her arms and legs. All of her bravery and resilience seemed to melt away in that hug, and a font of emotions she didn't know she had began to well up in the maternal embrace.

"I found you!" her aunt whispered in her ear.

She felt the tears begin to pool in her eyes, but she was resolute. She would not cry. Crying was a sign of weakness. She was not weak. She was of House Furtius stock, and she would follow her aunt's example. Of course, her aunt did not seem to have the same fortitude, she discovered.

Aunt Beah was weeping on her shoulder, and the tears dripped down her arm. Gatina tightened her embrace. She wanted her aunt to know that this was real.

"You found more than me; you found four new crewmen," Gatina said, trying to be stalwart as she broke the embrace. "One of whom I think has an eye for Pia," she added, quietly. Matros and her cousin had yet to ascend the ladder, and she wanted to give her aunt some warning before she met him.

"Oh, *does* he?" Beah said, jolted out of her emotional state.

"Don't worry; she likes him too," Gatina confided. "He's nice. A fit mariner," she added. "But he's been wounded. We had to take an arrow out of his shoulder, and she's been nursing him back to health ever since."

"I . . . see," Beah said, wiping her eyes quickly. "Well, we'll be glad to have him on crew when he's back to fitness. The other two hands you rescued know their craft. Seksus has been working them in the search, and he's had little complaint."

She did have to admit how much it both irritated and surprised her that her aunt would have given up the search so quickly, but she tried to put it out of her mind for the moment. She understood that the mission comes first—it always did. But that was something she realized she would need to discuss with her parents. None of them had taken a pirate attack, the daring rescue and surprise squall, then the shipwreck and subsequent search into account in the planning of this trip. Such things happened at sea, she was learning. But for the moment, things were as normal as they had been since they left Dras Ferman with their cargo hold full of fruit.

To her credit, Beah did not break down weeping again when her daughter finally appeared over the railing of the sloop, though she did hold her embrace for a while. Then she met Matros and Genver, and a more businesslike expression came over her.

"Welcome aboard the *Daydream*," she announced. "I believe you already know Handur and Jarspur," she said as the crewmen greeted their old comrades and slapped them on the back, much to Matros's discomfort. Each man waved as his name was spoken.

"They've both been a tremendous help," Aunt Beah added. "In fact, after talking with them and Seksus, I think we have a good chance of quickly reaching the *Legacy*, assuming she has not left port.

"But I need to say a few words," Aunt Beah said. "First off, I am eternally grateful to the Shipwrecker for keeping you safe and helping us find you." Gatina watched as her aunt made a symbol, drawing an X over her heart, then her lips, then in front of her forehead. The four mariners made the same motions.

"And I want to say that if it were left to me, I would not have waited much longer to search for you," Aunt Beah explained. "That is not because I do not love or cherish you.

"This entire voyage, for the most part, centers around the delivery of shipments to our clients," she said evenly. "We were delayed initially in Pluhalia when the storms slowed the shipments. And now we are even further behind."

Gatina swallowed. She was happy they had continued the search, but she understood the dilemma. She did not feel terribly bad to be delayed, but for Beah and her company, it could mean the difference between profit and ruin. And there were no guarantees that they would not face further delays. The only thing they could do now is make haste in their travel.

"Now we must hasten our trip," Aunt Beah said. "With these new hands to help, we can put to sail in good order. I think the odds of catching the *Legacy* are very good." Beah glanced at the four men and each nodded their agreement, even Matros, who, to Gatina's eye, was clearly not yet ready to take on normal sailing duties.

"We will push the *Daydream* as fast as she can go in an effort to reach Pluhalia and the *Legacy*," her aunt continued. "We do run the risk of missing her in port, which would put us further behind, but I see no other option. We will need more supplies than we have if we have to sail the *Daydream* all the way to Vaxel," her aunt decided.

"You're going to Vaxel?" Genver asked with interest. "The Anchorage?"

"That's our goal," Beah agreed. "We have a contract for citrus with a schooner bound for Remere. *If* we can get there in time. And there is still a pirate ship in the vicinity," she reminded them. "We passed it yesterday, and I think we can slip by them today, but we must be ready to crack on sail at a moment's notice to do so. Once we get to port, we can swear out a warrant for them to the magistrate, but we have to make it to port first."

"Captain, that ship is seeking its lost crew. They have two who were shipwrecked with us," Gatina suggested. "They said they saw its sails."

"They might be less dedicated to such a search than you suspect," she countered. "After three days, it's customary to abandon a search for men overboard. Assuming the *Venjanca* crew can count to three—and that's a big assumption—we can still put a day between us and them. They *told* you they saw it?"

"When Pia and I found the Shipwrecker's shrine, the pirates had found it first," Gatina reported. "We invoked the truce. They weren't . . . belligerent," she said, recalling Darrick's charming ways.

Her aunt gave Gatina a long look, as if she were appraising her judgement or assessment. After considering what Gatina said, Aunt Beah nodded.

"I see. That is indeed good news," she agreed. "That fat caravel will have a much harder time getting close to the island than we did to rescue their castaways. Are you girls aware of the duties you must perform to make peace with the Shipwrecker, now that you're both castaways?"

Gatina sighed. "There's a curse, isn't there?" she asked, concerned.

"Of a sort, or so it is said," Aunt Beah said. "It's just a silly ritual. We'll discuss it at supper—once we are on course." She turned to Seksus. "Weigh anchor," she ordered the bosun. "Set course toward Pluhalia at once. And put every scrap of sail up you can. It's time we were underway."

Luncheon aboard the *Daydream* was a feast, in honor of the rescued castaways. Captain Beah cooked it herself, insisting that the rescued take the time to get some sleep before they ate.

Upon Gatina's request, she eschewed the usual thick stew and instead grilled a large tuna that had gotten entangled in the drag nets the sloop dangled in its wake. In addition, she simmered a pot of peas seasoned with dried leeks, vinegar, salt, long pepper and wine, and served with butter; for dessert, she prepared a thick pudding with raisins and dates, topped with fresh oranges from the cargo hold. As a special treat, she dipped into the small store of rum spirits and prepared a spiced grog, though she limited each crewman to one cup apiece of the powerful drink.

The meal was well appreciated by those who had endured the hardships of shipwreck. Genver and Matros devoured the food as if they had never eaten before. Gatina and Pia nearly matched them, wolfing down everything in their bowl—even the ship's biscuit that had been soaked in wine and grilled over the coals.

As a celebratory feast, it won high praise, even if it seemed modest fare by landsmen's standards. Indeed, the castaways from the captured caravel pronounced their service on the *Daydream* to be far superior, and flattered

Captain Beah incessantly with their gratitude and appreciation of her generous nature. To be taken from the depredations of pirates and the despair of being marooned and given decent work—and decent pay—aboard such a fine sloop as the *Daydream* was far beyond their expectations.

With both the current and the winds aiding them, the sloop made excellent speed across the Bay. All sails were furled, and the beneficial direction of the winds kept them from having to tack incessantly. By the end of the luncheon feast, they had already covered many miles toward Pluhalia. Any fear of pirates intervening was soon dismissed as the sloop sped across the Bay at more than fifteen knots. Gatina worked with her aunt in the pilothouse to ensure that they were, indeed, crossing the waves as rapidly as they guessed. There was no way the larger, heavier caravel could possibly catch the swift *Daydream*.

Gatina had not realized how exhausted she was until she crawled back into her bunk at twilight on her aunt's orders after the woman had applied a balm to her skin. It was a welcome and warm spot, dry and blessedly bereft of sand. And it was safe. She was protected there, she knew.

Sleeping on the beach had been different. There had been no blankets, no pillow, and no bunk on which to lie. Instead, she had tried to smooth out the sand as best she could and remove sharp shells and rocks before she'd laid her head down for sleep.

Though the sound of the waves breaking on the beach had been peaceful, she had to remain aware of predators or pirates or the possibility of a passing ship, which had kept her slumber from being restful. The noises of the island—the birds and the insects—had provided an interesting background, but her sleep was never deep, nor was it peaceful, because she was always on her guard.

But there, aboard her family's ship, knowing that there was a competent officer at the tiller and a clear course plotted, sleep came easily. Pia, likewise, was sent to take some rest after she'd tended to her patient. Gatina mumbled a goodnight to her cousin, but from the breathing pattern she heard in the darkness, it sounded like Pia had succumbed to slumber the moment her head hit the bunk.

As she drifted off to sleep, a vision of the red-headed girl from the cove danced through her mind. The strange girl's words of instruction about the Chapel of the Eight Bells and her prophecy of meeting her husband there floated to her memory, giving her something meaningful to contemplate. Gatina didn't even know what the Temple of the Eight Bells was or where it was, and she certainly had no interest in finding a husband, but she did wonder about the prediction. It seemed too apt to be mere happenstance.

A loud hammering on the cabin's door woke her long before she was rested. She wanted to sleep for six more days. She really missed the box beds at Palomar Abbey, she realized, as they provided the silence and darkness she craved. She ignored the knocking and tried to cling to slumber.

As she rolled onto her side to face the wall, her sticky, tight skin burned with the effort. A few minutes later, the pounding returned to the door, along with Jordi's tired voice. It took Pia's jostling in the bunk above her to finally pull Gatina from sleep. Then her cousin's feet hit the floor with a soft *thud*.

"Maranka, it's time to wake up," she said, softly at first. Gatina ignored her. "Gatina, *wake up!*" Pia's voice was louder the second, then third times she spoke.

When Gatina kicked herself free of her bed cover, she slowly eased herself from her cot. Her skin was suddenly awash in pain. Every limb seemed enflamed and burned with every move.

"This *hurts*," she complained. Indeed, her face, neck, arms, and legs felt like they had been boiled in seawater.

Pia nodded sympathetically, holding up her own sunburned arms. Her broad face was also a bright pink. "It will until it heals. We've just been in the sun far too long," she determined, with a frown. "Unfortunately, there's not a spell for sunburn, just a bunch of balms and aloe. We're burned like a bun in an oven that's too hot." She picked up a jar of the ointment Aunt Beah had used earlier. "Turn around and I'll apply it. Then you can do me. It will promote healing and numb your skin a bit. It will help, I promise," she said, as she opened the tin.

Gatina was aggravated by her situation. Her arms, hands and shoulders were a bright, angry red, as were her nose and forehead. Every motion she made hurt her. Pia's skin was far more bronzed, the product of many days under the sun, and she did not seem as badly injured. But Gatina traditionally worked at night and avoided sunlight. Even when she was working the rigging, she kept her face shaded whenever possible. Now she felt like a ship's biscuit left on the coals far, far too long. The cream felt cool on her skin, and it instantly soothed the sting.

"Darkness does not leave me burned," she grumbled as she pulled the clean shift over her head, gently, after the cream had soaked into her skin. "I'm more of a night person."

"More sleep will help," Pia promised. "I feel half dead myself. My turn!"

When Gatina ventured abovedecks, she was pleasantly surprised that there was very little for her to do to aid in the navigation. Matros was already there, his arm in a sling, studying the charts. He revealed that he was very knowledgeable about the western Great Bay, the currents and winds, and the astronomical paths overhead. He had apparently altered their course and was explaining it to her aunt as she walked into the cockpit.

She listened to his briefing as he explained how they could take advantage of a northern current that curled through the Bay. If the southern winds continued to favor them, they could make it to Pluhalia by the end of the next day. Gatina did the math in her head. Their trip back should be two days—which is how long she and Pia had been missing. This was the start of day three, so as of that moment, they were only one day behind schedule.

It was good news. And her aunt agreed.

"We shall press on, then," Beah said to the new crewman. Her aunt had not seen her yet, but when she did, she gasped. "Maranka! You are burned from head to toe! You're on sick call. No labor for you—at least not yet."

Sick call did not mean she didn't work. But instead of helping the rest of the crew run lines, change sheet directions, or swab the *Daydream*'s deck, Gatina found herself under the cockpit's roof, taking over the observations and recording them and occasionally working the tiller—light duty, as Matros explained. He, too, was too injured to be considered fit, and aided in piloting the ship instead.

Aunt Beah filled a bucket with cold seawater and instructed Gatina to put her feet in it as she charted, and laid a cool cloth on the back of her neck. Her aunt said the saltwater would draw out the sting of the burn. As soon as did as instructed, she shivered.

Gatina had to admit that she felt better after half an hour. Her skin was not as hot to the touch, though it was still very stiff. She compared it to a sheet hanging on the clothesline, drying in the sun and getting stiff.

Pia made a point of stopping by the cockpit several times, ostensibly to check on them both. But she gave Gatina only a cursory glance and spent most of her time with Matros, she noticed. She could not blame her cousin's interest in the mariner, but she found it a little annoying. Matros was healing, and his wound didn't need *that* much attention.

When Aunt Beah returned to check on her a few hours later, she seemed satisfied with the treatment. "Your skin has cooled. The cold water and aloe have helped," she said as she sank onto the bench beside Gatina, who was still watching the pair take a reading of their speed at the rails as the sloop streaked across the waves. Both of them were smiling excessively.

Beah followed Gatina's line of sight. "Ah. Yes. My daughter seems to have taken to this young man," she said, quietly bemused.

In fact, Gatina was fairly certain that Pia had said his name softly in her slumber.

"I think he's pretty taken by her as well." Gatina sighed. "He was terribly grateful to us both when he woke up finally. He called us gifts from the gods, the answer to his prayers. But he doesn't look at *me* that way." She hadn't meant to sound bitter or disappointed when she said it, but her aunt put a consoling hand on her shoulder. "Not that I wanted him to," she said hurriedly. "He's not a mage, so . . . well, I'm happy for her. For them."

"I'll reserve judgement on that matter. He seems stalwart enough." Beah nodded. "He knows his seamanship. He's literate. He's ambitious. Indeed, he reminds her a bit of her father. The same confidence, the same intelligence, the same politeness. But only time will tell." She sighed. "Many men hide their true selves when a pretty maid is in sight."

Maybe he was Pia's future husband, as the strange girl had predicted. She hadn't mentioned that to anyone, but it seemed to be coming true.

When Pia and Matros returned to the cockpit, Matros logged the reading and refigured the chart. He quickly found their location and plotted it on the map with a charcoal pencil. But he winced as he jostled his shoulder.

It was clear to Gatina that the simple bit of movement of tossing the log line overboard and hauling it back in had hurt his bandaged shoulder. Even in the sling, it was painful. Pia noticed, too, and was by his side in an instant. She reached for and adjusted his sling so that she could have a good look at the wound. Aunt Beah's posture stiffened as she watched her daughter examine the man so intimately.

As Matros studied the map, Gatina studied Pia, who was studying Matros. She noticed her aunt's concerned but amused look. She had a crooked smile on her lips. It was not quite a smirk, but it was close. Matros did not seem self-conscious about her daughter's obvious interest.

"Where did you learn to plot a course, Matros?" Gatina asked, curious. It was not a skill many mariners possessed, she had learned.

"My second cruise," he admitted. "A barque out of Brisomar called the *Acorn*. The pilot fell ill, and the captain tried each of us at the task. I fared better than most. But I learned my letters at an abbey in Glavores."

"You did a fine job. We've gained hours now that I know about that current. So, Matros, what are your plans when we reach port?" Beah asked casually, when she was satisfied with his charting.

"Captain," Matros said, after a moment's thought, "I think my first business will be to go to the temple, find a magistrate, and swear out a complaint of piracy against the *Venjanca* for what they did to my ship and my fellow crewmen. Then I suppose I'll have to find a berth on another ship."

Beah considered. "You know, I have a small fleet, back in Prejestia. We're always looking for good men—fit mariners I can depend on. I place a premium on loyalty."

"Well, you will find no man more loyal than I," Matros suggested. "I owe my life to your daughter, and therefore I owe you my allegiance. I am a journeyman mariner, and I have been at sea for four years, down in Caramas. I have my credentials—or did, before I lost my ship."

"You wouldn't mind working in the Eastern Bay?" Beah proposed. "For a minor house with a scandalous reputation for mixing with magi?"

"I have no kin left in Glavores," Matros admitted. "That's one reason I went to sea. A prosperous life once. I've made many voyages. But these waters have grown too dangerous since I was a squid. Caramas seems to attract corsairs. In four years, this was the first time I've had pirates actively pursuing and attacking my ship."

"Things have gotten chaotic since the Duke died." Beah nodded. "They are not much better in the Eastern Bay than they are in the west. But there are more opportunities, I think, with more ports and more ships near the Mandros. Of course, with the scourge of slavery rising, things are likely to get worse before they get better. They made that Rat Jenerard the Master of the Waves," she added. "That man is no mariner, he's a gangster, and he sees the office as an opportunity for corruption, not regulation. Things could get quite rough in the next few years," she warned.

"Storms come and go." Matros shrugged—which made him wince. "If you're on a good-enough ship, you can weather them. My mates and I spoke earlier this morning. I think we'd rather have a good berth with folk we trust than take our chances in port. If you'll have us," he added.

Beah considered the matter. "Let's get through this voyage to Vaxel and then assess your standing. But the loyalty I expect requires a great deal of discretion along with it. I do not want my business discussed with anyone. It is . . . complicated and delicate. I'm a mage, after all, and we have our secrets. Can you and your mates keep your mouths shut about matters you might not understand?" she asked pointedly.

Matros looked around, his eyes lighting on Gatina for a long moment.

"I confess, I've had little experience with the magi," Matros admitted, "but by reputation, you are a secretive folk. I can respect that. As far as my mates, they're good fellows who only demand decent pay, good work, and good food. If you can fulfill that obligation—and keep us from pirates—then I think you will not be disappointed."

Matros was skilled in subtext, Gatina saw. She knew the man was well-spoken and seemed to have some education. Not many mariners went to abbey schools or even knew how to read and write. He and his friends had been helpful aboard the *Daydream*, and that impressed Aunt Beah, who was a much harsher critic than she.

"Then we will take your oaths when we get back to the *Legacy*; you can sign the log, and I'll have you integrated with my proper crew—once you meet with Captain Armandus, of course, and seek his approval. If you can sail with us for the rest of the voyage, then I think you will be well satisfied when we return east. If not . . . well," she said, cocking her head. "There are plenty of islands I can leave you on."

Gatina realized that Aunt Beah was pretty skilled in subtext as well.

As the day continued, it became obvious to Gatina that Matros was just as smitten with Pia as she was with him. But she did not think he was trying to sweet-talk his way into her aunt's good graces. In fact, he seemed determined to impress her with his industry.

Even though Matros was still weak, he was healing well enough to do small jobs, such as mending and splicing line, things that did not require much effort. He helped Beah with cooking duties, too. And while he could not swab or climb the rigging, he was happy to call the shanties used in timing those duties in his deep voice. He was the first to volunteer to assist with any task, no matter how trivial. Especially if it involved her cousin.

Over the course of the day, his actions caught not only Pia's attention but everyone else's as well. In fact, when Jordi commented at luncheon on how attentive the man was to not just the boat but also his big sister, Pia blushed. Though she was embarrassed, there wasn't much she could say, because it was true.

When they had been on the island, Gatina felt uncomfortable with that attention. The man had talked and joked with both of them, but when she realized that his affections were toward her cousin and not her, she relaxed, and that allowed her to observe him more objectively. And more carefully.

The clanging of the bell rang inside Gatina's ears. It took her several moments to realize that what she was hearing was real and not a dream. She understood that a bell was an alarm, but she had forgotten where she was and what a bell ringing on a boat might mean. Then the pounding on the cabin door began. With a sense of alarm, she snatched up her shadowblade from behind her pillow and threw open the door, ready to fight.

Jordi was caught off guard by a naked black sword being pointed at him by his cousin when he opened the door.

"Maiden's mercy, Kitten!" he protested as he stared at the blade, eyes wide. "There's no need for that!"

"Sorry," Gatina mumbled. "I heard the bell. I thought we were under attack."

"No, but we did spy a sail," he informed her. "That's what I came to tell you."

"Pirates?" she asked worriedly.

"We thought so at first, but your brother used magesight and ruled that out. It's the *Legacy*," he explained.

"The . . . *Legacy*?" she asked, confused.

"Yes, apparently, they were headed toward Dras Ferman while we were headed to Pluhalia. I think they were searching for us. Only dumb luck that we sighted them, I suppose, but they're about a half-mile ahead and closing. Mother didn't want to wake you, but Cat thought you might want to know."

"Thank you!" Gatina said, excited at the prospect of seeing her parents again. Indeed, there was a kind of desperate need in her to do so. Her burnt skin, her many adventures, and her pure exhaustion made her want to seek the comfort of her mother. And she never felt safer than when her father was around. "Wait, if they were coming after us, that means we won't be heading to Pluhalia, right?"

"Correct," Jordi nodded. "We'll have to change course. I don't know where we're headed to yet—that will be up to the captains—but we can likely get on our proper way again. But Cat wants you on deck when the *Legacy* arrives, so your absence doesn't give your mother a fit," he explained.

"Aye," Gatina nodded, putting her blade back in her bed and tying on a headscarf. Even that motion hurt, with her shoulders burned like bacon. "I certainly don't want to do *that*."

CHAPTER EIGHTEEN
EYES ON THE HORIZON

Politics has long been the bane of the Sea Lords, both their own and that of the landsmen they encounter. By nature of their many houses, havens, and companies, with alliances and rivalries shifting with the inevitable changes in the marketplace, it has always been difficult for them to consolidate their considerable power enough to establish themselves as a true commercial empire. Further, the unavoidable role that authorities ashore play in their commerce and society frequently muddy the waters. Yet if the Sea Lords lack a practical means of coming together in a meaningful way, their many seasonal councils, held under the auspices and clergy of their divine sovereign, the Storm King, seek consensus about important topics sufficient to allow them some sense of unity, even when their factions are at open war.
—*from* **Sea Lords, Their Cults, Religious Customs, and Traditions**

THE FIFTH TIME THAT GATINA CAUGHT HER MOTHER STUDYING HER, SHE sighed, exasperated, and glared right back.

"I am *fine*, Mother! I promise!" she proclaimed, irritated.

The reunion of the *Legacy* and the *Daydream* had been joyful, an unexpectedly benign conclusion to what had been a frightening delay. When the *Daydream* had gone two days late, Captain Armandus had elected to wait no further and go in search of the sloop.

Gatina had no doubt that her parents had been instrumental in his decision—Mother, especially, could be quite persuasive. They had sailed from Pluhalia the previous day, and it was only luck that they had selected a similar course to Beah's. When the ships pulled up side by side, the expressions of relief and gratitude were followed with a detailed accounting of the *Daydream*'s eventful journey from Dras Ferman.

Her parents were horrified to learn how close they came to losing their only daughter at sea, of course. But they quickly recovered—their Kitten did have a way of getting herself into and out of such predicaments.

But ever since then, Gatina found herself feeling like a mark being studied whenever her mother was around. Of course, if done correctly, a mark would never realize they were under surveillance. But her mother's constant gaze made her so uncomfortable that she sought solitude by climbing the mast of the *Legacy* under the pretense of seeing if her shoulders and limbs were yet healed enough to resume normal duties. It was a painful exercise and did not give her the answer she wanted. Climbing hurt.

However, when she returned to the deck, she realized that her attempt had caused her mother to worry even more. Gatina decided it was time to address her mother's concerns directly.

No sooner had she returned to the deck than her mother confronted her.

"Are you sure you are well?" Minnureal asked.

"Well enough to climb the mainmast," Gatina assured her. "It still hurts, but . . ."

"Keep putting the ointment on it," she counseled. "We were very worried about you, you know," she added. "We knew something was wrong when you didn't return in time."

"We managed," Gatina reported. "Squalls, pirates, shipwreck . . . that's just the life of a mariner. I've been in danger before," she dismissed.

"You are far more than a mere mariner," her mother reminded her. "But the danger of the sea is different from a heist. We had no control over the situation this time. I had a bad feeling the moment you left. And now that we find out what happened, it is so much worse than we imagined."

"But I'm fine!" she insisted, annoyed at her mother's lack of confidence in her. "I was able to contend with everything the sea could throw at me!"

Her mother sighed and shook her head. "I know you and Cat are capable—we've done everything we can to ensure that you are. But this . . . it was terrifying to know that you were out there, somewhere, and we had no idea what was happening. And every idea of what could have gone wrong."

"You know, I won't be a child forever," Gatina pointed out. "In a few years, I will complete my apprenticeship and be off on my own. Will you still worry about me this much then?" she asked skeptically.

"Only if you run away to sea." Her mother chuckled. "But yes, I will still worry. You may no longer be a child, but you will always be *my* child."

It was unusual for her mother—and father—to be overcome with a case of parental nerves, given their line of work. Gatina had never been known for a sense of caution in her missions, and that had always been a source of concern. But this wasn't a mission. It was a mishap at sea, a storm, something entirely out of their control.

Gatina wisely chose not to roll her eyes. Instead, she stared back at her mother indignantly. "Mother, I am fine. I just wanted to see if I was fit for deck duty. I'm not," she said, answering her own question. "But considering we don't know where we're going yet, that doesn't seem to be a concern."

"Your aunt and Captain Armandus are discussing our course with your father now. Our plans have changed since Pluhalia. We . . . received some intelligence there that has altered them. We should have a course plotted to somewhere by this afternoon."

"So, what do you think of Matros?" she asked, attempting to change the subject.

"The mariner? The one who clearly likes your cousin? I'll tell you after I've had a chance to learn who he is—who he *really* is."

Gatina was confused. "You think he's a spy or something?"

"No, no—well, he could be," she conceded, "but that's very unlikely. No, I mean that I need to find out what kind of *man* he really is. Anyone can be on his best behavior around a girl's family when they first meet. It's what he does when he thinks no one is looking that's important."

"So, you're going to spy on him?" Gatina asked, intrigued.

"Observe more than spy," her mother corrected. "But yes. It's my duty as Pia's aunt. Just as your relatives will investigate the young man you eventually marry."

The mention of marriage startled Gatina. It reminded her of Pippa's prediction. "Who said *I* was getting married?" she asked defensively.

"Oh, I'm sure you'll find a worthy wizard who is intelligent enough to meet our standards, Kitten," Minnureal dismissed. "If he is a man of worth and character, then he should not suffer overmuch. It might be difficult to find such a man, but we have every confidence in you."

"As if I'll *ever* find a man you'll find worthy—with *rajira!*" Gatina snorted. "I suppose I can always just take holy orders and live out my life as a spinster . . ."

"Kitten, don't despair," her mother soothed. "Just keep your eyes on the horizon. These things just have a way of playing out. I never thought I'd marry, myself," she revealed.

"Really?" she asked in surprise. She couldn't envision her mother without her father.

"I was proud, I was motivated by other matters, and I had no desire for such entanglements when I had greater ambitions for political change," she explained. "Yet I met your father—in a *very* unusual circumstance—as if the gods ordained it. I met a man so worthy that I adopted his house and bore his children, children I didn't even know I wanted but who have become the most precious thing in the world to me. He was intelligent. He was educated. He was kind. He was wise. He was dashing—so dashing!" she said fondly.

"It's kind of a family curse," Gatina agreed.

"I could have easily become a Practical Adept and pursued my interests without him, you know. But he wooed me, and eventually I knew there was no better man in all the world for me. When you know what your heart says, you should listen."

"My heart isn't saying much," Gatina said doubtfully. "And now I'm officially cursed! By a capricious goddess devoted to chaos!"

"It will, Kitten," her mother assured. "And don't worry about the curse. We Furtiusi navigate such things all the time. Often, they only have the power over you that you let them—and you are a very determined girl," she reminded Gatina.

"Now," she continued, "while it is Shadow's news to share, I will let you know that we faced disappointment in Pluhalia. It turns out our prime contact with the Sea Lords that Master Thinradel directed us to was forced to ship out the day before we landed, which has complicated things. Apparently, he is being pursued by agents of the Five Counts on suspicion that he is . . . plotting against them."

"He *is* plotting against them," Gatina pointed out. "So are we."

"Which is why he's being pursued so aggressively. Including by Censors," her mother informed her, causing Gatina's eyes to widen. "He moved to a different location to escape their grasp, so we may have to alter our course, or split up the *Daydream* and the *Legacy* again, before we make Vaxel. That is what your father, your aunt, and the captain are discussing."

"This mission seems to be fraught with chaos," Gatina sighed.

"Every mission is, Kitten." Her mother sighed. "We just try to shield you from most of it, as much as we can, and only give you what you need to complete your portion. That's all an apprentice should expect. Once you are a journeyman, you can make your own decisions, plan your own heists, and take your own risks. And then you'll truly see what *chaos* means!"

Before Gatina could pursue her line of questioning, Atopol interrupted them at the rail.

"Ah, Kitten, you're back from your spy mission," he teased, nodding his head toward the mainmast. "Father has asked that we join him in the captain's cabin. For an update on Shadow Council affairs," he informed them.

The mention of the family's rebellion sent Gatina's pulse racing. She had not forgotten about the mission, of course, but she had been occupied with survival, pirates, and the daughter of a highly impulsive divinity. But somehow, Atopol's announcement brought the importance of the voyage back to her. It wasn't about making a profit from citrus, or dodging pirates, or learning the intricacies of Sea Lord culture and mythology. It was about overthrowing a tyrant who had the worst possible intentions. That was what was most important.

Gatina had never been to the captain's cabin, of course—only the bosun and Aunt Beah came there regularly. It was not a large room, to her surprise; indeed, the cabin she had shared with Pia on the *Daydream* was slightly larger. But there was a table affixed to the deck, a few stools, and a large bunk that doubled as a bench. A modest brass lantern hung from the ceiling. There was little in the way of ornamentation or decoration—Captain Armandus had a humble sense of décor—but there was a small shrine to the Fairtrader nailed to the bulkhead, and a single painted tapestry devoted to the night's sky that she could see was reasonably accurate tacked to the space above his bed. But otherwise, the cabin was austere.

Her father was already seated, as was Aunt Beah. Captain Armandus stood and paced nervously as he regarded his companions. Atopol and her mother led her into the room, and her brother immediately ceded the remaining empty stool to his mother.

"So, this is the rest of the cabal," Armandus said, regarding her and her family suspiciously as they entered.

"More of a conspiracy than a cabal," Minnureal said as she took her seat. "We are agents of the Shadow Council, which is opposed to Count Vichetral and his cronies." Gatina was shocked—ordinarily, they did not discuss such matters with outsiders. Something must have compelled her father to bring him into the knowledge of their true mission, she concluded. The captain did not seem happy about it, either. She sought a stool in a corner, out of the way, while she listened to them argue.

"Politics and the sea never mix well," the captain asserted.

"The sea is the common field on which politics is always expressed," her father argued quietly. "Every ship that sails owes allegiance to some power ashore," he pointed out.

"That doesn't mean we have to like it," Armandus murmured. "I suspected that something was odd when Beah took on the *Daydream* and . . . *you*," he said suspiciously. "The family has always been wary of unnecessary complications with landsmen. I can see why now."

"We work in the service of the duchy and its peoples. Including you. Do you think Count Vichetral's policies will advance your trade?" Minnureal asked pointedly. "Forcing you to a choice between becoming slavers or privateers?"

"No," he admitted. "I mislike the directives of the Master of the Waves of late. The old duke was fair enough, but this count is a landsman pretending to be a mariner and doesn't understand our ways."

"So, appreciate that some landsmen are working to restore Alshar's maritime might and just and responsible regulation," Hance said firmly. "The Wave and the Wood both owe Vichetral as an enemy. We either cooperate to hold him to account, or we both see our worst fears come to pass."

"I take no issue with your fight with the Count of Rhemes," insisted Armandus. "I just object to being a party to a fight between Coastlords."

"No one has the luxury of being ambivalent anymore," her mother said flatly. "Either you reject tyranny and join the fight, or you deal with the consequences of your hesitancy. These are the stakes we fight for."

Armandus paused for a longish time until he finally sighed. "So be it. If I must choose, I choose the side of liberty and reason. No matter how inconvenient it may be. Or how deceitful," he added pointedly. Gatina nearly blushed. She was used to keeping secrets as part of her family legacy. She was not used to being called out for it by a self-righteous stranger to their ways. It was a harsh rebuke from an honest man, and it stung her more than she anticipated.

"We use our deceit as a weapon against a man who sits on a stolen throne. Trust that the gods of both land and sea will not see a tyrant prosper," Minnureal assured him. "Vichetral recruits the worst of both to do his bidding. We find the best to counter him. The Shadow Council has been a watchman against tyranny for more than four hundred years."

"And the Sea Lords have been watchful for it for more than six hundred," Armandus argued, defiantly. "We strove against the Archmage. Against the dukes when they were thrust upon us. And against this count who has too high an opinion of himself. We will strive against you, too, should you prove faithless in your struggle," he reminded them. "It matters not what highborn Sea Lords you might recruit to your cause. We see who the tyrants are," he declared.

"Then take a seat and help us prevail, Captain," Minnureal said, respectfully, gesturing to the final open stool. "We are at a crucial point in our plotting. All could rest on whether or not we are successful. Your assistance would help ensure that. Some of your countrymen—if I may use that term—have decided that liberty is worth a struggle. Your sister-in-law has deemed it worthy and committed herself. Are you counted among them?" she asked pointedly.

It was a direct challenge to the man's character, Gatina realized. And not entirely fair.

She had come to know that honest merchantmen like Armandus were far more focused on the expectation of profit than any political ideals. Those were landsmen's concerns, in their minds, and only worthy of note when they had an effect on maritime issues. While some mariners were proud of their countries of origin, the Sea Lords had always held themselves a people apart, with the sea as their nation. The nature of the maritime trade encouraged a more-international perspective that focused on the general brotherhood of the sea, not the interests of any one nation ashore.

But she was surprised when Captain Armandus grunted and took the final stool at the table. "This may all see us hanged," he pointed out with a sigh.

"A great many things could happen," Beah affirmed. "But if we let those greedy lubbers dictate our fortunes to us, then a simple hanging might be preferable to what results."

"We come away from Pluhalia with ill news," Hance began, once it was clear Armandus was finished with his objections. "I met my contact there to introduce me to our mark, only to find that we had missed him by a day. Indeed, the Council of Counts has made a special point to send their agents to root out the sedition they see among the Sea Lords and make an example of them," he related. "It is being ordered by Baron Jenerard, who may have been involved in the assassination of Duchess Enora in Vorone. He has been named Master of the Waves and tasked to bring the Great Houses of the Sea Lords in line with Vichetral's vision for Alshar."

"A right bastard, that Jenerard," conceded Armandus. "He's a Rat, nasty and ambitious."

"He's ruthless as well—something that's common in Vichetral's court," her mother agreed. "If the count put him to a task, it is a test of loyalty and competence. Without the support of the Sea Lords, his council will not be able to hold power indefinitely.

"The good news is that Jenerard is loathed by a great many of those whom he's wronged over the years," Beah informed them. "The Brotherhood has interfered in the workings of the docks across the Great Bay and oft used Jenerard as their face in 'negotiations' with the gangsters. His corruption insults the sensibilities of honest merchants.

"But there are also those who are pragmatic enough to understand the utility and profit of a renewed slave trade," she continued. "Or who see the elimination of smaller competition in warfare a boon to their own fortunes. Sadly, piracy and commerce raiding can be incredibly profitable. More, it threatens the smaller companies who do not have the means of defending themselves and makes them more likely to assent to pressures from the larger companies."

"Thankfully," her father picked up, "there are plenty of houses that understand the dangers of such trade and realize how it is being used against them. I have heard more than once how there will only be a handful of great companies controlling all of shipping in the Great Bay in a few years, if these policies are adopted."

"Aye, that's true," Armandus conceded sadly.

"Many houses are rebellious toward the idea of accepting the usurper's authority if it leads to such a course. They favor Duke Lenguin's line, his policies, which encouraged competition and were generally fair—for a landsman. Those houses have formed a kind of loose alliance that extends from Falas to Vorone, Castal, Farise, and beyond. They are ready to resist the Council of Five."

"Are they, now?" Armandus asked, skeptically. "A handful of small houses and havens? Against the likes of House Venjancar? House

Amporos? House Ramarith?" he asked, naming three of the largest and most powerful Sea Lord families on the Great Bay.

"That's who we are trying to form an alliance with," Hance explained reasonably. "If we can secure their aid and bring them into our operations, it would give us increased leverage in our resistance. Nor are they overly fond of the new 'kingdom' formed by Castal and Remere. They still hold Farise and interfere with operation of that great port. Without a voice for Alshar influencing their policies, Alshari-flagged ships encounter poor circumstance there. I was to meet one of their representatives suggested by our former Court Wizard. Alas, he was forced to flee Pluhalia ahead of an expedition sent by Vichetral to arrest him and his associates."

"So, how does this affect our plans?" Atopol asked thoughtfully.

That raised Captain Armandus's bushy eyebrow. "You allow your *children* to speak in council?"

"Children? Cat and Kitten have been some of our most effective agents since the Shadow Council reconvened," their mother answered proudly. "They are tolerably well informed on our operations, our goals, and our methods. We value their insights on matters such as this."

Gatina blinked her violet eyes in shock. This was the first she'd heard of this. To her mind, she had been kept ignorant and largely left out of important Shadow Council matters. Perhaps Atopol had some influence with their parents, but she felt more like an ungainly tool than a valuable counselor.

"It means we have to change course and meet with him in a different port," their father said in answer to her brother's question. "From what my contact said, he fled on a sloop to Manahar, where he has some allies. It is a small port but a lively one and on the way to Vaxel."

"It's not my preferred course," grumbled the captain. "I like to take the southern fork of the delta and sail up that way. It's wider and deeper."

"But Manahar is close enough to Vaxel so that taking the northerly route does not add too much time to our journey," Beah reasoned. "It will take but two days to get there, if the winds aren't against us too much, and then we can sail directly to Vaxel in time for the Anchorage to begin. If we can pick up your man in a timely manner, he can accompany us there."

"Why is Vaxel Anchorage so important? What is it, exactly?" Gatina asked, earning a sharp look from the captain. She ignored it.

"The Anchorage has an interesting history. It is one of the larger gatherings of the merchant fleets all year," Beah explained. "It first began when the sugar ships from the Shattered Isles made their way into port in summer and required cargo to fill their empty holds. It grew into an opportunity for the Sea Lords to gather in council and discuss matters important to them. And then the dukes used it as an opportunity to assess the value of the ships who made anchorage there, for taxes and regulation, as well as inspect them for safety. Since then, it has become a general fair and gathering for mariners of all types, Sea Lords, Coastlords, and others. It is assumed that this contact we're picking up has some plan or scheme to be conducted at the Anchorage—one which the Shadow Council may be of service to."

"There are many high nobles and important captains at the Anchorage," agreed Armandus. "It is one of the great councils. A lot of commerce is discussed and arranged there. High court cases are heard before the magistrates of the Storm Lord. And the Master of the Waves traditionally gives speeches and recruits ships of war for ducal service there."

"So, whatever the rebel Sea Lords have planned could be terribly important for our rebellion," Hance concluded. "Establishing our alliance and assisting them—as well as coordinating our efforts—could be what we need to start undermining Vichetral's rule. Having to contend with both the Brotherhood and the Censorate makes things far more difficult for both of us.

"So, we're planning on making port in Manahar in two days, taking on enough additional cargo to fill our holds to overflowing, fetching our contact, and then proceeding to Vaxel."

"To what end?" demanded Atopol. "I like a day at the fair as much as anyone, but this all seems entirely too vague to be useful to us."

"I don't know what kind of mission this will end up being," her mother told them almost apologetically. "We won't know that until we make contact. So, I want you both to prepare for anything. From now on, I need you to focus on your training more than your seamanship. With the additional hands we've acquired, we have enough manpower to sail both ships instead of towing the *Daydream*, and that should allow you suitable time to prepare. You'll both be transferred there until Manahar, so you'll be ready. For anything."

BEAH CONTINUED TO COMMAND THE SLOOP, BUT HER MOTHER, FATHER, AND cousins were also aboard to run the sail, along with Matros and Genver, who took over as bosun of the *Daydream*. Gatina wondered, too, if the threat of four shipwrecked souls on one ship was bad luck. Pia, Matros, and Genver must also complete the Shipwrecker's ritual, just as she would, she knew. But Pia was a Sea Lord and Matros a mariner; neither seemed as concerned about the matter as she was.

Gatina sat with her back to the mast sail, under the wide berth of shade it provided after both ships began the voyage northwest toward Manahar. A gentle breeze danced across her shoulders, which were still red but no longer an angry purple-red from her time on the island. Aunt Beah had provided her with a tin of salve that had taken the sting from her burn and encouraged healing, but she had cautioned Gatina to apply it frequently. Minnureal had been diligent in enforcing that directive.

Minnie joined Gatina, while Atopol slid onto the bench opposite. Hance stood. Now that the ships had been reunited, everyone was able to sleep a full night or day, depending on the duties they had drawn. But for now, they were enjoying a moment alone as a family. A family that was planning to challenge a vile usurper's rule.

"It wasn't just our Sea Lord contact we tried to make in port," Hance revealed. "The Shadow Council used magic to get word to your mother in Pluhalia regarding the full plan of the Council of Five. Vichetral is using pressure on the independent Sea Lord families," Hance explained. "Through emissaries and agents, the counts are seeking an agreement or fealty with at least five of the larger houses and countless smaller ones. Their goal is to grant their favorites beneficial rights and prerogatives at the expense of the weaker houses that do not pledge their loyalty. And they are using the Censorate to do that, among other unsavory tactics."

That was troubling news. The black-and-white checkered cloaks of the Royal Censors were the last thing she expected to see this far from Falas. Gatina scanned her father's face, trying to find either a trace of worry or a sign of confidence. She only saw his face as neutral, the mask he often presented in public and, more recently, she realized, to her.

Her brother shared her concern. "The Censors?" Atopol asked. "Really? Against the Sea Lords? The seamagi aren't going to like that," he predicted.

"They usually left the seamagi alone, in Lenguin's day," their mother agreed, "but they are empowered to regulate them harshly under Vichetral's rule."

"Vichetral is willing to use whatever device he has to secure their loyalty. That is why he's sending his dog Jenerard to bark at them. But he won't be alone. From what we've learned, he is planning on bringing several crews of Rats to disrupt the Anchorage and intimidate the Sea Lords as well."

"They don't seem like the kind of folk to be easily intimidated," Gatina pointed out.

"The minor houses are like any small business," her father argued. "No matter how proud the culture, they have to face the realities of their situation. This Sea Lord council at Vaxel will be important. More than a hundred houses will be represented there, many bearing proxy votes from those who could not attend. Those are who Jenerard will be attempting to bribe, threaten, or frighten into compliance. And they are the ones we will be attempting to influence, I think," Hance revealed.

"They don't seem like the kind of folk to be easily influenced, either," Atopol said doubtfully.

"Let's hope we can perform better than Jenerard, then," their mother agreed. "Because if they gain that acceptance, Vichetral and the counts will have control over more than just the waterways. The Council of Counts is looking for full control over the merchant and shipping families, Sea Lord and Coastlord, across the Great Bay. With that control they stand to dominate the duchy's economy in a way that will keep him in power until he dies."

Minnureal's nostrils flared as she huffed out an angry breath. Gatina was relieved that her mother's ire was directed at someone else. She was all too familiar with her mother's temperament, having tested it herself many times in the past.

"If that comes to pass, we will have precious little left to use as leverage," she continued. "Therefore, the overall goal of this mission is to sway those very same houses to join the Shadow Council or at least reject Vichetral's embassy," she reminded them. "Historically, Sea Lords do not cater to the whim of landsmen's politics. Instead, they look to the economics. But a handful of smaller houses alone simply cannot stand against the power of the Great Houses if they have support and recognition of the palace. Regardless of who lives there."

She nodded to Hance, who was ready to continue the discussion.

"Vaxel is where we present options for those independent houses," he explained. "One of those options involves something of great value to the Sea Lords that we hold in our possession. And that is something with which we can bargain." Hance looked to Minnie and nodded. Gatina was irritated that Father did not elaborate on what exactly was in House Furtius's possession that could be used as leverage. Atopol was likewise aggravated by the tease of information and lack of details. Secrets, she knew, were part of their legacy. What was not known could not be told.

Still, it was irritating.

"Manahar, if you recall, is a port city in southern Rhemes," Minnureal reminded them, her tone shifting from aggravation with the Five Counts and their plans to a more academic tone. "The city is larger than Pluhalia but less than half the size of Vaxel. It is a small but major trading hub for inland products. As such, we will reprise our aliases as minor Sea Lords in order to collect our informant. We should be able to do so alone, but just in case, you two will tour the city with your cousins and be available for assistance if needed." Minnie turned her head and looked at Gatina. "There will be *no* incidents on this trip. Am I clear? Manahar is no Sea Lord haven; it's a Coastlord port that has made Rhemes wealthy. Rhemes is from where Count Vichetral hails," she reminded them. "His spies and supporters will be everywhere, so it's best to be extremely cautious. No unnecessary entanglements, no impulsive thefts that might attract attention. Am I clear, apprentices?"

Gatina's face drained of the deep sunburn shade as she swallowed and nodded.

"The fact that Manahar is technically in Rhemes is actually beneficial for us. While you're there, try to listen in to the conversations between people of all stations. Manahar will be filled with ships on their way to the Anchorage. Many will be off their guard and may let something slip that could be important to our eventual mission. Mind also what is *not* said—the subtle looks, for example, between merchants, beggars, or even the most elevated Sea Lords. Spies come in all guises. The truth often lies in between the words, as we have often seen. Your observations will help inform our strategy, so it is essential that you pay attention."

"So, just . . . wander around and listen?" Atopol asked, surprised.

Hance looked at Atopol, then Gatina. "I trust your judgement. You have both proven capable in surveillance, among the other tasks with which you have been entrusted, and you are clever enough to realize what is important and what is not. Until then," he said, opening a locker on the deck that held the wooden practice swords, "prepare yourselves."

Later that evening, once the sun had set and the stars were high above, Hance suggested lessons. And while he offered Gatina options other than calisthenics, she chose to do what her brother was doing, stiff skin or not. While her skin no longer felt like Briga's hot coals, it did feel tight.

"I suspect that the more I move, the better it will feel," she assured her father, who looked worriedly at her as she winced her way through her exercises. "Don't worry, Father; I won't crack," she joked.

But the more she worked, the more she began to wonder about that. It wasn't her muscles. Her skin protested the simplest of movements. The motion of raising her arms overhead in jumping jacks had her suck her breath in sharply until she adjusted to the squeeze across her shoulders and upper back. After those were finished, he had them climbing the masts. That did not bother her as much.

But then sword practice with first the wooden scimitars the mariners favored and then their shadowblades. That was particularly grueling with her sore skin. Every touch by the wooden blades was agony. She opted to take out revenge for her sunburn on her brother, who was not expecting a vicious attack. He was startled by her initial blows, but Atopol quickly regained his composure and answered each strike gallantly. Finally, her father called an end to the drills for supper. But their lessons did not stop then.

"Have you ever used a sextant?" Hance asked as he picked up the navigational instrument made of brass and mirrors. Atopol shook his head.

"Aunt Beah showed me some basics when we were sailing to Dras Ferman," she admitted.

"It's an advanced form of navigation, taught in the later years at Palomar for those students who seek a life on the sea. And for Sea Lords and maritime Coastlords and other mariners, it's taught in the journeyman training," he said.

"It's one of the secrets of deep-water navigation," Hance continued as he hung the device around his neck with a lanyard. "Without it, a clock of some sort, and accurate charts, we could never sail out of sight of land.

"The sextant is used to determine the angle between the celestial bodies overhead and the horizon. We use it to figure latitude and longitude." It was shaped like a triangle, but instead of a flat bottom, it was curved, and the curve was numbered from zero to one hundred twenty. "The angle measures sixty degrees here and one hundred twenty here." He pointed to the arc along the bottom. "As you can see, the design is one-sixth the size of a circle, hence the name. Our ancestors have used this for centuries. This is one of the Ancient designs that miraculously survived the Inundation. And with its survival, the understanding of how to use it," he said, taking the device back from Gatina.

"The sextant principle is both mathematical and scientific, and uses a double reflection principle," Hance said as he held the metal device. Gatina groaned mentally at the mention of math. She had no trouble with the basics, the geometrical or the angles, but some of the material introduced at Palomar Abbey had simply frustrated her to tears. "In it, when a ray of light is reflected by two mirrors"—he pointed to both fixtures—"the angle between the incoming ray of light and the outgoing ray is twice the angles between the mirrors. And these filters protect our eyes from the sun when it's bright. Ever wonder why so many mariners wear eye patches?"

Gatina looked at her father questioningly. "You mean it's not from fighting at sea?" She had always assumed that.

Hance smiled and chuckled softly. "I am certain some of them have had eye injuries from fights or accidents, but the majority stared too long into the sun." He handed the device back to Gatina, who brought it to her eyes and adjusted the index bar. While she did that, he explained which parts of the device she was using and how it worked. "The piece you're moving is called the index bar and it has the index mirror affixed to it. The second mirror, the horizon mirror, does not move. You look through the telescope and adjust the index bar to obtain the measurements, then we use an equation to gauge location."

"Math?" Gatina finally said aloud. "More math." That had been her least-favorite class at the abbey.

Atopol laughed. "I told you it would come in handy."

Hance smiled. "Yes, more math. And the sextant is useful for more than the celestial navigation. Mariners also use the sextant to determine the distance between fixed objects, like land or an anchored ship."

"Does the sextant work at night? To sight the lights overhead?" she asked.

"It does. We can sight the moons and the stars, and there's no need for the filters after dusk. The important thing is the *horizon*," he explained. "A mariner always keeps his eyes on the horizon. That's good advice in any trade."

Minnureal joined the three of them on deck as Hance let each of them use the brass instrument.

"Don't drop it; always use the neck lanyard," she advised, as the piece nearly slipped from Gatina's fingers. "Besides, if you break it, it's considered bad luck."

"I don't need any more bad luck after being shipwrecked." Gatina sighed as she put the loop of string around her neck. "I've been cursed by the Shipwrecker, and Aunt Beah said Pia, Matros, Genver, and I have to do some ritual to break the curse and regain the Shipwrecker's blessing. Otherwise, I'll be bad luck for every voyage I ever take." The words tumbled from Gatina's mouth without any regulation from her brain. She'd held her worry inside for the days since she was rescued.

She hadn't meant to sound so miserable about it, but her complaint apparently inspired Minnureal's sympathy. Her mother pulled her into a protective embrace. This time, though, it was Gatina who began to weep.

"Such superstitions do not concern us," she assured. "We are not of Sea Lord stock."

Hance agreed with an indulgent smile. "Your mother is correct, Kitten," he said, softly. "Darkness is our patron divinity. A curse, some have said, but we see it as a blessing to be given the gifts we have, the legacy we have, and the tradition that has sustained us for centuries. Consider your family curse dominant over the Sea Lord curses. Their deities are locked in eternal struggles inside their own belief structure. We have a higher mission. Neither you nor your brother are bound by any Sea Lord tradition."

When Minnie released her, she reached for Gatina's chin and tilted her face up so that she could see her eyes. "You are of House Furtius stock. You are the scion of Kiera the Great. You are a shadowmage. You are not bound by any curses set on ignorant mariners. Do you understand me? This is *not* something for you to worry about."

Gatina nodded, but in her heart of hearts, she knew she would have to contend with the Shipwrecker and her curse.

CHAPTER NINETEEN
THE WITCH OF MANAHAR

The remarkable thing about the Sea Lord religion is that despite the culture having outposts from Merwyn to Alshar, including far-flung ports across the Shattered Sea, it has been remarkably unified in its pantheon. The gods and goddesses don't have proper names, there are few additional contributions from sympathetic cultures, and there is little variance in belief or practice among them. The mythology, ritual, and structure of the religion have been largely unchanged since its inception in Cormeer despite the lack of sacred texts. It is a religion of custom, based on the demands of the sea alone, with almost no dissenting sects among the six cults. Compared to the religions of the Magocracy, the Narasi knights, or the thousands of tribes across the world, the Sea Lords have been steadfast in their devotion to their ancient creed.

—*from* **Sea Lords, Their Cults, Religious Customs, and Traditions**

As the *Daydream* and *Legacy* neared the port of Manahar, the number of ships they passed increased dramatically. Manahar was one of the main ports for the sprawling county of Rhemes and a good deepwater port that allowed ships to come and go without regard for the tides. This made it popular with smaller ships that might have difficulty finding a berth in Vaxel or Gavina or Brisomar, the three larger ports nearby that attracted the long-distance trade from Remere or Merwyn. It was also more popular with the maritime Coastlord houses, who found it more comfortable than the larger ports.

But what was disturbing to Gatina was the number of warships they passed as they crossed the buoys delineating the port. Great galleons, fitted with deck engines designed to sink or damage other ships, well-armed carracks with crenelated forecastles, and even sloops and barques outfitted for war sailed past the *Daydream* as she sought a berth in Manahar. Indeed, Gatina had never seen so many ships of war in her journey. Only a few of them flew the ducal standard, indicating their service to the duchy. Some of them could well have been part-time pirates or privateers seeking employment as escorts, she reasoned. After all, the Anchorage was where such ships were recruited to take the Duke's colors.

Gatina was gratified that she made no mistakes as she helped her aunt guide the *Daydream* into the port slip it had been assigned—a slip that Gatina thought was far too narrow for the wide ship to fit. As the crew worked to moor the ship, her Aunt Beah paid the port master's agent their docking fees. While she had the pay chest out, she also gave Gatina, Atopol, Pia, and Jordi half of their accumulated pay, according to her accounts, before they were sent ashore.

It wasn't as much as Gatina thought; despite her hard work and dedication, the nine pieces of silver and handful of coppers she was disbursed seemed paltry. She had more in the stolen pirate's purse she'd taken in Pluhalia. It wasn't that there was anything she particularly wanted, but when she could have made thrice as much in one night of burglary as she had in weeks of toil on deck, it put her opinion of honest work into perspective.

"And here is a list of items we need to stock up on while we're here," her aunt said as she handed a scrap of parchment to Pia. "I'll handle securing more rations and purchasing a new gig for the *Daydream*, but we need thread, needles, blank parchment, ink—we've used up a lot of that—some oilskin, two bailing buckets, a whetstone—I can't believe we sailed without one—two new mops, and a load of charcoal. You should be able to get all of that at Mormont Supply. You do remember where that is?" she asked, an eyebrow raised.

"Yes, Captain," Pia said, resigned. "Just past the docks on the right."

"Exactly. Go ahead and pay for delivery, and they should have it to us by this evening. Then stop at House of Frey Spice Merchants and get us some salt, long pepper, cardamom, garlic, cinnamon, dried aloe . . . well, it's all there on the list," she said. "I don't want to pay the prices for such things at the Anchorage. Vaxel prices are always high, and even more so during the festival. Best we load up on what we need here, where it's cheaper."

"Is that going to give us enough time to look around?" Atopol asked.

"Oh, yes," Jordi answered. "Manahar is better laid out than a Sea Lord haven. Coastlords tend to be more practical and less bound by tradition. It should only take an hour or so, and then we'll be at liberty."

"All of you draw down swords from the armory," Beah ordered before they left. "I don't expect any more trouble, but with this many men o' war in port, it's best to appear armed to avoid it. Besides," she added, "if Hance and Minnie get into trouble, I want you four to be prepared with good arguments."

As soon as Gatina stepped onto the dock, she realized that this was unlike any of the other ports she had visited. She also realized that her view of the ports was rather limited, as she hadn't been to many, but she had not imagined the smells and colors she took in as she walked down the dock to the cobbled street; there were flowers in shades of red, blue, purple, and yellow as well as lush green plants everywhere. Some of these flowers were taller than she was, and all of them gave off an earthy, spicy scent unlike anything she had smelled.

She was instantly relaxed despite the well-ordered turmoil around her. It wasn't the type of chaos she had experienced in Cadena and Pluhalia. Here, it was more frenetic. There was money to be made here, and people were busy pushing carts and rushing to and from dock slips or to and from vendor stalls. She liked the dockworkers' energy. This was not a slow-paced port for them. There were easily twice the number of porters and stevedores there, and she heard a lot more of the flat accents of Rhemes than the Sea Lords' lilting speech.

"Welcome to Manahar," Jordi said as they made their way to the end of the dock. "Pia and I visited last year. It's an interesting place. You can find pretty much anything you are looking for here as well as items you didn't know you needed." He swept his arms wide, careful to avoid hitting any passersby. "And I am very happy to report that one thing they don't have here is a slave market, and that's a good thing in more ways than one." Jordi looked pointedly at Gatina.

Instead of replying, Gatina scanned the vendor stalls scattered in front of her. She was surprised by the variety of goods on display. She spotted a baker's cart, but Atopol saw it first. Before she could say anything, her brother made a beeline for it. It was predictable. She shook her head and followed him, as Pia and Jordi fell in behind her.

"Martijne! You just can't run off," she said quietly when she caught up to him.

"It's fresh bread!" he protested. "I've only had hardtack for weeks! You know how I love baked goods," he said. Gatina shook her head and smiled to herself.

While her brother made his many selections, Gatina contented herself with a half dozen apples from another vendor, paying a copper penny for them. In Falas, she could have had a dozen for that price, she realized.

Pia found the supply store quickly enough, secured the items on the list with no difficulty, and arranged for their delivery. The spice dealer was more difficult, as a good third of the items listed on the parchment were either in short supply or out of stock entirely. That was unusual—this port was known for spices—but the merchant explained that the great galleons from Farise that usually brought the more exotic items to port were being interdicted by the kingdom now. She made a few substitutions before paying the bill and giving the merchant the dock and slip number for the *Daydream*.

As they were leaving the spice merchant, they were surprised to run into Matros, Genver, and the other mariners they'd rescued. That wasn't unusual—every mariner liked to get his feet dry after even a few days at sea—but where they were going was not a tavern or alehouse.

"We're going to the magistrate to swear out a warrant against the *Venjanca* for piracy with the port authorities," Matros explained. "We'll do the same in Vaxel. That will prohibit them from docking here, and once word spreads, it will make them a target for the ducal fleet. There are rewards for capturing pirates."

"Won't that also make you a target?" Beah asked, concerned.

Matros shrugged. "I'm a free mariner. That already makes me a target. I'm not concerned about retribution. It's my duty to my lost ship and mates. I want them gone from the Great Bay."

"He's so brave," Pia sighed when they took their leave of the mariners.

"Mother is going to swear a warrant too, as a witness," Jordi pointed out with a scowl. "It's just what you do after an incident like that. It's rare that sort of thing happens so soon after an attack, though. Maybe doing it quickly will keep that scummy galleon from preying on anyone else. If they're smart, they'll flee the Bay entirely."

The four found a small table in a nearby ale tent, where they purchased cups of watered-down ale and more landsman's food for luncheon while they planned the rest of their day.

"Are you planning to eat all of that now?" Pia asked, her eyes on the pile of sweet biscuits, rolls, bread, and tarts stacked in front of Atopol.

Atopol shook his head. He already had food in his mouth. When he finished chewing, he said, "No, of course not. I'll take it back to the ship. This is for later, too." He looked around. "This is an unusual port," he decided. "Charming but different."

It was then that Pia and Jordi explained how the community and Manahar came to be so unique.

"Many people arrive here by ship as we did," Jordi said as he tore into his pork-and-cheese pie to let it cool off. "It was one of the earliest settlements to challenge the primacy of the Sea Lords, back in the Magocracy. Unlike the Sea Lords, the magelords settled the interior, conquering the local tribes for the empire, and became the Coastlords. It became the main port to service the Farisian spice fleets, forestalling Vaxel. By the time the Narasi showed up, the Coastlords had made it one of their strongest military ports for the western Bay." He brought a bit of the pie to his mouth but set it down quickly. "Still too hot, but it smells so good!"

"I'd bet that's the spices," Pia said. "Manahar is known for exotic spices and unusual flowers. I'm sure you noticed the bright colors?" Gatina nodded.

"Yes, they're beautiful!"

"A lot of them came from Farise, along with the spice ships," Pia informed her. "They don't really grow well other places around the Bay. Manahar is also known for its Calrom settlement," she said mysteriously. "Have you ever seen the Calrom?"

"No, but I've heard of them. I think they're prohibited from Falas by ducal order," she recalled.

Jordi spread his hands out as if to motion to their specific region. His mouth was full, but once he swallowed his pie, he said, "They're strange folk. They're tribal, but without a homeland of their own. They live apart from everyone else in camps wherever they can find a place that won't kick them out. They're mostly tinkers, horse traders, and vagabonds. They're often accused of thievery. Very mysterious and very colorful. They're very common here in Manahar, though. I think they're tolerated because they amuse visiting mariners."

"The Calrom are a nomadic tribe, but they do have a somewhat permanent encampment here, just east of the port, in tents, wagons, and a few cottages," Pia agreed. "It's one of the things that make Manahar interesting. We visited last time we were here, and it was fascinating. Would you like to go?" she asked, her eyebrow cocked.

"Aren't they the tribe that practices some sort of prophecy?" Atopol asked curiously between bites.

"They tell fortunes," Pia corrected. "That's especially popular in a port town, where there's a constant stream of visiting mariners. In fact, there's an old woman who calls herself a witch there who will tell you your fortune—who you'll marry, or what great fate awaits you. Mother wouldn't let me do it, last time we were here, but I managed to sneak away to visit one of the witches, just for a bit. I wonder if she is still at the settlement." Pia smiled as she stared into space—she wasn't focused on anyone at the table.

Jordi rolled his eyes at his sister's dreamy look. "Absolute rubbish, if you ask me," he said. "They just make up a bunch of nonsense and take your silver. What a waste of coin!"

Pia glared at him. "Nobody asked you. Besides, it could be fun to have our fortunes told," she suggested. She looked pointedly across the table to Gatina and Atopol to gauge their interest.

Prophecy was something Gatina avoided. It wasn't that she was frightened of it, exactly. In her family's line of work, she thought it best not to get too comfortable with prediction, accurate or not. Lady Silk, her magic teacher back in Falas, had often dismissed prophecy and prediction as dangerous. At best, it was unreliable, she'd always maintained. At worst, it could lead to false assumptions and misplaced feelings of confidence. If she was told something—a heist—was meant to be, then she might get overconfident and not pay attention, and that might lead to mistakes or getting caught.

But the idea of even a charlatan making up predictions would be entertaining, she decided. Gatina was in disguise, after all. There was no way that some old witch would be able to guess at her real life as a thief, the one she led as Kitten of Night. It might be amusing to hear her guess wrongly about it.

Besides, it seemed that Pia really wanted to do it. Gatina smiled despite herself. Clearly, her cousin was interested in some indication of where her feelings toward Matros might lead her. As she considered Pia's suggestion, Jordi was still explaining why prophecy was pointless, but he was mostly talking to himself.

"That might be fun. If the Calrom are thieves, perhaps I'll meet a girl. What else is Manahar known for?" Atopol asked.

"Actually, this is one of the most successful of the commercial cities in Rhemes," Jordi said. "And it has been that way since long before its count took power." He cast a glance around them but saw nobody overtly watching or listening. "The counts of Rhemes prohibited any of their trade to go through the larger Sea Lord ports and forced it through Manahar."

"Shipbuilding and ship repair are both important too." Pia agreed. "There's a big shipyard west of the town. And there are a lot of forests within a day's journey inland, something a lot of Sea Lord ports lack. In fact, Manahar is the last viable port until travelers reach Vaxel, so if you are low on supplies, you would stock up here before continuing your journey."

"Is there a shrine of Eight Bells here?" Gatina asked hopefully.

"No, not that I'm aware of," Pia admitted. "There are about a dozen around the Great Bay, but they tend to be in smaller places. Technically, they're dedicated to the Salt Crone or Shipwrecker and are usually built by retired mariners or men too sick or wounded to sail anymore. Don't worry; we'll find one," she said encouragingly. "We have an entire year before the curse begins."

That was disappointing. Most of the other tasks she'd heard of to escape the Shipwrecker's Curse were easy enough, but finding a shrine of Eight Bells was going to be tricky, apparently.

Jordi let out a deep sigh. "And here we go with talks of curses. First witches and prophecies, now curses. Aren't you two supposed to be properly educated scholars? It's all superstitious nonsense."

Gatina didn't let him goad her. Instead, she turned the Sea Lords' religious beliefs on him. "Aren't you superstitious? You are a Sea Lord, after all, Jordi," Gatina said to him. "I'm not saying I believe in curses. I'd just prefer to take care of ridding myself of one before anything bad happens," she reasoned.

Jordi just smirked and shook his head. "Of course, I am little superstitious, but I also have common sense. Besides, I like to think that I use good judgement."

"I DON'T KNOW ABOUT YOU ALL," ATOPOL SAID, FINISHING HIS ALE, "BUT I'M just happy to be off the ship for a couple of hours. Let's go see the market and maybe get our fortune read. And listen to people," he added, reminding them of why they were there. They returned their mugs to the bin and began their tour.

Gatina couldn't have agreed more. She knew she needed to engage in people-watching to help her complete her very, very unnuanced Sea Lord alias. It encouraged her that she might pass as authentic to the folk of Manahar, who were mostly of Coastlord descent. But it might prove instructive in her alias and disguise creation to mingle among them. The only real experience she had with Sea Lords was with her cousins and the crewmen on the *Legacy*. She needed more inspiration.

Creating an alias was hard work. In addition to researching the clothing, mannerisms of the locals in each class, and speech style, she needed to learn all she could about the political structure, economy, and customs. Something as seemingly innocent as inflecting the incorrect syllable might reveal her as a fraud. So, studying the villagers was necessary. Besides, this was the largest mission she had participated in. She wanted to impress her parents. She knew Atopol was getting close to the end of his apprenticeship.

Part of her apprenticeship included creating her alias and disguise for this mission. Her parents would provide a name and a bit of detail about the history—always purposefully vague, but it was her responsibility to complete the dossier and disguises to make them believable. This was the first time she had been tasked with the creation of an alias in their enemy's home county. This was a much-higher-stakes situation than when she was undercover as a nit and tasked with infiltrating the Brotherhood of the Rat during her first mission in Falas.

As they wandered the vendor stalls in the market, Gatina quickly realized how boring life must be in this sort of village. The only source of excitement that she could see came from when ships came into port. Unfortunately, all the market's stalls were similar to those she'd seen in the other ports around the Great Bay. Farm stalls, food vendors, knife and blade sharpeners, fabric merchants, fishing supplies, net weavers, and artisans hawking cheap bracelets and strands of beads—none appealed to her.

She did find one merchant who sold art supplies. She was on her way to his cart when a man with a bushy mustache, dressed in a long cape and an elaborate, silly hat stood on a wooden box outside the largest of the ale tents to raise his head above the passers-by. He brought a small horn to his lips and blew into it. The jarring blare caused everyone to stop what they were doing.

"Ahoy, ahoy!" he shouted. "Master Sangarlan will present *The Strongest Girl in the World and the Beast of Turtle Island!* At second bell behind this very tent!" The man took his hat off and gave a deep bow, then fumbled for a moment before displaying a small puppet of what was supposed to be a horrible monster, with scaly breast, wings, and one horribly hairy eyeball. On his other hand, he revealed a smaller puppet on but one finger—a little girl with red hair, including two ridiculously long braids, freckles, and a striped dress. "A tale of romance, adventure, and outrageous drama for a mere two copper pennies! Remember, the second bell at the small stage behind this merchant's tent!" he yelled.

There was nothing special about the barker—plenty of merchants used such means to lure you into a tent, usually promising unparalleled value at incredible bargains. Even minstrels of a certain quality could rent a space and perform for a paying crowd rather than passing a hat or waiting for passers-by to reward them. And while this was the first time Gatina had ever seen such a thing for a puppet show, that was not what made her gasp.

"Pia!" she said, grabbing her cousin's arm. "That puppet! It's . . . it's the girl I saw on the island!" she said in a whisper.

"What?" Pia asked, confused. "What girl— Oh!" she said, recalling the brief episode. "Oh!" she repeated with more emphasis, her eyes widening. "You mean, you saw . . . Pippa? *That* Pippa? The strongest girl in the world?"

"Yes!" Gatina said excitedly. "I didn't tell you she called herself that, but she lifted a boulder the size of a gig and pulled a ship's anchor out of the sand all by herself! The one on the way to the cove!"

Pia stared at her in disbelief, as if she thought Gatina was trying to fool her. But a moment later, she shook her head. "Pippa is supposed to be the Shipwrecker's daughter. She's ancient but looks like an extremely strong young girl. The tale is that she's the result of the goddess and a lonely ship's captain who was marooned. It's, ah, an indelicate story." She blushed. "But Pippa was the result. She has a bunch of adventures associated with her. But she's always seen as a kind of comical children's character in most of them."

Gatina looked at Pia. "Is this something we should do? Will it help with the curse?"

"Again with the curse!" Jordi scoffed. "They're capitalizing on your fear. It's just a puppet show!"

Atopol turned to look at Jordi. "Puppet show?" he asked. Atopol wore a confused expression on his face. "A puppet show? Not a theatrical production? "

Atopol was unaware that puppet shows were an important part of the culture to the Sea Lords. Gatina only knew because Pia had explained it to her after she found the finger puppets on the island.

"Sea Lords and coastal villagers alike use the puppets and puppet shows as folks in Alshar would use the theater," Gatina explained. "The finger puppets are very affordable and accessible for everyone."

"Would you like to go? We have time. We could shop and then go to the show, then visit the witch."

Gatina noticed that when Pia mentioned the witch this time, Jordi just shook his head. She realized that he was either resigned to it or had given up his argument.

"No, let's just get to the Calrom encampment," Gatina suggested. "I'm finished with looking in the market. I'm suddenly very interested in what my future holds," she confessed.

Instead, she wandered the stalls while the others shopped. As they moved from vendor to vendor, Gatina studied the people around her. She watched the merchants and how they engaged with their clientele. She studied the Sea Lords and their mannerisms, and observed that they were able to blend in with the crowd as well as maintaining an air of detached superiority.

She also noticed that mariner after mariner was greeted enthusiastically by vendors. It was as if the seafaring folk ranked in a higher social class than the coastal villagers and even those Sea Lords who were ashore permanently as merchants or artisans. Going to sea enriched you socially there.

Actual mariners were easy to spot: the most flamboyantly dressed of all at the market. Despite the heat, they wore breeches, leather boots or shoes, striped tunics, richly embroidered waistcoats, and sashes, as well as wide-brimmed leather hats.

But the Sea Lords among the mariners had a distinctive style. They favored coats, not mantles or cloaks, and wide belts on which swords were usually hung, as well as feathers in their hats or braided in their hair. They displayed more jewelry than common mariners and often displayed small crests representing their houses sewn onto their right shoulders, sometimes with the name of their ship if they were an officer.

For the most part, the majority were men, but there were some women among them who dressed similarly but with their jackets heavily brocaded and their well-pleated, shoe-length dresses stylishly cut at the hem in a variety of interesting wave-like patterns—sometimes with a provocative slit up one side.

It was a daring look and attracted some attention from the men in the market, but it wasn't wise to get fresh with a Sea Lord lady dressed in such a manner. They moved with confidence and purpose, proudly investigating the wares on the tables and blankets and carts without fear of insulting behavior. For in addition to heavy bracelets, amulets, necklaces, and a host of rings, each one of them wore a small, curved dagger on the small of her back, either on a belt, in a sash, or as part of her dress. And every such lady was assumed to have a large family or ship's crew willing to run to her aid at a moment's notice, if she did not handle matters herself.

There were many words to describe the women who dressed such a way; *demure* was not one of them. Gatina could well imagine any of them calmly stabbing a mariner who got fresh with them without regret and then going back to their shopping. She made a point of remembering that look.

THE CALROM ENCAMPMENT WAS NOT FAR FROM THE MARKET—INDEED, THE two were connected by a simple lane that led between two large stone buildings. The field beyond had been given over to their use, and while there were large tents, wagons, caravans, and even small shacks farther away from the lane, along the road was a riot of colorful stalls and tents dedicated to the Calrom's crafts. The farthest section had been fenced as a corral that was half-filled with horses they were buying, selling, and shoeing—being a farrier was apparently a popular profession among the swarthy-skinned tribe.

But so was being a tinker, a seamstress, or a tinsmith, she realized, as they wound their way past a number of each of them. Most worked out of the back of covered wagons or carriages, while others merely set up a blanket near the road along with their tools. Others sold leather goods, or baskets, or woolen caps knitted by their women. All of them had black hair that seemed to drink the light and tanned skin with a sort of golden hue to it. And every dark eye along the street affixed itself to the four of them the moment they came into sight.

Gatina realized that she was being sized up as a mark—she had done it so often herself, it seemed a bit of a novelty to be the victim of such appraisals for once. She ignored it, of course, as any Sea Lord woman would. But she watched her purse.

Their clothing was hard to ignore. It was a continuation of the bright colors and patterns of all sorts of flowing fabrics, seemingly put together with little regard for matters such as taste or aesthetics. The favorite garment for both men and women seemed to be scarves: worn as sashes, or around the neck or waist, or tied on their heads. It was as if some monster had devoured an entire cloth market and vomited everywhere.

Pia led them to the next row of tents and awnings behind the ones facing the road, where other services were provided more discreetly. They had no clear signs advertising whatever wares outside of them, just colorful banners with strange sigils on them—and Gatina was no stranger to codes. Pia found one with a brightly painted red eye on a yellow triangle of silk.

"I've traveled to many ports, but this is the only one I've seen with a settlement," Pia explained as they walked. "Manahar has a temperate climate, and it seems that those who settle here are either elders or those with young families. But their seers are famous for their ability to glimpse the future, it's said."

Jordi nodded but seemed unimpressed. "Yes, they are a good ally to cultivate, too, as they are familiar with many different ports and cultures, for many different activities," he emphasized. "But they use all that to pull you in with their mystical nonsense."

"Kohni Ceija isn't like that!"

Jordi rolled his eyes again. "Ah, yes. Kohni Ceija. She is such a fraud. I can't believe you're going to take them to see her."

"Hush. You're going, too," Pia said. "Kohni Ceija has been in the encampment for years, according to what everyone says. For a few silver pennies, she'll tell you your future—good or ill. But I'm excited to see her again."

"Again?" Gatina asked.

"Oh, yes, I snuck away from Mother last time we were here. I only had a few pennies, but she promised me a life of adventure. I'd say she's passing accurate. If you're worried about the curse, Kohni Ceija will put your mind at ease, Gatina," Pia suggested. "I think this is her," she mumbled as she approached the open door of the tent. There was smoke wafting from it, Gatina saw, and her nose told her that it was incense and pipe smoke. Before her cousin could stick her head in, a short wisp of a Calrom woman appeared.

"You want your fortune told, younglings?" the wizened crone asked in a croaking voice, the pipe between her teeth not moving perceivably as she spoke. "I tell you who you marry, who is your enemy, how many babies, even when you die!" she promised.

She was tiny, probably Gatina's height, but plump. Not heavy but not someone who had missed many meals. The woman looked up expectantly as they approached her.

"Ah. I know *you*." She pointed a plump finger at Pia. "We've met before. Last year. How fares your life of adventure, girly? Come, sit." She motioned to the pillows scattered on the ground with her bracelet-covered arm. Gatina noted that her voice matched her face—calm.

"Hello, Kohni Ceija. I am gratified that you remember me," Pia said, startled. "Yes, I did have a recent adventure. Quite the adventure, actually. That's why we are here. Do you have the time to talk about our futures?"

"If you have the silver, I have the time," she said, waving magnanimously at her tent. "Four silver pennies each," she demanded, her palm sticking out.

"I'll not spend my pay on that," Jordi said, shaking his head.

"You don't have to," Gatina said, pulling the pirate's purse she'd been carrying out of her dress. "Baramel the Rat will pay for this. I want us all to do it," she decided, counting out sixteen small pieces of silver from the pouch into Kohni Ceija's wrinkled palm. As it was stolen money, Gatina didn't really think of it as hers. She was just its custodian for a time. Her own purse was at her belt, filled with her wages. For some reason, they seemed more precious to her.

The witch looked up at her suddenly and cocked her head. "You're in the trade," she accused quietly.

"What?" Gatina asked in surprise. "I'm a mariner! An apprentice, but—"

"An apprentice, yes," the witch said, curtly, closing her fingers around the silver. "But not as a mariner, despite your pretensions. Worry not, little cat; Kohni Ceija does not go sniffing to magistrates or Watchmen. Stolen silver spends just as easily in the market as wages. Who is to be first?"

"I'll go!" Pia said quickly. Eagerly, she entered the tent with the witch pulling the flap down. For nearly ten minutes, things were quiet inside, although occasionally there were gasps or yelps from her cousin's lips that she could hear through the fabric. When Pia emerged, she looked excited.

"What did she say?" Gatina asked, curiously, as her brother went in next.

"That I'm to marry a mariner—most likely Matros, by her description. And soon—within the year!" She beamed. "She said other things about where we'll live and our children, but she promised a long and intriguing life."

"I could have told you all of that for only two silver pennies," Jordi pointed out. "It's rubbish, all of it. Every young girl wants to know who she'll wed—and a mariner's daughter marrying a mariner is hardly difficult to predict."

"It was kind of fun," Pia admitted. "Thank you for paying for me, Maranka!"

"What about the curse?" Gatina asked anxiously.

"I . . . I forgot to ask about that. Sorry!" her cousin said guiltily.

When Atopol emerged, he looked thoughtful. "I'm supposed to become the greatest thief in the world," he revealed with a sheepish grin. "I'm to meet a powerful wizard, perform the greatest heists in history, go on grand, dangerous adventures, become a nobleman of high esteem, and eventually marry a beautiful princess and rule over a distant, exotic land." He chuckled. "Really!"

"Rubbish," snorted Jordi as he went to take his turn inside. "Pure rubbish!"

"Then how did she know my name was Cat?" he asked his cousin.

"Because you look like a bloody great cat," Jordi sneered as the flap closed over the door.

It was nearly twenty minutes before he emerged. When he did, Jordi looked disturbed and reflective. He didn't seem to want to brag about his prediction or how it was rubbish. Indeed, he seemed subdued.

"She said that Father is still alive," he finally revealed after he exhaled a great sigh. "He's alive and he'll return to us someday." He no longer dismissed the predictive powers of the witch, Gatina noted, and even seemed disturbed about their conversation.

"Your turn, Kitten," Atopol said, nudging her toward the tent, where Kohni Ceija awaited her. "Go handle your curse. I got a princess and professional acclaim. I'm curious to see what you get."

Suddenly, Gatina's feet didn't seem to want to work, and she wasn't as eager to go into the tent. But she forced herself to move forward until the tent flap closed behind her.

It was surprisingly dark within, and the cloying smell of smoke hung in the air like a shroud. The old witch took a seat on a pile of pillows in front of a small glass dish that had been painted black. It was filled with water. The witch tossed it on the floor and refilled it with water from an elaborate green glass ewer.

"So, the kitten comes to hear her fate," the witch croaked. "A thief you are, like your brother and your sires. A very good thief," she praised. "Not like these bravos in camp, who steal pennies and think they're masters of the art. Here," she said, producing a tiny little dagger with an elaborate bronze hilt. "One drop of blood will let me see your future," she promised.

Wordlessly, Gatina held out her hand, and the old witch pierced her fingertip with a long-practiced stab. A single drop of blood welled up as her ancient fingers squeezed it, until it was heavy enough to drop into the dish of its own accord. "Now give me a moment to see," Kohni Ceija urged. "Speak not until I have spoken to you."

She set down her pipe, heaved a great sigh, and bowed her head over the scrying bowl. She was at it for several minutes, long enough for most people to grow impatient. But Gatina said nothing and did not move. She knew how to hold a freeze for hours if necessary.

"The Kitten in the Darkness," Kohni Ceija finally pronounced in a wavering voice. "Daughter of the great. Greatness inspires you; greatness infuses you," she said, not looking up. "A mage you are. You will yet rise great in their company. You will own many slaves," she said, to Gatina's horror, "and you will redeem the duchy for its rightful master. You and your husband will become great lords at the Duke's court," she promised. "You will come to know the greatest wizard in the world and enjoy great wealth and prosperity."

"My . . . *husband?*" Gatina asked with morbid curiosity.

"A northman, it appears. A scholar. A warrior. A knight. A wizard of great power and authority. He comes from the humblest of beginnings yet will prove to be one of the wisest of his age. He will match you as a glove matches the hand it is fitted for. You will love him from the moment your eyes are set on him. Passionately," she emphasized. "He has a great heart, yet discipline and honor are his watchwords. A kind man. Handsome, too. If a bit short." She shrugged.

"How short?" Gatina blurted out.

"Taller than you—and we are all the same height when we lie down," she pointed out. "But he is your match in every way. The adventures you've had until now pale in comparison to what you will have in his company. He will spurn you at first, but you will be relentless in pursuing him. You will help him achieve his greatest desires. He will become yours. Together, you will face foes you cannot imagine," she predicted.

"And . . . what of the curse?" Gatina asked, in a whisper. That sparked an unexpected peal of laughter from the old witch.

"The curse of the Shipwrecker?" she cackled. "My dear, you have the determination of a badger and the wits of a vixen. No mere goddess is going to impede your progress. The curse is for mariners, not thieves. You will break it easily. And when you do, your future will unfold for you like a banner unfurled. You will restore the duchy," she promised. "You, not armies or wizards or even the gods. And you do it for the young man who appears after the bells are rung. That is all," she said, covering the bowl with her hand. "Kohni Ceija is tired. And well paid for her efforts. Get back to your ship and prepare for your future. It is going to be . . . interesting," she pledged.

THE FOURSOME WALKED IN SILENCE FROM KOHNI CEIJA'S TENT, AND LITTLE was spoken as they walked back to the docks.

What could they say? Gatina wondered. The meeting had been unlike anything she had experienced. The woman had never met three of them before, yet had accurately provided information, however small in some cases, that was just enough to make Gatina question her initial belief about prophecy.

Finally, Jordi broke the silence. "Well, that was certainly strange," he said. "I can see why she is so popular. She tells a good story," he said.

"I think a lot of it might be wish fulfillment," Atopol said. "I have never had plans outside of living up to my full potential, which, of course, includes becoming the greatest thief in the world. But who couldn't predict that?"

"Greatest *male* thief," Gatina corrected. "I'll be right there beside you. Marriage? Me? No, thank you. I don't think a man like she predicted even exists in this world," she said despondently.

As the four reached the ramp leading up to the *Daydream*, Gatina saw Aunt Beah on the deck with her parents and a stranger.

He was a tall, blond man dressed as a Sea Lord—young, handsome, fit and virile, and dressed in well-appointed finery. He surveyed all four of them critically as they walked up the gangplank.

"Children," her father announced, "I would like you to meet Sea Lord Lancellus of House Luxosar. He is the contact we've crossed the Great Bay to meet. And he has news," he added ominously.

CHAPTER TWENTY
SEA LORD LANCELLUS

The problem with conspiracies is that it is difficult to choose your allies. But the depredations of tyrants raise defiant voices in all manner of places, and we take what assistance we can from wherever we can. It has been generations since Coastlords and Sea Lords have joined in common cause for the betterment of the Duchy. Now I see why.
— *from Gatina's Heist Journal*

THAT EVENING, A PRIVATE SUPPER WAS HELD IN THE CAPTAIN'S CABIN. The meal of roasted lamb with tubers and vegetables, along with fresh bread, two varieties of cheese, wine, and fruit tarts had been brought from the port. Service was performed by Taruk, the bosun, who left as soon as the meal had been plated and only returned when the bell was rung. This was an official meeting of some sort. One that included the newcomer, and her mother and brother, Aunt Beah, Pia and Jordi. And Ginny the cat, who had not left Gatina's side since she reboarded the *Legacy*.

As Gatina joined the others in the dining area, she realized this was the first time in nearly five weeks that she had sat down at a proper table, dressed in her own gown as herself, not as a character with an alias or as thief, to enjoy a meal. She shifted in her chair until the slip under her gown cooperated enough that she could sit flat on top of it instead of sitting on the lumpy, scratchy crinoline.

Once she was seated, the cat immediately settled herself underneath her chair. The only disadvantage to wearing the lavender gown was the tightness of the bodice. She was suddenly very aware of how her body had developed and just how the boning in the dreadful device forced her to sit straight. She was never much of a sloucher, but the bodice allowed not even the tiniest amount of movement. She was very aware of each breath she took. She would be happy to take it off later.

But she knew she looked comely in it. She hoped the handsome Lord Lancellus would think so.

While she waited for everyone to be served, Gatina glanced across the round table, expecting to see Captain Armandus. Instead, she saw her father. The captain was nowhere to be seen. And that was when she was certain that this was indeed an official meeting of the Shadow Council.

After the final plate had been placed on the table and Taruk had left the cabin, Hance brought his fork to his wine cup and tapped it hard enough to generate a ringing sound loud enough to gain everyone's attention. And once everyone heard it, the low rumble of conversation quieted.

"Thank you all for joining us for this small but urgent meeting," he said. "It is important that we formally introduce our new friend Sea Lord Lancellus, of House Luxosar. Lord Lancellus has been our covert informant for nearly a year, apparently. He has the highest confidence of Master Thinradel. It is largely with his help that we have been able to determine which houses may be agreeable to joining our cause."

Gatina had been instantly drawn to Lancellus when her aunt introduced him to her earlier that day. She was surprised by her attraction to him. Yes, he was handsome and charismatic. And tall. He was so tall that she had to tilt her head back to look at his face. She liked to look at his face, too. He had an interesting face, she decided.

He was not much older than Atopol. He wasn't as darkly complected as most Sea Lords, but his face had the rugged complexion wrought by a life at the sea and in the sun. He was tan and already wore slight wrinkles at his eyes. His hair indicated that his ancestry, at least, was not pure Sea Lord strain, but the proud manner in which he carried himself left her no room to doubt.

But his eyes were what drew her attention. Those were mesmerizing. They seemed to change shades of blue or blue gray, depending on the light. His mouth, if she was being honest, also drew her attention and perhaps curiosity. He had full lips. And she wondered what being kissed by those lips might feel like.

But she put that thought away for later. He was no mage, so there was no need to dwell on such things. She had her duty. And right now, she was doing that a disservice by thinking such thoughts about the man's lips. Gatina shook her head to focus on what her father was saying.

"Lancellus is the youngest son of House Luxosar, which is known for trading among all the Sea Lord Houses—small and large," Hance said.

"Indeed, House Luxosar owns more than a dozen galleons and twenty caravels, and sails from four of their own havens. In addition to trading, they have two companies of shipwrights, which specialize in trading barques, sloops, and caravels. That positions it to be an asset as we work to sway smaller and medium-sized Sea Lord families to join our cause.

"House Luxosar was a great friend to the late Duke Lenguin. His father was one of Lenguin's close advisors. He bears news from his family's contacts abroad and has plans to expand our efforts. He will explain what he has learned and how that can help our efforts. And by all means, please eat," Hance said, noticing that no one had touched the first course yet.

By the time Gatina had finished the second course of her meal, she was ready to push Lord Lancellus overboard. Despite a pleasant voice, intriguing eyes and luscious-looking lips, she found his descriptions to be both condescending and arrogant. But she listened politely and gave him her full attention. If her parents thought he was of value to the mission, then he had the information she needed.

"Thank you for allowing me to speak to you directly," he began, his eyes flashing around the room. "First, my news, for it puts context to all else I speak of: The so-called King Rard of Castalshar—an abomination of a construct—has allowed the ducal heir, Anguin son of Lenguin, to be crowned with the coronet of Alshar. His Grace was confirmed by the Coronet Council."

That caused the usually silent family to murmur in surprise. It wasn't generally thought that Rard would allow such a thing and would keep young Anguin in his pocket as a hostage before laying claim to Alshar directly.

"That is an intriguing development," Aunt Beah nodded. "To what purpose?"

"We know not the mind of the King," Lancellus admitted, "but it appears that the Duke of Remere would not approve of allowing such an important post to be left vacant when the heir was of an age to take his throne. The Dukes of Vore and Merwyn agreed, and installed the lad to his title, if not his estate. They call him the Orphan Duke at Rard's court."

"What of his sisters?" Gatina's mother asked, concerned.

"They remain wards of the so-called Royal Court," Lancellus answered, sneering at the idea. "As was last known, they are safe in abbeys of great repute in Castal, receiving an education on their duties. His Grace has celebrated his investiture with a summer of jousting and tournaments in Gilmora," he reported.

"So . . . he is *free?*" Atopol asked.

"He is constantly attended by all manner of Castali gentlemen," corrected Lancellus. "Thankfully, there are some loyal expatriate Alshari who are also allowed to accompany him—a few good Sea Lords who remembered their duty even as their liege was slain and his heir taken into exile. His Alshari chaplain has remained with him constantly. He is accorded the respect and dignity of his title but holds no real power beyond the few Gilmoran possessions he inherited. There is no doubt he is watched closely by Rard and Grendine. But he is now . . . exposed," Lancellus agreed.

"Does that really change our plans?" her mother asked. "Even if Anguin has been elevated to his father's seat, he remains in exile. There is little chance he could raise an army to challenge Vichetral without Rard using it as an excuse to seize control over the duchy. The control of the Council of Five grows greater every day. It is up to us to counter their efforts until Anguin is in a position to return."

"I bear news of that as well." Lancellus grinned fetchingly. "One of the scions of House Luxosar, Sire Grenvaden of Inmar—"

"Inmar?" Gatina burst out. "That's not on the coast—that's leagues and leagues inland!"

"He was granted lands in the region by Duke Lenguin, early in his reign, and has adopted a landsman's life," Lancellus admitted, looking a bit embarrassed. That was something else Gatina had learned about Sea Lord culture: the mariners who had adopted Coastlord or Narasi customs and titles, or who were granted estates inland and lived as knights, had a poor reputation among their maritime kin. Common fishermen were held in higher esteem than their landbound cousins.

"Yet he knew his duty well enough to follow Anguin into exile," Lancellus continued. "Sire Grenvaden has informed us much on Anguin's doings and made observations at Rard's court. From that vantage he and some other notable scions of Sea Lord houses have conceived a plan to convince Anguin to return to Alshar by sea and declare himself," he said proudly.

It was clear that he expected the news to be greeted with more enthusiasm than it was. Gatina could understand why. Count Vichetral and his allies had tremendous forces on land upon which to call to uphold his power. Each count who was admitted to the Shadow Council had pledged to resist King Rard and his schemes against Alshari sovereignty, which Vichetral would accuse Anguin—Duke Anguin, she corrected—of being. Even if he suddenly appeared and raised his banner, Gatina had no doubt that he would be quickly seized by Vichetral and imprisoned at the palace in Falas.

She was not the only one who was suspicious of the scheme. Hance looked at the Sea Lord thoughtfully.

"My lord, what would that accomplish, save to put the Duke in danger?" he asked. "Without support positioned to take advantage of such a bold move, I fear that treachery and calamity would arise quickly and make our situation worse."

"You prefer to see our duke in the hands of the Castali?" Lancellus asked sharply.

"No, but a holiday of jousting in Gilmora isn't exactly imprisonment," Beah argued. "Indeed, many of his ancestors enjoyed the tournament circuit there, if I recall. Unless there is sufficient support on land and sea for him when he returns, then we court disaster."

"That is why we are meeting," Hance agreed. "To build that support. Already the Vale Lords tire of Vichetral's edicts and imperious ways, even as their counts participate in his council. We are attempting to build a coalition there as well as among the Sea Lords toward that end. Perhaps you should explain your house's position, Lancellus, and why you can provide the leadership we need to reach that goal."

"Very well," conceded Lancellus with a nod. "You must know already that there are well over two hundred recognized houses of Sea Lords in Alshar, most around the Great Bay, where our ancestors first settled the coast. Most of these trace their lineage back to Cormeer, during the Golden Age, when we strove against the tyranny of the Magocracy in an effort to trade and raid as we saw fit," he said proudly.

"Yes, well, how did that resolve?" Minnureal asked sarcastically. Gatina's ancestors were the ones the Sea Lords struggled with and eventually capitulated to. Lancellus did not take the bait, to his credit.

"Among that two hundred, about thirty or forty are wealthy and powerful enough to be considered great, with the others enjoying honorable but lesser positions," he continued. "House Luxosar is among them, but only just. The largest have fleets of hundreds of ships, the galleons and deep-sea freighters which ply the Shattered Sea and the Shallow Sea from here to Unstara and the Ten Kingdoms."

"Does House Luxosar?" asked Atopol.

"We are not that large," the man admitted, in a rare display of humility. "But we are not without resources. For comparison's sake, all of House Luxosar's galleons are larger than the *Legacy*," he boasted. It was the third time he had done so in her hearing, Gatina noted. "We have a fair-sized fleet but have concentrated our efforts more in shipbuilding than trade. Our yards produce more than six vessels a year, though of smaller sizes—like this ship," he noted once again.

"That puts us in a position to court favor with smaller as well as medium-sized houses. It allows us to remain a power in the Great Bay shipping industry. We are able to maintain our status and finances, we enjoy great credit with the larger houses who need our barques and sloops to bring their galleons cargo, and we are well respected across the Bay as a result. More, we have good relationships with Coastlord fleets and trading houses, which extends our influence into areas where our more conservative fellows are unwilling to follow."

He paused to take a sip from his cup. "Excellent wine," he said. "From our haven in Sangsara, we have access to the best wine merchants. And many others. We hear news—a lot of unofficial news—especially when the fleets return after completing their voyages. As we primarily trade along the coasts of Castal and Remere and in Enultramar and Farise, my father believes we are well positioned to be of service to the Shadow Council—and it to us," Lancellus said, finally getting closer to his drawn-out point.

Gatina sighed into her napkin as quietly as she could. Aggravation aside, Lancellus was otherwise pleasant, she decided. And he was handsome. But he was not a mage, she reminded herself. And the fact that he was not a mage made it easier for her to find him irritating. He was good at making offhanded comments about the *Legacy*'s size and his own house's greatness. His arrogant manner made it difficult to endure him, despite his pretty eyes.

But he had information she and her family needed, and that made him an asset.

"House Luxosar, along with several of the smaller Sea Lord Houses, maintains a neutral policy toward landsmen's politics on most issues," the man continued. "However, that doesn't mean that we turn a blind eye to issues that will impact our business interests.

"While we prefer to remain far removed from the issues of inland politics, my house is sensitive, as are most Sea Lords, about the change in policy regarding slavery and piracy. You should be aware that there is a strong faction within the smaller trading houses that is growing to hate Vichetral's regime because of the legitimization of slavery and endorsement of piracy that puts their own ships at risk. We Luxosari find both to be repugnant and extremely bad for business. We prefer to make our coin off legitimate trade."

"In that, we are in full agreement," Beah said as she sipped Lancellus's wine. "We've had a brush with corsairs recently."

"Our primary rival is House Venjancar, a much-larger trading house oft associated with . . . unsavory elements. They provide warships for the ducal service but also clandestinely raid when no one is looking. They are heavily invested in the slave trade that is emerging. They were clandestine allies of the old Doge of Farise when he was raiding with the Mad Mage. And they are closely aligned with Count Vichetral and one Baron Jenerard, which means—"

"They are run by the Brotherhood of the Rat," Gatina finished.

Lancellus looked at her, really noticing her for the first time despite their earlier meeting, it seemed to her. "Yes, well done—Gatina, was it? Yes, The Brotherhood of the Rat," he agreed. "A more disreputable gang of thugs and villains than Enultramar has ever seen.

"House Venjancar has quietly embraced Vichetral's maritime policy and is trying to rally the other Sea Lord houses to his banner—by bribery, if they can, and coercion if they must. And unfortunately, given Vichetral's influence over this region, the call to legitimize the banner of the Five Counts is gaining traction."

"Jenerard's appointment as Lord of the Waves was confirmed by Vichetral." Hance nodded. "We have learned that he has been tasked to bring the rest of the Sea Lords in the Bay to heel under their banner. Which would mean the secret domination of the Brotherhood and their policies."

"That cannot be endured," Lancellus agreed. "We have learned that a secret council of those Sea Lord houses friendly to Vichetral is planned for the Vaxel Anchorage and Assessment. They will meet there with Jenerard, where he will attempt to convince them to conspire to dominate the other Great Houses and subvert the lesser houses to their will. That most likely will be staged as a private party in the Stormfather's Temple. That building has several rooms that can be used for private events. We would have a chance to disrupt that effort, should we join forces.

"The actual Anchorage will be led by the current high priest of the Storm King in Vaxel, the patriarch of the Sea Lord pantheon," he said. "He's a decent fellow and his position is ceremonial. But he will have much sway over the smaller trading houses. It is our belief that if the Venjancari prevail and the Sea Lords unite behind Vichetral, the nature of the Sea Lords of Enultramar will change irrevocably for the worse, as merchant ships will be forced to carry slaves instead of proper cargoes or be pressed into service as warships to fight the Castalshari," he finished.

Gatina looked at her father, hoping to see some sort of reaction across his face, but as usual, she saw nothing. Hance was known for his ability to both vanish in plain sight and show no emotion in his expression. It was admirable, if not a bit strange, she thought. But when she glanced at her mother, she saw that she was struggling to remain calm.

But before her mother could speak, her aunt did, breaking her own reserved calm.

"Lord Lancellus, I appreciate the information you have shared with us," Beah said. "I find it absolutely disheartening that any of the Great Houses would support Vichetral's policies. They are an affront to traditional Sea Lord customs and guidance. These policies are an insult to the Stormfather!" Her aunt was only a few octaves away from yelling, Gatina noticed. She had had several cups of wine. Before she became more upset, Hance put a steadying hand on top of her arm, while Minnie poured her a fresh cup of wine. This seemed to calm her.

"I could not agree more, Lady Beah," Lancellus said. "I have the leave from my father to express House Luxosar's support of your endeavor to stop Vichetral and his regime.

"I confess I had never heard of your Shadow Council, though it sounds akin to the Farisian Contramara. But once my father educated me on our family's lore, it seems we have worked together, in years past, several times. Though we had to consult the house's library to verify the accuracy of my claim."

He passed a document to Hance. "This should prove helpful, should you doubt my details. This is an account of the times my house and the Shadow Council of Coastlords have partnered, though none of those arrangements have been during our lifetimes," he explained. "The most recent record dates to several generations ago, perhaps our great-grand-sires' times during the reign of the Black Duke. I believe my ancestors helped yours move some *questionable* antiquities."

Gatina nearly giggled when he said *questionable*. What he *really* wanted to say was *stolen*, she imagined. *Would that make House Luxosar one of our fences?* she wondered, curious about both the items transported and how recently the two houses had worked together.

Hance was examining the document, which he passed to Minnie, and then she passed it to Beah. "This does indicate a significant association," he agreed. "Our private histories likewise show a relationship—which is why I was eager to take Master Thinradel's advice and seek you out."

Gatina suspected that all three of the adults were aware of the Houses' shared history. If they were not, Lancellus would not be there. Her parents did not employ random nobility without reason, she knew.

"We will discuss this after we conclude your portion of the meeting, Lancellus," Hance said. "To your point about the Anchorage and Assessment, is that not but in a few days' time?"

"The opening ceremonies commence the day after tomorrow, my lord," Lancellus confirmed.

"And that is the best way to reach the largest number of Sea Lord Houses at once?" her father asked.

"Yes, one of them. It is the annual council in Vaxel, where many new deals are struck, promotions are announced, and new policy is conceived. I am certain you are aware that Vaxel has a distinguished history as an important port. Its location on the western coastal trading route has helped secure that status. Originally, it was known as the city with the best access to the fruit-growing regions inland, but its deep, natural harbor gave it access to larger seacraft, and the land formations helped protect it from tropical storms and raiders. And those conditions exist today," he reminded them.

Gatina shifted in her chair. The crinolines were sticking to her legs, and she desperately wanted to stand up and shake out her gown, but she knew that would not be appropriate. So, instead, she tilted her head toward the long-winded Sea Lord as he continued his lecture about the great stronghaven of Vaxel. She did learn a few things.

The Bay was deep enough to allow the ancient Early Magocracy galleons and the Sea Lord freighters to sail into port without anchoring out in the Bay. It was one of the few great ports of Enultramar who could provide a haven for the deep-ocean vessels at any time of year.

"And what happened when the Coastlords took over the inlands?" Atopol asked when Lancellus paused for a sip of wine. Gatina knew that her brother was aware of that answer, but she welcomed the interruption.

"Ah, Atopol, that is a fascinating question. Vaxel remained a key port in the trading routes, and despite the Coastlords' control, the port maintained a Sea Lord culture, at least toward the southern end of the city. The best way to determine the influence is by examining the architecture. And that southern portion is home to four of the major havens, which helped Vaxel secure its position as one of the five largest Sea Lord settlements in the Great Bay. And that is also why Vaxel, or more specifically Vaxelhaven, is home to the ducal Assessment," he said, proudly.

"It is a lovely facility," her aunt agreed. "I've been to the Anchorage twice before. They have a bit of everything there—shopping, food, trade fair, recruitment—"

"And culture," Pia added, looking at Gatina. "They may even have the Chapel of the Eight Bells. They seem to have temples to all the other deities."

Lancellus shook his head. "No, not that one. It's considered bad luck for a port. But the cultural celebration can be exciting—and expensive," he cautioned. "A lot of business is conducted at Vaxelhaven's Anchorage. The duchy contracts warships there for defense, the various ecclesiastic orders hold rites for the fallen and the lost, the values of ships and cargoes are assessed, seamagi are raised in their station, new captains are announced, trade partnerships are struck, and all manner of competitions are held," he explained.

"Wasn't it the site of an insurrection or two?" Jordi asked. Gatina noted that his elbows were on the table, and he was very intent on hearing every word Lancellus uttered.

"Well, not insurrections," Lancellus admitted, "but close. Vaxel has a tradition of rebellious behavior and was the focus of two different armed oppositions to the navies commanded by the Magocracy," Lancellus clarified. "Then, when the Archmage's rule was established, it became a central location for the rebellion led by the Magelords—who are now the Coastlords, of course. That led to a bit bad feelings on the Sea Lord families, which worsened when the Magocracy took over the festival and turned it into an assessment.

"That was when the practice of setting the value of ships and cargo for taxation purposes was established. Eventually, the Sea Lords accepted the policy. And when the Narasi became sovereigns in Alshar, that practice continued as ducal policy. So, you can understand why the Vaxel Anchorage remains an important gathering for Sea Lord houses each year. And, as I said, it is only one of a few such meetings," he said, reaching for his cup.

Aunt Beah took that as her cue to take the conversation back for the moment. "Yes, Lancellus has been kind enough to prepare maps of the Vaxelhaven compound with us," she said as she stood and cleared away some items to lay the large map down in the center of the table. "As an overview, here is the rendering. Vaxelhaven is a walled compound of about fifty acres. One side is along the coast and the others are land-facing. Vaxelhaven is basically a city within the city of Vaxel proper. The four houses that control this compound have used the Anchorage as a means to wield power in the form of control over the sea routes and to generate coin for their holdings. And though they have invested money back into the compound, I would say they make more profit from one day of the Anchorage than they do from any of their other business ventures."

After Beah finished speaking, she rolled up the map. It was then that Hance was ready to offer some input, Gatina thought. She expected that they would be attending this gathering. But instead of committing to the mission, he deferred to Minnie.

"Lancellus, you say this is the best way to reach a majority of the Sea Lord houses. My lady wife, what are your thoughts?"

Gatina watched her mother's expressions and mannerisms. She seemed lost in thought, but she recognized that her mother was calculating a plan or an idea for a way in.

"My only questions concern access and security," Minnie said. "How strict is it? Will we be able to move freely once we are inside? And can we find a trusted location as a base of operations?"

"Security is manageable. You will need documents, of course. I'd wager that with the Lord of the Waves in attendance, things might be tighter than last year. But for folk with your reputation for such skills, you'll be fine."

Gatina remembered that her father had said Baron Jenerard had brought Censors with him. She wondered if the magical police force might become a problem.

"As I said earlier, the priest of the Storm King is a reasonable man. If we can gain his favor, then he will share his opinion with the smaller houses. That might save us time and gain us support quickly," Lancellus explained. "As for the other houses who will be voting on great matters ... I am open to suggestions."

AFTER THE MEETING HAD ENDED, GATINA FOLLOWED PIA FROM THE ROOM quickly. She wanted her cousin's help in unfastening the stays on her dress. But before she was able to ask, Pia ducked into a small cupboard. Gatina was about to walk behind her, but then she heard her cousin's laughter and Matros's voice.

And that's when she backed up quietly and turned around. Gatina knew Pia and Matros had gotten close, closer even since their time on the island, but she had not realized it was *that* serious. She thought to Kohni Ceija's prediction. Clearly, Matros was the mariner that Pia might well marry. It appeared that they were getting started early with that plan.

As Gatina climbed into her bunk, she wondered about the Calrom witch's predictions for herself.

Who was this mysterious mage she might marry? When would she meet him? Where? There was no chance of marriage until Anguin was put onto the throne and this mess with Vichetral was cleaned up, she knew.

She also thought about Lancellus. He was long-winded and aggravating, yes, but he was also handsome, intelligent, and invested in the same cause as she. And now that he was to become part of the Shadow Council, she would be working a bit closer with him.

Gatina smiled at the thought as Blessed Darkness washed over her and she fell asleep. She didn't have to marry him to admire him.

CHAPTER TWENTY-ONE
A DUEL ON THE DECK

Adaptability is just as important as stealth when it comes to a heist. Approaching a conventional job with typical insight may prove fruitful, but the whims of Fortune and the unexpected turns of fate often require us to adapt to circumstance that we did not—cannot—envision. That requires imagination and sets the superior thief above those who know only one manner in which to achieve their goals. The thief who can adapt will certainly prevail. The thief who cannot will inevitably fail.

—from **The Shield of Darkness**,
written by Kiera the Great

THE NEXT MORNING, JUST BEFORE SUNRISE, GATINA LAY IN HER BUNK ON THE *Legacy*, waiting for Pia to leave the forecastle. She wasn't ready to face the day yet, but she knew she must be on deck soon to attack her duties. She simply wanted a few moments to herself to think about everything that had happened since they'd left Falas.

When she finally rolled herself off the bunk and took care of her morning needs, she realized it was likely time to clean their cabin. She hadn't been aboard the *Legacy* in a few days, but it looked like it needed freshening. That duty fell to her and Pia, she knew, as the most junior members of the crew. But she realized that chore would depend on what was assigned that day, and the only way to know that was to venture abovedecks.

Gatina stretched her arms up over her head and quickly worked through a brief set of motions Lord Steel had taught her using the wooden scimitar that she had tucked away under her bunk. The activity felt good and helped wake her stiff muscles. Then she washed her face in the basin and tucked her hair under a plain white scarf.

By the time she joined her brother and cousins on the *Legacy*'s deck, the sun was already spreading magnificent magenta and orange rays across the waves. It had become part of her routine to take stock of the situation the moment she emerged from the forecastle—a habit all good mariners adopted, she knew.

The ship was underway, headed northwest at about ten knots, by her estimation. With a full hold, it was unlikely that she could do much better even with a tailwind and a full sail. She could see the *Daydream* off the starboard stern easily keeping pace with her. The sloop looked elegant and beautiful in the distance. The weather was clear, with just a few clouds aft and no feeling of rain in the air.

It was a glorious day at sea, and Gatina took just a moment to inhale the air and admire the view at the starboard rail. The *Daydream* really was beautiful.

"Maranka!" Seksus bellowed at her. "Gather at the foremast with your crewmates! Duty assignments!"

Heaving one last sigh, Gatina returned her focus to the ship she was on. They were still serving as crew under Seksus and Taruk's watchful eyes, even as they prepared for the mission in Vaxel, and there was plenty to do even with the sails full and the rigging trimmed.

But Gatina did not mind. She found her time spent in this role useful, instructive even. It allowed her to observe how the professional mariners worked, dressed, spoke, and otherwise interacted with each other. She knew enough to fool a landsman, she knew, but she wanted to master the craft of sailing adequately enough to convince a professional that she could be a fit mariner.

All four of them were on first watch and would be until noon when luncheon was served. Then two of them would be on the dogwatch afterward for a few hours, with two of the mariners from the second watch, which was already headed to sleep after a bite of breakfast. Seksus was dividing up the chores the quartermaster had decreed needed to be done, when Gatina approached the foremast. Her brother and cousins had already gathered there, and the bosun was impatient.

"About time, Lady Maranka," he said sarcastically. "We've no time for daydreams today. Vaxel is but two days hence, and the captain wants this ship scrubbed from the crow's nest to the waterline before we get there. That means all of you need to look lively. There will be hundreds of ships there, potential clients and vendors, and if we're not the most impressive caravel in the port, then the captain will want to know why!" he bellowed.

Gatina didn't take the bosun's harsh words personally. It was his job to execute the orders of the captain and quartermaster, and he spared none of them from his attention. Rarely did he give an order that wasn't bracketed with suspicion and even insults. He was just as gruff in his praise when it was sparingly doled out. But his sense of discipline was important for how the ship was run, she had realized. A soft-spoken bosun would make her doubt the confidence in the captain and crew of any ship she sailed on.

"Jordi and Martijne, turn to and clean Captain Armandus's quarters and cockpit—dust from top to bottom, then mop the quarterdeck to the foremast," Seksus instructed. "But be mindful not to just slosh water around and walk away—*scrub*, this time, you lazy squids, and make sure it's dry when you're done. Captain hates a wet deck in his cabin," he said with emphasis.

"Pia, Maranka, you two get the entirety of the deck from the mainmast aft. It gets swabbed, every bit o' brass polished, and every iron fitting oiled before luncheon," he directed sternly. "I want to see those elbows jiggling, not your eyes gazing over the rails while you dream. I catch that, you'll be surveying the bilge for leaks!"

"Aye, bosun!" Pia called in unison with Gatina. No other response was expected or would be tolerated.

"After the luncheon bell, you two squids will be on dogwatch. You will be cleaning out every locker on deck: I want lines coiled properly, sails folded right, fire buckets and lamps filled, ashes dumped, privies cleaned, and everything gleaming before you're done!" he added. Gatina suppressed a groan. She had hoped Atopol and Jordi would get dogwatch their first day back aboard the *Legacy*.

"All four of you will transfer to the *Daydream* tonight after your watch," he continued. "We'll get two crew in return. But expect to be back here by dawn tomorrow, where you'll do anything you skimped on today. Now step to it!" he commanded. "And look lively!"

"Aye, bosun!" they responded together, jumping to their feet.

Atopol smiled at her as they assembled around the mop locker. "Dinner meeting or mission meeting, I wonder?" he asked. "Any idea what's on the menu?"

Gatina suspected it had to do with their mission, so she too was curious about that. She was not concerned about the menu, though.

"Not a clue, I'm sorry to say," Pia said. "I just know we've all been requested to attend. But that's long hours away from now."

"And we'll be exhausted by then," Gatina agreed. "Dogwatch? Did we do something wrong?" she complained. That was something else mariners were expected to do. No one liked swabbing, but if you didn't complain about it, there was something amiss with you.

"Let's just bloody get it done," Pia said moodily, and grabbed a bag of sand and a bucket. She nearly stomped away toward the forecastle.

"What's wrong with her?" Atopol asked. Usually, their cousin was cheerful—especially lately.

"Captain caught her with Matros," Jordi explained in a low voice. "They were kissing in a cupboard or something. He dressed her down and then sent Matros over to the *Daydream* last night."

Gatina winced at the revelation. "I guess that's why I'm on dogwatch now." She sighed and grabbed two mops and a bucket.

"They were just kissing," Jordi said defensively, "but the captain doesn't like fraternization in his crew. Even in their off time. He's within his rights," he admitted.

"I just feel sorry for Matros," Atopol offered as he collected his supplies. "He just got booted off a ship for kissing the daughter of the captain of the ship he's been transferred to. That's going to be an awkward conversation."

Gatina quickly fell into step with her cousin as they began hauling seawater from over the rails and splashing it on the deck.

"So . . . late night, last night," she observed casually as she sprinkled sand across the deck.

"You heard?" Pia asked, almost accusingly. "It wasn't anything. I just wanted to talk to him before I turned in, and . . . well, we ran out of things to talk about," she admitted. "Our lips just kept moving. They didn't need to send him away." She pouted.

"Don't worry; you can swim," she teased.

"I really like him, Gatina," she confessed in a low voice as they began to vigorously swab the deck. "He's smart and kind and witty . . ."

"He's a fine fellow," Gatina agreed as she mopped. They had done it so many times that they fell into an easy rhythm. "What does your mother think of him?"

"She says she likes him, but she won't really discuss it with me. I suppose I can understand that. She's just getting to know him, after all."

"Don't worry," Gatina offered, "my mother is going to grill him about every detail of his life and test him in so many ways that your mother won't even get a chance."

"She is?" Pia asked, surprised.

"It's her duty," Gatina reminded her. "She's not only suspicious of everything, but she's also really good at being suspicious. It comes with being a shadowthief. But I don't think you have to worry," she consoled. "I have a good feeling about Matros."

"I did too," she agreed. "Then the captain found us."

"If he was really angry, he would have just chucked him overboard or had him flogged or something. I think he just doesn't want you distracting each other right now. We have a mission," she reminded her. "And a cargo to get into a busy port."

"I know, I know," her cousin groaned. "We'll get to spend some time together in Vaxel, I hope. There's a lot to do there. And we should be in port for several days. I guess I just have to be patient."

They began polishing the *Legacy*'s hardware on the main deck. Gatina had not realized just how quickly the Bay water could tarnish the brass and metal fixtures—or just how many fixtures were on the ship. Doorknobs, hinges, hooks, brackets, and clamps, not to mention all of the fastenings. All had to be wiped down with a greasy cloth after a thorough scrubbing with ashes and lye. There was a lot to polish. Fortunately, this chore was done every other day, and that made the time go a bit faster.

"How are *you* doing?" Pia asked her. "I saw you staring at Lancellus at dinner."

"Me? I am faring well, I suppose," Gatina said as she worked the ash solution onto a stubborn stain. "And I was not staring. I was *observing*," she emphasized. "That's something shadowthieves are good at, too."

"So, what did you observe?" Pia asked as she refilled the bucket to rinse the deck.

"He's tall, has pretty eyes, and he thinks quite well of himself," Gatina reflected. "His voice is so lovely, he has to hear a lot of it. Intelligent but arrogant, dedicated but entitled . . . a typical Sea Lord," she suggested.

"His family is quite wealthy," Pia reported. "It's too bad he isn't Talented."

"I'm glad he's not," Gatina said as she went back to swabbing the water off the deck.

"You know, you don't *have* to follow the family custom," Pia reminded her. "Mother didn't."

Gatina sighed. "Our house has these rules for a purpose," she said, shaking her head. "I'm too proud of my legacy to abandon them lightly. Besides, from what that witch said, I won't meet my husband until after the curse is lifted."

Pia did not laugh at her, thank Blessed Darkness. Instead, Gatina watched as her cousin chewed on her bottom lip, as if lost in thought. Finally, when she spoke, Gatina found a bit of relief in the answer.

"You're placing entirely too much importance on that," she insisted. "Cursed? No. It's just an old superstition," she insisted. "Mother does not take to curses, and Father did not put much faith in them either," she admitted. "I think your fortune is what you make of it."

Gatina stared at her cousin, wide-eyed. "You *aren't* going to try to break the curse?"

"Well... I also think it's not wise to snub a custom or a religion. So, the first chance I get, I'll find a temple and make it right by the Shipwrecker. It can't hurt. But I think a lot of it is what you make of it. If you think you're cursed, you're more likely to draw bad luck. But I don't particularly feel cursed," she added shooting a smile at the *Daydream* in the distance, where Matros was stationed. "Except maybe for drawing dogwatch."

Gatina went back to her swabbing as she considered what Pia had said. Perhaps she had a point. There was, as yet, no tangible sign of a curse in her life. Certainly, Pia seemed to be enjoying the results of the shipwreck, she noted. She could see her point, especially about making your own luck, good or bad.

Besides, if Kohni Ceija knew her business as well as Pia said she did, there was no way anything bad was going to happen to them. The old witch would've seen it and likely told them, she reasoned. She had heard comments—mainly sarcastic ones from Jordi—about how some of these witches would predict great things for their marks but then speak of a problem that must be removed—usually by investing in incredibly overpriced candles that had been blessed in a certain way, or pricy mystical amulets that could aid the querent toward their desires—for a price.

But while she suspected the witch of being a charlatan, there were too many things she'd said that had rung true in her ears. She had guessed that she and Atopol were thieves, for one, and even guessed her professional name. She recalled Jordi had changed his perspective a bit when the old woman had mentioned his father was still alive and would return someday. Also, to Kohni's credit, she did not press them for more silver, not that Gatina would have hesitated to part with it. It wasn't really hers, after all. It was loot.

It was a confusing situation. Especially when she took the mysterious Pippa's predictions into account. She had to admit that the girl had foreseen Pia's infatuation with Matros when he was still unconscious. Matros and Pia did seem to have a very strong connection, one she herself could not explain.

But was it love? Gatina wasn't sure she understood what love was—or why there was so much fuss over it. She had no interest in that—or this supposed handsome wizard, either. To her mind, love and duty should go hand in hand, as it had with her parents.

Instead, she decided to finish her chores as quickly but diligently as she could. Swabbing the deck was not fun, but it did give her something to focus on other than curses, missions, pirates, and witches.

GATINA FOUND JORDI IN THE FORWARD SAIL LOCKER ON THE QUARTERDECK after she'd completed most of her duties on deck. He was securing the spare bolts of sailcloth in neat bundles and then stowing them each on their own shelf. She overheard him telling her brother about the Storm King's Tower at the Vaxelhaven compound.

"It's one of the biggest on the Great Bay," he assured him. "It's said you can see its beacon on the horizon for miles. It's also one of the older ones, built before the Magocracy took over."

She could not resist jumping into their conversation.

"How tall is the tower? Is there only one?" Gatina asked, hoping she'd be able to climb it.

"Probably a hundred and fifty feet, maybe more if you count the beacon house atop it," Jordi said after he thought about it for a moment. "It's only six floors high, I think. But I've never seen it in person."

"Is it like the other Sea Lord fortresses we've seen?" Atopol asked, curiously.

"The same basic design—an elongated pyramid, I guess you'd call it—but much, much bigger. It's likely a small fortress inside the larger compound, like a castle's keep is within its bailey. And by that I mean it is well fortified. Most Sea Lords keep a bunch of warriors around to hold their havens. And since it also houses the High Priest of the Stormfather of Vaxel, you can bet that there will be additional security," he assured.

"That's a tall tower," Atopol said, nodding appreciatively.

"That's got to be a lot of stairs," Jordi said, shaking his head. "I don't much like stairs."

"Stairs?" Atopol laughed. "We're the Cats of Enultramar. We don't take the stairs."

"It *would* be fun to climb," Gatina agreed.

Jordi looked to his cousin, then to Gatina. "You're serious? You'd scale the tower?"

"Of course we would, if we need to," Gatina assured him. "It's the most direct route to the top, and there won't be guards that high on the tower walls. Half of being a thief is avoiding routes with too many guards." She was looking forward to scaling a proper tower after spending so much time on the ship's rigging, nets, and lines.

"I doubt we'll end up doing that, though," Atopol said, disappointed. "If there is something up there we need, Father will probably get to steal it. But I guess we'll learn all of that at tonight's meeting on the *Daydream*. That's where Lancellus will give us our briefing. He and Father have been over there in his cabin all morning, planning it out. What did you think of him, Kitten?" he asked with a smirk.

Gatina tossed her head dismissively. "He's handsome enough, but he's just another arrogant Sea Lord too used to being in charge of things. Oh, he seems dedicated enough to the cause—but I'll be surprised if he ever voices an original thought."

"He's pretty typical of the higher class of Sea Lord," Jordi confirmed. "Intelligent, educated, wealthy, and obnoxiously self-assured. They all think of themselves as great pirates, adventurers, and merchant princes, but they're usually just glorified counting men."

"He brought a heavy satchel with him on board with his other baggage," Atopol revealed. "It was filled with parchment, and he protected it like it was treasure. That's probably where his information is stored."

"But can we trust him?" Jordi asked suspiciously. "I mean, Sea Lords have a reputation for treachery . . ."

"Jordi! You're half Sea Lord and there isn't a treacherous bone in your body!" Gatina said, shocked.

"So, I'm only partially treacherous," he reasoned. "My point is that if you study the history of the Bay, you'll see various Houses switch around their allegiances for all sorts of stupid reasons. I just don't want us to commit to something and then find out that he and his House have been blowing wind on both sides of the sail."

"He was vouched for," Atopol assured him. "My father doesn't take that lightly. Nor would he blindly enter into an agreement unless he'd done his own investigations. Besides, it isn't healthy to cross the Shadow Council," he said ominously. "It typically ends poorly."

IN THE LATE AFTERNOON, THE FOUR FINALLY TOOK THEIR LEAVE OF THE *Legacy* and rowed over to the *Daydream*, as instructed. As they climbed the rope ladder to the sloop's railing, Matros and Genver were waiting. They were to be deployed back to the *Legacy* while the family was preparing for their mission. Pia had to content herself with a smile and a fawning look at Matros as he rowed away from her.

Their parents, Aunt Beah, and Lancellus were gathered around the mainmast when they arrived. Her father had a serious expression on his face, she saw, and her mother looked preoccupied. The four of them sat on the deck when bidden and learned what the mission had in store for them.

"This is going to be complicated," Hance began. "The goal of the mission is to convince enough of the important Houses to reject Jenerard's proposals and the Council of Five altogether. That is going to mean a mixture of persuasion, argument, and even coercion and extortion if need be. And since there are so many of them, we're going to have to split up and approach our marks individually.

"Lancellus and I have spent all day figuring out which people will require what kind of argument and tried to fit each of you with a target we think you're best suited for. Sometimes, you will have more than one. But the situation in Vaxel could well prove . . . fluid," he said, carefully selecting his words. "That's why it's complicated. We won't have a lot of time to prepare the way we usually do for a heist. And we'll each be working our own marks and will only be able to help each other if we get into a pinch. I don't want there to be any pinching," he added sternly.

"Your mother and I will each have two targets," he continued. "Beah will have three, but they're all considered fairly easy to convince, and one of them she already knows personally. She will work from our safe house, a booth she's rented at Vaxel to dispose of her cargo. That's perfect cover for the kind of casual conversation she'll need to discuss the matter without attracting too much attention. Jordi and Pia will be supporting her there as well as running errands and doing some reconnaissance and lookout work."

Pia looked at her brother. "What, we don't get an assignment?"

"We need support on this mission more than we need additional agents," Gatina's mother assured her. "As helpful as you and Jordi have been, this is not something that should be undertaken lightly, nor by untrained people. But don't underestimate the importance of your roles," she warned. "We rely on our support staff when it comes to completing our missions. They often make the difference between success and failure." That seemed to soothe her cousin.

"I will be attempting the two most important marks," Hance continued. "One is the High Priest of the Stormfather himself. The other is the head of a company that controls much of the financing for shipbuilding in the Bay. Lady Night will have two similarly important assignments. Cat, you get two of the medium-sized houses to convince. They hold no less than eight proxies between them. Kitten, you get one, but we have two more that can be approached if you complete your first one in good order."

"So, what do we do to convince them?" Atopol asked.

"Whatever you have to," Minnureal answered flatly. "Appeal to their reason, their honor, their loyalty to Alshar. If that fails, persuade them that there is something sinister arising that they are unaware of—no one likes being on the wrong side of that sort of thing. See if they are open to a bribe and what kind. If that fails, then resort to threats and extortion. Most of these Sea Lords have secrets they would prefer to remain hidden, and others are quite fearful that their positions will be compromised in some way. All of these people have something important they don't want to lose. So, find out what it is and use that as leverage," she advised.

"What is the landscape going to look like?" Gatina asked. It was a term-of-art in their profession that described the general environment the heist or mission was taking place in.

"Crowded," her father answered. "There will be more than ten thousand mariners descending on the Anchorage, and hundreds of ships in port from all over the world. An easy place to get lost in," he predicted. "Plenty of opportunities for distraction and misdirection. Everyone will be focused on their own business, or enjoying the entertainments, or getting blind drunk.

"As far as the layout, I will defer to Lancellus, who is familiar with Vaxelhaven and has made several good sketches we can use to prepare," he said, nodding toward the Sea Lord. The man straightened and handed a parchment to her mother, indicating she should pass it around to each of them.

"Vaxelhaven is a city within a city," he began in a businesslike manner. "Imagine the temple from Pluhalia but four times as large. That's about the size of the main festival area. There will be a lot of activity, as most of the Great Houses are represented for the various councils and meetings underway. The haven is divided into a compound dedicated to each of the six divinities, with a seventh for the Lord of the Waves and the ducal contingent. There are important meetings running in each of them for the entire length of the Anchorage," he reported.

"Most of the attention will be on important court cases at the Storm Lord's temple or the actual assessment being conducted by the officials of the Lord of the Waves. But there will be thousands of other meetings as deals, future voyages, and transfers and promotions get underway. That means that most of our important contacts—sorry, our *targets*," he corrected self-consciously, "will be around the compounds of the Storm King and the Fairtrader. The lesser targets will likely be around the Maiden's temple complex, and in one case, the Corsair's."

Gatina studied the map carefully when it was passed to her. It was drawn in a neat and precise hand, she saw, and drawn to scale, according to the legend. The Storm King's tower was indeed a massive element of the haven, but as large as it was, it was but one of a score or more of other great buildings and dozens of smaller ones. The market area alone looked to be almost a mile long, easily, stretching from one end of the long haven to the other.

The entire place was surrounded by a long, non-crenellated wall that separated it from the rest of the vast port complex. She did her best to memorize the layout in the few moments she held it before passing it to her brother.

"It will be especially important to master your disguises as Sea Lords for this mission," her mother lectured. "In addition to planning your missions, you will spend the next two days working with Lancellus to perfect them. That starts tonight. He is going to examine how you fight with scimitars, how you walk, how you move. Then on to your accents, mannerisms, and appearances. We will give you the dossiers on your marks afterwards. I think it will be a most instructive evening."

GATINA WAS ALWAYS READY TO PRACTICE SWORDPLAY. SHE LOOKED FORWARD to the exercise as she gripped the hilt of her wooden practice sword. She had practiced a few times, but she knew she needed to work with the scimitar. It was the signature weapon of the Sea Lords, as the Rat Tail was to the Brotherhood or mageblades were to warmagi.

The curved blade was still mostly foreign to her mind and novel in her hand. It required an entirely different style from those blades she was familiar with. She had only begun using it in earnest over the past few weeks, and while she had adjusted to it, she welcomed more time with the weapon. What she really wanted was to watch others fight with it, to observe their stances and styles.

Each of them was issued one of the practice blades and warmed up a bit before Lancellus paired them up. After a few bouts on their own, he stopped them for a moment and addressed the basic flaws he witnessed.

"These blades are not designed for thrusting, despite the point at the end," he explained. "They are used almost exclusively for slashing—and in a particular way. Instead of a static guard and individual strikes, the scimitar requires everything being done in *circles*," he said, taking a guard position and demonstrating with the practice sword. Gatina was surprised how smoothly his form flowed from one position to another, and his footwork seemed adequate and well practiced. His hips gyrated in an almost-musical fashion.

"The maritime scimitar is designed to be short and heavy, the kind of blade that can hew through a line holding a sail or hack a boarding ladder to pieces if necessary. It is short, to contend with the crowded decks where you might not have a lot of room to swing. That means you must get closer to your opponent than you're used to," he said, demonstrating with Atopol.

The two dueled for a few moments with Atopol beginning to pick up the rhythm of the fight and the style before Lancellus stopped once again. "It's far more dependent on the wrist and elbow for its efficacy, and less dependent on the shoulder," he continued, using Atopol's arm to demonstrate. "You want to use the momentum of the blade not just to attack but to be in a position to defend when you complete the circle. Jerking movements are counterproductive. Once you get the blade moving, you want to keep it moving as constantly as possible." Once again, he and Atopol took their guards, and Gatina could see her brother adopting the style.

Then they broke up again and tried on their own. Gatina was paired with Jordi this time, and the two of them made several passes at each other. She began to see the advantages to using the blade in the Sea Lord style—and some disadvantages. It was fine for blocking another scimitar, for instance, but she knew the point on her shadowblade would likely give her the means to tear apart any authentic Sea Lord duelist with thrusts.

Footwork was also very important to the style, she realized. It emphasized keeping not just the sword in motion but also your feet. As many of the situations where it might be used would happen on the deck of a ship that might be rolling at sea, she could appreciate that. It also encouraged you to use another weapon in your off hand, she quickly figured out, not just for blocking or an opportunistic attack but for balance. Balance was vitally important to using the scimitar.

"That was . . . adequate," Lancellus pronounced, after switching up the partners a few times and watching them work. "Jordi, your elbow is not held high enough. Atopol, quit trying to manage a thrust and focus on the edge of the blade. Pia, stay light on your feet and keep them moving," he advised.

"What about me?" Gatina asked, realizing that she wanted his criticism.

"You're doing . . . well," he admitted. "I didn't expect you to be so quick with the blade as you are. But I'm concerned that you will tire quickly with it, and once that happens, you could be in trouble."

Gatina snorted and rolled her eyes. "I wouldn't place a wager on that," she said.

"Then take on Pia, this time, and fight for as long as you can," Lancellus directed.

Gatina and her cousin took their guards after touching their wooden blades together in salute. From the moment Pia's sword began to move, Gatina moved faster, twirling herself in a circle while snaking her way within her cousin's clumsier guard. She delivered two light taps on her arm, then shifted around and struck her shoulder from the other side. Pia nearly landed a blow in return, but Gatina had learned the trick of visualizing the end of the circle she was drawing and parried it easily. Then Pia surprised her by reversing the direction of her blade and connecting with Gatina's neck.

Lancellus directed Pia to practice with Attie while he offered feedback to them and provided greater insight and instruction directly to Gatina.

But as Pia began to demonstrate the attack and defensive maneuvers with Atopol, Lancellus had had enough, Gatina saw. He stood up and walked over, giving them a wide berth to where they were practicing. His attention was fully on Atopol. He circled around, his eyes tracking each strike and dodge. Finally, Lancellus spoke.

"Be a little more aggressive, Martijne. That's it," he encouraged. "Be more aware of your opponent's range, Maranka; how far out can she strike? How wide is the arc of her arm? Now use that to your advantage," he coached.

Atopol and Jordi were both listening to his advice too. Gatina suspected her brother found it aggravating because of the Sea Lord's imperious attitude, but this *was* Lancellus's weapon of choice, and he was far more practiced in it than they were, she knew.

"Excellent work, Pia, good, keep her on the defensive," Lancellus coached. Gatina felt a sweat break across her forehead as Pia pressed her attack. She blinked to keep it from trickling into her eyes. Eventually, she knew Pia would give up. She hoped. She knew she wouldn't. When it seemed as though neither would relent, Lancellus called a halt to their duel.

"That's not bad," Pia said when they took a break. "Would you like me to show you the attack for that defensive move?" Gatina had quickly learned that for every offensive measure, there was a defensive measure, so if Jordi was defending, he also had a way to attack.

Gatina and Pia worked until Lancellus called another pause, and then critiqued them both on their footwork and their patterns of attack during the precise dance, which is how Gatina came to view scimitar work. Then they switched partners, and she was facing her brother.

They worked long after her arms no longer stung from the overhand swinging and exertion. Once again, Lancellus stopped them from time to time to criticize. He again cast doubt on Gatina's stamina.

"If you think I'm too weak to fight a duel, perhaps you'll entertain me?" she asked, her chest heaving.

"I will try not to be too hard on you," Lancellus agreed, taking his guard position: blade extended, knees bent, feet lightly planted on the deck. "I've been studying swordplay since I was eleven. *Go!*" he commanded, and immediately started a sweeping attack from his shoulder, whipping the sword around with great force toward her torso.

It wasn't a surprise to Gatina—she'd seen him use the same opening move in nearly every demonstration. She took half a step back and let the blade pass harmlessly in front of her before she stepped in, turned quickly to her right, and swept her own sword across the Sea Lord's back.

Of course, he had also moved, so his back wasn't where it was supposed to be, and he caught her blade on his. For the next several minutes, they danced back and forth, with Gatina usually making smaller, tighter circles in her footwork that forced Lancellus to correct for a smaller opponent. It was a little more difficult than she expected, because her bust seemed to have grown since the last time she'd done any serious swordplay, and it was throwing off her balance just a hair. Twice she dropped to the deck and allowed his blade to pass overhead. That seemed to startle him. When he overcorrected, it threw him off-balance, and she brought her blade down on the back of his left thigh.

"I've been studying swordplay since I was *nine*," she informed him, as he rubbed his leg.

"You . . . you are a credit to your master," he conceded. "Still, most mariners are larger than me and would seek to bowl you over with pure physical force in a real fight. You may not have the opportunity to dance around like that."

"If it was a real fight, I wouldn't have to," she dismissed. "Nor would I be limited to just my blade to defend myself. Shall I demonstrate?"

Lancellus rolled his shoulders and assumed the guard position once again. "Let's see if you can stop this," he suggested, and rushed her with his blade swinging viciously fast. He also stomped his boot hard onto the deck, something that she'd seen street duelists do to distract their opponents.

She didn't fall for the ruse. She kept her eyes on his and predicted where his blade was going to be before it got there. Sidestepping his aggressive attack, she stuck her left hand in his face and activated a cantrip that produced a small, brief magical flare of light. Then she whirled, reversed direction, and slashed his left arm. He countered too late as he struggled to see anything with his blighted vision, and in her next whirl, Gatina circled close in before slapping his right thigh and then his shoulder from behind as she rotated around him.

"Halt!" he called, shaking his head. "That was three solid strikes. What devilry did you do to my eyes?" he complained.

"Just a little magic to make things interesting." She smiled. Then she opened her left hand. "And while I was at it, I stole your purse," she said, revealing the pouch in her palm. "That's what I'd do in a real fight, too."

"That's what you get for fighting a shadowthief," Atopol laughed. "Another pass and she'd have your rings, your boots, and your belt, too. Don't worry about your eyes; it will clear up in a moment."

"Well done, Maranka," Lancellus praised despite himself as he rubbed his eyes. "You are fiendishly quick with that thing. And you don't seem to tire as much as I would expect you to."

"My swordmaster believes in a rigorous training schedule," she agreed, returning his purse to him. "I've been hauling up sails and swabbing the decks for weeks. I've fought for my life on more than one occasion. And I *don't* like to lose," she added confidently.

Lancellus gave her a long, thoughtful look. "No, I wouldn't imagine you would."

CHAPTER TWENTY-TWO
PLANNING THE MISSION

Cracking a heist has become one of my favorite parts of the process. I used to dislike the procedure when I began my apprenticeship, but I have come to value the security that comes with knowing everything I can about what I'm about to crawl into: the landscape, the people, the assets, and the liabilities. Even then, as Kiera often said, things will inevitably go awry. But by knowing as much as you can about the job, you can sometimes anticipate how they will go awry, and include that in the plan.

— *from Gatina's Heist Journal*

GATINA BARELY TASTED HER MEAL THAT NIGHT, ALTHOUGH IT WAS MORE plentiful and flavorful than her usual rations. She was too excited by the prospect of planning her mission.

It had become, with swordplay and magic, one of her favorite parts of a mission she'd learned during her apprenticeship. Where once she felt constrained by the plans her parents put forth, when they had begun instructing her how to break apart the mission goals and determine which steps needed to be taken to achieve them, planning—or "cracking," in the family parlance—a mission was almost as exciting as executing one. Each portion was like a small puzzle to be solved or a lock to be picked. There were endless possibilities at this point, as well as endless challenges.

The family and Lancellus gathered in the captain's cabin once the light fell, and Hance distributed one or two small scrolls to each of them. These held the details of their individual assignments as he'd identified them, as well as suggestions copied down in his meticulous hand.

"If I might have your attention," he said, as they sat to eat and conspire in lamplight. "Thanks to Lancellus, we have several very detailed maps of the Vaxelhaven temple complex where the Anchorage and Assessment meeting will take place in a few days' time." He motioned toward the larger piece of parchment he'd tacked to the back of the cabin door.

"This shows the entire complex overview. It is a rather large facility, roughly fifty acres, and is one of four different Sea Lord havens surrounding the city of Vaxel proper. It is owned and controlled by House Grellius, an ancient and distinguished Great House ruled by Viscount Esperius. He will be the master of the festivities—rather, his staff will. The good viscount is the official host of the Sea Lord council held in conjunction with the Anchorage.

"For centuries, the Anchorage has been one of the chief sources of revenue and a reflection of the importance of House Grellius in status among the other Great Houses. The current High Priest of the Stormfather, not coincidentally, is the viscount's cousin. Between the two of them, they wield a lot of power. This is their big festival, and they want there to be no trouble. Both of them will be in or around the temple for most of the week, hosting parties, receptions, and officiating at ceremonial events. They will entertain the Lord of the Waves when he arrives and listen to his traditional speech on the palace's policies in regard to the Great Bay.

"The Sea Lord house controlling Vaxelhaven has used the assessment as an opportunity to wield power and generate income. They don't do that by holding parties. They instead offer a plethora of activities for the thousands of merchants and mariners who will be in Vaxelhaven for the Anchorage.

"Expect to find a bit of everything. Vendors will sell everything from drinks and food to fabric and weapons—and the viscount gets a cut of each transaction, one way or another. Those vendors and booths will reach beyond the walls of the haven to cater to the mariners from the great gathering of ships, but the official activity is all within the walls. Our safe house will be here," he said, pointing to the map with an iron skewer. "Beah has arranged for a booth with a small cottage attached from which she'll sell the *Legacy*'s cargo. It's enclosed, relatively private, and should be a place we can sleep and eat when we're not working."

"Yes," her mother agreed. "And to complete your individual missions successfully, you must know each of those areas—plus the seventh, the ducal pavilion. You must be able to blend into any of those areas. Thankfully, with so many travelers there for the first time, you won't look out of place if you get misdirected or confused—there should be plenty of that there. Learn the main routes between each section, as well as any shortcuts or escape routes you can imagine that you might need.

"Lancellus has prepared documents to instruct you about who you are targeting in this mission," Minnie explained as she opened her own scroll. "Within you will find details about your mission, your target, and your alias," she informed them. "Get familiar with those details and formulate a plan to complete your mission. If you have general questions, ask them now. You will present your plan to Shadow and myself in private for approval before we get to Vaxel. And to ensure that you cannot inadvertently interfere with each other's missions, keep the details of your task to yourself. What you don't know—"

"You cannot tell," Atopol and Gatina replied together, startling Lancellus.

There was little chatter as everyone opened their scrolls and began to read. As Gatina skimmed through the files, she kept glancing up at the big map to place each detail in context in her mind. It was fascinating reading, almost like reading a book.

Her target was a young woman called Lady Bomaris of House Crenalsar. The house was led by Viscount Botylyn of Lagosta, the dossier informed her. House Crenalsar had a good-sized merchant fleet of more than twenty caravels, twice as many barques, and four large galleons that made the overseas run to Farise and Remere. They specialized in shipping wine, olive oil, and cotton, and had small havens in Remere and Castal, in addition to Enultramar.

The house had been on tolerably friendly terms with the late Duke Lenguin and was considered one of the more progressive and less traditional institutions among the Sea Lord nobility. They were particularly devoted to the Fairtrader and had financed many shrines and temples to the divinity over the years. The viscount also had alliances and good relations with his Coastlord neighbors and had even enjoyed several beneficial partnerships with them over the years.

The good viscount was supposed to go to the Anchorage himself to participate in the council this year, according to Lancellus's notes, but he had suffered an injury. His leg was broken in two spots. It was severe and recent enough that he was still in a wooden splint, confined to bed in Lagosta. Instead, his eldest daughter, Lady Bomaris, would attend and represent the house in his place—and carry three other proxies of closely allied houses.

Gatina immediately saw why she had been chosen for this particular target. The girl was only a few years older than she was. Lady Bomaris was nearly sixteen years old. She was young, but she had been well educated in the temples and counting houses, and she was considered very intelligent. She was likely to be accompanied by a priestess or an older relative, Gatina reasoned. A Sea Lord was unlikely to allow his lady daughter to travel alone during the troubles in the Great Bay, even when she was headed to a haven. Indeed, she might have a small entourage.

In addition to her father the viscount, House Crenalsar represented a coalition of small merchant houses in the Eastern Bay who supplied cargo for their ships, and that put a lot of pressure on the young woman. She must not only present herself well on behalf of her father but also ensure that everyone's interests were met during any negotiations or risk alienating her clients and vendors. That was the source of her proxies.

She would likely be traveling on her father's private sloop, the *Viscount's Fortune*, the document informed her—and included several specifications that only a Sea Lord would find helpful. By tradition, the family held a suite of rooms in the main complex, which was where she would be lodging with her staff. She was expected to conduct several meetings and attend many prominent functions, including the Lord of the Waves' customary speech. Bomaris had already been seen as a rising star of the Eastern Bay in negotiations, the dossier reported. Her two older brothers were already at sea, so the responsibility to represent the House fell to her.

Then came her favorite part: her alias. Gatina saw that she would be portraying a Sea Lord named Lady Foscombra, one from the minor house of Verac, from Torventos, in the southeast portion of the Bay. That connection to the larger house might present her with a greater opportunity to be near Lady Bomaris, she realized. There were not as many southeasterners who attended the Anchorage, the dossier noted, as the autumnal version of the meeting held at nearby Argarus every year. Nor did House Crenalsar have much contact with House Verac, it noted.

She eagerly read the details of her new persona and began to absorb them into her memory as completely as possible. She memorized her fictitious father and mother's names, her imaginary siblings, details about their estate in Torventos, their small but proud fleet of barques and sloops, and a list of local features all Torventoi would be familiar with. It wasn't as detailed as she would prefer, but Gatina knew that the information she was given was reliable. If questioned, she should be able to improvise and misdirect well enough to pass as Foscombra.

But that left a lot of detail for her to provide, she knew. Her Maranka alias was relatively simple. She was a mariner from a low estate. A Sea Lord noblewoman, however, would require more specific details to pass herself off as authentic. One by one she began to fulfill them: what Foscombra liked to eat, her favorite pastimes, her ambitions and fears, her personal mannerisms. Many Gatina cheerfully looted from previous aliases because it was just easier that way. Others she invented on the spot, and she began to knit the alias together.

Meanwhile, the others began to call out questions. Atopol looked up with a quizzical expression at one point.

"What kind of atmosphere should we expect at the Maiden's Haven?" he asked.

"The Maiden's Haven portion is dedicated mostly to hospitality," Beah answered. "That's where the majority of the beer tents, taverns, and entertainment will be found, along with the common sort of mariner. It's really the only section that welcomes non–Sea Lords—and their coin. All manner of entertainers perform here—musicians, clowns, singers, jugglers, puppet shows, that sort of thing. It's a bawdy place, and fights break out there all the time, despite the Watchmen posted there."

"Is it the kind of place you can blend in with a crowd?" he asked, thoughtfully.

"Oh, absolutely," she agreed. "Even the high-born Sea Lords drop by to see the entertainment or recruit mariners for their ships."

"Excellent!" her brother said and went back to his work.

"How far is it between the duchy's pavilion and the Temple of the Stormfather?" Hance asked curiously as he gazed at the map. "Can I walk it in less than half an hour?"

"That depends on the time of day," Lancellus answered after a moment's consideration. "And what day it is. If it is crowded, you may find it more challenging. The Stormfather's Temple and its court are where all criminal and civil cases are heard, and depending on the case, there could be hundreds of plaintiffs, defendants, witnesses, clerks, scribes, and lawbrothers crowding its entrance and spilling out into the street. Other cases will see it almost empty."

"What happens with the prisoners?" Minnie asked.

"The building includes a small jail and an area for executions or maimings, as deemed necessary by law," Lancellus explained. "Those found guilty are subject to imprisonment, fines, or the other sentences, but many are held here pending their hearings."

Gatina thought what he described sounded abhorrent. Maimings! Executions she understood, but *maimings?* That sort of punishment was forbidden by Luin's Common Law, she knew, but it had been once practiced in certain parts of the Magocracy, and it was sometimes employed by the maritime courts. She shuddered again, then she shook it away. That did not concern her. She knew that Lady Bomaris would not be found near that area—unless she needed to file official business. And she doubted the girl's father would send her there alone to do that without a lawbrother by her elbow.

"Where is Jenerard going to be speaking?" her father asked a moment later. That produced a scowl from Lancellus as he shuffled through his notes.

"His Excellency will be providing the central address at the opening of the council of Sea Lords," he finally answered when he found the notation. "That is traditionally where the Duke's representative communicates policy from the coronet to the captains and great lords. There is a festive reception and ball right afterwards, traditionally. He speaks again two days later at the Stormfather's Blessing of the Fleets, then spends the rest of the day judging the contests over at the Corsair's Quarter. That night, he addresses the captains who have taken ducal service and appoints the Admiral of the Fleet for the year."

"And who might that be?" her father prompted.

"It has been Admiral Rumaris for the last four years," Lancellus supplied. "A seasoned veteran of the Farisian campaign. But he was closely allied with the late duke. I doubt he will be appointed once again," he said sadly.

"Where is Jenerard staying while he's in Vaxel?" Atopol asked.

"The Lord of the Waves has a small villa in the Landsmen's Quarter for his official business, along with a private dock for the flagship and escort vessels. That's the complex where his officials inspect ships and render official tax valuations on those vessels. Traditionally, this is where Duke Lenguin would recruit privateers, hire ships, and levy all of the annual taxes. He would also recruit ships for the Alshari Navy from the Landsmen's Quarters," Beah answered. "But he is only assured of being there at the closing ceremonies when he hosts the Ball of the Waves for senior officials, admirals, captains, and certain high nobles from influential Great Houses."

Things went like that for a while, with the questions becoming less frequent as everyone figured out their basic plan for meeting and then persuading their marks.

Gatina's approach was relatively simple: find a compelling way to get Lady Bomaris alone and then make an impassioned plea to her. From what she could see from the proposed schedule in her dossier, there would be several opportunities between meetings and official events that might provide a chance to do so.

Gatina made her plan to move in on Bomaris early and take no chances. If the Sea Lord maiden was supposed to be one of the easiest marks, she wanted every possible chance at her.

The meeting broke for a few short moments so that everyone could refresh themselves. Gatina was very thankful for the opportunity to move around. Sitting for so long was exhausting. As she meandered along the deck under the night's sky, she considered the Vaxelhaven compound and its various areas. She thought she had the basics of a strong plan, and that made her both excited and happy. She was finally going to have a role in this mission.

She rejoined the group as her mother called everyone back inside. After finding her seat, the discussion quickly turned to security and attendance. It seemed someone had asked Lancellus what to expect in matters of security.

"Well, while there will be security, it will not be as tight as at a proper castle, or the palace in Falas. Mostly the Watch from Vaxel, the Storm King's private guards, and a few companies of young naval infantry. But with Baron Jenerard in attendance, expect the unexpected. That is my best advice."

"I would wager that he will have members of the Brotherhood with him," Hance reasoned.

Gatina shifted uncomfortably in her seat. She was not fond of the Brotherhood of the Rat, and she wanted to make sure that she didn't run into any of them, but she also knew that was not up to her.

"Many would find that an affront to the dignity of the Anchorage," Lancellus informed them. "Even those who have a history of piracy themselves. The Brotherhood are considered landsmen by most of my people, the worst sort of thug who threaten everyone's livelihood. The Lord of the Waves is supposed to be fighting that sort of criminal, not employing them. I know not why Duke Lenguin ever appointed the man."

"You can blame Duchess Enora," Minnureal said darkly. "Jenerard flattered and bribed his way into her circle at court and then convinced her to propose him as a candidate. Her Grace was insistent on him. I think Lenguin made the appointment to appease her, but he was searching for a replacement when he died."

"How easy would it be to infiltrate into the opening remarks by the man?" Atopol asked. "Could a well-dressed, handsome young Sea Lord noble bluff his way in?"

"That's more or less accurate," Lancellus said. "The Grand Meeting is theoretically open to all Sea Lord houses in good standing. There will be guards, of course, but they will only be there to keep the drunks from the Maiden's Haven from coming in and disrupting the place."

"What about our safe house?" Gatina asked. "Will there be guards between the main complexes and that we have to contend with?"

"Last time, we were placed in a compound nearer the water's edge. We were in a smaller two-room apartment. There was limited security in that area, but it still seemed difficult to get in or out unless you were an invited guest or someone who should be there," she said. "The Watch wasn't checking documents, but they were asking our business the first few times we passed. But I was there under House Gavina's banner, for official business, so there was no problem."

"Thank you!" Gatina called, and returned to her own file. As she read through the dossier a third time, she found something she had missed: House Crenalsar was located in the Viscounty of Cadena but also had holdings on Segal, an island viscounty. Both were near Prejestia, and according to the document, the house had connections to the big wine merchants in Bikavar.

That, she knew, must be lucrative. She had seen how many ships it had taken to supply the citrus trade this voyage. She could only imagine how many more it would take to contend with wine at that scale. It seemed that House Crenalsar, while on the minor side, had influence with other small houses. They were able to create a merchants' coalition to contract wine shipments all over the Eastern Bay, giving them an outsized authority. She found that to be fascinating—and difficult to maintain. They had garnered support from other small holdings and used that to amass a bit of power.

Gatina began to devise a plan, though she made a few minor notes on the parchment. As her alias, she would slip into the Maiden's Haven and wait for Lady Bomaris to walk by. She wanted that time to observe the girl. The trick would be determining when she would arrive. And learning what she looked like. The notes Lancellus provided indicated that the girl had dark-colored hair, green eyes, and tan skin and she was slight of build. Unfortunately, that described at least one in four Sea Lord women she had encountered.

She had more luck with her livery: a sun in a light blue sky over a slanted crest of waves, a small anchor in one corner. Like most Sea Lord maidens in their finery, she would likely wear it on a sash, jewelry, embroidered directly on her clothing, or as a decorative motif.

Or, she reasoned, she could just ask around and find out who she was and what she looked like.

When Hance cleared his throat to get everyone's attention, Gatina was startled. She had become engrossed in her planning.

"At this point, we know that nine major figures will be in attendance at Vaxelhaven. Each one is a target of our operation. Our primary goal is to convince them to reject Jenerard's proposal of alliance. Our secondary goal is to recruit them to join the Sea Lords aligned with the Shadow Council."

Gatina felt her father's eyes on her as he glanced around the table at everyone. He took a sip of wine before continuing.

"In some cases, you might be able to make a reasoned argument against the proposal, maybe stoke your target's sympathies or morals, perhaps discuss the issues of slavery and piracy, for example, by explaining where these slaves actually come from and how they are sold," he suggested. "In other cases, it might not be as clear. As such, you might need coercion, blackmail, misinformation, or bribery—or perhaps a mixture of all. That might well be the case for our larger, better-known targets."

As her father spoke, Gatina glanced at Atopol's document. His target was a Sea Lord named Bracomel. He was an influential middle-range broker and agent who shipped wine and olive oil—more counting man than mariner. She wondered if Bracomel had any connection to Bomaris.

"Each of you will develop your plans separately," Hance continued. "Then, tomorrow, after mastering your alias, you will present your strategy to us for approval, including any special equipment, props, or resources you might need. Try to keep them reasonable—we're far from our usual support, and securing anything too unusual may prove difficult. I urge you to consider using the sources of information you have at your disposal in Lancellus and Beah, who have both participated in the Anchorage over the years and have some experience with the site. And each has a different level of knowledge and intuition about how the Sea Lords and the various houses operate."

"This may aid your goal," Lancellus announced. "This information was not conveyed in writing, because I received word of it only in Manahar before meeting up with you. We learned that Baron Jenerard has permission from Count Vichetral to raise the annual assessment fee dramatically, as well as various docking and passage fees," he revealed. "More, he is empowered to arrange special privileges for the Sea Lords who agree to support the council."

"What kind of special privileges?" Beah asked suspiciously.

"He is authorized to grant special docking permits, abatement of taxation, and lower fees to those in open support of the Council of Five's policies. Such special favor is in direct violation of Sea Lord custom and will cause a great deal of irritation, especially among the minor houses. He has also been commissioned to expand the current ducal fleet by a tithe. The Council of Five wants another score of heavy warships and twice that in light corvettes."

"That isn't a good sign," Hance said, shaking his head. "It means he prepares for war."

"It's worse than mere war," Lancellus insisted. "The larger the ducal fleet, the smaller the pool of fit mariners and seaworthy craft for commerce. It will make our people angry. Especially when they learn that any who complain will be offered the same bargain . . . *if* they take a letter of marque and reprisal. It is possible that we can use this to persuade the Storm King's priests to help our cause," he suggested. "They mislike such corruption and should be against it on moral grounds. It does provide us with a bit of leverage."

"What is a letter of marque and reprisal?" Gatina asked, confused, when her cousins and aunt gasped at the news.

"It's official permission to make war on the nation's enemies without consequence," Beah said, solemnly. "In this case, the term *enemy* might mean the Castali fleet—pardon, the Castalshari fleet . . . or it might mean dissidents within the Great Bay. It's an invitation of piracy," she summarized. "Merchantmen would only be given the same privileges as the Great Houses if they abandon commerce and become men o' war."

"Imagine the *Legacy* converted for war," Pia explained. "All the cargo bulkheads torn out, twice the crew complement, and sent into battle against experienced warriors. We'd be sunk in a month," she condemned.

"But if that's the only way you can afford to pay your crew, then that's what you'd be forced to do . . . while the Great Houses monopolize shipping in the Bay and beyond," agreed Jordi, who looked particularly angry at the news.

"It is an easy way for the Council of Five to sow division among the Sea Lords and maritime Coastlords," Lancellus agreed. "Give their supporters trade advantages and force their opponents into warfare . . . or rebellion."

Gatina quickly considered the options. She wasn't sure how they would spread such information or even if they could, but it would certainly be useful. Getting the crowd worked up might prove beneficial, she considered. She had seen what could happen when the masses got angry. If enough people heard about it, she thought, then there might be some possibility of action among the smaller houses.

"This arrangement that Jenerard is proposing means that the smaller houses will be shut out of the major port cities," Lancellus said. "It will dramatically alter the nature of our councils. That is why it is especially important to influence their votes in the Anchorage."

"This will not stand," Beah said calmly but firmly. "The Great Houses are less than a quarter of the total of our folk. The maritime Coastlords follow us in most ways, as they share our fortunes in the Bay. The smaller houses will not sit idly by while the larger houses benefit financially and politically and we are ruined."

And that was when the missing piece of her plan to sway Lady Bomaris fell into place.

SHADOW ADJOURNED THE MEETING A LITTLE PAST MIDNIGHT, ENCOURAGING them all to get some rest. Gatina wasn't quite ready to head for her bunk yet, however. She lingered at the rails on the quarterdeck, staring out over the calm seas and enjoying the starlight and the nearly full moon. She was unsurprised when her brother joined her.

"So, what do you think of the mission?" he asked as he leaned against the rail.

"It's not as exciting as I thought it would be," she admitted. "I was anticipating some clever heist or perhaps listening in on Jenerard's plans. Instead, I'm convincing a teenaged girl that she should be angry about something. It's hardly a challenge."

"I know what you mean." Her brother chuckled. "I'm actually going out of my way to make my mission more challenging. I plan on using some shock, a threat, and a bit of thievery to convince my mark. That should be easy. My mark is a coward. He's a picture of fear and avarice. I think Mother and Father kept the interesting missions for themselves."

"Still, it's better than pretending to be a deckhand," Gatina considered. "I just wish that it was something that would lead to an end to all of this. Not just a strategic little push in a long, overly complicated game of politics."

"That's not for us to decide," Atopol said sullenly. He paused, his gaze fixed on the nighttime horizon. "Do you want to see something interesting?" he asked unexpectedly.

It took Gatina by surprise, but she trusted her brother when it came to that sort of thing. If Cat thought it was intriguing, usually she agreed. She nodded.

"Come see what I found when we were out searching for you," he said conspiratorially. He led her down the ladder to the main deck, then up to the bow and the bowsprit. Without a bit of hesitation, he leapt upon the bowsprit and clamped his legs around it before shimmying out a few feet. Gatina wasn't worried about him plunging into the sea below—she trusted Atopol on the rigging more than she trusted herself.

He reached down and pulled something off the bow of the hull and then shimmied back to her.

"What is it?" she asked, fascinated.

"It's a name plate for the ship," he explained when he dropped down onto the deck again. He presented it to her. "I found it and pried it up, because I was curious, and I steal things. It's the original name plate. I asked Jordi about it. It's kind of the shipwright's signature for the vessel, his certification that it is complete and inspected. It has the ship's name and his name on it, binding them together."

"So?" Gatina asked, still intrigued.

"You know this sloop was acquired by . . . *professional* means," he said delicately. "Of course, it was renamed and probably repainted . . . and then hidden in a boat house for over a decade. *Daydream* is just the sort of whimsical name our parents would give it. But this plate carries her *original* name. Take a look," he encouraged.

She turned it over in her hands, and finally had to use magesight to see it clearly. Engraved on the foot-long brass plate in flowing Narasi script was the legend THE YELLOW ROSE, followed by A GIFT FROM VISCOUNT ENVELLITUS and SHIP'S HUSBAND MASTER RONVELUS, ARGARUS SHIPYARD.

"What's a ship's . . . husband?" Gatina asked, confused.

"I didn't know either. Jordi told me it was the master shipwright who oversaw her construction. Argarus is the main military port in the center of the Bay and an ancient Sea Lord stronghold. I have no idea who this Viscount Envellitus is. But that's not the interesting part."

"What's the interesting part?" she asked after a few moments of confusion.

"Kitten, who uses yellow roses in the heraldry?" he prompted.

"I don't . . . Oh. *Oh!* OH!" Gatina said, her eyes getting larger with every word.

"Exactly." Atopol nodded. "That is the symbol adopted by Duchess Grendine of Castal. Now Queen Grendine of Castalshar. Kitten," he smirked, excitedly, "this was probably her ship. And Mother and Father . . . *stole it!*"

CHAPTER TWENTY-THREE
HEIST PRESENTATION

Oft the difference between a successful heist and a failure is rooted in a few essential details. What kind of dog is guarding the property? What kind of shoes is the mark wearing? Is the Watchman colorblind? Is the mark left-handed or right-handed? Preparation and conditioning are important, craft skills are vital, but the best thief in the world may fail at a heist because he overlooked a detail. Which details are most important? All of them.

—*from* **The Shield of Darkness**,
written by Kiera the Great

"No, no, you're doing it all wrong!" Lancellus objected with a scowl as Gatina walked across the deck in front of him.

"I'm . . . *walking* wrong?" she asked, confused and surprised.

"You look like a Coastlord pretending to be a Sea Lord," he advised, his voice taking a quiet but urgent tone that captured Gatina's attention. "As if you were a stage actor playing a role."

"Which is essentially what I'm doing," Gatina riposted. "Where am I failing?"

"You're supposed to be the scion of an ancient house of mariners," he said patiently. "You are the legacy of generations of yearning, of bittersweet memories of family lost at sea, or drowned in storms, or dying by some violent means. The burden of grief lies heavily on your shoulders, and you've spent your entire life learning how to bear it. Even if it's been decades since that happened, you carry it with you always. You are proud—so keep your chin up!" he insisted. "That is how a Sea Lord woman approaches everything, every day. Even when she's just walking through the market."

Gatina nodded, took a moment to include that fact into her mindset, and turned to try again. She hadn't anticipated her alias requiring that much subtlety.

As soon as the planning meeting had ended, Gatina had begun working in earnest on her own specific mission. She had her target and her alias. She also now had a much better understanding of the Vaxelhaven compound and how it was configured. That, combined with the information about the role the Anchorage and Assessment played, helped her considerably. She had a fair idea of what the fictitious Lady Foscombra would think and feel about her attendance there. That should help considerably with the mission, she reasoned.

At least with her portion. She knew enough of the entire operation, at least the parts she was meant to understand. She also knew that her parents had not divulged the entire mission to anyone in the room. Everyone had their part to play. There was just enough coordination with each other at important points to be able to shift priorities, enact a rescue, or provide assistance in an emergency, but not so much that they could endanger each other under interrogation. It also forced each of them to concentrate fully on their role and not become preoccupied with the success or failure of the others.

She had considered her part as fairly simple: Gatina would masquerade as Lady Foscombra, a maiden from a minor but prosperous Sea Lord holding from the Eastern Bay but not too near her mark's home haven.

The details were vague, and she preferred to keep it that way. To her mind, this was a one- or two-day assignment. Nobody needed to know that much about Foscombra. And if she did her duty, nobody would remember ever meeting her, except for Lady Bomaris.

She designed her alias accordingly, using the specifications in the dossier. She had thought it was a reasonably straightforward approach: Lady Foscombra, it seemed to her, was an ambitious young maid, proud of her lineage and position, who followed her betters around much like a puppy, seeking opportunity beyond her fairly humble origins.

But as Lancellus had observed—and rather harshly, she thought—there was more to portraying the fictitious girl than she had anticipated.

She had considered her wardrobe carefully, within the limited options available. Back in Falas, Shadow House had rooms of costumes, shoes, jewels, and cosmetics from which to select. The *Daydream*'s stores were far more limited. While her mother had brought some supplies and costumes in preparation, the variety was constrained by the nature of the mission.

She was gratified when she returned to her shared cabin and found one large wardrobe case set on her bunk. Gatina threw it open and began sorting through it to see her costume options but soon got discouraged at their limitations.

She found four gowns in different colors—cornflower blue, yellow, green, and orange. The yellow was clearly meant for formal occasions, she could see, while the blue and green were more businesslike and the orange was much more whimsical.

After much consideration, she decided that the green gown would do best for her needs and height. It was loose-fitting and demure enough to wear her working blacks underneath undetected, and came with a smart-looking half-jacket that left her lower arms bare. The pleated skirt was full enough to conceal her shadowblade and, quite honestly, a small village.

At the bottom of the wardrobe she found two wig boxes and removed both. She opted for a deep brown wig that was already braided. The other was darker, almost black, and outrageously curled—again, something for a formal occasion. The lighter brown seemed humbler and more casual, she decided.

She set that beside the gown and then considered the footwear options. Instead of selecting shoes or slippers, Gatina decided that her boots might be a better choice. Plenty of Sea Lord ladies wore ankle-high or calf-high boots, well waxed against the elements. The modest heel would add almost an inch to her height but did not make her feet hurt or present a danger from tripping, she reasoned. A girl from a smaller house who was used to working alongside her brothers and father on the docks and the decks of her haven would likely continue to wear her best pair of boots, even to a somewhat formal function, she reasoned. The customary curved dagger was another essential accessory, and she opted for the plainer of the two provided for consideration. She added it to the pile she had started.

Then she opened the smaller box mounted to the side of the wardrobe. That was where the costume jewelry was stored. She selected a fine chain with a small anchor pendant to indicate her devotion to the Maiden—modest, unpretentious, and meaningful.

Sea Lord women were even more infatuated with jewelry than Coastlords, to the point of ostentation, but they were far more concerned about it as a symbol than a mere display of wealth. A girl from a minor house would cherish such a piece far more than a ruby pendant or a necklace of pearls. Indeed, though pearls were prized among the Sea Lords, they were traditionally reserved for more mature women and often were used in conjunction with symbols of their station and affluence like pendants or amulets. She picked three modest rings and a simple bracelet to complement the necklace.

Lastly, she chose from the three hats her mother had stacked on top of the wigs. The wide-brimmed leather one would be fine if she were accompanying her aunt to purchase supplies on the dock, she decided, but not for a festival. She opted instead for a well-made stiff brown straw hat with a colorful band that matched her dress somewhat and sported a dashing feather that was not too gaudy—just the kind of inexpensive accessory a relatively poor young maid might sport to attract a little attention.

Satisfied with her costume selection, Gatina considered her reflection in the looking glass included in her kit. Using the spell she had learned years before, she darkened her eyes to a grayish blue. She realized a bit of light cosmetics would transform her now-pink complexion to a more olive tone, allowing her pale skin to appear more natural. She wanted darker hair, dark eyes, and a rich skin color for this mission.

That was Lady Foscombra looking back at her in the looking glass, she decided. She looked nothing like Gatina at all, and the feather in her high-crowned hat made her look taller. She practiced introducing herself over and over in the looking glass until she could rattle off her complete name, haven of origin, and details about her family as casually as she could in real life.

She felt gratified the next morning when both Aunt Beah and Lancellus approved her wardrobe choice with some minor modifications. Beah added a small scarf to the hat to protect her neck from the rays of the sun, and Lancellus had suggested an additional earring. His explanation was informative.

"No young maiden from a small house is going to attend the Anchorage without the idea of attracting a fine husband," he explained to her critically. "It's an opportunity for her to expose herself to some of the finest and wealthiest mariners and businessmen in the Great Bay. Lady Foscombra will be trying to subtly catch the eye of such a man by her dress as well as her demeanor. A single earring invites the eye to your face," he concluded, "and is a subtle indication that you are, indeed, considering marriage."

"Really?" Gatina asked, intrigued.

"He's correct," admitted Aunt Beah during her inspection. "I wore a sea dragon earring my mother gave me when I met my husband. I'm giving it to Pia now—not that she needs the help. Once I was wed, I put it away and got pearl earrings in both ears for special occasions."

"But I'm not *trying* to attract attention," she protested. "Indeed, I'm trying to avoid it!"

"But you'll look like you're trying to avoid it if you don't look like you're trying to attract it," Beah assured her. "The Anchorage will be filled with hundreds or thousands of young maids like your Lady Foscombra. If you're the only one there who isn't seeking a husband, at least ostensibly, it will be noted."

Then came the walking, which Gatina had thought she had mastered. But that was when Lancellus' criticism really started to bite. She had managed a bit of the swagger that seemed to be the legacy of all Sea Lords, male and female, but as she pranced back and forth across the deck, the man's reviews became more and more harsh.

"That's a little better," he conceded after she repeated the walk with her chin stuck well forward. It forced her eyes and face up and into the light, she knew—a much different presentation than she was used to. Indeed, she was usually trying to avoid showing her face as much as possible to escape notice and identification. Coastlord noblewomen kept their chins down, demurely, while members of the lower classes tended to bow their heads a bit in deference due to their station. "But there's still something amiss," Lancellus said, his hand on his chin. "Do it again."

Suppressing a sigh, she turned and made the seven-step walk in front of him once again. As she completed it, he snapped his fingers.

"I know! You aren't swinging your hips at all. Or your shoulders. Sea Lord noblewomen tend to do that a lot more than Coastlords. They are bold. You are walking timidly. And the humbler a maiden's origins, the more boldly they are apt to display that in their gait. The skirt on that gown was designed to twist and billow as you walk, and it's barely moving even in the wind," he criticized. "Turn your hips more when you move, and counterbalance with your shoulders to give it more of an effect. Move confidently but constantly."

"In circles, like using a scimitar," she suggested.

"Yes! Exactly!" he agreed. "There's a rhythm to it. And it is anything but dainty. Your hips should roll like the waves on the sea, not glide."

It took some effort to incorporate the advice into her presentation, but she had spent enough hours practicing swordplay to be very aware of how her body worked—even if her increasing height and bust tended to betray her from time to time. She managed to get the roll in her hips and shoulders incorporated with the swaggering steps that came from life at sea by the third attempt, producing a kind of elegant snap to the way her skirts billowed as she walked.

It annoyed her to no end that Lancellus was able to determine her errors in presentation better than she was, but it did increase her respect of the arrogant Sea Lord. He was no mere mariner, she decided. He had the intelligence and attention to become a good agent.

"Better," he conceded grudgingly as she danced by again, her skirts doing what they were supposed to do. "Do three circuits of the deck that way until it's as natural as breathing. Martijne is next," he said, dismissing her.

Gatina returned to her bunk, sank onto it, and spent a moment pulling off her boots and reflecting on the frustration of being criticized by a mere amateur—and being forced to agree that he was right. With a sigh, she began to study the folio once again.

In reviewing the report that Lancellus had provided, she thought it would be best to put herself in proximity with Lady Bomaris as quickly as possible. She reasoned that if they saw each other a few times without interacting, then it would be less suspicious when Gatina was close enough to her to take action. That was key to her plan.

It began with a simple bit of pickpocketing. Not for personal gain, but to ensure that she made personal contact with the maiden. She could easily steal something from the woman, but she also knew that she must put herself into a position where such an action was natural, as natural as stealing could be. Her goal was to steal a ring or bracelet or hairpin, something of sentimental value to Lady Bomaris—and then seek to return it personally. That would give her an opportunity to speak with her at length, in private, without concocting some story about a fictitious business proposal or an elaborate lie about long-lost relatives. Those sorts of strategies were weaker than a straightforward encounter.

She was using the Sea Lord women's perspective on jewelry to her advantage. Most of the pieces they wore had deep sentimental or spiritual value and were given as gifts or inherited from revered ancestors and proudly displayed as a token of their histories and legacies. Losing such a piece in a strange place like the Anchorage would doubtlessly inspire a deep emotional reaction. The opportunity to regain the lost piece would be irresistible, she reasoned. It wouldn't matter what the cost or the value of the piece was; the tie between the woman and the jewel was strong enough to compel action.

She looked back at the document on her lap. The woman was a Sea Lord who'd likely grown up in the Maiden's Haven and was likely dedicated to that cult more than the Fairtrader or the others at this stage of her life. It was akin to the role Ishi's temple played in the lives of Coastlords and Vale Lord women.

Gatina was willing to wager that Bomaris owned an anchor charm of some sort, a gift to symbolize her coming of age in society. That would work best, she realized. The religious symbol of the Maiden was an anchor and a chalice, a common motif in the society. No respectable maiden would be found without it. Even her cousin Pia wore an anchor bracelet engraved to mark her entry into womanhood. That's what she would prefer to steal, then, Gatina decided.

And then she would arrange it so that she could return it. She knew she could "find" the bracelet or item, then alert the guards or authorities and ask them to let Lady Bomaris know that it had been found and she would offer to return it—in some private setting. That would grant her access to the girl's suite of rooms, she figured.

But how would she manage to *find* the girl? There would be hundreds of people at the Assessment. That might prove the most challenging part of the mission, she realized. She knew she needed a way to both stand out and blend in. But she also wanted the girl to remember her or at least remember seeing her so that she would seem familiar enough to become physically close to her. Caution was needed, too, because she did not want to alarm Bomaris. You never wanted to make a mark suspicious before the moment of contact.

Gatina worked through several scenarios of how she could put herself in a position to come into initial contact with Bomaris. Her dossier included the itinerary for the entirety of the gathering. According to Lancellus's notes, there would be an informal gathering of Sea Lord houses, a kind of general reception sponsored by the haven, called the Registry reception, on the opening day at the third bell. That gathering was planned for the stronghold's keep, an outdoor plaza in front of the Storm King's temple. It was a wide, public area directly in the center of the compound and adjacent to the primary hospitality area, the Maiden's Haven. She mentally plotted the route Bomaris would likely take to reach the reception and found her best chance at making contact.

It was a wide expanse along the thoroughfare that ran through the middle of the compound. Each house representative should be easy to recognize as they passed by. The wide avenue was a prime location for vendors, she understood. She reasoned that if she arrived early enough, she could buy a cup or a snack and position herself close enough to the main thoroughfare to afford a good perspective on those heading from the residential quarters to the reception.

The protocol was for the haven's purser to loudly call out the name and house of each visitor as they entered the compound, much like a herald did at a court function. That would give her a positive identification of her mark. When House Crenalsar was called, Bomaris would step forward for recognition and Gatina could identify the woman.

Then it would just be a matter of quick footwork and positioning to get close to her. That would give her the chance to gauge several things, including layout, opportunity, and security.

Gatina was wary of being spotted in such a public place, but she assumed that any spies who would be lurking in the shadows would not take one more moderate-status maiden gawking at her betters as anything remarkable. She fully expected that she would not be the only agent of some power or other along that route. Indeed, she hoped their curiosity might send them into the daylight to see who was in attendance, and thus identify them.

Besides, it would be one of the few opportunities she had to see the layout in daylight. While she preferred operating mostly in darkness, seeing things in the sunlight allowed her to better assess the environment. And that might come in handy. Maps were helpful but of limited value, she knew from experience. Seeing the compound for herself might save her life.

Vaxelhaven was massive. She needed to view it and figure out the best places she could hide in daylight or nighttime. Such knowledge could be critical, should she need to escape. She knew firsthand how quickly simple missions turned chaotic and dangerous. She did not want to rely on her *rajira* as much as her skill in this setting. That meant understanding the buildings, the material used to construct those buildings, the landscape, and even something as simple as the type of trees she might use to climb or hide behind.

That was the difference between Lancellus and her, she consoled herself. He might have a good eye for detail and an awareness of his surroundings, but he lacked the thoroughness of her training and experience. He might be a competent spy someday, but Gatina was already one, not to mention an accomplished shadowthief. That gave her some solace about his critique as she practiced swinging her shoulders and hips around the deck.

That night, when Gatina presented her plan, she was greeted with unexpected and challenging questions from her mother and her father. She had not thought through everything as well as she thought she had, it seemed. Fortunately, she was good at thinking on her feet.

She began by appearing in their cabin fully costumed, made up, and in character. She endured a barrage of rapid-fire questions after she introduced Lady Foscombra with the traditional Sea Lord formal bow—one arm folded in front of her stomach, the other folded behind her back. It was more a bob than a bow and seemed rather curt than the more graceful and elaborate curtsies of the Coastlord noblewomen.

She responded to the questions easily, even the strange ones she hadn't anticipated. In short order, she claimed the details of her ancestry, her family, her home haven, the notable features of that port, the names of the fictitious ships in her house's tiny fleet, and the various companies they held stake in—she delivered every answer without hesitation, in a reasonably good Sea Lord accent.

That seemed to satisfy her parents. But as she related the details of her plan, the true critique began.

"I appreciate the elegance of a simple pickpocketing, Kitten, but how will you avoid being caught?" Minnie asked. That particular question caught her off guard. She had *never* been caught while stealing a bauble. A burglary, yes, technically, but not while she was lifting purses or jewels. She had a deft touch and a talent for misdirection. She'd stolen keys from the belts of guards and golden rings encrusted with gemstones. Nor could she imagine a scenario where that would happen.

"By being very, *very* careful and particularly stealthy, Mistress," she said, shifting into her professional mode as an apprentice. "There will be hundreds of people present. It will be crowded, and we will be packed in tightly. A casual bump, a bit of misdirection, and it should be fairly easy to steal something without being noticed."

Hance smiled before he began to question her. "To your point, as it will be very heavily attended and crowded, how exactly do you plan to position yourself near Bomaris without arousing undue suspicion? You do not want to be obvious by lurking around, so what is your plan?" he asked, as she poured herself a small glass of wine from their bottle.

Instead of stammering or showing frustration, Gatina took a moment to think through her father's question. Of course, she already had her plan and knew the answer. She reached for a sip of her watered wine and let the flavor roll over her tongue. It wasn't that she did not have an answer. She simply did not wish to rush to that answer.

"I don't, necessarily. I plan to arrive early enough to sit near the promenade, at one of the wine merchants or beer tents, near where the house representatives will be called forth. I will take a table and a morsel near the Maiden's Haven ostensibly to view handsome young Sea Lords from distinguished houses I might chance to marry. From there, I will identify Bomaris when she is called forth as House Crenalsar's representative when she enters the Registry reception by the purser. As she leaves the threshold, I will make my way toward the crowd and follow closely behind her, with two to three people and ostensibly in their company."

"That means she might see you," her mother pointed out.

"I *want* her to see me but not to notice me or see me as a threat; just as another Sea Lord maiden hopeful for a handsome lord's attention."

"That could work," her mother conceded. "What happens if you get one?"

"Then I do a very bad job of flirting, ask a few embarrassing questions that make me clearly unsuitable for matrimony but clearly overeager for such, and embarrass either the man or myself enough to effect an escape," she replied, with a small smile. "Believe me, I am far better at flirting badly than at flirting well. I anticipate no difficulties. If the gentleman persists, then I will flee in a fit of feminine offense or embarrassment and seek Lady Bomaris's company as a means of refuge." That was an almost universally respected tactic in social situations, she knew.

"And then?" her father prompted.

"And then as I get closer to her, I will find an opportunity to steal one of her baubles. I assume she will be wearing an anchor bracelet or necklace, in honor of the Maiden. That's my preferred loot." She lifted her arm to show the one she was wearing. "The bracelet is symbolic to her," she suggested. "It will have some sentimental value, and she will eagerly seek its return. Enough so that she will be happy to meet with a slightly familiar woman to retrieve it."

Gatina studied her parents' faces before continuing. So far, they were paying attention to her, and she saw no indication of concerns. "As Lady Foscombra, I will contact the festival authorities before the next bell, just about the time she realizes it is missing, and let them know that I have 'found' the missing bauble. I will generously offer to return it to Lady Bomaris in her quarters at a predetermined time—just after the Registry reception ends, about fifth bell."

"Late afternoon." Her mother nodded approvingly. "People will be moving through the streets, on their way from their day's activities toward some sort of supper or entertainment."

"Exactly," Gatina assured. "She should be relieved to know her bauble has been found and will likely rush back to get it. That should give me a second point of contact," she reasoned. "Either I will speak to her there or make arrangements for a lengthier conversation. In either case, I will be able to present my arguments and gauge her reactions."

"And if she is unpersuaded?" her father asked pointedly.

"Then I shall discover what her weakness is and formulate a plan to counter it," she said confidently.

Hance pursed his lips before he spoke. "And if your Bomaris wears no jewelry? What shall you do then?"

Gatina was not prepared with an answer to that question. She had never seen a Sea Lord maiden not wear jewelry. Instead of admitting that she hadn't thought of that to her father, she quickly said, "Then I shall steal her purse."

Her answer seemed to satisfy him. He nodded. "Very well, then your heist plan has been approved." Hance nodded to her mother. Before Gatina could speak, Minnureal voiced additional concerns.

"I agree that it's a decent plan. However, I have reservations about your disguise and your ability to remain in character should certain situations arise. Therefore, I strongly encourage you to continue to work with Lancellus. There is simply far too much at stake for you not to perform flawlessly."

Gatina gave another Sea Lord–style bow. She was not overly excited by her mother's pronouncement. While Lancellus was knowledgeable about the culture—his own—and intelligent, she also found him to be vexing. He could come across in one instance as kindhearted and sympathetic and in another as arrogant and dismissive.

Gatina resigned herself to her fate. Fortunately, she knew they would arrive in Vaxel soon, and that limited the amount of time she would have to spend with him.

After the meeting, Gatina approached Lancellus. She was determined to make quick work of the task at hand, though she had hoped for a meeting later that evening with him; instead, he suggested they meet at once on the deck, away from the others.

His instruction began when he asked her to introduce herself as her alias. Gatina quickly determined that he wanted to hear her accent, inflection, and delivery. Fortunately, she had been studying the Sea Lord accent since she arrived at her family's house.

"Good day, sir. My name is Lady Foscombra, of House Verac, out of Torventos," she said, minding her accents and how she rolled the *brah* sound at the end of her name. Lancellus winced.

"The *s* is softer. Again," he directed. The next time, his facial expression was not as pronounced, but he was still not pleased. "Fasz-CAHM-brah. Say it with me," he instructed as he led her through the pronunciation of her alias. "Good, again. Again." He drilled the name into her mind, not relenting until she had mastered it.

"Your inflection should be more lilting and fluid," he said. "The enunciation should run together, like a melody," he explained, "instead of sounding harsh as it had when you said it."

Gatina practiced it in her head several times before trying it again aloud. The more she repeated it, the wider Lancellus's smile grew. After what seemed like the five hundredth time, he smiled and nodded. "Yes! Yes, that's it. Perfect," he said, pleased. "Now tell me about the weather at home?"

Gatina thought that was a strange request, but she reasoned that it was a fair one, given that Sea Lords' livelihoods depended on decent sailing weather. She recognized that it was also a test of her enunciation, and she was careful to keep the lilting tone in her voice.

"At home, we've had mild temperatures and favorable westward breezes. Torventos is a rainy place, but with few squalls to bedevil us. Our fleet sails with limited trouble," she reported as her tutor studied her.

"That's good," he said. "Now, what can you tell me about where you live? People will expect details—minor details," he suggested when he prompted her to think more about her alias and backstory. "What is the best story to have in your mind ahead of time? Keep that one and keep it simple," he suggested. Of course, she had already created a slight story of her background and heritage. Smiling, she nodded.

"Our fleet in Torventos fares well. We have had much success. Our caravels can transport more than seven hundred casks of good Bikavar wine each, many for the larger houses. We've also profited from our specialization in transporting religious statuary when the wine trade slackens," she reported, her voice lilting with the Sea Lord accent.

She looked at Lancellus's expression while she was explaining what her house transported. He did not seem happy with her answer.

"There's still something amiss," Lancellus said, shaking his head and chewing his lip. "Ah! Try again," he instructed.

She nodded and repeated her story. Suddenly, Lancellus reached out and grabbed her hands with his much-larger ones. That took her by surprise.

"That's it!" he said, shaking his head. "Sea Lords often use gestures when they speak. Their hands are rarely still when they are talking about something they're excited or proud of. When they engage in normal conversation, they range from here to here—between the shoulders and belly," he explained, moving Gatina's hands in that region. "If they are very excited, their hands rise above the shoulders for emphasis. And when they are being demure, persuasive, or apologetic their hands still move, but more gently, and below the hips," he said, pulling her hands down to her waist. "Especially the womenfolk."

"Are you certain about that?" she asked skeptically.

"I was raised in a haven with three sisters and five female cousins," he revealed. "I've watched them all try to convince my father and mother over the years. Believe me, this is a mannerism that will appear authentic," he assured. "Try again, this time using your hands."

Gatina took a deep breath, reluctantly pulling her hands from his, and repeated the story a third time, this time using her hands to gently emphasize what she was saying. She realized as she spoke that she had indeed seen her aunt and cousins use their hands for emphasis when they spoke casually. Something clicked inside her head, and suddenly, it seemed like the most natural thing in the world for Lady Foscombra of House Verac to do.

"Our fleet in Torventos fares well. Each of our caravels can transport seven hundred casks of good Bikavar wine during the season. We've also found much profit by shipping religious statuary," she repeated, this time using her hands to gracefully emphasize her words.

"That's much, *much* better." The Sea Lord grinned. "Now you can pass for a proper Sea Lord maiden. From a distance. For a short time."

"Thank you, my lord." Gatina curtsied sarcastically.

Then he suddenly looked at her face closely, a bit too closely for her taste. "But I think it will be appropriate if you wipe off a good amount of the cosmetics. Remember, Lady Foscombra is merely a girl, mayhap your age or younger. If you want to vanish into the crowd, you'll have an easier time as a girl than as—"

"As someone wearing far too many cosmetics and a dress out of her station?" Gatina asked hotly. "How do you think girls prepare themselves for such occasions? We wear the best possible gowns and present ourselves in a manner which we think will most call subtle attention to ourselves. And we frequently use too many cosmetics in that endeavor," she pointed out.

Lancellus sighed. "I was not trying to hurt your feelings, nor was I trying to denounce your effort. I just think you're prettier without all of that paint on your face, I suppose."

The admission took Gatina aback—no one had ever called her pretty before. Not when they were speaking of her as opposed to one of her aliases. She sighed.

"Trust me on this part," she insisted. "When a girl goes to a ball or an important function, we usually adhere to what we think the socially acceptable presentation is. The younger we are, the less subtle we are about it. A maiden like Foscombra, from a crappy little port at the arse end of the Bay, would use every trick she could to make herself appear comelier. You said you have sisters—do they not do this?"

"Well, yes," he admitted. "In any case, you have mastered the important elements. I think you can pass as authentic. I'm just worried. You must understand. There is more at stake here than you realize. This is my life, my family's livelihood at stake. Everything, everyone must be perfect for us to meet our goal."

It was obvious that he was worried about the mission. She was not as worried. Her part was small compared to the parts she was uninformed about. But she knew each person would play a vital role. "What else do you suggest, Lancellus?" she asked. She wanted to succeed. And that required working together.

He smiled, and that set her at ease. "Nothing at the moment. I confess, you and your family are remarkable at what you do—more so than I had expected. Go and practice while I work with your brother. You did well today."

Gatina bowed again, and remaining in character, she headed slowly back to her cabin, swinging her hips and arms as she'd been instructed. She should have been proud at the praise the handsome Sea Lord had given her.

Instead, she found herself reflecting on just how strong and well-formed his hands had been when they'd grabbed hers.

It would be an interesting mission.

CHAPTER TWENTY-FOUR

THE VAXEL ANCHORAGE AND ASSESSMENT

Nothing prepares you for adventure except adventure. There comes a moment when all of your careful preparation is past and you find yourself in the moment where you realize that everything is now at stake. It's the excitement of the heist, the manifestation of the mission, where you realize the immediacy of your task. If you do not embrace it, you have already failed.
— *from Gatina's Heist Journal*

THE NEXT MORNING, THE TWO SHIPS SAILED INTO THE NORTHERN CHANNEL OF the river that led to Vaxel—and they were not alone.

It seemed an entire fleet had appeared around them in the night, though she knew that they had merely begun the approach to a busy port, where hundreds of vessels were also traveling. She had rarely seen more than two or three ships around them at a time on this entire journey, but when she peered over the rail that morning, she could spot a dozen, at least. Many were barques, sloops, or caravels, but there were also galleons and frigates sailing up the deep river before and aft of the *Daydream*. Flags and banners from many ports and nations flew from their masts, and some had painted sails with the arms of their house or the company they were owned by as they struggled against the sluggish river current.

After weeks at sea, it was a novelty to see land on either side of them as they entered the mouth of the river. They passed a few fishing villages and smaller havens and depots along the way, where local spectators had congregated along the docks and banks to witness the fleet of ships headed to the Anchorage.

The only disturbing thing on that bright, clear morning was the large number of warships that accompanied them in the channel. Some flew the ducal banner—the famed Anchor and Antlers of Alshar—while others bore the red-and-white striped standard that indicated they were currently between commissions and looking for work. They made her nervous after her brush with the *Venjanca*. Many of the warships had uncovered their deck engines, the clever machines they used to fight against other ships, in a naked display of their power.

There was a great variety of those, she saw as she scanned their decks with magesight. Some would send entire volleys of arrows at their foes, while others were designed to cast stone projectiles with great force, like a trebuchet, or hurl sea axes at the hulls and riggings of their enemies. Great ballistae capable of firing heavy bronze spears lined the rails of many, and nearly all of them had protected forecastles where mariners and marine infantry could hide and shoot at their opponents with crossbows. Usually, the warships would keep their valuable and expensive engines covered with oilcloth to protect them from the elements, only revealing them when it was time for action. To see so many brazenly displayed made her anxious.

They were just advertising, she realized, demonstrating their abilities in combat to lure potential clients. The duchy wasn't the only such employer, she knew; many of the larger companies hired warships as escorts for security of their merchant fleets, both in the Bay and beyond. Showing off how powerful your warship was would be a good way of inviting such inquiries, she reasoned.

Gatina was awake early that morning. The excitement ahead of the mission had made it difficult, not impossible, for her to sleep. But she had managed a few hours' rest before dawn, when she began climbing back into her disguise. She did not apply her cosmetics yet, but she did wear her working blacks under the gown. By the time she was ready, dressed as Lady Foscombra, the *Legacy* and *Daydream* were near the very crowded port of Vaxel.

She found her mother in the captain's cabin, studying the maps once again as she drank a mug of tea and broke her fast with cheese and fruit.

"Good morning, Lady Foscombra," her mother said, upon seeing her in her costume. "I see your lessons with Lancellus were of benefit. You look every part a Sea Lord maiden," she praised.

"Good morning," Gatina replied with a Sea Lord–style curtsy. Her mother was dressed in a much finer gown, as her alias had her mingling with wealthier Sea Lords. Her mission involved some of the absolute elite of society, and her expensive gown reflected that.

"Mother, is there a way to dampen the residual arcane energy that I pick up from others?" she asked as she cut a bit of cheese off the wheel. "I just wonder if it would make it easier for me to focus on my mark if I were able to do that."

While she waited for a response, Gatina gathered an orange and a bit of biscuit that had been soaked in wine and fried. The magical question had occurred to her while she was dressing. She was still concerned about identifying Lady Bomaris once she arrived, and had been seeking a way to simplify matters.

She had good experience with picking up energy from crowds. So far, that had proven helpful in a number of situations. She had managed to avoid riots and protests in the streets of Falas many times by "reading" the crowds. She knew from her studies that the ambient emotional energy of a mass of people produced a subtle arcane effect, if you knew what to look for. She had wondered if she could reverse the process, dampening that energy to the exclusion of just one set of ambient feelings.

Her mother stopped what she was doing and considered her thoughtfully. "That's a pretty subtle distinction, Kitten. Especially for a mark you've never met. The answer is yes, but it would take practice and experience to do so. It's pure Blue Magic to filter out the emotional ambience of a crowd—a lot more difficult than absorbing their collective feelings and intent. Have you had a problem with that since Falas?"

Gatina shook her head. "No, but I haven't been around a large crowd since then, either," she said. "Not more than a port marketplace."

After a pause, her mother suggested a solution. "An intriguing thought. It is worth exploring," she conceded. "Perhaps you can focus on one thing at a time. Some emotional element that your target presents that is at odds with the rest of the crowd. But I wouldn't rely on such a thing in the field until you've perfected it in practice. We can work on it after this mission," she proposed.

Gatina nodded as she considered the advice. "How close are we? Are we nearby? When shall we reach the dock?" She was eager to get the mission underway and knew that she needed to be in position at the Maiden's Haven as soon as she could be. Her plan depended on that.

"I spoke to Beah this morning about that," she answered. "A lot will depend upon the harbormaster's dictates. The port is so crowded that Captain Armandus opted to take anchorage farther away at a wharf he had used in the past," Minnie explained. "It's about a mile and a half from the Vaxelhaven compounds. The *Daydream* will remain anchored in the Bay after we unload the cargo. You will be inserted into Vaxel then, the first of us to be on site. You can make your way to the safe house from there. The sloop will be anchored close enough to row a boat to it if we need to. That way, we will be ready to sail if we need to make a quick escape."

Gatina frowned at her mother, wondering if that was cause for concern. "It's fine, Kitten," her mother soothed. "There is so much traffic, we felt it best to only bring one ship to port. And it's never a bad idea to have a means to get away quickly if we need to."

Satisfied, she tried to relax. A walk through Vaxel would be fine, she reasoned, and allow her to get into character and see the port itself before she reached the compound.

"I just wish this thing wasn't so bloody warm," she complained. She stretched, but the gown's stays were still a bit too tight. Her mother took note and stood to help her.

"It's a greater distance by foot but faster by sea," her mother explained as she helped Gatina adjust the gown. "You'll need your range of motion. I just hate that you have to wear your blacks underneath in this heat, but it can't be helped. If it's any consolation, we're all sweating in our blacks. You have sufficient coin?" she asked, as she patted her shoulders.

Gatina jingled her purse in response. There was plenty of silver and copper in there, she knew. And she could always steal more if she needed to.

"When will you and Shadow be on site?" she asked.

"Various times. We don't want to arouse any suspicion, of course. Your father and I will be hiring separate carriages for our journey into the compound to meet our marks. Your brother will be in disguise as a messenger. Beah and your cousins will operate as they normally do and set up the safe house. Lancellus will be meeting a contact in town before he heads into the compound to meet his targets. But we should all be there by late this afternoon if the gods cooperate."

"You mean the ones that cursed me?" she asked sarcastically.

"It won't be the Shipwrecker who fouls our plans." Her mother chuckled. "Darkness will protect us, as it always does. But if I were you, I'd invoke the Maiden of the Havens. She works best with your alias. Remember, you are Lady Foscombra and that is the only name you answer to on this day," she cautioned. "As long as the mission goes to plan, you will return to our safe house. If it doesn't, well, then steal a horse and race to the *Legacy*. Captain Armandus knows we might have to break away at any time. He'll be prepared," she assured.

Gatina made a face. She'd stolen a horse before. It hadn't worked out well. But stealing a horse might be her best way to get out of there quickly if something were to go awry. Or perhaps a boat. As usual, she had several mental plans and contingencies in mind. She had spent the evening studying the temple maps. She had figured four different ways to extract herself if everything went into the chamber pot.

"Do we have any idea of who might befoul the plan?" she asked. "Besides the gods, that is?"

"You can expect that Baron Jenerard will have plenty of agents at the Anchorage," her mother revealed. "Both open and clandestine. Likely some of his Ratty friends, but Vichetral has plenty of other agents as well, from all social classes. They could be anyone or look like anyone.

"From what Lancellus tells us, this is a vital mission for the Council of Five to consolidate their power over Alshar. Without the Sea Lords firmly under his control, there will always be a question of his power. He will leave nothing to chance, and he will take every opportunity to squash any resistance to his plans."

"So, a fun day at the fair, filled with spies and cutthroats." She smiled.

Her mother did not smile. "This is a dangerous mission, Kitten, for all of us. And an important one. And a complicated one. So complicated that it would be unreasonable to expect it to go smoothly. Be prepared to improvise if you're forced to. And be prepared to escape if you must," she warned.

Gatina knew that if worse came to worst, she could climb the Storm King's Tower and from there take to the rooftops. Or she could just take to the rooftops. Or steal a boat. Or change her disguise and lurk in the shadows until danger had passed. She was comfortable whichever way things evolved.

But she couldn't help but worry about her family. As good as they were at what they did, the universe had a perverse way of making such missions far too interesting.

As the *Daydream* neared the wharf later that morning, towed by two longboats hired for the purpose, Gatina was amazed at the number of ships already docked in Vaxel. There were so many masts in sight with their sails furled that they looked like a forest. As far as the eye could see, there were ships of all colors, shapes, and sizes arriving for the Anchorage, far more than she'd ever seen at once in any port. It was breathtaking in a way; she couldn't begin to imagine all the places that they'd voyaged to.

She had her forged documents in her purse, as well as enough coin to get her through the day. Her documents were not as good as those her cousin Onnelik would have crafted, but they would do fine for this mission. They identified her, her fabricated house, and her business in Vaxel. There was even a short letter of introduction from her fictitious father that had been penned by her real father, asking the recipient to extend his daughter all possible hospitality.

She departed the *Daydream* as soon as possible; by all appearances, she was merely a paying passenger who had booked passage on the sloop, and as soon as the gangplank was lowered and the holds opened to remove the cargo, she made her way down the dock.

Lancellus had explained the significance of the Vaxel Anchorage and Assessment on his first night aboard the *Legacy*. But she had no true idea of the event's massive scale until she got to the wharf. She had to wait nearly a full hour before she was able to depart the *Daydream*.

The great wharf was mobbed. There were carts, horses, carriages, vendors, and people—*everywhere*. A small army of porters, stevedores, and mariners rushed to load and unload cargo from every dock. It was loud and chaotic and jarred her ears. She had not seen that many people in one place in weeks. She wasn't sure where to look first. Or where to step. She was mindful of her gown, of course, but there was nowhere to go. The crowd pressed forward slowly and orderly, but it was very much a slow-moving group and every person in it was headed to the same place, Vaxelhaven.

She had taken her leave of the ship and boldly marched down the docks, her satchel in hand. It contained the rest of her clothing and a few hidden items she might need. Her shadowblade was strapped to her thigh under her voluminous skirts, and as she walked down the docks, she could feel its hilt under her clothes with her left wrist. That gave her a feeling of security.

She appreciated that more and more as she departed the docks proper and started the long walk toward the Anchorage. There were plenty of fit mariners filling the streets, of course, most dressed in what passed for finery for the festival.

But she also noticed plenty of less-reputable-looking men—not common mariners but hard-eyed brutes who seemed to be everywhere. She recognized the kind of thug she'd fought in Falas so often. Most of them carried scimitars or long knives, as if they were expecting a fight. She would not be surprised if they also carried Rat Tails concealed somewhere on their persons.

The streets of Vaxel reminded her of the other Sea Lord ports she'd been to, only on a much, much grander scale. Most of the buildings she passed were hundreds of years old, their gray stone facades washed by countless storms and their steeply pitched rooves towering three or even four stories overhead. They were not as grand as the mansions and townhouses of Falas, and far plainer, but then, the Sea Lords were not typically given to a lot of architectural ornamentation.

It was easy for her to lose herself in the crowds; she was just one more maiden wandering towards the festival, after all, no more noteworthy than a stray dog. She felt a thrill of anonymity and independence as she walked the cobbled streets, gawking at the shops that catered to mariners on leave.

There were rows and rows of them, offering everything from lodging to food to less-savory products. There seemed to be no end of taverns catering to the trade. It seemed as if every other shop was an alehouse or a vendor of spirits. Even this early in the day, there were already men staggering from one such house to another, singly or in small groups. She steered clear of them when she could, and when she couldn't, she gave them a bold smile and a challenging nod. Lady Foscombra was not to be trifled with.

She could not even see the Storm King's Tower yet. She suspected she was in for a long walk and was more than a bit jealous of her parents and their carriages. Her working blacks underneath did not help. It was growing warmer every minute. She questioned the decision to wear the gear. But she knew it was too late to change her mind.

Gatina had plenty of time to think about where she might find Lady Bomaris during her long walk. She also had a lot to take in by the time she approached the Anchorage proper. She was no longer concerned with her dress. Women wore all sorts of gowns—from casual to formal—and many carried palm-frond fans with them against the heat and cloth parasols against the sun as they trudged along in the twenty-person-wide processional to the compound's gates. The lines were well formed and moved slowly to allow everyone's pace. The vendors on the sides yelled out their wares: *"Wine! Tea! Ale! Sugar spirits!"* Gatina heard those calls more times than she could count. She ignored them and just moved with the crowd.

When she tired of mentally reviewing the details of her alias, Gatina began studying the strangers she walked with. She watched. She listened. She learned.

Apparently, the Lord of the Waves in the Landsmen's Quarter was hiring privateers, and that was a topic of discussion among young boys and men wherever she went. That did not bode well for the end of piracy, she thought. From what she could make of the boastful conversation, none of the boys had ever sailed beyond their home ports, though they used very colorful language in their bragging.

She also learned that the women surrounding her thought it was dangerous that so many disreputable-looking fellows had flooded the town unexpectedly. The Maiden's Haven welcomed common mariners, but there was a great number of seedy-looking men who had arrived as well. Some of them were quite dangerous-looking, openly wearing their weaponry and all but leering at them. But, based on the tittering comments, many of the women were also intrigued by that idea.

She took her mother's advice and found one thing to focus on during the walk. There was a large, feathered hat several rows in front of her. Every time its owner moved, the feather bobbed. At least twice, the owner of the hat had stumbled, causing the feather to dip down and snap back up. Gatina found that to be entertaining, and that was how she passed the time until the gates of Vaxelhaven came into view.

She saw the gates as she crested the hill, and beyond the gates, she finally caught sight of the Storm King's Tower. It wasn't as impressive as she had imagined, which was disappointing. It looked almost identical to every other Sea Lord stronghold she'd seen, a tall, plain-looking square tower that narrowed slightly with every ascending story until it culminated in a pyramid.

The only differences she could see were the sheer size of the Storm King's Tower and the faded gilt that colored the pinnacle. The exterior was plain and unadorned, with occasional windows or balconies that seemed to have been added as afterthoughts, not intrinsic to the design. But it would still be a fun climb, she decided.

The queue to enter the festival was long and crowded, as everyone tried to enter at once. There were guards standing by, anxiously looking for any sign of trouble and occasionally finding it as some mariner who had overindulged too early got into an argument or two groups from rival ships called insults and comments at each other. No one seemed to be checking for identification credentials, she noticed, but she still removed her documents and prepared to answer any questions. The first two sets of guards waved her through without comment or even looking at them.

But it still seemed to take forever. It was nearly second bell and she was long past ready to be inside the compound and in place for her mission.

As she followed the crowd closer to the gate, she was unexpectedly startled. She noticed the black-and-yellow banner of the *Venjanca* being carried by one of its crew, followed by a handful of rough-looking mariners who were singing loudly and badly as they pushed their way through the crowd as a group. Fortunately, she did not recognize the crewman carrying the flag, but she made it a point to avoid direct contact with him and his fellows.

The *Venjanca* was a declared pirate ship, after all. She knew Aunt Beah and Matros and his mates had all made complaints before the magistrate to that effect at Manahar, but she reasoned that the news had not yet gotten to Vaxel—or that things were simply too busy and chaotic for the authorities to take action. Or it was another example of the corruption implicit in Vichetral's rule. If the Lord of the Waves was in bed with the Brotherhood of the Rat, then looking the other way for one of their pirates was to be expected.

It made her a little bit nervous to know they were so near. They didn't act as if they were looking for her or anyone in particular. They didn't even seem particularly belligerent, compared to the other mariners in the crowd. They were just flexing their muscles, boasting of their prowess, and showing their presence. Nor were they the only band of scruffy-looking thugs in the crowd. In fact, the more she walked, she saw banners from other warships, which helped alleviate her worry.

Gatina also took note of the city watch who were in charge of security, who all wore blue baldrics with yellow sea axes embroidered on their shoulders. There didn't seem to be nearly enough of them for the size of the crowd. She counted at least twenty Watchmen as she drew closer to the gates, but a goodly sized group of drunks in the crowd could have overwhelmed them. She was not sure if they were local or had come from other ports to assist with the meeting, but they seemed more tense than she would have expected.

"So many corsairs here this year!" she heard one older woman complain as she neared the gates. "It's as if there's a war on!"

"It's that Castali king they're worried about," another replied in a hushed whisper. "He's barred the port of Farise from Alshar, and they think he's coming for Count Vichetral next. The Lord of the Waves wants a grand fleet to meet him if he does," she speculated. "That's why there are so many warships in port. And so many corsairs at the Anchorage."

Gatina filed that information away for later use. It made sense that the Council of Five was worried about the new kingdom they'd formed in opposition to. The conquest of Farise had paved the way for it, but now the rebellious counts were rejecting King Rard's authority, and that had consequences.

Instead of allowing people easy access into the compound, ropes had been set up to create a series of four queues, each overseen by a pair of guards alert for any troublemakers. As she scanned the towers, she also noted guards on top of the gatehouse, though they did not appear to be armed beyond their swords. Of course, they could easily have crossbows concealed, she reasoned.

As she passed through the gate, Gatina noticed images carved into the stone of the structure, and the closer she got, the better able she was to discern that they were representations of the various Sea Lord divinities. She studied those images until it was her turn at the checkpoint. Instead of reviewing her papers, as she thought he would, the old guard nodded and motioned her into the compound. She was surprised how easy it was.

But that was the last bit of security she saw. She was inside now. She had made it without incident.

As soon as Gatina stepped into the compound, she was overcome by a sense of amazement. The transition from orderly queue to the chaos of the festival was jarring. Her senses were overwhelmed simply because there was so much to see everywhere she looked. There were food vendors, artisans, musicians, barkers, bands of mariners singing shanties or shouting at each other. People were wandering around, looking for their lodgings, while porters bearing handcarts full of baggage tried to fight their way through the crowds. Everywhere she turned, something was happening.

The participants weren't all Sea Lords, either. There were plenty of Coastlords and common folk who had business at the Anchorage, or at least wanted to enjoy the festivities. Merchants and monks mingled with maidens and musicians as different folk continued to pour through the gates and into the compound, each seeking their far-flung destinations. She passed four somberly dressed nuns dedicated to the Salt Crone who seemed to be in a kind of ritual procession. Street musicians played gitars or pipes or accordions for tips. Well-guarded money changers converted foreign coins to Alshari money nearby, while acrobats entertained a small band of onlookers who were breathless at their antics.

Despite the chaos, Gatina tried to keep her mind on the mission. She merely needed to find the Maiden's Haven quickly and pick her spot to surveil the thoroughfare. Being there was much different from studying a map of the place. For a moment, she was turned around and found herself walking toward the Corsair's Quarter before she realized her error. Fortunately, she also noticed pictorial signs directing visitors to the various quarters. Without those markings, she realized how chaotic it might have become for any visitor.

Thankfully, she reoriented herself quickly, realized where she needed to be, and found the line of ale tents and pushcart vendors she'd predicted would make a good spot to see the crowd without being consumed by it.

Once she purchased a skewer of grilled shrimp and a cup of weak ale, Gatina edged her way to a table nearest the interchange between the Maiden's Haven and the Storm King's Tower complex, where she expected to eventually see her mark.

Based on her understanding of how the presentation of representatives worked at the Registry reception, she knew that Lady Bomaris would be greeted and announced formally. Gatina positioned herself just as she had planned. And then she waited.

And waited. The third bell rang. She watched hundreds if not thousands of Sea Lord ladies pass her by. She used magesight to examine them each while she pretended to gawk at their finery.

When the serving girl returned with a second cup of ale, the trumpets inside the tower blared, announcing the beginning of the Registry, which would record which noble houses had chosen to attend the Anchorage and Assessment this year—and the festivities began.

A press of well-dressed Sea Lords and their entourages began to make their way to the gates of the complex. The tower's purser blew his whistle and announced the name and title of each one, along with their illustrious house. It wasn't dissimilar to a courtly function at the palace at Falas, she decided, although the ceremony and the manner of dress were different. There were far less cloaks and far more coats and jackets, and the cosmetics the Sea Lord ladies used were applied far more liberally than their Coastlord counterparts. Huge, wide-brimmed hats seemed to be the fashion of the day, and abundant displays of cleavage that would make a Coastlord noblewoman blush were commonplace.

One after another, viscounts, admirals, commodores, and haven lords were announced, along with their wives and children, in order of rank. A piercing whistle from the bosun's lips preceded each announcement. Then various officials with the office of the Lord of the Waves, prominent clergy of all six cults, and Coastlords with maritime interests were announced. Finally, the lesser houses presented themselves, one by one.

But there was still no sign of the woman she sought. If she had already passed by her position, Gatina had not seen her, which irked her no end. But she kept watching.

She had a third cup of ale and waited some more, thankful the beverage was weak. She had to pee, but she was reluctant to abandon her post for a privy in case she missed her mark. Indeed, she waited for another full bell to ring. From her vantage point, Gatina watched countless minor lords and ladies be introduced, listening to their names being called out by the purser. After they were presented, instead of returning to the crowd, they were escorted off the small landing and led down to a private entrance to the plaza.

When Lady Bomaris of House Crenalsar was finally presented, Gatina's head whipped around as she furiously tried to glimpse the woman.

And there she was: a pleasant-looking young girl just a few years older than she, in a smart-looking dark green gown and a handsome hat secured by a white scarf. For one glorious moment, her face was locked into Gatina's memory, with her sun-and-anchor crest displayed on a yellow sash across her shoulders confirming her identity. She was late, but that was her. It *had* to be.

Her eyes tracked the woman as she was directed to the private entrance, a confused expression on her face. She seemed to have two retainers, an older woman and a middle-aged man, both wearing the same yellow sash. That, at least, made it easier to keep track of them in the crowd once she knew what to look for. Then they disappeared inside.

Abandoning her cup of ale and her seat, Gatina prepared herself for action. She slipped through the crowd toward the main entrance—her alias was not high-status enough to warrant the special door reserved for great lords. She even had a chance to use the privy inside the courtyard and prepare herself before Lady Foscombra emerged into the vast outdoor space in front of the temple set aside for the Registry reception.

It was time for the Kitten of Night to go to work.

CHAPTER TWENTY-FIVE

LADY BOMARIS

Sometimes, the direct approach is the best option.
— from Gatina's Heist Journal

THE COURTYARD IN FRONT OF THE TEMPLE OF THE STORM KING WAS FILLED with the elite of the Sea Lords, and the Registry reception was designed to cater to their tastes and predilections.

There were trestle tables set up around the perimeter of the compound, offering raw oysters, grilled scallops, skewered fish, smoked pork, and other delicacies, along with wine, ale, brandy, and the sugar spirit known as rum, as well as confections of sugar, treacle, and the mysterious dark, bittersweet delicacy known as chocolate that hailed from the even more mysterious island of Unstara. Musicians played elegant music from behind carved wooden screens while liveried servants moved back and forth around the growing crowd of Sea Lords.

Statues of the Storm King twenty feet high and carved from white marble looked down on the gathering with an imposing glare. There was no hatred or antipathy in the expression, Gatina decided, simply the inevitability of tempests and the stern manner required to meet them bravely.

Her prey was much less imposing; Bomaris was stumbling through the crowd, doing her best to carry herself with the dignity and authority of a young woman asked to represent her revered father and generations of bold ancestors while surrounded by the elite of her society. She did not seem up to the task.

Gatina's sympathy instantly went to the girl as she watched her try to stand with the greater lords of the Great Bay and get snubbed the moment they realized that she was not among the most powerful. The strutting aristocracy that ruled the seas did not see beyond her youth and the diminished station of her house. One glance at the sigil on her baldric caused more than one sniff and dismissing shrug.

Gatina grew more and more irritated at the purposeful rejection of her mark. Every time Lady Bomaris tried to strike up a conversation with one of the senior members of the aristocracy, she was treated like a peasant or servant—or at least a minor consideration, worthy of no more than a few polite words and an excuse to leave her company.

Gatina was sympathetic but understood implicitly the social situation. Her many missions and heists around Falas had shown her all strata of society and how they interacted under different circumstances. Her mother had encouraged her to study such things for the benefit of her aliases and a general understanding of how people acted toward each other.

As noble as her house was, Gatina knew, and as important it was in the Eastern Bay, the Registry reception was designed to allow the Sea Lords to demonstrate their comparative status—by dress, by accessory, by pure presentation—but mostly by the interpersonal relationships they could flaunt among their peers. She had seen much the same thing in Falas at the various balls, parties, and feasts that occurred in spring around Ishi's Day, when the elite from across Alshar opened the social season in the capital. She'd infiltrated a few of them last year to steal Viscountess Leverly's ruby necklace.

Bomaris might be from an old and distinguished house, but this was her first time in such company, Gatina noted. Nor did she seem to have much in the way of an entourage to guide her, nor a mentor to make introductions. The people around her often had old and deep ties of commerce, family, and education. A young girl from a backwater standing alone and trying to get noticed was easy enough to brush past. They might regret it later, she reflected, when they discovered how much official weight she'd have in council, but for now she was merely an unfamiliar face.

It was painfully awkward to see. Indeed, Gatina watched with horrid interest as Bomaris grew more and more anxious. Every now and then, she'd find someone to exchange more than a few words with and successfully introduce herself, but no one seemed particularly interested in a young girl from the provinces.

Gatina followed the young woman closely enough to keep her in sight, but she was mindful to keep enough distance to avoid raising any concern. Given the number of people surrounding her, she was not worried about that. When you weren't trying to attract attention at a party, you were just another pretty dress walking by in the background.

Lady Bomaris wound her way through the backside of the reception, keeping close to the dais and the buffet tables that had been laid out. A huge pewter ship lay on one, filled with brandy punch that seemed to flow from the top of the mast and onto the flooded deck below by some means unseen but which attracted a small crowd around it. Bomaris hesitantly tried to shoulder her way through it to the punch.

Gatina decided that this was a good opportunity to do her first pass. There were two approaches you could try when attempting to pickpocket a mark. The first was to do it with extreme stealth so that the mark wasn't even aware that you were there. The other was to make contact with your mark and establish enough familiarity so that suspicion evaporated during the second pass.

Gatina politely weaved her way through the tangle of brocaded jackets, gilded scimitars, and raw silk cloaks without much trouble—crowds that weren't trying to kill you were easy to navigate once you knew how—and managed to get in front of Bomaris in line in short order. She poured one of the little tin cups on the table full with one of several ladles hanging over the sides of the pewter ship like oars, and then started to turn away from it while she sipped. She arranged to face Bomaris for just a moment, before the cup came to her lips.

Recognizing the expression of frustration on her mark's face, Gatina glanced at her cup, caught the Sea Lord's eye, smiled briefly, and offered her the cup. Bomaris took it gratefully, without a word exchanged. Then Gatina poured herself another cup of punch and retreated through the crowd as swiftly as she'd entered.

No word was exchanged between them, but that brief moment—and especially the smile—was all she needed. In Bomaris's mind, her face would be associated with kindness and generosity, not fear or suspicion. She faded back into the larger crowd, assumed an unassuming pose, and continued to watch her mark from afar while sipping the deliciously cool, delightfully sweet punch.

She needed to wait a few moments before attempting the second pass—the one in which she would contrive to steal the bauble from her mark. The memory of her face needed time to fade into her mark's subconscious, leaving only the emotional associations.

Bomaris wandered out from the crowd around the punch bowl eventually and made her way slowly over to the snacks arrayed at the other tables. She picked a few things up and looked around, almost forlornly, for someone else to talk to. No one seemed particularly interested. Then she wandered over to the area directly in front of the dais that had been set with chairs and a few small tables to allow the assembled nobility to listen to speeches or merely socialize at length. From the look of the officials skulking around the edges of the garden, that would not be for a while, it seemed. Bomaris chose a position relatively close to the front, Gatina noted.

A few moments later, she found a seat behind the girl, where it might be difficult to notice her due to the trio of middle-aged ladies gossiping at a table between them.

From there, she studied her. So far, Gatina had not noticed anything ostentatious about her mark. Bomaris wore a simple but elegantly cut pale green cotton gown under a light green short jacket. It was the color of a forest or an estuary, she observed. And it complemented her green eyes.

But Bomaris was disappointingly plain in her accessories for a Sea Lord. She wore no large necklaces or earrings, from what Gatina could see, nor ornaments in her hair or hat. Her slender fingers were bare of rings. She had really thought Bomaris would at least wear some jewelry. There was a purse at her waist on her right side, she noted—but that was not as compelling a theft as something personal.

As she sat there and considered her options, Gatina watched Bomaris take a sip of her punch. That's when she saw a glint on the girl's left wrist and recognized that she was wearing a bracelet: a thin circlet of brass and silver.

Gatina smiled into her own cup and gave thanks to Blessed Darkness, relieved that this would not become complicated. She quickly reviewed her plan again in her mind. She would need to make a few adjustments, she realized. She could bump into her in a crowd, as she had initially planned. But she might also visit the table and use simple misdirection to take the bracelet off Bomaris's wrist. Or she could simply wait for an opportunity to present itself. She'd spent enough time in the garden to understand the ebb and flow of servers and drunkards. It was only a matter of time before something she could take advantage of happened.

As it turned out, she didn't have long to wait. A ruckus from the other side of the roped-off portion of the garden distracted her—and others, she quickly saw—from her thoughts.

A group of very drunk mariners was attempting to gain access through one of the lesser gates to the stately gardens where she and the others were seated. It was a large crew, she saw, and though they were dressed in their portside finery, it was clear that they were from the lower stations of Sea Lord society . . . and very intoxicated.

The servants and petty officials in charge of security began arguing with them, but the mariners were rudely insistent. A uniformed guard approached and began to angrily deny them entrance, but a large brute of a mariner leveled him with a swift punch to the jaw. In moments, a wave of them invaded the serene garden where the Registry reception was underway. There were cries of surprise and outrage as the common crewmen swept through the reception. Loud arguments broke out as the leaders of the drunken mob faced guards and officials trying to remove them. The men somehow felt entitled to address some grievances with some of the parties within the enclosure.

And that was her cue to action. The flow of drunkards, she knew, would provide enough distraction to allow her to unfasten the bracelet. She slipped through the sudden onslaught of surly seamen until she was not ten feet from her mark.

But, before she could act, Lady Bomaris stood and backed away from her table. One very tall mariner with an exaggerated paunch and a long, bushy beard had suddenly accosted her and was drunkenly demanding he accompany her to his duel.

"If I'm to die, it'll be in fair company!" he bellowed as he sized her up. "Aye, you're a comely one; you'll do fine," he slurred in her face. Bomaris looked shocked and clearly intimidated by such a large, belligerent man as he menaced her.

Before Gatina had even considered her options, she acted. She stuck out her foot and tripped the drunken sailor by kicking the heel of his boot from the side as he pressed past her and closer to Bomaris. The sudden and unexpected shock challenged his balance, already impaired by drink, and it sent him staggering. He tried to grab onto Bomaris for balance and managed to grab the woman's arm before he fell flat.

Gatina really did feel bad for her mark about the situation. The poor thing looked terrified. But then Bomaris grabbed the man's fat wrist to hold him in place and kicked him squarely in the groin. The mariner dropped to his knees with a loud moan, all the breath knocked out of him. He fell face first into pavers at their feet.

Gatina was on her feet and by Bomaris's side in an instant.

"Here, let's go over this way," she coaxed, gently leading Bomaris toward the edge of the garden as chaos slowly erupted around them.

The unseemly gang of drunkards was enjoying their invasion, while the high-born Sea Lords responded with indignation and disgust. The mariners leered at the ladies present and arrogantly challenged and swore at the men, occasionally striking blows or tormenting them with insults. It seemed contrived to disrupt the affair, she decided, as they ducked around belligerent seamen and outraged noblemen. While they walked, Gatina's fingers nimbly unfastened the bracelet, and she allowed it to slip into her palm, then into her gown. It was gone before they reached the safety of the wall.

"Always keep your back to something in a riot like this," Gatina advised into her ear as they made it to the gray stone blocks. As Bomaris regained her composure, she cast a long look into Gatina's eyes.

"Thank you," she said, gratefully. "I am called Bomaris."

Gatina nodded and smiled. "A pleasure. I am Foscombra. It's best for a lass to be mindful of where you step," she advised, careful to put Lancellus's dialect lessons to use as she pulled her behind a planter. "There seem to be a lot of drunkards about, even this early in the day."

Bomaris nodded, smiled, and glanced over her shoulder at the man who had accosted her. He was still sprawled under the table, his fat legs sticking out. If he had a duel scheduled, he was likely to be late, Gatina decided.

She waited until Bomaris was distracted by someone getting thrown into the pewter ship full of punch before she nodded and backed into the crowd, which had gotten a lot more hectic. Her mission was accomplished. The bracelet was secure inside her sleeve. Instead of returning to her table, Gatina wound her way back through the chaos and toward the gate. Her work there was complete, for now. She had what she needed to move her portion of the mission forward.

She merely needed to bide her time until Bomaris discovered the loss. She could do that from anywhere inside Vaxelhaven. And there was plenty to see, she knew. There was something deliberate about the invasion of the Registry reception, she suspected. The way the rogues had blatantly assaulted the guests did not seem like a mere spontaneous event; it had the feel of a calculated move. She was immediately suspicious of it, no matter how handy it had been for her, personally.

Gatina found her way back to the wine tent near the main thoroughfare where she had begun her mission, and chose a different table and purchased a new cup. From her location she was able to observe the traffic to and from the Storm Lord's Temple, which now included a squadron of Watchmen with clubs dispatched to get the reception back under control.

But she was also able to observe the number of mariners who were seemingly being recruited by cup after cup offered by sly-looking men at the cheaper sort of grog stands lining the route outside of the Maiden's Haven complex. That got her notice.

That, of itself, wasn't unusual, from what she understood. Aunt Beah had explained that the Maiden's Haven compound served food and drink around the clock during the Anchorage. It was where a man went to spend the pay he accumulated at sea on the comforts of rich food and strong drink, song, and all manner of entertainment.

But the men buying drinks at the stalls appeared to have unending purses, she noted after fifteen minutes. They seemed to be buying any and all who were interested as much as they wanted—for no better reason than to get them drunk. Perhaps that would not be unusual, late into the evening, but it wasn't even late afternoon yet.

She sipped her drink and observed discreetly for an hour, and witnessed a large line of prisoners being marched from the Storm Lord's Temple after their riot was brought under control. She saw six other fights break out between individuals and two between rival crews. She twice saw her brother, still dressed in his messenger disguise, running back and forth through the thoroughfare, and once caught sight of Lancellus in Sea Lord finery, complete with a feathered hat, with a pretty maiden on his arm. He needed no disguise; he was representing his own house. And she had to admit he looked even more handsome in his stylish garb. She almost envied the girl he escorted.

While she sat at the table, Gatina examined the bracelet she had stolen. It was a simple circle of brass with a silver anchor charm attached to it. She felt the thrill she always had after a successful theft; practicing her Art was a reward of its own, a celebration of her skills regardless of the value or the nature of the loot.

The bracelet was not particularly valuable. It was nothing extravagant, the sort of jewelry given as a gift to a young person to encourage their devotions. It was inscribed inside: *to Bomaris from Your Mother. Good Voyages Ahead!* It indicated Bomaris's devotion to the goddess known as the

Maiden of the Havens, the Sea Lord divinity in charge of hospitality, provision, security, and abundance.

Despite her satisfaction with the theft, she felt a bit uneasy about stealing a religious item, especially after her recent brush with the Shipwrecker. But it was part of the mission and for the greater good, she rationalized. And she intended to return it.

She just hoped the Maiden felt that way about it. She didn't need any trouble from another Sea Lord goddess.

AFTER FINISHING HER DRINK, GATINA MADE HER WAY TOWARD THE QUARTERS for the smaller houses with the intention of finding her family's safe house in daylight, and the residence halls rented to the visitors to the Anchorage were on the way.

She also wanted to observe the pathways—on the ground and overhead—and was gratified to see several shortcuts through both if she needed them.

The roofs of the compound were a mixed lot; the more permanent structures were steeply pitched, due to the frequent rains, but they were also sturdy and covered with tiles of terra cotta or slate. The temporary structures, and those more cheaply built, were less steep and often had architectural decorations that could provide cover or leverage if she had to flee undetected. It was an important observation. She knew she would meet Bomaris at some point that night, and she needed to see her routes to and from the apartments.

She paused in her journey, just for a moment, and heaved a deep and satisfied sigh. After spending weeks sailing and learning seamanship, it felt good to be back at work.

The residential area reserved for the smaller Sea Lord nobles was quaint and small. Beyond the stalls and booths along the main thoroughfare, there were scores of them, from grand-looking townhouses closer to the center of the compound to multi-flat buildings of assorted construction to glorified shacks and even tents and pavilions at the far end of the complex. Lady Bomaris and her delegation were staying in one of the smaller apartments in the better-appointed section.

She made a languorous circuit of the quiet complex as if she were returning to her own residence, which gave her an excellent opportunity to scout out the place. She made it a point to be friendly to everyone she encountered. After all, part of blending in was being seen pretty much everywhere and nowhere. Her dress was nondescript. There were plenty of other maidens in the same cut and shade of green. Her hair was decidedly mundane. Her braids were simple and utterly forgettable. She passed through the district unnoticed, if not unseen.

The buildings were no taller than three floors and clumped together in groups of four, it seemed. She could visualize the layout by examining the windows from afar. If Bomaris's apartment was any indication, each property varied in size from one to three bedrooms with a small seating area. Some of the apartments included garden-level terraces, while others had small balconies with large, shuttered windows.

Security was laughable. None of the windows had any sort of bars, she saw; they were perfectly open—as good as a doorway to a thief. And a ground-to-rooftop trellis affixed beside each balcony might as well have been a ladder. That was fortunate.

While she explored the residential quarters, Gatina also paid attention to the sounds she heard. She was particularly aware of laughter and shouting coming from a number of small, private parties that seemed to be springing up in the residential area itself as old friends and new acquaintances gathered over drinks. Shouting might indicate trouble, whereas laughter was more favorable. To her, laughter indicated good cheer, and good cheer might indicate more agreeable—and less vigilant—neighbors.

Satisfied with her observations, she made a short stop at the safe house to check in with Aunt Beah, who was busy entertaining two clients who may or may not have been her marks. Gatina freshened herself in the rear of the little shack before making her way once again toward the main complex.

As she wandered back toward the Maiden's Haven, Gatina watched with interest as the Watch began carting away some of the drunken mariners who were infesting the street. Some of them were belligerent, while others were so drunk, they could barely stand. Many were singing—badly. When one Watchman stopped directly in front of her and pulled an unconscious man out of a puddle, she decided that enough time had passed since she had stolen the bracelet.

She located a festival warden and let him know that she had found a bracelet belonging to Bomaris. She caught the man off guard as he was sitting down to a quick bite to eat. Fortunately, he was agreeable.

"Excuse me, Master Warden," she said to the tired-looking man with overeager politeness and a perfect Sea Lord curtsy, "I believe Lady Bomaris of House Crenalsar lost something at the Registry reception today. I found it. I would like to return it to her in her quarters this evening, if you can direct me there. Is there a way you might relay that message to her? I can be there at the fourth bell."

She offered the man her sweetest, most innocent smile. And pushed a silver penny in front of his plate. His eyes shot down to it, and he gently pushed his plate forward to cover it with an exhausted sigh.

"Aye, my lady. I'll send the message as soon as I've eaten. How about you run over and let the housing warden know? He's in the blue tent just next to the Topsail Tavern. He can tell you where to find Lady Bomaris's quarters, if you like," he said, dismissing her.

"Thank you for your assistance, Master Warden," she said, nodding meekly at the overworked man before turning to leave.

"Watch yourself, my lady," the warden warned as he quietly pocketed the silver penny. "It's rough at the Anchorage this year. More than I've seen in all my days. Bunch of rats and thugs this year, getting everyone worked up with cheap grog and whispers. Keep your eyes open and your dagger handy," he suggested sympathetically. "My men can't be everywhere at once."

"Thank you for the warning." She nodded with a smile. She patted the knife on her back in front of him, to assure him that she wasn't unarmed. Gatina did not mention the shadowblade strapped to her thigh under her skirts, of course. Any ruffian who mistook her for easy entertainment would regret it instantly.

She made her way to the housing quarters a second time. This time, she knew where to go. She found the housing warden quickly, in the blue tent that had been indicated, and after she explained the situation, he gave the precise address of her mark from his registration book. There was no sign that the man suspected she wasn't who she claimed to be. Gatina had learned how to be persuasive. The words of her mother came back to her as they spoke: *a pretty girl's smile can open doors that a battering ram can't.*

As she finished with the man, the fourth bell rang. Once again, Gatina realized that she had plenty of time on her hands. But instead of wandering around Vaxelhaven, she decided to remain in the housing quarters and observe the area in preparation for her meeting. She found a little stone bench under an arbor where she could see the second-floor flat

Bomaris had rented. She could perhaps spot Bomaris as she returned to the quarter and then follow her to her apartment, she reasoned. Despite the heat, it was a pleasant day, and she spent the time hanging spells she might need later.

That was a delicate process that required a lot of attention and control but one she could do subtly enough to escape notice. To anyone walking by, she was just a tired young girl taking a moment to herself. Unless they gazed at her with magesight, there was little to indicate that she was preparing magic, drawing power, and hanging spells to be ready at her command.

As luck had it, Bomaris returned earlier than Gatina had hoped. Shortly before the fifth bell, she watched the girl hurry up the lane toward her residence, though she stopped once to get her bearings in the strange place. Gatina was in position outside of the apartment for the appointed meeting. After the bell chimed the fifth time, Gatina counted to one hundred, then emerged from her secluded little bench. She took a deep breath and knocked on the door to Bomaris's second-floor apartment. On the third knock, Lady Bomaris opened the door.

The girl looked startled, then relieved—Gatina's earlier appearances had built up some level of trust in her mind, she saw. She favored the Sea Lord with a smile.

"Ah! It's you!" Gatina said, feigning relief.

"Oh, hello," Bomaris said, eyes widening in recognition. "I was wondering if I would see you again. You found my bracelet?"

"I didn't know it was yours," Gatina lied, holding up the bauble triumphantly. "But I'm glad it was. I found it after that scuffle at the Registry," she assured.

"That was so strange!" Bomaris confessed. "Not at all what I expected. Oh, do come inside," she said, holding the door open to Gatina hospitably. "It was Foscombra, yes?" Bomaris asked as she led her into the small sitting room that was sparsely decorated with a settee and floor pillows.

Gatina examined the whitewashed room at a glance: respectably appointed by shabby furniture, nondescript paintings on the walls depicting famous ships or important Sea Lords, with a filigree of ocean waves painted in blue near the ceiling overhead. Fresh air skimmed her neck, thanks to the open balcony. The floor-to-ceiling curtains framing the balcony fluttered in the breeze. An easy exit, she decided. But then she quickly turned her attention back to her mark.

"Yes, I am Foscombra," Gatina said, offering her a Sea Lord curtsy. "I wasn't expecting to get accosted at such a fine event, myself. You would think they'd keep the forecastle hands at bay during such an important occasion. It was definitely odd," she agreed.

"It was more than odd; it was criminal," Bomaris agreed as she escorted Gatina into the small sitting room. "My sire cautioned me that the Anchorage could get rough, but he stressed to be wary at night—that was not yet noon!"

"This Anchorage is odd, by all accounts," Gatina agreed. "I was frightened by the incursion myself, and it made me . . . excitable," she said, affecting an appropriately guilty expression. "But you handled yourself well enough, my lady," she praised. "I'm just sorry you lost your bracelet in the fray."

"And I thank the Maiden you were good enough to return it to me," Bomaris assured her. "I thought for certain some thief or ruffian made off with it in the invasion. It was a gift from my late mother, and irreplaceable," she explained.

"As I suspected when I saw the inscription," Gatina said sympathetically. "Such heirlooms are not lightly missed. Not in my family, at least."

Bomaris smiled, this time not as nervously. She motioned for Gatina to have a seat on the small settee and poured them both a cup of wine from a carafe.

"A vintage from Caramas," she explained. "I'm used to the bold red Bikavars, but I like a little variety, and the Anchorage has wines from all over the world. And it's not watered," she warned. "Father only permits me watered wine, but after today . . ." she said, handing a goblet to Gatina.

"Thank you, my lady." She nodded before taking a sip. "This entire day has been a bit overwhelming for me, too," she added. "This is my first time away from my haven on my own. I'm representing my house this year," she boasted.

"As am I!" Bomaris beamed. "I have been sent as my father's proxy in council while he is ill," she confided as she sipped. "Representing both my house and our other business interests. Father assured me it would be a boring affair overall. And you?"

"Much the same," Gatina lied as she had another sip of the oversweet wine. "We're a small house but proud. Our fleet is at sea for the season, and so my sire sent me in his place while he contended with business. He thinks it will be a good experience for me and educate me in commerce before he marries me off to some decrepit old mariner," she complained.

"You think he would do that?" Bomaris asked, wide-eyed with concern.

"Not really," Gatina admitted. "At least, I don't think so. But a girl has to be prepared for anything." She sighed.

"In truth!" Bomaris smiled widely as if some secret were now out. "I am a bit flustered and more than a bit overwhelmed myself," she admitted. "I've been helping to direct the fleet for a year now, since Mother died, but this is the first time I've been sent off on my own. My father was injured and could not make the voyage himself. He assures me that he trusts my judgement, but . . . it's . . . frightening," she confessed. "I walked past the chiefs of houses who have a hundred times the worth of my own today and realized that they could buy or sell me and my kin a hundred times over without learning our names," she said, shaking her head. "That's . . . disconcerting."

"There are mighty merchant princes here," Gatina agreed. It seemed like an appropriate time for her to begin her campaign of persuasion. "Of course, not all of them profit from honest commerce. At least . . . my sire is not pleased with the markets of late. Since the Duke died," she said with a sigh. It was a risk, of course, as was talking politics in any situation.

"You mean the slavers," Bomaris nodded, finishing her cup. "And the corsairs."

"We have had losses," Gatina lied convincingly. "One of our barques was taken this spring. We fear to put our ships at sea even on the Bay, much less beyond. No man wants to end up in chains as his payment for honest service."

"That has become a troubling tale, and one I've heard too often," agreed Bomaris sympathetically. "One doesn't have to be a counting man to realize how badly business has suffered since the straits are closed to regular commerce. Politics," she said, shaking her head and refilling her glass.

"Politics," Gatina agreed, holding out her cup for a refill. "My sire suggests that this count—this Council of Counts—does not have the best interests of our people in mind when they make their policies."

"A change in ruler means a change in policies," agreed Bomaris with a sigh. "Not all of them are favorable. Tell me, how does your house view the new regime?" she asked, suddenly serious.

"We are . . . not in favor," Gatina admitted, knowing she took a risk. "Nor should any small haven fail to see the hazards that will arise if Vichetral's rules are to be implemented. Forgive me if I presume, but none of our people have had much kind to say about the rumors we've heard."

"Nor have we," agreed Bomaris. "But we won't know for certain until the Master of the Waves makes his proposals in council," she added. "Perhaps it is not as dire as we have heard. 'Whispers make poor counselors,'" she said, quoting from some Sea Lord hymn, Gatina figured.

"From what I have heard, no less than Baron Jenerard will make the presentation," Gatina said with a sniff. "My father does not respect the man, despite his fancy titles and mighty friends. He believes Jenerard wishes to see us smaller houses end up subordinate to his cronies among our folk. Jenerard wants to see us all as desperate privateers, flinging our ships against the Castali and Remerans while his cronies take over all trade in the Bay!" she accused.

"Interesting," Bomaris nodded, sipping her wine.

"Jenerard has a reputation for corruption. The man consorts openly with pirates and dock rats," Gatina continued indignantly, "and if the councils don't stand up to him, we'll all end up in chains of one sort or another!" she insisted.

"You think there is a real danger?" Bomaris asked curiously.

"I am certain of it, my lady," Gatina said with confidence. "A house like yours should pay attention to such things. Your sire, especially, else an injury will be the least of his concerns. House Crenalsar doesn't have the resources of its rivals—particularly House Venjancar—and if Vichetral and Jenerard have their way, it could well imperil you."

"That is a dangerous position to take these days, my lady," Bomaris observed.

"Only if you are unwilling to stand bravely against pirates and slavers," Gatina continued persuasively. "The Council of Counts desires to see the slave trade flourish and prepares for war against this new kingdom," she explained. "Baron Jenerard seeks to turn the smaller Sea Lord houses into slavers and warships and grind them away whilst his friends in the larger houses dominate trade in the Bay and beyond. Even now, he is preparing to propose a slate of policies that will see our people diminished greatly!"

As she explained the situation, Bomaris's expression firmed, and turned wooden, making it difficult for Gatina to determine how successful she was being. Her words clearly were having an effect—she had strong feelings about the subject, based on her posture and the look in her eyes.

"It is a difficult situation," the noblewoman conceded thoughtfully.

"It is more than difficult—it will lead to the destruction of scores of Sea Lord houses and secure Count Vichetral the throne of Alshar in all but name," she continued. "I would wager that Jenerard is responsible for the rough characters who invaded the Registry," she reasoned. "He has brought all manner of ill-behaved men to the Anchorage—pirates, Rats, even Royal Censors. All to pressure the Sea Lords' council to accept Vichetral's policies."

Bomaris heaved a great sigh, as if she were carrying a heavy burden. Gatina was hopeful—it seemed as if her words had a strong effect.

"I have heard some of this," Bomaris finally admitted after a long pause. "It seems too great a matter for the daughter of such a small house as Crenalsar. Indeed, all of this seems overwhelming," she admitted. "Perhaps that was why I was so preoccupied that I lost my bracelet. I fear I was not paying as close attention as I should've been in the Registry reception."

"You cannot blame yourself for that," Gatina assured her. "That was merely bad luck. Though I suppose bad luck is not good in our families' endeavors."

"I suppose not," she agreed. "Are you here alone or with your family? I'm sorry; that was forward of me. I am alone, save for a servant and a single advisor. This is my first Assessment where I am solely representing my house. My father was hurt," she added again.

Gatina put a hand to her chest. "I am so sorry to hear that. Is he healing?" She found this bit of acting to be forced, even though it was needed.

"He is. He is on the mend," Bomaris reported. "His absence put me in the position of being our representative to the Anchorage, and it's a bit unusual and . . . overwhelming. What about yourself? You're alone too, you said. Are you representing your house as well?"

Gatina shook her head. "No, some of my family is here," she said, finding truth in that statement. It was time for her to get away from politics, she decided, and reestablish a more personal collection. "I come from a very small house, but we have partnered with larger ones where needed. We don't even have a vote on the council. But that's not why I'm visiting you. I found your bracelet," she reminded her, pulling it from her pocket and holding it up.

Bomaris looked at the bracelet that was hanging from Gatina's fingers, then she glanced at her naked wrist.

"I tried to find you when I realized what happened, but I wasn't sure where you had gone," Gatina explained. "And then, everywhere I turned, there were fights. So, I found a warden and he told me to bring it to you myself." As Gatina spoke, she watched the woman's facial expressions carefully.

"It's very unusual for it to get lost like that," Bomaris admitted, rubbing the empty spot on her wrist. "The clasp is very tight. I've worn it every day since my mother gave it to me. She was a woman of profound intuition," she revealed sadly. "I miss her very much."

"I figured that it was valuable to you," Gatina said sympathetically.

"It is one of my most prized possessions. I thank you for returning it to me. That was very kind of you. Here, let me get you something to reward you," she said, standing.

"My lady, that is not necessary!" Gatina insisted. "I did it out of kindness, not hope for reward!"

"It would be callous of me not to repay that kindness," Bomaris insisted. "Bide."

Bomaris stood and walked to the carafe. Gatina thought she was going for more wine, but she crouched behind the small couch instead.

A moment later the woman rose, a short, ladylike scimitar raised and resolutely pointing at Gatina.

"I'd like to think I inherited some of Mother's intuition. It has never steered me wrong, in business or in life. That clasp hasn't come undone once in six years, even in a tempest. You seem awfully well informed about politics for a minor Sea Lord from a small haven. And you mentioned my father's broken leg before I did.

"But that's not who you really are, is it, Lady Foscombra? My intuition is screaming at me that you are not who you say you are," Bomaris declared, the point of her sword never wavering. "So, who *are* you? Who are you *really?*"

CHAPTER TWENTY-SIX
A PRODUCTIVE MEETING

In a fight or a duel, always seek the high ground. That might be a rope, a tree, a rooftop, or a settee. It seems odd in the moment, but staring someone down from a higher position confuses your opponent and gives you an advantage.

—*from Gatina's Heist Journal*

Gatina was shocked—not by Bomaris's sudden production of a sword, but by her own failure to predict that she was preparing to draw it. The Sea Lord had given no indication that she was suspicious of her—until there was a blade in her face. She had to admire that—there were not many who could successfully sneak up on one of the Cats of Enultramar.

Gatina realized that she had two choices: she could come clean and reveal herself and her mission, or she could defend her alias as Lady Foscombra. Family doctrine was to protect your alias until you couldn't and then escape. This was a tricky situation. She decided the wisest course of action was to try to maintain her alias, so she stood and raised her hands up toward her chest, her cup of wine still clutched in one.

But she shifted her feet into a fighting stance. And as she drew up her left elbow, she nudged open the small opening in her skirt that gave her access to her shadowblade.

"My lady!" she said with alarm. "I have no idea what you were talking about!" She tried to affect an innocent-sounding and convincing voice, and her eyes went wide in shock and surprise. "I was just trying to return your bracelet, and you draw a blade? You're frightening me right now!" She added a bit of a catch to her voice. She thought that might help undermine Bomaris's confidence.

Unfortunately, the Sea Lord was as unwavering as her blade. "I think you do!" Bomaris pronounced as she pressed forward a few inches, her sword's point closer to Gatina. "I know not who you are, my lady, or who you work for, nor to what purpose, but I know you are deceiving me. I want to know why!"

Bomaris sought to threaten Gatina further as she gestured with the tip of her sword—it was a formal weapon, she saw as it got all too close to her face, with an elegant brass cup guard filigreed in silver in the design of a mermaid. The blade itself was honest steel, highly polished, and visibly sharp. Not the sort of thing she wanted near her throat.

So, Gatina shifted her plan—and her feet. As the sword point came closer, Gatina spun and dropped into a crouch, drawing her shadowblade from its hidden sheath with one smooth motion. It clashed against the scimitar soundly and threw Bomaris's blade far out of line.

Instead of pressing her attack and threatening the woman, Gatina dropped back into a guard position. Despite the sudden appearance of steel, there might be a way to salvage this mission yet, she reasoned, as her blood pumped in her ears and her breath raced with adrenaline.

"I had hoped you were not the sort to strike an unarmed woman," Gatina said, maintaining her Sea Lord accent and speech patterns.

"You seem to be armed," Bomaris said, raising her scimitar once again. "I can only guess that you work for House Venjancar," she accused. "You seek to coerce my vote in council!"

Gatina realized the young woman knew more about the sordid portions of the politics of the Assessment than she had suspected. Bomaris might be young and inexperienced, but she was informed.

"Quite the contrary," Gatina insisted, as they faced off against each other, the points of their swords hanging in the air mere inches apart. "Venjancari are little better than pirates. But you were correct that I was not entirely what I seemed," she agreed as she swiftly beat down Bomaris's blade again. Still, she did not attempt to strike.

Bomaris answered with a lunge of her own, which Gatina easily parried. "Then who are you?" she demanded as she recovered her position.

"That's complicated," Gatina admitted as she withdrew toward the table, hoping to keep the woman talking and not hacking at her. "But the fact that I'm not stabbing you right now should tell you I wasn't sent to harm you."

"Says the assassin I took by surprise!" Bomaris laughed. "You will not find it easy to kill me." She advanced boldly and forced Gatina to parry a few tentative blows.

"If I was an assassin, we wouldn't be chatting, would we?" Gatina pointed out. "Besides, how do I know *you* haven't sold out to House Venjancar and Baron Jenerard?" she asked as she batted away the scimitar again. Gatina used footwork and misdirection to confuse Bomaris. She would seem to lunge to her right but then, once Bomaris had committed, switch direction. Bomaris was a competent swordswoman, but she did not have Gatina's practice or skill. All the while, Gatina continued frequent and vocal denials. But Bomaris did not believe her.

"How dare you! My house will not bow to you and yours!" Bomaris insisted as her blade came up and down quickly then swooped from side to side as she tried to advance in traditional Sea Lord style. Thanks to Lancellus's recent tutoring, Gatina was able to sidestep every move without much effort. She had committed the footwork to memory.

But Gatina realized her gamble had failed. Instead of confusing the Sea Lord, she had aggravated her even more. So, she tried empathy. And that was fairly close to the truth.

"There is much I can't tell you," she admitted as she defended herself. "But I assure you, Lady Bomaris, I am not allied with the Venjancari or Jenerard or Count Vichetral. I *oppose* slavery. My house opposes slavery," she insisted, backing away from the scimitar, with what she hoped was a look of worried horror on her face. None of this was going according to her plan. She would need to decide on a course of action quickly. "I was sent to speak to you—that was all."

"And what a delightful conversation we are having!" Bomaris said as she pushed her way around the table to reach her. Gatina vaulted over it, using her left hand as a pivot, and landed on the other side in a fighting stance.

"It's not going the way I'd anticipated," Gatina conceded. "But it need not end in bloodshed. At least tell me your stance on the subject!"

Bomaris lodged a different attack from the opposite angle, circling the table. "We oppose slavery and everything the Council of Counts is seeking to do," she proclaimed angrily, clearly frustrated with her ineffective attack. "We've been under pressure from Venjancari and other houses to take up such trade, and we've refused!"

"Then why are we fighting?" Gatina asked as she parried over the table.

"Because you seem to know far more about the subject than you revealed," Bomaris explained, her blade still extended. "Indeed, it was a closely held secret that Baron Jenerard would even appear at the

Anchorage this year until a few days ago. Only those affiliated with the Venjancari and their cronies would know that!"

"We've known for weeks," Gatina conceded. "Long enough to construct a plan to stop him."

"Why should I trust you?" Bomaris demanded. "It is not beyond the Venjancari to send a pretty assassin with soothing words to get close enough to me to kill me," she reasoned.

"They seem more the type to send brutal thugs to your door, don't you think?" Gatina challenged. "I came to talk, my lady, nothing more!"

"Bearing a hidden blade? To what purpose?" she asked. She began moving her sword in circular motions, which—given the scimitar's design—was the best way to maintain its momentum. It was also designed to be intimidating in a duel. But it limited the possibilities of her strike to a few specific attacks. That's when Gatina decided offense would be her best option. It was time to put Bomaris on the defense.

"I am not a threat, Bomaris," Gatina insisted, though she beat away her scimitar with every word, putting the woman in a far more defensive stance. "As for why I am armed, the agents of Vichetral are everywhere," she explained as she advanced. "They hunt for me. Because I am a threat to them," she said, withdrawing from her attack instead of pressing it. "I could have already killed you five different ways if I wanted to. I haven't. That should give you a reason to trust me."

Gatina knew she was the more experienced swordswoman. Bomaris's swordswomanship was strong, but Gatina was better practiced and had been in actual duels for her life. She doubted Bomaris could say the same.

Instead of answering, Bomaris began another slashing attack. It was one that Lancellus had shown Gatina on the *Daydream*. One she had committed to memory after repeatedly practicing it with him. She knew this foot pattern well—and its counter.

Gatina quickly refocused, matching her footsteps to Bomaris's and anticipating the scimitar's inevitable attack. It really was a beautiful bit of art—the dance of the scimitar—but so was countering it decisively. Gatina answered each of Bomaris's attacks with the counterattack. With one swift and unexpected motion, Bomaris was disarmed, the pretty sword clattering to the floor as Gatina passed by her opponent—and Gatina was crouched on the table, her blade inches from Bomaris's face. She had the high ground now, and her opponent was unarmed.

If the young Sea Lord was surprised by Gatina's maneuvering, she did not allow it to show on her face. Nor did fear. But she did not lunge for her lost sword.

"If you're not with Venjancar, then explain how you know so much about what is happening," she demanded instead.

Gatina sighed. She was tired of repeating herself. One thing she had learned in observing Sea Lords: they were a stubborn people.

"I have you at an advantage, and I am not pressing it," she pointed out, lowering her shadowblade. "That should earn me some trust."

"A fair point," conceded Bomaris, her eyes locked on Gatina's. "Yet it doesn't explain your knowledge—knowledge only my enemies would know."

"Perhaps you have allies you have not yet met," Gatina countered. "I would suggest that is the case. And that is a subject for a lengthy conversation," she proposed. "We need to talk. Swordplay will not help us come to an understanding."

"Who in five hells *are* you?" she demanded insistently. "And who do you work for?" That was when Gatina realized she may have done a bit too much. The woman already did not trust her and had thought the worst of her. Now she may have given her additional cause for concern. "You're no maiden of a proper Sea Lord family, despite your appearance," Bomaris continued, as she stared up at Gatina quizzically. "You say you aren't working for the Venjancari. So, who are you?"

"I just want to talk. Truce?" Gatina proposed as she shifted her feet. She did not step to the floor yet; she needed Bomaris to agree to end the fighting before she gave up the higher ground. Gatina knew she must explain more than she had hoped in order to gain Bomaris's trust. She curiously monitored Bomaris's body language, looking for any signs of tension that might indicate a return to fighting.

But the woman was still not calm and still extremely wary. Her chest was heaving from the exertion and sweat appeared on her brow. Gatina was barely winded.

"Yes, yes, fine. Truce," she agreed, as she kicked her scimitar away from reach and sank onto the settee. Cautiously, Gatina stepped down from the table and sat in a chair across from her.

Bomaris slowly reached down to the floor and retrieved her wine cup from where she'd set it before she'd drawn her sword. However well practiced Bomaris was at swordplay, she had also been fueled by her emotions.

Anger and fear fed her adrenaline. Gatina was familiar with those emotions, of course, but knew that a good swordsperson did not yield to the temptation of using them. They provided strength, but they could not sustain you in a fight and they exacted a toll on your body, Master Steel had always insisted. A proper swordsman dueled with a dispassionate heart. Bomaris drained the cup in one swallow.

When she set down her empty cup, Bomaris repositioned herself so that she faced Gatina. "You are not who you appear to be, Foscombra. That is clearly not your real name."

"Let us continue using it for the sake of convenience," Gatina proposed. "My real name is unimportant."

"So, how do you know so much about what's happening—things nobody else should know?" Bomaris's tone was no longer demanding, but it was insistent. Gatina sighed. But before she could answer, there was a heavy, ominous pounding on the door. A muffled male voice demanded entry.

Alarmed, they both looked at the door.

"Are you expecting someone?" Gatina asked, her eyes wide with surprise.

Bomaris shook her head as the pounding began again. "My servants are occupied elsewhere and won't return until tonight. But we might have attracted attention with our sparring," she pointed out.

Gatina stood. "Then we should postpone our discussion and avoid any uncomfortable explanations. Meet me at the Fairtrader's Shrine at midnight. In public, to allay your suspicions. I will return your bracelet to you then, and I will explain all that I am able to then. Will you meet me?"

Bomaris paused, staring at her intently, then nodded once.

"I shall see you then, my lady. I would mention none of this to anyone," Gatina advised, "for both our safety." She stood, secured her shadowblade back in its sheath and gave a brief Sea Lord curtsy before sprinting to the open window that led to the balcony.

Behind her, the pounding resumed, and Bomaris called with a frustrated sigh, "I will be there in a moment!"

GATINA CLIMBED THROUGH THE WINDOW AND STEPPED ONTO THE STONE balcony silently, but her pulse was pounding in her ears. Things had not gone according to plan, and she began chastising herself for her incompetence even as she heaved herself onto the rooftop from a conveniently located trellis outside the balcony.

She glanced around and saw nothing unusual or alarming. Most folk were enjoying the festivities of the Anchorage, not wondering about the sound of steel being crossed in the residential quarter. That worked to her advantage.

She considered her options: She could climb up or down. She reached over to the trellis. The roof was the safest choice, she knew, even if the sun was still beating down and illuminating her escape. The roof provided options the ground did not.

As she climbed, she realized how much better she had gotten at the task and how much easier it was. She had been a good climber before, but working on the *Legacy* and the *Daydream* had made her stronger and quicker and more certain of herself at heights. All the time she had spent climbing the ropes and nets had built her muscles and endurance.

But climbing in a gown with her working blacks underneath presented a different challenge. The gown bunched up between her legs and got under her feet more than a few times. She had to be mindful of it so she didn't tear it. She wanted to listen as best she could, to make sure Bomaris was not in trouble.

But she heard no shouting below. As she neared the top of the trellis and slipped onto the roof of the flats, she considered her next steps. The heat of the day was bearing down on her. She wanted to strip down to a shift and jump in the Bay for a swim to cool down, but that was not an option, she knew. She decided instead that a well-ventilated tent and a cool drink in her hand might be a better course.

She knew her mission was in peril, thanks to her mistakes. Bomaris should never have been able to see beyond her alias, and she had. That stung Gatina. Lady Foscombra had been the most challenging alias she had ever developed. She had worked hard to perfect the Sea Lord dialect and mannerisms, yet Bomaris had seen clear through all of it. That was a critique of her craft that she could not endure.

Worse, she had been confronted with a sword when she had not anticipated it. That was just unprofessional, she chided herself in her mind. It was one thing to see your cover discovered; it was quite another to allow complacency to let a mark get the advantage of her. That was unacceptable.

As she pulled herself over the ledge to the roof, she mentally recounted the fastest route to the safehouse. It was relatively close at hand and would provide her an opportunity to regroup and recover from the unexpected turn of events.

She felt at home on the rooftops, though they were much more steeply pitched than the rooves of Falas she was most used to. There was something peaceful about being up there, on the heights, able to peer down on the normal routes below without being seen. No one expected someone to be up there, she knew from experience. It was as good as a private road across the compound if you knew what you were doing. Once she had gotten out of the immediate area, it was a quick walk to the thoroughfare that led to the safe house, or she could blend in with the crowd for the next few hours.

Her mind was racing with questions as she made the leap between buildings. Who was at Bomaris's door? What did they want? How was Bomaris so well informed for a daughter of a minor house from a backwater on the Bay? She did not wonder why Bomaris was upset—that made perfect sense to her. Would she see the woman again at the appointed time? It had to be halfway near the sixth bell now, and she had hours until their appointed meeting time at midnight.

The rooftops seemed a homely place as she sank down on the roof for a few moments' rest. She surveyed the rooftop with a practiced eye. As she massaged her shoulders and arms, she visualized the apartment building layout she had absorbed from her observations. From her airy vantage, she saw that the roof connected Bomaris's building to two additional buildings.

Each was separated by a covered breezeway that led to courtyard gardens with seating behind each of the buildings. Gatina decided to travel by roof as far as she could, then climb down the back of the building and arrive in the garden before she made her way—calmly!—through the crowds. She ran through that plan several times in her mind, mapping out her course and secondary options while she continued to stretch her sore muscles.

When Gatina reached the end of the roof, she took a deep breath, then lowered herself over the ledge and began her descent. She landed silently in the empty, shaded garden and shook her gown off and out, hoping to remove any leaves or scuffs from it. She strolled placidly through the garden gate, down the lane, and into the main thoroughfare without anyone taking note of her. She was unworthy of notice. As she made her way through the breezeway, she decided to venture to the Maiden's Haven on her way back to the safe house. She was hungry. And the sausages smelled delicious. It was time to lose herself in a crowd.

Gatina spent the late afternoon wandering in and out of the various Vaxelhaven quarters, purposefully confusing any who might be following. She did not shop, nor did she steal. The only things she purchased were food and drink, though she found an artisan's booth and was tempted to purchase a fresh quill and ink—her afternoon adventure begged to be recorded in her heist journal. But she knew that was not practical during a mission left half-done.

So, she watched and she listened as she made her way to the safe house by a circuitous route. She learned no secrets along the way, only that most of the patrons of the Maiden's Haven enjoyed ale and sailing, many ladies were on the hunt for a husband, many mariners were pursuing less formal affairs, and there were, indeed, pirates openly roaming the Assessment without fear.

That was, of course, the most foreboding of observations; to permit such outlaws free rein in the Assessment was a travesty. But what she found most fascinating, though, was the group of ladies searching for husbands. She did not fully understand why they would seek a match so desperately at such a young age. She assumed they were a year older than she, and she was certainly not ready for such nonsense yet, Duty or not.

But then, when Lancellus had held her hands . . . and Pia and Matros were always sneaking off . . . what if she did find someone who caught the attention of her heart, she wondered? Someone whom the gods and prophecy had foretold? A mage who was also a warrior, kind and intelligent and fair of face? Was she no better than the cackling girls in the Maiden's Haven who made eyes at strong-limbed mariners and well-dressed Sea Lords? The thought appalled her.

Yet the prospect intrigued her. Despite the importance of the mission, the idea of someone waiting for her at its conclusion was . . . enticing. She had never admitted that to herself before, and she had no idea why it was suggesting itself now. But as she ate her sausages and drank her beer, the idea of a man in her life beyond her father and brother started to seem . . . interesting.

Darkness, Kitten! she chastised herself. *You're mooning about a man who doesn't exist when you've nearly bungled your mission!*

She shook her head to clear her mind. That kind of daydreaming was dangerous. What if she were kidnapped because she lacked focus on her mission? What if she missed an important detail because she was just as flighty as any daft maid in the Bay? She finished her meal guiltily, then resolved to return to the safe house.

She briefly wandered through the Salt Crone's Quarter, led by a morbid curiosity for the depressing divinity. Lancellus had explained what took place in this area, she recalled. Medical treatment could be had there, as the physicians who attended to the larger ships were trained in the Salt Crone's service. But most of the complex was devoted to less-hopeful possibilities. She knew about the life insurance and burial arrangements, but it was fascinating to hear how the process was explained. One could pay a set fee and be guaranteed that their families would receive a payment when they died or lost a limb at sea. It was a morbidly useful service, she could imagine. She wondered if thieves had that option somewhere—or magi, for that matter.

After that, she spent a few moments watching the knot-tying contests sponsored by the rescue and salvage corps the cult supported, which were surprisingly entertaining. There were boys and girls younger than her as well as Sea Lords older than her competing at various levels as they demonstrated their skill. She sat close enough to the small stage to see how quickly the rope flew through their fingers, back and forth, over and under, until a knot was finished.

It was seductively instructive as well. As she watched a hitch-tying competition, she was surprised to see a quicker way to complete the knot than she knew, one she would be sure to use when she was back as a crewmember.

She soon meandered to the scimitar duels taking place at the front of the Corsair's pavilion. This, she knew, would be even more informative. Despite having performed well against Bomaris, she appreciated the opportunity to observe others plying the distinctive blade.

She settled onto a bench near the front as the match began, and she was mesmerized by the competitors using blunted weapons in a variety of settings: large area, corridor, stairs, and rigging, which was the most exciting. The duels followed the standard three-point rules but with some intriguing differences to the duelists she'd faced. And the fluidity of the fights was hypnotic, an elegant dance of steel and sheer balance. She quickly decided that she did enjoy the scimitar, not because of the blade itself but because of the intricate footwork needed to execute the moves. It was graceful.

After that, she made her way back to the safe house near sunset. Her cousins were both there—and both exhausted by their day. Aunt Beah looked pleased as she welcomed Gatina into the nondescript shack and offered her bread and tea.

"How fares your mission?" she asked, lightly, as Gatina buttered her bread.

"It . . . faltered," Gatina admitted. "My mark discovered my subterfuge and called me on it. But I recovered," she offered in her defense as she added a fig jam to the bread. "We are meeting at midnight at the Fairtrader's Shrine. I hope to finish the mission then."

"There seems to be a lot of that going around." Her aunt frowned. "You aren't the only one who has encountered difficulties. Minnie reported seeing Censors in the crowds today," she warned. "A lot of them."

"Censors?" Gatina asked, alarmed, just before she was about to bite into the bread. Her aunt nodded.

"They're scouring the place. And there's plenty of Rats about, too, according to your brother. Fights abound. There have been two dead so far, just from the scuffles," she revealed. "Both high-born Sea Lords lured into street fights."

"That's . . . not good," Gatina realized.

"No, Kitten, it is not," Beah agreed grimly. "And it is bound to get worse. Vichetral wants to ensure that the Sea Lords are cowed, and he thinks these base attacks will do that. He's openly flouting the traditional law and authority of the Assessment by doing this, and he doesn't care."

"What if his side carries the vote on the Master of the Wave's proposals?" Gatina asked as she chewed the tough bread.

"Even if our side carries it, there will be trouble," Beah predicted with a sigh. "This is a bold move on your family's part, but even if it succeeds there will be consequences. Our best hope is that the Sea Lords will resist ducal authority when there is no sitting duke—at least, not one Vichetral can recognize. There is some legitimacy in that," she suggested.

"We can only do our parts," Gatina sighed as she finished her bread and gulped her tea. "I'm going to take a nap and then change my gown before I go out. Wake me up in a few hours," she requested.

"I will, Kitten," Beah promised. "Just be careful. Take your sword with you tonight. I have a bad feeling about this evening's work."

By the time she had made it to the Fairtrader's Shrine shortly after the eleventh bell, Gatina's stomach reminded her of just how sparing she'd been today. Despite the sausages at supper and the bread before her nap, her stomach was complaining that it was well past time to eat something again.

Thankfully, the Fairtrader's Shrine offered some late-night fare to facilitate the deals negotiated after twilight. In addition to kaffa, tea, and brandy, there were some morsels available when she chose her table—not too near the main entrance, and with a good view of the main chamber of the temple. She ended up ordering a sausage-and-potato pie, two baked apples, and two cups of wine for herself and Bomaris.

While she waited for the Sea Lord and the meal, Gatina scanned the room. She liked the quieter, more elegant surroundings of this temple than the frantic, boisterous atmosphere of the Maiden's Haven.

The Fairtrader's Shrine offered a more comfortable venue designed for discussing business and commerce. The music was slower, softer, and designed to relax, not to excite, she noted. The chairs were cushioned with feather pillows, and the tables were much sturdier and grander. The decorations were tasteful and elegant, not gaudy and crude like the ones the Maiden's Haven boasted. The Fairtrader's Shrine was clearly an expression of the vast wealth the Sea Lords represented, she realized, a sanctuary from the gritty realities that paid for such luxuries.

And when her meal was finally delivered, it came on a pewter plate instead of a mere trencher, and the ales were in ceramic mugs. The sausage-and-potato pie was generously large and delicious, and she devoured it in moments.

While she sat and ate and waited for her mark to arrive, Gatina watched the transactions and conversations unfold all around her. She saw several houses, notable by their crests, arrive and depart to meet with their fellows in the elaborate and elegant quarter.

She noted a number of small pictographic signs designating different commodities hanging discreetly from the thick wooden posts that supported the lofty ceiling: wine, oil, spices, citrus, silver, timber, pig iron, wheat, cotton, hemp, and others she did not readily recognize were represented, and men and women quietly met under them to arrange their bargains and secure their profits. Her ears picked up on numbers she had only previously associated with her studies of the stars.

Much was said in code, she realized, or in jargon specific to a particular industry that she was unaware of. But it all intrigued her.

There were other sections of the large hall dedicated to merchant discussions, family gatherings, traders' meetings, and other matters. From her vantage point, she could see areas devoted to shipbuilding, salvage, insurance, sale, design, and mapmaking. Each area was its own little hub of activity.

Then she was startled as she saw her brother, still dressed in his disguise as a messenger, running notes back and forth across the room. Within the hour, Gatina also saw her mother and father at separate times as they pursued their own missions in disguise. They were seemingly conducting business as they met with other Sea Lords in the various meeting areas. None of her family lingered there long, unfortunately. The Fairtrader's Shrine was a popular place for spies tonight, she was amused to see.

But that was to be expected. This was the commercial heart of the Assessment, arguably the most important aspect of the entire event. This is where the deals were struck that affected thousands, where the commerce that fed the appetites of millions was decided. By her estimations, millions of ounces of gold had changed hands since she'd ordered her pie. That meant it was also where the powerful Sea Lord families met to discuss plans and strategies. It was not unpredictable for it to be the best place to meet a powerful mark.

She suddenly regretted sitting so far away from the other tables, but eavesdropping was not her mission. Gaining Bomaris's allegiance was.

As the time for her meeting neared, Gatina stood to stretch her legs. She also signaled the attendant for a second cup for herself. Tea this time; she didn't want wine to dull her senses this late in the evening. As it was delivered, Gatina again caught sight of Atopol, who was now leaving the hall with a determined stride. He passed Bomaris as she arrived, her flamboyant sea-green skirt causing enough of a swoosh to gain his attention, much to Gatina's irritation and amusement. She was more intrigued by the sword the lady bore on her hip than her gown. She watched as Bomaris surveyed the room, looking for her. Gatina waved. The noblewoman walked purposefully to the table as soon as she recognized her.

"Lady Bomaris! I'm so happy you were able to come!" Gatina said as she stood, genuinely happy to see her. She had been worried about who had been at the woman's door.

"I would not miss the opportunity," Bomaris said, with special emphasis as she returned Gatina's curtsy. "I've had the most unpleasant afternoon and was looking forward to your company as a result," she said, biting her lip. "In truth, I know not to whom else to turn at the moment."

"Have a seat," Gatina encouraged. "I think we can come to some solution for whatever it is that disturbed you. I took the liberty of ordering tea," she pointed out as she sat across from the noblewoman. "But if you'd prefer kaffa, wine, or brandy, I'd be honored to treat you."

"You're most generous," Bomaris said with a sigh. "I'm looking forward to a calm, quiet, peaceful explanation of just what in five hells is going on."

Gatina was about to reply as she saw Sea Lord Lancellus saunter through the entrance, dressed in a sharp-looking leather doublet and a handsome hat she didn't recognize, his scimitar carried jauntily on his hip. He seemed relaxed as he waved toward a group of fellows he seemed to know seated at a table in the merchant area, and began to walk toward them.

He didn't seem to notice that he had been followed by a group of five corsairs who arrived only a moment later, all of whom were armed with scimitars and seemed to be ready for a fight. More mariners pushed through from behind them, all of them seeming to search for someone in the crowd. There was a clear look of determination in their eye.

Gatina's heart sank. She suspected that they were looking for Lancellus, though she had no proof of that. That was not the sort of thing she needed right now.

"My lady, I will certainly give you an explanation," she assured Bomaris as she watched the corsairs at the door. "But I cannot entirely guarantee that it will be calm, quiet . . . or peaceful."

CHAPTER TWENTY-SEVEN
PIRATE'S PROVOCATION

Awareness of your circumstances is essential. The master thief must constantly be aware that even the most obvious of situations contain nuances that you ignore at your peril. A softly spoken word, a casual glance, a shift of the eye can all lead to disaster if you fail to recognize and respect them.

—from ***The Shield of Darkness***,
written by Kiera the Great

THE ATMOSPHERE IN THE FAIRTRADER'S SHRINE WAS TENSE ALL OF A SUDDEN. The unexpected appearance of the ruffians startled the large number of high-born merchants gathered there; men of means who were negotiating deals worth thousands if not millions of ounces of gold were suddenly confronted with surly men, common mariners, and agitators, well-plied with spirits and a sense of outrage over the well-born men and women who controlled their financial fates.

Gatina could appreciate the sense of injustice the common mariners felt; she had seen first-hand what they endured and how little they were paid for their labors and risks. Yet without the Great Houses and wealthy lords who arranged the voyages that built and employed their ships, there would be no need for mariners—they would become little better than glorified fishermen, which the Sea Lords universally looked down upon. There would be no great voyages across the Shattered Sea or the Shallow Sea and beyond if these high-born men and women did not make the arrangements and undertake the financial risk to seek a profit.

The two classes had a history of conflict, she knew—roughly half of the famous pirates she'd heard about during her voyage were the result of crews mutinying against tyrannical captains employed by heartless companies. The Great Houses made a point of aggressively pursuing and punishing such mutineers and even pursued their families in an effort to keep them under control. But usually, when grievances grew too great the institutions of the Sea Lords intervened and negotiated a reasonable settlement between the parties.

But that didn't keep both sides from harboring deep-seated feelings about each other. For the Sea Lords to see their serene sanctuary in the Fairtrader's Shrine invaded by ruffians inspired a decided reaction among them.

The scimitars they wore on their belts were usually mere ornaments, accessories to their outfits that demonstrated their authority and position. Indeed, it was almost expected that a lady or gentlemen of the aristocracy would bring the sword to the temple to indicate their seriousness during the evening discussions, particularly if they were military in nature. Gatina had secured her own blade from her baggage at the safe house, and it dangled from her belt on her left, just over her hidden shadowblade. Bomaris, too, had worn her sword. Gatina saw many a smooth hand drop near the ornamented hilts of their swords as the mariners began to filter through the room.

Once Lady Bomaris had settled into her chair, Gatina resumed her own seat. Immediately, she produced the bracelet and pushed it across the table to her.

"Your bracelet," she pronounced. "I am truly sorry about the earlier ... misunderstanding. I thought I would begin our discussion with its return as a sign of good faith."

"Thank you!" Bomaris said sincerely, examining the jewelry before returning it to her wrist, where she caressed it. "That returns a bit of trust to our relationship, I think. So, what should I call you? Foscombra?"

"It's as good a name as any, for our conversation," Gatina conceded. "But you were correct: it is not my own. I am in disguise at the moment," she revealed. "Purposefully to find you, get close to you, and to discuss certain matters with you. But it was never our intent to harm you in any way," she promised.

"*Our?*" Bomaris noted, her eyebrows rising. "So, you are not working alone?"

Gatina shook her head. "I can only tell you so much," she warned, her eyes glancing around the room, "and I'd best do it quickly. But I will tell you what I can. No, I am not working alone. I am working on behalf of a certain group of Coastlords who have been seeking to undermine the reign of the usurper," she said, without naming Vichetral. That was the sort of name that would get noticed even in a crowded, noisy room.

Bomaris nodded, her eyes studying Gatina intently. "Go on," she prompted.

"This . . . society is secret, ancient in origin, a legacy of dark times in our past," she continued, choosing her words carefully. "It was recalled to duty once again upon the death of Duke Lenguin and the rise of the Council of Counts. It seeks to restore Alshar to prosperity and legitimate rule." She watched the Sea Lord more carefully than before, gauging her reaction.

"That seems a noble pursuit," Bomaris said quietly. "But what does that have to do with me?"

"A fair question," Gatina conceded. "Your name was one of several Sea Lords we were guided to in order to encourage an alliance between us toward that end," she explained. "The Anchorage gave us an opportunity to contact you, and at a particularly important time."

"The Sea Lords' council." Bomaris nodded.

"Yes," Gatina agreed sympathetically. "What happens in that council is going to shape the politics of the duchy for years—decades, perhaps. Our organization is contacting several such parties in an effort to influence the outcome of the council. Alas, the forces of Count Vichetral are aware of us, and he has sent hunters to seek us out and stop us. And exercise their own influence over the council."

While she spoke, her eyes continued to scan the room and keep watch for the situation evolving around them. The rough-looking mariners had spread out across the temple floor, brazenly ordering drinks or sitting down—uninvited—at tables with their social betters and daring their occupants to do something about it. Some were lingering quietly by the doorway, she could see, allowing a few more of their fellows to trickle in against the wishes of the priestesses.

She kept her eye on Lancellus, who was sitting with a group of younger, well-dressed Sea Lords about his own age. The man was also aware of the situation; she could see by how he sat and where his eyes lingered. Despite his easy smile, she could tell he was alarmed by the ruffians. Indeed, it looked like an operation preparing to do—*something*. It was far too well organized to be happenstance. It put Gatina on her guard.

"That would explain the unusual visitor who interrupted our earlier discussion," Bomaris sighed. She leaned over the table, just close enough for Gatina to hear her. "You'll never believe who was at my door," the Sea Lord said, her voice barely above a whisper. "It was a man in a black-and-white checkered cloak, and he was asking the strangest questions. A Royal Censor. From Falas."

Gatina's jaw nearly dropped. She understood the significance of the cloak but was surprised that Bomaris did. "What do you know of the Censorate?" she probed.

"That is someone—a wizard—who polices the magi," Bomaris replied. "I've heard stories of them, though I never expected to meet one." She took a long drink from her cup. "I assume that he was looking for you and your compatriots."

"Were you afraid? What did he want? Are you all right?" Gatina had no nuance to the questions, though she hoped her voice and tone came off as curious and not terrified. She felt badly that the Sea Lord had been subjected to any questions at all. The Censors were masters of intimidation. She had been very careful and, as far as she knew, had blended into the crowds before they could have detected her, she guessed. Gatina certainly didn't want to run into anyone in a black-and-white checkered cloak ever again. She hated the bloody Censors.

"He was cordial," Bomaris admitted, "but he was very direct and abrasive. Intimidating," she pronounced.

"That is the most powerful magic they have," Gatina agreed. "Perhaps they served a purpose once, but since King Rard expelled them from his kingdom, they have taken service with Vichetral and his cronies. They still police the magi—but only the magi opposed to Vichetral. What did he tell you?" she asked carefully. "And what did you tell him?"

The woman took another sip of her wine. When she set her cup down, she placed both hands on the table in front of her, and then she explained. "He said he was here on behalf of the Council of Counts, and that he and his fellows were investigating possible threats to the peace at the Vaxelhaven Anchorage by certain criminal wizards who sought to disrupt the event. He wanted to know if I knew anything about any magi . . . and then he wanted to know my house's position."

"Your position on what?" Gatina asked, rocking back into her chair. That was an unexpected complication. "What did you say?"

Gatina was torn between listening to Bomaris and keeping a watch over Lancellus and the men who were clearly following him. *He knew he was followed*, she thought. *So, why allow them to join him here instead of slipping away and losing them in the crowds? What was he up to?* she wondered.

"Well, I said that I'm just a simple maiden ignorant of such things and that my opinion did not necessarily reflect my sire's. My intuition told me to tell them nothing. I gave the man very little information. I told him it was unbecoming for him to interrogate a maiden without a chaperone, and I eventually feigned outrage and slammed the door in his face." She was matter-of-fact in her retelling of the interview, enough so that Gatina believed her.

"Good," Gatina exhaled. "Well done. He had to have tracked me somehow," she admitted guiltily.

"You work for magi, then?" Bomaris asked, surprised.

Gatina inhaled and decided, daringly, to reveal a little more to the girl. She whispered the mnemonic that temporarily abated the spell that colored her eyes, and let it stay down for a long moment. Enough to startle Bomaris, at least. Then she resumed it, returning them to the sea foam color she'd chosen.

"You could say that," Gatina agreed.

The Sea Lord's eyes grew wide. "You're . . . you're *one* of them!"

"It's a family legacy. But unimportant to our discussion. I do appreciate you not telling him anything, though. That might have made things . . . awkward."

"You were trying to return my bracelet. And you didn't try to kill me when you could have. And you were never rude," Bomaris added. "Even if we crossed blades, my intuition told me you were not a threat to me and my house."

"I'm not," Gatina agreed. "I just wanted to talk to you and convince you to reject Jenerard's proposals tomorrow. With the proxies you bear, you could have an influence on the outcome of events."

"So, did you use magic to find my bracelet?" Bomaris asked, curiously.

"I did not find it; I stole it," Gatina confessed. "But always with the intention of returning it to you. I needed a way to meet you without a formal introduction. And a means of gaining your trust."

She watched Bomaris's face, hoping that opting for truth was the right decision. She could quite easily take offense at the admission. Thankfully, she was more pragmatic.

"Reasonable," she conceded finally. "If cynical. As it turns out, I am entirely inclined to reject the Master of the Waves' proposal. As is my sire and our partners."

"You . . . you are?" Gatina asked, hesitantly.

"He's trying to convince the larger houses to join forces with him and a few large houses to support the council's return to piracy, slavery, and kidnapping as common practices," she said, frowning. "We've been under such pressure for months, and it is irritating. No decent mariner would support that."

"I am gratified to hear that, my lady," Gatina said sincerely, realizing that despite the problems she'd encountered, her mission was a success. Bomaris was an ally. "I hope that your house will support us in this fight. It seems we have common interests after all. Or at least common enemies."

Bomaris did not make her wait long for an answer. She spoke quietly, fingering the bracelet on her wrist. "My house will support the effort. We and our folk have suffered greatly since Duke Lenguin's death," Bomaris explained. "Ordinarily, such matters are left to the landsmen, and we do our best to ignore landsmen's politics. But to be honest, we have never trusted Vichetral, and when he took power and confirmed Jenerard as the Master of the Waves, we were not surprised. But not happy. We've long been aware of who the baron represents."

Gatina sighed, relieved at last to have completed her mission. She signaled the attendant to order more tea while she and Bomaris spoke about the Assessment and their hopes for the duchy's future.

"The Brotherhood of the Rat," Gatina answered, nodding. "I think some of these new 'guests' in the shrine tonight are likewise affiliated with them," she said, glancing pointedly around the room.

"I noticed that," agreed Bomaris, her eyes narrowing in disgust. "We hate those bandits. Honestly, seeing young Anguin on the throne would bring much happiness to my father," she assured. "He has been devastated since the Duke's death and all of the chaos that's happened." She took a moment to glance around, making sure that they were not being overheard. "Several of the smaller houses are conspiring to rescue Anguin from Castal and place him on the throne," she whispered.

Gatina was pleased that Bomaris shared these details. She was aware of the effort already, but this confirmed it. She knew that it would only help their effort to recruit the smaller houses to cause.

A moment later, however, another group of rough-looking mariners—at least a dozen—barged into the temple to join their fellows, much to the consternation of one of the priestesses on duty. A number of arguments began to break out, raising the background noise in the temple significantly. Gatina started paying attention to the placement of the ruffians in the room. There seemed to be quite a lot of them now.

As the harried-looking attendant arrived with their tea, she quickly guided the conversation to something less controversial while the harried servant was in earshot—you could not be too careful. "I don't know; I think the silk gowns have been quite lovely this season," she said to Bomaris, who understood the change in topic. "A longer cut that I prefer with my figure, but stylish." Gatina handed the barmaid a few coins. Once she had left, she extended her hand to Bomaris and whispered, "On behalf of the Shadow Council, I am pleased to extend an alliance to you." She was gratified that Bomaris shook her hand firmly.

Behind her, she saw one of the mariners break off from the group, sauntering through the tables and leering at the artwork on the walls and ceilings. The man appeared to be drunk, Gatina noted, except for how his feet moved. They were precise and careful in their step, not the sloppy gait of a drunken sailor.

Gatina watched as the man quickly and quietly took a position near Lancellus, out of his direct line of sight. He scavenged a cup of brandy abandoned by a frightened patron and appeared to lounge against a pillar.

But Gatina could sense that his left hand, under his cloak, concealed a piece of metal. Likely a knife or dagger, she reasoned. Apparently, the arrival of the newest crowd had been the signal for action. Indeed, the minute after the two girls shook hands, all hell broke loose in the Fairtrader's compound.

It began with a loud argument near the entranceway, where a pair of bleary-eyed mariners were insisting on entering when a priestess had forbidden them to. Gatina was startled to recognize them: they had been shipwrecked on the same island together. Darrick and Baramel. The last time she'd seen them, they'd been sleeping in the Shipwrecker's shrine. She was astonished to see that they had been rescued, and by their ornaments and livery, they had rejoined the crew of the *Venjanca*... and made their way to the Anchorage.

That confirmed her suspicions. This was indeed a setup. The men were too widely dispersed in the room for a mere drunken lark at the expense of the nobility. There was serious purpose in the eyes of the thugs.

"What are they on about?" Bomaris asked in a murmur, her head turning toward the doorway.

"They are pirates, and they are about to start trouble," Gatina warned quietly. "I've been watching them. Prepare yourself for action, my lady," she advised.

"Really? *Here*? This is *sacred ground*!" Bomaris protested, appalled by the notion.

"Really, my lady." Gatina nodded sadly. She saw the man near Lancellus shift his position when everyone's eyes were distracted. His left hand drew back, preparing himself to strike. "Now pardon me a moment."

"Foscombra!" Bomaris said, her eyes widening in shock. "You aren't going to—"

"I'm going to intervene before they are ready," she revealed. "One of our agents is here, and he's in danger. When things start happening, draw your blade and stand with your back toward the wall."

"When things start . . ." Bomaris asked, confused.

"You recall what happened at the Registry reception?" she reminded the Sea Lord. "It's going to be like that, only . . . bloodier. Wish me luck!" She smiled, rising from her seat.

Bomaris stared at her incredulously as she boldly strode up to the man who was stalking Lancellus. He looked startled as she quickly came within range of his face.

"Hey!" she said loudly in an accusatory voice. "What are you hiding under there?"

"Wha—" the ruffian asked, confused.

"Under that great stinking cloak of yours!" Gatina continued, emphasizing her Sea Lord accent. "You look like you're about to stab someone!"

"Begone, girl!" the man directed her angrily, keeping his left hand concealed. "Lest you get far more than you bargained for!"

"By the Fairtrader's invisible hand, all my bargains are fair!" dismissed Gatina. "But you don't look like the sort who—"

That was when things in the temple went from tense to chaotic. Someone sent up a cry, and suddenly several of the ruffians drew their weapons—belaying pins, scimitars, clubs, daggers, and more than one Rat Tail appeared, all at once. The man she faced growled and tried to push past her toward Lancellus.

Gatina was prepared for that. As he passed, she tripped his left foot and gave him a shove that sent him sprawling on the floor. The Rat Tail he had concealed skipped across the floor.

"To arms!" she shouted, drawing her scimitar and waving it overhead.

It seemed to be the call that the nobility needed to hear. Lancellus glanced at her, recognized her, and stood with his own blade drawn in a flash. Many around him did likewise as a reflex, and suddenly, the entire temple was brawling in earnest.

Gatina very carefully stomped her raised heel on the outstretched hand of the Rat at her feet and kicked him in the face for good measure before turning to face whatever danger lurked behind her. She was quick enough to avoid a charging ruffian with a club in his fist. She whirled and gave him a slash across his right calf as he passed by.

Cries of anger, outrage, and pain filled the air a moment later. While many of the aristocracy were retreating toward the far corners of the room, many others had elected to fight with the disreputable gang that had invaded the sacred temple. Their ornamental blades came out in defense.

Lancellus was not the only target, however—within seconds, several Sea Lords clutched their bellies or their backs as their would-be assassins struck at them. It was indeed a deliberate fight, an assassination under cover, she realized. In such a brawl, no one would question how some lord got stabbed or by whom. And no one would ask about their politics. No doubt most of those bearing the brunt of the Rats and ruffians, pirates and drunken mariners would have opposed Jenerard's proposals on the morrow.

She spent the next few moments avoiding a direct fight with anyone, instead glancing around at the threats and dangers evolving in the battle and seeing where she could do the most good. She began with Lancellus and his friends, who were being hard pressed. A trio of *Venjanca* pirates drew their scimitars on Lancellus and began to press forward in an attack.

Though Gatina had not planned to fight, she had very little say in the matter. She couldn't very well let Lancellus fall without giving him aid. She made a point of twirling near one of the three pirates and smashing the bell of her scimitar into his nose when he wasn't looking. Then she kicked him hard enough behind his knee to send him tumbling backward onto Bomaris's table, spilling the wine and knocking over their table.

To her credit, Bomaris was on her feet before he landed, her own blade in one hand and her lady's dagger in the other.

Gatina glanced up and saw Lancellus nod at her before he was attacked by the other two men. One of his friends moved to take one of them while Lancellus concentrated his efforts on the other. The pirate had an intense look on his face as he tried to kill his target. It was less intense a moment later when Gatina threw an empty carafe into it—hard.

The man was stunned and took a moment to find his feet. He held on to the table to pull himself up. Bomaris moved quickly to join Gatina before turning to face the sprawling ruffian. Before he could return to join his mates, both girls engaged in defensive measures and blocked his path. Gatina was relieved she knew Bomaris's fighting style. That helped. She was better able to focus on the fight, knowing that Bomaris was able to defend herself. They both glared down at the disheveled man.

"I'm not fighting a couple of lasses!" he spat as he raised his battered scimitar. That was when Gatina noticed a Rat Tail hanging from his belt and resolved not to get close. Things would get dangerous, likely deadly, very soon. He made a halfhearted swing with his sword as if trying to wave them away with mere intimidation.

Bomaris's blade rang firmly against it as she batted his sword out of line and returned to a high guard position.

"What makes you think you have a choice?" she asked coolly as Gatina stood beside her and followed her motion. She admired the Sea Lord's bravery, but she knew they needed to end this quickly.

"Fine! It is fairer with the both of you," he said hotly. His breath smelled of cheap spirits and he was missing a few teeth. The man began defending strongly, but he was not watching his step. Gatina saw a chair on the floor just behind him. That was handy.

Bomaris executed a low spinning move, and though her blade was parried, she kicked him hard in his knee. Instead of wincing, the man uttered a wicked laugh.

"That's hardly ladylike, now, is it?" He growled and began to fight in earnest, pushing them backward as he advanced with great, sweeping strikes. He bore a much heavier blade than their dainty scimitars, she recognized, and while they were able to keep his sword from biting, it took both of their efforts. In a moment, he had the initiative in the duel through sheer strength.

Gatina knew they needed to change that. She attempted to weave within the reach of his blade, and then she lunged forward, praying the surprise move might catch him off guard.

It didn't. He grabbed her by her shoulder with his left hand and tried to hold her at bay. And that was a mistake. Not only did he anger her, but he also gave her an advantage. She plucked the Rat Tail from his belt and jammed it into his thigh as hard as she could.

The pirate howled and pushed her away like he was trying to escape an attacking dog. That gave Bomaris the opportunity to slash at his face, producing an ugly cut above his eyebrows.

Gatina was graceful and used her training to avoid falling. Instead, she used the momentum to her advantage, dropping her scimitar and finding a more decisive weapon. She spun around and picked up the fallen chair, swinging it at his back as hard as she could. He staggered at the unexpected blow. Then she struck him in the stomach with it, shattering the chair. When he was bent over in pain, she grabbed a wine jug from a nearby table, still full, and hit him at the base of his skull. He crumpled to the ground. She reasoned he would be unconscious awhile—long enough for them to get to Lancellus and escape.

She recovered her scimitar and stepped over him to rejoin Bomaris.

"It has been lovely, my lady, but I think our evening here is done!" Gatina had to shout to be heard.

"That it is!" Bomaris agreed. "This has gotten out of hand. Has no one sent for the Watch?"

Gatina realized she could no longer see Lancellus. The Fairtrader's sanctuary had turned into a bloody and boozy brawl, and heated cries of pain and anger filled the smoky air around them.

"I need to find my friend," she announced to Bomaris loudly, and pointed toward where she last saw him—right in the middle of the fighting. She turned to Bomaris with a smirk and shrugged as the Sea Lord stared at her in disbelief.

"Is that wise?" she asked doubtfully as they surveyed the chaos.

"No, but it's necessary," she insisted. "We need to get him and get away."

Their path was stopped when another Rat fell at their feet, gutted by a scimitar. He looked shocked and screamed as the wide wound in his abdomen began bleeding profusely. It was a gruesome scene.

"That looks rather permanent," Bomaris noted thoughtfully before she vomited on his body. The shouts from all around them muffled the sound of her predicament, and Gatina turned away to guard her new friend while she recovered.

The gangsters and ruffians seemed to have the advantage at the moment. Though they were outnumbered by the aristocrats they were attacking, too many had fled rather than fight, and the thugs were using the surprise and shock of their assault to their gain. There were as many highborn noblemen sprawled on the floor, wounded, dead, or unconscious, as there were pirates. Gatina wondered how many of them would have voted against Jenerard in council.

She scanned the chaotic scene with a purposeful eye and finally found Lancellus in the crowd. She spotted the Sea Lord across the room, fighting for his own life against a very familiar-looking Rat: Darrick.

Gatina sighed, irritated to see him again. She had hoped he was still on that island. Instead, he was pressing with his scimitar and a dagger against Lancellus, both men trying to step around the bodies that were starting to litter the floor. Her friend looked exhausted and pale, and his shirt was soaked in blood. While he held his own against the pirate, it was clear that he was starting to falter.

Quickly, she considered the options and the escape routes. All of the exits were blocked by men and women who were either fighting for the love of the fight or fighting for their lives. There was no sign of the Watch as of yet—more than likely, they'd been bribed or coerced into staying away from this attempt at slaughter, Gatina reasoned.

Her attention returned to Darrick. He had a leer on his lips while he fought that turned his handsome face into a sinister expression.

"That's where I need to go," she warned Bomaris. "That pirate is fighting my friend!"

"He's huge!" Bomaris pointed out.

"He's both a Rat and a pirate, which is worse than being one or the other," she explained as she watched the duel. "He's a killer. We've met before." She knew Lancellus was trouble. Darrick was pressing him backward toward another group of Rats near the main entranceway, who were ready to kill him. She was sure of it. There were already a few bloody bodies at their feet.

Gatina tugged on Bomaris's hand as the duel spun them around until Lancellus faced her for a moment. She heard Bomaris gasp at the sight of him.

"That's my friend. Follow my lead and I'll get you both out of here!" She pulled Bomaris behind her, just as both combatants paused in the midst of their duel and took stock of each other. Then she put on a performance she only wished her cousin Huguenin could see.

"My lords! My lords! By the Maiden, help us! We can't find a way out," she wailed, panic in her voice. She looked at both men as she gently kicked Bomaris's foot. Bomaris began to sob on cue, affecting a terrified maiden in despair. She held her sword out of sight, behind her skirts.

The distraction proved effective and allowed Lancellus a brief moment to catch his breath as well as notice the Rats waiting behind him. He turned to engage them, one hand pressed to his bloody abdomen. Darrick, meanwhile, looked mystified and confused by the appearance of two well-dressed young ladies begging for his assistance—and standing between him and his intended foe.

"Sir, won't you help us?" Bomaris pleaded to Darrick as she stepped between him and his prey. Gatina prepared to strike at him the moment he raised his blade at her. Instead, he shoved her out of his way and made his way toward Lancellus.

But Gatina swiftly raised her scimitar into guard and blocked his path, something the pirate did not expect. Darrick's facial expression told her everything she needed to know. Perhaps he had displayed decency back on the island, under the Shipwrecker's Truce, but no more. That scowl showed there would be no going back, not for him.

He raised his sword threateningly as she protected Lancellus's back. She did not flinch. Indeed, she welcomed the chance to fight him.

"Why are you doing this, lass?" he asked, genuinely curious.

"Why are *you*?" she asked in return. "Is the Shipwrecker's Curse acting on you already? You could be enjoying a cup of wine in the Maiden's Haven; instead, you're fighting a maiden with murder on your mind!"

Instead of answering, the pirate shrugged and made a sincere attempt at slicing Gatina's head off. She parried well enough, but there was strength behind the blow that indicated the serious nature of his threat. He seemed surprised at how easily she struck back, and within a few passes, he recognized that this was a serious fight, not a sparring match.

They continued the dance, and Gatina felt a rush of adrenaline flood her body. Perhaps it was the attraction she had once felt for this man, barely older than her brother, or the desire to protect Lancellus. But the energy permeated her limbs and she felt vitally alive as she drew strength from it and used it. Her limbs had been conditioned with long hours of hard labor at sea, and they moved with lithe alacrity. She was facing an opponent she had every reason to want dead, and she did not particularly feel a sense of restraint as they locked eyes over their crossed blades.

"You're good," he grunted as they spun against each other. "Would you care to have a drink with me after the brawl?" he asked, tilting his head with a cocky grin. That infuriated her.

"I'm better than you, Darrick," she said in a growl, "and I don't think you would find me the best of company!"

He looked startled when he heard his name, she saw, and she took some satisfaction in that. He hadn't reacted to her comment about the curse, nor did he recognize her, she realized. She didn't mean to give him a chance to. Her rage and her frustration led her feet and guided her hand and her blade. She was meeting every strike with the proper counter. Twice she nicked his wrist above the bell guard as they traded blows. He seemed hesitant to fully commit to the fight, and she used that to her advantage.

But she knew she needed to end it. She had to get Lancellus and Bomaris to safety. Soon. Escape was her goal, after all. But if she could inflict some damage on Darrick on the way out, she could live with that.

Alas, her chance at ending his life did not come. Both of them were distracted by other factors around them—a man holding the bloody stump of his wrist and screaming wildly, a trio of older Sea Lord ladies howling in a corner though no one was menacing them, calls for assistance, cries of pain and outrage, and vile curses. Though they continued to trade blows, Gatina never let herself get close enough to be hit—but that also kept her from striking decisively.

In a moment, Bomaris joined the attack, which was helpful. The two girls circled around him, alternating their strikes before attacking him at the same time so he wouldn't know where to strike or defend. Bomaris drew blood from him, slicing him in his bicep. Then Gatina slashed him in the leg. Neither wound was fatal. But she knew they didn't have time to keep this up, especially when she saw Lancellus take a wound to the thigh. It was time to end this fight.

Fortunately, Ifnia was on their side. A fight beside them spilled over between the combatants, as someone threw a wiry little Sea Lord across the room, his limbs flailing. Gatina and Bomaris quickly moved out of the way, leaving Darrick to face off with two other Sea Lords who seemed eager for the contest. But he had the poor judgement to turn his back to the girls, taking up a wide stance as he faced more serious opponents.

She didn't stab him in the back—that seemed unsporting. But before he could attack either man and while he was still very distracted with his predicament, Gatina kicked him squarely in the groin. After that, he didn't fight so well.

Satisfied, she rushed to Lancellus's side, pulling Bomaris behind her. The gang of ruffians guarding the door was taking turns beating at him with their cudgels as he tried to get past. She scanned for other exits again, but when Lancellus stumbled under their blows, Gatina realized she needed to make her own exit.

She commanded their attention for a moment with a sharp whistle, which got all of their eyes on her. She raised her hand, drawing all of their eyes. Then she whispered a mnemonic that released the flashing cantrip she sometimes used as a distraction in a fight. It was an intensely bright light that appeared between her raised fingers. It lasted only for a moment, but in the dim conditions of the temple, it was bright enough to temporarily blind and confuse her foes. They cried with dismay as they rubbed their eyes in confusion.

"Time to go!" she insisted, grabbing Lancellus's arm and pulling him toward the doorway, pushing past the stunned pirates. Bomaris was right behind him, slashing at the dazed ruffians just enough to keep them from pursuing.

Though there were a few more thugs outside, they seemed more concerned about the approach of the Watch than keeping anyone from escaping. Indeed, a grim-looking squadron of soldiers was assembling outside the temple, she could see, and the pirates waiting there were clearly rethinking their evening plans.

Gatina pushed through them without pause, her friends close behind her. She did not stop until they were safely out of their reach.

"Are you badly hurt? Can you walk?" she asked Lancellus as they stumbled to a halt. He clutched his side and had wounds on his thigh and his shoulder. His pretty shirt was ruined beyond repair. Lancellus nodded as he caught his breath, but after a few steps, he slowed down.

"It's mostly other people's blood," he said bravely, but she could tell it hurt him to speak.

"Undoubtedly," Gatina agreed as she looked at his belly wound. Thankfully, it was not deep, nor did it seem to be spurting blood, which would have indicated a serious wound. It might hurt, but it was superficial, she decided. He had been lucky. Half an inch deeper and he would have been very unlucky. But he wasn't going to be moving quickly on his own.

Gatina sheathed her scimitar and motioned for Bomaris to take an arm, and they each helped him move past the guards who were preparing to invade the temple and put down the brawl. No one questioned them or stopped them, she was grateful to see. They paused again at the corner, where she tore a strip from her skirt hem and folded it into a pad to place over Lancellus's wound.

"How about you, Bomaris?" Gatina asked. "Were you injured?"

"Just my sense of decorum," she said as she sheathed her own blade and looked at Lancellus with concern. "The nerve of attacking people in a temple!"

"They're nothing more than pirates," Lancellus agreed. "They're being paid to disrupt the peace and hurt people in an attempt to bully the Sea Lord's council. Some are out for murder," he added darkly. "They seek to slay any who might have weight in council against them. My people don't like being told what to do," he said through clenched teeth as he put pressure on the wound.

"Well spoken, my lord!" Bomaris approved as she put her hand over his on the bandage.

Gatina realized that introductions were in order. "Lady Bomaris of House Crenalsar, may I present to you Lord Lancellus of House Luxosar," she said with a resigned sigh.

"A pleasure, my lady," Lancellus gasped as he looked up at Bomaris's face. Despite being in a brawl and vomiting a moment before, Gatina was impressed that her cosmetics still looked near perfect. Lancellus apparently thought so too. "And the Maiden's own grace on you for lending us your aid."

"The pleasure was mine," Bomaris assured him in a smooth voice that took Gatina by surprise. "Where to? A physicker?" she asked anxiously.

"My wounds are not critical," he insisted. "But we must get off the street as quickly as possible. They are hunting me, specifically, among others. And this is not the only brawl they have planned," he revealed. "Indeed, this night will be filled with such attacks. Jenerard has brought every thug and gangster he could to Vaxelhaven to intimidate the council. Those who won't be cowed will end up with their throats slit in some alley or dead in some meaningless fight. That's what they intended for me," he added grimly. "I sought the Fairtrader's Shrine because I didn't think they'd dare to pursue me there. I was mistaken. They had planned to attack there anyway."

"Let's head for your quarters, Bomaris," Gatina decided. "They are much closer than ours, and no one will be looking for him there."

"Of course," Bomaris agreed as she helped Lancellus to gently stand. Gatina suppressed the desire to roll her eyes and failed.

They made their way through the darkened streets as quickly as they could. Gatina was forced to use magesight to navigate through the disorder that seemed to cling to the streets in the darkness. As loud as it had been inside the Fairtrader's Shrine, it was much louder outside, where there seemed to be brawls everywhere, even inside the Salt Crone's Quarter.

They avoided more than one such fight as they wove through the streets until they were at the familiar entrance to the residential complex. She glared effectively enough at the few folk still skulking in the darkness to keep them at bay. She felt more and more anxious as they approached Bomaris's apartments. Thankfully, there was no one lurking outside in wait for her.

Gatina knew she had to make her way to the safe house to tell her family what was happening and assure them of her safety, but she did not want to leave Lancellus injured and alone. He was exhausted, had lost some blood, and his scimitar dangled almost uselessly from his hand. And she wanted to get Bomaris to safety, too. It would reflect poorly on her to have completed her mission only to lose her mark to a street fight.

"I think you will both be safe here," she said when they had made it up the stairs to the door of the residence. "Just keep the lights low and don't open the door for anyone you don't know until morning," she advised.

"My servants will be able to help," Bomaris agreed as she pushed open the door and looked around. "They should be back by now. I will tend to my lord's wounds and keep away from trouble," she promised.

"You have my utmost appreciation for that, my lady," Lancellus said graciously as he stumbled through the door. "My labors are over for the day, if I have any say in the matter. Now, if there is a place I can sit for a few moments . . ." he said as they helped him to the settee. Lancellus winced as he collapsed onto it but nodded gratefully. "I know you must leave, Lady Foscombra, but I thank you for your assistance. I know you need to meet your . . . contacts."

"That would be best, under the circumstances," Gatina agreed.

"Please tell them that I was completely successful in my endeavors, but that they should leave here before the council meets, lest they be discovered. I learned that they are aware of our efforts to intervene and even have some idea of who you are. They plot to capture you or worse."

"Then we should flee." Gatina sighed. At least she could take solace in being successful in her mission.

"I am convinced that our success depends on it," Lancellus agreed. "I will survive well enough here until I do my duty in council," he decided, glancing up at Bomaris. "But you and your associates should flee."

Gatina shook her head. "I don't want to leave you behind. But you are right. If they have a hint of who we are and where we are, we're in danger. So are you. The Rats are on an assassination mission. If they recognize you out in the streets tonight, they will strike."

"They will not keep me from appearing at council tomorrow and voting my conscience," he assured her.

"Nor me," Bomaris agreed as she helped him lie down on the short couch. "Don't worry. I will keep him safe in my quarters until morning and bind his wounds. We will not leave until daylight, and with guards, if necessary. You have my word," she assured Gatina. "I am no stranger to the medical arts. I have cared for my father and my brothers and our retainers. I can take care of him, too. And when we have heard the Master of the Waves, done our duty, and voted our conscience, I will be happy to take him away from Vaxel on the *Viscount's Fortune*," she promised.

She spent a moment summoning her two frightened-looking servants from their room and set them to light a fire, boil some water, and tear sheets into bandages while she took a closer look at the wound in his belly by taper light.

"No, it's not serious," she agreed when he pulled the bandage reluctantly away from the wound. "With some thread and a needle, I can put it right for now. A splash of rum over it will keep it from festering. Lady Foscombra . . . may I speak to you for a moment before you go?" she asked, biting her lip.

"What is it?" Gatina asked, when the girl pulled her aside.

"You must be careful," she insisted when they were out of Lancellus's earshot. "I am concerned that you will be attacked on your way back to . . . wherever it is you must go. I really think it best you stay here."

"That is not possible," Gatina said, shaking her head. "I have duties to attend to, especially on a night like this. You heard what he said: they know we are here, somehow. I have to warn my folk. Our work is done here now. Just keep Lancellus safe. He is valuable to our efforts."

"And quite . . . handsome," Bomaris admitted quietly, glancing back at the resting Sea Lord. "Dashing, even."

"In an arrogant, egotistical Sea Lord sort of way, I suppose," Gatina conceded in a grumble.

"There is some appeal to that." Bomaris smiled. "Really, this evening did not end up as I expected it to. But it hasn't been entirely unpleasant."

"This evening is far from over," agreed Gatina. "But your part, I think, is done. Go tend to Lancellus and be at the council on time. Do your duty. And thank you for your alliance. Lancellus is instrumental to that too."

"House Luxosar is well known for its influence and wealth," Bomaris admitted. "Tell me, has he been pledged in marriage?"

"I haven't the faintest idea," Gatina said, surprised at the question. How could Bomaris think of such things when the entire Anchorage seemed beset by chaos and destruction? "You'll have to ask him yourself. That should give you something to talk about while you are stitching him back together," she suggested.

"In either case, I want to thank you," Bomaris said, pulling Gatina into a sudden embrace. "I don't think I would have survived the day without your bravery and quick thinking. I came to Vaxel feeling hopeless and alone, but now I think I have a few stalwart friends to depend upon."

"As do I," Gatina said sincerely as she broke the embrace. "You two settle in and stay quiet. My night, alas, is just beginning, I fear."

"May the Storm King and all his daughters protect you," Bomaris said, giving her the Sea Lords' blessing.

"It will be Darkness that does that," Gatina shrugged. "Farewell!"

With that, she faded into the shadows of the night. Bomaris's apartment was closer to the Stormfather's Temple than to the safe house, and she had more than a mile to walk through the bloody streets to get there.

As Gatina wound her way back to the safe house, she was on her guard by necessity, her hand never straying from the hilt of her scimitar. She could hear fights and squabbles from all over the place, cries of fear and outrage ringing out between quick clashes of steel or other commotions. She wanted no part of it.

There was far too much going on tonight. Knowing that the Brotherhood was active and infiltrating the Anchorage was one thing, but to see it in action was something else. Something very frightening. It was somehow worse than the riots she'd witnessed in Falas—those had been among the common folk, or the dueling clubs, or the occasional gang. The Rats in Vaxel seemed to have more sinister purpose—this wasn't a riot as much as a street battle. She clung to the shadows while the unnerving shouts and screams seemed to come from everywhere.

She prayed to Blessed Darkness that her parents and brother as well as aunt and cousins would be safe back in Aunt Beah's unassuming shack.

But as she neared the Maiden's Haven, another brawl spilled out from the vast tent onto the walkway. It was, perhaps, less bloody than the fight in the Fairtrader's Shrine but far larger and no less violent. The weapon of choice between combatants seemed to be clubs, not swords, at least.

Gatina tried to make her way around the group instead of pushing through. Several were already on the ground, fighting with their fists. Others used belaying pins or cudgels. Only occasionally were swords or daggers being employed. She dodged one pair of duelers nimbly as they hurled curses at each other and drunkenly slashed around with their scimitars. But while they seemed to be exceptions, there were plenty of other fights going on.

She was almost through the brawl when Gatina unexpectedly heard a familiar voice: her cousin Jordi's. And he was in distress.

She stopped her progress and quickly scanned the darkened streets with magesight. She knew if one of her cousins was there, the other was probably nearby.

She was relieved when she saw them both of them together . . . except they were being confronted by a pair of drunken mariners who looked no better than Rats themselves, each holding a short, brutal-looking cudgel.

With a sigh, she drew her scimitar and began her third fight of the night.

CHAPTER TWENTY-EIGHT
SHADOWBLADE UNSHEATHED

A good thief has to know when it is time to take their leave, or they won't be a good thief for long.
— from **The Shield of Darkness**,
written by Kiera the Great

GATINA CIRCLED THE BRAWL CAREFULLY IN THE SHADOWS, HER SCIMITAR IN hand and ready for action should any come her way. The crowd was anxious and belligerent, she could sense, and the number of individual fights that kept breaking out sounded more the result of drunkenness than any malignant plot—something to preoccupy the Watch while more-sinister plans were carried out, Gatina decided.

As soon as one scuffle broke out, there were several men who would try to drag the combatants away from each other. The attention of the Watch was divided, after all, with the fight up at the Fairtrader's Shrine and the other brawls she'd witnessed. They couldn't police the thousands of people crammed into the Maiden's Haven complex. Not without causing a real riot.

Some of the acrimony there was due to rival crews facing off after too much drink, she could see. Other fights seemed to be about women, insults, or money. But she could see the same sort of foul fellows squinting in the shadows, encouraging the chaos while swigging from bottles or smoking pipes while they watched the violence unfold around them. They seemed to delight in the number of brawls threatening to become a general riot.

Few of them involved blades, she was happy to see, but the cudgels and belaying pins that seemed to be the weapon of choice were deadly in their own right. There was a feeling of danger and alarm in the air so thick she could taste it. She could still hear her heart pounding; it felt like her head was being hammered by the sound. She had remained on alert since she parted with Lancellus and Bomaris and thought the worst of the night was past her. But now she had to rescue her cousins as well.

This fight would most definitely grow larger than the one inside the Fairtrader's complex, she could see. There, it had been a few dozen rascals with a plan and an agenda. This was less sinister but had a greater possibility of tumbling completely out of control. There were thousands of visitors packing the broad expanse of the complex, so many that they spilled out into the street. In places, minstrels tried in vain to distract with their music, which gave the scene a kind of eerie character as more fights broke out.

They were still contained. But she could tell that the majority of instigators were either pirates or Rats. If not fighting between themselves, they seemed to be egging on common mariners with insults and challenges.

It was easier to gain access to the Maiden's Haven, after all, as it had no proper guards at the gateway—a rickety wooden affair that was more canopy than an entrance. There was no secure barrier stopping anyone who really wanted to get in from doing so. And there was no one in authority who was trying to break up the gathering. A few individuals had taken it upon themselves to protect the innocent, and a few Watchmen were screaming for calm, but they were outnumbered, and the situation was deteriorating fast.

This was part of the baron's plan, Gatina realized. More of the baron's plan, she corrected. Jenerard had targeted the entire stronghold, not just the wealthier quarters.

She had learned about the political power of riots in Falas over the years. They were excuses for unreasonable restrictions on behavior, she'd found, or a reason to round up whatever "undesirables" the regime wanted to be suppressed.

More, they frightened the common folk who were most affected by them into inaction, when bravery was called for. A bad riot could disturb a town for months or years and give rise to all sorts of unfortunate results. The dueling societies had only risen in prominence in Falas after the first severe riots, she recalled. She suspected Baron Jenerard planned the same sort of thing here, with Rats and pirates instead of brash young aristocrats as his soldiery.

Yes, she needed to get Jordi and Pia to safety and then find her parents. They needed to know what was happening, she thought, though they probably already knew, she realized. There wasn't much that Shadow did not know.

And then they had to get out of there. If the Censors were closing in on them, it was time to depart Vaxelhaven with all possible speed.

Weaving through the outskirts of the crowd was easier for her than most—she was little and lithe, and few regarded her as a threat, despite the scimitar she carried. She kept aware of everything around her, not merely the people she was pushing past. She used other people to block her from the possibility of conflict as she moved closer and closer to her cousins.

The *clang* of blades right in front of her jarred her from her thoughts. Two men were dueling far too close for her comfort, so she stepped back and paused for a moment to find her cousins again, her back to a wall of a crumbling tavern. She suppressed the desire to shout out their names—there was already plenty of shouting and tumult happening around her. Instead, she wished they would shout again so she could find them.

She saw multiple fights, from duels to fisticuffs, but most didn't last long. She had little desire to get involved in those. Instead of diving back into the crowd, Gatina opted to observe and bide her time for the perfect moment. When it came, she navigated through the crowd as quickly as she could, not stopping unless she had to. She did her best to avoid engaging with anyone unless absolutely necessary; of course, Brotherhood members and pirates did get special attention and treatment, most notably elbows, knees, and vicious kicks to their shins or groins. When someone turned to menace her, she gave a fierce expression and raised her scimitar in front of her in a warning. No one challenged her after that. These were drunks on a rampaging lark, not real warriors.

But she was careful to avoid the majority of the violence. Her dress was stepped on several times, leading to more rips. The entire hem was already ruined after providing a bandage for Lancellus, and it was coming undone in the front, she saw as she stepped back again.

But her gown was the least of her worries. The shouting from Sea Lords and Rats was incredibly loud—and rude—as they fought. At least three had been gutted by scimitars, though she wasn't sure if the blades were held by pirates or Sea Lords. The wounded were carried out by their friends or left to moan and bleed on the street while they got trampled.

She counted at least fifteen skirmishes scattered around but no further sign of her cousins yet. That had her worried. She was certain that it was Jordi's voice she'd heard. Her next priority was her cousins' safety.

She caught sight of pale hair through the crowd and thought it might be Jordi, for one precious moment. That's when one of the ruffians grabbed her around her waist with a wild cry and swung her around before setting her down. She was treated to a leering unshaven face bearing a look of drunken triumph and breath like a burning distillery.

He did not know what he had done. Gatina's frustration from the evening's events seemed to coalesce all at once in response to the indignity, though it had caused her no harm. She greeted him with a punch in the nose with the bell guard of her scimitar before kicking him squarely in the groin. He went down to his knees, his eyes wide, and she continued through the crowd.

She heard Pia before she saw her—and her cousin was screaming.

Gatina was startled and appalled at the sight of Pia slung over the shoulder of a burly mariner, wearing a fiendish grin on his face as he tried to bear her away. Her cousin Jordi, his face already streaked with blood, was pursuing her abductor valiantly, an expression of determined rage on his face. He threw a few blows with his fist but was wary of hitting his sister.

Gatina didn't even think about it first; she leaped to intercept the drunken mariner, her scimitar in hand and dire necessity powering her stride. In a moment, she had bounded into his path and took a guard stance that would see the man impaled on the point of her blade if he did not stop.

"Enough!" Gatina snarled angrily. "Put her down!" she commanded.

The mariner was startled but skidded to a stop with a challenge so direct and potentially deadly—he was not *that* drunk, apparently.

"Leave us be, lass!" the man pleaded as Jordi caught up with him. "It's just a little fun at the Anchorage!"

"Have you considered bleeding might be fun?" Gatina countered contemptuously as she whirled her scimitar around in a warning. "That's my *cousin*," she explained in an even voice as her steel cut the air. "And she's betrothed to an absolute madman. Matros the Mighty. By the Crone, that's a drink of bilgewater you do *not* want," she advised intently.

As Jordi was now standing at his shoulder, glaring at the man with blood pouring down his face, the mariner realized he was not just outnumbered but possibly in real danger. He considered the matter carefully.

"Not fond of bilgewater," he admitted, and, with great ceremony, set Pia down gently on her feet. "No harm done, lass," he assured her, pretending to brush dust off the shoulder of her dress. "Just having a little fun after a long voyage and a few drinks. Things just got rowdy. A fellow needs a little recreation when he's been at sea."

"Perhaps you should take up Rushes, then," Jordi said through clenched teeth. "Let's go, Pia!" he insisted, putting his arm protectively around her shoulder.

"Enjoy the rest of the festival," Gatina said with an affected smile and a final flourish of her sword before she followed behind her cousins as they walked away.

"Head toward the safe house," she hissed into Jordi's ear as she caught up. "Are you injured?"

"Just a bash to the head from a bottle," Jordi admitted. "Someone threw it. I have no idea why. I'll live," he grunted.

"Thanks for intervening," Pia said earnestly. "I would have used a Gutbuster spell on him, but I already used it on someone else tonight and didn't have time to cast it again. I didn't even see him coming. It's like everyone went mad tonight!"

"It's part of a larger plan," Gatina informed them grimly. "This is only one of many brawls. Why were you at the Maiden's Haven, anyway?"

"We were tasked to deliver a package to your brother and were just passing by," Pia related as they rounded a corner far enough away from the riot to stop for a moment. "He's climbing the spire of the Storm King's tower tonight. Well, climbing down," she corrected.

"What?" Gatina snapped, stunned. "*Cat* gets to climb it?"

"It's part of his mission plan," Pia revealed. "He needs to make a speedy escape. So, he's rappelling down the side. We were supposed to meet him at the bottom and give him this," she said, indicating a small bundle tied up with a bit of line that was slung over Jordi's shoulder.

"What is it?" Gatina asked, confused.

"No idea," admitted Jordi. "But he said he needed it, and your mother prepared it, so . . . we were also supposed to take whatever it was he was stealing and give him this. Then come back to the safe house."

"He's *stealing* something? *And* climbing the tower?" Gatina asked, appalled. "That lucky . . . *feline!*" she said, nearly snarling.

"How did your mission go?" Pia asked hesitantly.

"Fine, fine, I convinced her to do what she was going to do anyway," Gatina grumbled, suddenly dissatisfied with her mission. "I just made her feel better about it. And possibly improved her romantic prospects."

"Didn't you steal something?" Jordi asked, confused. "I thought that was part of your plan."

"It was and I did, but I gave it back to her, so it *hardly* counts," Gatina fumed. "And I barely got to climb *anything*. Oh, a few sword fights and a rescue, but that's it!"

"You have the strangest family I have ever known," Pia said solemnly after giving Gatina a thoughtful stare.

"And you and Cat are the most competitive siblings I've ever seen," Jordi agreed. "He was snickering about the climb all day. I don't even think he really needed to do it; he just thought it would be dramatic if he was fleeing pursuit."

"He would!" Gatina said with a disgusted snort.

Then she took hold of herself. It was already late, and there were still things to take care of—getting angry with her brother was not helping any of that. If they were supposed to meet him and they didn't show up, what would that mean for his mission or for him? She knew it wouldn't be good.

"Look, I will take the package and finish your mission. You two return to the safe house and have Aunt Beah see to that cut," she advised, taking the bundle from Jordi. She exchanged it for her scimitar, which he took gratefully in hand. "I'll meet Cat and give this to him. Oh, and tell Beah that Lancellus was successful with his mission, I was successful with mine, and he's currently undercover with a friend. It's a long story," she added when her cousins both looked at her curiously.

"It sounds like you had an eventful day," Pia finally said.

"Very," Gatina agreed, slinging the package over her shoulder. "A pack of rogues invaded the Registry reception, I got in a duel with my mark in her apartments, I was almost discovered by a Censor, and then we both fought off the gang of Rats and pirates that was stalking Lancellus. I'll tell you all about it later. Where are you supposed to meet Cat?"

She was far more confident in her own skills as a Shadowmage than Pia's ability as a seamage. And Jordi was skilled, of course, but he had no *rajira* and little knowledge of spycraft. It wasn't that she didn't trust her cousins. They lacked the years of training under House Furtius's rigid guidelines that she had enjoyed. No, she knew this was something she needed to do. If only to hiss at Atopol for his daring plan.

Fortunately, neither Pia nor Jordi seemed bothered by her suggestion. Indeed, they seemed relieved. Both looked as though they had had enough excitement for the evening.

"He said to meet him at the base of the eastern side, near the northern corner—he assured me that it would be deserted," Pia explained. "There are apparently bushes there. But he also suggested that he might have someone after him after the theft and might need support. Or a distraction. Say! You can't go back through all of that without a sword!" she objected when she realized Gatina had given up her scimitar.

"I've still got my shadowblade and plenty of spells hung," Gatina dismissed. "I'll be fine."

"Oh! And there was one more thing," Pia continued, biting her lip. "We got a message from your fa— from Shadow. He says that things might get hot and you should be prepared for an early withdrawal. Mother says you would know what that meant."

Unfortunately, she did: it meant that her father's mission may have turned sour—and that was not good news. Her parents' multiple marks were considered the highest-value for the mission overall as well as the most dangerous. She had very little idea of who they were or how they were approaching their tasks, but if things were going awry enough to consider a quick escape, that was bad news.

"Thanks for letting me know," she murmured. "I'll collect Cat and his loot, and see you back at the shack. Darkness protect you!" she bade as they prepared to leave. Jordi hefted the scimitar in his hand while Pia prepared another spell, but they both paused to give her a quick hug before they headed back to the safe house.

She watched her cousins as they cautiously threaded their way back through the darkened streets, Pia using her magesight to guide them. Once they were out of her sight, Gatina dipped deeper into the alley, where her dress hem caught on a corner of the building and tore it even more.

"Darkness!" she swore, staring at the tattered skirt. Instead of ripping it, she opted to remove it entirely. Her working blacks would better suit this task, anyway. Trying to go back through the chaotic streets in disguise could make her late or subject her to more unexpected adventures, she reasoned. She could make much better time going by rooftops. She found a dark and shadowy spot and began her transformation from Lady Foscombra into the Kitten of Night.

She figured out her best route to the base of the tower from her memory of the maps as she quickly unfastened the ruined gown and allowed it to drop at her boots. By her reckoning, if she scaled one of the nearby residences and moved in a more or less straight line, she could avoid the crowds, guards, and riots of the streets and get there reasonably quickly.

Her boots followed before she rolled down the leggings to cover her shins. As she wiggled the flattened working boots out of their pockets in the thighs of her working blacks and slipped them on, she tried to mentally recount just where the worst of the crowds were and where the Watch might be deployed. Then her scarves, hat, belt, and accessories joined the pile. She balled up her disguise and tucked it into a rain barrel before she moved the scabbard of her shadowblade from her leg to across her back. Lastly, she slung her brother's package across her back and secured it tightly.

As she made her way through the alley toward the great tower, she sought the right wall to climb. She wasn't sure how much time she had before Atopol's mission would be completed, but she knew she'd better hurry.

Gatina remained safely in the shadows as she climbed up the worn bricks and onto the tiled roof of the first building and began making her way to the Storm King's tower. Her heart sang as she moved comfortably through the darkness, the sharkskin soles of her boots barely making a sound as she passed. This was her element, her favorite place to be, slinking through the Blessed Darkness on a mission. There was little light up there, and what there was only cast better shadows. Even in the city, with thousands of people around, this was a world apart.

The complexities of navigating a strange rooftop at night, with only magesight to guide her, soothed her like a tonic. The buildings in Vaxelhaven were delightfully close together, and making the leap from one to another was simple, despite the occasionally severe pitch of the roof. She was surprised at how quickly she made progress—perhaps her legs had grown a bit since she last skipped over the rooftops in Falas, she reasoned.

It was peaceful up there, the only noise coming from the ruckus in the streets. Apart from bats, a few birds, and the occasional night web, there wasn't anyone else to witness her passage—until she came to the very last building.

There she was surprised to meet a cat—a black-and-white kitten, actually—who was sitting balled up on the edge of the roof, watching the tumultuous scene below with interest.

"Well, hello, kitten!" Gatina said, smiling under her veil. "Lovely night, isn't it?"

The kitten did not scamper away, afraid, so Gatina took a moment to pet it. It replied with a strong purr. She could no more resist petting a willing cat than Atopol could resist a sweet roll fresh from the oven.

She figured it was a good omen. She needed one. There was a large avenue between the building she was on and the much-larger Storm King's tower, and it was filled with people screaming, cursing, shouting, singing, and fighting.

Many had been lured to the area by more-serious riots, she knew, their drunken curiosity overwhelming their good sense. There were precious few guards around, she noted, but plenty of armed mariners, some with lamps or torches. And she noticed an empty guard station at the tower base. She would wager they had been sent up as reinforcements for the fights that seemed to be everywhere inside the stronghold. It would be tricky for her to make her way through them once she returned to street level.

Using her magesight while she continued to pet the kitten, she spotted the rope her brother was using to descend the tower and followed it to a window high on the fifth floor. She imagined he used it to climb up, too, though he could have gone in by disguise. It took her only a moment to spot him, despite the spells he was using, as he rappelled slowly down the side of the tower.

"Time to go to work, kitten," she said, giving the cat one last affectionate scratch under its chin. Then she found a good place to climb down and spent the next few moments weaving from one spot of shadow to another, ensuring that she had no witnesses. The corner of the tower at the bottom of the rope was planted with a thorny holly hedge designed to deter bystanders, but it served just as well as cover.

When her brother landed, pushing out nimbly over the hedge, she was waiting.

"Hello, Cat," she said in greeting as he landed gently on the ground like his namesake. He was wearing his own working blacks, his shadowblade slung over his shoulder. She took note of the large black sack he was carrying—a loot bag. "Find what you needed?"

Atopol glanced at her, but his violet eyes did not appear startled. She knew it took a lot to rattle her brother.

"Perfectly, Kitten," he said, a note of triumph in his voice. She liked that when they were working, they always used their working names for each other. And they spoke in a low tone that made it more difficult for anyone to identify them. "Where are our friends?"

"Safe. There has been a change in plans. They got caught in a riot and I volunteered to finish their task."

"Are they well?" he asked, concerned, as he set the bag on the ground and took the bundle from her.

"Jordi's got a cut on his head from a thrown bottle, and Pia's a little shaken up, but other than that, they're fine," she said, as he opened the bundle and revealed a costume. "I don't think you'll need your disguise," she counseled as she glanced around to see if they were being observed. "I don't think any of us included riots and fights and brawls in our plans. We should probably go back to the safe house by the shadows."

"I heard some noise while I was setting up," he admitted as he fished a few things out of the bundle and put them into pockets. "I saw a few things happening as I started the climb. There was a bit of a disturbance."

"Actually, it's a very large disturbance. A few of them," she explained. "It turns out that our friend the baron brought his friends the mice and the swashbucklers to the party this evening, and they had entirely too much to drink. Things have gotten very interesting very quickly. Guards were called in, people got stabbed and beaten, it's been an entertaining evening. By the way," she added ruefully, "you have some nerve, climbing that big thing all by yourself!"

She could feel his grin under his veil. "What, that little thing?" he chuckled, glancing up at the spire. "It was pretty thrilling," he admitted. "Better than the temple spires in Falas. You can see most of the harbor from up there. Jealous?"

"Entirely," Gatina agreed. "What did you steal? Money? Jewelry?"

"A small library," he revealed as he opened his sack and showed her several account books. "These can be used as leverage against the good baron's offer. Blackmail," he said, his eyes bright. "Shadow let me know that Lord Bracomel has been stealing money from his customers and vendors, showing them one accounting while keeping his actual accounts secret in these.

"He gets a lot of correspondence, so I sent him some from a mysterious stranger who knew about the entire affair and delivered it myself. I made him nervous with messages all day, until he moved the books to where I could get to them. Then a distraction, a break-in, and I was out the window. I left a tersely worded note that he would not recover them unless the council vote failed and implied we would give them to the authorities instead. We think this is the leverage we need," he explained as he tucked the books safely back into the sack.

"Well done and clever—if boring," Gatina praised with a cock of her head. "Shall we go?"

"Now you know why I wanted to climb down the tower. Ready for our shadow run? I'll follow your lead," he agreed, nodding toward the buildings on the other side of the street.

They made quick work of their climb to the nearest apartment building, though Gatina was sad that the kitten had left its spot. From there, they raced along the roof's ridge before leaping to the next with practiced ease.

They had a fine view of the continued fighting along the way and of the guards who were trying—and failing—to stop the many skirmishes between gangs, factions, and different crews of rival ships who were venting their ire on the streets. The guards were badly outnumbered, Gatina could see, and that was never a good sign.

But it thrilled her to be above it all with her brother. They were, indeed, the Cats of Enultramar, and together they could sneak through anywhere, she reflected proudly as they ran through the shadows on the rooftops, unobserved by any but the stars.

When they were nearly to the safe house, they scaled the steeply pitched roof of a decrepit tavern on the crossroads between the more permanent and more temporary buildings and paused to watch from the peak. This was where the cobbles ended and the streets turned into mere hard-packed dirt.

Things were quieter there near the temporary quarters than they were near the center of the compound. They would have to descend to cross the way—there weren't any buildings close enough by to permit them to leap over—and it was a good time to pause and take stock of the situation. Thankfully, there weren't any fights apparent in the area, just a few small groups of revelers clustered here and there as people trickled back from the troubled spots toward their quarters.

"Look, there's the Fairtrader's Shrine." She pointed in the distance. "I think that's where all of this started tonight. Then it spread to the Maiden's Haven."

"You seem awfully well informed," her brother noted. "At least it's not so bad here."

"We were there—Bomaris and I, then Lancellus arrived with a gang of Rats from the *Venjanca* following him. They—the Rats, not Lancellus—started it."

"In a temple? That seems extraordinarily unwise," Cat observed as he lowered his veil.

"I don't think they were concerned with curses. They're on a mission to target specific Sea Lords, I think. And intimidate or kill the ones who won't side with Jenerard and Vichetral in the council. Like Lancellus."

Atopol nodded. "That's not a fair fight at all. There are more Rats and rogues than guards—and they fight dirty. The guards don't know what they're up against. They'll need the City Watch from Vaxel proper to contain all of this."

Gatina was about to answer him when she saw something on the streets that made her blood freeze in her veins. She was using magesight to peer through the darkness when a man moved out of the shadows for a moment—revealing his black-and-white checkered cloak.

Gatina gasped through her veil and grabbed Atopol's arm while she pointed.

"Censors!" Atopol spat. "What are they doing there?"

"What does it look like they're doing?" Gatina asked rhetorically.

"They're . . . waiting," her brother observed. "There's another on the opposite side of the street. Oh! And one over there!" he said, pointing out a third checkered-cloaked man who was lingering behind an empty cart.

"How many more?" Gatina wondered aloud as she frantically scanned the area again with fresh urgency. Between the two of them, they were able to pick out three more at the crossroads.

"Half a dozen seems . . . unreasonable," Atopol said quietly. "They usually work in pairs." That had been Gatina's experience, too. "They would only send that many if they were expecting a lot of trouble from a powerful mage. Like one of us," he pointed out.

"They've been tracking us somehow," Gatina agreed. "One of them showed up to Bomaris's quarters while I was there."

"I ran into two of them outside of the Salt Crone's compound," Atopol informed her. "They were looking for someone but didn't see past my disguise."

"This isn't good, Cat," she said grimly, as she watched the hidden Censors staking out the intersection. "Six is a lot to try to sneak by. Ordinarily, I'd say we could use shadowmagic, but—"

She was interrupted by a shout from below—from a familiar voice. Her father's voice. She heard rapid footsteps and the clash of steel, but she couldn't see anything yet. But Shadow's voice was unmistakable to her ear. And it sounded like he was in trouble.

Without hesitation, she put her stomach flat on the ledge and peered over, knowing her brother would not allow her to fall should she lose her balance. She was just in time to see the dark cloak of a man swirl by as he fled and fought with a familiar style, even if his face looked nothing like her sire. She did not need magesight to see her father dueling against a pair of guards—led by one sinister-looking Royal Censor.

She pushed herself back to the rooftop. "It's Shadow!" she explained breathlessly. "He's fighting two guards and a Censorate warmage. He needs our help," she said as she prepared to climb down.

"Wait!" Atopol put a firm hand on her arm. "We can't just go diving in—that's *seven* Censors in total! And a couple of swordsmen! If we're going to do something, we must be prepared. What is the plan, Kitten?"

"I propose we climb down silently and surprise them from the shadows," she said as she listened to the swords clanging. "They must think they trapped him here, all alone. They won't be expecting a couple of cats appearing suddenly," she reasoned as she refastened her veil over her face. All thought of danger was gone from her mind. The six waiting Censors who had seemed so impassable a few moments before faded in importance compared to their father's life.

She looked at Atopol. He nodded grimly.

"You take the southern corner, I'll take the northern," he suggested as he prepared himself for action. "Move to an oblique position and attack them from behind—before they can get to Shadow!"

"Darkness protect us," she agreed, giving her brother one last meaningful look before she crept into position.

Then they both launched themselves off the roof from different directions, Atopol choosing to bounce off the wall once to slow his descent before he landed on his toes and rolled into the shadows, drawing his shadowblade as he did so.

Gatina silently swung herself over the edge and caught a wooden shutter to one of the upper-story windows. It swung her neatly around on its leather hinge until she could drop gently to the street below. She slid behind a rain barrel and drew her shadowblade from over her shoulder.

The sword felt good in her hand—an extension of her arm and hand, the promise of dangerous retribution for anyone who dared attack her father. The short, light blade was a welcome change from the scimitar. She was good with the Sea Lord weapon, but she was excellent with the shadowblade. And it was much more familiar.

Suddenly, an appropriate name came to her mind for it: Kitten's Claw. That went extraordinarily well with Atopol's name for his blade, Cat's Whisker, Gatina realized. She grinned to herself under her veil as she looked for opportunities to intervene in the fight.

Her father's disguise did nothing to hide his unique style of swordplay. He was using a Sea Lord scimitar in one hand and a long, wickedly curved dagger in the other, and fought with both of them with admirable precision. The guardsmen he faced were armed with straight-edged short swords, though they carried cudgels in their off hands.

Behind them was the Royal Censor, his sinister checkered cloak thrown back to reveal stout armor and a grinning face. He bore a long mageblade in his hand, but he was depending on his underlings to control the battle and cheering them on enthusiastically.

"Come on, come on!" he was shouting. "You've nearly got him! Recall that he's a mage and watch for tricks!" he reminded them.

"That's why you're here!" grunted one of the guards as he was forced to fall back by Shadow's aggressive attack. "Can't you do something with him?"

Every time her father engaged, he was falling back, Gatina realized as she watched him fight. But he did not know about the other Censors—or at least she didn't think he did. She did not know how they had caught his trail and followed him, but it was clear he had fallen into a trap. And now he was backing into a bigger one.

She glanced around and saw that the closest Censor hiding was starting to inch forward to spring the trap from behind a two-wheeled cart. The donkey it had been attached to was long in its stable, and it leaned down on its shaft, granting the foe excellent concealment from its raised aft end.

Gatina didn't hesitate. Her mind automatically chose her route, and her body responded the moment she saw an opportunity. She raced across the street, ran up the shaft and the bed of the creaky old cart, grabbed the heavy rear gate—and vaulted over it feet-first. Both of her sharkskin boots collided against the unsuspecting Censor's lantern jaw in the same instant, sending him reeling into the darkness.

She did not stop moving when she landed. The next Censor was thirty feet farther up the street and was so fixated on the fight in the crossroads that he had not noticed his comrade's sudden fall. He was just emerging from the covered doorway of a darkened shack when Gatina's silent footsteps brought her up behind him.

There were many ways to incapacitate an opponent when they were unaware of your presence, she knew from long practice and experience. She was not tall enough to properly choke the man with a garrote or stab him in the throat—but his armor only covered his torso. His knees were an ideal target. She could incapacitate him and remove him from the fight without killing him.

Two swift and sudden passes of Kitten's Claw's razor-sharp blade cut through the man's trousers just above his boot tops. She felt the blade bite through to his flesh with each strike as she passed, but she did not stop. Indeed, she was a dozen paces away by the time the man fell to his knees with a painful cry. Two down. Four to go.

She spared a glance at the duel in the crossroads. Her father was still holding his own, and one of the guards had dropped his club and was clutching his sword arm while he defended himself from sharp, relentless blows. But her father was still falling back two steps for every one he advanced.

". . . spent two days tracking you all over town," the Censor was saying as he followed the guards. "We knew you were here—the Lord of Shadows, they call you," he sneered.

"I have no idea what you are talking about!" Shadow lied.

"We know *exactly* who you are!" the Censor insisted. "And what you've been doing. It's the noose for you, by Vichetral's order!" he pronounced.

That thought made Gatina's blood turn cold—and sharpened her resolve. Before she could move, however, her father called back in a wry chuckle as he fought.

"You have to catch me to hang me," he sneered back as he executed a sweeping parry. "And these two fellows don't seem to be up to the challenge. Nor do you," he added contemptuously. He punctuated his response with a flare cantrip—the same one Gatina had used earlier in the evening. It made the wounded man cry out and shield his eyes, allowing her father to slash successfully across his arm.

"You think I'm alone?" the Censor asked, amused, as he raised his mageblade. "We've been following you across the Bay for *weeks*. I did not come unprepared. Now!" he announced loudly as he lunged at Shadow with his mageblade.

The Censor's weapon was unusually shaped and purposefully constructed to be as much a tool of magic as a weapon of war. The tip of the blade was widened, with a hole cut in the center of the blade and filled with glass—thaumaturgical glass, she knew. Master Steel had explained the weapon to her thoroughly when the Censorate began throwing their weight behind Count Vichetral. That glass contained spells and enchantments that made it as powerful as a wand, in the right hands. And it was still a formidable weapon without it.

But not so formidable that her father couldn't parry it easily—and release another flare in the other guard's face.

The call from the Censor had summoned his reinforcements from the shadows, however. A few checkered-cloaked figures emerged from the gloom, their own mageblades drawn. Just not nearly as many as the Censor had expected. Of the six that they had identified from the rooftop of the tavern, only two more appeared at his summons.

That meant that Cat had taken care of at least two on his own. Gatina felt a twinge of frustration that they had equaled one another again.

"Where are the others?" the first Censor called out in confusion as he faced off with Shadow alone, both his guards incapacitated.

"Did your allies desert you?" her father mocked as he took a firm dueling stance with both of his blades raised.

"Three of us is more than enough to handle one filthy thief!" the man snarled and began to aggressively attack. Gatina crept closer to the duel, knowing that she would be called for shortly. Sure enough, after a few sharp passes between the men, Shadow glanced over his shoulder toward the approaching Censors behind him.

"But what if there are more in the shadows?" her father asked loudly. That was enough of a cue, Gatina figured, and she quickly padded to her father's side, her shadowblade raised. Atopol, too, bounded into the center of the street with his own blade drawn. "I think you have badly miscalculated the odds, my friend!" Shadow chuckled apologetically.

"I have more men on the way!" promised the breathless Censor as he realized his plan was failing.

"But not in enough time to save you, I think," her father observed, backing away. Gatina and Atopol moved to guard his back from menace. The Censor paused in his attacks as he waited for his men to move into position. "Nor your master's mission. The vote will not go in your favor now, I'm afraid."

"I don't give a damn about the blasted Sea Lords!" the Censor snapped. "This was just an opportunity to lure you into the open. You and your filthy rebels have violated the Bans on Magic for years, and now you're going to answer for it!"

"The Censorate has abused its authority for years," countered Shadow. "Now that you have aligned yourself with a tyrant, it is you who can expect to be held accountable when he falls. If you are wise, you and your fellows will leave Alshar before that happens," he proposed.

"The Censorate answers to no mere lords," the man dismissed—and Gatina was startled that she recognized him now that she was closer. Censor Captain Stefan, the one who had pursued her so relentlessly back in Falas and at the abbey. He looked a little different now, but it was decidedly him. "We answer only to the king's law!"

"Which king? Kamaklavan, who has been dead for four centuries? Or King Rard?" Shadow asked. "He's assumed Kamaklavan's authority, hasn't he? And didn't he order you expelled?"

"He is illegitimate!" Stefan barked. "We do not recognize his authority! He has unleashed the hell of unregulated magic on this land!"

Shadow shrugged. "On that, at least, we can agree. But, politics aside, you have lost this round. We will be gone by morning," he predicted, "and you will have to contend with the mess we've left behind for you once again. I doubt your patron will be happy about that."

"The only thing that concerns me is eliminating a pack of shadowthieves who misuse magic to steal and kill," Stefan declared proudly. "That is the oath I swore. Lay down your weapons now, and I will perhaps be merciful in my judgement."

The other two Censors were almost within striking range now as they tried to surround the three of them. But as they raised their mageblades, a new voice rang out in the street—a female voice.

"Spare us! There isn't an ounce of mercy in your soul!" it declared bitterly, as a dark figure appeared between—and behind—the two approaching Censors. She reached out to touch each of them on the neck behind their ears, and before either one realized that they were being attacked, a spell went off—and both men began to convulse uncontrollably. "Your pursuit of us ends here," she continued as she glided between the thrashing bodies in the street.

It was Lady Night—their mother, she realized. Gatina hadn't even seen her with magesight.

Stefan's eyes widened in surprise as he realized that he was now alone in facing down his prey. Shadow smiled and advanced, his scimitar raised. Gatina shifted her feet to face him—and then realized that one of the guards was trying to rise once again. She stepped forward and smacked his temple hard with the flat of her shadowblade. He slumped into the dirt once again.

Stefan looked around, a hint of panic in his eyes as he saw he was overmatched and about to be assailed by four opponents at once. Perhaps he didn't have her father's confidence in facing such odds, Gatina reflected, or maybe he wasn't as skilled a swordsman as he boasted.

But he was no fool. Without another word, the Censor turned and took to his feet, running back toward the central compound as fast as his boots would carry him.

"That," Shadow pronounced tiredly as he watched the retreating foe, "was enormously satisfying. They must have cast the tracking spell on me when I met with one of my marks," he admitted guiltily.

"He said he had more men on the way," Atopol reminded his father as he sheathed his blade.

"And Shadow said that we would be away by dawn," their mother reminded him as she dropped her black veil. "Both are true. We have been revealed here. Our missions in Vaxelhaven are done, for good or ill, and it is time for us to withdraw."

CHAPTER TWENTY-NINE

DAYDREAM SETS SAIL INTO THE SUNSET

As we sail away, I still don't understand all this fuss about love.
Pia found someone. Lancellus found someone.
But why? Where's the glory in love?
The glory is in the mission.

— *from Gatina's Heist Journal*

OF COURSE, IT WASN'T AS SIMPLE AS WALKING AWAY FROM THE DARKENED battle. Gatina's mother and father sought to dispel the tracking spell the Censors had laid on him, so that they could not follow. Shadow stripped off his disguise and revealed his working blacks. Gatina and Atopol policed the field, removing the mageblades from each of the fallen Censors and putting them on the roof of the tavern, just to annoy and complicate their lives before retrieving Atopol's loot. But as the sky began lightening in the east, the four of them walked quietly back to their safe house.

After her third rescue of the evening, Gatina was exhausted. She'd been up for almost an entire day straight, she'd engaged in multiple swordfights and three rescues, and her body was struggling to keep upright as they made their way through the streets. There was nary a noise in the distance at this time of night—or day, she corrected—and it seemed as if most of the riots had ceased. But that did not mean they let down their guard.

They were silent on their walk. Even though they were in the shadows, they did not risk unnecessary noise—explaining how four folk dressed entirely in black were skulking through the darkness at this hour would have been unnecessarily awkward. By the time they finally entered the shack, they found Aunt Beah pacing the main room fretfully.

"Oh, thank the Darkness!" Beah cried when the four of them appeared. "I was getting so worried. It sounds like five hells were breaking loose out there. Pia and Jordi told me what happened."

"They only saw a small part of it." Gatina grinned tiredly. "It was chaos. Pirates, Rats, Censors, and drunks."

"Swordfights, brawls, thievery, and magic," Atopol agreed, pulling his cowl from his head with his own grin. "Shadow was nearly caught," he added.

"It's true," Hance assured her as he removed his mantle. "I was facing two guards and a Censor when these two jumped in to help. They set up an ambush at the crossroads. I didn't expect the Cats to be there to ambush them back."

"Pure luck," Atopol admitted.

"We returned by rooftop," Gatina bragged. "Cat just completed his mission; I'd already finished mine and figured I'd assist him. We were just about to head back to the safe house when we saw the Censors hiding and heard your voice."

"They followed me since the concourse and tried to capture me when I crossed the main road," Shadow related. "I knew they were there, but I could not shake them. They were tracking me."

"That's when the hidden Censors tried to intervene," Atopol added.

"And then Minnie joined in at the last moment. It was really quite dramatic," he said as he smiled fondly at his wife.

"When Pia and Jordi told me what happened in the Maiden's Haven, I got concerned," their mother agreed. "I figured I would be in reserve for you, should you run into trouble. As you do," she said pointedly.

"Both of my missions were, nonetheless, a success," her father revealed. "Commodore Werskin will be putting the full weight of his house against Jenerard's proposal now. And the high priest of the Stormfather will not support it either. That should manifest in dozens of votes against it."

"I have the account books from Lord Bracomel, who appears to be a more-ambitious thief than we are. With that leverage, we can be certain he will not do anything we don't want him to—and he had twelve full proxies in his portfolio," Atopol announced proudly as he patted the black bag filled with the books he'd stolen.

"Lady Amorset will likewise do our bidding, lest her noble husband receive proof of her long-hidden lover." Minnureal nodded. "And that fool Master Lomray and his idiot sons will now be entirely opposed to Count Vichetral's plans to legalize slavery, lest they find their own necks in chains themselves."

"My three marks all agreed to cooperate," Beah agreed. "They didn't need much coaxing, but they feared being alone in their dissent until I assured them that they could count on support from other quarters. That's five votes we can count on."

"I convinced Lady Bomaris to join us," Gatina offered. "She was rather enthusiastic, if suspicious. Lancellus told me that he was successful in his persuasion as well—enough so that he attracted a pack of Rats and pirates to chase him. He was lightly wounded by the encounter. He's hiding out with Bomaris now, until the vote takes place," she explained. "They seem to . . . to be quite fond of each other," she admitted.

"By my reckoning, that should be more than sixty votes against Jenerard," Hance said thoughtfully. "If not more. I just hope it's enough to carry the day."

"Whether it is or not, we have made good connections here and learned quite a lot," her mother pointed out. "But while they are required to vote in council, we would be foolish to linger in Vaxelhaven with this many Censors around. The next few days here are going to be . . . contentious," she predicted.

"I agree; it is time for us to withdraw," Hance said, looking at his cousin apologetically. "You and your house have been of good service here, Beah. Thank you."

Gatina's aunt smiled. "And we nearly broke even," she admitted. "I sold our entire cargo out yesterday, and at a good profit. It will be close, but even with paying the extra hands we took on, I think we'll make the enterprise worthwhile."

"You'll do better than that," Minnureal insisted, dropping something into Beah's hand. It was a heavy gold necklace thick with sapphires. "A donation from a very dignified Sea Lord matron who made a very unkind remark about my gown," she explained. "I decided that she didn't need such a pretty necklace anymore. Use it as payment for services rendered on this voyage. We could not have done it without you."

Beah stared wide-eyed at the expensive piece of jewelry, her lip quivering. "I could buy another caravel with how much this is worth!"

"You can keep paying your people properly during a very difficult time," Hance corrected. "Which might last longer than we anticipated. Even if the vote goes against him, Jenerard will not stop in his quest to dominate the Bay. Nor will Vichetral lightly give up his stolen throne. It could well be years before you are free from their influence, Beah," he warned.

"But where can I sell this?" Beah asked suddenly. "I haven't gone to a fence in years!"

"I know someone who knows someone who sometimes works with Master Sensidat," Gatina's mother suggested. "From what I understand he's always looking for something pretty like that. You'll get a good price for it, and no questions asked."

The five of them continued to discuss the details of their missions and their various adventures for nearly an hour as the sun began to brighten the sky in earnest. But the longer they waited, the more anxious Gatina was getting. At least seven Censors were still out there—those who had recovered—looking for them. Lingering in a safe house was fine, but the longer they tarried there, she knew, the higher the chance that they would be discovered by magic. And she was far too tired for another fight.

She was gratified when both her cousins came into the room dressed in working clothing—sailing, not stealing. Jordi's head was well bandaged, and Pia looked as fresh as a peach. Gatina tried not to resent the few hours of sleep her cousin had undoubtedly grabbed while Gatina was out skipping across rooftops and dueling in the streets.

"I took the liberty to arrange a boat for you at dawn," Aunt Beah explained. "Jordi and Pia will row you out to the *Daydream* where it's anchored in the harbor. I didn't want to risk you staying here if the Rats, Censors, and pirates decide to conduct a more-thorough search."

"Excellent idea!" Gatina agreed. "They are certainly looking for us now. The Censors interrupted my meeting in Lady Bomaris's apartment earlier. That's why I was at the Fairtrader's Shrine when the fighting started," she explained. "Then Lancellus arrived. He was followed by a bunch of Rats—including Darrick—"

"From the island?" Pia asked, surprised. "The handsome one?"

Gatina nodded. "He didn't look so handsome on the floor and nearly senseless. We had to defend ourselves, after all. By then, pretty much everyone inside the main temple sanctuary was fighting. It was rather violent," she admitted.

As she heard herself speak, Gatina began to realize just how dangerous her evening had been. But it would be over soon enough, she realized gratefully.

Everyone looked at her when she had finished. In fact, the room was silent.

"You said you left Lancellus with this girl?" Beah asked curiously.

"Yes, Bomaris said she could tend his wounds and hide him until the council," Gatina replied, now curious herself. As aggravating as she found the young Sea Lord, she had grown fond of him, she realized. "Indeed, they seemed very friendly together, so I thought . . . Was that wise?" she asked, suddenly doubting herself.

Her aunt's laughter struck Gatina as strange. "Yes, Kitten, it's perfectly fine. He's been studying House Crenalsar for the past month. He figured them for allies. But it sounds as if he found more than just a collaboration. It wouldn't be a bad match, considering their houses," she admitted.

Gatina felt a pang of jealousy when she realized that Lancellus was in *very* capable hands with a charming and beautiful woman who shared much in common with him. Indeed, she could visualize them together all too well: from what she had seen, Bomaris had a spirit to match Lancellus's cocky arrogance, and they were from similar backgrounds. Still, it cut at Gatina's heart that the handsome Sea Lord had not paid more attention to her—even if she didn't want it. Alas, Pia picked up on where her mind had wandered.

"Don't worry; I didn't like him for you anyway," she whispered.

Gatina's eyes went wide. "*Pia!* I never—"

"He's not a mage, anyway, is he?" her cousin continued. "He's far too tall for you. And so arrogant! I'm certain there are better things in store for you than the likes of him," she assured.

"I am not even thinking about that sort of thing!" Gatina lied.

"Weren't you?" Pia challenged.

"Pack up all of your things," her father suddenly ordered. "Let's get to the boat. Once we're on the water, we can relax. They'll never be able to figure out where we went when there are this many ships in port. Come now, before the tide starts to turn!" he directed.

It didn't take long to bundle up their belongings and their loot and erase any trace of their residence in the shack. Before long, they were dressed in Sea Lord clothing, their working blacks packed away, and saying farewell to their beloved aunt. Gatina was so tired that she barely recalled climbing into the longboat from the *Daydream* where it was moored in the crowded harbor.

The water seemed incredibly peaceful after her hectic night. Pia and Jordi had been told to row them, and she was grateful for that. Her arms and legs felt sore and stiff after the long night's activities, and even the thought of exerting herself at the oars was exhausting. When they finally came alongside the *Daydream*, Matros was waiting for them.

"Is he going with us?" Gatina asked in surprise as she climbed up the ladder.

"He and one of his mates," her father agreed. "That way, we won't have to rely exclusively on you and Cat to get us back home. And that way, he will be waiting for Pia when she returns on the *Legacy*," he reminded her with a grin.

"That's going to be the longest voyage in my life!" Pia complained as she followed behind Gatina.

Once aboard the sloop, Gatina did start to relax a little. After all, there were hundreds of ships in Vaxelhaven, and even with magic, it would be difficult for the Censors to figure out which one they'd fled to. From afar, the *Daydream* looked like any other ship—perhaps a little prettier than some but not particularly distinguishable from a common merchantman. And when the winds and the tides turned in a few hours, they could sail blithely away from the Anchorage without raising suspicion.

Pia, at least, wanted to make the most of her time with her paramour, and Gatina was happy to leave her to it. The only lover she wanted at the moment was blessed slumber. She made her way to her cabin. Atopol was fast behind her, yawning in that annoying way he did that made her yawn, too. She knew she only had a few hours until they departed, but she collapsed onto her bunk and fell fast asleep instantly.

The gentle rocking of the sloop coaxed a storm of dreams into her sleep. The events of the previous day seemed to explode in her sleeping mind as scenes of riots, rooftops, flashing blades, and sinister Censors all strove to capture her in her dreams. Rats and pirates chased her through rubble-strewn streets while she desperately sought to find her family. The blessed darkness seemed no refuge in her dreams; indeed, it seemed to conspire to reveal her to her enemies every time she thought she was safe.

Bomaris and Lancellus featured prominently—the arrogant Sea Lord seemed to pay attention to her until the beautiful Bomaris appeared, and then he lost all interest. The pirate Darrick manifested long enough to mock her and threaten her with a Rat Tail. Censor Stefan pursued her relentlessly through the streets of Falas, or Vaxelhaven, or Inmar, always just a few steps behind her. And the ghostly laugh of the Shipwrecker seemed to haunt every discordant scene in her sleeping mind.

She awakened only when Pia shook her by her shoulders. Gatina blindly scrambled for a knife or sword until she realized that it was her cousin who was touching her, not Stefan's cold, cruel hands.

"Gatina!" Pia whispered harshly. "Wake up! You're having a nightmare!"

"Sorry!" Gatina pleaded as she shook off the lingering memory of the dream. "I had a long day and a longer night."

"I know." Pia sighed, looking at her with sympathy. "But you managed magnificently. You're safe aboard the *Daydream*," she reminded her. "I just wanted to say goodbye before we left. Jordi and I are returning to Vaxelhaven on the *Legacy* to help Mother finish up buying a cargo."

Gatina rose, stretched, and moaned quietly as her aching muscles protested. The rush of adrenaline and excitement that had propelled her through her mission was long gone, but the reminders of her strenuous evening were still there.

"I'm sad that you're leaving," Gatina admitted. "This has been . . . a lot of fun. Well, mostly," she corrected with a grin.

"It has been an adventure." Pia smiled in return. "I am going to miss you, too. And your brother. We've heard about your family all of our lives, but to actually meet you and get to know you has been . . . well, an adventure. Not one I'll ever forget. Of course, I'm not bound to forget the girl who saved my . . . my husband," she said sheepishly.

"Husband?" Gatina asked in surprise. "When did this happen?"

"Matros just asked me," Pia revealed with a shy smile. "Of course, I said yes. I really do love him. But don't tell anyone just yet. I haven't. Only you."

Gatina felt honored but couldn't understand why Pia would only confide in her alone. "Why? Don't you want anyone else to know?"

"Not yet. We want to be safely back at Prejestia before we announce it. But I had to tell someone, and I know you're very good at keeping secrets."

"It's pretty much all I do," Gatina agreed.

"Exactly. But there will be much to sort out before we get married. Mother will want him to prove himself, and watch him like a hawk, and Jordi . . . well, my brother is going to have a hard time with it, I know. Even if he respects Matros, he's already suspicious of him."

"That's just how brothers are." Gatina nodded. "I hate to think what Attie will do to whatever man I end up with. If I end up with one," she corrected. Suddenly, the very idea of meeting a man who might marry her seemed foolish. Somehow, Pia's announcement about her wedding had put things into perspective. It didn't matter if gods and witches predicted that someone would come into her life, she realized. The likelihood of meeting a powerful wizard who would be willing to court a girl like her seemed small.

Pia made a face. "Of course you will!" she insisted. "And not because some old Calrom witch said you would. You're pretty, you're smart, and you're . . . you're the most interesting girl I've ever met. How could any man resist you?"

"Lancellus did," Gatina reminded her glumly. "No, I wasn't seriously interested in him, but . . . well, it's just a little discouraging that he wasn't interested in me."

"He's a Sea Lord," Pia dismissed. "He won't take any girl seriously unless she's heir to a good-sized fleet."

"Like Bomaris," Gatina agreed as they headed out of the cabin and onto the deck. It was midmorning now, and the deckhands were preparing to raise sail. "I suppose I'm happy for them, but it's still a little disappointing."

"In a month, you won't even be thinking about him," Pia encouraged. "You'll be off on some other mission, in some amazing disguise, doing dangerous things and flirting with mysterious gentlemen while you rob them blind. Lancellus will be the last thing on your mind. Trust me. You live too interesting of a life to get obsessed with someone like him."

"Well, I am very happy for you and Matros," Gatina admitted, pulling her cousin into an embrace. "He seems like a good man. I hope he makes you happy."

"He does!" Pia assured her, beaming broadly as they joined the rest of her family on the deck. "And I make him happy, for some reason." Her cousin's eyes were sparkling like sunlight on the Bay.

"Well, he has been at sea a long time," Gatina pointed out. "He was wounded. He was shipwrecked. That could lead to a kind of desperation . . ." she teased.

Pia burst into laughter at that, and the two of them stumbled to the rail where Jordi was waiting. He looked at his sister suspiciously.

"What's so funny?" he asked, an eyebrow cocked.

"Nothing. Nothing you need to concern yourself with," Pia assured him.

Gatina embraced both of her cousins repeatedly before they departed, and her parents thanked them profusely for their stalwart assistance on the mission. Gatina and Atopol lingered at the rail as their boat rowed back to the docks.

"I'm going to miss them. One last voyage," Atopol remarked. "Then back home." He sounded relieved. "I like the sea, but I think I prefer land."

"Is that where we're going?" Gatina asked, curious.

Atopol shrugged. "I'm not certain. Father says he'll discuss our plans once we're under way—and after he's had more sleep. Apparently, he learned some things on this mission that may have an effect on the Shadow Council. He said he'll explain later."

"More sleep would be welcome," Gatina agreed as she watched the distant boat get smaller and smaller. "Indeed, I could sleep for a week."

"Don't count on it," Atopol warned. "Once we're under sail, we'll be deckhands again until we make it back to Prejestia. But at least it will be a straight voyage this time. We shouldn't be making any stops along the way. As long as we can avoid pirates and squalls, we should be back in a few days at the most."

"Then expect me to sleep every moment that I'm not working," Gatina insisted. "And maybe a few that I am."

Gatina did her best to fulfill her promise: she returned to her tiny cabin and collapsed back into her bunk the moment she could. This time, her dreams weren't nightmares—but they were undeniably strange.

She dreamt of the future, a time when all of Alshar was held by young Duke Anguin, and piracy and slavery were vanquished. She dreamed of a time when the Brotherhood of the Rat was held to account for their many crimes, where Count Vichetral and his cronies were soundly defeated, and where the Royal Censorate of Magic was disbanded and scattered. She dreamed of the powerful young wizard that Kohni Ceija had spoken of—but instead of seeing his face, she felt his presence, his heart. He was a good man, in her dreams.

But she was pulled from her dreams too soon. Atopol woke her for supper. The *Daydream* was well under way, and Vaxelhaven was nearly out of sight. There were no ships in pursuit. Whatever else happened at the Anchorage, it was behind them. They were safe.

Supper was held in the captain's cabin—her parents' cabin, she corrected—with just the four of them. Matros was on the tiller, and the great sails were taking them eastward and south, toward the center of the Great Bay. The windows in the cabin let the graceful light of sunset illuminate their meal—salt pork, beans, rice, and a pudding—but the wine was good. Excellent, in fact.

When everyone had settled in, Hance called an impromptu meeting of the Shadow Council to order.

"I think it is safe to say that our visit to Vaxel was a success," he began, "even if things did not go entirely to plan. All of our missions were a success. I'm confident we won over enough votes to keep Baron Jenerard from taking control of the Sea Lords. We had the unexpected benefit of the chaos and the fighting to show just how untrustworthy Count Vichetral's leadership is."

"Unfortunately, a few of the most vocal opponents to the Council of Five were . . . eliminated in the chaos," her mother added sadly. "But that's not going to work in their favor, in my estimation. The Sea Lords are picky about that sort of thing. They do not play the Game of Whispers. Extortion is one thing; assassination is something entirely different."

Gatina looked around the table and saw that everyone was in agreement. Sea Lords preferred a fair fight—or at least an honest one. Their culture did not favor the kinds of skullduggery that Jenerard had brought to the Anchorage.

"More importantly, we were able to establish some important alliances," her father continued. "Master Thinradel was correct: there is great potential in the Sea Lords to aid our cause. They have incredible capabilities that can add greatly to the Shadow Council's efforts. They just require a little guidance and organization."

"Or a little bribery and coercion," Minnureal countered, cocking her head. "They are a bold people but lack sophistication. I think with a little effort, we can bring them into the fight against Vichetral and put Duke Anguin on his rightful throne."

"But how long will that take?" Atopol demanded suddenly. "We've been at this for years now, and we're no closer to chasing that rascal from the palace than we were when we started!"

"Toppling a regime takes patience," their father answered thoughtfully. "And persistence. I can't tell you how much longer it will take, because I've never done it before," he confessed. "You two have performed admirably in this effort. You've done everything we've asked of you, and you've excelled at every task we've set. In the process, you've become two of the best shadowthieves in the history of our house. That is to be commended.

"But this isn't just about you—or even about us," he reminded them. "All of Alshar is depending on us, whether they know it or not. Anguin might have been crowned in exile, but until he sits on his own throne in Falas, we will not be done. And if we fail, that day may only come when King Rard finally invades—and leaves all of Alshar a mere fief of his empire."

"And then we start all over again, fighting against him," Gatina concluded with a frown.

"Mayhap," her mother conceded. "Sometimes peace, stability, and prosperity are elusive. You have to fight for it. But we've done well so far, and I think the day when Alshar is free and under its proper ruler is within sight."

"I don't share your optimism," Atopol admitted glumly. "I think we'll be fighting against Vichetral forever."

"You aren't privy to the same secrets we are," their mother said, a little defensively. "We did learn a lot at the Anchorage. We have new allies, new resources, and new challenges that derive from them. But we are making progress," she insisted.

"Slow, steady, almost-imperceptible progress," Atopol said bitterly. "I dislike complaining, but I don't see any end in sight. We'll still be fighting against Vichetral's grandchildren fifty years from now at this rate."

"And if we are, then we will be just as dedicated to the fight then as we are now!" their father insisted, giving her brother a sharp look. "We have no choice. Regardless of whether or not the vote at the Anchorage fails, men like Jenerard will keep preying on ships and men to fill slave auctions. They will abuse the peasants, cheat the merchants, and rob the artisans with taxes and fees. It might seem a hopeless task, but if no one undertakes it, it will be. The only solution is to restore Alshar to its proper ruler and ensure that he is as fair and judicious as his father."

"And when will that happen?" Atopol asked with a scowl.

Their parents gave each other a searching look. Then her father spoke.

"Perhaps sooner than you think," he admitted. "One of the valuable things we learned in Vaxelhaven was that the current high priest of the Storm King there is helping plot the rescue of Anguin from King Rard's grasp. Many of the Sea Lords feel that Vichetral would not be able to stand if Anguin is on Alshari soil once again. After a rather intense discussion, I convinced him that we were in favor of such a thing and offered to help. He is suspicious of our aid—and he has every right to be, with Vichetral's spies lurking everywhere—but he requires a show of good faith on our part before he cooperates. I was coming back to the safe house with the news when that Censor began to chase me."

"What kind of show of good faith?" Gatina asked, curious.

"We need to locate and then acquire a certain . . . cup," Hance answered. "It's called the Chalice of Storms—an ancient holy artifact that has been lost since the time of the Black Duke. Well, not lost, actually—the Storm King's high priest at the time pawned it, and it hasn't been seen since. The high priest I spoke with is willing to work with us if we can return it to him."

The Chalice of the Storms, Gatina remembered from her book, was a priceless relic of the Sea Lord pantheon that represented the Storm Lord's fury. It was supposed to be able to summon great tempests—or quiet them. It had vanished generations before, as her history on the Sea Lord culture had mentioned. The Sea Lords had a kind of obsession with ancient artifacts and relics, the way the Narasi had one with swords. The book she had read described it as a golden chalice, bejeweled in green and blue stones. It sounded impractical and gaudy to her.

"That doesn't seem so hard," Gatina admitted. "Any idea where it might be?"

"Yes, actually," their mother supplied. "Thanks to one of my marks, we found out that it is currently in the possession of . . . the Brotherhood of the Rat. We think it is in one of their lairs along the Great Bay. They know how valuable it is to the Storm Lord's temple, and they've been using it as leverage against the clergy for years now. It's one of the things that has allowed them to exert so much influence over Alshar for the last few decades."

"Why would the priesthood care about some old cup?" Atopol asked.

"Because it's one of the three sacred artifacts of the Sea Lord religion," Hance explained. "The other two are the silver Sea Axe scepter that's a part of the Alshari crown jewels and an ancient anchor that was lost in the Great Bay centuries ago. Legend has it that when it is recovered finally, the Great Houses of the Sea Lords will unite once again."

"And that when all three are together again, they will rise together and retake Cormeer, their ancestral homeland, with a mighty armada," their mother smirked. "Since Cormeer is firmly under the rule of Merwyn, on the other side of the continent, I find that doubtful. But that's what the prophecy says, according to my sources."

"Prophecy?" Gatina asked, her eyebrow raised. "I don't like the sound of that."

"Prophecies, like curses, often turn out to be false, if history is any guide," her mother explained. "Have you any idea how many anchors have been lost in the Great Bay over the centuries? The likelihood of that one special, ancient anchor ever rising from the rock it was hidden under is . . . small. Impossibly small. I think the Duke of Merwyn can rest easy that Cormeer is safely in his possession."

"Under . . . a rock?" Gatina asked, confused.

"That's the story," her mother nodded. "It's supposedly the anchor from the Storm King's own ship. Legend has it that whoever owns the anchor holds the fate of all of Alshar in their hands, so it was an important ceremonial symbol back then. My mark told me that it was hidden from the Coastlords during the Early Magocracy so that they could not use it against the Sea Lords. It was taken to some secret location on some uninhabited island and buried under a huge boulder where even the magi could not find it. Then everyone on the ship that carried it perished in a tempest on the way back to their temple. So, it's lost forever, now."

Gatina's eyes went wide with understanding as she recalled the red-haired little girl who had dug up the anchor on the beach . . . *and then gave it to her.*

If the legends were correct, then Gatina held the fate of all of Alshar in her hands.

The very idea was laughable, of course, and made the Calrom witch's prediction about meeting her future husband seem reasonable in comparison. How could knowing where an old anchor was have any bearing on the future of the entire duchy? Did an anchor given to her by an imaginary little girl—the strongest girl in the world, supposedly—have any bearing on the course of history? It made her want to giggle at the thought.

"So, we have to steal this mystical cup from the Brotherhood of the Rat, then?" Atopol asked skeptically, while Gatina tried to grapple with the intricacies of fate and magical anchors. Her parents looked at each other once again, and after a long pause, her mother nodded to her father.

"Actually, we aren't," he finally said. "*You* are."

"Me?" Atopol asked in surprise.

"Yes," their mother agreed. "Your father and I have been talking. We think it is time that the Cat of Enultramar perform his journeyman heist—alone," she pronounced. "To that end, we've agreed that you shall be the one who steals the Chalice of Storms to prove your mastery of our craft."

"It won't be easy," her father continued as Gatina and her brother stared at him, their mouths agape in surprise. "The last rumor we have heard was that the Brotherhood had acquired it and took it to one of their lairs in a little port called Solashaven. It's in the eastern end of the Bay, and the port has almost completely silted up over the years, but that's the last clue we have about it. The good news is that the nearby town of Pearlhaven would serve as an excellent staging ground for the heist. And it happens to have a Chapel of Eight Bells," he mentioned to Gatina. "I understand you need one to break that silly curse you're obsessed with."

"A . . . Chapel of Eight Bells?" Gatina asked in a whisper.

"You . . . you want me to do my journeyman heist?" Atopol said, shaking his head in disbelief. "You think I'm ready?"

"You're better at your craft than I was at your age," admitted Hance. "You and Kitten have been so eager to best each other in your training that you've far surpassed where I was when I was sent into the palace after the Sea Axe. You're certainly ready for this."

"If anyone can find it and steal it, you can. We are masters of our Art," Minnureal reminded him. "We've taught you well. It's time you demonstrated what you can do. If you steal this successfully, you will be a journeyman—your own man," she emphasized.

"What about me?" Gatina asked. "I'm just as good as Cat! Better!" she insisted proudly.

"Your time will come, Kitten," her father assured her. "But you still have some things to learn. This particular heist seems well suited to Cat's skills, and it came along at just the right time. No doubt, when you are ready, the Blessed Darkness will grant you a journeyman heist worthy of you."

"Until then, I want you to study more shadowmagic." Her mother nodded. "When we get back, you can work with Lady Silk until your brother is ready for his heist. You've become accomplished with a shadowblade, but you are still weak in matters arcane."

Gatina felt a little disappointed at the news, but she knew she shouldn't be. She was two years younger than Atopol, after all, and she had to admit that—perhaps—he might be the tiniest bit better than she in a few ways.

"So, I'm going to be a journeyman," Atopol reflected an hour later as they both stood at the stern of the sloop and gazed at the beautiful sunset.

"Only if you actually get to steal the stupid cup," Gatina pointed out.

"It will be easy," her brother dismissed. "It's just a bunch of Rats."

"Bloodthirsty, violent, murderous Rats," she corrected. "Guarding a precious relic."

"What could possibly go awry?" He shrugged.

"At least I'll be able to get rid of this curse." She sighed.

"You know that's just superstition, don't you?" he asked. "I haven't wanted to give you any grief about it, but you're really putting too much stock in that old mariners' tale. You got shipwrecked for like a day. You survived. There's no curse."

"Maybe. Still, just to be on the safe side . . ." She shrugged. "Who knows what will happen if I break it? Or if I don't?"

She didn't mention to her brother the old witch's prediction of meeting her future husband at the Chapel of Eight Bells, nor the fact that she had been given an ancient mystical anchor by an imaginary little girl that put the fate of the entire duchy in her hands. If he didn't believe in the curse, there was little chance he'd think highly of such things.

But she was used to keeping secrets. It was her legacy, she knew, just like fighting for her country and magic and stealing were. Kiera the Great had established that for their house centuries before, and her ancestors had kept faith with that rule.

The setting sun was bright, but it was energizing. She enjoyed the warmth as it offset the strong breeze that promised cooler weather to come. The sky was cloudless. The ship was headed east, directly toward Prejestia, and if the wind was any indication, they would have favorable sailing conditions for a while.

She leaned over the railing and enjoyed the peace she found in the sound of the water. The sea had come to be meaningful to her. Whether it was placid or turbulent, the sea, like the Blessed Darkness or the eternal stars, brought her peace. It gave her a bit of relief.

So much was changing, so quickly, and she wasn't sure what it meant or where she fit into it all. She was glad this mission was over, but she would miss the sea. She was happy for Pia and Matros, she was happy for her brother's new quest, and she was happy she was going home to Falas. She was going to miss the *Daydream*—the *Yellow Rose*, she corrected herself—but she was eager to pursue new adventures, too.

"Hey!" Matros called from the tiller. "You two lazybones had better change into your deck clothes! You're on watch in a quarter hour," he reminded them, "and a night watch, too. Best be prepared!"

"We're the Cats of Enultramar!" Gatina called back to the mariner with a wide grin after glancing at her brother. "We do our best work at night!"

ABOUT THE CREATORS

Terry Mancour is the *New York Times*–bestselling author of more than thirty books, under his own name and various pseudonyms, including *Spartacus* (Star Trek: The Next Generation Book 20) and the Spellmonger series (twelve books and counting), among other works. Terry was born in Flint, Michigan, in 1968 (according to his mother) and in 1978 wisely relocated to North Carolina, where he embraced Southern culture and its dedication to compelling narratives and intriguing characterizations. He attended the University of North Carolina at Chapel Hill, majoring in religious studies.

Emily Burch Harris grew up reading Nancy Drew and Susan Sand mysteries before diving into fantasy and horror novels. Born in Maryland and raised there as well as North Carolina and West Virginia, she has a knack for finding cold spots in rooms, legends about witches, lost objects, and folks who like to talk. She worked as a journalist before deciding fiction was far more fun than the stark reality of the news. Emily is the editor and writing partner of Terry Mancour.

CONNECT WITH TERRY MANCOUR

Get updates
http://spellmongernewsletter.com/

Check out the Spellmonger series
https://spellmongerseries.com/

Join the Spellmonger Discord
https://discord.gg/68txXKR

Follow him on Amazon
https://www.amazon.com/Terry-Mancour/e/B004QTNFOO

Like his Facebook page
https://www.facebook.com/spellmongerseries/

CONNECT WITH EMILY BURCH HARRIS

Visit her website
https://emilyburchharris.com

Follow her on Amazon
https://www.amazon.com/Emily-Burch-Harris/e/B017Y87Q7U

Like her Facebook page
https://www.facebook.com/avalonschoice/

Follow her on Instagram
https://www.instagram.com/emilyburchharris

Follow her on Twitter
https://www.twitter.com/emilydbharris

Sign up for Terry's newsletter for the latest musings, updates, and release information from the Archmage himself!

Head to the link below and enter your email to stay connected.

http://spellmongernewsletter.com/

DISCOVER STORIES UNBOUND

PodiumAudio.com

www.ingramcontent.com/pod-product-compliance
Ingram Content Group UK Ltd.
Pitfield, Milton Keynes, MK11 3LW, UK
UKHW041304180426
11947UKWH00009B/666